THE RED AND
THE BLACK

STENDHAL

THE RED AND THE BLACK

A CHRONICLE OF 1830

A new translation by Burton Raffel

Introduction by Diane Johnson

Notes by James Madden

THE MODERN LIBRARY

NEW YORK

2003 Modern Library Edition

Biographical note copyright © 1995 by Random House, Inc.
Introduction copyright © 2003 by Diane Johnson
Translation copyright © 2003 by Burton Raffel
Notes copyright © 2003 by Random House, Inc.

LIBRARY OF CONGRESS CATALOGING-IN-PUBLICATION DATA
Stendhal, 1783–1842.
[*Rouge et le noir.* English]
The red and the black: a chronicle of 1830 = *Le rouge et le noir* / Stendhal; a new
translation by Burton Raffel; introduction by Diane Johnson; notes by James Madden.
p.   cm.
ISBN 0-679-64284-6
1. France—Social life and customs—19th century—Fiction.   2. Young men—
France—Fiction.   I. Title: *Rouge et le noir.*   II. Raffel, Burton.   III. Madden, James.
IV. Title.

PQ2435.R7 E5 2003
843'.7—dc21
2002040798

Modern Library website address: www.modernlibrary.com

Printed in the United States of America on acid-free paper

2 4 6 8 9 7 5 3 1

STENDHAL

Marie-Henri Beyle—later known as Stendhal—was born in Grenoble on January 23, 1783. His mother, whom he idolized, died when he was seven, and he was raised by three people he detested—his bourgeois father, a prosperous lawyer; a jealous maiden aunt; and a tyrannical Jesuit tutor who inspired in him lifelong feelings of anticlericalism. The only person he felt any closeness to was his maternal grandfather, a respected physician who embraced the culture of the Enlightenment. In 1799, at the age of sixteen, the young man left for Paris to study mathematics at the École Polytechnique, but became a dragoon in Napoleon's army the following year. The invasion of Italy took him to Milan, the city he came to love above all others; over the next decade he served as an aide-de-camp in Bonaparte's campaigns in Germany, Austria, and Russia. In between wars he flourished in Parisian drawing rooms and devoted himself (unsuccessfully) to writing plays, all the while keeping elaborate journals that chronicled his travels and love affairs.

Following Napoleon's fall in 1814, Beyle retired permanently from the army and settled in Milan, where he began to write in earnest. He soon produced *Lives of Haydn, Mozart, and Metastasio* (1814), followed by the two-volume *History of Painting in Italy* (1817). His next book—

a travel guide entitled *Rome, Naples, and Florence in 1817* (1817)—was the first to bear the pen name Stendhal, the most famous of the more than two hundred pseudonyms he employed in his lifetime. During this period he fell in love with Matilde Dembowski (née Viscontini), who served as the basis for his heroines. Suspected of being a French secret agent and of involvement in left-wing plots, the writer was expelled from Italy in 1821 by the Austrian police.

Upon returning to Paris, Stendhal immediately resumed *la chasse au bonheur* (the pursuit of happiness) and writing. He quickly finished the semiautobiographical treatise *On Love* (1822), the critical study *Racine and Shakespeare* (1823), and *Life of Rossini* (1824). *Armance,* the author's first novel, appeared in 1827. *A Roman Journal,* a guidebook that marked Stendhal's first real success, came out in 1829. Then in October of that year he began a novel based on a case reported in the *Gazette des Tribunaux:* the trial of a young man charged with the attempted murder of an ex-mistress. Published in 1830, *The Red and the Black* shocked the public with its incisive portrait of Restoration France, along with its probing psychological study of the complex protagonist, Julien Sorel. ("A novel is like a bow, and the violin that produces the sound is the reader's soul," Stendhal like to remind his audience.)

Following the July Revolution of 1830, which brought Louis-Philippe to the throne, Stendhal returned to government service. In 1831 he was appointed consul to the port of Civitavecchia, some forty miles from Rome, where he spent many of his final years. During the 1830s Stendhal began two novels, *Lucien Leuwen* and *Lamiel,* both of which remained unfinished and were not published until long after his death. He also undertook two autobiographical works, *Memoirs of an Egotist* and *The Life of Henri Brulard,* which likewise appeared posthumously. In 1835 Stendhal was awarded the Legion of Honor for services to literature; the following year he returned to Paris on an extended leave of absence. There he started a biography of Napoleon and completed *Memoirs of a Tourist* (1838), a popular travel guide to France. Then, between November 4 and December 26 of 1838, the author dictated his last great novel, *The Charterhouse of Parma* (1839), a tale of political intrigue set in Italy. In failing health, he lived long enough to rejoice in Balzac's generous praise of it. Stendhal died in Paris, following a series of strokes, on March 23, 1842, and was buried the next day in the cemetery of Montmartre.

"I will be famous around 1880," Stendhal once predicted. Indeed, at about this time he began to attract widespread attention, and many of his previously unpublished books appeared—including *A Life of Napoleon* (1876), *Journal of Stendhal* (1888), *Lamiel* (1889), *The Life of Henri Brulard* (1890), *Memoirs of an Egotist* (1892), and *Lucien Leuwen* (1894). In the twentieth century such writers as Paul Léautaud, André Gide, and Paul Valéry have acclaimed Stendhal's work. "We should never be finished with Stendhal," said Valéry. "I can think of no greater praise than that."

FOR REUVEN ELIEZER PRIDE

CONTENTS

Part Two

INTRODUCTION

Diane Johnson

I always think that Stendhal, the name Marie-Henri Beyle chose as his *nom de plume,* would have preferred to be Lord Byron, the prototypical romantic hero of the early nineteenth century, handsome, gifted, aristocratic, and rich. The two men met a time or two in Milan, and Stendhal greatly admired *"le joli homme de génie."** Though Byron, the younger, was long dead by 1830, when Stendhal's great novel *Le Rogue et le Noir* was published, Stendhal's tone often reminds one of Byron in his letters, or in *Don Juan,* a work which Stendhal cites in epigraphs to his chapters.

Like Byron, Beyle had a masculine life of action. He served in the military under Napoleon—between 1800 and 1813 in Italy as a second lieutenant, and with the campaigns in Germany, Russia, and Austria as aide to the Napoleonic general Michoud. At other times he lived in Paris, where he exerted himself to lead a strenuous, somewhat rakish life about town, and would become a diplomat—a French consul-general—in Civita Vecchia, Italy, the country he most loved and appreciated. His years there seem to have been happier than those he

---

* See Jonathan Keates's entertaining account in his biography *Stendhal* (Carroll & Graf, 1997). A member of Byron's party in Milan found Stendhal "a fat and lascivious man."

spent in Paris, where, as a provincial born in Grenoble, he perhaps did not quite fit in, being neither handsome enough (plain, short, and plump) or rich enough to cut a swath in the society he would have preferred.

The period of Beyle's lifetime (1783–1842), one of the most turbulent in European history, included the French Revolution, the Terror, the reign of Napoleon, Napoleon's wars, the subsequent restorations of Louis XVIII and Charles X, and upheavals caused by various factions struggling to make France a Republic. Altogether, in France alone during this period there were at least six political regimes, culminating in 1830 with the July Revolution, which put an end to the Bourbon rule, and instead of fulfilling the author's republican hopes, brought to the throne a new king, Louis-Philippe, who would still be ruling at Beyle's death. And when we consider the upheavals in Italy, so long dominated by Austria, and by 1830 divided into various papal and other states, it is not surprising that politics play an important part in Stendhal's books, as in his life. The period covered in *The Red and the Black* is almost coextensive with the moment it was being written.

But the contradictions involved in leading a life of fashion as well as the life of a writer were something else he shared with Lord Byron. At the same time that the Marie-Henri Beyle side of his nature was drawn to *mondaine* life in the military and social worlds, Stendhal was a sober intellectual and writer. It is fortunate that as both a provincial bureaucrat in Italy and a Parisian dandy he would have had considerable leisure time, during which he wrote critical essays in French journals, articles which were translated for English magazines, wrote extensively on painting, music, and opera, as well as travel pieces, stories, and of course his five novels, of which the most famous are *The Red and the Black* and *The Charterhouse of Parma*. By these efforts he supplemented his small private income.

Today Stendhal is secure in the smallish pantheon of the greatest French novelists (Flaubert, Balzac, Stendhal, and Proust), but he is not uncontroversial, and some of his qualities, especially his natural, almost conversational style, invite comparisons with Flaubert, always to Stendhal's disadvantage. Flaubert, an exquisite stylist, is, at the moment at least, the undisputed *roi* of French prose, but for many, Stendhal is the more enjoyed, and is above all a greater creator of characters, perhaps excepting Madame Bovary.

An American reader is most likely to have encountered *The Red and the Black* at about the age of its protagonists, Julien Sorel and Mathilde de La Mole, who are eighteen or nineteen when we meet them. The other important figure, Madame de Rênal, is "about thirty, but still quite pretty." As with many novels, to take it up again at an older age is to experience a different book. At first reading, you are caught up in Julien's precarious career, with his love affairs and mishaps, and with the adorable, tempestuous Mathilde and poor Madame de Rênal. We are drawn to Julien's egotism, so like our own, laugh when Julien falls off his horse or fights a duel, and are generally swept along by the story and the brilliance and candor of its understanding of human motivation. American literature has not produced a writer like this, though the reader may think of Twain's similar mixture of irony and romanticism.

We were not apt to be distracted by the character of Stendhal himself, his cynicism, social perspicacity, the complexity of his attitude toward Julien, and his inability to hide his writerly cards. What on first reading had seemed a tone expressive of the dawn of the romantic period, we now find to be heavily ironic, often patronizing, even sarcastic and impatient, and to owe a lot to Voltaire and the eighteenth-century *philosophes,* as well as to romantic ironists like Byron. This is especially true at the beginning of the novel, as Stendhal sets off on his task of recounting Julien Sorel's rise and fall. We see as the novel progresses that the author softens toward his hero, even identifies with him, and puts a lot of his own experience into a tale that began more objectively. The reader then may become fascinated by the character of Stendhal, who positions himself in the tale as a presiding intelligence without ever seeming to be in charge of what happens; he always makes it clear that it is the characters themselves who direct their fates, reacting in the light of the corrupt realities of their society.

Julien Sorel's story was taken from the actual case of Antoine Berthet, reported in the *Gazette des Tribunaux* in December 1827, whose career and crime become Julien's. At first one senses that Stendhal felt constrained by the story he had chosen: a bookish boy, son of a brutal peasant who beats him and whose family doesn't understand him, sees a way out of his situation by studying for the priesthood and taking a job as a tutor in a prosperous bourgeois family, the Rênals. Here he has an affair with Madame de Rênal, and in other ways furthers his career, learning manners and something of the world. He is intelligent and good-looking, the epitome of a romantic hero with his large, dark eyes and tousled curls. More important, he has "an unshakable determination to undergo a thousand deaths rather than fail to achieve success."

This accounts for the side of Julien that is calculating, flattering, insincere, and inwardly hostile even to people who intend to help and love him—indeed, he is an early example of an antihero of whom, at first, even Stendhal cannot approve. But there is a side of Julien that is loving despite himself, that is deservedly proud of his superiority to many, if not most, people in the ranks above him, and who takes pleasure in the pleasures of life with natural spontaneity. It is his most admirable side, when he finally becomes truthful and sincere and listens to his own heart, that dooms him, an outcome that of course reflects Stendhal's own cynical view of a world where hypocrisy, scheming, wealth, and rank are necessary to success.

Unlike Byron, Stendhal himself was far from irresistible to women, at least as a lover, and there is some suspicion that he was rather too direct and clumsy in his approaches to them, or unrealistically romantic, or self-protective in that he more often than not fell in love with married women. In any case, despite his innumerable love affairs, perhaps complicated by having syphilis (like many other figures of the period), he never married, and confessed to occasional homosexual impulses.

By all accounts, however, he was a delightful friend to women, admiring those with intelligence and learning, qualities warmly appreciated by French men in this time of famous salons and witty hostesses. This was generally an eighteenth-century frame of mind, which was in part to disappear in the covert misogyny of later nineteenth-century writers.

That Stendhal liked women helps explain why he is such a great portrayer of women characters. His portrait of Mathilde de La Mole in *The Red and the Black* is clearly drawn by a man who understood women—he had a beloved sister—and Mathilde is a woman the modern reader can understand without having to allow for the attitudes of an earlier time. Unlike the heroines of certain English novels, who are apt to be clinging, frail, and doomed like Clarissa or Tess, to die at the least transgression, Stendhal's heroines are witty, rational, responsible for their own actions, and willing sometimes to sacrifice our pity for our respect. Above all, they are women in a French novel, which is quite a different tradition, always franker about sex and infinitely less censorious. Almost more than his racy, vernacular style (very well rendered in this new translation), defying the developing taste of his period for a more florid style of prose (Victor Hugo found him horribly prosaic, and Henry James "unreadable"), his portraits of women seem utterly modern.

But Julien Sorel is, of course, his greatest creation, perhaps because Stendhal himself embodied some of the contradictions of Julien's nature. At pains to demonstrate Julien's muddle of inexperience, romantic delusion, ambition and naïveté, pride and timidity, Stendhal sometimes betrays his own exasperation with these qualities, but by the time Julien is installed in the splendor of the aristocratic Parisian de La Moles' mansion, Stendhal's scorn turns instead on the fashionable Royalist society to which they belong, an attitude reflecting his republican views. The long scene where Julien sits in on the Royalist discussion is a masterly precis of the political climate of his day.

Here Stendhal falls under the spell of his own, perhaps rather autobiographical, creation. It is easy to imagine as least some of Julien's misadventures in Parisian society to have come from actual experience, whether Stendhal's own or that of others he observed floundering in that exacting setting. Stendhal's friends said Julien reminded them of him; in other words, as the novel progresses Julien becomes more like Stendhal, and hence his creator comes to like him better.

Perhaps this is why he spares us a harrowing account of Julien's end, a fate the present reader may passionately resent, as this one did at first reading. For, alas, things are to end badly, leaving Madame de Rênal to die of grief, and poor Mathilde pregnant, though far from ruined. What is one to make of Julien's fate? Was Stendhal bound by the actual case, in that Antoine Berthet was executed? Is it an ultimately cynical statement about the futility of life and ambition, or a concession to the concepts of romantic tragedy, or the ultimate expression of Stendhal's ambivalence about his hero, or a moment of high, ironic comedy that laughs at human absurdity, the culmination of which is found in Mathilde's Gothic plans for Julien's grave?

Though Julien, Madame de Rênal, and Mathilde de La Mole are themselves creatures of the romantic period, they were formed by someone with a foot in each world, which explains the savagery with which their conflicted creator will turn on his characters at unexpected moments. In any case, it is the harshness of Julien's fate which has sealed posterity's view of Stendhal as a severe, even bitter realist rather than the romantic he struggled to hide, and who emerges despite himself. For what, finally, is more romantic, in the largest sense, than the ending of this remarkable work?

DIANE JOHNSON is the author of ten novels—most recently *Le Mariage* and *Le Divorce*—two books of essays, two biographies, and the screenplay for Stanley Kubrick's classic film *The Shining*. She has been a finalist four times for the Pulitzer Prize and National Book Award.

Translator's Note

Stendhal was largely misunderstood in his lifetime (when he was noticed at all), and has continued to be misperceived in the century and a half since his death. Translating—as opposed to reading—*Le Rouge et Le Noir* has given me new respect for the virtuosic brilliance of Stendhal's prose, and for the passionate intensity that makes this novel a profound and moving tragedy.

My text has been the 1972 Gallimard Folio edition, which is based on but has been updated from the Pléiade version, edited and annotated by Henri Martineau in 1932.

The meaning of the book's title has been disputed. The best short account of the various interpretations seems to me that of Professor René Ternois:

> The title *The Red and the Black* was not understood by [Stendhal's] contemporaries. A great deal has been written to explain it, and many silly things have been said. Probably the "red" symbolizes dreams of glory, in the revolutionary or in the imperial armies, and the "black" [symbolizes] ecclesiastical ambition—in short, the dilemma created for Julien Sorel, or, more likely still, the impossible dream versus the sad necessity. It is very possible that the title concerns the two colors in the game of roulette; life

itself is a game; Julien hesitates for a long time before placing his bet; he bets on the red, and loses. At a different point, he would have bet on the black, and might have won. He did not have the chance.

(translated [and at one point corrected] from *Le Rouge et Le Noir,*
vol. I, Paris, Larousse, 1937, p. 8)

The epigraphs placed by Stendhal before each of the book's many chapters, until the dramatic final chapters (which have been given no epigraphs), are frequently, deliberately, and notoriously unreliable. Many were written by Stendhal himself, and ascribed ironically to highly unlikely sources. With one exception, I present them, here, as he wrote them. When Stendhal attributes to Virgil a passage written in fact by Horace, I have added a correction. *Caveat lector.*

The many different currencies in use, in Stendhal's France, have here been converted (mostly in due proportion) to more readily comprehensible francs. Famous names, battles, and the like have more often than not been explicated, in the text proper, by an added word or two. M., the standard French abbreviation for *monsieur,* has without exception been given its full form. In conversational passages, *monsieur* has usually been translated as "sir." And so on. Or, as Stendhal would say, and I have been careful to let him say, *etc., etc.*

NOTICE

This book was about to be published when the great events of July turned our minds away from mere fictions. There is reason to believe that the following pages were written in 1827.

PART ONE

Truth, bitter truth.
DANTON

CHAPTER ONE

A SMALL TOWN

Put thousands together
Less bad,
But the cage less gay.
—HOBBES

The little town of Verrières might be one of the prettiest in all Franche-Comté. Its white houses with their sharp-pointed roofs of red tile stretch down a hillside, every faint ripple in the long slope marked by thick clusters of chestnut trees. A few hundred feet below the ruins of the ancient fortress, built by the Spanish, runs the River Doubs.

To the north, Verrières is sheltered by a great mountain, part of the Jura range. The first frosts of October cover these jagged peaks with snow. A stream that rushes down from the mountains, crossing through Verrières and then pouring itself into the Doubs, powers a good many sawmills—an immensely simple industry that provides a modest living for most of the inhabitants, more peasant than bourgeois. But the sawmills are not what brought prosperity to the little town. It was the production of printed calico cloth, known as "Mulhouse," which ever since the fall of Napoleon has created widespread comfort and led to the refinishing of virtually every house in Verrières. Just inside the town, there is a stunning roar from a machine of frightful appearance. Twenty ponderous hammers, falling over and over with a crash that makes the ground tremble, are lifted by a wheel that the stream keeps in motion. Every one of these hammers, each and every day, turns out I don't know how many thousands of nails. And it's pretty, smooth-cheeked young girls who offer pieces of iron to these enormous hammers, which quickly transform them into nails. This operation, visibly harsh and violent, is one of the things that most astonishes a first-time traveler, poking his way into the mountains separating France and Switzerland. And if the traveler, entering Verrières, asks who owns this noble nail-making factory, deafening everyone who walks along the main street, he'll be told, in the drawling accent of the region, "Ah—it belongs to His Honor the Mayor."

If the traveler spends just a moment or two on Verrières's grand thoroughfare, which ascends along the bank of the Doubs right up to the top of the hill, the odds are a hundred to one he'll see a tall man with an air both businesslike and important.

As soon as he appears, every hat is respectfully raised. His hair is grizzled, he's dressed in gray. He wears the insignia of several knightly orders; his forehead is lofty, his nose aquiline, and taking him all in all there's a certain orderliness about him. At first sight, one even feels that he blends the dignity of mayoral status with the sort of charm still often to be found in a man of forty-five or fifty. But it does not take long for a Parisian traveler to be struck, most unfavorably, by clear signs of self-satisfaction and conceit, topped off by who knows what limitations, what lack of originality. Finally, one is aware that his talents are confined to making sure he is paid exactly what he is owed, while paying what he himself owes only at the last possible moment.

This then is Monsieur de Rênal, mayor of Verrières. Crossing the street with solemn steps, he goes into City Hall and disappears from the traveler's sight. But if the traveler keeps on walking, no more than another hundred paces up the hill he will see a distinguished-looking house and, if he looks through an adjoining wrought-iron gate, a very fine garden. Beyond that, he will see a horizon shaped by Burgundian hills, which seems to have been put there expressly for the purpose of pleasing the eye. This view will help the traveler forget the foul smell of petty financial transactions, which had begun to asphyxiate him.

He is informed that this house belongs to Monsieur de Rênal. The mayor of Verrières owes this fine, just-completed dwelling, built of cut stone, to the profits earned by his noble nail factory. His family, it is explained, is Spanish, ancient, and (as the story is told) settled in the region long before Louis XIV conquered it.

Ever since 1815, his status as an industrialist has embarrassed him. It was 1815 that made him mayor of Verrières. The terrace walls around the different parts of this magnificent garden, holding in place each of the different levels descending almost to the Doubs, are yet another reward for Monsieur de Rênal's iron-trade business acumen.

Nowhere in France can you hope to find the picturesque gardens surrounding Germany's manufacturing towns—Leipzig, Frankfurt, Nuremberg, etc. In Franche-Comté, the more walls you put up, the more your property bristles with rocks heaped one on top of another, the more claim you have on your neighbors' respect. Monsieur de Rênal's gardens, packed with walls, are even more admired because he bought—for just about their weight in gold—the bits and pieces of land on which they lie. For example, the sawmill located so strangely right on the bank of the Doubs, which caught your eye as you entered Verrières, and on which you noticed the name SOREL, written in gigantic letters on a board protruding over the roof, until six years ago had stood exactly where, at this very moment, they are building the wall for the fourth terrace of Monsieur de Rênal's garden.

For all his haughty pride, Monsieur de Rênal had been obliged to make a good many overtures to old Sorel, a tough, stubborn peasant; he had to count out a stack of handsome gold coins before the old man agreed to move his business elsewhere. As for the *public* stream that had powered the sawmill, Monsieur de Rênal relied on the influence he enjoyed in Paris to have it diverted. This official favor had come to him after the elections of 182-.

To get one acre, he had given Sorel four, situated five hundred paces farther down the bank of the Doubs. And even though the new location was far more advantageous for his trade in pine boards, Père Sorel (as they call him, now that he's a rich man) knew how to play on his neighbor's pressing impatience, and his *land-owning mania,* squeezing out a sale price of six thousand francs.

To be sure, the transaction was criticized by wiser heads in the area. Once, about four o'clock on a Sunday, coming home from church, dressed in his mayoral robes, Monsieur de Rênal saw in the distance old Sorel, surrounded by his three sons, watching him and smiling. That smile proved fatally illuminating to the mayor: he realized, from then on, that he could have bought the land for less.

To earn a public reputation in Verrières, the essential thing—while of course building a great many walls—is not to adopt some design carried across the Jura gorges by Italian stonemasons, in their spring-time pilgrimages to Paris. Any such innovation would earn the impru-dent builder the unshakable taint of *rebel;* he would be forever after ruined in the eyes of the wise, moderate folk who parcel out reputa-tion in Franche-Comté.

In truth, these wise fellows wield an incredibly wearisome *despotism,* and it is precisely this wretched word that makes small towns unlivable for those who have been successful in that great republic we call Paris. The tyranny of opinion—and such opinion!—is every bit as *idiotic* in the small towns of France as it is in the United States of America.

CHAPTER TWO

A MAYOR

Importance! My dear sir, isn't that worthless? The respect of donkeys,
the astonishment of small children, the rich man's jealousy and the wise
man's disdain.

—BARNAVE

Happily for Monsieur de Rênal's reputation as an administrator, a huge *retaining wall* was required for the public walkway running along the hillside, roughly a hundred feet above the Doubs. This wonderful location gives it one of the most picturesque views in all France. But every spring the rains had regularly furrowed the walkway, digging out gullies and rendering it impassable. This inconvenience, which af-fected everyone, placed Monsieur de Rênal under the fortunate obli-gation of immortalizing his administration by a wall twenty feet high and well over two hundred feet long.

The upper portion of this wall—on behalf of which Monsieur de Rênal had been compelled to make three trips to Paris, because the former minister of the interior had declared himself the mortal enemy of Verrières's walkway—the upper portion of this walkway had now grown to be four feet above the ground. And as if to chal-lenge all the ministers, present and past, at this very moment slabs of cut stone are being put in place.

How many times, dreaming about Parisian balls long left behind, with my chest pressed against those great blocks of stone—a lovely gray streaked with blue—has my glance plunged down into the valley through which the Doubs runs! Out there, along the left bank, five or six valleys go meandering, the eye easily able to distinguish small streams tumbling through them. Having splashed through one waterfall after another, one sees them pouring into the Doubs. The sun is powerful, in these mountains: when it shines directly overhead, a traveler's daydreaming, as he stands on this raised earthwork, is sheltered by magnificent plane trees. They owe their rapid growth, as well as their beautiful foliage, green tinted with blue, to the earth brought by the mayor and deposited behind his huge retaining wall, for in spite of the Municipal Council's opposition, he had enlarged the walkway by more than six feet—I commend him for this, although he is a monarchist and I a liberal—and indeed that is why, in his opinion and that of Monsieur Valenod, the fortunate director of the Pauper's Bureau in Verrières, this raised earthwork can bear comparison to that of Paris's Saint-Germain-en-Laye.

For myself, I find only one thing to object to, about LOYALTY WALKWAY. One can read this formal title in fifteen or twenty places, on marble plaques that earned Monsieur de Rênal an extra star on his official medal. But what I disapprove of about Loyalty Walkway is the barbarous way the authorities cut and clip those vigorous plane trees, down to the very quick. Instead of looking as if their heads were bowed low, plump and round and debased like the most vulgar of garden vegetables, they ask only to be granted the magnificent shapes one sees them assume in England. His Honor the Mayor is a despot, and twice a year all trees belonging to the town are shorn without pity. Those of liberal belief pretend (though they exaggerate) that the town gardener's hand has become even more severe since Father Maslon decided to impound for church use the profits from this shearing.

This young ecclesiastic was sent out from Besançon, some years ago, to keep watch on Father Chélan and several other priests in the neighborhood. An old surgeon-major, a veteran of the Italian wars who had retired to Verrières, and who in his lifetime had been (according to His Honor the Mayor) both a Jacobin and a Bonapartist, actually had the nerve to complain to the mayor about the periodic mutilation of these beautiful trees.

"I like shade," replied Monsieur de Rênal with the arrogant tone so appropriate when speaking to a surgeon and member of the Legion of Honor. "I love shade, and I have *my* trees cut so they provide shade, nor can I conceive of any other use for trees, especially when, unlike the useful walnut, they *bring in no revenue.*"

And there you have the mighty words that, in Verrières, decide everything: *bring in no revenue.* This phrase alone is representative of the habitual views of more than three-quarters of the inhabitants.

Bring in no revenue, then, explains every decision taken in this little town, which seemed to you so pretty. The arriving traveler, seduced at first by the beauty of the deep, green valleys all around, fancies that these are people who appreciate the *beautiful;* indeed, they're constantly chattering about the loveliness of their countryside, nor can one deny that they in fact appreciate it—but simply because it attracts outsiders whose money fattens up innkeepers, which in turn, via the local tax system, *brings in revenue.*

One fine autumn day Monsieur de Rênal strolled along Loyalty Walkway, his wife on his arm. While listening to her husband, who addressed her in serious tones, Madame de Rênal's glance anxiously followed the movements of her three little boys. The oldest, who might have been eleven, kept coming over to the stone wall, clearly thinking about climbing up on top. Her gentle voice called out, "Adolphe," and the child gave up his ambitious project.

Madame de Rênal seemed to be about thirty, but still quite pretty.

"He's going to regret it, this fine gentleman from Paris," said Monsieur de Rênal, obviously offended, his cheeks even paler than usual. "I'm not entirely without friends at the castle...."

But though I propose to tell you about provincial life for some hundreds of pages, I will not barbarously submit you to the prolixity, the *wise heavy-footedness* of country conversation.

This fine gentleman from Paris, so unbearable to the mayor of Verrières, was none other than Monsieur Appert, who two days earlier had found a way not only to push himself into both Verrières's prison and its Pauper's Bureau, but also into the hospital, which the mayor and the principal landowners administered free of charge.

"But," said Madame de Rênal timidly, "what harm could this gentleman from Paris possibly do you, since you look after the welfare of the poor with such scrupulous integrity?"

"He's come here just to *dig up* scandal, and then he'll have articles appearing in the liberal newspapers."

"You never read them, my dear."

"But people talk to us about those Jacobin articles; it's distracting, *and it keeps us from doing good.** And as for me, I'm never going to forgive the parish priest."

CHAPTER THREE

A PRIEST

*A priest who's virtuous and not a schemer is a heavenly gift
to a small town.*

—FLEURY

You need to know that Verrières's parish priest, an old man of eighty, who owed his health and his iron will to the brisk air of these mountains, had the right to visit the prison, the hospital, and even the Pauper's Bureau at any time he wished. Monsieur Appert, who had been recommended to the parish priest by people in Paris, had the good sense to arrive in this gossipy little town at exactly six o'clock in the morning. And he went straight to the rectory.

Father Chélan read the letter from Marquis de La Mole, a French nobleman and the largest landowner in the province, then sat quietly contemplating it.

"I'm an old man, and well loved here," he finally murmured. "They wouldn't dare!" Quickly looking up at the gentleman from Paris, his eyes were gleaming, despite his age, with a special consecrated fire that showed how delightful he found it, plunging himself into something both good and rather risky:

---

* A direct quote [Stendhal's note].

"Come with me, sir, and in the presence of the jailer and, above all, of the superintendents at the Pauper's Bureau, please express no opinion whatsoever on the things we will be seeing." Monsieur Appert understood that he was dealing with a high-minded man: he followed the venerable priest, went to the prison, the old people's home, the poorhouse, asked a great many questions and, in spite of some extraordinary responses, did not allow himself the slightest indication of criticism.

These visits lasted several hours. The priest invited Monsieur Appert to dine with him, but the gentleman from Paris pretended to have letters to write: besides, he did not want to compromise his generous companion-in-arms. About three o'clock the two men went to inspect the Pauper's Bureau, then returned to the prison. There, they found the jailer standing at the door, a tall, bow-legged giant of a man; fright had transformed his ugly face into something truly hideous.

"Ah! Monsieur," he said to the priest, the moment he saw them, "this gentleman I see here with you, isn't he Monsieur Appert?"

"And?" said the priest.

"It's just that, as of yesterday, I have the most precise orders, sent by the chief of police and delivered by a gendarme who had to gallop all night, that Monsieur Appert mustn't be allowed into the prison."

"Let me inform you, Monsieur Noiroud," said the priest, "that this traveler, here with me, is Monsieur Appert. Remember that I have the right to enter the prison at any hour, day or night, accompanied by whomever I choose."

"Yes, Father," said the jailer, his voice low, bowing his head like a bulldog obliged to do as he is told, but reluctantly, for fear of the stick. "It's just, Father, I've got a wife and kids, and if anyone squeals on me I'll be a beggar. All I've got to live on is my job."

"I'd be just as sorry to lose mine," said the good priest, his voice increasingly emotional.

"But what a difference!" the jailer answered quickly. "You, Father, everyone knows you've got an income of eight hundred francs a year, good land under the warm sun. . . ."

These are the things that, for two days—gossiped about, exaggerated twenty different ways—stirred up malignant passions all over the little town of Verrières. Just now, they were serving as the text for a little discussion Monsieur de Rênal was having with his wife. That morning, accompanied by Monsieur Valenod, director of the Pauper's Bureau, he had gone to see the parish priest, bearing witness to the liveliest sort of dissatisfaction. No one was there to shield Father Chélan; he alone bore the weight of these gentlemen's remarks.

"Well then, gentlemen! At eighty years of age, I'll become the third parish priest to be dismissed in this district. I've been here fifty-six years; I've baptized virtually everyone living in the town, which was no more than a farmers' market when I arrived. Day after day I marry all the young people, just as I've long since married their grandparents. Verrières is my family—but what I said to myself, seeing this stranger from Paris, was: 'Perhaps this man is in fact a liberal, we see all too many of them. But what harm can he do our poor folk and our prisoners?' "

Monsieur de Rênal's harsh words, and especially those of Monsieur Valenod, as director of the Pauper's Bureau, grew more and more strident.

"Well then, gentlemen, dismiss me," the old priest cried, his voice trembling. "I'm still going to live here. Everyone knows that, forty-eight years ago, I inherited land that brings in eight hundred francs. I will live on that. I don't put away anything from my salary, which may be why I'm never frightened when there's talk of taking it away from me."

Monsieur de Rênal got on very well with his wife, but he had not known how to reply when she'd asked, timidly, "What harm can this gentleman from Paris do to the prisoners?" He was about to grow angry when, suddenly, she choked back a cry. Her second son had just climbed to the top of the wall around the terrace, and was running along it, although it soared more than twenty feet above the vineyard on the other side. Fear of frightening her child, and causing him to tumble down, had kept her from calling out. Finally, laughing at his success, the boy looked over at his mother, saw how pale she was, and, jumping down to the walkway, ran over to her. He got a good scolding.

This minor episode changed the whole course of their conversation.

"I've really got to bring that Sorel into the house," said Monsieur de Rênal. "The sawmill operator's son. He'll keep an eye on the children: they're getting to be too much for you. He's a young priest, or very nearly, an expert Latinist, and he'll help the children make good progress, because Father Chélan tells me he's a solid sort. I'll give him three hundred francs and his board.

"I had some doubts on the question of morality, because Sorel was the favorite of that old surgeon, the one who was a member of the Legion of Honor and who came to live with the Sorels, under the pretense that he was actually related to the family. The man might very well have been, after all, a secret agent for the liberals. He used to say that our mountain air was good for his asthma, but who knows if that was true or not? He was with *Buonoparté* on all his Italian campaigns, and once, I've heard, he even voted against the Empire. This liberal taught Latin to young Sorel, and left him all the books he'd brought with him.

"Also, I would never have dreamed of having someone right out of a sawmill here in the house, around our children, but Father Chélan—actually, just the night before the quarrel that has estranged us forever—told me Sorel had been studying theology for three years, planning to enter the seminary, so he's no liberal: he's a Latinist.

"This would be a sensible arrangement in more ways than one," Monsieur de Rênal continued, while watching his wife with a diplomatic air. "Valenod's terribly proud of that pair of Normands he just bought, for pulling his fancy carriage. But his children don't have a tutor."

"He might very well steal ours."

"So you like my plan?" said Monsieur de Rênal, thanking his wife, with a smile, for the excellent idea she'd just had. "All right, then. It's decided."

"Ah, good Lord! My dear, how quickly you make up your mind!"

"It's because, me, I know what I'm doing—and our parish priest has seen that. Let's be completely open about it: we're surrounded by liberals, here. All these calico dealers are jealous of me, I'm quite sure of it; two or three have gotten rich—well now! I'm going to be powerfully pleased when they see Monsieur de Rênal's children passing by, on their way to the walkway, accompanied by *their tutor.* That's going to make an impression. My grandfather always used to tell us how, in his youth, he had a tutor. This one will cost me a hundred gold crowns, but we must see this expense as something necessary to preserve our social standing."

This sudden decision left Madame de Rênal distinctly pensive. She was a tall, well-made woman, who had been the local beauty, as people in these mountains put it. There was a distinct straightforwardness about her, and in the youthful spring of her walk: indeed, to the eyes of a Parisian such unspoiled charm, as innocent as it was lively, might even have seemed suggestive of a sweet sensuality. Had she been told this was the sort of effect she produced, Madame de Rênal would have been deeply ashamed. She had never in her life been tempted either to flirtation or any manner of affected behavior. Monsieur Valenod, the wealthy director of the Pauper's Bureau, was said to have tried making advances to her, quite without success, which threw her virtue into high relief, for he was a tall young man, strongly built, with a florid face and great black whiskers—one of those coarse creatures, shameless and loud, that they call, in the provinces, good fellows.

Madame de Rênal, terribly shy and equally moody, was above all else disturbed at Monsieur Valenod's incessant moving about, and the blaring of his voice. Her antipathy to what Verrières called pleasure had gotten her a reputation for snobbishness. No such thing had ever crossed her mind, but she'd been perfectly happy to see fewer and fewer townsfolk calling at her house. Nor should we hide the fact that, in the eyes of the town's *ladies,* she was an outright fool, since with not the slightest regard for proper management of her husband, she passed over the loveliest opportunities for buying beautiful hats from Paris or Besançon. But if they just let her wander about in her fine garden, she never complained.

This was, in short, an artless soul who had never so much as thought of passing judgment on her husband and admitting to herself that he bored her. It seemed to her, though not in so many words, that no relationship between husband and wife could be any better. She was especially fond of Monsieur de Rênal when he spoke to her about his plans for their children, the first of whom he meant to make a soldier, the second a judge, and the third a priest. That is, she found Monsieur de Rênal less boring than any other man she knew.

Nor was this marital opinion an irrational one. His Honor the Mayor of Verrières owed his reputation for wit and, above all, for good breeding to half a dozen jokes he had inherited from an uncle. Old Captain de Rênal, before the Revolution, had served in an infantry regiment commanded by the Duke d'Orléans, and when he'd been in Paris had been entertained in the prince's drawing rooms. There, he had seen Madame de Montesson, the celebrated Madame de Genlis, and Monsieur Ducrest, who had redesigned the Royal Palace. These personages kept popping up, over and over, in Monsieur de Rênal's stories. But little by little this echo of events exceedingly ticklish in the telling became laborsome for him, and after a time he repeated his anecdotes about the House of Orléans only on great occasions. Besides, since he was extremely polite, except when the topic was money, he was very properly thought of as the most aristocratic person in all Verrières.

CHAPTER FOUR

A FATHER AND SON

And am I to blame
If that's how things are?
—MACHIAVELLI

"My wife really has a head on her shoulders!" the mayor of Verrières said to himself, at six o'clock the next morning, as he walked down to Père Sorel's sawmill. "Though I told her I had, so as to maintain my natural superiority, it really had not occurred to me that if I didn't hire this little priest—who's said to command Latin like an angel—the director of the Pauper's Bureau, that restless soul, might very well have had the same idea and stolen him away. With what self-satisfaction he'd have talked about his children's tutor!... Will my tutor, once he's in the house, wear a cassock?"

Monsieur de Rênal was pondering this question when he saw, in the distance, a peasant, a man nearly six feet tall, who from the first light of dawn had apparently been hard at work, measuring lengths of wood laid out along the bank of the Doubs. The peasant did not seem particularly pleased to see His Honor the Mayor coming toward him, because his timber was blocking the towpath and had been put there in violation of town laws.

Père Sorel, for it was indeed him, was very surprised—and even more pleased—by the strange arrangement Monsieur de Rênal proposed for his son. All the same, he listened with that air of downcast discontent, and absolutely no interest, which the shrewd inhabitants of these mountains understood only too well how to drape over themselves. They had been enslaved, ever since the days of Spanish domination, and they preserved this physiological trait of the *fedayin* of Egypt.

Sorel's first response was merely a long recitation of all the formulas of respect, which he knew by heart. While he was repeating these meaningless words, with a stupid smile that nicely supplemented the look of dishonesty, even of roguery, so profoundly natural to him, the old peasant's lively spirit tried to figure out what could have led so important a man to take in his good-for-nothing son. He was totally disillusioned with Julien—and here was Monsieur de Rênal offering the incredible salary of three hundred francs a year, plus food and board, and even clothing. This last claim, which Père Sorel had the quick wit to suddenly include, even before negotiations had been concluded, was agreed to by Monsieur de Rênal just the same.

The mayor had been struck by the demand. "Since Sorel is hardly delighted and gratified by my proposal, as in the nature of things he ought to be," he said to himself, "it's clear that he's had offers from elsewhere, and from whom could they have come, if not from Valenod?" Monsieur de Rênal urged Sorel to settle things on the spot, but he would not: the wily old peasant stubbornly refused, saying he had to consult his son—as if, in the countryside, a wealthy father ever consulted a penniless son, except for the sake of appearances.

Water-powered sawmills are sheds on the banks of a stream. The roof sits on a frame built around four big wooden pillars. At a height of eight or ten feet, in the middle of the shed, one sees a saw rising and coming down, while an extremely simple device pushes a piece of wood against the blade. A wheel turned by the running stream is what operates both parts of the process, the ascending and descending saw and the mechanism that gently guides wood toward it, after which it is cut into boards.

Walking over to his factory, Père Sorel bellowed for Julien; there was no response. All he could see were his older sons, giantlike fellows who, armed with heavy axes, were squaring up fir-tree trunks, then lugging them to the saw. Completely occupied with following exactly the black line drawn on the wood, with each swing of the axe they would pare away enormous chips. They could not hear their father's voice. Sorel went into the shed and looked in vain for his youngest son, in the spot next to the saw where he was supposed to be. He found him, finally, five or six feet higher up, sitting on one of the roof beams. Instead of carefully watching over the working of the machinery, Julien was reading. For old Sorel, nothing could have been more objectionable; he might have forgiven Julien his small size, hardly suited for hard labor, and utterly unlike his older brothers, but he himself could not read, and this mania for reading was repulsive to him.

He called Julien two or three times, without being heard. More even than the noise of the saw, the young man's intense focus on his book blocked out his father's terrible voice. At last, despite his age, Sorel jumped onto the tree trunk being fed into the saw, and from there got up to the roof beam. A violent blow sent Julien's book flying into the running water; a second blow, just as powerful, struck the young man on top of his head, making him lose his balance. He was about to drop some twelve or fifteen feet, right onto the machine's moving levers, which would have beaten him to a pulp, but his father grabbed him with his left hand, even as he fell.

"Well, lazybones! You're always reading your damned books—and you're supposed to be in charge of the saw? Read them tonight, when you're wasting time with the parish priest—fine, fine!"

Stunned by the force of the blow, and bloodied all over, Julien went back to his official post, on the platform next to the saw. There were tears in his eyes, less from the physical pain than for the loss of his book, which he dearly loved.

"Get down here, you pig, so I can talk to you."

The noise of the machine was loud enough to keep Julien from hearing the command. His father, who had already jumped down, had no interest in climbing back up, so he went to fetch a long stick used for cracking nuts and smacked his son on the shoulder. Julien's feet had barely touched the ground when old Sorel began shoving him roughly along, in the direction of the house. "God only knows what he's going to do to me!" the young man said to himself. As they proceeded, he looked sadly at the stream into which his book had fallen: it was the one he loved best in the world, *Memories of Napoleon on Saint-Helena.*

His cheeks were purple, his eyes cast down. He was a small young man, eighteen or nineteen years old, not appearing very strong, with irregular but delicate features and an aquiline nose. His large black eyes, which at peaceful moments indicated thought and passion, were at the moment sparkling with wild hatred. His dark chestnut hair, worn very long, covered much of his forehead and, when he was angry, gave him a wicked look. Among the innumerable varieties of the human face, there may well be none more striking. His slender, compact form was more indicative of light quickness than of power and energy. Even when very young, his extremely thoughtful air and his pallor had convinced his father he would not live, or if he did that he'd be a burden on his family. Everyone in the house despised him; he hated his brothers and his father; when the children played in the public square, on Sunday, he was always beaten up.

He was barely a year old when his beautiful face began to make friends for him, among the little girls. Looked down on by the entire world as a feeble creature, Julien was adored by the old surgeon, he who had had the nerve, one day, to speak to His Honor the Mayor about the butchered plane trees.

Sometimes the surgeon paid Père Sorel for a day's working time, and taught his youngest son Latin and history, or what he himself knew of history: Napoleon's Italian campaign of 1798. When he died, he'd left his Legion of Honor medal to Julien, as well as whatever was owing from his half-pay military pension, plus thirty or forty books, the most precious of which had just leaped into *the public stream*, diverted into new channels by the influence of His Honor the Mayor.

They'd hardly gotten into the house when Julien felt his father's powerful hand take hold of his shoulder; he trembled, waiting for the blows to follow.

"Answer me and without any lying," the old peasant's rough voice cried in his ears, while his hand turned the young man around as a child turns a toy soldier. Julien's large black eyes, flowing with tears, found themselves staring straight into the small, gray, rascally eyes of the old carpenter, who seemed determined to read his son's soul, straight down into its depths.

CHAPTER FIVE

A NEGOTIATION

Taking it slowly fixes everything.
—ENNIUS

"Answer me without lying, if you're able to, you son of a *lizart*: Where did you meet Madame de Rênal? When have you spoken to her?"

"I've never spoken to her," Julien answered. "The only time I've ever seen the lady is at church."

"But you've stared at her, you barefaced rascal?"

"Never! As you know, at church, all I ever see is God," Julien added, a bit hypocritically, yet a fair and decent maneuver, as far as he was concerned, for warding off his father's blows.

"Anyway, there's something behind this," replied the sly peasant, and then he was silent for a moment. "But I'll never learn anything from you, you damned hypocrite. But I'm going to be rid of you, and that's a good thing for my sawmill. Somebody, the parish priest or someone else, has gotten you a good job. Go and get yourself packed, and I'll take you to Monsieur de Rênal's house, where you're going to be his children's tutor."

"And what would I be paid?"

"Food and board, clothing, and three hundred francs a year."

"I'm not interested in being a servant."

"Pig, why are you jabbering about being a servant? Would I want my son to be a servant?"

"But who will I be eating with?"

This question embarrassed old Sorel, who felt that if he spoke about such matters he might say something rash: he grew fiercely angry at Julien, piling insult after insult on him, accusing him of being a glutton, and then ended by walking away to consult with his other sons.

Julien saw them, before too long, leaning on their axes and conferring. After watching them for a long time, and realizing that he could not predict what would happen, he went and set himself on the far side of the saw, to keep from being surprised. He wished he were capable of thinking about this unexpected news, which was going to change his destiny, but he felt unable to think sensibly. His mind was entirely absorbed in trying to imagine what he would find inside Monsieur de Rênal's fine mansion.

"I've got to get away from all this," he said to himself. "I'd sooner run off than be reduced to eating with the servants. My father will try to force me; I'd rather die. I've saved up more than fifteen francs, I'll escape tonight; in two days, using back roads where I won't have to worry about gendarmes, I'll be at Besançon, and there I'll sign up as a soldier, and if I have to I'll cross over into Switzerland. But that will be the end of getting ahead in the world: no more ambition for me, no more of that fine priestly status, which can lead to everything."

The horror of eating with the servants was not something natural to Julien; to make his fortune he would have done other things equally unpalatable. He had learned his repugnance from Rousseau's *Confessions,* which was the only book that in any way helped him imagine the great world. That, plus a collection of Grand Army bulletins and *Memories of Napoleon on Saint-Helena,* completed his personal Koran. He would have died for these three books. He would never believe in any others. As the old surgeon-major had once said, he considered every other book in the world a pack of lies, written by swindlers trying to get ahead.

Together with his fiery soul, Julien possessed one of those stunning memories so often linked to stupidity. To win over Chélan, the old parish priest, on whom he saw very clearly his future depended, he had learned by heart the entire New Testament in Latin; he also knew

Monsieur de Maistre's *On the Pope*—and had no more belief in the one than in the other.

That day, as if by mutual agreement, Sorel and his son avoided speaking to each other. In the evening, Julien went to the parish priest for his theology lesson, but it seemed to him risky to say anything about the strange proposal made to his father. "Maybe it's a trap," he said to himself. "I'd better act as if I'd forgotten all about it."

Early the next day, Monsieur de Rênal summoned old Sorel, who first kept the mayor waiting for an hour or two, then at last appeared, and as he came through the door made a hundred excuses, mixed with as many shows of respect. By pressing all sorts of objections, Sorel learned that his son would be eating with the master and mistress of the house; on days when they had company he would dine with the children, in a separate room. Always inclined to quibble, in exact proportion as he sensed His Honor the Mayor anxious to really move forward, and also bristling with defiance and genuine astonishment, Sorel asked to see the room where his son would be sleeping. It was large, furnished most properly, but into which they were already moving beds for three children.

This was like a flash of light to the old peasant: he immediately, and with great confidence, asked to see the clothing his son was to be given. Monsieur de Rênal opened his desk and took out a hundred francs.

"With this, your son can go to Monsieur Durand, the tailor, and get a complete black suit."

"And even if I took him away from you," said the peasant, suddenly forgetting his fawning and scraping, "he'd still keep his black suit?"

"Of course."

"Fine, fine," said Sorel languidly. "So there's only one thing left, to have everything arranged: how much you're going to pay him."

"What!" cried Monsieur de Rênal indignantly. "We agreed on that yesterday. I'll pay him three hundred francs, which seems to me quite enough—and perhaps too much."

"That was what you offered, I can't deny it," said old Sorel, speaking even more slowly—and then, with a stroke of genius that would astonish only those who do not know the peasants of Franche-Comté, he added, looking fixedly at Monsieur de Rênal: *"We can do better elsewhere."*

At these words, the mayor's face registered immense shock. He recovered himself and, after a weighty conversation that lasted two full hours, in which not a single word was casually uttered, the peasant's shrewdness prevailed against that of the rich man, who did not need to be shrewd to make his living. All the many conditions and stipulations that would regulate Julien's new existence were settled, and not only was his salary set at four hundred francs a year, but it was to be paid in advance on the first day of each month.

"Good!" said Monsieur de Rênal. "I'll give him thirty-five francs."

"To round the sum off, for a man as rich and generous as Your Honor the Mayor," said the peasant *coaxingly*, "why not make it thirty-six francs?"

"So be it," said Monsieur de Rênal, "but that's enough."

The mayor suddenly sounded decisive. The peasant saw that no more could be gotten out of him. Then it was Monsieur de Rênal's turn to push ahead. He flatly refused to give the first month's thirty-six francs to old Sorel, who was anxious to have it on his son's behalf. Monsieur de Rênal realized, too, that he was going to have to inform his wife what he had agreed to.

"Let me have back that hundred francs," he said pleasantly. "I have a certain credit on Monsieur Durand's books. I'll go with your son, to get the black suit."

After this forceful gesture, Sorel prudently returned to his fawning formulas; this occupied a full quarter of an hour. Finally, seeing there was absolutely nothing more to be gained, he left. His last respectful declaration was completed by these words:

"I'll send my son to the château."

This was how those who served in the mayor's administration referred to his house, when they wanted to please him.

When he got back to his factory, Sorel could not find his son. Worried about what might happen to him, Julien had gone off in the middle of the night. He wanted a safe place to leave his books and his Legion of Honor medal. So he had brought them to a young timber merchant, a friend named Fouqué, who lived up on the high mountain towering above Verrières.

And when he came back:

"God knows, you cursed lazy dog," his father told him, "if you'll ever be honorable enough to pay me the price of your raising, all I've spent on you for so many years! Take your rags and go to the mayor's house."

Amazed not to be beaten, Julien left as quickly as he could. But as soon as he was out of his terrible father's sight, he began to walk more slowly. He thought that making a stop at church would be important to his hypocrisy.

The word surprises you? Before arriving at so horrible a conclusion, the young peasant's soul had traveled a long road.

In his early childhood, he'd seen dragoons from the Sixth Cavalry, home from the war in Italy, with their long white cloaks, wearing helmets that dangled plumes of black horsehair, and watching them tie their horses to the window grille, at his father's house, made him desperate to be a soldier. Later, he listened in ecstasy as the old surgeon-major told him tales of the battles at Lodi bridge, at Arcoli, and at Rivoli. He was struck by the old man's passionate glances at his Legion of Honor medal.

But when Julien was fourteen, they began to build a church at Verrières, and one that could be called magnificent in such a small town. There were four marble columns, the sight of which especially fascinated him; they became famous all over the region, for the mortal hatred they caused between the justice of the peace and the young vicar, considered a spy for the Congregation of the Holy Virgin. The justice of the peace was about to be dismissed—or so most people thought. Hadn't he dared to quarrel with a priest who, just about every second week, traveled to the regional capital, Besançon, and there reported (it was said) to His Grace the Bishop?

In the meantime, the justice of the peace, father of a large family, was responsible for several punitive sentences that seemed unjust; all of them were against readers of the liberal newspaper, *The Constitutional.* Those who were on God's side had won. True, it was all about trifling sums, no more than three or five francs, but one of these petty fines had to be paid by a nail maker, Julien's godfather. In his anger, the man exclaimed, "What a changed man! And for more than twenty years we thought the justice of the peace was such a decent fellow!" By this point the surgeon-major, Julien's friend, was dead.

All of a sudden, Julien stopped talking about Napoleon, declaring he would become a priest; in his father's sawmill he could be seen, day after day, memorizing a Latin Bible lent him by the old parish priest. That good man, amazed at the youngster's progress, spent whole evenings teaching him theology. In his presence, Julien expressed nothing but pious sentiments. Who could have imagined that this girlish face, sweet and pale, concealed an ineradicable determination to risk a thousand deaths rather than fail to make its fortune!

For Julien, making his fortune meant, first of all, leaving Verrières: he hated his hometown. Everything he saw there chilled his imagination.

Beginning in early childhood, he had had moments of exaltation. He dreamed of the delights he'd experience, one day, being introduced to the pretty ladies of Paris: he would know how to attract their attention by some brilliant act. Why shouldn't he become the beloved of one of them, like Bonaparte while he was still poor, but loved by the sparkling Madame de Beauharnais? For many years there had not been a single hour when Julien did not say to himself that Bonaparte, an obscure, poverty-stricken junior officer, had conquered the entire world with his sword. This notion comforted him for misfortunes that, to him, seemed very great, and redoubled his pleasure, when there was any for him to enjoy.

Construction of the church, and the justice of the peace's decisions, struck him like lightning: he had an idea that turned him half crazy for weeks, and finally seized him with all the supreme force of the first idea that an impassioned soul feels it has ever invented.

"When Bonaparte set people to talking about him, France lived in fear of invasion: military skills were both necessary and fashionable. Today, we see forty-year-old priests with salaries of a hundred thousand francs—that is, three times as much as Napoleon's famous generals. And they have to have assistants. Here's the justice of the peace, such a good fellow, such a thoroughly honest man—until now: old as he is, he's forced to disgrace himself for fear of displeasing a young vicar of thirty. So the thing is: become a priest."

Right in the middle of his newfound piety, when he had been studying theology for two years, Julien had once betrayed himself by a sudden eruption of the fire devouring his soul. It was at Father Chélan's, a dinner party of priests where the good Father had introduced him as an educational prodigy, and Julien managed to praise Napoleon in wild terms. So he bound his right arm to his chest, pretending he had dislocated it while moving the trunk of a pine tree, and for two months carried it in that awkward position. After this personal punishment, he pardoned himself. And there we have the young man of nineteen, in appearance so slight and weak that he would not have been thought more than seventeen, who—carrying a small bundle under his arm—walked into Verrières's magnificent church.

He found it dark and empty. When there was a holy day to be celebrated, all the casement windows were covered with crimson cloth. When the rays of the sun shone through, this produced a dazzling light, deeply impressive and profoundly religious. Julien shivered. All alone in the church, he seated himself in a strikingly attractive pew. It bore Monsieur de Rênal's coat of arms.

Kneeling on the prayer stool, Julien noticed a scrap of printed paper, flattened out as if for reading. He leaned forward and read:

Circumstances attending the execution and the last moments of Louis Jenrel, executed at Besançon on the . . .

The paper had been ripped. On the back could be made out the first words of a line, which read: *The first step.*

"Who could have put this bit of paper here?" thought Julien. "Poor wretch," he added with a sigh, "his name ends just like mine . . ."—and then he crumpled the paper.

Leaving the church, Julien thought he saw blood near the basin of holy water, but it was only sanctified liquid that someone had spilled. The play of light through the red curtains over the windows made the water seem like blood.

Now Julien was ashamed of his secret terror.

"Am I turning into a coward!" he exclaimed to himself. *"Forward march!"*

These words, so often recited during the old surgeon-major's battle stories, were heroic to Julien. He walked rapidly toward Monsieur de Rênal's house.

But for all his noble resolutions, when he got within twenty paces of it he was gripped by an invincible timidity. The ironwork gate was open; to him it seemed magnificent, and he had to go in there.

Julien was not the only one whose heart was troubled, as he arrived at the house. Madame de Rênal's extreme shyness was shaken by the thought of this stranger, who, by the very nature of his job, was going to find himself constantly with her and her children. She was in the habit of having her sons sleep in her room. That morning, the tears had flowed abundantly, seeing their little beds carried into the room that was now the tutor's. She could not persuade her husband to have the youngest child's bed, Stanislas-Xavier's, carried back into her room.

Madame de Rênal carried feminine delicacy to an extreme. She fashioned for herself the most obnoxious of images, a gross and un-kempt creature paid to snarl at her children, and all because he knew Latin, a barbarous language for the sake of which her sons were going to be flogged.

CHAPTER SIX

BOREDOM

I no longer know what I am,
Or what I'm doing.
—MOZART'S *FIGARO*

With the grace and vivacity natural to her, when she could not be seen, Madame de Rênal was leaving the drawing room, going out the French window leading into the garden, when near the main doorway she noticed a young peasant, really still a child; he was extremely pale and had obviously just been weeping. He wore a very white shirt, and under his arm was carrying an absolutely spotless jacket of violet rat-teen.

The little peasant's complexion was so pale, his eyes so gentle, that Madame de Rênal's sometimes romantic spirit thought, at first, that this could be a young girl in disguise, coming to ask a favor of His Honor the Mayor. She felt sorry for this poor creature, held motion-less at the entryway, clearly not daring to lift his hand toward the doorbell. Madame de Rênal went over, forgetting for a moment the bitter grief she'd been feeling as she contemplated the tutor's coming. Julien, facing the door, did not see her approaching. He shivered when her sweet voice said, so close to his ear:

"What have you come for, my child?"

Julien turned quickly and, struck by the charm of Madame de Rênal's expression, lost a bit of his shyness. And then, stunned by her beauty, he forgot everything, even what he was doing there.

Madame de Rênal repeated her question.

"I've come to be the tutor, madame," he finally replied, deeply embarrassed by the tears he'd been wiping away as best he was able.

Madame de Rênal was silent, bewildered; they were standing very close, looking at each other. Julien had never seen anyone so beautifully dressed, especially a woman with such a dazzling complexion, speaking to him in so sweet a voice. Madame de Rênal looked at the heavy tears on the young peasant's cheeks, which had been at first so exceedingly pale, and which were now so rosy. And then she began to laugh, with all the foolish gaiety of a young girl, scoffing at herself; she could not believe how happy she was. This, this was the tutor she had imagined as a dry, badly dressed priest, snarling and beating her children!

"Really, my dear sir?" she finally said. "You really know Latin?"

Being addressed as "sir" so astonished Julien that, for an instant, he hesitated.

"Yes, madame," he answered shyly.

Madame de Rênal was so overjoyed that she actually dared to ask him:

"You won't snarl too much at my poor children?"

"Me, snarl at them?" Julien said, astonished. "Why?"

"Indeed, sir," she added, after a small silence and in a voice more and more emotional, "you'll be good to them, you promise me?"

Hearing himself again spoken to as "sir," and perfectly seriously, and by a lady so elegantly dressed, went beyond any of Julien's expectations: even in the castles in Spain he'd built as a child, he'd never contemplated that any lady of fashion would condescend to speak to him at all, until he was wearing a handsome uniform. For her part,

Madame de Rênal was utterly beguiled by his fine complexion, his great black eyes, and his lovely hair, which was curlier than most men's—since, to freshen up, he'd just plunged his head into the waters of the public fountain. To her deep pleasure, she'd seen the shy demeanor of a young girl in this fateful tutor, though on her children's account she'd dreaded his harsh surliness. For so quiet and peaceful a soul as Madame de Rênal, the contrast between her fears and the reality she saw in front of her was a great event.

She finally recovered from her surprise. She was amazed to find herself standing at the door to her own house, so close to a young man virtually in his shirtsleeves.

"Shall we go in, sir," she said with a patently embarrassed air.

In all her life, no purely pleasant emotion had ever so deeply moved Madame de Rênal; never had an apparition so charmingly superseded her worst, most troubling fears. So: Her pretty children, of whom she'd taken such loving care, were not to fall into the hands of a peevish, dried-up priest. They had barely walked into the hall when she turned toward Julien, who was timidly following along. The wonderment in his face, seeing so fine a house, was to her yet another charming trait. She could not believe her eyes, especially since she'd thought a tutor had to be wearing black.

"But, sir," she said to him, stopping once again, powerfully afraid—because she had been made so happy—of being deceived, "is it really true that you know Latin?"

Julien's pride was aroused by these words that demolished the fairy-tale world in which, for a quarter of an hour, he had been living.

"Yes, madame," he said, trying to take on a distant, chilly tone. "I know Latin quite as well as our parish priest, and sometimes he even says I know it better than he does."

Madame de Rênal realized that Julien, who had stopped barely two steps behind her, was speaking quite cuttingly. She came closer to him and said, in a hushed voice:

"But really, these first days you won't whip my children, will you, even when they don't know their lessons?"

So sweet, even so suppliant a voice, coming from such a beautiful lady, made Julien instantly unable to think of what he was owed, arriving in this house with such a splendid reputation as a Latinist. Madame de Rênal's face was close to his, he breathed in the perfume of a woman's summer clothing, an amazing sensation for a poor peasant. He grew very red and said, with a sigh and a weak voice:

"Have no fear, madame, I will obey you in everything."

This was the precise moment when Madame de Rênal, her concern for her children completely dissipated, felt herself struck by Julien's unusual beauty. His almost feminine features, and his embarrassment, did not seem in any way ridiculous to a woman herself so extraordinarily shy. The masculine ways people thought necessary, for a man to be handsome, made her afraid.

"How old are you, sir?" she said to Julien.

"I'm about to be nineteen."

"My oldest son is eleven," Madame de Rênal went on, completely reassured. "He'll be almost a comrade for you; you can reason with him. His father started to beat him, once, and the child was ill for an entire week, but it was only a very tiny blow."

"How different from me," thought Julien. "Just yesterday, my father was beating me. How happy these rich people are!"

Madame Rênal had already become aware of the slightest nuances the tutor was feeling deep in his soul; she took this swell of sadness for shyness, and wanted to encourage him.

"What is your name, sir?" she asked, with a lilt and a graciousness that utterly charmed Julien, though he could not have said why.

"I'm Julien Sorel, madame. I tremble, coming to a strange house for the first time in my life: I need your protection and for you to pardon me for all sorts of things, in my first days here. I've never gone to school, I'm too poor; the only men I've ever spoken to are my cousin, a surgeon-major and a member of the Legion of Honor, and our parish priest. He'll tell you good things about me. My brothers have always beaten me, so don't believe a word they say, if they tell you bad things. Pardon my faults, madame: they will always be unintentional."

Julien was studying Madame de Rênal as he delivered this long speech, and he felt a good deal more comfortable. This is always the effect of perfect graciousness when it springs from natural roots, and above all when the person displaying it never dreams of doing so.

Julien, who was an excellent judge of female beauty, would at that moment have sworn that she could not be more than twenty. He suddenly, then and there, had the rash notion of kissing her hand. He was immediately afraid of his own idea. A moment later he said to himself: "It would be sheer cowardice not to do something that might prove distinctly useful to me—and would lessen the disdain this beautiful lady probably feels for a poor workman only just now freed from his saw." Perhaps Julien was encouraged by the words *handsome boy,* which for six months he'd been hearing, every Sunday, from young girls. As he was silently debating with himself, Madame de Rênal made a few instructive comments on how to begin his work with the children. The violence of his inner struggle once again turned him exceedingly pale. Speaking stiffly, he said:

"Never, madame—I'll never beat your children, I swear to God I won't."

And as he spoke, he boldly took her hand and carried it to his lips. She was astonished by the gesture and, as she thought about it, shocked. Since the weather was very warm, under her shawl her arm was bare and, as Julien lifted her hand, the arm was completely uncovered. After a moment, she reproached herself for not having, with proper rapidity, registered her indignation.

Monsieur de Rênal, having heard them talking, came out of his study. With the same imposing, paternal air he put on when, as mayor, he solemnized marriages, he now addressed Julien:

"It will be important that I speak to you before the children see you."

Taking Julien into a room, he gestured to his wife—who had preferred to leave them to themselves—to come in, as well. The door once shut behind them, Monsieur de Rênal seated himself, most formally.

"The parish priest has informed me that you are dependable: everyone here will treat you honorably, and, if I am satisfied, when you come to leave us I will help you set up on your own. I prefer that you entertain no visits from either relatives or friends, their manners not being suitable for my children. Here, then, are thirty-six francs for the first month—but I require your word that not a cent will go to your father."

Monsieur de Rênal was annoyed at the old peasant, who in this business had been the sharper of the two.

"Now, *sir*—and I have ordered that everyone here will so address you, and you will become aware of the advantages of entering a household where everyone acts properly—now, sir, it's not right for the children to see you wearing a jacket. Have the servants seen him?" he asked his wife.

"No, my dear," she replied contemplatively.

"So much the better. Put this on," he said to the surprised young man, giving him a full-length frock coat. "Shall we pay a visit to Monsieur Durand, the tailor?"

More than an hour later, when Monsieur de Rênal returned with the new tutor dressed all in black, he found his wife sitting exactly where he had left her. She felt herself soothed, now, by Julien's presence; as she considered him, she forgot to be afraid. Julien did not think of her at all: in spite of his distrust for fate and men alike, at this moment his soul was nothing but a child's. He felt that it had been years since, three hours earlier, he had knelt in the church, trembling. He noted Madame de Rênal's distant air; he understood she was angry because he had dared kiss her hand. But the pride he felt, touching these new garments, so different from those he was used to wearing, threw him sharply out of equilibrium, and he tried so hard to hide his pleasure that everything he did became abrupt; he took on a distinctly foolish air. Madame de Rênal watched him, amazed.

"A certain sobriety, sir," Monsieur de Rênal told him, "if you wish to be respected by my children and by my domestics."

"Sir," replied Julien, "I am troubled, embarrassed, wearing these new clothes; a poor peasant like myself has never worn anything more than a jacket. With your permission, I'll close myself in my room."

"So," said Monsieur de Rênal to his wife, "what do you think of this new acquisition?"

By a process essentially instinctive, and of which she certainly had no conscious awareness, Madame de Rênal hid the truth from her husband.

"I'm hardly as enchanted with this little peasant as you are: your kindness will turn him into such an impertinent that, after a month, you'll have to send him away."

"So be it! We'll send him away, I'll lose the hundred francs he'll probably have cost me, and Verrières will have gotten used to seeing Monsieur de Rênal's children with a tutor. This could not have been accomplished had I left Julien in workman's clothing. If I send him away, of course, I'll keep the new black suit I've just ordered for him at the tailor's. All he'll keep will be the ready-made clothes I found at Monsieur Durand's shop, for which I've paid."

To Madame de Rênal, the hour Julien spent in his room seemed like so many seconds. The children, who had been told about their new tutor, overwhelmed their mother with questions. Finally, Julien appeared. It was a different person who returned to them. To say of this man that he was somber would be a misrepresentation: he was sobriety incarnate. He was introduced to the children, to whom he spoke in a manner that astonished even Monsieur de Rênal.

"I have come here, gentlemen," he told them as his finished his introductory comments, "for the purpose of teaching you Latin. You already know how to recite your lessons. Here is the Holy Bible," he explained, showing them a small, pocket-sized book, bound in black. "What you have, here, is the detailed story of Our Lord Jesus Christ; this is the part of the Bible known as the New Testament. I will often oblige you to recite your lessons: let me recite mine."

The oldest, Adolphe, had picked up the book.

"Open it at random," Julien went on, "and tell me the first word of the paragraph. Until you ask me to stop, I will recite from memory this holy book, our rule of conduct in everything."

Adolphe opened the book, read out a word, and Julien recited the entire page with the same facility he would have had in speaking French. Monsieur de Rênal gave his wife a triumphant look. Seeing their parents' astonishment, the children opened their eyes wide. A servant came to the door of the room; Julien continued to recite in Latin. The servant remained, at first motionless, and after a time left. Soon Madame de Rênal's chambermaid, and also another woman, the cook, came and hovered near the door. By then, Adolphe had opened the book in eight different places, and Julien went on reciting with unchanged ease.

"Ah, my God! What a handsome priest," said the cook, loudly; she was a thoroughly good girl and deeply devout.

Monsieur de Rênal's self-esteem was disquieted. He had absolutely no interest in examining the tutor, being totally concerned with rummaging about in his memory for Latin words. At last, he was able to recite a line from Horace. The only Latin Julien knew was the Bible. Knitting his eyebrows, he replied:

"The holy ministry for which I am meant will not permit me to read a poet so profane."

Monsieur de Rênal quoted quite a number of imaginary verses from Horace. He explained to his children just who Horace was, but the children, smitten with admiration, hardly heard a word he said. They kept watching Julien.

With the servants constantly coming and going at the door, Julien felt he ought to prolong his demonstration.

"Monsieur Stanislas-Xavier," he said to the youngest child. "You choose a passage from the holy book."

Little Stanislas, terribly proud, read out the first words of a paragraph—reading rather better than worse—and Julien recited the whole page. To complete Monsieur de Rênal's triumph, while Julien was intoning, Monsieur Valenod—he of the noble Normand horses—came in, along with Monsieur Charcot de Maugiron, deputy governor of the district. The episode earned Julien the title "sir": the servants themselves would not dare refuse it to him.

That evening, all of Verrières crowded into Monsieur de Rênal's house to glimpse the marvel. Julien spoke somberly to all of them, keeping them at a distance. His fame grew so rapidly, all through the town, that not many days later Monsieur de Rênal, fearing someone might steal him away, suggested he sign a contract for two years.

"No, sir," Julien replied coolly. "If you should want to send me away, I would be obliged to leave. A contract binding me, without exacting anything of you, does not seem fair, so I can't agree."

Julien handled things so well that, less than a month after he'd come to the house, he'd won the respect of Monsieur de Rênal himself. The parish priest having broken relations with both Monsieur de Rênal and Monsieur Valenod, nobody could betray Julien for his old Napoleonic passions. Whenever he spoke of Napoleon, he did so with horror.

CHAPTER SEVEN

ELECTIVE AFFINITIES

They can only touch the heart by breaking it.
—A CONTEMPORARY

The children adored him, he had no affection whatever for them; his mind was elsewhere. Nothing these urchins could ever do made him impatient. Cold, fair, impassive, and yet loved, because somehow his coming had banished boredom from the house: he was a good tutor. He felt only hatred and horror for the high society into which he had been admitted—at the foot of the table, to be sure, which might perhaps explain the hate and the horror. During some formal dinners he was barely able to contain his hate for everyone around him. Once in particular, on the Feast of Saint Louis, when Monsieur Valenod was monopolizing the conversation at Monsieur de Rênal's table, Julien came very close to betraying himself; he was saved only by hurrying out to the garden, pretending he had to look in on the children. "What panegyrics on probity!" he silently cried. "You'd think it was the one and only virtue of virtues—and even apart from that, such vulgar respect for a man who has obviously doubled and tripled his fortune, ever since he got to be in charge of the poor! I'd bet he even makes money on the fund for foundlings—those poor children whose misery is the most sacred of all! Ah! Monsters! Monsters! And me, I'm also a kind of foundling, detested by my father, by my brothers, by my entire family."

A few days before the Feast of Saint Louis, Julien had been all alone and saying his breviary prayers, walking in a small wood called the Belvedere, which overlooked the Loyalty Walkway. He'd been trying unsuccessfully to avoid his two brothers: he had seen them from a distance, approaching along a deserted path. The jealousy of these huge workmen was so excited by his fine black clothes and eminently proper appearance, and by their brother's open contempt for them, that they'd beaten him until he was unconscious and lying prone, bloodied all over. Madame de Rênal, walking in the wood with Monsieur Valenod and the deputy governor of the district, stumbled on him, quite by accident; she saw Julien motionless on the ground and thought him dead. Her shock was so intense that it aroused Monsieur Valenod's jealousy.

His alarm, however, had sounded entirely too soon. Julien found Madame de Rênal wonderfully beautiful, but because of her beauty he hated her: that loveliness was the first reef on which his fortune had almost foundered. He spoke to her as little as possible, to wipe out the memory of that ecstatic rapture which, on his first day, had led him to kiss her hand.

Elisa, Madame de Rênal's chambermaid, had had no trouble falling in love with the young tutor; she spoke of him, often, to her mistress. Miss Elisa's love had earned Julien the hatred of one of the menservants. One day, Julien overheard this man saying to Elisa: "You don't want to talk to me anymore, since this filthy tutor's come to the house." Julien did not deserve this insult; nevertheless, with a handsome young fellow's instincts, he paid even more attention to his appearance. Monsieur Valenod's dislike grew in equal measure. He said publicly that so much coquetry was unsuitable for a young ecclesiastic. Aside from not wearing a cassock, this was indeed how Julien dressed.

Madame de Rênal noticed that he spoke more often than usual with Elisa, and learned that these conversations were caused by the extraordinary poverty of Julien's wardrobe. He had so little underclothing that he was regularly reduced to washing it, away from the house; for these petty attentions Elisa was useful to him. This utter poverty, which she had not suspected, moved Madame de Rênal; she wanted to give him gifts, but did not dare; and that inner conflict was the first painful feeling Julien caused her. To that point, Julien's name and a feeling of chaste, completely intellectual happiness had become synonymous in her mind. Tormented by the idea of his poverty, Madame de Rênal asked her husband to give him a gift of underclothes.

"What foolishness!" he replied. "How now! Give gifts to a man with whom we are perfectly satisfied, and who is serving us very well? That would make sense only if he were negligent and we needed to stimulate his zeal."

This kind of perspective humiliated Madame de Rênal; she would never have so much as noticed it, before Julien's coming. Every time she saw the utter propriety of his clothing, which was also so extremely plain, she asked herself: "This poor boy, how can he possibly manage it?"

Little by little, instead of being shocked she felt pity for everything Julien lacked.

Madame de Rênal was one of those provincial women one might very well take for stupid, for the first fifteen days one knew her. She had no experience of life, and conversation held no interest for her. Endowed with a refined and haughty soul, the natural instinct toward happiness possessed by all creatures led her, most of the time, to pay no attention to what was done by the grosser folk in the middle of whom chance had thrown her.

She might have been distinguished for spontaneous vivacity, had she received any sort of decent education. But as an heiress, she had been raised in a convent by nuns who were passionate worshipers of the Sacred Heart of Jesus, and driven by violent hatred for French enemies of the Jesuits. Madame de Rênal had enough sense to quickly forget, as utter absurdity, everything she had learned at the convent, but she set nothing in its place and ended by knowing nothing. The flattery showered on her from an early age (as heiress to a large fortune), and a pronounced leaning toward impassioned devotion, helped shape her as someone who lived a life entirely interior. Given her perfect air of condescension, and a renunciation of self-will (which the husbands of Verrières held up to their wives, as an example, and which made Monsieur de Rênal swell with pride), she lived her life as loftily as she possibly could. A great princess, famous for her pride, devotes infinitely closer attention to what the gentlemen around her are up to than this provincial woman, so sweet, always so visibly modest, but paying absolutely no attention to whatever her husband might say or do. Until Julien's arrival, indeed, she had not truly paid attention to anyone or anything except her children. Their little hurts and ills, their sorrows, their little pleasures, filled to the brim the emotional existence of a soul which, in all her life, had adored only God—though that was when she was still at Sacred Heart, in Besançon.

Although she would not admit it, not to anyone, when one of her sons had a fever she was reduced to the same state as if he had died. In the first years of their marriage, confidences about these kinds of fears and sorrow, forced out of her by immense need, had been met by her husband with a bout of coarse laughter, a shrug, and some platitude about the foolishness of women. Such displays of wit, especially when the health of their children was at issue, twisted a dagger into her heart. This was what she had gotten, in exchange for the eager, honey-sweet flattery she'd known, as a girl in the Jesuitic convent. Her education had been shaped by sadness. Too proud to speak of these afflictions, even to her friend, Madame Derville, she fancied that all men were like her husband, and Monsieur Valenod, and the deputy governor, Charcot de Maugiron. Coarseness and the most brutal insensitivity to everything not connected with money or the power of being decorated with medals; blind hatred for every argument opposing their views—these seemed to her natural attributes of the male sex, exactly like wearing boots or felt hats.

Long years later, Madame de Rênal had still not gotten used to these men of money, among whom she was obliged to live.

All of which explains what went on with the little peasant, Julien. She discovered sweet pleasures and all the glowing charms of novelty in the affectionate ways of this noble, fierce soul. Madame de Rênal often had to excuse his extraordinary ignorance, which was yet another charm, as well as the coarseness of his manners, which she tried to correct. She learned that he took the trouble to listen to her, even when they spoke of the most ordinary things, like a poor dog run over, as it was crossing the street, by a peasant's cart going quite fast. Seeing such small tragedies made her husband laugh his grossest laugh, whereas she could see the furrowing of Julien's handsome, beautifully arched black eyebrows. Generosity, nobility of soul, humanity, little by little appeared to her to exist nowhere but in this young ecclesiastic. It was only for him that she felt the sympathy, even the admiration, that virtue arouses in well-born souls.

In Paris, Julien's position vis-à-vis Madame de Rênal would have been quickly resolved, but in Paris love is born out of the pages of romantic fiction. The young tutor and his shy mistress could have found enlightenment for themselves in three or four of these novels, and even in high school poetry. The novels would have outlined what roles to play, giving them models to imitate, and sooner or later, perhaps without much pleasure, and even sullenly, vanity would have compelled Julien to play out the game.

In small towns off the Mediterranean coast, or in the Pyrenees, the very slightest of occasions would have turned decisive, given the climate's burning intensity. Under our quieter, darker skies, an ambitious but poor young man, moved to ambition only by the refinement of his heart, which obliges him to seek some of the pleasures money can supply, can go on spending every day with a deeply prudent woman of thirty, busy with her children, without finding any of the guides to behavior provided by romantic fiction. Things go very slowly, in the provinces; everything happens naturally, bit by bit.

Frequently, while daydreaming about the young tutor's poverty, Madame de Rênal would find herself moved to the point of tears. Julien came upon her, one day, just as she suddenly burst out weeping.

"Eh, madame! Something unpleasant must have happened to you!"

"No, no, my dear," she answered. "Call the children and we'll take them for a walk."

She took his arm and leaned against him, in a way that seemed to him strange. It was the first time she had ever spoken to him as "my dear."

As they neared the end of the walkway, Julien observed that she was noticeably blushing. She slowed her steps.

"You'll have heard," she said, not looking at him, "that I'm the sole heiress of a very rich aunt who lives in Besançon. She's always giving me presents. . . . My sons are improving . . . quite astonishingly . . . so I'd like you to accept a small present as a mark of my gratitude. It's just a few francs so you can take care of your clothing needs. But . . ." she continued, blushing even more, and then saying nothing else.

"But what, madame?" said Julien.

"It would not be useful," she went on, her glance turned down, "to mention this to my husband."

"I am humble, madame, but I am not base," replied Julien, looking at her, his eyes bright with anger. He drew himself up to his full height. "This is something you have not sufficiently considered. I would be less than a manservant if I involved myself in concealing from Monsieur de Rênal anything whatever concerning *my wages.*"

Madame de Rênal was thunderstruck.

"His Honor the Mayor," continued Julien, "has five times paid me thirty-six francs, in the time I have been in his house. I am ready to show my record of expenses to Monsieur de Rênal and to anyone else, even Monsieur Valenod, who hates me."

After this outburst, Madame de Rênal was left pale and trembling; their walk ended without either of them able to find an excuse for renewing the conversation. To love Madame de Rênal became more and more an impossibility, in Julien's proud heart; for her part, she respected him, she admired him, she had been scolded by him. Giving herself the excuse that she could make up for the humiliation unwittingly caused him, she let herself offer him the tenderest of attentions. For an entire week, the novelty of such things was sheer happiness for Madame de Rênal. And to some degree, they quieted Julien's anger; he had not the slightest notion that there might be anything remotely resembling personal feeling in all this.

"So there," he told himself, "this is what these rich people are like. First they humiliate you, then they think they can make it all up to you by monkey business!"

Madame de Rênal's heart was too full, and as yet too innocent, for her not to inform her husband of the offer she'd made to Julien, despite all her resolutions to the contrary; she told him exactly how it had been declined.

"What?" replied Monsieur de Rênal, distinctly annoyed. "How could you tolerate such a refusal from a *servant?*"

And when Madame de Rênal protested against the use of that word:

"I speak, madame, as did the late Prince de Condé, in presenting his chamberlains to his newly married wife: 'All these people,' he said to her, 'are our servants.' I have read you the passage in Besenval's memoirs, so indispensable for the understanding of social precedence.

Anyone not a gentleman, living in your house and receiving a salary, is your servant. I'll have a few words with Monsieur Julien, and I'll give him a hundred francs."

"Ah! my dear," said Madame de Renal shakily, "at least let it not be in front of the servants!"

"Indeed, they might be jealous, and with reason," said her husband as he left her, thinking about tax aspects of the sum he had mentioned.

Madame de Rênal dropped into a chair, almost fainting with sorrow. "He's going to humiliate Julien, and it will be my fault!" She covered her face with her hands, horror-struck by her husband. She promised herself never to take him into her confidence again.

When next she saw Julien, she was trembling all over; her chest was so constricted, she could not manage to say a word. In her embarrassment, she caught hold of his hands and squeezed them.

"Well, my dear!" she finally said. "Are you happy with my husband?"

"How could I not be?" answered Julien with an ironical smile. "He gave me a hundred francs."

Madame de Rênal looked at him, doubtful.

"Give me your arm," she said at last, more forcefully than Julien was used to hearing her speak.

For all the frightfully liberal reputation of the store's proprietor, she was courageous enough to walk, with Julien and her children, right into the bookstore in Verrières. There, she picked out, for two hundred and fifty francs, volumes which she gave to her sons. But these were books she knew Julien had been wanting. She required that, right there in the shop, the children inscribe their names in the volumes given them. Although Madame de Rênal was happy with the kind of amends she'd been able to make to Julien, he was astonished by the quantity of books he saw. He had never dared go into a place so profane; his heart beat wildly. Far from having any notion of what Madame de Rênal was feeling, he longed for a way that would allow him, as a young theology student, to obtain some of these books.

And then he thought, if he did it skillfully, he might be able to persuade Monsieur de Rênal that he ought to set his sons, as a subject for the writing of themes, the lives of celebrated gentlemen born in the province. After a month of careful preparation, Julien worked out the idea, and to such a point that he risked raising, while speaking to Monsieur de Rênal, a matter which might well have been, in different circumstances, distressing to the noble mayor—namely, the notion of contributing to a liberal's fortune by taking out a subscription at the bookstore. Monsieur de Rênal certainly agreed that it would be sensible to give his oldest son a *visual* impression of books he might hear mentioned in conversation, once he was attending military school. But Julien saw that His Honor the Mayor had dug in his heels and would go no further. Julien suspected some hidden reason, but could not imagine what it might be.

"I've been thinking, sir," he said to his employer one day, "that it really would be very unseemly to have an upright gentlemanly name like Rênal appear on the dirty accounts of this bookstore."

Monsieur de Rênal's forehead cleared.

"It would be almost as bad," continued Julien, his voice wonderfully humble, "for a poor theology student, should someone discover, one day, that his name had been on the accounts of a bookstore that rented out volumes. Liberals could accuse me of having requested the most infamous of writings. Who knows, they might even go so far as to write after my name the titles of these perverse books."

But Julien let it go at that. He could see the mayor's face taking on, once again, an expression of embarrassment and irritation. Julien stayed silent. "I've hooked my fish," he said to himself.

Some days later, the oldest of the boys asked Julien, in their father's presence, about a book he'd noticed in the monarchist newspaper, *The Legitimist.*

"In order to avoid such subjects as the triumph of the Jacobin party," said the young tutor, "while in the meantime giving me information needed to reply to Monsieur Adolphe, perhaps we could have the very least of your people take out a bookstore subscription."

"Not a bad idea," said Monsieur de Rênal, obviously very pleased.

"However, it would be necessary to specify," said Julien, with a certain somber and almost miserable air that works so well with certain people, when they witness the success of some long-desired business, "it would be necessary to specify that the servant is forbidden to borrow any novel whatever. Once in the house, these dangerous volumes might corrupt madame's maids, and the servant himself."

"Don't forget political pamphlets," added Monsieur de Rênal loftily. He would have liked to conceal the admiration he himself felt for this middle way, concocted by the tutor of his children.

Julien's life was thus composed of a series of petty negotiations, and their success concerned him far more than the signs of special affection he could have read in Madame de Rênal's heart, if only he had bothered.

The moral position he had occupied all through his life was renewed, in his post with His Honor the Mayor of Verrières. Just as in his father's sawmill, he had the most profound contempt for the people he lived among, and hated them. Every day he witnessed tales told by the deputy governor, by Monsieur Valenod, or by other friends of the house, relating events they had just seen, and realized how little their ideas resembled reality. Things that to him seemed admirable were precisely those censured by the people around him. His silent response was always: "What monsters, what fools!" He was glad, and proud, that often he understood nothing they were talking about.

In his entire life, the only person to whom he had ever spoken honestly was the old surgeon-major, whose limited stock of ideas concerned either Bonaparte's campaigns in Italy, or surgery. Julien's youthful fortitude delighted in reciting the old man's most painful surgeries, assuring himself: "I've never blinked."

The first time Madame de Rênal tried having a conversation with him, having nothing to do with the children's education, he began to talk about surgical procedures; she turned pale and asked him to stop.

Julien knew nothing about anything else. Accordingly, living in the same house as Madame de Rênal, the most peculiar silence developed when they were alone together. In the drawing room, no matter with what humility he behaved, she saw in his eyes how intellectually superior he felt to everything he encountered in her house. If she found herself alone with him, even for an instant, it was not hard to see how embarrassed he became. This troubled her, because her woman's instinct told her that there was no tenderness in this embarrassment.

Based on some idea or other, formed by a tale of high society narrated by the old surgeon-major, as soon as Julien was anywhere with a woman, and no one was speaking, he felt himself humiliated, exactly as if the silence was his fault. This feeling was a hundred times more painful when they were alone. His imagination sprouted the wildest Spanish-style notions as to what a man ought to say, finding himself alone with a woman: all the ideas presented him by his troubled mind were utterly impossible. No matter that his soul soared in the clouds, he was unable to break the humiliating silence. And so his severe bearing, on the long walks he took with Madame de Rênal and her children, was intensified by the cruelest kind of inner suffering. He found himself disgusting. If some ill luck forced him to speak, he managed to say the most ridiculous things. Worse yet, he saw how absurdly he was behaving, and then exaggerated it still further, but what he did not see was the expression in her eyes, so lovely and revealing so ardent a heart that, just as a good actor does, it gave meaning to words that had no meaning. She noticed how, alone with her, he never said anything worth saying except when, distracted by something unforeseen, he wasn't trying to turn a well-phrased compliment. Since the friends of the house did not spoil her with new and brilliant ideas, she found Julien's flashes of insight thoroughly delightful.

Ever since Napoleon's fall, provincial manners rigidly suppress anything that smacked of gallantry. People are afraid of being dismissed from office. Rogues turn to the Congregation of the Holy Virgin for support, and hypocrisy has made excellent progress, even among the liberal classes. Boredom grows and grows. The only pleasures left are reading and farming.

At sixteen, Madame de Rênal, rich heiress of a devoted aunt, was married to a well-bred gentleman, having neither experienced nor witnessed, at any time in her life, anything that resembled in the slightest the world of love. Her confessor, the good parish priest, Father Chélan, had barely mentioned love to her, and then only in connection with Monsieur Valenod's attempts, and had created in her mind a picture so disgusting that the very word had come to represent nothing but the most wretched debauchery. What she saw in the very small number of novels chance had placed in front of her eyes seemed purely exceptional, even completely unnatural. Thanks to this state of ignorance, Madame de Rênal was able, perfectly happily, to think constantly about Julien and yet remain quite remote from anything worthy of even the slightest censure.

CHAPTER EIGHT

MINOR OCCASIONS

Then there were sighs, the deeper for suppression,
And stolen glances, sweeter for the theft,
And burning blushes, though for no transgression.
—BYRON, *DON JUAN*, CANTO I, STANZA 74

The angelic sweetness that came from Madame de Rênal's very nature, and from her genuine goodness, was not in the least affected when she thought about her chambermaid, Elisa. Coming into some money, the girl admitted to her confessor, the parish priest, that she hoped to marry Julien. Monsieur Chélan was delighted by his young friend's good fortune, but was extremely startled when Julien told him, most determinedly, that Mademoiselle Elisa's offer did not suit him.

"Be careful, my son, of what's happening in your heart," said the old priest, knitting his brows. "I congratulate you on your religious vocation, if it is that and that alone to which you owe this contempt for a more-than-sufficient fortune. Fifty-six years have rolled since I came to officiate in Verrières, but so far as I can see, I am going to be deprived of my parish. This grieves me, even though I have an income of eight hundred francs a year. I want to share these details with you, so you have no illusions as to what awaits you as a priest. If you dream of paying court to men of power, your eternal damnation is guaranteed. You could make a fortune, but you'd have to tread on the poor, flatter the deputy governor of the district, and the mayor, and all other men of substance, and assist them in their passions. For a layman, such conduct, which the world calls knowing how to live, is not incompatible with salvation. But with the likes of us, a choice has to be made: it's a question of making your fortune in this world, or in the next. There's no middle ground. Go now, my dear friend; consider; and come back in three days to tell me what you've decided. I have a troubled glimpse, deep down, of a dark ambition which does not speak to me of the temperance, the perfect surrender of worldly advantages, which a priest must have. I see good things in your spirit—but permit me to tell you," added the good old man, tears in his eyes, "for you as a priest, ah, I tremble for your salvation."

Julien was embarrassed by his own emotions: for the first time in his life, he felt himself loved, and he wept with delight as he went away, hiding his tears under the great trees high above Verrières.

"Why am I in this state?" he finally asked himself. "I know I'd give my life, and a hundred times over, for this good Father Chélan, even if he's just proved to me that I'm nothing but a fool. He above all is the person I need to deceive, and he sees right through me. The secret ambition he senses is my plan to make my fortune. He doesn't think I'm worthy of becoming a priest—and that at the very moment when sacrificing an income of a thousand francs ought to have given him the highest opinion of my piety and my vocation.

"From now on," Julien continued, "I'll only depend on tested aspects of my character. Who could have known that I'd be glad to shed tears! That I'd love the person who proves me nothing but a fool!"

Three days later, Julien invented the excuse he should have found the very first day: it was slanderous, but what did that matter? He swore to the old priest, with much pretense of hesitation, that there was something he could not explain, because it would be damaging to a third party, which had from the first dissuaded him from agreeing to the marriage. It was as good as an accusation against Elisa. Monsieur Chélan felt a certain worldly warmth underlying his behavior—not what ought to be inspiring a prospective priest.

"My friend," he told Julien once again, "become a good rural bourgeois, worthy and well educated, rather than a priest without a vocation."

Julien replied with new explanations, which were all well and good, but just words: he used the same phrases a fervent young seminarian might have employed, but the tone with which he spoke them, and the badly hidden light burning in his eyes, worried Father Chélan.

But there is no need to prophesy terrible things for Julien: he had nicely created language appropriate to a crafty, prudent hypocrite. At his age, this was hardly wickedness. And as for his speech, the gestures he relied on, he lived among country folk, he had never had the opportunity to watch the great models. Later, as soon as he'd been given the chance to mingle with these gentlemen, he would become equally polished in both gesture and word.

Madame de Rênal had been amazed when her chambermaid's newfound wealth did not make the girl happier. She saw her constantly going to the parish priest, and returning with tears in her eyes; finally, Elisa talked to her about her marriage.

Madame de Rênal thought she must be ill; a sort of fever kept her from sleeping. She felt truly alive only when she was watching either her chambermaid or Julien. She could think of nothing but them and the happiness they had found in the Rênal household. The wretchedness of Elisa's little house, where they'd have to exist on a thousand francs a year, she pictured to herself in ravishing colors. Julien might very well become a lawyer at Bray, a local office of the district government, in which case she'd sometimes see him.

Madame de Rênal believed most sincerely that she was going mad; she said so to her husband, and then, finally, she fell sick. That same evening, as her chambermaid was attending to her, she noticed the girl crying. At that moment she loathed Elisa and was rude to her; then she begged the girl's pardon. Elisa's tears fell still faster; if her mistress would give her permission, she said, she'd explain just why she was so miserably unhappy.

"Tell me," answered Madame de Rênal.

"Well then, madame, he's refused me. Nasty people told him terrible things about me, and he believes them."

"Who refused you?" said Madame de Rênal, barely able to breathe.

"And who else, madame, but Julien?" replied the chambermaid, sobbing. "Father Chélan couldn't make him change his mind, because Father doesn't think he ought to turn down a good girl just because she's been a chambermaid. After all, Monsieur Julien's father is nothing but a carpenter. How did he himself make his living before he came here with madame?"

Madame de Rênal heard nothing else the girl said; overflowing happiness very nearly cost her the power of thought. She told herself, several times, that Julien's refusal had been definitive, which fact would no longer permit of a more sensible decision.

"I'll make one last try," madame told the chambermaid; "I'll talk to Monsieur Julien."

The next day, after lunch, Madame de Rênal treated herself to the delightful pleasure of pleading her rival's cause, and for a solid hour seeing Elisa's hand, and her fortune, refused over and over again.

After a while, Julien's responses grew more formal, and he finished with a lively rebuttal of Madame de Rênal's eminently sensible suggestions. She could not suppress the torrent of happiness that overwhelmed her soul, after so many days of despair. Suddenly, she felt ill. When she'd been taken back to her room and put to bed, she sent everyone away. She felt a shock of the most profound order.

"Have I fallen in love with Julien?" she finally asked herself.

At any other time, this discovery would have plunged her into all manner of repentance and a profound agitation, but now it seemed to her no more than a bizarre display, but of no particular significance. Her soul, exhausted by all she'd been going through, had no spark of sensitivity to enlist in passion's cause.

Madame de Rênal wished to attend to her responsibilities, but fell into a very deep sleep; awaking, she was not as worried as she ought to have been. She was far too happy to feel concern about anything. Innocent and naïve, this good provincial woman had never tortured her soul, trying to tease some new shade of feeling, or of misfortune, out of any sensory moment. Before Julien's coming, she had been entirely absorbed in that massive heap of things-to-be-done that, outside of Paris, is the fate of a good mother: Madame de Rênal was used to thinking of the passions as we think of the lottery—guaranteed deception and a happiness sought only by fools.

The bell sounded for dinner; hearing Julien's voice, as he led in the children, Madame de Rênal blushed. Made more skillful by love, she explained her reddened face by a frightful headache.

"Like all women!" Monsieur de Rênal answered her, laughing uproariously. "There's always something in need of repair, in those machines!"

No matter how accustomed she was to this sort of nasty joking, his tone of voice shocked her. To distract herself, she looked over at

Julien's face: he could have been the very picture of ugliness, and at that moment he would have delighted her.

Quick to copy the ways of court gentlemen, at the coming of the first fine days of spring Monsieur de Rênal transferred his family to Vergy, the village made famous by the tragic old love story of Gabrielle. A few hundred steps from the wonderfully picturesque ruins of an ancient Gothic church, Monsieur de Rênal owned an old château, with four towers and a garden made to look like that of the Tuileries; it had thick boxwood borders and alleys lined with chestnut trees, trimmed twice a year. An adjoining field, planted with apple trees, provided an excellent place for civilized strolling. Eight or ten magnificent walnut trees grew at one end of the orchard, their immense branches rising perhaps eighty feet in the air.

"Each of those damned walnut trees," declared Monsieur de Rênal when his wife admired them, "costs me the harvest of half an acre: grain can't grow in their shade."

The view of the countryside seemed fresh and new to Madame de Rênal; her pleasure came very close to ecstasy. She drew courage and determination from the feelings it inspired in her. Two days after their arrival in Vergy, Monsieur de Rênal having gone back to the city on official mayoral business, Madame Rênal hired workmen—at her own expense. Julien had given her the idea of a little graveled walkway, encircling the orchard and running under the shade of the great walnut trees: this would allow the children to take morning walks without the dew wetting their shoes. The idea was carried to completion less than twenty-four hours after its conception. Madame de Rênal happily passed the entire day, together with Julien, giving orders to the workmen.

When the mayor of Verrières returned from the city, he was distinctly surprised, seeing this walkway in place. His arrival surprised Madame de Rênal, too: she had forgotten his existence. For the next two months he amused himself, remarking on the boldness with which, quite without his having been consulted, so important a *repair* had been accomplished. On the other hand, Madame de Rênal had paid the whole cost, out of her own funds, and this made him feel a bit better.

She spent her days running in the orchard with the children, and hunting butterflies. They made oversized nets of clear muslin, with which they captured the poor *Lepidoptera,* this being the barbarous name Julien had taught Madame de Rênal. For she had ordered, from Besançon, Monsieur Godart's handsomely illustrated volume, and Julien read her the fascinating accounts of these poor little beasts.

With no compassion whatever, using pins, they stuck the trophies of their hunt onto a big cardboard box; this too had been set up by Julien.

At last, there was something for Madame de Rênal and Julien to talk about: he was no longer exposed to the ghastly torture inflicted by moments of silence.

Indeed, they talked to each other constantly, with profoundly keen pleasure, though always about completely innocent matters. This active life, busy and cheerful, pleased everyone except Miss Elisa, who found herself overloaded with work. "Not even in carnival season," she said, "when there's a ball at Verrières, has madame ever paid so much attention to her wardrobe. She changes her clothes two or three times a day."

Since it is our intention to flatter no one, we will not deny that Madame de Rênal, who possessed superb skin, had her dresses made so that they left her arms, as well as her breasts, quite open to view. She had a fine figure, and this way of showing it off was wonderfully becoming.

"You've never been *so youthful,* madame," her friends from Verrières told her when they dined at Vergy. (This is of course the way they talk, out in the countryside.)

An unusual fact, which I know will seem quite incredible among us, is that Madame de Rênal paid so much attention to her wardrobe without the slightest conscious purpose. It pleased her and, without thinking of anything more, whenever she wasn't with the children and Julien, chasing butterflies, she was helping Elisa make her mistress's dresses. The only errands that took her to Verrières were the necessity of buying the new Mulhouse summer dresses, which were just ready.

She brought to Vergy a young woman, a relation. Since her marriage, Madame de Rênal had gradually become quite close to Madame Derville, who in earlier days had been with her at Sacred Heart.

Madame Derville used to laugh heartily at what she called her cousin's crazy ideas. "All by myself," she used to say, "I'd never have thought of such things." These unexpected notions, which in Paris would have been called flashes of wit, made Madame de Rênal feel embarrassed, when she was with her husband; but Madame Derville's presence gave her courage. She spoke her thoughts, at first, in a timid voice, but when the ladies were alone for any length of time, Madame de Rênal's spirits rose, and a long day to themselves went by like an instant, leaving the two friends wonderfully merry. When she came, this time, Madame Derville found her cousin much less merry but a great deal happier.

For his part, ever since beginning their stay in the country Julien had lived like a genuine child, as happy chasing butterflies as were the children he taught. After living under so many constraints, with so much subtle maneuvering, being alone and away from other people's eyes and, instinctively, no longer afraid of Madame de Rênal, he gave himself up to the pleasures of existence, so very lively at his age, and there in the middle of the most beautiful mountains in the world.

The moment Madame Derville came, Julien took her for his friend. He hastened to show her the view at the end of the new walkway, under the giant walnut trees, for in fact it was the equal, or even superior to, the most striking view to be seen in Switzerland and the Italian lakes. If you climb the steep ascent, starting only a few steps farther on, you'll soon get to great cliffs, bordered by a forest of oaks growing almost down to the river. It was at the heights of these almost perpendicular boulders that Julien, happy, free, and even more than happy and free, felt himself the king of the household, escorting his two friends and rejoicing in their appreciation for such sublime sights.

"For me," said Madame Derville, "it's like Mozart's music."

His brothers' envy, the presence of a despotic father bursting with bad temper, had spoiled the countryside around Verrières for him. He had no bitter memories in Vergy; for the first time in his life there were no enemies anywhere in sight. When Monsieur de Rênal was in the city, as he often was, Julien was not afraid to read. Soon, instead of reading only at night and being careful, still, to hide his lamp under an inverted flower vase, he was able to let himself sleep; during the day, in the intervals between the children's lessons, he brought a book to these great rocks, which were the sole supervisor of his behavior and the object of his immense delight. He found there, all combined, happiness, ecstasy and, in moments of discouragement, consolation.

Certain things said about women, by Napoleon, several discussions of the value, under his reign, of fashionable novels, gave Julien, for the first time, ideas that any other young man of his age would have had a long time before.

Summer heat arrived. They got into the habit of spending their evenings under a huge lime tree, a few steps from the house. The darkness, there, was profound. Julien spoke brilliantly, one night, relishing the delights of speaking well, and to young women; while gesturing, he happened to touch Madame de Rênal's hand, which was lying on the back of one of the painted wooden chairs they had brought to the gardens.

The hand was withdrawn, and quickly, but to Julien it seemed his *duty* to arrange matters so that this hand would not be drawn back when he touched it. This notion of a duty which he was required to accomplish, and a sense of being ridiculed, or more likely made to feel inferior if he could not accomplish what he wanted to, instantly drove all pleasure from his heart.

CHAPTER NINE

An Evening in the Country

Monsieur Guérin's painting of Dido, an exquisite sketch.
—Strombeck

The next day, when he again saw Madame de Rênal, he looked at her very strangely, seeing her as an enemy with whom he was required to do battle. This look, so different from the night before, made Madame de Rênal's self-possession waver: she had been good to him and he was apparently angry at her. She could not look away.

Madame Derville's presence allowed Julien to speak less and spend more time alone with his thoughts. His only occupation, the whole day, was to strengthen himself by reading his inspired book, which made him more determined.

He cut the children's lessons short, and then, when Madame de Rênal's presence suddenly forced him, once again, to thoughts of conquest, he resolved that, come what may, tonight she was going to let her hand remain in his.

The setting sun, and the decisive moment coming nearer, made Julien's heart beat in the most remarkable fashion. Night fell. He saw, with a joy that lifted an immense weight from his heart, that it was going to be exceedingly dark. Heavy clouds filled the sky, blown by a hot, sticky wind: a storm seemed to be coming. The two women walked and walked, and it grew late. Everything they did on this night struck Julien as bizarre. They toyed with time: for certain sensitive souls, this appears to magnify the pleasures of love.

They sat down, finally, Madame de Rênal next to Julien, and Madame Derville beside her friend. Caught up in what he was planning to attempt, Julien had nothing to say. Conversation faltered.

"Will I be trembling and miserable like this, when I face the first duel I have to fight?" Julien asked himself, having too much contempt both for himself and for others not to be aware of the state of his soul.

In this mortal anguish, any perils seemed to him preferable. He kept wishing that something would come up and Madame de Rênal would be compelled to go back into the house, and abandon the garden! So powerful was the violence he was forcing upon himself that, inevitably, his voice became profoundly different. Soon Madame de Rênal's voice began to tremble, too, but he was totally unaware: the frightful battle he had to wage against timidity was far too painful for him to notice anything outside himself.

After a final anxiously hesitating moment, during which flooding emotion seemed to set Julien somewhere out of his own body, ten o'clock sounded on the clock above his head. Each fatal stroke reverberated in his breast like some physical force.

At last, while the sound of the final stroke had still not died away, he put out his hand and grasped Madame de Rênal's, which was immediately withdrawn. Without knowing quite how he did it, Julien took her hand again. Although shaken inside, he looked down, with a glacially frozen glance, at the hand he had seized, pressing it with convulsive power. She made a last effort to pull it away, but in the end her hand stayed in his.

Happiness flooded across his heart: it was not that he loved Madame de Rênal, but the horrible torture was over. Madame Derville saw nothing, so he felt obliged to go on talking; his voice became bright and strong. Madame de Rênal's, on the other hand, shook with such emotion that her friend thought she was ill and suggested she return to the house. Julien sensed the danger: "If Madame de Rênal goes back to the drawing room, I'm going to tumble into the frightful position I've been in all day. I haven't held this hand captive long enough for the victory to count."

Just as Madame Derville was again proposing a return to the drawing room, Julien gave a hard squeeze to the hand that had surrendered to him.

Madame de Rênal, who was already starting to stand up, sat down once more and said, in a faint voice:

"I do really feel a bit ill, but the open air does me good."

Her words confirmed Julien's happiness, which right then was extraordinarily full: he talked, he forgot to forge and counterfeit; both listening ladies found him the most amiable of men. But still, in the midst of his eloquence, he felt a sudden sinking fear. He was mortally afraid that Madame Derville, tired of the wind, which in advance of the storm was growing stronger, might want to go back to the drawing room by herself. And then he would be left face-to-face with Madame de Rênal. Almost accidentally, he had had enough blind courage to do what he'd meant to do, but he felt it was utterly out of his power to say the simplest word to Madame de Rênal. No matter how gently she might reprove him, he was going to be beaten in battle, and the advantage he had just won would be annihilated.

That night, luckily for him, his forceful, affecting words found favor with Madame Derville, who quite often had thought him as boorish as a child, and not at all amusing. As for Madame de Rênal, with her hand in Julien's she did not think anything, she simply gave herself over to being alive. The hours spent under the great lime tree, which local legend said had been planted by Charles the Bold, were for her a veritable epoch of happiness. She listened with delight to the wind wailing in the tree's dense foliage, and the sound of occasional drops falling on leaves in the lower branches. Julien had not noticed something that might have reassured him: Madame de Rênal, obliged to withdraw her hand when she stood up, helping her cousin restore a flower vase the wind had blown over, right at their feet, had barely seated herself again when, almost without any objection, she gave him her hand once more, rather as if this were something they had already agreed upon.

Midnight had been tolled long before; it was finally necessary to leave the garden; they separated. Carried away by love's happiness, Madame de Rênal was so uneducated in love's ways that she said virtually nothing reproachful. Happiness kept her from sleeping. A leaden sleep seized Julien, mortally exhausted by the struggle in his heart, all day long, between shyness and pride.

He woke at five the next day, and it would have been painfully cruel for Madame de Rênal, had she known it, but he barely gave her a thought. He had done *his duty, performed a heroic act.* This made him exceedingly happy, and he proceeded to shut himself in his room, where he read about his heroes' exploits with a new pleasure.

By the time the bell for lunch sounded, he had forgotten, absorbed in the bulletins of Napoleon's Grand Army, all the gains of the night before. As he descended the stairs, he told himself, casually: "I have to tell this woman I love her."

Instead of loving looks, which he had expected to encounter, he met with the severe face of Monsieur de Rênal, who had arrived from Verrières at ten that morning, and was not hiding his displeasure, finding that Julien had spent the whole morning without paying any attention to the children. Nothing could be as ugly as this important man in a foul mood and thinking himself empowered to display it.

Her husband's every bitter word pierced Madame de Rênal's heart. As for Julien, for the last few hours he had been so deeply immersed in ecstasy, and was still so absorbed in the Great Things that had been passing in front of his eyes, that at first he could barely descend far enough down even to hear the harsh questions Monsieur de Rênal was asking him. He replied at last, rather crisply:

"I was ill."

The tone of this response would have annoyed a less vulnerable man than the mayor of Verrières; he thought about an instant reply, chastising Julien then and there. The only thing that stopped him was his rule that, in business, he should never hurry himself.

"This young fool," he said to himself after a moment, "has after a fashion earned himself a reputation, here in my house, and Valenod might take him into his, or else he might well marry Elisa, and in both cases, deep down in his heart, he might scoff at me."

Despite his prudent reflections, Monsieur de Rênal's dissatisfaction did not blaze any the less brightly in the stream of vulgar comments that followed; they gradually began to irritate Julien. Madame de Rênal was at the point of dissolving in tears. Lunch was barely over when she asked Julien to give her his arm for a walk, and she leaned on him, affectionately. But to everything she said, he was only able to reply, half muttering:

"That's what rich people are!"

Monsieur de Rênal was walking quite near them; his presence irritated Julien. He realized, suddenly, that Madame de Rênal was leaning on his arm in a markedly noticeable fashion; this filled him with horror, and he pushed her away, violently, and pulled back his arm.

Luckily, Monsieur de Rênal did not see this new rudeness, though it was observed by Madame Derville, who also saw her friend break down and weep. Just then, Monsieur de Rênal began to chase away, with a volley of stones, a small peasant girl who had chosen a forbidden path, cutting across a corner of the orchard.

"Monsieur Julien, please," Madame Derville said quickly. "Remember that we all have our moments of ill humor."

He looked at her coldly, his eyes showing a sovereign contempt.

This astonished Madame Derville, and she would have been even more surprised if she had understood that look's real meaning: she would then have seen there a still unformed longing for vengeance of the most atrocious order. Who could deny that such humiliating moments have given us the Robespierres of the world?

"Your Julien is remarkably violent; he frightens me," whispered Madame Derville to her friend.

"He's right to be angry," was the reply. "Given the amazing progress he's made with the children, what difference does it make if he spends a morning without speaking to them? You'll agree, surely, that men can be remarkably harsh."

For the first time in her life, Madame de Rênal felt something like a desire for vengeance on her husband. And Julien's profound hatred for the rich was rising to the surface. Luckily, Monsieur de Rênal called to his gardener and stayed busy, along with him, in closing off the orchard's forbidden path with pine branches. During the remainder of the walk, the ladies addressed a host of courteous observations to Julien; he responded to none of them. Monsieur de Rênal was barely out of sight when, on the pretext of fatigue, they each requested the support of his arm.

Placed between these two women, whose red, embarrassed cheeks plainly showed their high distress, Julien's somber, steady appearance formed a striking contrast. He was contemptuous of both women, and of all their tender sentiments.

"Lord!" he said to himself. "Not even five hundred francs a year to finish my studies! Ah, I'll tell him where to go!"

Completely caught up in these fierce ideas, the kindly words of the two ladies—what little of them he bothered to make out—annoyed him: they were senseless, foolish, weak-minded and, in a word, *feminine.*

Obliged to talk for the sake of talking, and to find some way to keep the conversation going, Madame de Rênal chanced to say that her husband had come back from Verrières because he'd contracted, with one of his farmers, for the purchase of corn straw. (In that region, corn straw is what mattresses are stuffed with.)

"So he won't be rejoining us," she added. "He and his valet, and the gardener, will be busy refurbishing all the mattresses in the house. This morning they've already done all the beds on the first floor, and they're moving on to the second."

Julien's face blanched. He looked at Madame de Rênal strangely, and began to walk faster, so he could be more or less alone with her. Madame Derville let them walk on ahead.

"Save my life," Julien told Madame de Rênal. "You're the only one who can do it: you know your husband's valet detests me. I confess, madame, that I have a picture, a portrait; it's hidden in my mattress."

At these words, Madame de Rênal too turned pale.

"Right now, madame, you're the only one who could walk into my room. If you don't see it, investigate the corner of the mattress closest to the window; you'll find a black cardboard box, small and smooth."

"And there's a picture inside!" said Madame de Rênal, barely able to stay on her feet.

Her dejection was obvious, and Julien immediately made use of it.

"I have a second favor to ask of you, madame. I beg you not to look at the picture: it's my secret."

"It's a secret," Madame de Rênal repeated, her words barely audible.

Still, no matter the well-born folk among whom she had been raised, people proud of their fortunes, their emotions roused only by money, love had already set a degree of generosity in her heart. Cruelly wounded as she was, Madame de Rênal asked Julien the necessary questions, speaking from pure devotion, and resolved to do for him exactly what he asked of her.

"So," she said, as she began to move toward the house, "a small round box, black cardboard, very smooth."

"Yes, madame," replied Julien with the stiff manner men often assume in times of danger.

She climbed to the château's second floor, as pale as if she were walking to her death. To add to her misery, she felt she was on the point of becoming ill, but having to be of service to Julien gave her strength.

"I've got to get that box," she said, walking still faster.

She heard her husband say something to his valet: they were right in Julien's room. Luckily, they went through it, into the children's quarters. She lifted the mattress and thrust her hand through the straw with such violence that she scratched her fingers. She was usually enormously sensitive to minor pain of this sort. But she was not even aware of what she had done, because just then she felt the smooth surface of the cardboard box. She took it and quickly walked off.

The moment she was no longer afraid of being surprised by her husband, the horror of this box made her very sure she was going to be ill.

"Julien is in love, and I've got his beloved's picture!"

Collapsing into a chair in the entryway, Madame de Rênal was seized by all the terrors of jealousy. However, her utter ignorance was of use to her at that moment, for astonishment balanced the scales against sorrow. Julien appeared, grabbed the box, not uttering a word of thanks, not saying anything, and ran into his room, where he made a fire and quickly burned the whole thing. He was pale, stupefied; he dramatized the dangers from which he had just escaped.

"A portrait of Napoleon," he said to himself, shaking his head. "Found hidden in the rooms of someone who spouts such hatred for that usurper! Found by Monsieur de Rênal, such a monarchist, and already so angry at me! And to make matters worse, the white cardboard behind the portrait shows some lines written in my handwriting! And from which no one could possibly doubt my admiration! And every one of these ecstatic declarations dated! There's even one from yesterday.

"My reputation completely destroyed, annihilated on the instant," he told himself, watching the box burn, "and my reputation is all I have, it's the only thing that can earn me a living . . . and yet, what a way of living, oh dear God!"

An hour later, his weariness, and the pity he felt for himself, led him to feelings of tenderness. He found Madame de Rênal and, taking her hand, kissed it with more sincerity than ever before. She blushed with happiness and, virtually instantaneously, repulsed him, angry with jealousy. Julien's pride, so recently wounded, turned him into a fool. All he could see in Madame de Rênal was a rich woman: he let her hand fall, disdainfully, and walked away. He went for a solitary, pensive walk in the garden; before too long, there was a bitter smile on his lips.

"Here I am, walking as calmly as if I were a man whose time was all his own! I'm not taking care of the children! I'm risking Monsieur de Rênal's humiliating scorn—and he'd be right." He ran directly to the children's room.

The caresses of the littlest one, to whom he was deeply attached, partially eased his burning grief.

"This one doesn't despise me anymore," Julien thought. But soon he reproached himself for this easing of his sadness, treating it like yet another weakness. "These children caress me the way they caress the little hunting dog they got yesterday."

CHAPTER TEN

A LARGE HEART AND A SMALL FORTUNE

But passion most dissembles, yet betrays,
Even by its darkness; as the blackest sky
Foretells the heaviest tempest . . .
—BYRON, *DON JUAN*, CANTO 1, STANZA 73

Monsieur de Rênal, after going through all the rooms in the house, came back to the children's room, together with the servants carrying the straw matting. His sudden entrance acted on Julien like the single drop of water that makes a vase overflow.

Paler and darker-looking than usual, he sprang toward his employer. Monsieur de Rênal stopped and gave a quick glance at his servants.

"Sir," Julien declared, "do you think that, with any other tutor, your children would have made progress equal to what they've enjoyed with me? If you answer no," said Julien, not giving Monsieur de Rênal a chance to speak, "how dare you reproach me for neglecting them?"

Monsieur de Rênal, not having quite conquered his fear, decided that the peculiar tone the little peasant was taking stemmed from some better offer, which he had in his pocket, and he was about to resign. Julien's anger grew as he spoke:

"I can live without you, sir," he went on.

"I'm truly grieved to see you so upset," replied Monsieur de Rênal, stuttering a bit. The servants were ten paces away, busily arranging the beds.

"That's not what I want to hear, sir," answered Julien, beside himself. "Think of the disgraceful words you spoke to me—and, mind you, in front of women!"

Monsieur de Rênal understood only too well what Julien was asking of him, and a painful struggle tore at his soul. And then Julien, essentially crazed with anger, shouted:

"I know where to go, sir, when I leave you."

At these words, Monsieur de Rênal saw Julien established at Monsieur Valenod's house.

"Ah well, sir," he said at last, with a sigh and the same demeanor as when he asked a surgeon not to make things more painful than strictly necessary, "you'll have what you want. Starting the day after tomorrow, which will be the first of the month, I'll give you fifty francs a month."

Julien felt like laughing; he stood where he was, stunned. His anger had vanished.

"I can't feel too much scorn for this beast," he told himself. "Surely, here's the most extravagant apology so vulgar a soul could possibly utter."

The children, who had been listening to this scene, openmouthed, ran down to the garden to tell their mother that Monsieur Julien had really been angry, but he was going to get fifty francs a month.

Strictly from habit, Julien followed after them, without a glance at Monsieur de Rênal; he left him deeply annoyed.

"That's a hundred and sixty-eight francs," the mayor told himself, "Monsieur Valenod has cost me. I've really got to say a couple of strong words to him, about his contract for supplying the foundlings."

The next minute, Julien came back into the room:

"I've got to make my confession to Father Chélan: I have the honor to inform you that I will be away for several hours."

"Eh, my dear Julien!" said Monsieur de Rênal, laughing terribly insincerely. "Take the whole day, if you like—the whole day tomorrow, my good friend. Take the gardener's horse, for traveling to Verrières."

"Off he goes," Monsieur de Rênal said to himself, "to give Valenod his answer. He hasn't made me any promises, but it's better to let this young man's head cool down a bit."

Julien escaped quickly, proceeding up the wide wood through which one went from Vergy to Verrières. He did not want to get to Father Chélan's house too early. Far from wanting to commit himself to a new hypocritical scene, he needed to be ready to see clearly into his soul, and to pay attention to the thronging feelings that were shaking it.

"I've won a battle," he said to himself as soon as he was well into the wood, where no one could see him. "I've really won a battle!"

These words nicely summed up his whole position, and gave his soul a modicum of peace and calm.

"So now I've got a salary of fifty francs a month: Monsieur de Rênal must have really been afraid of something. But of what?"

Thinking about what could have frightened this man, only an hour earlier so happily powerful in dealing with him that he fairly boiled with anger, helped clear Julien's soul. He became almost aware of the ravishing beauty of the wood through which he was walking. Some enormous chunks of bare rock had fallen down the mountainside, right into the middle of the forest. There were huge beeches, reaching almost to the height of these boulders, and their shade gave off a delightful freshness, barely three steps away from places where the sun's powerful rays would have made it impossible to pause.

Julien caught his breath, for a moment, in the shadow of these great rocks, then set himself to climbing once more. Soon, following a narrow path, plainly almost never used except by goatherds, he found himself standing on a huge boulder: without any question, now, he was separated from all other men. To be in this position, physically, made him smile, for it was exactly where he so desperately yearned to be, morally. The pure air of these high mountains breathed serenity and even joy into his soul. In his eyes, the mayor of Verrières had always represented all the rich and insolent men on earth. But despite the violence he had displayed, he felt that the hate which had so recently stirred him was in no way personal. If he could stop seeing Monsieur de Rênal, in a week he would have forgotten him—him, his château, his dogs, his children, and all his family. "I forced him, God alone knows how, to make the greatest of all sacrifices. Hah: more than fifty gold crowns a year! And yet, just a moment before I pulled back from the most awful jeopardy. So: two victories in a single day; there is no merit attached to the second one, which I still need to understand. Well, such a painful investigation can wait for tomorrow."

Standing on his huge rock, Julien looked out at the sky, lit by an August sun. Crickets sang in the field below; when they were quiet, he was surrounded by absolute silence. He could look over twenty leagues of countryside. From time to time he saw sparrow hawks launch themselves from the rocks over his head, and watched their noiseless circling. His eyes followed the birds of prey, mechanically. The hawks' quiet, powerful movements impressed him; he envied their strength; he envied their utter isolation.

That had been Napoleon's destiny. Would it be his, one day?

CHAPTER ELEVEN

AN EVENING

Yet Julia's very coldness still was kind,
   And tremulously gentle her small hand
Withdrew itself from his, but left behind
   A little pressure, thrilling, and so bland
And slight, so very slight that to the mind
   'Twas but a doubt.

BYRON, *DON JUAN*, CANTO 1, STANZA 71

Yet he had to show himself in Verrières. As he was leaving Father Chénal, it was Julien's good luck to meet Monsieur Valenod, to whom he quickly conveyed the good news of his increased salary.

Returning to Vergy, he didn't go into the garden until darkness had settled down. His soul was weary, after all the powerful emotions he had been experiencing that day. "What will I say to them?" he thought uncomfortably, wondering about the two ladies. He had no idea that his soul functioned precisely at the level of petty events, which usually so preoccupy women. Often, Julien made no sense to Madame Derville, and even to her friend, and he himself understood no more than half of what they said to him. This was due to the power and, if I may speak in those terms, the grandeur that had been turning this young, ambitious man's soul upside down. For this strange creature, almost every day was a stormy season.

Walking into the garden that evening, Julien was quite prepared to listen to the pretty cousins. They had been waiting impatiently for him. He took his usual place beside Madame de Rênal. The darkness had long since deepened. He'd wanted to take the white hand he'd been watching as it lay, near him, along the back of a chair. The hand had hesitated a bit, but in the end had been withdrawn, and in such a fashion that the lady's vexation had been demonstrated. Julien was willing to let it go, and to continue happily chatting, when he heard Monsieur de Rênal approaching.

Julien could still hear, as if ringing in his ears, the vulgar words spoken to him that morning. "Now," he asked himself, "wouldn't it be a way of laughing in this creature's face, this man so stuffed with all the advantages of wealth, if I took possession of his wife's hand, precisely in his presence? Yes, I'll do it, I will, so he can see my scorn."

And, at that very moment, the calm so unnatural to Julien was swept away: he desperately wanted—with such anxiety that he could think of nothing else—for Madame de Rênal to give him her hand.

Monsieur de Rênal talked politics, and angrily: two or three Verrières industrialists, grown far richer than he, planned to oppose him in the next election. Madame Derville was listening. Julien, annoyed at this bland bluster, came nearer to Madame de Rênal's chair. Darkness hid his movements. He was bold enough to put his hand very near the pretty arm that her dress left uncovered. He was so upset he hardly knew what he was doing: putting his cheek against the pretty arm, he ventured to set his lips against it.

Madame de Rênal quivered. Her husband was four steps distant; hurriedly, she gave Julien her hand, and simultaneously pushed him away a little. As Monsieur de Rênal went on insulting worthless men, Jacobins who were enriching themselves, Julien covered the hand he was holding with passionate kisses—or, at least, kisses that seemed passionate to Madame de Rênal. But now the poor woman had the proof, that fatal evening, that the man she'd silently adored was in love with her! The whole time he'd been away, she'd been seized by a dreadful illness, which had forced her to ponder.

"My God, I've been in love," she said to herself, "I've experienced love! Me, a married woman, in love! But," she told herself, "I've never felt this sort of melancholy madness for my husband; I can't stop thinking about Julien. After all, he's just a boy; what he feels for me is immense respect! This craziness will pass. What difference does it make to my husband that I can have these feelings for a young man? Monsieur de Rênal would be bored by my conversations with Julien, all about matters of the imagination. He's busy thinking about business. I'm not taking anything away from him and giving it to Julien."

No hypocrisy intruded on the purity of this naïve soul, distracted by a passion it had never experienced. She was deceived, but all unawares, although a virtuous instinct took fright. These were the struggles still shaking her when Julien appeared in the garden. She heard his voice almost at the same moment she saw him sit down beside her. And her soul felt itself soaring, lifted by the bewitching happiness that, for two weeks, had seduced but had, even more, astonished her. For her, it was all unknown. However, a few moments later she asked herself: "Is Julien's presence enough to wipe away all his wrongdoing?" She was frightened; that was when he had taken her hand.

His passionate kisses, the like of which she had never experienced, made her suddenly forget that perhaps he loved another woman. In her eyes, he was no longer guilty. Throbbing sadness, daughter of suspicion, died away, and a happiness, about which she had never so much as dreamed, brought her love's ecstasies and a wild gaiety. It was a charming evening for them all, except for His Honor the Mayor, who could not forget those industrialists, grown so terribly rich. Julien was no longer thinking of his black ambitions, nor of his painfully difficult plans. For the first time in his life, he was carried away by the power of beauty. Lost in a vague, sweet reverie utterly foreign to his nature, he was pressing the hand that seemed to him loveliness incarnate; he half heard the rustling of the lime leaves, stirred by a light night breeze, and the dogs of a mill along the Doubs, barking in the distance.

But this was pleasure, not passion. When he got back to his room, he did not think only of his happiness: he picked up his favorite book. At age twenty, the sense of the great world and what could be achieved there was all that mattered.

But soon he set down his book. In thinking about Napoleon's victories, he had discovered something new about his own. "Yes, I've won a battle," he said to himself. "But I must consolidate my gains, I must crush the pride of this proud gentleman while he is still retreating. This is unadulterated Napoleonism. I need to ask for a three-day leave so I can visit my friend Fouqué. If he says no, I'll demand his consent. But he'll agree."

Madame de Rênal could not close her eyes. She felt as if, till that moment, she had never lived. She could not stop thinking about the happiness of feeling Julien cover her hand with burning kisses.

Suddenly, a word frightened her: *adulteress.* She could see it. The worst things that the vilest debauchery could stamp on the notion of sensual love swarmed into her mind. These ideas were trying to stain the glow of the tender, divine image she had constructed, both of Julien himself and the happiness of loving him. The future was painted in ghastly colors. She saw herself as contemptible.

This was deeply frightening; her soul had penetrated unknown places. She had tasted, that evening, a brand-new happiness; now she found herself plunged, all of a sudden, into atrocious misery. She knew nothing of such suffering, which threatened to unhinge her mind. For a moment, she thought she would confess to her husband, tell him she was afraid of falling in love with Julien. At least, she would be talking about him. Luckily, she remembered a warning her aunt had given her the night before her marriage. It was about the dangers of confiding in a husband, who was after all a woman's master. Racked by pain, she wrung her hands.

She was caught up, completely at random, by contradictory and miserable images. As much as she feared never being loved, the frightful idea of sin tortured her just as if, the next day, she were to be exposed on the public pillory, in the central square at Verrières, wearing a sign that identified her adultery for all who passed by.

Madame de Rênal had no experience of life. Even in the full light of day, and with complete control of her faculties, she could not have seen any distinction between being guilty in God's eyes and being branded, in public, with the most burning general contempt. When the horrible idea of adultery—and of all the scorn that, as far as she was concerned, this sin brought in its wake—allowed her a few moments of rest, and she began to daydream of the sweetness of living innocently alongside Julien, as they had been doing, she found herself lurching into the equally horrible idea that he loved another woman. She could still see how pale he became, when he was afraid of losing that woman's portrait, or of compromising her by letting anyone see it. It was the first time Madame de Rênal had ever seen fear on that calm, that noble face. He had never shown such emotion for her or for her children. This new sorrow pushed her to the boundary of misery sustainable by the human soul. Without realizing it, she screamed so loudly that her chambermaid awoke. Suddenly, Madame de Rênal saw a light shining near her bed, and she recognized Elisa.

"Is it you he loves?" she screamed in her madness.

Overwhelmed by her mistress's frightful disorder, and her obviously troubled mind, the chambermaid, most fortunately, paid no attention to these strange words. Madame de Rênal became aware of her imprudence. "I have a fever," she said, "and I think I've been a bit delirious. Stay with me." Completely wakened by having to contradict her own words, she felt better: reason gave her back the self-control taken away in her half-waking sleep. To escape from the attentive, watching eyes of her chambermaid, she directed her to read the day's newspaper, and the girl did so, in a droning monotone, sounding out a long article from *The Legitimist,* while Madame de Rênal made up her mind, most virtuously, to treat Julien, when next she saw him, with absolute coldness.

CHAPTER TWELVE

A JOURNEY

In Paris one finds elegant people; in the provinces one can find
people of character.
—SIEYÈS

At five o'clock the next day, before Madame de Rênal made her appearance, Julien had obtained a three-day leave from her husband. He had not expected to, but he wanted to see her again; he kept thinking about her exceedingly pretty hand. He went down to the garden, where Madame de Rênal was usually waiting for him. Had Julien actually been in love with her, he would have looked up and seen her, behind the half-closed shutters on the first floor, her forehead leaning against the glass. She watched him. Finally, for all her good resolutions, she decided to go down. Her habitual pallor had given way to the most lively color. This entirely unsophisticated woman was plainly upset. A feeling of constraint and even of anger had changed her expression of intense serenity; she appeared totally divorced from all the vulgar concerns of her existence; and the net effect was to add fascination to a celestial face.

Julien went over to her at once, admiring the beautiful arms, revealed by a hastily thrown on shawl. The freshness of the morning air seemed to add an additional glow to a complexion already showing, after her long, troubling night, an extraordinary range of reactions. Her beauty was modest as well as touching, and even when heavy with thought—as one never saw among the lower classes—was apparently able to quicken in Julien aspects of his soul he had never before sensed. Too busy admiring these surprising charms, his eyes most attentive, Julien never gave a thought to the friendly greeting he was expecting. He was thus even more than astonished by a glacial coldness, which she seemed determined to convey, and in which, also, he thought he could even read an intention to put him in his place.

The smile of pleasure died on his lips; he remembered his worldly status, especially as compared to a rich, noble heiress. All one could see in his expression, just then, was arrogance and anger at himself. He felt a deep regret at having delayed his departure for more than an hour, all for the sake of being greeted by so humiliating a reception.

"Only a fool," he said to himself, "gets angry at others. A stone falls because it's heavy. Am I going to be forever a child? When will I acquire the good habit of giving these people my soul, only and exactly to the extent they pay me for it? If I want to be valued by them, as well as by myself, it must be by demonstrating to them that my poverty is doing business with their wealth, and yet that my heart is a thousand leagues distant from their insolence, set in a sphere too high to be affected by their petty displays of either disdain or approval."

While these sentiments came crowding into the young tutor's soul, his mobile face took on an expression of proud suffering and ferocity. Madame de Rênal was deeply troubled. The virtuous frigidity with which she had meant to greet him gave way to an expression of concern, a concern stirred by the abrupt changes she had just witnessed. All the empty words people employ, in the morning, about health and the fine day we're having, simultaneously dried up in them both. Julien, whose judgment was not in the least troubled by passion, quickly found a way to show Madame de Rênal how little he believed in friendly relations with her: he said nothing about the little trip he was taking, told her good-bye, and went away.

As she watched him go, struck dumb by the somber arrogance she could see in his look, so very friendly only the night before, her oldest son, running up from the end of the garden, hugged her and said:

"We're on leave. Monsieur Julien's going on a trip."

Hearing this, Madame de Rênal felt herself gripped by a mortal chill. Virtue made her miserable, and weakness made her even more miserable.

This new development completely occupied her mind: she was swept far beyond the sensible resolutions she owed to the horrible night just experienced. It was no longer a matter of resisting this wonderfully amiable lover, but of losing him forever.

She had to join the others for lunch. To add to her sorrow, all that Monsieur de Rênal and Madame Derville talked about was Julien's departure. His Honor the Mayor had noted a bit of insolence in the firm tone Julien used, in requesting a leave.

"This little peasant surely has a pocketful of offers from someone. But this someone, perhaps Monsieur Valenod, must be a little discouraged by the sum of six hundred francs a year he's now going to have to pay him. It used to be, back in Verrières, that one could insist on a delay of three days in order to think about such things, but this morning, to keep from having to give me a response, our small gentleman left for the mountainside. Having to bargain with a miserable workman who's become insolent—oh, that's where we've come to!"

"Since my husband, who says nothing about how deeply he's wounded Julien, now believes Julien intends to leave us, what should I believe?" Madame de Rênal asked herself. "Ah! It's all over and done with!"

So she could at least weep freely, and not answer Madame Derville's questions, she said she had a frightful headache and put herself to bed.

"That's the way it is, with women," said Monsieur de Rênal once again, "there's always something wrong with these complicated machines. And *he* went away, laughing at us."

While Madame de Rênal was lying, cruelly gripped by the dreadful passion into which chance had drawn her, Julien went cheerfully on his way, in the middle of the most gorgeous scenery mountains can offer. He had to cross the high range north of Vergy. The path he was following, which rose gradually through towering beech trees, zigzagged back and forth along the slopes of the prominent great mountain, north of the Doubs valley. Soon, as he passed above the lesser hills through which, on its way south, the Doubs flowed, he could see all the way to the fertile plains of Burgundy and Beaujolais. Although not markedly sensitive to this sort of beauty, the ambitious young man could not help stopping, from time to time, to contemplate so vast and imposing a spectacle.

He finally reached the summit of the great mountain, near which the route he was following would take him, leading down to the isolated valley in which lived his friend, the young timber merchant, Fouqué. Julien felt no urgency about seeing him, neither him nor any other human being. Hidden like a hunting hawk amid the bare rocks crowning the mountain, he could spot from a long way off anyone who might be approaching him. He found a small cave set in the virtually vertical slope of a boulder. He climbed up and was soon settled in this hideaway. "Here," he said, his eyes shining with pleasure, "no one could ever hurt me." It occurred to him that he might linger, free to write out his thoughts, otherwise so risky if set down on paper. A square rock became his desk. His pen flew: he was not aware of where he was. Finally, he realized that the sun was setting behind the mountain range that went all the way to Beaujolais.

"Why don't I spend the night here?" he said to himself. "I've got some bread, and *I'm free!*" The echoes of these wondrous words rang in his soul: hypocrite that he was, he could not be free even with Fouqué. His head in his hands, Julien felt happier, in his cave, than he had ever been in his life, stirred by his wandering thoughts and by the sheer happiness of freedom. Not aware that he was watching, he saw the twilight slowly spreading. In the middle of vast darkness, his soul lost itself in thoughts of what it might be like when he got to Paris. First of all, there would be a woman, both good and beautiful, and with a mind finer than anything he had found in the countryside. He would love her passionately, and he would be loved. If he had to go away, though not for long, it would be to cover himself with glory, thus deserving her love even more.

Even endowing him with an imagination like Julien's, a young man brought up among the sad truths of Paris society would snap out of the novel he'd been reading, restored by the coldest irony: all the noble deeds would have vanished, along with any hope of accomplishing them, and they would be replaced by the familiar saying, "If you leave your mistress alone, alas, what you risk is being betrayed two or three times a day!" Our young peasant saw nothing blocking him from the most heroic deeds, except the opportunity to perform them.

Now the darkness of night had replaced the day, and he still had a good six miles to go before he reached Fouqué's village. Before he left the little cave, Julien lit a fire and carefully burned every scrap of what he'd written.

He startled his friend, knocking on his door at one o'clock in the morning. Fouqué was busy doing his accounts. He was a tall young man, quite sufficiently ugly, with gross, hard features, a nose of infinite length, and a large store of goodwill hidden under his repulsive appearance.

"Are you here, on the spur of the moment, because you've broken with your Monsieur de Rênal?"

Julien told him, carefully presenting matters as he preferred they be perceived, what had happened the night before.

"Stay here with me," Fouqué told him. "I see you quite understand Monsieur de Rênal, and Monsieur Valenod, and the assistant governor, Maugiron, and the parish priest, Chélan. You have a nice understanding of the fine points of these people's characters, you've readied yourself to handle all sorts of negotiations. You know more about arithmetic than I do; you could easily handle my accounts. I'm doing extremely well. Because I can't possibly do everything by myself, and I'm terrified of meeting up with a scoundrel, if I take someone into the business, I'm losing good opportunities every day of the week. Less than a month ago, I passed a deal to Michaud, from Saint Armand, and he made six thousand francs. I hadn't seen him in six years: we met, just by chance, at an auction in Pontarlier. Why couldn't you have made—yes, you—those six thousand francs, or three thousand, anyway? Because if I'd had you with me that day, I could have bid for that timber cutting, and nobody could have stopped me. So be my partner."

The offer did not please Julien: it got in the way of his craziness. All during dinner, prepared by the two friends themselves (as the Homeric heroes had), since Fouqué lived alone, he showed Julien his account books, and demonstrated for his benefit what an opportunity the business offered. Fouqué had the loftiest notions of Julien's mind, and of his character.

When Julien was by himself, in his little pinewood room:

"It's true," he told himself, "I could make thousands of francs out here, and then I'd be in a better position to become a soldier, or a priest, whichever would be better, whatever's more in fashion, then. The modest savings I'll have accumulated would remove all the petty details and difficulties. Alone up on this mountain, I'll be freed from some of that awful ignorance I suffer from, all those things high society people take so seriously. But Fouqué doesn't plan to get married, yet he keeps telling me that being alone makes him miserable. The real reason he'd take in a partner, someone who has no money to invest in his business, is the hope that he'll find himself a companion, a person who'll never leave him.

"Am I capable of deceiving my friend?" Julien asked himself peevishly. This being, for whom hypocrisy and an absence of all sympathy were the usual methods of protecting himself, could not bear, this time, the thought of the slightest trickiness in dealing with a man for whom he had friendly feelings.

And then, suddenly, he was relieved, he had found a good reason for refusing. "What! Me turn coward and give up seven or eight years? I'd be twenty-eight, by then—but at that point Bonaparte had done the greatest of things! Having hidden myself in obscurity, and made a bit of money by selling timber and earning favors from assorted rascally underlings, who can say if I'd still have the sacred fire you need, if you're going to make a name for yourself?"

Next morning, Julien coolly and confidently gave his answer to his good friend, who had thought the partnership idea was all settled. His sacred vocation at the holy altar would not allow Julien to accept. Fouqué could not believe it.

"But just think," he kept repeating. "I could either make you a partner or, if you like that better, I could pay you four thousand francs a year! And you'll go back to your Monsieur de Rênal, who looks down at you like mud on his shoes! When you've got four thousand francs in your hand, what's going to stop you from going into the seminary? And let me tell you something else, I'll make sure you get the best parish in the whole region. Let me tell you," Fouqué added, lowering his voice, "I supply firewood for Monsieur ———, and Monsieur ———, Monsieur ———. I give them the best oak, and let them pay me as if it were ordinary white pine—but there's no better investment anywhere."

Nothing could prove victorious over Julien's vocation. In the end, Fouqué thought him slightly insane. The third day, early in the morning, Julien left his friend; he would spend the day walking, surrounded by the great mountain's rocks and boulders. He located his little cave, but the peace he had brought there the first time had vanished: his friend's proposals had swept it away. Like Hercules, he felt himself poised in the balance—not between good and evil, but between the mediocrity of an assured livelihood and all his heroic, youthful dreams. "I have no real steadiness," he told himself, "which makes doubt all the more dangerous. I'm not made of the wood from which great men can be carved, so I worry that eight years spent earning my bread might deprive me of the sublime energy which makes extraordinary things possible."

CHAPTER THIRTEEN

FISHNET STOCKINGS

A novel: It's a mirror you take for a walk down the road.
—SAINT-RÉAL

Seeing the picturesque ruins of the ancient church at Vergy, Julien realized it had been two days since he'd had so much as a stray thought of Madame de Rênal. "When I was leaving the other day, that woman reminded me of the immense distance separating us; she treated me like a workman's son. Of course, she wanted me to see how much she regretted having given me her hand, the previous night. . . . But still, she's so pretty—and her hand! What a bewitching thing! And there's such nobility in her eyes!"

The thought that he could have made money with Fouqué brought a certain ease to Julien's mind: it was not so regularly corrupted by irritability and the strong sense of his poverty, his inferior status in the world's eyes. Located as if on a high promontory, he was able to evaluate and, one might say, rise above both extreme poverty and the extreme comfort that, still, he called wealth. He was by no means possessed of a fully elaborated philosophy, but he had enough insight to feel himself different, after his short trip up the mountain.

He was struck by the signs of deep disturbance, as Madame de Rênal listened to the brief recital of his journey, an account she had requested of him.

Fouqué had had marriage plans, he had had unfortunate love affairs; long, intimate confidences on this subject had filled the two friends' conversation. After finding happiness far too soon, Fouqué had become aware that he was not his lover's only love. All these stories had astonished Julien: he learned a good many new things. His solitary existence, all his fancies and defiant mistrust, had kept him shut away from everything that might have illuminated him.

While he'd been away, Madame de Rênal's life had been nothing but a string of ever-changing tortures, all of them unbearable; she had been truly ill.

"Above all," Madame Derville told her, when she saw Julien returning, "sick as you are, you must not go down to the garden tonight. The dampness will make your illness a great deal worse."

Madame Derville had seen with great surprise that her friend, always criticized by Monsieur de Rênal for the plainness with which she dressed, had begun to wear fishnet stockings and delightful little shoes, fresh from Paris. For the last three days, Madame de Rênal's only amusement had been to cut out and have sewn by Elisa, in great haste, a summer dress made from a pretty little fabric, eminently fashionable. The dress had been finished only moments after Julien's return; Madame de Rênal immediately put it on. There was no more reason for her friend to wonder. "She's in love, the poor thing!" Madame Derville said to herself. She understood, now, all the peculiar symptoms of her friend's illness.

She saw her speaking to Julien. Madame de Rênal's surging color gave way to pallor. Her eyes, fixed on those of the young tutor, clearly showed anxiety. She expected that, at any moment, he was going to declare himself and announce whether he was leaving the house or staying. Julien had no interest in saying anything on this subject, which had not crossed his mind. After frightful struggles, Madame de Rênal at last had the courage to say, in a trembling voice in which all her passion could be heard:

"Will you be leaving your students, for a place somewhere else?"

Julien was struck by Madame de Rênal's shaky voice, and by the look in her eyes. "This woman loves me," he told himself. "But after this transitory weakness, of which her pride disapproves, once she's no longer afraid of my leaving, she'll go back to being proud and haughty." This insight into their respective positions was, for Julien, as quick as lightning. He answered, hesitantly:

"I would be sorry to leave such pleasant children, *so well born*, but it may be necessary. There is also the duty one owes oneself."

Speaking the words *so well born* (one of the aristocratic phrases Julien had recently acquired), he conveyed a sense of deep resentment.

"In this woman's eyes, of course," he told himself, "I'm simply not well born." As she stood listening to him, Madame de Rênal was admiring his mind, his beauty; her heart was pierced through by the possibility of his leaving, which he had conjured up for her to see. All their Verrières friends who'd come to dinner, while Julien was away, had complimented her, enviously, on the amazing man her husband had been fortunate enough to dig up. It was not that they hadn't understood the children's progress. Knowing the Bible by heart, and in Latin, had struck the inhabitants of Verrières with such wonder that it might well last for a century.

Julien, who spoke to no one, had no knowledge of all this. Had Madame de Rênal retained even a bit of composure, she would have complimented him on the reputation he had won, which would have comforted his pride and made him mild and friendly to her—even more so, because the new dress was wonderfully becoming. Madame de Rênal, who was also pleased by her pretty dress, and what Julien had said to her about it, wanted to walk about in the garden, but soon had to admit she was in no condition to continue. She had taken the traveler's arm and, far from strengthening her, the feeling of her arm touching his had completely drained her.

It was night. They'd just seated themselves when Julien, exercising his former privilege, was bold enough to set his lips on his pretty neighbor's arm and take her hand. He thought of Fouqué's daring and how well it had worked with his mistresses; he did not think of Madame de Rênal. The words *well born* still weighed heavily on his heart. He was supposed to squeeze her hand; it gave him not the slightest pleasure. Rather than feeling proud, or at least recognizing the signs of her emotion, betrayed that night by perfectly obvious signs, neither her beauty, her elegance, nor her freshness made much impression on him. Her soul's innocence, and the fact that she had never experienced hatred, had surely helped prolong her youthfulness. It is in the face that age first shows itself, in most women.

Julien was sullen and moody all night. He had only been angry, before, at fate and at society; now that Fouqué had offered him a vulgar way of achieving comfort, he was out of sorts with himself. Totally wrapped in his own thoughts, though from time to time he addressed a few words to the ladies, Julien ended by letting go of Madame de Rênal's hand, not even knowing he'd done so. This shook the poor woman's soul; it seemed to her a demonstration of her fate.

Had she been sure of Julien's affection, perhaps her virtue could have summoned the strength to resist him. Shaking from fear of losing him, her passion came to the point of reaching for his hand, which in his self-absorption he had left lying along the back of a chair, and taking it in hers. This revived his youthful ambition. He would have preferred that what she had done be witnessed by all those terribly proud, noble folk who, with patronizing smiles, had looked down at him, seated with her children at the foot of her husband's table. "This woman can't really despise me, not now. In that case," he said to himself, "I ought to be impressed by her beauty. I owe it to myself to be her lover." Such a thought would never have occurred to him, before his friend's ingenuous confidences.

The sudden decision he'd just taken provided a pleasant distraction. He said to himself: "I have to have one of these two women." It would be distinctly nicer, he noted, paying court to Madame Derville, not because she would be more enjoyable, but because what she had seen was a tutor honored for his learning—not simply a workman, a carpenter, carrying a ratteen jacket under his arm, as Madame de Rênal had first seen him.

And it was indeed precisely as a young workman, blushing to the whites of his eyes, standing at the front door of the house and not daring to pull on the knocker, that Madame de Rênal fancied he was at his most charming.

Continuing this review of his situation, Julien realized that he could not dream of a conquest of Madame Derville, who was more than likely aware of the fondness Madame de Rênal had shown for him. Obliged to return to the latter of the two women, he asked himself: "What do I know about this woman's nature? Just this: Before my trip, I took her hand; she withdrew it. Today, I withdraw my hand, and she grasps it and squeezes it. What a wonderful opportunity to repay her for all the contempt she's shown me. God only knows how many lovers she's had! Perhaps she picked me only because it's so easy to meet."

This, alas! is the curse of overcivilization! At age twenty, a young man's soul, given some degree of education, is a million miles from spontaneity, without which love is often the most boring of responsibilities.

"And besides," continued Julien's petty vanity, "I owe it to myself to succeed with this woman, because if I ever make my fortune, and someone brings up my vulgar post as a tutor, I can explain that love threw me into this position."

Once again, Julien withdrew his hand from Madame de Rênal's, then took hers and squeezed it. As they walked back to the drawing room, just before midnight, Madame de Rênal asked him, her voice lowered:

"You're going to leave us, you're going to go away?"

Sighing, he replied:

"I have to go, because I'm passionately in love with you, which is a sin—and such a sin for a young priest!"

Madame de Rênal leaned on his arm with such abandon that her cheek felt the warmth of his.

Neither of them had experienced the same night. Madame de Rênal felt exalted by the loftiest of virtuous delight. A young flirt who falls in love, early on, gets used to love's difficulties, so when she reaches the age of true passion the charm of novelty has vanished. Since Madame de Rênal had never read romantic fiction, every last shade of her happiness was, for her, brand new. There was no sad truth to chill her, not even the specter of the future. She imagined herself quite as happy, ten years on, as she was right now. Even the idea of virtue, the faithfulness she had sworn to Monsieur de Rênal, which some days earlier had troubled her, presented itself in vain: she sent it away like an unwelcome guest. "I'll never have to give Julien anything," she told herself. "We'll go on living just as we have, this last month. He'll be my friend."

CHAPTER FOURTEEN

English Scissors

A young girl of sixteen had a rosy complexion, and wore rouge.
—Polidori

For Julien, Fouqué's offer had effectively destroyed his happiness: he could not decide which way he should go.

"Alas! Maybe I lack sufficient character; I'd have been a poor soldier for Napoleon. At least," he added, "my little affair with the mistress of the house might distract me a bit."

Luckily for him, even in this minor matter his soul, at bottom, could not accept such cavalier language. Her pretty dress made him afraid of Madame de Rênal. In his eyes, this dress represented the very latest in Parisian fashion. Pride kept him from leaving any part of the campaign to chance or to the inspiration of the moment. Having heard Fouqué's revelations, he combined them with what little he had read about love in the Bible, and drew up a singularly detailed battle plan. Since—though he would not admit it—he was seriously apprehensive, he wrote the plan out in full.

The next morning, in the drawing room, he was left alone, for just a moment, with Madame de Rênal.

"Don't you have any other name but Julien?" she asked.

Our hero had no idea how to respond to this flattering question. This was not a detail anticipated by his plan. Without the foolish plan, Julien's lively spirit would have served him perfectly well: surprise would simply have increased the liveliness of his insights.

He was inept, and then exaggerated just how inept he was. Madame de Rênal was quick to forgive him. She took his bungling for charming candor. And to her eyes, what was particularly lacking in this young man, possessed of such genius, was precisely a lack of candor.

"Your little tutor makes me seriously distrust him," Madame Derville sometimes told her. "It seems to me he's always thinking, and all he thinks about is clever maneuvering. He's a sneak."

Julien could not shake his profound humiliation, remaining quite miserable at not having known how to reply to Madame de Rênal.

"A man like me has got to reverse this defeat"—and seizing a moment when they were going from one room to another, he fancied himself obliged to give Madame de Rênal a kiss.

Nothing could have been less productive, nothing less agreeable and, for him as for her, nothing more reckless. They were very nearly seen. Madame de Rênal thought he'd gone crazy. She was frightened and, above all, shocked. Such clumsy stupidity reminded her of Monsieur Valenod.

"What would have happened to me," she asked herself, "had I been alone with him?" Her sense of virtue was fully restored, because love was fading.

She was careful to see to it that one of her children was always nearby.

The day turned boring for Julien: he spent it trying, clumsily, to carry out his battle plan for seduction. He never looked at Madame de Rênal—not once—without question marks in his eyes. However, fool that he was, he could not help seeing that he was not doing well, trying to be agreeable, and even less well, trying to be seductive.

Madame de Rênal could not recover from her astonishment, finding him so clumsy and at the same time so bold. "It's the natural shyness of love, for a man of such spirit!" she finally concluded, rejoicing exceedingly. "Can it be that my rival never loved him!"

After lunch, Madame de Rênal returned to the drawing room, where she was being visited by Monsieur Charcot de Maugiron, deputy governor of the Bray district. She was working at a small tapestry loom, raised to a good height. Madame Derville was beside her. Which is how things stood, in the bright light of day, when our hero deemed it appropriate to set his boot in motion and press it against Madame de Rênal's pretty foot, whose fishnet stockings and pretty Paris shoes had obviously made an impression on the gallant deputy governor of the district.

Madame de Rênal was absolutely terrified. She let her scissors drop, and her ball of woolen yarn, and her needle, and the forward movement of Julien's boot was able to pass for a clumsy attempt at breaking the scissors' fall, since he'd seen them sliding down. Luckily, the scissors, made of English steel, managed to shatter, and Madame de Rênal kept voicing her regret that Julien had not been standing closer.

"You saw them falling before I did: you could have stopped them. Instead, all your eagerness did was give me a really good kick in the foot."

All this quite deceived the deputy governor of the district. But not Madame Derville. "This pretty boy has awfully stupid manners!" she thought. "Even the sophistication of a provincial capital would not tolerate such mistakes."

Madame de Rênal found an opportunity to say to Julien:

"Be careful. I command you."

He saw how clumsy he had been and was in a surly mood. He considered for some while whether or not he ought to be angry about those words: *I command you.* He was enough of a fool to think: "She's entitled to say 'I order you,' if it's something about the children's education. But in dealing with my love, she's got to treat me as an equal. How can I love without *equality*...?" And then his mind got busy, trying to track down commonplaces about equality. He repeated, angrily, a line from Corneille that Madame Derville had taught him a few days earlier:

Love creates equalities, it doesn't search for them.

Stubbornly, he went on playing Don Juan—he who in all his life had never had a mistress. All day long, he was a ridiculous fool. He had only one good idea: bored by himself, as well as by Madame de Rênal, he was frightened at the prospect of sitting next to her in the garden that evening, in the darkness. He told Monsieur de Rênal he was going to Verrières, to see his confessor; he left after dinner, nor did he return that night.

At Verrières, he found Father Chélan in the process of moving. He'd finally been forced out of office, and Father Maslon had replaced him. Julien helped the old priest, and had the notion of writing to Fouqué that the irresistible vocation he'd felt for the sacred ministry kept him, at first, from accepting his friend's considerate offer, but that he'd just witnessed such an act of injustice that, perhaps, it would be better for his own salvation not to take holy orders.

Julien congratulated himself on the dexterity with which he would make use of the old priest's dismissal, leaving a door open through which he might return to a life of commerce, should melancholy prudence prevail, in his heart, over deeds of heroism.

CHAPTER FIFTEEN

COCK CROW

Latin's spelling turns *amour* to death:
amor, à mort—since love will stifle breath,
informing us of what our death can cause:
pain, tears and losses, hell, profound remorse.
—*BLASON D'AMOUR*

Had Julien been capable of just a bit of the shrewdness which, for no good reason, he was sure he possessed, he could have congratulated himself the next day on the effect produced by his trip to Verrières. Absence had wiped away his ineptitudes. He was abundantly moody all that day, and that night a ridiculous idea came to him, with which unusual daring he communicated to Madame de Rênal.

Hardly had they seated themselves in the garden, and without waiting for darkness to truly settle in, Julien put his mouth to Madame de Rênal's ear and, at the risk of horribly compromising her, said:

"Madame, at two o'clock I will come to your room. I have something I need to tell you."

Julien was very afraid that his request would not be agreed to. His seducer role weighed on him so horribly that, had he been free to do as he wished, he would have locked himself in his room for days and never looked at these ladies. He understood that his heavy-handed behavior, the night before, had ruined all the promising signs of the previous days. Really, he had no idea to what saint he ought to be praying.

Madame de Rênal responded to Julien's rude announcement with genuine indignation, not in the least exaggerated. He thought he could hear a certain scorn in her brief reply. He was positive that, though she spoke very softly, he could make out the words *don't be a fool*. Pretending he had something to tell the children, he rose and went to their room, and on his return seated himself next to Madame Derville, as far away from Madame de Rênal as he could get. He thereby relinquished any possibility of taking her hand. They were discussing weighty matters and Julien performed extremely well, aside from intervals of silence during which he sat racking his brain. "Why can't I devise some fine maneuver," he asked himself, "and compel Madame de Rênal to show signs of the undoubted affection that, three days ago, she convinced me she truly felt!"

He was totally bewildered by the desperate state into which he had thrown his affairs. Nothing, however, would have embarrassed him more than success.

Analyzing matters, back in his room after midnight, his pessimistic perspective led him to believe that Madame Derville was contemptuous of him, and things were probably not much better with Madame de Rênal.

In a truly foul mood, and deeply humiliated, Julien could not sleep. He had absolutely no intention of giving up his dodges and devices, or of abandoning his plans and living from day to day alongside Madame de Rênal, happy as a child with the pleasures each day brought him.

He wearied his brain, creating complicated schemes; the next moment he found them completely absurd. In a word, by the time the château's clock sounded two in the morning, he was utterly miserable.

The bells woke him as the crowing of the cock woke Saint Peter. He felt himself on the verge of a horribly painful episode. He had not given a thought to his rude proposal, from the moment he'd made it. How badly it had been received!

"I told her I'd be there at two o'clock," he said to himself, rising from his bed. "Maybe I'll be clumsy and gross, the way they think a peasant's son can't help but be—Madame Derville certainly said as much—but at least I won't be weak."

He was correct to appreciate his courage: never had he squeezed himself into so painfully tight a position. Opening his door, he shook so violently that his knees gave way beneath him, and he had to support himself against the wall.

He wore nothing on his feet. He went to listen at Monsieur de Rênal's door, through which he could hear snoring. He was dreadfully disappointed. Now he had no reason at all not to go on. But, good God, what would he do in there? He had no plan, and even if he had, he was so shaky that he would have had no likelihood of adhering to it.

At last, suffering all the pain he might have experienced had he been marched along to a firing squad, he reached the small antechamber that led into Madame de Rênal's room. He opened the door with a trembling hand, making an incredible amount of noise.

There was light: a small lamp was burning in front of the fireplace. He hadn't anticipated this fresh bad luck. Seeing him enter, Madame de Rênal quickly leaped out of bed.

"Wretch!" she cried.

There was a degree of confusion. Julien forgot his useless plans and returned to his natural role: not to please so bewitching a woman seemed to him the greatest of all misfortunes. His only answer to her accusations was to throw himself at her feet, hugging her knees. Since she addressed him in extremely harsh terms, he dissolved in tears.

Several hours later, when Julien left Madame de Rênal's room, one might have said, as they say these things in romantic novels, that he had nothing else to desire. In fact, it was the love he had inspired, and the unforeseen effect of her seductive charms, that produced his triumph: nothing in all his inept conniving had brought it about.

Still, amid those sweetest of all moments, he remained a victim of his bizarre pride, pretending to be a man accustomed to subjugating women. He made unbelievable attempts to spoil what was lovable. Rather than being mindful of the ecstasies he evoked, and the guilty remorse which heightened their intensity, it was the notion of *duty* that gripped his attention. He was afraid of frightful remorse and of perpetual scorn, should he discard the ideal model he was intending to follow. In short, it was exactly what made Julien a superior being which kept him from enjoying the happiness that had come his way. He was like a young girl of sixteen, with a magnificent complexion, who before she goes to a ball is foolish enough to daub herself with rouge.

Mortally afraid that Julien might indeed come as promised, Madame de Rênal had been in the clutch of cruel anxiety. Julien's tears and his despair profoundly upset her.

Even when there was nothing left to refuse him, she pushed Julien away, her indignation very real, and then threw herself into his arms. There was no reason or consistency in her behavior. She saw herself damned for all eternity, and tried to hide hell's images from her eyes by endlessly caressing him. In a word, our hero's happiness was complete, not excluding even the burning response he had elicited from the woman—had he been able to enjoy it. Even Julien's departure did not stop the ecstasies that, in spite of herself, were shaking her, or the battles with remorse that tore her apart.

"My God! Happiness—love—that's all there is to it?" This was Julien's first thought, as he came back to his room. He was in that state of shock and restless uncertainty into which souls fall, having just attained what they've so long craved. A soul accustomed to desiring now has nothing left to desire, but has not as yet acquired memories. Like a soldier newly returned from military review, Julien was busily examining all the details of his conduct. "Was there anything lacking, anything I owed it to myself to do? Did I play my role to the fullest?"

And what role was that? Why, that of a man in the habit of brilliant performances with women.

CHAPTER SIXTEEN

THE DAY AFTER

He turned his lip to hers, and with his hand
Called back the tangles of her wandering hair.
—BYRON, *DON JUAN*, CANTO 1, STANZA 170

Luckily for Julien's glory, Madame de Rênal had been deeply upset, deeply astonished, to realize that the man who, in a flash, had become the whole world to her, was an idiot.

As she was persuading him to leave, seeing dawn was near:

"Oh God!" she said. "If my husband's heard anything, I'm lost."

Having had the opportunity to prepare a few choice phrases, Julien called this one to mind:

"Would you regret your life?"

"Ah, very much, right at the moment. But I wouldn't regret having known you." Julien thought it better suited his dignity to leave her in broad daylight, with an infinite recklessness.

The perpetual care he lavished on even the most minor aspects of his life, while indulging himself in the craziness of appearing to be an experienced man of the world, had a single advantage: when next he saw Madame de Rênal, at lunch, his conduct was a masterpiece of prudence.

As for her, she was unable to look at him without blushing to her eyelids, but neither could she live for a second without looking at him. She was aware of the problem, and redoubled her efforts to conceal it. Julien looked at her once and once only. At first, Madame de Rênal was grateful for his prudence. Soon, seeing that this single glance would not be repeated, she was alarmed: "Doesn't he love me anymore?" she said to herself. "Alas, I'm surely too old for him. I'm ten years his senior."

As they left the dining room for the garden, she squeezed Julien's hand. Startled by so extraordinary a sign of love, he looked at her passionately, for at lunch he had thought her wonderfully pretty, and when he'd kept his eyes lowered, he'd spent the time rehearsing her charms. His look soothed Madame de Rênal. It did not completely quiet her anxieties, but on the other hand her anxieties virtually wiped out the remorse she felt toward her husband.

At lunch, her husband had noticed nothing. Not so Madame Derville, who believed her friend was on the point of succumbing. All through the day, her resolute and mordant friendship did not hold back, but spoke words of wisdom to Madame de Rênal, determined to show her, and in hideous colors, the dangers she was running.

Madame de Rênal was burning to be alone with Julien; she wanted to ask him if he still loved her. For all the unchangeable sweetness of her nature, more than once she came close to telling Madame Derville exactly how anxious she was.

In the garden that evening, Madame Derville managed things so well that she located herself between Madame de Rênal and Julien. Madame de Rênal, who'd been indulging in delightful anticipation of squeezing Julien's hand, and bringing it to her lips, could not so much as speak a word to him.

Disappointment made her even more upset. Remorse began devouring her. She'd scolded Julien so harshly for his reckless visit, the night before, that she worried he would not come this night. She left the garden early, and settled herself in her room. But unable to bear her impatience, she went and put her ear to Julien's door. Despite the uncertainty and passion gnawing at her, she did not dare go in. That seemed to her the most degrading thing anyone could do (as the provincial proverb puts it).

The servants were not all in bed. Prudence finally forced her to go back to her room. Two hours of waiting were, for her, two centuries of torture.

But Julien was so faithful to what he called his duty that he'd never have failed to carry out the plan he'd formulated, point by careful point.

Just as one o'clock was sounding, he made a stealthy escape from his room, sure that Monsieur de Rênal was deeply asleep, and came to Madame de Rênal. He found real pleasure in her love that day, since he was less concerned with the role he was supposed to be playing. He had eyes to see with, and ears that heard. What Madame de Rênal told him about her age helped put him at his ease.

"Alas, I'm ten years older than you! How can you love me!" she repeated rather senselessly, and because it weighed on her.

Julien had not thought of this misfortune, but he saw it was real, and forgot virtually all his fear of being laughed at.

His stupid notion of being seen as an inferior lover, because of his inferior birth, also disappeared. And as Julien's ecstasy reassured his timid mistress, she began to recover both happiness and her capacity for thinking more clearly about her lover. Luckily, he had almost entirely lost, that night, the false assumption that had transmuted their rendezvous the night before into a victory rather than a delight. Had she been aware of his careful role-playing, that mournful discovery would have forever destroyed for her every possibility of happiness. All she could see was a faintly wistful effect caused by the disproportion in their ages.

Although Madame de Rênal had paid no attention to speculation about love, it happens that differences in age, next to differences in wealth, are one of the great themes of provincial wit, whenever the conversation turns to matters of love.

Nor was it more than a few days before Julien, restored by the ardor natural to his age, became a wildly passionate lover.

"I must admit," he told himself, "that hers is a soul of angelic goodness—and how could she be any prettier?"

His notion of playing a role had very nearly vanished. In a moment of abandon, he had confessed to her all his anxieties. This intimate avowal carried to its very fullest the passion he had inspired. "So I've never actually had a lucky rival!" she said to herself, delighted. She was brave enough to ask about the picture, so important to him; he swore that the painting had portrayed a man.

When Madame de Rênal was calm enough for reflection, she was no longer astonished that such happiness existed, and that she had ever doubted it.

"Ah," she said to herself, "if only I had known Julien ten years ago, when I could still pass as pretty!"

Julien had no such thoughts. Ambition was still his central passion: that was indeed his pleasure in possessing—he, such a poor creature, so unlucky, so despised—a woman as aristocratic as she was beautiful. His adoration of her, his ecstasies at the sight of his beloved's charms, finally reassured her, at least a little, about the difference in their ages. Had she possessed some of the sophistication a woman of thirty has long since come to enjoy, in any of the world's more civilized countries, she would have been quiveringly concerned about the durability of a love that apparently thrived only on astonishment and the raptures of vanity.

When he forgot ambition, briefly, Julien was extravagantly pleased even by Madame de Rênal's hats and by her dresses. He could not get enough of the pleasures he took in her perfume. He opened her glass cabinet and spent hours on end admiring the beauty as well as the placement of everything he found. His beloved, leaning against him, watched him as he looked at her jewels and her frills and laces, the presents that, before a marriage, fill the wedding baskets set out on display.

"I should have married a man like him!" Madame de Rênal sometimes thought. "What a burning soul! How ravishing life would be, with him!"

Julien had never found himself so close to these awesome instruments of feminine artillery. "It's not possible," he said to himself, "that Paris could have anything more beautiful!" And then he could see nothing objectionable in his happiness. Quite often honest admiration, and his mistress's ecstasies, made him forget the empty theory that, early on in this relationship, had tied him into knots and made him very nearly ridiculous. There were moments when, despite his habitual hypocrisy, he discovered a wonderful sweetness in confiding to this noble lady, for whom he had so much admiration, his ignorance about all manner of society's little ways. His mistress's rank seemed to lift him equally high. As for Madame de Rênal, she found the sweetest and most moral of sensual pleasures in teaching him about this abundance of trifles—he, a young man of genius, widely regarded as someone who, one day, would go far. Even the deputy governor of the district, and Monsieur Valenod, did not hesitate to admire him; they struck her, because of that, as less stupid.

Madame Derville could not have agreed, not at all. Depressed by what she thought she was seeing, and finding her wise advice hateful to a woman literally out of her mind, she left Vergy without any explanation—which, indeed, no one bothered to ask of her. Madame de Rênal shed a few tears, and soon realized that her happiness had vastly increased. With Madame Derville gone, she could spend almost the entire day alone with her lover.

More and more, Julien as well gave himself up to the sweet society of his beloved, though when he spent too long alone with her Fouqué's fateful offer came to mind, upsetting him all over again. There were moments, during the first days of this new existence, when he, who had never loved, who had never been loved by anyone, took such delicious pleasure in being honest that, indeed, he very nearly confessed to Madame de Rênal the ambition which, until then, had been the absolute essence of his being. He would have liked to consult her about the strange attraction he felt for Fouqué's offer, but a small episode occurred which put an end to all candor.

CHAPTER SEVENTEEN

THE FIRST DEPUTY

O, how this spring of love resembleth
The uncertain glory of an April day:
Which now shows all the beauty of the sun,
And by and by a cloud takes all away!
—TWO GENTLEMEN OF VERONA

One evening at sunset, seated beside his beloved at the far side of the orchard, too distant for any interruption, he was daydreaming most profoundly. "Do such sweet moments," he wondered, "last forever?" Trying to find the right profession was an intense preoccupation; he regretted that great, fast-approaching misfortune that ends childhood and ruins the early years of young men without money.

"Oh," he exclaimed, "God obviously sent Napoleon for the youth of France! Who can take his place? What will they do without him, those miserable ones—richer by far than me—who have precisely enough money to get themselves a good education, but not enough, at age twenty, to pay off the right people and push themselves into a career! Whatever we do," he added with a deep sigh, "this fateful, imperishable memory will forever keep us from being happy!"

Suddenly he saw Madame de Rênal frowning. She took on a cold, disdainful air: that way of thinking seemed to her better suited to servants. Raised with the idea that she was extremely rich, it pleased her to assume that Julien had been, too. She loved him a thousand times more than life itself, and never gave a thought to money.

Julien had no idea what she was thinking. Her frown brought him back to earth. He had enough presence of mind to be careful how he spoke, explaining to the noble lady seated so close beside him, on the grassy slope, that the words he'd just repeated were ones he'd heard on his visit to his friend, the timber merchant. This accounted for the profanity.

"Well then! Don't have anything more to do with those people," said Madame de Rênal, not yet abandoning the cold look that, all of a sudden, had replaced her glances of the liveliest tenderness.

Her frown, or rather the regret he felt for his own carelessness, was the first blow suffered by the illusion that had been sweeping him away. He said to himself: "She is good and sweet; her liking for me is strong; but she's been raised in the enemy camp—and they're quite right to be afraid of high-minded men with good educations, yet without the money to launch themselves on careers. What would become of them, these aristocrats, if we were allowed to fight them on equal terms! Me, for example: If I were mayor of Verrières, I'd be well meaning and honest, the way, at bottom, Monsieur de Rênal is! But how I'd sweep away Father Maslon and Monsieur Valenod, with all their thievish trickery! How justice would triumph in Verrières! It's not their ability that's stopping me. They bungle along, that's all they do."

That day, Julien's happiness had been close to stability. All that was missing was for our hero to have the courage of honesty. He needed the courage to do battle, but *right on the spot*. Madame de Rênal had been stunned by Julien's words: upper-class people are always saying that we could certainly see Robespierre's return, precisely because of the lower-class people who are being elevated far too high. Madame de Rênal's coldness lasted a long time, and seemed to Julien unusually obvious. And the fear of having spoken unpleasantly to him, even indirectly, was followed by her disgust at what he had said. Unhappiness was clearly displayed on her face, so cloudless and simple when she was happy and untroubled.

Julien did not dare, now, to daydream unguardedly. Calmer, and less loving, he thought it unwise to go to her room that night. It would be better if she came to his: if a servant saw her hurrying through the house, there would be twenty different excuses for so quick paced a walk.

But this arrangement, too, had its difficulties. Fouqué had sent Julien volumes that he, as a student of theology, had never been able to ask for, at a bookshop. He dared open them only at night. He was deeply pleased that no visitor could interrupt him; before the little episode in the orchard, any such expectation would have rendered him unable to focus on what he was reading.

Madame de Rênal had shown him an entirely new way to understand these books. He had ventured to ask her a horde of questions: they were all about small issues, but ignorance of them simply checked the mind of a young man not born into good society—no matter the natural genius he seemed to have.

This education, administered by love and given him by a wonderfully ignorant woman, was sheer happiness. Julien immediately began to perceive society as, today, it actually is. His insights were not blurred by an account of what it had once been like, whether two thousand years ago or merely sixty years, in the days of Voltaire and Louis XV. To his inexpressible pleasure, a veil dropped away from his eyes: he at last understood what had been going on in Verrières.

To begin with, there were complex machinations, set in motion two years earlier by the governor at Besançon. These had the support of letters from Paris, written by men at the very highest levels. It was all about arranging for Monsieur de Moirod—the most pious man in the whole region—to be the first (not the second, but the first) deputy to the mayor of Verrières.

He was in competition with a certain very wealthy manufacturer, who absolutely had to be shoved down into the post of second assistant.

This allowed Julien to understand, at last, the hints he'd overheard when the region's high society came to dinner at Monsieur de Rênal's. These men of privilege were deeply concerned with who got the first deputy's post, though neither the rest of the town, and above all the liberals, suspected even the possibility of such an issue. What made this so important a matter, as everyone knows, was that the eastern side of Verrières's main street needed to be moved back a good nine feet, that thoroughfare having been designated a national highway.

Now, if Monsieur de Moirod, who owned three houses that would have to be moved to widen the road, should manage to become first deputy, he would automatically become mayor, should Monsieur de Rênal be elected to the Chamber of Deputies, and he would close his eyes, and the houses jutting out into the public road would be quietly and invisibly repaired, in assorted small ways, so they could stay where they were for another hundred years. For all Monsieur de Moirod's well-known probity, and his reputation for high piety, there was no doubt that he *would go along*, because he had a great many children. Nine of the houses scheduled to be moved were owned by the best people in Verrières.

To Julien, this plotting was far more important than the history of the Battle of Fontenoy, an event he'd become aware of, for the first time, in one of the books Fouqué had sent him. There had been things that astonished Julien, in the five years since he'd begun studying, at night, with the parish priest. But circumspection and humility being primary qualities for a student of theology, it had always been impossible for him to ask questions.

One day, Madame de Rênal gave an order to her husband's valet, Julien's enemy.

"But, madame, today's the last Friday of the month," the man replied rather strangely.

"All right, go," said Madame de Rênal.

"Oh, fine," said Julien, "he's going to that hay warehouse, the one that used to be a church and, not long ago, was put back into some sort of churchly service. But what's he going to do there? This is one of those mysteries I've never been able to unravel."

"It's a completely respectable institution, but very odd," replied Madame de Rênal. "Women are not allowed in. All I know is that everyone is on familiar terms with everyone else. For example, that servant will meet Monsieur Valenod, and that proud, stupid man won't be in the least put out to hear himself addressed, intimately, as 'Saint-Jean,' and he'll answer the servant just the same way. If you're really interested in finding out, I'll ask Monsieur de Maugiron and Monsieur Valenod for the details. It costs us twenty francs for every one of the servants, to keep them from cutting our throats, some fine day."

Time flew on. Thoughts of his mistress's charms distracted Julien from his dark ambitions. Although he did not realize it, the fact that he was required not to say anything about sad or rational matters, since they were each on different sides, added both to his happiness and to the power she had acquired over him.

When the presence of very perceptive children forced them to speak only in the language of cold reason, Julien watched her with the glowing eyes of love and, perfectly docile, listened as she explained how the world worked. Often, in the middle of her narrative of some masterly bit of knavery, having to do with constructing a road or providing supplies, Madame de Rênal would suddenly forget herself, losing control almost to the point of frenzy, and Julien would have to speak sharply to her, for she was allowing herself familiarities with him, exactly the sort of intimate gestures she used with the children. And there were days when she imagined loving him as if he were her child. Didn't she always have to answer his simple-minded questions about a thousand elementary things, matters of which no well-born child of fifteen would be ignorant? The next minute, she adored him as her master. His genius almost frightened her: she thought herself able to see in this young ecclesiastic, each day more clearly, the great man of the future. She could see him as the pope, she could see him as prime minister, like de Richelieu.

"Will I live long enough to see you in your glory?" she would say to Julien. "There's a place all ready for a great man. The monarchy and the Church both need him."

CHAPTER EIGHTEEN

A KING IN VERRIÈRES

Is that all you're good for, to be thrown away, like the corpse of a
country, having no soul and your veins bloodless?
—SERMON BY THE BISHOP, AT SAINT CLEMEN'S CHAPEL

On the third of September, at ten o'clock at night, a gendarme woke
up everyone in Verrières, galloping up the highway. He brought the
news that His Majesty, the King of ———, was arriving on Friday
next, and would be staying till Tuesday. The head of the district
authorized—that is, ordered—a guard of honor to be assembled:
every possible pomp and ceremony was to be exhibited. A mounted
courier had been dispatched to Verrières. Monsieur de Rênal arrived
that night and found the town all aflutter. Everyone had ambitions;
those with the least pretentions were renting their balconies for observing the king's entrance.

Who would command the guard of honor? Monsieur de Rênal saw
at once how vital it was, on behalf of those whose houses might have
to be moved, that Monsieur de Moirod should be the commander.
This could establish his claim to be first deputy. There was no difficulty about Monsieur de Moirod's piety, which was beyond all comparison, but he had never before ridden a horse. He was a man of
thirty-six, profoundly fearful, and equally terrified of tumbling off
and becoming an object of ridicule.

His Honor the Mayor paid him a call at five the next morning.

"Please be aware, monsieur, that I come seeking your advice, exactly as if you already held the post that all upright people wish you
to have. In our unfortunate town, industrialists are becoming wealthy,
liberals are turning into millionaires: they long for power, they know
how to capitalize on every chance. Let us consider the interests of the
king, of the monarchy and, above all, of our holy religion. How would
you feel, monsieur, if you were offered command of the guard of
honor?"

In spite of the terror that horses inspired in him, Monsieur de Moirod finally accepted the honor, as a form of martyrdom. "I know how to behave properly," he told the mayor. There was barely enough time to put the uniforms in order: they had last been used seven years before when a prince of royal blood passed through.

At seven o'clock, Madame de Rênal arrived from Vergy, together with Julien and the children. She found her drawing room filled with liberal ladies, preaching amalgamation of the two political parties, and asking her to persuade her husband to grant them, too, a place in the guard of honor. One of them pretended that if her husband was not chosen, grief would drive him into bankruptcy. Madame de Rênal quickly sent them all away. She seemed much preoccupied.

Julien was astonished but, even more, angered that she was making a mystery of whatever might be troubling her. "I thought as much," he told himself, bitterly. "The joy of receiving royalty in her house drives love from her mind. All this fussing simply dazzles her. She'll love me again, when these class-inspired notions stop bothering her brain."

What truly amazed him was that, on these accounts, he loved her even more.

Decorators began pouring into the house; he tried in vain to find an opportunity to say anything to her. He finally managed, just as she was coming out of his room, carrying off one of his suits. He tried to speak to her. She refused to listen. "I'm really a fool to love a woman like this: ambition turns her just as crazy as her husband."

She was crazier. One of her greatest longings, which she had never confessed to Julien, for fear of shocking him, was to see him out of his dreary black garments, even if only for a single day. With a dexterity quite remarkable in a woman so straightforward, first she got Monsieur de Moirod, and then the deputy governor of the district, Monsieur de Maugiron, to agree that Julien should be included in the guard of honor, in preference to five or six young men, sons of very wealthy industrialists, two of whom, at least, were of exemplary piety. Monsieur Valenod, who planned to loan his dashing light carriage to the prettiest women in town, and get them to admire his handsome Normands, agreed to let Julien have one of his horses, though he loathed him. But all the honor guards would have, or would borrow, gorgeous sky blue outfits with two silver colonel's shoulder-pieces, last put on glittering display seven years earlier. Madame de Rênal wanted a new costume, and it took her no more than four days to send to Besançon, and to receive from there an entire uniform, complete with sword and cap, and everything else belonging to a guard of honor. Amusingly, she thought it unwise to have all this made in Verrières. She wanted to surprise him, him and the whole town.

Once he had behind him the tasks of creating the guard of honor, and of building public spirit, the mayor was able to busy himself with a great religious ceremony. The King of ——— would not want to pass through Verrières and not visit the famous relic of Saint Clemens, preserved in Upper Bray, not far from the town proper. It would be desirable to have as many clerics as possible, but this was the hardest thing to arrange. Father Maslon, the new parish priest, wished at all costs to avoid including Father Chélan. Monsieur de Rênal tried to explain to him that this would not be wise, but in vain. The Marquis de La Mole, whose ancestors had for so long been royal governors of the entire province, had been appointed to accompany the King of ———. He had known Father Chélan for thirty years. He would surely ask for news of him, when he got to Verrières, and should he find that the old priest was out of favor, and out of office, he was exactly the sort who would call on the old priest, in the little house to which he had retired, and bring with him everyone he could from the whole attending train. What a slap in the face!

"I would be dishonored both here and in Besançon," declared Father Maslon, "if he were included among my priests. Good Lord, he's a heretic!"

"No matter what you say, my dear Father," replied Monsieur de Rênal, "I cannot expose the administration of Verrières to an insult from Monsieur de La Mole. You're not familiar with him: though he's a courtier of considerable weight, out here in the countryside he wields a singularly wicked tongue, always trying to embarrass people. He's quite capable, simply for his own amusement, of covering us with ridicule in every liberal's eyes."

It was only between Saturday night and Sunday morning, after three days of bargaining, that Father Maslon yielded to the mayor's fear, which was evolving into courage. A sugared letter had to be written to Father Chélan, seeking his assistance for the reliquary cere-mony at Upper Bray, provided his great age and his physical limita-tions would allow him to come. Father Chélan requested, and received, a letter of invitation for Julien, who was to accompany him, as a sub-deacon.

Beginning Friday morning, thousands of peasants, tumbling down from the surrounding mountains, inundated the streets of Verrières. The weather was bright and sunny. At last, toward three o'clock, the crowd was suddenly aroused: a great fire had been seen on a high rock about three miles from Verrières. This announced that the king had just crossed the department's borders. Immediately, the ringing of all the bells, and repeated salutes fired by an old Spanish cannon owned by the town, signaled the collective joy on this grand occasion. Most of the inhabitants climbed onto rooftops. The women were all on bal-conies. The guard of honor was set in motion. The glittering uniforms were admired; everyone recognized a parent, a friend. Monsieur de Moirod's fear was laughed at: he rode with his wary hand ready, at any moment, to clutch at his saddlebow. But one sighting made everyone forget all the others: the lead horseman in the ninth rank was a very handsome young fellow, very slender, and at first totally unrecognized. Soon a cry of indignation from some quarters, and silent astonishment from others, proclaimed universal astonishment. The horseman, mounted on one of Monsieur Valenod's Normand steeds, was per-ceived to be young Sorel, the carpenter's son. With a single voice, all of them, and especially the liberals, cried out against the mayor. Just because this little workman, disguised as an ecclesiastic, tutored his brats, he'd had the audacity to include him in the guard of honor, to the prejudice of so-and-so and so-and-so, wealthy industrialists! These gentlemen, declared a lady banker, really ought to publicly snub this impudent little meddler, who'd been born on a dung heap.

"He's a sneaky sort, and he's wearing a sword," said a man nearby. "He's vicious enough to slash them across the face."

The aristocracy's remarks were deadlier. The ladies wondered if it had been the mayor all by himself who'd perpetrated this gross im-propriety. Most of them knew the mayor's contempt for those of low birth.

While he was the subject of so much chatter, Julien was the happiest of men. Naturally bold, he handled himself better on horseback than did most of the young men of this mountain town. He could tell from the women's eyes that they were talking about him.

His silver shoulder-pieces shone more brightly, since they were new. His horse kept rearing and bucking; he was overflowing with joy.

But his happiness knew no bounds when, as they passed beneath the walls of the old fort, the sound of the little cannon made his horse jump out of line. By great good luck, he did not fall, and from that moment he felt himself a hero. He was an artillery officer in Napoleon's army, he was charging at an enemy battery.

There was one person still happier. She had first seen him as he passed the town hall's casement windows. Then, riding in a light carriage, and quickly making a large detour, she arrived just in time to shudder as his horse drove out of the line. Finally, her carriage dashing at full gallop, heading out one of the other town gates, she managed to reappear at the spot where the king was to pass, and proceeded on just behind the slowly advancing lines, no more then twenty paces distant, in the middle of all the noble dust. Ten thousand peasants shouted when the mayor had the honor of speechifying for His Majesty: "Long live the king!" Another hour afterward, when all the speeches had been listened out to the very last word, the king actually entered the town and the little cannon began to fire like mad. Alas, then came an accident—not to the cannoneers, who had proven their worth at Leipzig and Montmirail, but to the future first deputy, Monsieur de Moirod. His horse threw him off, and he landed, gently, right in the only pool of mud along the whole route, which was scandalous, because he had to be hauled out of there before the king's carriage went by.

His Majesty descended in front of the beautiful new church, which that day was decked out with its crimson banners. The king then had to eat his dinner, and immediately thereafter get back into his carriage so he could venerate the relic of Saint Clemens. The king had barely reached the church when Julien came galloping toward Monsieur de Rênal's house. There, with regret, he took off his lovely sky blue outfit, his sword, and his silver shoulder-pieces, in order to reassume his usual shabby black garments. Climbing back onto the horse, he was soon at Upper Bray, which lay along the heights of a singularly lovely hill. "Enthusiasm multiplies these peasants," he thought. "Verrières is totally clogged, but here are more than ten thousand more, swarming around this old church." Half ruined by revolutionary vandalism, it had been magnificently rebuilt, since the Restoration of the Monarchy, and there was already talk about miracles. Julien found Father Chélan, who first sharply rebuked him, and then gave him a cassock and a white overrobe. Julien quickly dressed himself and followed Father Chélan, who went looking for the young Bishop of Agde. He was Monsieur de La Mole's nephew, recently elevated to the post, and was supposed to display the relic to the king. But the bishop could not be found.

The priests grew impatient. They awaited their leader in the old church's dark, Gothic cloister. Forty-eight priests had been brought together, thus figuratively reconstituting the old Canonical Chapter of Upper Bray, which before the Revolution had been composed of forty-eight members. After three-quarters of an hour discussing the bishop's youthfulness, the priests thought it appropriate that the dean of the chapter seek out the lord bishop, informing him that the king would soon be arriving, so he had better come to the cloister right away. Father Chélan's great age had made him the dean. Despite his restiness to Julien, he indicated that the young man was to accompany him. Julien wore his surplice extremely well. Employing a style of ecclesiastical grooming about which I know nothing, he had smoothed down his beautiful hair so that it lay entirely flat, though by an oversight (which increased Father Chélan's ill humor), under the long folds of his cassock he was visibly still wearing his guard of honor spurs.

When they reached the bishop's chamber, the great man's servants, festooned with decorations, curtly replied to the old priest that His Lordship could not be seen. And they made fun of him, when Father Chélan tried to explain that, given his status as dean of the noble Canonical Chapter of Upper Bray, he was entitled to be admitted to the presiding bishop's presence whenever he liked.

Julien was too haughty not to be shocked by these lackeys' insolence. He began to go from one door to another, through the old church's interior, trying every door he met with. One small door opened at his touch, and he found himself in the middle of an anteroom full of His Lordship's valets, all wearing black and wearing gold chains around their necks. Seeing how urgent he was, these gentlemen thought he'd been sent for by the bishop and allowed him to proceed. A few more steps, and Julien found himself in a huge Gothic hall, extremely dark, paneled in black oak; with a single exception, the high-pointed Gothic windows had been bricked over. There had been no attempt to disguise this coarse bricklaying, which was in sad contrast to the archaic beauty of the woodwork. The two longer walls of the hall, famous among Burgundy's antiquarians, and which Duke Charles the Bold had erected, about 1470, in expiation of one or another sin, were furnished with wooden stalls, richly carved. All the mysteries of the Apocalypse were there, portrayed by wood painted in various colors.

Julien was moved by this melancholy magnificence, so disfigured by bare bricks and untouched white plaster. He stopped, silent. At the far end of the hall, near the one window through which daylight penetrated, he saw a large swing-mounted mirror, framed in mahogany. A young man in a purple cassock and a lace overrobe, his head bare, was standing three steps from the glass. It seemed an odd furnishing for such a place; clearly, it had been brought from town. Julien noted how the young man was frowning; the mirror showed him making the sign of the cross with his right hand, in utter gravity.

"What is this all about?" he thought. "Is it some preparatory ceremony this young priest is performing? Perhaps he's the bishop's secretary. . . . He'll be just as insolent as the other lackeys. Ah well, no matter: let's give it a try."

He walked carefully down the length of the hall, his eyes focused on that one window, watching the young man, who went on giving the benediction, slowly, but over and over, never resting for a moment.

As he grew closer, he saw quite clearly the young man's irritated face. The richness of his lace overrobe caused Julien to stop, still some steps from the magnificent mirror.

"It's my duty to speak," he told himself, at last. But the hall's beauty had moved him, and he felt himself already wounded in advance by the harsh words he expected to hear.

The young man saw Julien in his mirror, turned around, and immediately dropping his air of irritation, spoke in the gentlest tones:

"So, sir! Is everything finally ready?"

Julien stood there, stunned. As the young man had swung toward him, Julien had seen the great cross hanging on his breast. This was the Bishop of Agde. "So young," thought Julien, "no more than six or eight years older than me!..."

And he was ashamed of his spurs.

"My lord," he replied shyly, "I have been sent by the dean of the chapter, Father Chélan."

"Ah! He comes very highly recommended," said the bishop, his courtly manner redoubling Julien's fascination. "But I must beg your pardon, sir. I took you for the person who was supposed to fetch my miter. They did a ghastly job of packing it in Paris: the silver foil toward the top is horribly damaged. It would be a most ugly sight," the young bishop added sadly, "so I still have to wait!"

"My lord, I'll go fetch your miter, if Your Grace will allow me."

Julien's beautiful eyes had their effect.

"Do go, sir," replied the bishop, with charming politeness. "I must have it at once. I am desolated, being thus obliged to keep the gentlemen of the chapter waiting."

When he got to the middle of the hall, Julien turned back toward the bishop, and saw him once again giving benedictions. "What could that be?" he asked himself. "Surely, some ecclesiastical ceremony required by the ceremony that's going to take place." Back in the valets' antechamber, he saw they had the miter in their hands. Yielding to Julien's imperious look, in spite of themselves they gave him their lord's miter.

He was proud to carry it. Crossing through the hall, he walked deliberately, holding it with respect. The bishop was sitting in front of the mirror. But from time to time his right hand, no matter how tired, kept making the sign of the cross. Julien helped him set the miter in place. The bishop shook his head from side to side.

"Ah! It will stay on," he said to Julien happily. "Would you step back a bit?"

Then the bishop walked, extremely quickly, to the middle of the chamber, after which he came back toward the mirror, his stride very deliberate. He'd gone back to frowning and, most solemnly, making the sign of the cross.

Julien was immobilized by astonishment, trying to understand, but unable to risk it. The bishop paused and looked at Julien, his face rapidly losing its grave appearance:

"What do you think of my miter, sir? Will it go all right?"

"Very well indeed, my lord."

"It's not set too far back? That would look rather silly. But it won't do, either, to wear it down over the eyes, like a policeman's cap."

"It looks exactly right, to me."

"The King of ———— is accustomed to older priests, and surely more somber ones. I would not want—especially because of my age—to seem too frivolous."

And the bishop set himself to walking, once more, and to the giving of benedictions.

"It's obvious," Julien told himself, finally daring to face the fact. "He's practicing how to make the sign of the cross."

A little later:

"I'm ready," said the bishop. "Go, sir, and alert the dean and the gentlemen of the chapter."

Soon Father Chélan, followed by two very old priests, entered the hall by way of a great, sculpted doorway that Julien had not noticed. But now he remained where his rank placed him, last of them all, unable to see the bishop except above the shoulders of all the priests crowding through the door.

The bishop came slowly down the hall; when he reached the doorway, the priests fell into line. After a brief moment of disorder, the procession began, the marchers intoning a psalm. The bishop was at the rear, between Father Chélan and another exceedingly old priest. Down the long corridors of the Upper Bray church they went; in spite of the bright sunshine outside, they walked in dark and dampness. Finally they reached the portal leading into the cloister. Julien was thrilled by such a beautiful ceremony. The ambition quickened in him by the bishop's youth was at war, in his heart, with the delicacy and exquisite politeness of the young prelate. This politeness was utterly unlike that of Monsieur de Rênal, even at his very best. "The more you ascend toward the highest rungs of society," Julien said to himself, "the more charming become the manners you find."

They entered the cloister through a side door. Suddenly a terrible noise shook the church's ancient vaults; Julien thought they might collapse. But it was the old cannon, once again. Pulled by eight galloping horses, it had just arrived, and, barely on the ground, had been quickly maneuvered into position by the cannoneers of Leipzig, who were firing five times a minute, just as if they were facing the Prussians.

But this wonderfully worthy sound no longer had any effect on Julien; he was no longer dreaming of Napoleon or of military glory. "So young," he thought, "to be Bishop of Agde! But where is Agde? And how much does the job bring in? Maybe two or three hundred thousand francs."

The bishop's servants appeared, with a splendid dais. Father Chélan grasped one of the supporting rods, but in fact it was Julien who did the carrying. The bishop seated himself. He had actually begun to look older: admiration for our heroes knows no bounds. "What couldn't be accomplished, with skills like that!" Julien thought.

The king entered. Julien had the pleasure of seeing him up close. The bishop made an elegant, impressive speech, not forgetting a touch of exceedingly polite agitation, as a mark of respect for His Majesty.

There is no need to go into the details of the ceremony at Upper Bray: for two weeks it filled the columns of every newspaper in the province. From the bishop's speech, Julien learned that the king was descended from Charles the Bold.

One of Julien's subsequent duties was to audit the ceremony's accounts. Monsieur de La Mole, having secured a diocese for his nephew, also wanted, courteously, to pay the expenses. The ceremony at Upper Bray, all by itself, had cost three thousand eight hundred francs.

After the bishop's speech, and the king's response, His Majesty ascended the dais, after which he showed his deep devotion by kneeling on a pillow near the altar. The choir encircled the stalls, which were raised a good two steps above the floor. It was on the higher of these steps that Julien was seated, at the feet of Father Chélan, and alongside a train bearer, similarly posted at the feet of a cardinal from Rome's Sistine Chapel. There was a Te Deum, and waves of incense, and endless volleys of muskets and artillery; the peasants were drunk with happiness and piety. A day like this undid the work of a hundred issues of Jacobin newspapers.

Julien was six paces away from the king, who in fact was praying fervently. Then he noticed, for the first time, a little man with a spiritual face, wearing virtually no ornaments. But there was a sky blue decoration underneath his very plain garments. Julien was closer to him than he was to most of the other lords, whose clothing was so heavily ornamented that—as Julien put it—the cloth itself could not be seen. This little man, as he soon learned, was Monsieur de La Mole. He struck Julien as proud and even arrogant.

"This marquis can't be as polite as my nice bishop," he thought. "Ah! Being a cleric makes you sweet and wise. But the king is here to venerate the holy relic, and I don't see any relic. Where would they keep Saint Clemens?"

A low-ranking priest, his neighbor, informed him that the venerable relic was housed high in the church, in a *burning chapel.*

"What is a burning chapel?" Julien asked himself.

But he did not want to seek an explanation. He redoubled his attention.

When it was a sovereign ruler who paid a visit, protocol specified that canons not accompany the bishop. But as they started toward the burning chapel, the bishop summoned Father Chélan, and Julien boldly followed along.

Having climbed a long staircase, they came to an exceedingly small door, but with a Gothic frame, magnificently gilded. The paint looked as if it had been applied just the night before.

Assembled in front of the door, on their knees, were twenty-four young girls, from Verrières's most distinguished families. Before opening the door, the bishop knelt in the middle of these pretty girls. As he prayed in a firm voice, they seemed unable to help admiring his beautiful lacework, his graceful bearing, his young and very gentle face. Whatever remained of our hero's rationality left him, as he saw this spectacle. At that moment, he would have gone to war for the Inquisition, and with deep conviction. Suddenly, the door opened. The small chapel seemed to be covered in light. On the altar stood more than a thousand candles, divided into eight rows separated from one another by bouquets of flowers. The sweet smell of the purest incense swept through the doorway like a whirlwind. Newly gilded, the chapel was very small indeed, but wonderfully exalted. Julien noticed that some of the altar candles were more than fifteen feet high. The girls could not restrain a cry of admiration. The only ones allowed into the chapel's tiny vestibule were the twenty-four girls, the two priests, and Julien.

Soon the king arrived, followed only by Monsieur de La Mole and his high steward. The guards stayed outside, on their knees, and presenting arms.

The king knelt so hastily that his knees fairly thumped on the prayer stool. Only then was Julien, glued to the gilded door, able to make out, underneath one of the girls' bare arm, the charming figurine of Saint Clemens. He was lying on the altar, dressed as a young Roman soldier. There was a large wound in his neck, from which blood seemed actually to be flowing. The artist had surpassed himself: the dying eyes, brimming with grace, were half closed. A budding mustache decorated the delightful mouth, half shut but seeming still to be praying. Seeing the statue, a girl standing next to Julien wept hot tears, one of which fell on his hand.

After a moment of the most profoundly silent prayer, disrupted only by the distant sound of bells, from villages thirty miles around, the Bishop of Agde asked the king's permission to speak. He delivered a brief sermon, deeply moving for its plain language; the effect was obvious.

"Never forget, young Christian ladies, that you've seen one of the greatest kings in the world down on his knees, here among the servants of God the All-Powerful and Awesome. These feeble servants, persecuted, murdered on earth, as you can see by the still-bleeding wound of Saint Clemens, have their triumph in heaven. Isn't this a sight, young ladies, you'll remember all the rest of your days? Hate the impious. Be forever faithful to this God—so great, so awesome, but so good."

At these words the bishop rose, authoritatively.

"Do you promise me that?" he said, holding out his arms as if inspired.

"We promise," said the girls, weeping.

"I receive your promise in the name of God Himself!" the bishop continued, in a voice of thunder. And the ceremony was over.

Even the king was weeping. It was a long time before Julien had the nerve to ask where the saint's bones were, those bones sent from Rome to Philip the Good, Duke of Burgundy. He was told they were hidden in the charming wax figurine.

His Majesty graciously permitted the young ladies who had accompanied him into the chapel to wear a red ribbon, inscribed HATE THE IMPIOUS, ETERNAL ADORATION.

Monsieur de La Mole had ten thousand bottles of wine distributed among the peasants. That evening, in Verrières, the liberals had ten thousand times more reason to light up their houses than did the royalists. Before his departure, the king paid a visit to Monsieur de Moirod.

CHAPTER NINETEEN

THINKING LEADS TO SUFFERING

Everyday events are so grotesque they keep you from seeing the very real misfortune of our passions.

—BARNAVE

Restoring everyday order to the furnishings, in the room Monsieur de La Mole had occupied, Julien found a very thick sheet of paper, double folded. He read the bottom of the first page:

To His Excellency, Marquis de La Mole, Peer of France, Knight of the King's Orders, etc., etc.

It was a petition written in the clumsy handwriting of a cook:

MONSIEUR MARQUIS,

I have been a religious man all my life. I was at Lyons, during the siege, in constant danger from mortar shells, in '93, of wretched memory. I receive communion; every Friday I go to mass in our parish church. I've never failed to do my Easter duty, not even in '93, of wretched memory. In my kitchen I had plenty of people, before the Revolution; my kitchen was always meatless on Friday. I enjoy a universal good reputation in Verrières, and I daresay I deserve it. I carry the dais in processions, alongside monsieur the parish priest and His Honor the Mayor. On high occasions, I carry a great big candle, bought at my own expense. All of which matters are on file in Paris, at the Ministry of Finance. I ask the marquis for the Lottery Bureau at Verrières, which will soon be vacant, one way or another, the current holder being very sick, and besides is someone who votes for the wrong side, etc.

De Cholin

In the margin of the petition was a note signed "De Moirod," which began: "I had the honor, *yesterday,* to speak to the good subject making this request, etc."

"So even that imbecile De Cholin shows me the path that needs to be taken," Julien told himself.

A week after the king passed through Verrières, what remained afloat, for all the innumerable lying stories, stupid explanations, ridiculous debates, etc., etc., which had focused, successively, on the king, the Bishop of Agde, Marquis de La Mole, the ten thousand bottles of wine, de Moirod's pitiful tumble—which, in the hope of a medal, kept him from leaving his house for a month after his fall—was the incredible indecency of Julien Sorel, a carpenter's son, having been *shoveled* into the guard of honor. You should have heard, on this subject, the wealthy industrialists, manufacturers of printed calico cloth, who, evening and morning, made themselves hoarse, in the cafés, preaching equality. That haughty woman, Madame de Rênal, was responsible for the abomination. Why? The beautiful eyes and lovely, fresh cheeks of the little ecclesiastic, Sorel, said all that needed to be said.

Not long after their return to Vergy, the youngest of the children, Stanislas-Xavier, developed a fever. Madame de Rênal immediately fell into a frightful state of remorse. For the first time, she criticized her love affair rationally; she seemed to understand, as if by some miracle, what an enormous sin she had allowed to sweep her away. No matter how profoundly religious her nature, until this moment she had not realized how great was her crime in the eyes of God.

Earlier, at the Sacred Heart convent, she'd loved God with a passion; even then she had feared Him. The struggles now lacerating her heart were even more frightful, because her fear had no basis in rational thought. Julien had learned that any attempt at rationality, far from calming her, proved inflammatory: she saw in it the language of hell. However, since Julien himself was very fond of little Stanislas, it was easier for him to talk to her about the child's illness, which soon became serious. And then remorse kept pushing sleep away from her bed: all she could do was lie in a grim silence, for if she opened her mouth at all, what emerged were confessions of her sins against God and man.

"I beg you," said Julien, whenever they were alone, "say nothing to anyone. Let me be the sole confidant of your pain. If you still love me, don't speak: all your words can't take away our Stanislas's fever."

But this was cold comfort and had no effect. He had no idea if Madame de Rênal had gotten it into her head that, to appease the anger of a jealous God, she either had to hate Julien or see her child die. Her inability to hate her lover, which she knew she could not do, was what made her so wretched.

"Go away from me," she said to Julien one day. "In the name of God, leave this house. It's your presence here that is killing my son.

"God is punishing me," she added in a low voice. "He is just. I worship His justice. My sins are frightful, and I have been living without remorse! All this was the first sign of God turning away from me: I need to be doubly punished."

Julien was deeply moved. There was no hypocrisy in her, no exaggeration. "She believes that, in loving me, she is killing her child, and yet the miserable woman loves me more than she does the child. No question, I cannot doubt it: remorse is killing her, and thus the sublimity of her emotions. But how could I have inspired such a love—me, so poor, so badly raised, so ignorant, sometimes so clumsy and so inept?"

One night, the child grew still sicker. At about two in the morning, Monsieur de Rênal came to see him. Consumed by fever, the child was severely flushed and did not recognize his father. Suddenly Madame de Rênal threw herself at her husband's feet: Julien saw that she meant to tell him everything and ruin herself forever.

Luckily, her strange behavior annoyed Monsieur de Rênal.

"Good-bye! Good-bye!" he said, starting to walk away.

"No, listen to me," his wife cried, on her knees in front of him, trying to hold him back. "Hear the whole truth. I'm the one who's killing my son. I gave him life and I'm taking it away from him. Heaven is punishing me, in the eyes of God I am guilty of murder. I must abandon myself, I must humble myself. Perhaps this sacrifice will appease the Lord."

If Monsieur de Rênal had been a man of any imagination, he would have known everything.

"Romantic notions," he exclaimed, pulling away from his wife, who was trying to wrap her arms around his knees. "All that is just romantic gush. Julien, the moment it's light outside, call the doctor."

And he retired to his bed. Madame de Rênal dropped back on her knees, half fainting, and pushed Julien away with a convulsive movement, when he tried to help her. Julien stood there, stunned.

"So here's the adulteress!" he said to himself. "Could it be possible that these tricky priests . . . might be right? Those who commit a multitude of them, may earn the true comprehension of sin? How incredible! . . ."

For twenty minutes after Monsieur de Rênal left, Julien watched the woman he loved, her head resting on the child's little bed; she was completely motionless and virtually unconscious. "Here's a woman of superior intellect reduced to a bundle of misery, and all because," he told himself, "she's come to know me."

Time sped by. "What can I do for her?" He had to make up his mind. "It's not a question, anymore, just about me. What do people and their dull affectations mean to me? What can I do for her? . . . leave her? But I'd be leaving her alone, and in the grip of the most dreadful grief. This automaton of a husband does her more harm than good. He'll speak harsh words to her, because he's a clod. She might go mad, throw herself out a window.

"If I leave her, if I stop watching over her, she'll tell him everything. And who knows? Maybe, for all the wealth she's brought him, he could turn her into a slave. She's capable of telling the whole thing, good Lord! to that son of a . . . that priest, Father Maslon, who'll use the death of a six-year-old child as an excuse for moving into this house, and never leaving, nor will that be an accident. In her grief and her fear of God, she'll forget everything she knows about the man, and all she'll see will be the priest."

"Go away," Madame de Rênal suddenly said to him, opening her eyes.

"I'd give my life a thousand times over," answered Julien, "if I knew what would be best for you. I have never been so loved, my dear angel, and perhaps only at this very moment have I begun, as never before, to adore you as you deserve. Should I go away from you, knowing you're miserable because of me! But my pain shouldn't matter. Yes, my love: I'll leave. But if I do leave you, if I stop watching over you, always putting myself between you and your husband, you'll tell him everything, you'll ruin yourself. Think: He'll drive you from the house, in disgrace; all Verrières, all Besançon, will be chattering about the scandal. All sorts of horrible things will be laid at your door; you'll never recover from the shame. . . ."

"This is what I'm asking for," she cried, standing up. "I'll suffer: so much the better."

"But what you'll do, if you create that kind of scandal, is spread your misery to him, too!"

"But I'll humble myself, I'll throw myself down in the mud—and maybe, doing that, I'll save my son. Humiliation like that, completely in the public eye—maybe that's public penance? Even more than having my weakness publicly judged, isn't that the greatest sacrifice I can offer to God? . . . Maybe He'll look down and accept my humiliation, and leave me my son! Show me a more painful sacrifice, and I'll hurry toward it."

"Let me be punished. I'm as guilty as you are. Do you want me to shut myself up in a Trappist monastery? The strict severity of a life like that might appease your God. . . . Ah, heaven! Why can't I take Stanislas's sickness on myself?"

"Oh, you love him, you do," said Madame de Rênal, standing once more and throwing herself into his arms.

And even as she did so, she pushed him away in horror.

"I believe you! I believe you!" she went on, after dropping onto her knees. "Oh, my one and only love! Oh, why aren't you Stanislas's father! Then this wouldn't be the horrible sin of loving you better than I'd love your child."

"May I stay here, if I love you only like a brother? That's the only rational atonement; it might appease the Almighty's anger."

"And me," she cried, standing up and taking Julien's head in her hands, holding it not too far from her eyes. "And me, will I love you as if you were my brother? Could I ever love you like a brother?"

Julien began to weep.

"I'll obey you," he said, falling at her feet. "I'll obey you no matter what you order me to do. That's all I'm capable of. My soul is crooked with pride; I see no other way. If I leave you, you'll tell your husband everything; you'll be ruined, and so will he. He'll never be in the Chamber of Deputies, not after such shame. If I stay, you'll think I caused your son's death, and you'll die of grief. Do you want to see what happens, if I do leave? If you like, I'll go and punish myself for our sins, leaving you for a week. I'll spend that week in a retreat—anywhere you like. At the church in Upper Bray, perhaps. Just promise me you'll confess nothing to your husband when I'm away. Consider: If you said I shouldn't, I'd never return."

She promised, he left, but after two days was called back.

"Without you, I cannot keep my promise. I will speak to my husband unless you're always here, your looks ordering me to stay silent. Every hour of this disgusting life seems as long as a whole day."

At last, heaven had mercy on this miserable mother. Little by little, Stanislas passed out of danger. But the ice had been broken, her mind had grasped the extent of her sin; she could no longer recover her equilibrium. Remorse remained, as it had to in so honest a heart. Her life turned into heaven and hell: hell when she was not looking at Julien, heaven when she was at his feet. "I'm not deceiving myself," she said inwardly, even when she dared surrender fully to her love. "I am damned, irremediably damned. You're young, I seduced you and you yielded: heaven can pardon you. But me, I'm damned. I have absolute proof of that. I'm afraid: who wouldn't be afraid, looking down into hell? But in my heart of hearts I feel no repentance. If I were given the chance, I'd commit my sin all over again. May heaven not punish me here and now, while I'm in this world, and not punish me through my children, and I'll deserve nothing more. But you, at least, my Julien," she cried aloud at other times, "are you happy? Do you think I love you enough?"

Julien's mistrust, and his wounded pride, which had above all else required a sacrificial love, could not withstand so exceedingly great a sacrifice, so clear and plain and so constantly renewed. He worshiped Madame de Rênal. "She's had every opportunity to be noble, and I'm a workman's son—and she loves me. . . . When I'm with her, I'm not just a kind of valet, responsible for a lover's duties." With that fear banished, Julien fell into all the insanity of love and its mortal doubts.

"At least," she cried, when she thought she saw him unsure of her love, "let me make you very, very happy, for the few days we have to spend together! Let's hurry: tomorrow, perhaps, I'll no longer be yours. Should heaven strike me through my children, there would be no possibility of trying to live just so I could love you, not knowing it was my sin that was killing them. I couldn't survive that blow. If I wanted to, I still couldn't; I'd go mad. Ah! If I could only take your sin on me, as you so nobly offered to take Stanislas's burning fever!"

This great moral crisis changed the quality of Julien's feeling for his mistress, as well as the nature of their mutual bond. His love was no longer merely admiration for her beauty, but pride in possessing someone like her.

Yet their happiness had become something altogether superior; the flame that devoured them had grown far more intense. They experienced wild, ecstatic fits. The world might have thought their happiness had much increased. But they never recovered the delicious calm, satisfaction without clouds, the easy happiness of their love's first periods, when Madame de Rênal's only fear had been that Julien did not love her enough. Sometimes, their happiness took on all the appearance of sin.

In their happiest moments, and apparently the most tranquil ones: "Ah! God in heaven! I see hell," cried Madame de Rênal, seizing Julien's hand with a convulsive movement. "What ghastly tortures! I've thoroughly deserved them." And she embraced her lover, attaching herself to him like ivy against a wall.

Julien tried, but in vain, to calm her quivering soul. She took his hand and covered it with kisses. Then she fell into a dark and dream-like musing: "Hell," she said, "hell will be good for me. I'll still have the few earthly days I spend with you—but a hell here on earth, my children's death. . . . But still, perhaps at that price my sin might be for-given. . . . Oh Almighty God! No, don't pardon me at that price. These poor children haven't offended against You, not in any way: me, me, I'm the only guilty one: I love a man who's not, not my husband."

Julien observed how, after this, Madame de Rênal would reach mo-ments of apparent tranquillity. She was groping for her inner self: she loved him, she had no desire to poison his life.

Amid these fluctuating times of love, of remorse, and of pleasure, the days went by, for them, at the speed of light. Julien lost the habit of reflecting, of pondering.

Miss Elisa went to Verrières, having some small legal matter to deal with. She found Monsieur Valenod deeply annoyed at Julien. She hated the tutor, and spoke of him often.

"You'll ruin me, sir, if I told you the truth! . . ." she said to Monsieur Valenod one day. "When it comes to really important things, employ-ers always take the same position. . . . None of you ever forgives a poor servant who tells you certain things. . . ."

Starting from such conventional phrases, which Monsieur Valenod's impatient curiosity knew how to compress and shorten, he learned things infinitely mortifying to his self-esteem.

This woman, the most distinguished in the entire region, around whom he had so carefully and solicitously hovered for six years, un-fortunately in the full sight, and the full knowledge, of the whole world—this woman, so proud, whose contempt had so often made him redden all over, had just taken as her lover a petty laborer disguised as a tutor. And to complete his vexation, the director of the Pauper's Bu-reau also learned that Madame de Rênal adored her lover.

"And," the lady's maid added, sighing, "Monsieur Julien scarcely had to lift a finger to achieve this conquest. She's had no effect at all on that fixed coldness of his."

Elisa had not known for sure, till they'd gone to the country, but she suspected the affair dated back a good deal further.

"That's got to be the reason," she added spitefully, "for his refusing to marry me. And I, like an idiot, I went to Madame de Rênal for advice, begging her to speak to the tutor."

That very evening, along with his newspaper, Monsieur de Rênal received a long anonymous letter, informing him in great detail of what had been going on under his roof. Julien saw him turn pale, reading this letter, written on bluish paper, and looking up at the tutor with malevolent glances. And the whole evening, His Honor the Mayor never let go of what was bothering him; Julien wasted his breath, trying to please him, asking about various genealogical details concerning the best families in Burgundy.

CHAPTER TWENTY

ANONYMOUS LETTERS

Do not give dalliance
Too much the rein: the strongest oaths are straw
To the fire i' the blood.
—SHAKESPEARE, *THE TEMPEST*

At midnight, as they were leaving the drawing room, Julien was able to say to his beloved:

"We can't see each other, tonight. Your husband is suspicious. I could swear that long communication he was reading, sighing the whole time, was an anonymous letter."

Luckily, Julien locked himself in his room. Madame de Rênal had the crazy idea that his warning was just a pretense, that he did not want to see her. She absolutely lost her head, appearing in front of his door at the usual time. Having heard sounds in the corridor, Julien immediately snuffed out his candle. Someone tried to open the door: Was this Madame de Rênal, or was it a jealous husband?

Quite early the next day, the cook, who had always watched over Julien, brought him a book, on the cover of which he read the following, written in Italian: *"Look at page 130."*

Shuddering at her rashness, he found page 130, and there discovered, attached by a pin, the following hastily scribbled letter, bathed in tears and badly written:

You didn't want to see me tonight? It's times like this when I think I've never read your soul down to the bottom. Your glances frighten me. I'm afraid of you. My God! Haven't I loved you enough? If that's the way it is, let my husband learn all about our love, and let him shut me up forever in some country prison, far away from my children. Maybe that's what God wants, too. I'll die quickly enough. But you'll be a monster.

Don't you love me? Are you tired of my craziness, my confessions, and my guilt, you who utterly lack faith? Would you like to destroy me? Here, I've given you an easy way to do it. Go on, show this letter to everyone in Verrières, or better yet just show it to Monsieur Valenod. Tell him I love you—but no, don't say anything so blasphemous. Tell him I adore you, that my life never began until the day I saw you, that in the wildest moments of my childhood I never so much as dreamed of the happiness I owe you, that I've sacrificed my life for you, that I sacrifice my soul for you. You know that I'm sacrificing much, much more for you.

But what does that man understand about sacrifice? Tell him—tell him, just to make him angry, that I defy all the wicked, and there's no longer any ill fortune left in the world, for me, except to see changes in the only person who's keeping me alive. What happiness it would be to lose that life, to offer it as a sacrifice, and never again have to fear for my children!

Surely, my dear, if there is an anonymous letter, it comes from that disgusting being who, for six years, has pursued me with his awful voice, his stories about how well he jumps, on horseback, his conceit, and the unending enumeration of all the money he makes.

Was there an anonymous letter? My naughty one, that's what I'd like to discuss with you—but no, you did the right thing. Holding you in my arms, perhaps for the last time, I could never have been able to talk sensibly, as I do when I'm alone. From now on, happiness won't be so easy for us. Will that bother you? Yes—on days when you won't get any amusing books from Monsieur Fouqué. It's now all settled: tomorrow—whether there was or wasn't an anonymous letter—I'm going to tell my husband that I've received an anonymous letter, too, and he has to immediately offer you some fantastic sum, and figure out a decent excuse, and send you, at once, back to your father.

Alas, my dear! We'll have to be apart for two weeks, perhaps a month! But see? I'll do you justice, you'll suffer as much as I will. But in the end, it's the only way to counterbalance the effect of that anonymous letter. It's not the first my husband's received, and always about me. Alas, how I used to laugh at all that!

My sole objective will be to persuade my husband the letter came from Monsieur Valenod. I don't have any doubt he was in fact its author. If you leave the house, be careful to find yourself a place in Verrières. I'll make sure, somehow, that my husband plans to spend two weeks there, to prove to all the fools that there's no coldness between us, he and I. Once you're in Verrières, be sure to be friendly to everyone, even the liberals. I know all the ladies will be after you.

Don't be angry at Monsieur Valenod. Don't cut off his ears, as you said you would, one day. On the contrary, be terribly nice to him. The important thing they have to believe, in Verrières, is that you're going to work for him, or for someone else, as a children's tutor.

Now there's what my husband will never allow. And suppose he does? Fine! At least you'll live in Verrières, and sometimes I'll see you. Oh Lord! I think I love my children more, just because they love you. What a blow! How will all this end? . . . I'm wandering. Anyway, you know what you have to do. Be sweet, be polite, don't be nasty even to the most vulgar people—I beg you on my knees. They're going to decide our fate. Never forget for a moment that my husband doesn't in any way agree with you, when it comes to what he likes to call *public opinion*.

You're going to supply me with the anonymous letter. Arm yourself with patience, and a pair of scissors. Take a book and cut out the words you need. Then use light glue and stick them on the sheet of bluish paper I've enclosed: it came to me from Monsieur Valenod. Expect that your room will be searched, so burn the pages from which you've cut words. If you can't find the words you want, be patient and put them together, letter by letter. To save you trouble, I've made the anonymous letter very short. Alas! If you don't love me anymore, as I fear, this letter will seem to you very long!

ANONYMOUS LETTER

MADAME,

All your petty intrigues are known, but those who have an interest in curbing them have been notified. Because of a lingering regard for you, I pledge to totally separate you from the little peasant. If you are sufficiently prudent for this, your husband will be given to believe that the notice he received was a deception, and its erroneous nature will be made plain to him. Consider: I have your secret; tremble, wretched woman. From here on you have to *walk the straight and narrow:* I will be watching you.

When you've finished pasting up the words that compose this letter (did you recognize Monsieur Valenod's way of speaking?), go out of the house: I'll meet you.

I'll go to the village, and I'll return with a mournful face, which is indeed how I will feel. Good Lord! What am I risking, and all because you *thought you'd guessed* there was an anonymous letter. In any case, with a hangdog look, I'll give my husband the letter, which someone I didn't recognize will have delivered to me. And you, you go walking under the tall trees, with the children, and don't come back till dinnertime.

From up on the rocks, you can see the roof of the pigeon house. If everything went well for us, I'll set out a white handkerchief. If not, there won't be anything.

You ingrate: Won't your heart compel you to find some way of telling me you love me before you go for that walk? Whatever may come, be sure of one thing: if we are forever separated, I won't survive for a single day. Ah, you wicked mother! I've just written two empty words, dear Julien. I can't feel them: right now, all I can think of is you. I only wrote them because I don't want you to scold me. Now that I can imagine losing you, what's the point to pretending? Yes! I'd rather you think my soul horrid, than lie to the man I adore! I've done only too much deceiving, in this life of mine. All right: if you don't love me anymore, I forgive you. There's no time for rereading my letter. To me it seems a trivial matter, paying with my life for the joyous days I've spent in your arms. You know that's not all I'll have to pay for.

CHAPTER TWENTY-ONE

CONVERSATION WITH THE HEAD OF THE HOUSE

Alas, our frailty is the cause, not we:
For such as we are made of, such we be.
—SHAKESPEARE, *TWELFTH NIGHT*

Julien spent an hour putting together the words, enjoying himself like a child. As he was leaving his room, he met his pupils and their mother. She took the letter with simple naturalness and courage, so calmly that it frightened him.

"Is the glue sufficiently dry?" she asked him.

"Is this the woman that remorse made so wild?" he thought. "What is she planning right now?" He was too proud to ask her, but—and quite possibly, never—had she been more attractive to him.

"If this goes badly," she added with the same cool self-mastery, "they'll take everything I have. Bury this box somewhere on the mountain: one day it may be all I have."

She handed him a glass box, covered in red morocco leather, filled with gold and diamonds.

"Now go," she told him.

She hugged the children, the youngest one twice. Julien did not move. She walked rapidly away, without glancing at him.

Ever since opening the anonymous letter, Monsieur de Rênal had suffered frightful agonies. He had not been so agitated since a duel he had just managed to avoid in 1816, and, to do him justice, the thought of being shot had made him less miserable. He scrutinized the letter in every possible way: "Isn't this a woman's handwriting?" he said to himself. "And if it is, what woman wrote it?" He reviewed every woman he knew in Verrières, without being able to settle on any suspect. "Could a man have dictated the letter? Who?" The unknowable factors remained the same. He was a jealous man, and certainly hated by most of those he knew. "I must ask for my wife's advice," he said to himself, out of pure habit, rising from the armchair into which he had sunk.

And, barely on his feet: "Good Lord!" he said, slapping himself on the head. "More than anyone, it's she I have to watch out for. Right now, she's my enemy." And anger brought tears to his eyes.

An appropriate reward for his flinty-heartedness, regarded by country people as wisdom's only practical path, was that the two men he most keenly mistrusted, at the moment, were also his two most intimate friends.

"And then, I have perhaps ten friends," and he thought about them, calculating what sort of consolation he could count on from each. "For all of them! For all of them!" he exclaimed furiously, "my ghastly luck will be an intense delight!" Luckily, he believed he was just as intensely envied, and with good reason. In addition to his superb town house, which the King of ———, by sleeping there, had just forever honored, he had built up, and most handsomely, his château in Vergy.

It had been painted white in front, and the windows decorated with lovely green shutters. For a moment, he felt comforted by the very thought of this magnificence. Indeed, this château was visible from a distance of ten miles or more, thus eclipsing all the country houses, or would-be châteaux, in the neighborhood, the humble hues of which had been allowed to go gray with age and weather.

Monsieur de Rênal could count on the tears, and the pity, of one of his friends, the parish churchwarden, but he was an imbecile who would cry about anything. Yet this man was his one and only resource.

"No one's as miserable as I am!" he cried angrily. "What horrible loneliness!

"Can it really be," the man actually started to whine, "can it really be that, with all my woes, I haven't got a single friend I can turn to for advice? Because my brain's unhinged, I know it is! Ah, Falcoz! Ah, Ducros!" he cried bitterly. These were two childhood friends his arrogance had forever alienated, in 1814. They were not aristocrats, and he'd wanted to break away from the spirit of equality in which they had lived since childhood.

One, Falcoz, a warmhearted, spirited man, a paper merchant in Verrières, had bought a printing house in the province's largest town and launched a newspaper. The Congregation of the Holy Virgin decided to ruin him: his newspaper had been closed up, his printing license had been revoked. In these difficult circumstances, he tried writing, for the first time in ten years, to Monsieur de Rênal. The mayor of Verrières felt it his duty to respond like an old Roman: "Had the king's minister done me the honor of asking for my advice, I would have told him: 'Have no pity on the printers in this province, ruin them all, and turn printing into a monopoly, exactly like tobacco.'" Monsieur de Rênal remembered the language of this letter to his old friend—which at the time had earned the admiration of all Verrières— with horror. "Who would have said that, for all my social standing, my wealth, my awards and decorations, I'd one day regret it?" He was in the midst of an angry frenzy, directed equally against himself and everything around him, since he'd spent a dreadful night. Luckily, however, he had not thought of spying on his wife.

"I'm used to Louise," he told himself. "She knows all my business:

if I were free to marry tomorrow, I couldn't replace her." So he soothed himself with the notion that his wife was innocent. This way of looking at things did not require of him any demonstration of character, and it set everything in good order. "After all, how many slandered women have we seen!

"What's going on here?" he suddenly exclaimed, while walking wildly up and down. "Why should I let her, and her lover, laugh at me as if I were a nobody, some barefoot beggar? Should everyone in Verrières be gloating at how good-natured I am? What haven't they said about Charmier (who was a local fellow, a notorious cuckold)? As soon as they hear his name, doesn't everybody start grinning? He's a fine lawyer: Whoever says anything about the speeches he makes? 'Ho, Charmier!' they say, '*Barnard*'s Charmier'—which is what they call him, since that's the name of the other fellow, the man who's disgracing him."

"God be praised," said Monsieur de Rênal, at other moments, "that I don't have a daughter: however I decide to punish the children's mother, that won't interfere with any doweries. Maybe I can catch the little peasant with my wife, and kill them both. That way, the tragedy might wipe away all the ridicule." This idea made him smile; he worked it out in full detail. "The penal code is on my side and, no matter what happens, the Congregation of the Holy Virgin and my friends on the jury will save me." He examined his hunting knife, which was very sharp. But the idea of blood frightened him.

"I could beat up this arrogant tutor, and run him off. But what a scandal in Verrières, and even in the whole province! After Falcoz's newspaper was shut down, and his editor in chief got out of prison, I was one of those who kept him from getting a job worth six hundred francs. They say this scribbler has had the nerve to show up in Besançon: he could thoroughly thump me, in print, and do it so skillfully I could not sue him. Sue him! . . . The arrogant fellow would find a thousand ways of hinting that everything he'd said was true. A well-born man who preserves his social standing is universally hated by the lower classes. I can just see my name in those ghastly Parisian newspapers. Oh God! What a bottomless pit! To see the ancient name of Rênal muddied with the muck of ridicule . . . If I ever traveled, I'd have to change my name. Ha! Give up this name, which has created my glory and my power! What a heap of wretchedness!

"If I don't kill my wife, just drive her away in disgrace, she has her aunt in Besançon, who'll back her with her entire fortune. My wife will go live in Paris, with Julien. Everyone in Verrières will know about it, and I'll still be taken for a stupid fool."

Then the miserable man became aware, by the thin light coming from his lamp, that dawn was coming. He went out to take a bit of fresh air in the garden. Right then, he had virtually decided not to create a scandal—mostly because a scandal would give such immense pleasure to his good friends in Verrières.

Walking in the garden calmed him a little. "No," he exclaimed inwardly, "I'm not going to deprive myself of my wife, she's much too useful to me." He pictured to himself, with horror, what the house would be like without his wife. He had no relative except the Marquise de R———, a widow, an imbecile, and ill-natured.

A wonderfully sensible idea began to come to him—but carrying it off would require a strength of character far superior to what the poor man actually possessed. "If I keep my wife," he told himself, "I know that, some day, if she provokes me, I'll reproach her for her sin. She's proud, we'll separate—and that will happen even before she's inherited her aunt's estate. Oh, how they'll make fun of me! My wife loves her children; in the end they'll go to her. But me, I'll be the talk of Verrières. 'What?' they'll say. 'Didn't he even know how to get revenge on his wife?' Wouldn't it better to be satisfied with being suspicious, and not go hunting for proof? But then I'd be tying my own hands, I'd never again be able to reproach her for anything."

The next minute, having revived his wounded vanity, Monsieur de Rênal recalled, in great detail, all the various tricks recited at Verrières's casino and at the gentlemen's club, when some sharp-tongued fellow would interrupt their play at billiards, amusing himself by cutting up a deluded husband. But, now, how cruel those witticisms seemed to him!

"God! Why isn't my wife dead! Then I wouldn't be open to ridicule. If only I were a widower! I'd go to Paris and spend six months in the best society." After a moment of happiness, inspired by the thought of becoming a widower, his mind began to toy with ways of finding out the truth. At midnight, once everyone was in bed, could he spread a thin layer of bran in front of the door to Julien's room? The next morning, at daybreak, he'd be able to see the footprints.

"But what good would it be," he swore to himself, suddenly and violently. "That slut Elisa would have seen it, and everyone in the house knows how jealous I am."

In another of the stories told at the casino, a husband guaranteed his misfortune by sticking a bit of wax, like a seal, on his wife's door and on that of her lover.

After so many hours of circling around and around, this way of shedding light on his fate struck him, decidedly, as the best of all, and he had begun to think how to work it out when the walkway curved and, coming toward him, there was his wife, whom he had hoped to see dead.

She was coming back from the village. She had gone to hear mass at the church in Vergy. A vague tradition, on which philosophers may cast cold eyes, but in which she had faith, maintained that the little church that served them today had once been the chapel of the Lord of Vergy. The idea so obsessed Madame de Rênal that she constantly went there to pray. She imagined, over and over, her husband out hunting, and killing Julien, as if by accident, then later that night making her eat his heart.

"My fate," she said to herself, "depends on what he'll think, listening to me. After that fatal fifteen minutes, perhaps I'll never speak to him again. He's not someone either wise or rational. With my own limited intelligence, I should be able to anticipate what he'll do or say. He will decide our shared fate; he has the power. But that fate hangs on my ability to direct such a temperamental creature's thoughts, blinded by anger, blocked from seeing half of whatever's there to be seen. Oh Lord! I'll need ability, I'll need self-control. Where will I get them?"

Entering the garden, and seeing her husband in the distance, she found that calm, as if by magic. His wild hair and rumpled clothing showed he had not slept.

She handed him the letter, unsealed but refolded. Without opening it, he stared at his wife with demented eyes.

"Here is an abomination," she told him, "handed to me by some shabby fellow, who pretended he knew you and you would recognize him, as I went by the notary's garden. I ask only one thing of you, which is that you send this Monsieur Julien back to his father, and without any delay." Madame de Rênal hurried to say these words, perhaps speaking a bit too soon, in order to free herself of the horrible prospect of having to say them.

She was thrilled, seeing the effect she'd had on her husband. From the fixed look with which he stared at her, she understood that Julien had guessed correctly. "Instead of torturing himself with so real a misfortune, what genius he showed!" she thought. "What perfect tact! And in a young man still of so little experience! Where won't he get to, later on? Alas, his successes will make him forget me."

Suddenly, this small tribute to the man she adored freed her of her difficulties.

She congratulated herself on this development. "I haven't been unworthy of him," she told herself, with a sweet and intimate delight.

Without saying a word, for fear of committing himself, Monsieur de Rênal looked over this second anonymous letter, written—as my reader may recall—in printed words, pasted on a light blue sheet of paper. "They're making fun of me in all sorts of ways," Monsieur de Rênal said to himself, worn out by fatigue.

"Still more insults to look at, and always on my wife's account!" He was at the point of shouting the most vulgar insults at her, hardly restrained by the thought of the Besançon inheritance. Consumed by the need to attack her for something, he crumpled up the second letter and set himself to walking very fast; he needed to get away from his wife. A few moments later, he came back to her, and more calmly.

"It's a question of making a decision and sending Julien away," she said to him at once. "After all, he's a workman's son. You can compensate him with a handful of gold coins, and, besides, he's a scholar and he can easily place himself elsewhere—for example, with Monsieur Valenod or at Monsieur de Maugiron's house; they both have children. That way, you won't do him any harm. . . ."

"You talk like the fool you are," shouted Monsieur de Rênal, in a frightening voice. "How can anyone expect good sense from a woman? You never pay any attention to rationality: How could you know a thing? Your indifference, your laziness, require you to do no more than chase butterflies—weak beings we're cursed to have in our families! . . ."

Madame de Rênal let him talk, and he talked for a long time. *He got over his anger,* as they say in the country.

"Sir," she finally said to him, "I speak as a woman whose honor has been violated—in other words, the most precious thing a woman possesses."

Madame de Rênal maintained unyielding self-control, all through this painful conversation, on which depended the possibility of her continuing to live under the same roof as Julien. She groped for ideas most capable of guiding her husband's blind anger. She'd paid no attention to all the wounding comments he'd addressed to her; she did not hear them; all she thought about was Julien. "Will he be pleased with me?"

"This little peasant on whom we have lavished kindness, and even gifts, may well be innocent," she finally said. "But nonetheless, he's at least been the occasion for the first insults I've ever received. . . . Sir! When I read that awful piece of paper, I promised myself that either he left our house, or I would.

"Do you propose to create a scandal, which will dishonor me, and you as well? You'll thrill the good folk of Verrières.

"It's true: there is universal jealousy for the prosperity your administration, in its wisdom, has attained for you, for your family, and for the town. . . . Well! I'll get Julien to see you about taking a month's leave, at that timber merchant's place on the mountain—a worthy friend for a little workman."

"Don't get excited," replied Monsieur de Rênal, now pleasantly calm. "What I ask of you, above all, is that you do not speak to him. You'll make him angry, and get me into a quarrel with him. You know how touchy this little fellow is."

"The young man has absolutely no tact," answered Madame de Rênal. "He may be a scholar: you know more about that than I do. But at bottom he's a genuine peasant. Frankly, I've never thought well of him ever since he refused to marry Elisa, which would have been a guaranteed fortune, and his excuse for so doing was that, in secret, she paid visits to Monsieur Valenod."

"Ah!" said Monsieur de Rênal, his eyebrows raised unusually high. "What, did Julien tell you that?"

"No, not exactly. He's always talked about his vocation, his call for the holy ministry. But believe me, the primary vocation for people like him is having enough to eat. He led me to understand, pretty clearly, that he couldn't ignore these secret visits."

"And me, I had to be ignorant of them!" exclaimed Monsieur de Rênal, flaring up once again, and stressing every syllable. "Things go on in my house that I know nothing about. . . . What's this? Is there something between Elisa and Monsieur Valenod?"

"Ha! That's old news, my dear," said Madame de Rênal, laughing, "and maybe nothing wrong happened. It was when your good friend Valenod wouldn't have been sorry if it were thought, in Verrières, that he and I were having—purely platonically, mind you—a bit of a love affair."

"Which is what I thought, once," cried Monsieur de Rênal, angrily slapping his head, proceeding from one discovery to another. "And you never said anything to me about it?"

"Is there any point to making two friends quarrel, just because of our dear Valenod's little flush of vanity? Show me the woman in society who hasn't received letters that were witty, and even a touch gallant?"

"He wrote to you?"

"He wrote a lot."

"Show me those letters—immediately. I command it." And Monsieur de Rênal grew six feet taller.

"I've kept them, indeed," she answered, with a sweetness verging on indifference. "I'll show them to you someday, when you're more sensible."

"Right now, by all that's holy!" Monsieur de Rênal shouted, made drunk with anger—and yet happier than he had been in the last twelve hours.

"Promise me," said Madame de Rênal seriously, "that you won't quarrel with Monsieur Valenod about these letters?"

"Quarrel or no quarrel, I can take the foundling home away from him. But," he went on, furious, "I want those letters right now. Where are they?"

"In a drawer in my writing desk. But you may be sure I won't give you the key."

"I'll damn well break it," he shouted, running to his wife's room.

He broke it, in fact, with an iron bar—a precious carved mahogany writing desk, brought from Paris, which he used to polish, often, with his coattail, whenever he thought he'd seen a little spot.

Madame de Rênal went running up the hundred and twenty steps to the pigeon house; she tied the corner of a white handkerchief to the little window's iron bars. She was the very happiest of women. With tears in her eyes, she looked out toward the great woods of the mountain. "Surely," she told herself, "from under one of those shaggy birches, Julien can make out this happy signal." She listened for a long time, then cursed the noisy monotone of crickets and birdsongs. Without these insistent sounds, a cry of joy, sent from the high rocks, would have reached exactly where she stood. Her greedy eyes devoured the huge, dark green slope, smooth as a meadow, shaped by the treetops. "Why hasn't he got the wit," she asked herself, waiting all expectant, "to think of some signal, so he can tell me his happiness is as great as mine?" She did not come down until she began to be afraid her husband might come looking for her.

She found him wildly angry. He tore through Monsieur Valenod's bland phrases, not meant to be read with so much emotion.

Seizing a moment when her husband's emphatic performance gave her a chance to be understood:

"I keep coming back to my idea," Madame de Rênal declared, "that Julien really ought to go on a trip. Whatever skill he may have at Latin, he remains, after all, only a peasant, frequently coarse and deficient in tact: every day, thinking himself terribly polite, he makes me exaggerated compliments, in poor taste, that he's learned by heart from some novel. . . ."

"He never reads them," Monsieur de Rênal exclaimed. "I guarantee that. Do you fancy I run this house like a blind man, who has no awareness of what's going on?"

"All right! If he hasn't read these silly compliments, then he makes them up, and all the worse for him. In Verrières, too, he must have spoken to me like that . . . and though I can't quite be sure," said Madame de Rênal, "he must have spoken to Elisa that way: it's how she must sometimes have talked to Monsieur Valenod."

"Ah!" shouted Monsieur de Rênal, shaking the table and the entire room by one of the fiercest fist-pounding blows ever struck. "The anonymous letter, with those cut-out words, is written on the same paper as Valenod's letters to you."

"At last! . . ." thought Madame de Rênal. She made herself seem thunderstruck by this discovery, and, not having the courage to add a single word, went to the sofa, far away at the other end of the drawing room, and sat down.

But the battle was already won. She had her hands full, stopping Monsieur de Rênal from going to the anonymous letter's supposed author.

"Why don't you see that making a scene, without full and sufficient proof, would be to give Monsieur Valenod a signal of the greatest possible clumsiness? You are envied, sir, and who is to blame? Your own abilities: your wise administration, the tasteful construction work you've had done, the fine dowry I brought you, and above all the large inheritance we can expect from my aunt—an inheritance which is made to seem far more important than it is—have made you Verrières's leading man."

"You forget my birth," said Monsieur de Rênal, smiling a bit.

"You are one of the most distinguished gentlemen in the province," Madame de Rênal emphatically reaffirmed. "If the king were entirely free, and able to do justice to high breeding, you could imagine yourself, without any doubt whatever, in the House of Lords, etc. And being in so magnificent a position, you propose to give jealousy an occasion for comment?

"To speak to Monsieur Valenod is to proclaim to all Verrières—no, what am I saying? to Besançon, to the whole province—that this minor shopkeeper, who has been admitted, perhaps unwisely, to intimacy *with a Rênal*, has found a way of insulting you. If these letters, which you've now obtained, were to prove I'd responded to Monsieur Valenod's lovemaking, you'd be obliged to kill me, and I'd deserve it a hundred times over—but not to confront him in anger. Think: All your neighbors need no more than an excuse, they've been waiting for revenge on your superiority. Think: In 1816 you played a part in certain people's arrest. That man who was hiding on his roof—"

"What I think is that you feel neither respect nor goodwill toward me," exclaimed Monsieur de Rênal, with all the bitterness that such a memory revived. "And I was never made a peer!"

"What I think, my dear," Madame de Rênal responded, laughing, "is that I will be richer than you, that I've been your companion for twelve years, and that on all these matters I'm entitled to have a voice, and above all in today's business. If you'd rather have Monsieur Julien than me," she added with poorly masked displeasure, "I'm prepared to spend the winter with my aunt."

She phrased it *masterfully*, displaying a steadiness that was acting as if it were struggling to wrap itself in politeness. It was decisive for Monsieur de Rênal. Still, observing country procedures, he went on talking for a long time, reviewing all the arguments; his wife allowed him to talk: there was still anger in his voice. In the end, two hours of pointless jabbering exhausted the strength of a man who had been dealing with anger the whole night. He settled the approach he would take to Monsieur Valenod, to Julien, and even to Elisa.

Once or twice, during this great scene, Madame de Rênal was close to some degree of compassion, on account of the man's very real misery: he had been close to her for twelve years. But genuine passion is egotistic. Besides, from minute to minute she'd been waiting for him to acknowledge last night's anonymous letter, and there had been no such acknowledgment. Madame de Rênal's safety was not certain, lacking information about what ideas might have been suggested to this man, on whom her fate depended. In the countryside, of course, husbands are in charge of opinion. A moaning and groaning husband covers himself with ridicule (though from day to day this becomes less of a risk, in France), but his wife, if he refuses her money, lapses into the condition of a workman making fifteen cents a day, and respectable people are not always willing to hire her.

A harem slave can surely love her sultan; he is all-powerful; she has no hope of stealing his authority by a series of small subtleties. The household sultan can wreak terrible, bloody vengeance, but soldier-like, gracious: one dagger thrust, and it's all over. But in this nineteenth century, husbands kill their wives with public scorn—that is, by having all drawing rooms closed to them.

Madame de Rênal's awareness of danger was vividly heightened as soon as she returned to her room. She was shocked by how chaotic everything had become. The locks on every single one of her pretty little boxes had been broken; several of the thin parquet floorboards had been pried up. "He's had absolutely no pity on me!" she said to herself. "Ruining this colored wood, which he loved so much: when one of the children came in with wet shoes, he'd turn red with anger. And now it's ruined forever!" Seeing this violence drove away, and quickly, the last of her self-reproaches on account of her overly swift victory.

A little before dinnertime, Julien returned with the children. When they were drinking coffee and eating cheese, and all the servants had left the room, Madame de Rênal spoke to Julien, exceedingly dryly:

"You expressed your desire to me, that you might be permitted to spend two weeks in Verrières. Monsieur de Rênal is quite agreeable to granting you a leave. You can go whenever you think best. But to keep the children from wasting their time, their papers will be sent to you, every day, for your corrections."

"To be sure," added Monsieur de Rênal, his manner distinctly sour, "I won't give you more than a week."

Julien noted, on his face, the anxiety of a deeply tormented soul.

"He still hasn't made up his mind," he said to his beloved, in the drawing room, when they were alone for a moment.

Madame de Rênal swiftly told him everything she'd done since that morning.

"I'll give you the details, later tonight," she added, laughing.

"Female perversity!" thought Julien. "What pleasure, what instinct, leads them to deceive us?"

"It seems to me you're both enlightened and blinded by love," he said to her rather stiffly. "What you've done today is admirable, but is there any wisdom in seeking to be together tonight? This house is packed with enemies: just think of the passionate hate Elisa feels for me."

"That hate much resembles the passionate indifference you apparently feel for me."

"Even if I were indifferent, I have the responsibility of saving you from the peril into which I've plunged you. If, by some chance, Monsieur de Rênal decides to speak to Elisa, she can tell him everything in very few words. Suppose he hides himself near my room, well armed. . . ."

"Ah! Not even courageous?" said Madame de Rênal, with the arrogance of a noble family's daughter.

"I won't ever stoop to discussing my courage," said Julien coldly. "That's beneath me. Let the world decide, when I've done what I will do. But," he added, taking her hand, "you don't understand how deeply attached to you I am, and how happy it makes me to have this chance of taking leave of you, before our cruel separation."

CHAPTER TWENTY-TWO

PATTERNS OF BEHAVIOR, IN 1830

Words have been given to men in order to hide their thoughts.
—R. P. MALAGRIDA

He'd barely reached Verrières when Julien reproached himself for being unfair to Madame de Rênal. "I'd have been as spiteful as a little girl, had weakness made her avoid that scene with her husband! She behaved herself like a diplomat, and here I am, sympathizing with the defeated fellow who's my enemy. I'm behaving like a petty shop-keeper. My vanity is affected, simply because Monsieur de Rênal is a man!—a member of that vast, illustrious guild to which I, too, have the honor of belonging. I'm nothing but a fool."

After removal from office drove him out of the rectory, Father Chélan refused lodgings offered him, for political reasons, by the most substantial liberals in the region. The two rooms he'd rented were piled all over with books. Julien, wanting to show Verrières what being a priest was all about, got a dozen pine planks from his father, and lugged them down the highway on his back. Borrowing tools from an old friend, he soon constructed a set of bookshelves, in which he arranged Father Chélan's books.

"I'd thought you corrupted by worldly vanity," the old man told him, weeping with joy. "This is a worthy redemption for that bit of childishness, that brilliant uniform for the guard of honor, which made you so many enemies."

Monsieur de Rênal had directed Julien to live in the Rênals' Verrières house. No one had any idea what had happened. On the third day after his arrival, Julien was visited in his room by no less a personage than Monsieur de Maugiron, the deputy governor of the district. Only after two long hours of insipid verbiage, and jeremiads about the wickedness of human beings, the dishonesty of those in charge of the public treasury, the dangers facing our poor France, etc., etc., was Julien able to catch a glimpse of the point to this visit. They'd already gotten to the staircase landing, and the poor, half-disgraced tutor was in the process of saying farewell, with all proper signs of respect, when the future governor of some lucky district was pleased to concern himself with Julien's well-being, praising his moderation in matters that affected his own self-interest, etc., etc. Finally, embracing Julien in the most fatherly way, he suggested to him that he depart from Monsieur de Rênal's service, and make his entrance into the household of a civil servant who had children *to educate* and who, like King Philip, thanked heaven not simply for giving them to him but also for having brought them into a neighborhood where Monsieur Julien dwelled. Their tutor would enjoy a salary of eight hundred francs—not payable from month to month, which would not be truly generous, said Monsieur de Maugiron, but quarterly, and always in advance.

It was Julien's turn, after an hour and a half of listening to boring prattle. His reply was utter perfection, and above all quite as long as a pastoral letter. It left everything up in the air, saying nothing specific. It included respect for Monsieur de Rênal, reverence for the people of Verrières, and acknowledgment of so illustrious a gentleman as Monsieur de Maugiron. The deputy governor, dumbfounded to find Julien more Jesuitical than he was, tried in vain to secure some concrete response. Delighted, Julien took the opportunity to give himself some exercise, and began his reply all over, cast in different language. No eloquent parliamentarian, taking advantage of the end of a legislative session (when the elective body seems often to stir itself), has ever said less and employed a greater quantity of words. Monsieur de Maugiron was barely out the door when Julien began to laugh like a crazy man. To make full use of his Jesuitical spirits, he wrote a nine-page letter to Monsieur de Rênal, explaining everything that had been proposed to him, and humbly requesting his advice. "But, all the same, this scoundrel never mentioned the name of the 'civil servant' making this offer! It has to be Monsieur Valenod, who sees in my exile to Ver-rières the consequences of his anonymous letter."

His missive sent on its way, Julien—feeling as satisfied as a hunter who, at six A.M. on a beautiful autumn day, comes upon a field full of game—went to ask Father Chélan's advice. But before he got to the good priest's lodgings, heaven—wanting to contrive joyous occasions for him—set in his path Monsieur Valenod, from whom he did not conceal that his heart had been lacerated. A poor boy like him ought to be completely devoted to the vocation heaven had placed in his heart, but in this unspiritual world vocation is not everything. To do worthy work in Our Lord's vineyard, and not to become entirely un-worthy of his wise fellow workers, instruction was obligatory. Two ex-pensive years must be spent in the seminary at Besançon; economies were therefore necessary; and that would be a great deal easier on a salary of eight hundred francs, rather than six hundred francs, which was eaten up, month by month. On the other hand, in placing him with the Rênal children, and above all by inspiring him with a special af-fection for them, wasn't heaven indicating that this wasn't the time to give up that educational process for a different one? . . .

Julien had attained so high a degree of perfection, in this sort of eloquence, which in our time has been substituted for the swift-moving action of the Empire, that he ended by boring himself with the sound of his words.

Coming home, he found one of Monsieur Valenod's servants, in splendid livery, who had been looking for him all over town. A lun-cheon invitation for that very afternoon was delivered.

Julien had never been to the man's house; only a few days earlier, all he had thought of was the best way to beat him with a stick, but in such a way that it would not become a matter for criminal prosecution. Although the time was specified as one o'clock, Julien thought it more respectful to present himself at the Pauper's Bureau office at twelve-thirty. He found his host displaying his importance, surrounded on every side by file boxes. His huge black whiskers, his enormous shock of hair, his Greek cap set crossways on his head, his immense pipe, his embroidered slippers, the fat gold chains crossing every which way on his chest, and all the apparatus of a provincial financier who considers himself a Don Juan, had no effect on Julien. It only made him think, once again, of the cudgeling he owed the man.

He requested the honor of being presented to Madame Valenod; she was at her dressing table and could not receive him. In compensation, he was given the favor of assisting in Monsieur Valenod's preparations. Then they went to her together and she presented her children, tears in her eyes. This lady, one of the most important in Verrières, had the coarse face of a man, onto which she had been applying rouge, in honor of this grand ceremony. She displayed quantities of maternal pathos.

Julien thought of Madame de Rênal. His mistrust was scarcely susceptible to anything except this sort of recollection, summoned by contrasts, but which then gripped him almost tenderly. These feelings were heightened by being inside the Valenod house. He was given a tour. Everything he saw was magnificent and new, and he was told the price of each item. But Julien found it rather disgraceful, smelling of stolen money. Everyone, right down to the servants, seemed to be setting their faces against contempt.

The tax collector, the man who handled indirect taxes, the chief of police, and two or three other government officials arrived, along with their wives. They were followed by several rich liberals. Lunch was announced. Julien, already in a distinctly black mood, began to reflect that on the other side of this dining room wall were the captive poor, from whose food they had probably been *chiseling away* to pay for all this luxurious bad taste that they expected would overwhelm him.

"They're hungry, over there," he told himself. His throat tightened. He could not eat and almost could not speak. It grew worse a quarter of an hour later: they could hear, as if from a distance, phrases from a popular song—more than a little vulgar, it must be admitted—being sung by one of the shut-in poor. Monsieur Valenod glanced at one of his people, wearing full livery, who disappeared; soon they heard no more singing. Just then, a servant brought Julien Rhine wine, in a green glass, and Madame Valenod took pains to explain that this cost nine francs a bottle, if bought locally. Julien accepted his green glass and said to Monsieur Valenod:

"They're not singing that ugly song anymore."

"Indeed! I quite believe it," he replied triumphantly. "I've imposed silence on the beggars."

These words were too much for Julien. He had acquired the manners, but not the heart, of his social status. For all his hypocrisy, so frequently practiced, he felt a heavy tear rolling down his cheek.

He tried to hide it behind the green glass, but it was absolutely impossible for him to do honor to the Rhine wine. *"To stop them from singing!"* he said to himself. "Oh my God! How can You allow it?"

Luckily, no one noticed his unacceptable emotionalism. The tax collector had been singing a royalist tune. As the refrain was roared out, in chorus: "There you are," said Julien's conscience. "The filthy fortune you're after, and the only place you'll get to enjoy it is like this, and in this kind of company! You'll have a post worth maybe twenty thousand francs, but then you'll find, while you stuff down your meat, that you'll have to stop your poor prisoners from singing. You'll give dinners with money you've stolen out of their miserable pittance, and even as you eat they'll grow more miserable!—O Napoleon! It was good, in your day, to climb to fortune by fighting battles. But to accumulate like a coward, from the sorrows of the miserable!"

I confess that the weakness that Julien demonstrates, in this monologue, gives me a poor opinion of him. He'd be worthy of joining ranks with those parlor liberals, in their yellow gloves, who convince themselves they're changing the whole way of life in a great country, but who can't possibly have on their consciences the tiniest, most harmless scratch.

Julien wrenched himself, violently, back to what he was supposed to be doing. He hadn't been invited to dine in such excellent company just so he could dream and not eat a thing.

A retired manufacturer of calico prints, a corresponding member of the Besançon Academy, and of that in Uzès, called out to him, from one end of the table to the other, to ask if it were true, as it was generally said to be, that he'd accomplished such astonishing things in the study of the New Testament.

Immediately, a profound silence fell. A Latin New Testament appeared, as if by magic, in the hands of this scholarly member of two academies. After Julien replied, a half sentence of Latin was read out, at random. He recited: his memory was found accurate, and the prodigy was admired with all the clamorous energy that flows at the end of a good meal. Julien looked at the beaming faces of the ladies; some of them were not bad. He noted the tax collector's wife, he who had sung so well.

"I am ashamed, really, to speak for so long in Latin, in front of these ladies," he said, watching her. "If Monsieur Rubigneau"—this being the member of two academies—"would have the goodness to read, at random, a Latin sentence, instead of proceeding to what follows in the Latin text, I'll venture on an impromptu translation."

This second demonstration raised his glory to new heights.

There were several rich liberals in attendance, also the happy fathers of children capable of being awarded scholarships, who in that capacity had become immediate converts, right after the last revivalist mission. In spite of such cunning tricks, Monsieur de Rênal had never cared to have them to his house. These honorable men, who had known Julien only by reputation, and because he had been seen on horseback during the visit by the King of ———, were his noisiest admirers. "When will these idiots grow weary of listening to biblical phrases, of which they don't understand a thing?" he thought. But rather than the language itself, what amused them was its oddity. It made them laugh. But Julien grew tired.

He stood up, gravely, as six o'clock sounded, and told them of a new theological discussion by Ligorio, which he had been studying for recitation, the next day, to Father Chélan. "Because my business," he added pleasantly, "is to hear lessons recited, and to recite them myself."

They laughed heartily; they admired him. This is how it is, in Verrières. Julien was already standing, so in spite of decorum all the others rose: this is the power of genius. Madame Valenod kept him for a quarter of an hour; he was required to hear the children recite their catechism; they committed the funniest mistakes, which he alone noticed. He could barely keep from correcting them. "What ignorance of religion's first principles!" he thought. He finally made his farewells and thought he might escape. But he had to weather a fable by La Fontaine.

"This is a highly immoral writer," Julien told Madame Valenod. "A fable he wrote on my lord Jean Chouart has the effrontery to pour ridicule on the most venerable of things. He has been roundly censured by the better critics."

Before he left, Julien received four or five invitations to dine. "This young man does honor to our region," the merriest guests shouted in unison. They went so far as to talk about a grant, from public funds, which would even allow him to continue his studies in Paris.

As this reckless notion was making the dining room ring, Julien nimbly got himself to the outer door. "Ah, scum! scum!" he exclaimed to himself three or four times, in a hushed voice, as he gratefully breathed in the fresh air.

At that moment he felt himself profoundly aristocratic, he who for so long had been so shocked by the contemptuous smile and haughty superiority he had discovered, under the polite phrases addressed to him by Monsieur de Rênal. He could not help being aware of the enormous difference. "Let's even put aside," he said to himself as he walked along, "that this is about money stolen from captive poor folk—and yet, to keep them from singing! Had Monsieur de Rênal ever thought of telling his guests the price of every bottle of wine he offers them? And this Monsieur Valenod, who keeps explaining what he owns, and never stops—why, when his wife is there he can't say anything about his house, his estate, etc., without saying *your* house, *your* estate.

"And this same lady, who seems so aware of the pleasures of ownership, just made a disgusting scene, as we were dining, with a servant who'd broken a stemware glass and *spoiled one of her dozens*. And the servant had replied with infinite insolence.

"What a bunch!" Julien told himself. "If they gave me half of everything they own, I couldn't live with them. Some fine day, I'll give myself away—I won't be able to hold back the contemptuous remarks they inspire in me."

All the same, pursuant to Madame de Rênal's orders he had to attend a number of very similar occasions. Julien was fashionable: his guard of honor uniform was forgiven—or perhaps that recklessness was the real reason for his success. Soon, nothing was more at issue, in Verrières, than the struggle to obtain this young scholar's services: Who would win, Monsieur de Rênal or Monsieur Valenod? These two gentlemen, together with Father Maslon, had for years formed a triumvirate that ruled the town with an iron hand. People were jealous of the mayor; he gave the liberals much cause for complaint. But he was, after all, a nobleman and destined to be superior, while Monsieur Valenod's father hadn't left him so much as ten thousand francs a year. He had to ascend, starting from the pity people felt for him as a youngster, on account of the ugly green apple clothes he'd always worn, to now, when he was envied for his Normand steeds, for his thick gold chains, for his Parisian-fashioned clothing, and for the whole of his current prosperity.

In all this world so new to Julien, he thought he'd come upon an honest man. He was a mathematician named Gros, with a reputation as a Jacobin. Julien, having pledged himself to say nothing except what was contradictory to his true beliefs, found it necessary to hold back a bit, in dealing with Monsieur Gros.

Great packages of his pupils' writing came to him from Vergy. He had been advised to visit his father, as often as possible, and though it was a sorry necessity, he obeyed. In short, he did a fine job of repairing his reputation, until one morning he was surprised to find himself being awakened by a pair of hands placed over his eyes.

It was Madame de Rênal, who had come into town and, climbing the stairs four at a time, leaving her children busy with a pet rabbit they'd taken on their trip, had reached Julien's room moments before they could. It was a delightful moment, but very short: Madame de Rênal had vanished by the time the children came, bringing their rabbit, which they wanted their friend to see. Julien gave them all a hearty welcome, including the rabbit. He felt as if he'd found his family once again; he felt full of love for the children, and happy to chatter with them. He was astonished by the sweetness of their voices, the simplicity and generosity of their little ways: he had to wash his mind clean of all the vulgar acts, the unpleasant thoughts, in the midst of which he lived and breathed, in Verrières. There was always the fear of having to do without, there were always luxury and misery at each other's throats. In the houses where he dined on their roast beef, everyone told secrets humiliating to themselves and nauseating to those obliged to listen.

"You're different, you're generous, you're right to be proud," he told Madame de Rênal. He recounted all the events at places where he'd dined.

"So you're all the fashion!" And she laughed heartily, thinking of the rouge that Madame Valenod felt herself bound to apply every time Julien was expected. "I suspect she has designs on your heart," she added.

Lunch was delicious. The children's presence, no matter how troublesome it might have seemed, in fact added to the general happiness. The poor children could not fully express their joy at seeing Julien again. The servants had not failed to tell them how Julien had been offered two hundred francs more, to *educate* the little Valenods.

In the middle of the meal, Stanislas-Xavier, still pale from his serious illness, suddenly asked his mother how much his silver plate and the goblet he drank from were worth.

"And why are you asking?"

"I want to sell them so I can give the money to Monsieur Julien, so he won't be *cheated* if he stays with us."

Julien hugged him, tears in his eyes. The boy's mother wept freely as Julien, who had taken Stanislas onto his lap, explained that he didn't need to use the word *cheated*, which when employed in this way was a servant's way of speaking. Seeing the pleasure he was giving Madame de Rênal, he tried to explain, using colorful examples at which the children laughed, what being "cheated" really meant.

"I understand," said Stanislas. "It's the crow who's stupid enough to drop his cheese, and that flatterer, the fox, picks it up."

Madame de Rênal, wild with happiness, covered the children with kisses, which she could hardly have managed without a bit of help from Julien.

Suddenly the door opened: it was Monsieur de Rênal. His dour, unhappy face was in strange contrast to the gentle joy his presence had driven away. Madame de Rênal grew pale: she felt unable to deny a thing. Julien took hold of the conversation and, speaking quite loudly, set himself to telling His Honor the Mayor about Stanislas and the silver goblet he'd wanted to sell. He was sure the story would not be well received. At first, hearing the word *silver,* Monsieur de Rênal raised his eyebrows, purely out of habit. "Any mention of this metal," he said, "is always prefatory to a draft drawn on my bank account."

But more than his concern with silver was involved: he'd experienced a surge of suspicion. For such happiness to be animating his family, in his absence, did not sit well with a man so dominated by prickly vanity. As his wife, for her husband's benefit, praised Julien's cheerful, lively way of broaching new ideas to their children:

"Yes, yes! I quite understand, he's making me hateful to my own children. He's entirely comfortable, being a hundred times more likable than me—I being, in the end, lord and master here. In our time, everyone likes to cast aspersions on *legitimate* authority. Poor France!"

Madame de Rênal did not concern herself with any subtleties, in her greeting to her husband. She had been contemplating the possibility, before he'd appeared, of spending twelve hours with Julien. She had an enormous number of things to buy in town, and declared her absolute intention that they dine at a café: no matter what her husband might say or do, her mind was made up. The very word *café* completely captivated the children—this word that contemporary prudes mouth with such pleasure.

Monsieur de Rênal left his wife, in order to pay some visits, when she went into the first drapery shop. He came back even glummer than before: he was convinced that the whole world was thinking of nothing but him and Julien. In fact, nobody had given him the slightest indication that, in the eyes of the public, he might be the offended party. Whatever had been recounted to His Honor the Mayor was exclusively concerned with Julien, and whether he'd be staying for six hundred francs, or accepting the eight hundred offered by Monsieur Valenod.

And Monsieur Valenod, when he met Monsieur de Rênal, *cut him cold*. Nor was this a spontaneous maneuver: almost nothing, in the countryside, is done without good reason. Genuine emotion is so rare, out in the provinces, that it gets pushed as far down as it can go.

Monsieur Valenod was what's called, three hundred miles from Paris, a *slick operator*, a man of natural, coarse brazenness. His triumphant career, since 1815, had reinforced these handsome characteristics. He ruled, in other words, subject to Monsieur de Rênal's orders, but being so much more active, never squeamish about anything, able to mix with the populace, always on the go, writing, speaking, brushing off humiliation, totally devoid of personal pretentions, he had come, in the eyes of the ecclesiastical power, to quite balance out his mayor. Monsieur Valenod had more or less said to the province's grocers: "Let me have the two most stupid among you." He'd said to the purveyors of justice: "Show me your two most notable ignoramuses." To the supervisors of health: "Tell me who are your two most crooked." And when he had gathered together the most brazen, in every business and profession, he'd said to them: "Let's rule together."

These people's methods had offended Monsieur de Rênal. Valenod's coarseness was offended by nothing, not even by the wild denunciations spouted against him, in public, by little Father Maslon.

Yet in the middle of all his prosperity, Monsieur Valenod felt the need to bolster his confidence by tiny, trivial acts of haughtiness, directed against the coarse truths he knew, quite well indeed, the whole world had the right to address to him. His activity had sharply multiplied since the fears he'd experienced, following Monsieur Appert's visit. He'd made three trips to Besançon; every courier who'd ridden out of town carried letters from him; he'd sent others by the hands of people, known to no one, who came to his house when darkness fell. He had perhaps been wrong to take old Father Chélan's office from him, for that vindictive proceeding had made him seem, to several devout people of good birth and breeding, a profoundly evil man. In addition, the clerical assistance rendered him, in this matter, left him absolutely dependent on the vicar-general, Monsieur de Frilair, and he'd already been asked to do some strange things. His political standing had reached this point when, indulging his personal pleasure, he wrote an anonymous letter. Even worse, his wife told him she wanted Julien to dine with them, a notion vanity had put into her head.

At this juncture, Monsieur Valenod expected a decisive scene with his old associate, Monsieur de Rênal. The latter had spoken harsh words to him, which did not bother Monsieur Valenod a bit, but de Rênal had the power of direct communication with Besançon, and even with Paris. Some royal minister's relative might suddenly drop down on Verrières and take over the Pauper's Bureau. Monsieur Valenod wondered about approaching the liberals, which is why several of them had been invited to the occasion at which Julien recited. He would have powerful support against the mayor. But elections might intervene, and it was all too obvious that directing a bureau and giving votes to the opposition were incompatible.

An account of these developments, very accurately puzzled out by Madame de Rênal, was passed along to Julien, as he lent her his arm and she went from shop to shop, until step by step they were brought to Loyalty Walkway, where they spent several hours almost as tranquilly as at Vergy.

While they were proceeding on their way, Monsieur Valenod was considering how to avoid a decisive scene with his former supporter and patron, taking a bold stance toward him. His approach worked, that day, but it further irritated the mayor.

Vanity, with the pincer grip given it by the petty worship of money, had never clutched more bitterly or more meanly, or thrown a man into a more wretched mood, than Monsieur de Rênal, as he walked into the café. But never, from the opposite perspective, had his children been happier and more joyful. The contrast annoyed him.

"I'm out of place in my own family, as far as I can see!" he declared at once, in a tone he meant to sound impressive.

His wife's only response was to take him aside and explain how badly they needed to send Julien away. The happy hours she'd just experienced lent her the confidence and steadiness required, so she could carry out the plan she'd been evolving for two weeks. At bottom, what most disturbed the poor mayor was knowing he'd become the butt of jokes all over town, because of his fondness for cash. Monsieur

Valenod was as generous as a burglar, and the mayor had behaved with more prudence than brilliance in the last five or six fund drives for the Brotherhood of Saint Joseph, the Congregation of the Holy Virgin, the Congregation of the Holy Sacrament, etc., etc., etc.

Among the squires of Verrières and its surrounding neighborhoods, whose gifts the fund-collecting friars neatly arranged in descending monetary order, Monsieur de Rênal's name had more than once been on the very bottom line. It was no use arguing, as he did, that he *wasn't making any money.* This is something the clergy cannot take lightly.

CHAPTER TWENTY-THREE

A CIVIL SERVANT'S SORROWS

The pleasure of carrying your head high, all year long, is more than paid for by having to endure certain fifteen-minute intervals.
—CASTI

But let's leave this petty man and his petty fears: Why did he bring a man of spirit into his house, when what he needed was someone with a servant's heart? Why doesn't he know how to pick people? The usual procedure in the nineteenth century is that, meeting a man of spirit, a powerful nobleman promptly kills him, exiles him, throws him into prison, or so humiliates him that he commits stupid acts and, deep in sorrow, dies for them. Here, by accident, it's still not the man of spirit who's been suffering. The great misfortune of France's small towns, and of places governed by elections (like New York), is that they can't escape from people like Monsieur de Rênal. In a city of twenty thousand inhabitants, it's these men who shape public opinion, and public opinion is a frightful thing in a country that has a constitution. A noble-souled, generous man who ought to be your friend, but who lives five hundred miles away, judges you by the public opinion of your city, which is formulated by fools to whom chance has granted noble birth, making them rich and safely moderate. But woe to the man who stands out from the rest!

After they had dined, the de Rênals went back to Vergy. But just two days later, Julien saw the whole family again in Verrières.

They had not been there an hour when, to his great surprise, Julien learned that Madame de Rênal was keeping something secret from him. She broke off her conversations with her husband, whenever he appeared, and almost seemed anxious for him to go away. There was no need to give that warning twice, not to Julien. He became distant, reserved; though Madame de Rênal was aware of it, she made no attempt to explain. "Am I to have a successor?" Julien thought. "Just two days ago she was exceedingly friendly! But I've heard that's how these great ladies operate. They're like kings: a government minister, without any warning, comes home after seeing his lord, and his letter of dismissal is there waiting for him."

Julien had noticed that the de Rênals' conversations, broken off so abruptly when he came near, were often about a mansion that the town owned, ancient but ample, and conveniently located, right across from the church, in the city's most commercial district. "What connection could there be," he asked himself, "between this house and her taking a new lover?" Morosely, he recalled François I's pretty lines, which to him were completely fresh, because only a month ago had Madame de Rênal taught them to him. And then, how many oaths, how many caresses, contradicted every single line!

> Women change their minds:
> Trust them, if you're blind.

Monsieur de Rênal took the mail coach to Besançon. The trip had been decided on only two hours earlier: he seemed deeply troubled. When he returned, he threw a large package, covered in gray paper, onto the table.

"There's that stupid business," he told his wife.

An hour later, the bill poster came and carried off the large package. Julien hurriedly followed after him. "At the very first street corner, I'm going to know the secret."

He waited impatiently, standing behind the bill poster. Taking up his big brush, the man spread paste over the back of the poster. It was scarcely fastened to the wall when, avidly curious, Julien found himself reading a detailed description of the huge old house that

Monsieur de Rênal and his wife had been discussing, and the announcement of a public auction. Bidding for the lease would take place in the town hall the very next day, at two o'clock sharp; it would end when the last of three candles had burned itself out. Julien was quite disappointed. The interval struck him as exceedingly short: How would all the potential bidders be notified in time? But the remainder of the poster, which was dated two weeks earlier, told him nothing more. He read it three times, from start to finish, in three different locations.

He went to look at the house. The porter, not seeing him, was quietly saying, to a neighbor:

"Bah! Bah! It's a waste of time. Father Maslon promised him he'd get it for three hundred francs, and since the mayor wouldn't go along, the vicar-general, Father de Frilair, sent it up to the bishop."

Seeing Julien apparently upset the two friends, who never uttered another word.

Julien would not have missed the auction. The dimly lit room was crowded, but everyone was inspecting everyone else in the oddest way. Then all eyes fixed on a tin plate, on which Julien noticed three candles burning. The bailiff shouted: "Three hundred francs, gentlemen!"

"Three hundred francs! Now that's going too far!" said a man, speaking softly to his neighbor. Julien stood almost between them. "The lease is worth more than eight hundred. I'm going to cover that bid."

"You're just spitting in the wind. What good will it do to get their backs up, Father Maslon, Monsieur Valenod, the bishop, the bishop's horrible vicar, Father Frilair, and all the others in that gang?"

"Three hundred and twenty francs," the other man called out.

"Dumb fool!" his neighbor responded. "And there's one of the mayor's spies," he added, motioning to Julien.

Julien quickly turned around to pay them back for this remark, but the two citizens of Franche-Comté paid him not the slightest attention. Their steady coolness revived his. Just then, the last bit of candle sputtered out, and the bailiff's dull voice announced that the house had been rented, for nine years, to Monsieur de Saint-Giraud, department chief in ——— district, and at three hundred and thirty francs.

The mayor having left the room, comments started up.

"There's thirty francs that Grogeot's arrogance is costing the city," someone said.

"But Monsieur de Saint-Giraud," said someone else, "will get back at Grogeot; he'll make him feel it."

"Disgraceful!" said a fat man to Julien's left. "I'd pay eight hundred francs for that house, eight hundred, and use it in my business—and it would be a good bargain."

"Bah!" answered a young industrialist, a liberal. "Monsieur de Saint-Giraud belongs to the Congregation of the Holy Virgin, right? His four children have scholarships, don't they? Oh, the poor man! The people of Verrières have to give him a bonus, five hundred francs every month. That's all there is to it."

"I hear the mayor couldn't stop it!" observed a third man. "Because he's an ultra, a real reactionary, all right, but he doesn't steal."

"He doesn't steal?" answered someone else. "No, it's the pigeons who steal, not the eagles. The whole thing goes into a big pot, and when the year's over, they all get their share. But that's little Sorel, right there. Let's go."

Julien was in a foul mood when he got back. He found Madame de Rênal just as sorrowful.

"You've been to the auction?" she asked him.

"Yes, madame, where I had the honor to be considered a spy for His Honor the Mayor."

"If he'd taken my advice, he'd have gone on a trip somewhere."

Just then, Monsieur de Rênal appeared. He, too, seemed very grave. They dined in absolute silence. Monsieur de Rênal directed Julien to return to Vergy with the children. It was a sad trip. Madame de Rênal consoled her husband.

"You need to get used to these things, my dear."

That evening, they were sitting around the hearth, still silent. The only sound came from the burning beech log. It was one of those grieving times that every family experiences, even the most harmonious. One of the children called out, joyfully:

"The doorbell! It rang!"

"Good Lord! If that's Monsieur de Saint-Giraud, coming to throw this thing in my face, pretending to thank me for it," exclaimed the mayor, "I'll tell him the truth. This is simply too much. He owes it all to Valenod, but it's being charged to me. What can I say, if these cursed Jacobin newspapers decide to make hay with such a tale, and turn me into a strawman monster?"

A very handsome man, with a thick black beard, came into the room, following one of the servants.

"Your Honor, I'm Signor Géronimo. May I present you with a letter given me, just before I made my departure, by the Chevalier de Beauvoisis, attaché to your ambassador in Naples? It is addressed to you—and that was only nine days ago," Signor Géronimo added pleasantly, looking at Madame de Rênal. "Madame, the chevalier is both your relative and my very good friend: he tells me you speak Italian."

The Neapolitan's high spirits changed a sad evening into a very happy one. Madame de Rênal decided that, without any question, he was to be asked to dine with them. She stirred up everyone in the house: at all costs, she did not want Julien thinking too much about being called a spy—for he had heard it twice that very day. Signor Géronimo was a famous singer, from good society and yet splendidly ebullient—qualities that, in France, are no longer entirely compatible. After they had dined, he sang a little duet with Madame de Rênal. He told charming stories. An hour after midnight, the children protested when Julien suggested they go to bed.

"Tell that story just once more," said the oldest.

"It's about me, young man," replied Signor Géronimo. "Eight years ago—at just your age, as I understand—I was a young student at the Naples Conservatory. Of course, I did not have the honor of being son to the illustrious mayor of so pretty a place as Verrières."

These words made Monsieur de Rênal sigh; he glanced at his wife.

"Signor Zingarelli," the young singer continued, exaggerating his Italian accent and making the children burst out laughing. "Signor Zingarelli, the director, was a terribly harsh teacher. He was not popular at the conservatory, but he wanted everyone to pretend he was. I got out as often as I could; I used to go to the little theater at San Carlino, where I heard music fit for the gods. But, oh Lord! How could I scrape up the price of a ticket in the back row? It was a lot of money," he said, making a face at the children, and the children laughed. "Signor Giovannone, director of the theater, had heard me sing. I was sixteen. 'This youngster's a treasure,' he said.

" 'Would you like me to hire you, my dear boy?' he said, coming over to me.

" 'What will I be paid?'

" 'Forty ducats a month.' Gentlemen, that's a hundred and sixty francs. I felt as if heaven had suddenly opened.

" 'But how,' I said to Giovannone, 'how can I get a hard man like Zingarelli to let me go?'

" '*Lascia fare a me.*' "

"Leave it to me!" cried the oldest child.

"Exactly, young man. Signor Giovannone said: 'My boy, we start with just a tiny engagement.' I signed a contract: he gave me three ducats. I'd never seen so much money. And then he told me what I had to do.

"The next day, I requested an audience with terrifying Signor Zingarelli. His old servant showed me in.

" 'What do you want from me, you good-for-nothing?' said Zingarelli.

" 'Maestro,' I told him, 'I repent my sins. I won't sneak out of the conservatory anymore, climbing over the fence. I'm going to work twice as hard.'

" 'If I wasn't worried about ruining the best bass voice I've ever heard, I'd lock you up for two weeks, on bread and water—rascal!'

" 'Maestro,' I answered, 'I'm going to be a model student, believe me. But I have to ask you a favor: if anyone comes to you, asking to let me sing anywhere else, don't say yes. Please, just say you can't do it.'

" 'And who the devil would come looking for a rascal like you? Do you think I'll ever let you leave the conservatory? Are you making fun of me? Clear out, clear out!' he said, trying to kick me on the rear end. 'Or else it's dry bread and a lock on the door.'

"An hour later, Signor Giovannone came to the conservatory office.

" 'I'd like you to make me a rich man,' he said to Signor Zingarelli.

'Let me have Géronimo. If he sings in my theater, next winter I'll be able to marry off my daughter.'

" 'Why would you want that good-for-nothing,' Zingarelli said. 'I won't let you; you're not going to get him; and besides, even if I agreed, he wouldn't leave the conservatory—he just finished swearing that.'

" 'If it's only a question of what he wants,' Giovannone said with a straight face, pulling out the contract I'd signed, 'here it is, in black and white! See his signature?'

"Absolutely furious, Zingarelli rang the school bell: 'Get that Géronimo out of the conservatory!' he shouted, boiling with anger. So they threw me out, and I laughed the whole way. That very same night, I sang 'The Multiplication Song.' Pulcinella was thinking of getting married, so he was counting—on his fingers—just what he'd need to buy for his house, and getting angrier and angrier the higher he counted."

"Oh please!" said Madame de Rênal, "please sing the song for us."

Géronimo sang the song, and everyone laughed so hard that they cried. Signor Géronimo didn't get to sleep until two, leaving the family enchanted by his fine manners, his agreeability, and his jolliness.

The next day, both Monsieur and Madame de Rênal gave him the letters he would need at the French court.

"So: Falsity is everywhere," Julien said to himself. "Here's Signor Géronimo going to London with sixty thousand francs guaranteed. Without the calm worldliness of the San Carlino's director, perhaps his divine voice might not have been known and admired for another ten years. Really, I'd much rather be a Géronimo than a de Rênal. The singer's not so honored in Italian society, but he doesn't have to experience the misery of auctions, like the one earlier today, and his life is merry."

One thing surprised Julien: the solitary weeks in Verrières, at Monsieur de Rênal's house, had been a period of happiness. He'd encountered disgust and distressing thoughts only at the dinners they gave for him. Couldn't he read, and write, and reflect without being troubled, here in this empty house? He was not constantly being pulled away from shining dreams by the cruel necessity of studying a base soul's behavior, and then to deceive him by hypocritical actions or words.

"Will happiness be something so close to home? . . . That sort of life is not expensive: if I chose to, I could marry Miss Elisa, or go into partnership with Fouqué. . . . The traveler who's just climbed a steep mountain sits down at the top, and finds perfect pleasure in resting. Would he be as happy, if were he forced to do nothing but rest?"

Madame de Rênal's mind had reached some fateful conclusions. In spite of all her resolutions, she'd confessed to Julien the whole business behind the auction. "He makes me forget all my vows!" she thought.

She would have sacrificed her life without hesitation, to save her husband's, and she had seen him in danger. Hers was one of those noble, romantic souls, for whom seeing the possibility of some generous deed, and not doing it, creates remorse every bit as strong as committing a crime. All the same, there had been deadly days when she could not keep from picturing the enormous happiness she'd taste if, having become a widow, she was able to marry Julien.

He loved her children more than their father did; in spite of his strict ways, they adored him. She was keenly aware that, in marrying Julien, she would be bound to leave this Vergy, a shady place very dear to her. She pictured herself living in Paris, continuing to provide her children with an education that all the world admired. Her children, and she, and Julien: they'd all be perfectly happy.

What strange effects marriage has, in the form practiced by the nineteenth century! The boredom of married life certainly kills love, if love has preceded marriage. But, says a philosopher, for those sufficiently wealthy not to need employment, marriage soon leads to a profound boredom with all balanced, calm pleasures. Nor is it only dried-up souls, among women, who have no passion for love.

These philosophical thoughts lead me to excuse Madame de Rênal—but she found no forgiveness in Verrières, and the whole town, though she was not aware of it, was devoted to nothing but the scandal of her love affair. That autumn, because of this intense business, the town did not suffer so much from boredom.

Autumn, and the first part of winter, went by rather quickly. It became time to leave the woods of Vergy. Verrières's high society became indignant, finding that their social excommunication had very little effect on Monsieur de Rênal. Less than a week later, certain sober folk, who like to compensate for their habitual seriousness by accomplishing this sort of task, expressed to him the most intensely cruel suspicions, though they phrased them in the most measured terms.

Monsieur Valenod, who had been playing everything close to the vest, had placed Elisa with an aristocratic family of high repute, which included five women. Elisa had been afraid, she'd said, of not finding a place all winter, so she asked these people for only two-thirds of what she'd been receiving at the mayor's house. Of her own volition, the girl had the excellent notion of making her confession to the former parish priest, Father Chélan, as well as to the new priest, in order to tell both of them all the details of Julien's love affair.

The day after his arrival, at six in the morning, Father Chélan had summoned Julien.

"I have no questions for you," the old priest said. "I ask you, and if I need to I will order you, to say nothing to me. I expect you, within three days, either to leave for the seminary in Besançon or for your friend Fouqué's home, he being still of a mind to arrange a magnificent place for you. I have anticipated everything, arranged everything, but you must leave and not return to Verrières for an entire year."

Julien made no reply. He was considering: Might his honor be thought offended by Father Chélan's efforts on his behalf? The old priest was not, after all, his father.

"Tomorrow, at this same hour," he finally said, "I will have the honor of seeing you once again."

Father Chélan, who had expected to effect matters with a high hand in dealing with this young man, said a great deal. Wrapped in a stance and a facial appearance of the deepest humility, Julien did not open his mouth.

Julien finally left, and hurried to warn Madame de Rênal; he found her in a state of despair. Her husband had just been speaking to her rather frankly. His natural weakness having been propped up by the expectation of the Besançon inheritance, he had decided to consider her completely innocent. He had approached her in order to acknowledge the strange condition of public opinion in Verrières. They were wrong, they were being misled by the envious—but what should be done?

Madame de Rênal had a fleeting notion that Julien could accept Monsieur Valenod's offer, and remain in Verrières. But she was no longer the simple, shy woman she had been the year before: her fatal passion, and her remorse, had instructed her. She soon experienced the sadness of acknowledging to herself, all the while listening to her husband, that at least some momentary separation had become inevitable. "Away from me, Julien will fall back into his ambitious plans, so natural when you have nothing. And me, great God, I'm rich! And so uselessly, when it comes to my happiness! He'll forget me. Lovable as he is, he will be loved, he will love. Ah, miserable woman . . . But what am I complaining about? Heaven is just. I haven't had the worthiness to stop sinning, and my sin destroys my judgment. To win Elisa over, all I had to do was pay her: nothing would have been easier. I didn't bother to stop and think, not for a moment: crazy love thoughts took up all my time. I will perish."

One thing struck Julien, when he told Madame de Rênal the terrible news that he was leaving: she made absolutely no selfish objection. She was obviously trying hard not to cry.

"We need to be strong, my dear."

She cut off a lock of her hair.

"I don't know what I'll do," she told him, "but if I die, promise me you'll never forget my children. Whether you're far or near, try to make them decent people. If there's another revolution, all the aristocracy will have their throats cut; their father will emigrate, perhaps because of that peasant, killed on a roof. Watch over my family. . . . Give me your hand. Farewell, my dear! These are our last moments. That great sacrifice having been made, I hope that, in public, I'll have the courage to think of my reputation."

Julien had expected despair. The straightforwardness of her farewell moved him.

"No, I won't accept your farewell like this. I'll leave; they want me to; you yourself want it. But three days after my departure, I'll come to see you, at night."

Madame de Rênal's life was changed. Julien loved her deeply, for it was he who'd had the idea of seeing her again! Her frightful sorrow was transformed into one of the liveliest floods of joy she had ever known. Everything became easy for her. The certainty of seeing her lover again wiped away, at these last moments, all the things that had been tearing them apart. Beginning at that moment Madame de Rênal's face, as well as her behavior, became noble, firm, and perfectly decorous.

Monsieur de Rênal soon returned; he was beside himself. He finally spoke to his wife about the anonymous letter received two months before.

"I'll bring it to the casino, to show everyone that it's from that disgraceful Valenod, the fellow I plucked out of poverty and made one of the richest bourgeois in Verrières. I'll shame him in public, and then I'll fight with him. This is simply too much."

"I might become a widow, good Lord!" thought Madame de Rênal. But at almost the same moment, she told herself: "If I don't stop this duel, as I certainly can, I'll be my husband's murderer."

Never had she managed her husband's vanity with such skill. In less than two hours she made him see, and always on rational grounds he had himself brought to light, that he had to show even more friendliness than ever to Monsieur Valenod, and even had to bring Elisa back to the house. It took courage for Madame de Rênal to decide on seeing this girl, who was the cause of all her misfortune. But the idea had come from Julien.

At last, having started three or four times to leave for the casino, Monsieur de Rênal realized, entirely by himself, that the very worst thing for him, fiscally, as well as the most personally disagreeable, would be for Julien, in the face of the excitement and babble going on all over Verrières, to remain in town as tutor to Monsieur Valenod's children. Obviously, the most rewarding thing for Julien was to accept Valenod's offer. But it would bring glory to Monsieur de Rênal, should Julien leave Verrières to enter the Besançon seminary, or the one at Dijon. But how could Julien be brought to make that decision, and how would he be able to live there, if he did?

Monsieur de Rênal, seeing the imminence of fiscal sacrifice, was more in despair than his wife. After that long conversational struggle, she was in the position of the man who, weary of life, has taken a dose of stramonium: he no longer reacts except by reacting, so to speak, and no longer feels any sense of direct interest in anything. Thus it happened to Louis XIV, when he was dying, and said: *"When I was king."* What a wonderful remark!

The next day, early in the morning, Monsieur de Rênal received an anonymous letter. It was in the most insulting style. The grossest words that could be applied to his situation appeared in every line. It was the work of some envious underling. This letter brought him back to thoughts of fighting with Monsieur Valenod. His courage soon reached the point of immediate action. He left the house alone and went to a gunsmith's shop to buy several revolvers, which he loaded.

"To bring things down to brass tacks," he said to himself: "if the harsh administration of the Emperor Napoleon were to return to the world, there's not a single stolen penny to hold against me. The most I've done is close my eyes, but I've got the proper letters in my desk, authorizing everything."

Madame de Rênal was frightened by her husband's cold anger; it recalled the fatal idea of widowhood she had tried so hard to push away. She shut herself in with him. For hours she talked to him, in vain: the new anonymous letter had decided him. Finally, she got to the point of transforming the courage required to give Monsieur Valenod a box on the ear, into an offer of six hundred francs to Julien, for a year's room and board as a seminarian. Monsieur de Rênal, cursing a thousand times over the day he had the fatal idea of bringing a tutor into the house, forgot about the anonymous letter.

He took some consolation in an idea he did not pass on to his wife: by means of his mature skill, and wielding it to overcome the young man's romantic notions, he hoped to get him to agree (for a small sum) not to accept Monsieur Valenod's offer.

Madame de Rênal found it very difficult to prove to Julien that, in acting according to her husband's convenience, and sacrificing the salary of eight hundred francs offered by the Pauper's Bureau director, he could without shame accept a bit of compensation.

"But," Julien kept saying, "I've never, not for a single second, intended to accept that offer. You've gotten me too accustomed to genteel living: the vulgarity of the people over there would kill me."

Cruel necessity, with its iron hand, forced Julien to bend his will. His pride offered him the illusion that he was accepting Monsieur de Rênal's offer only as a loan, and he gave the mayor a note pledging reimbursement in five years, with interest.

Madame de Rênal had kept thousands of francs, hidden in the little cave up on the mountain.

Trembling, she offered the money to him, feeling very sure he would angrily refuse.

"Is it your intention," said Julien, "to turn the memory of our love into an abomination?"

At last, Julien left Verrières. Monsieur de Rênal was extremely pleased: at the fatal moment, when it came to actually accepting the money, Julien found the sacrifice too great. He flatly refused. Monsieur de Rênal fell on his shoulder, tears in his eyes. Julien having requested a certificate of good conduct, the mayor's enthusiasm bubbled over into language magnificently exalting the tutor's behavior. Our hero had saved up a hundred francs, and expected to ask Fouqué for as much again.

He was deeply moved. But by the time he was two or three miles from Verrières, where he had left so much love, he was no longer thinking of anything but seeing the capital city, the great military center, that was Besançon.

During this brief three-day separation, Madame de Rênal fell victim to one of love's most cruel deceptions. Her life was bearable: all that existed between her and deep depression was the final meeting she'd have with Julien. She counted the hours, the minutes, that kept them apart. Finally, the third night, she heard from afar the agreed-upon signal. Having made his way through a thousand dangers, Julien appeared in front of her.

From that moment, she had only a single thought: "This is the last time I'll see him." Far from responding to her lover's eagerness, she was like a faintly animated corpse. When she forced herself to say she loved him, it was spoken so awkwardly that what it manifested was virtually the exact opposite. Nothing could free her from the cruel concept of eternal separation. For a brief moment, Julien's mistrustful nature made him believe he'd already been forgotten. The biting words with which he said this were met with nothing but silently streaming tears, and a clutching at his hand that was very nearly convulsive.

"But, good God! What do you want me to think?" Julien replied to his beloved's stiff protestations. "You'd show a hundred times more warmth to Madame Derville, who's just an acquaintance."

Petrified, all Madame de Rênal could say was:

"No one could ever be more wretched.... I hope I die.... I feel my heart freezing over...."

These were the fullest responses he could get from her.

When the coming dawn made departure necessary, Madame de Rênal's tears suddenly stopped. She watched him tying a knotted rope to the window, but said not a word, never kissed him. Julien's words accomplished nothing:

"So now we've gotten where you so much wanted us to be. From here on, you can live without remorse. You won't be seeing your children in their tombs every time they're the least bit indisposed."

"I'm sorry you couldn't kiss Stanislas," she said coldly.

Julien was powerfully affected by the cold embrace of this living corpse: for miles, he could think of nothing else. His heart had been cut to the quick, and before he crossed over the mountain, he kept turning around so he could see the steeple of the church in Verrières.

CHAPTER TWENTY-FOUR

A CAPITAL CITY

Such noise, so many people doing business! Notions of the future in a twenty-year-old head! What a way to keep from thinking about love!
—BARNAVE

He finally saw it, set on a distant mountain; its walls were black. This was the fortress of Besançon. "What a difference for me," he said with a sigh, "if I were coming to this great military center as a second lieutenant, serving in one of the regiments sent to defend it!"

Besançon isn't simply one of the prettiest towns in France: it holds an abundance of passionate, spirited people. But Julien was only a little peasant, who had no way of approaching these distinguished men.

When he'd been at Fouqué's, he'd taken to dressing as a bourgeois, and it was thus costumed that he crossed over the drawbridges. Knowing quite well the history of the siege of 1674, he wanted to see, before he closed himself up in the seminary, the ramparts and the citadel. Two or three times, he came close to being stopped by the sentries: he got into places forbidden to the general public, on grounds of military security, but in fact so the armies could sell hay, for twelve or fifteen francs a year. The walls' great height, the depth of the surrounding ditches, the frightening appearance of the cannons, had held his attention for some hours, by the time he went past the huge café on the rampart walkway. He stood looking at it, motionless in wonder. He could quite readily read the word CAFÉ, written in large letters above the two great doors; he could not believe his eyes. Shyness held him back, and then he risked going in, and found himself in a room thirty or forty feet long, with a ceiling at least twenty feet high. That day, it was all magical to him.

Two games of billiards were being played. Waiters called out the scores; the players hurried around the tables, about which spectators crowded. Billows of tobacco smoke, pouring from every mouth, wrapped them in a blue cloud. The men's height, their rounded shoulders, their heavy step, their enormous beards, the long frock coats they wore—everything attracted Julien's notice. These noble sons of ancient Besançon spoke only at the top of their lungs; they thought of themselves as terrifying warriors. Julien stood there, wondering: his mind was full of the immensity, the magnificence, of a great capital like Besançon. He did not feel entirely capable of ordering a cup of coffee, not from one of these gentlemen with their haughty looks, shouting out the billiard scores.

But the barmaid had spotted his charming face, this young bourgeois from the countryside, standing three steps from the stove, with his little bundle under his arm, contemplating a bust of the king in handsome white plaster. This tall Franche-Comté girl, with a good figure and dressed very fashionably (to enhance the café's reputation), had already twice said to him, in a soft voice meant for his ears alone, "Monsieur! Monsieur!" Julien's glance met her blue eyes, big and compassionate, and saw she'd been talking to him.

He went over to the bar, and to the pretty girl, quick-stepping exactly as he would have marched toward a hostile army. But in performing this notable maneuver, he dropped his bundle.

What pity for our country bumpkin would have sprung in the hearts of Paris high school students, who at fifteen already know how to make a polished, terribly distinguished entrance to a café. Yet these children, so eminently accomplished at fifteen, at eighteen turn *common*. The passionate shyness one finds in the provinces sometimes rises above itself, and then it shapes the will. Approaching this very pretty girl, who'd taken the trouble to speak to him, Julien—becoming courageous, precisely because he'd overcome shyness—thought: "I have to tell her the truth."

"Madame, I'm here in Besançon for the first time in my life. I should like to have, and to pay for, some bread and a cup of coffee."

She smiled, and then reddened: she worried that this handsome young fellow would bring down on himself, from the billiard players, sarcastic remarks and jokes. He'd be frightened and would not come again.

"Sit here, near me," she said, pointing to a marble table, almost completely hidden by the huge mahogany bar that projected out into the room.

The girl leaned down over the bar, allowing herself to show off her splendid figure. Julien noted it; all his ideas changed. The pretty girl had just set a cup in front of him, along with sugar and a roll. She was hesitating to call over a waiter, so he could have coffee, quite aware that when the waiter arrived, her tête-à-tête with Julien was going to end.

Julien was thoughtful, comparing this bright, blonde beauty with memories that frequently stirred him. Thinking of the passion he'd evoked was almost enough to drive away his shyness. The pretty girl had very little time; she understood what she saw in Julien's eyes.

"All this pipe smoke makes you cough. Come for breakfast, tomorrow morning, before eight: I'm almost always alone."

"What's your name?" said Julien, with a tender smile of happy shyness.

"Amanda Binet."

"May I send you, in an hour, a little package the size of this one?"

Lovely Amanda considered it.

"I'm watched. That could get me into trouble. All the same, I'll write my name on a card, so you put it on your package. Send it, don't worry."

"My name's Julien Sorel," said the young man. "I have neither family nor friends, here in Besançon."

"Ah! I understand," she said cheerfully. "You've come for the law school?"

"Alas, no," said Julien. "I've been sent to the seminary."

Utter dejection crossed her face. She summoned a waiter: now she had the courage. The waiter poured Julien's coffee without looking at him.

Amanda was busy at the bar, taking in money. Julien was proud of having dared to speak to her. A quarrel started, over at the billiard tables. The shouting and arguing echoed through the whole huge room, creating an uproar that astonished Julien. Amanda was sitting dreamily, her eyes lowered.

"If you like, miss," he said to her, suddenly confident, "I'll say I'm your cousin."

This touch of authority pleased her. "He's not a young nobody," she thought. Quickly, without looking at him, her eyes busily watching for people coming toward the bar, she said:

"Me, I come from Genlis, near Dijon. Say you're from Genlis, too, and you're my mother's cousin."

"Without fail," he said.

"Every Wednesday at five, during the summer, the seminarians go by, right here in front of the café."

"If you're thinking of me, as I go by, have a bouquet of violets in your hand."

She looked at him, very surprised. Her look turned his timidity to bravery, though he blushed quite deeply as he said:

"I think I already love you most passionately."

"Don't talk so loud," she told him, very frightened.

Julien tried to recall the words he'd read in a broken set of *La Nouvelle Héloïse*, which he'd found at Vergy. His memory served him well: for ten minutes he recited Rousseau to Miss Amanda, who was in raptures. He was delighted at his gallantry, when suddenly her face took on a glacial coldness. One of her lovers had just walked in.

He came over to the bar, whistling and swinging his shoulders. He glanced at Julien. Immediately, our hero's mind, always disposed to extremes, could not help brimming with thoughts of a duel. He turned very pale, shoved his cup away, set himself in a stalwart posture, and stared fixedly toward his rival. As this gentleman bent his head, leaning down on the bar and casually ordering a glass of brandy, Amanda looked at Julien, silently commanding him to turn away his eyes. He obeyed and, for two minutes, stayed as he was, pale, determined, and thinking of nothing except what was coming. At that moment, he looked resplendent. The rival had been startled by Julien's stare: tossing down his brandy, he said something to Amanda, stuck both hands in the side pockets of his long frock coat, and went toward the billiard tables, whistling and watching Julien. Our hero leaped up, wild with anger. But he did not know how to act the part of someone who's been insulted. He put down his little bundle and, strutting as well as he knew how, went toward the billiard tables.

Prudence spoke, but in vain: "Fighting a duel as soon as you get to Besançon, you throw away your career in the Church."

"Who cares? No one's going to say I put up with an insult."

Amanda saw his courage. It made a pretty contrast to the naïveté of his behavior. In a flash, she chose him over the tall young man in his frock coat. She got up and, acting as if she were looking at someone going by, out on the street, she quickly got herself between him and the billiard tables.

"Be careful with this gentleman. He's my brother-in-law."

"Who cares? He was looking at me."

"Do you want to make me miserable? Sure, he was looking at you, he may even have been thinking of coming over and talking to you. I told him you were my mother's cousin, just arrived from Genlis. He's a Franche-Comté hick who's never been anywhere past Dôle, on the road to Burgundy, so you can tell him anything you like and never worry about a thing."

Julien still hesitated. She quickly added, drawing on her barmaid's wit to supply all the lies she needed:

"Sure, he looked at you, but that was when he was asking who you were. This is a man who's *rude* to everyone: he didn't mean to insult you."

Julien was watching the fake brother-in-law. He saw him buying a number at the table where the most energetic billiard game was going on. He heard his coarse voice crying, in menacing tones, "It's my turn!" He stepped swiftly around Miss Amanda and took a step toward the billiard table. Amanda gripped him by the arm.

"First pay me," she said.

"That's fair," thought Julien. "She's afraid I'll leave without paying." Amanda was quite as excited as he was, and very red in the face. She gave him his change as slowly as she could, and kept repeating, in a soft voice:

"Get out of the café right away, or I'm finished with you, no matter how much you love me."

Julien did leave, but very slowly. "Isn't it my duty," he kept asking himself, "to take my turn and walk over, whistling, and stare at this rude fellow?" His doubts kept him on the street, in front of the café, for an entire hour, watching everyone who came out. The rude fellow did not appear, and Julien left.

He'd been in Besançon for no more than a few hours, and he'd already mastered one of his qualms. In spite of his gout, the old surgeon-major, once upon a time, had given him a few fencing lessons; that was the only knowledge Julien possessed, of which his anger could make any use. But that difficulty would not have mattered, had he known how to show his anger except by striking out with his hands—and, if it had come to a fistfight, his rival, an enormous man, would have thrashed him and left him lying flat on the floor.

"For a poor devil like me," Julien said to himself, "without protectors and without money, there won't be much difference between a seminary and a prison. I've got to store my clothing in an inn, where I can change into my black clothing. If I ever get to leave the seminary for an hour or two, I might very well—wearing my bourgeois clothes—get to see Miss Amanda again." It was all very logical, but Julien walked by every inn he saw, not daring to enter any of them.

At last, when he went by the Ambassador Hotel for the second time, his worried glance met that of a fat woman, still fairly young, very red-faced, who seemed cheerful and pleasant. He went over to her and told his story.

"Of course, my handsome little priest," she told him, "I'll hold on to your bourgeois clothes, and I'll even keep them well dusted. At this time of year, it's not a good idea to leave clothes untouched." She took down a key and personally conducted him to a room, suggesting he make a list of what he was leaving.

"Good Lord! How fine you look like that, Father Sorel," said the fat woman when he came down to the kitchen. "I'm going to give you a good dinner. And," she added in a soft voice, "it's only going to cost you twenty pence, instead of the fifty everyone else has to pay, because we really have to be nice to that little purse of yours."

"I've got two hundred francs," said Julien rather proudly.

"Ah, my God!" said the good lady, startled. "Don't talk so loud: there are lots of bad eggs in Besançon. They'd rob you of that in no time at all. Stay out of the cafés, especially: they're full of crooks."

"Really!" said Julien, her words giving him something to think about.

"Don't ever go anywhere but right here; I'll make you coffee. Remember, this is where you'll always find yourself a friend and a good dinner, and for twenty pence; that's saying something, it seems to me. Right? Now go sit down at the table, and I'll serve you myself."

"I couldn't eat a thing," Julien told her. "I'm too nervous. When I leave here, I'll go right to the seminary."

The good woman wouldn't let him go until she'd stuffed his pockets with food. Finally, Julien set out on his terrifying path. Standing in her doorway, she gave him directions.

CHAPTER TWENTY-FIVE

THE SEMINARY

Three hundred and thirty-six lunches at 83 pence, three hundred and thirty-six dinners at 28 pence, a cup of hot chocolate for those entitled to it: how much can I make on my bid?

—VALENOD, FROM BESANÇON

He could see, from a distance, the gilded iron cross over the door. He walked toward it, slowly. He felt as if his legs were giving way underneath him. "Here is hell on Earth, which I'll never be able to leave!" He finally decided to ring the bell. The sound echoed, as if in some lonely place. After ten minutes, a pale man, dressed in black, came to let him in. Julien looked at him and immediately lowered his eyes. The porter's face was exceedingly strange. His bulging green eyes were round as a cat's; the fixed line of his eyebrows proclaimed a complete absence of human empathy; his thin lips formed a tight semicircle over his teeth, which stuck out. These were not criminal features, but indicative of the total insensitivity which, for young people, can be even more frightening. The only emotion Julien's rapid glance could imagine on this narrow, pietistic face was profound contempt for anything anyone said to him, except words about heaven's eternal concerns.

It was hard for Julien to raise his eyes and explain, his heart throbbing and his voice trembling, that he'd like to speak to Father Pirard, director of the seminary. Without speaking a word, the black figure motioned him to follow along. They went up two stories, via a broad staircase with wooden banisters; the crooked steps slanted so sharply, on the side away from the wall, that they seemed about to collapse. A small door, hard to open—above it a great graveyard cross made of pine painted black—finally swung to, and the porter led Julien into a low-ceilinged, dark room, its whitewashed walls decorated by two large, time-blackened pictures. There, Julien was abandoned, deeply dismayed, his heart beating violently; had he dared, he would have wept. A silence like death prevailed all through the building.

A quarter of an hour later, which seemed to him an entire day, the ominous-looking porter reappeared, standing on the threshold of a door at the other end of the room; not troubling himself to speak, he signaled Julien to come. Our hero walked into a room even larger than the first, and even less well lit. Once again, the walls were whitewashed, but there was no furniture. Except that, in the corner nearest the door, Julien had seen a pine-board bed, two straw chairs, and a small armchair, also of pine, which had no cushions. At the far end of the room, near a small, yellow-paned window, there were some dirty flowerpots, and he saw a man in a shabby cassock, seated at a table. Apparently angry, he was plucking up a great many slips of paper, one after the other, writing a few words on each, and then arranging them on the table in front of him. He was not aware of Julien's presence. The young man stayed more or less in the middle of the room, motionless, exactly where the porter—who had now gone out and shut the door—had left him.

Ten minutes passed; the badly dressed man kept on writing. Julien's sense of shock, and his terror, mounted; he felt on the point of fainting away. A philosopher might have said, perhaps incorrectly: "This is the violent impression made by that which is ugly on a soul fashioned for the love of beauty."

The man who'd been writing lifted his head. It took Julien a moment to notice and, even after that, he remained as motionless as if the awful glance now directed at him had struck him dead. His anxious eyes could barely make out a narrow face covered with red spots, except on the forehead, which displayed a deadly pallor. Between the reddened cheeks and the white forehead shone two small black eyes, designed for frightening the bravest of men. The immense curve of the forehead was set off by a thick mop of straight hair, black as jade.

"Are you coming over here, yes or no?" the man said impatiently.

Julien took a shaky step and, finally, pale and ready to topple to the floor, as he'd never before been in all his life, he got within three feet of the little pine table covered with slips of paper.

"Nearer," said the man.

Julien came closer, stretching out his hand, as if trying to prop himself up on something.

"Your name?"

"Julien Sorel."

"You're good and late," he was told, and again the frightening eyes peered at him.

Julien couldn't endure this stare. He started to extend his hand, as if to keep himself upright, then fell full length on the wooden floor.

The man rang the porter's bell. Julien could not see, and he could not move, but he heard approaching steps.

He was picked up and set in the small white wooden armchair. He heard the awful voice saying to the porter:

"He appears to have had an epileptic fit. That's all we need."

When Julien was able to open his eyes, the red-faced man was writing; the porter had disappeared. "Be brave," our hero told himself, "and above all hide how I feel." He was feeling exceedingly nauseated. "If anything happens, God only knows what they'll think of me." Finally, the man stopped writing and, out of the corner of his eye, looked at Julien.

"Are you well enough to answer me?"

"Yes, sir," said Julien, his voice weak.

"Ah, that's good."

The man in black lifted himself partly out of his chair and impatiently rummaged through the drawer in his pine table, which creaked when he pulled on it. He found the letter he was looking for, slowly sat himself back down and looked at Julien, once again, as if to wrench out of him what little life he retained:

"You've been recommended to me by Father Chélan, who was the best parish priest in the whole diocese, a virtuous man if ever there was one, and for thirty years my friend."

"Ah! I have the honor of speaking to Father Pirard," said Julien, his voice fading away.

"So it would seem," replied the director of the seminary, looking at him testily.

The light in his tiny eyes grew brighter, and then there was an involuntary twitching of the muscles in the corners of his mouth. It was the face of a tiger, salivating as he contemplated devouring his prey.

"Chélan's letter is brief," he said, as if talking to himself. "*Intelligenti pauca*, good minds don't need a lot of words. The way things are going, these days, it would be hard to write briefly enough."

He read out loud:

"I send you Julien Sorel, of this parish, who twenty years ago I baptized, son of a rich carpenter who provides him with nothing. Julien will be a remarkable laborer in the vineyards of the Lord. His memory, his mind, are in no way deficient. He knows how to think. Will his vocation be an enduring one? Is it sincere?

"*Sincere!*" repeated Father Pirard, astonished, looking over at Julien. But his glance was already less empty of all human feeling. "*Sincere!*" he said once more, in a low voice, and then returned to his reading:

"I ask you to give Julien a scholarship. He will deserve it, once he's been given the required examinations. I have taught him some theology, the good old theology of Bossuet, of Arnauld, of Fleury. If he seems to you unsuitable, send him back to me: the director of the Pauper's Bureau, with whom you are well acquainted, has offered him eight hundred francs as a tutor for his children.

My spirit is tranquil, for which God be thanked. I am getting used to the terrible blow.

Vale et me ama, farewell, and think well of me."

Moderating his voice as he read the signature, Father Pirard sighed as he pronounced the word *Chélan*.

"He's calm," said he. "Indeed, his virtues deserve such a reward. May God grant me as much!"

He looked upward and made the sign of the cross. Seeing this sacred gesture, Julien felt a lessening of the profound horror with which, ever since he'd entered this building, he'd been frozen over.

"I have here three hundred and twenty-one aspirants for the holiest of professions," Father Pirard said at last, his voice severe but not unpleasant. "Only seven or eight have been recommended to me by people like Father Chélan. Accordingly, among those three hundred and twenty-one, you will be the ninth. But my patronage is neither favoritism nor indulgence, but redoubled carefulness and severity against sin. Go lock that door."

Julien forced himself to walk to the door, and then come back, without falling. He noticed that a small window, right alongside the door, opened onto country fields. He looked out at the trees; it did him good, like seeing old friends.

"*Loquerisne linguam latinam?* Do you speak Latin?" Father Pirard asked, when he returned.

"*Ita, pater optime.* Yes, kind Father," answered Julien, beginning to come back to himself. Surely, no man in the world had ever seemed to him less kind than Father Pirard, half an hour earlier.

The interview continued, in Latin. The priest's eyes softened; Julien began to recover his confidence. "How weak I am," he thought, "to let myself be imposed on by these shows of virtue! This man will be a rascal, just like Father Maslon." And Julien congratulated himself for having hidden almost all his money in his boots.

Father Pirard examined him in theology, and was surprised by the extent of his knowledge. His surprise was even greater when he examined Julien on the Holy Scriptures. But when he turned to questions about the teachings of the Fathers, he saw that Julien did not even know the names of Saint Jerome, Saint Augustine, Saint Bonaventura, Saint Basil, etc., etc.

"Really," he thought, "here is exactly that fatal tendency to Protestantism, for which I've always scolded Chélan: deep, deep knowledge—almost too deep—of the Scriptures."

(Julien had just been speaking, without having been questioned on the subject, about the *actual* dates at which Genesis, the Pentateuch, etc., had been written.)

"What's the point to this endless scrutiny of the Holy Scriptures," thought Father Pirard, "if it isn't an inquiry into *a person's conscience?* In other words, the most ghastly Protestantism. And in addition to this rash exploration, nothing from the Fathers that might counterbalance such tendencies."

But the director of the seminary was utterly astonished when, asking Julien about the pope's authority, and expecting to hear sayings of the church of ancient Gaul, the young man recited the entire book by the papal absolutist, de Maistre.

"What a strange man, that Chélan," thought Father Pirard. "Did he teach him this book so he could make fun of it?"

Trying to see if Julien took de Maistre's teachings seriously, he made further inquiries. In vain: Julien's responses drew only on his memory. And from then on, Julien felt really fine, and knew he was master of himself. After a very long examination, it seemed to him that Father Pirard's harshness was no more than a pretense. Indeed, had it not been for the settled rule of solemn austerity, maintained for fifteen years in dealing with his theological students, the director of the seminary would have thrown his arms around Julien, in the name of logic, for the abundant clarity, precision, and terseness of his answers.

"Here's a bold, healthy spirit," he said to himself. "But *corpus debile,* a weak body."

"Do you often fall down like that?" he asked Julien in French, pointing at the floor.

"That was the first time in my whole life. The porter's face absolutely chilled my heart," he added, blushing like a child.

Father Pirard came close to smiling.

"That's what comes of the world's empty shows. You've clearly gotten used to laughing faces, which are true displays of falsity and lies. Truth is austere, sir. But our task in this world is also austere, is it not? How important it is, keeping your conscience on watch for the weakness of *too much sensitivity to the world's empty charms.*

"Had you not been recommended to me," Father Pirard said, once more speaking in Latin, and with obvious pleasure, "if you had not been recommended to me by a man like Father Chélan, I would speak to you in the empty tongues of this world, with which you seem only too well acquainted. Obtaining the full scholarship you request, I must tell you, is the most difficult thing in the world. But Father Chélan would deserve very little, after fifty-six years of apostolic labor, if he could not command such a scholarship."

Having said this, Father Pirard enjoined against Julien's participation in any secret society, or congregation, without his consent.

"As to that, I give you my word of honor," said Julien, beaming like an honest man.

The director of the seminary smiled for the first time.

"We don't use those words here," he said. "They reek too much of the empty honor of worldly men, which lead them to commit so many errors, and often so many sins. According to paragraph seventeen of Pope Pius V's Bull, *Unam Ecclesiam,* I am owed your holy obedience. In this place, my very dear son, to hear is to obey. How much money do you have?"

"Here we go," Julien said to himself. "That's why I'm now his very dear son."

"Thirty-five francs, Father."

"Make a careful record of how you spend your money. You will have to account to me for all of it."

The whole painful performance had lasted three hours. Julien summoned the porter.

"Put Julien Sorel in cell number 103," Father Pirard told the man.

In a significant show of honor, he'd granted Julien quarters he had to share with no one.

"Bring down his trunk," he added.

Julien looked down and saw his trunk right in front of him. He'd been looking at the trunk for three hours, and never recognized it.

Number 103 was a tiny room, eight feet square, on the building's top floor. Julien noticed that it looked out on the fortress walls, and beyond that he could see the lovely plain, separated from the city by the Doubs.

"What a charming view!" he exclaimed to himself, and in saying the words he was not aware of what they expressed. All the violent emotions he'd been experiencing, in the short time he'd been in Besançon, had completely drained his strength. He sat down near the window, on the single wooden chair in his cell, and sitting there fell into a deep sleep. He did not hear the dinner bell, nor that for evening services. He had been forgotten.

When the first rays of the sun woke him, the next morning, he found himself lying on the wooden floor.

CHAPTER TWENTY-SIX

THE WORLD, OR WHAT THE RICH MAN IS MISSING

I'm alone in the world, no one bothers to think about me. All who I see
growing wealthy possess a boldness and a flinty heartedness I do not
feel. They hate me because of my easy kindness. Ah! Soon I'll die,
maybe of hunger, maybe at the sight of such hard men.

—YOUNG

He hurriedly brushed his cassock and went down. He was late. An assistant master scolded him sharply. Instead of trying to justify himself,
Julien crossed his arms on his chest:

"*Peccavi, pater optime,* I have sinned, kind Father, I confess my fault,"
he said with a contrite air.

His debut was a great success. The clever folk among the seminarians saw they were dealing with a man not at their profession's
starting line.

Recess came. Julien noted that he was the object of universal curiosity. But he was neither withdrawn nor silent. According to the principles he'd evolved for himself, his three hundred and twenty-one
colleagues were his enemies, the most dangerous of whom, in his eyes,
was Father Pirard.

A few days later, Julien had to choose a confessor. He was presented
with a list.

"Oh, Good Lord! What do they take me for?" he said to himself.
"Do they think I can't *take a hint?*" And he chose Father Pirard.

Although he did not know it, this was a decisive step. A small and
very young seminarian, a native of Verrières who from the first day
had declared himself Julien's friend, informed him that, had he chosen
Father Castaneda, the assistant director of the seminary, he might
have done better.

"Father Castaneda is Father Pirard's enemy. He suspects Pirard of
Jansenism," added the little fellow, bending close to Julien's ear.

Our hero considered himself wonderfully cautious, but all his first steps were, like his choice of a confessor, distinctly careless. Misled by the intense vanity of an imaginative mind, he took his intentions for accomplished facts, believing himself a consummate hypocrite. His foolishness went so far that he took himself to task for succeeding in this weaklings' art:

"Alas! It's my only weapon. In some other age," he thought, "I would have *earned my bread* by deeds that spoke for themselves, right in my enemy's face."

Satisfied with his own conduct, Julien looked around, seeing everywhere the appearance of virtue in its purest form.

Eight or ten of the seminarians lived as if already canonized, and had saintly visions like those of Saint Theresa, or Saint Francis when he received the stigmata of the Crucifixion, on Mount Verna in the Apennines. But this was a great secret, hidden by their friends. The poor young visionaries were almost always in the infirmary. A hundred of the others combined sturdy faith with indefatigable hard work. They studied, indeed, to the point of making themselves ill, though without learning much. Two or three were noteworthy for real talent, including one named Chazel, but Julien felt himself quite unlike any of them, and they shared that judgment.

The remainder of the three hundred and twenty-one seminarians were simply rough-hewn fellows, never quite sure they'd understood the Latin words they kept repeating all day long. Virtually all were from peasant families, and vastly preferred earning their bread by repeating a few Latin phrases than by sweating it out of the soil. Seeing this, quite early on, Julien was confident of swift success. "In every form of labor, people with brains are necessary," he told himself, "because when it comes down to it, there's work to be done. Under Napoleon, I might have been a sergeant. Among these future priests, I'll be the pope. All these poor devils," he added, "day laborers from their childhood on, have been living—until they got here—on sour milk and black bread. In their straw-roofed huts, they ate meat only five or six times a year. Like the Roman soldiers, for whom war was a peaceful time, these clumsy peasants are fascinated by the seminary's delights."

All Julien ever saw in their bleak eyes was sheer physical satisfaction, after the midday meal, and the physical pleasure of anticipating another meal. These were the people from whom he had to make himself stand out—but what Julien didn't know, and they were careful never to tell him, was that to place first in every class on dogma, on church history, etc., etc., was in their eyes nothing more than *the sin of vanity.* Ever since Voltaire, ever since the division of government into two chambers (which is fundamentally nothing but *mistrust and self-examination,* creating in the populace the destructive spirit of *suspicion*), the French Church appears to have understood that its true enemies were books. In its eyes, surrender of the heart is everything. Success in the acquisition of learning, even sacred learning, is for the Church highly questionable—and rightly so. What will keep superior men from going over to the enemy, as did Sieyès during the Revolution, or the liberal politician, Grégoire! Trembling, the Church clings to the pope as its only chance for salvation. Only the pope can put the fear of God into self-examination and, by the pious, ceremonious displays of the Papal Court, make an impression on the weary, sick spirits of people all over the world.

Half grasping these various truths (which everything said in his classes, however, tended to refute), Julien fell into a deep melancholy. He worked hard, and rapidly acquired things extremely useful for a priest, though in his eyes distinctly false and of no interest whatever.

"Has the whole world forgotten me?" he thought. He did not know that Father Pirard had already received, and thrown into the fire, several letters postmarked in Dijon, on the pages of which, despite their highly proper language, he perceived intense passion. Equally intense remorse appeared to struggle against that love. "So much the better," thought Father Pirard. "Certainly, it's at least better than having been in love with an impious woman."

One day, he opened a letter, apparently half erased by tears, which was an eternal farewell. "Finally," the writer said to Julien, "heaven has granted me its grace and given me hate—not for the author of my sin, who for me will always be that which is dearest in the whole world, but for my sin itself. The sacrifice has been accomplished, my dear. It has not been without tears, as you can see. The salvation of those for whom I am responsible, and for whom you felt such love, is what has accomplished this. A just but terrible God can no longer take revenge on them, for their mother's sins. Farewell, Julien: be just to everyone."

The last lines of this letter were absolutely illegible. There was an address in Dijon, but there was every expectation that Julien would not be replying, or at least that he would be making use of words that a woman returned to virtuous living could hear without blushing.

Julien's melancholy, aided and abetted by the poor nourishment of meals at eighty-three pence each, as furnished by the seminary's supplier, was starting to affect his mental balance when suddenly, one morning, Fouqué appeared in his room.

"I finally got in. I've been to Besançon five times, so help me, trying to see you. All I've gotten to see is that wooden face. I stationed a spy at the seminary door: Why the devil don't you ever go out?"

"It's a test I've inflicted on myself."

"You've really changed. Finally, I've actually seen you. Two shiny coins, worth five francs each, have just taught me I was an idiot for not offering them the first time."

The two friends talked on and on. Julien changed color when Fouqué told him:

"By the way, did you know this? Your pupils' mother has become wonderfully devout."

He spoke matter-of-factly, which hits very hard at a passionate soul, plainly bowled over, its dearest concerns affected.

"Yes, my friend, into the most exalted devotion. I've heard she goes on pilgrimages. But Father Maslon, who's been a spy on Father Chélan all these years, is eternally shamed, because Madame de Rênal won't go near him. She goes to Dijon, or Besançon, to make confession."

"She comes to Besançon?" asked Julien, his forehead reddening.

"Pretty often," answered Fouqué, questioningly.

"Have you got a copy of *The Constitutional*?"

"What are you talking about?" answered Fouqué.

"I asked you if you had a copy of *The Constitutional*," answered Julien in the calmest of voices. "They cost thirty pence an issue here."

"What? Liberals, even in the seminary!" Fouqué cried. "Poor France!" he added, imitating the hypocritical, sweet-toned voice of Father Maslon.

This visit would have had a profound effect on our hero, except that the next day, because of what he'd been told by the little seminarian from Verrières, who seemed to him so childlike, he came to make an important discovery. From the moment he'd entered the seminary, Julien's conduct had been simply a series of false steps. He made bitter fun of himself.

In truth, everything important in his life had been knowledgeably done, but he'd paid no attention to details, and those most skillful in seminary ways pay attention to nothing but details. In addition, his classmates had come to think of him as a *freethinker.* He had been betrayed by a host of tiny actions.

In their eyes he had been convicted of a monstrous sin: *he thought, he judged for himself,* instead of blindly following *authority* and example. Father Pirard had not been of the slightest help: outside the confessional, he had never addressed a word to Julien, and there too he listened more than he spoke. It would have been very different had he chosen Father Castaneda.

From the instant Julien became aware of his foolishness, there was no more boredom in his life. He wanted to know the extent of the damage and, to do this, he dropped a bit of the arrogance and stubbornness with which he had repulsed his classmates. And then they could take their revenge. His advances were met by a contempt that came very close to derision. He realized that, from the time he'd first come to the seminary, there had not been a single hour, especially during recess, that might not have had repercussions for or against him, that might not have either swelled the number of his enemies or won him the goodwill of the sincerely virtuous among the seminarians—or, at least, those less coarse than the others. The damage needing repair was huge; the task was extremely difficult. But Julien was painstakingly, ceaselessly on guard: he was at work designing himself a brand-new character.

His eye movements, for example, caused him serious difficulty. There was good reason, in a place like this, to keep one's eyes lowered. "How presumptuous I was at Verrières!" Julien told himself. "I fancied myself living; I was merely preparing to live. Now I'm finally in the real world, finding it exactly as I will go on finding it, until I've finished playing my part: surrounded by genuine enemies. What an incredible difficulty," he added, "this constantly evolving, never-ending hypocrisy! It makes the labors of Hercules pale by comparison. Our modern Hercules would have to be Pope Sextus V, for fifteen years in a row using his modesty to deceive forty cardinals who had seen him, throughout his younger years, both lively and arrogant.

"So: knowledge is nothing here!" he said to himself, resentfully. "Progress in dogma, in Church history, etc., only *seems* to make any difference. Talking about knowledge is a deliberate trap, meant for fools like me to fall into. Alas! All I've accomplished is a swift mastery of all this twaddle. Do they really judge these things at their true value? Do they think of them as I do? And I've been stupid enough to feel proud! All I've gained, for all my long, unending parade of academic honors, is fierce, relentless enemies. Chazel, who really knows more than I do, always throws a whopping blunder into his papers, so he drops into fiftieth place. If he ever takes a first, it's pure absent-mindedness. Ah! How useful one word, one single word from Father Pirard would have been!"

Once he'd had his eyes opened, the long exercises in aesthetic piety—saying the rosary five times a week, chanting canticles to the Sacred Heart of Jesus, etc., etc.—which had always struck him as mordantly dull, became the most fascinating things he did. In critically evaluating himself, and trying not to exaggerate his capacities, Julien did not aspire all at once—like those seminarians who served as models for the others—to make every single thing he did *significant,* or in other words to bear witness to a kind of Christian perfection. There is a way of eating a soft-boiled egg, in the seminary, that testifies to progress toward a life of devotion.

My reader may be smiling, but let him take the trouble to recall all the many errors committed, precisely in the eating of an egg, by Father Delille, when invited to lunch by a great lady of Louis XVI's court.

Julien first tried to reach a state of *non culpa,* or the negative virtue of comparative innocence, in which the young seminarian's walk, the method of moving his arms, his eyes, etc., revealed no worldly concerns, without as yet attaining to absorption in that other, eternal life, and its *pure nothingness.*

Julien was always finding, lettered in charcoal on the corridor walls, observations like the following: "What is sixty years of striving, balanced against either eternal delight or eternally burning in hell?" He no longer scorned them; he understood he had to keep them forever in front of his eyes. "What is it I'm going to do all my life?" he'd say to himself. "I'm going to be selling the faithful a place in heaven. How can I make them really see that place? By the difference between what they view when they look at me, and when they look at others like themselves."

After months of ceaseless effort, Julien still looked like a *thinker*. His way of moving his eyes and holding his mouth did not indicate implicit faith, a readiness to believe everything and endure everything, even martyrdom. Julien was angry, seeing himself inferior in this sort of thing to the coarsest of coarse peasants. They had excellent reasons for not looking like thinkers.

How hard he strove to achieve a face of fervent, blind faith, prepared to believe anything and suffer everything—the face so often found in Italian monasteries, and of which, among our nonecclesiastics, Guercino has left, in his religious paintings, such perfect models.

During high festivals, the seminarians were given sausage with sauerkraut. Those who sat near Julien, in the refectory, noticed how indifferently pleased this made him: it was one of his most serious offenses. His classmates saw it as an obnoxious trait of intensely stupid hypocrisy: nothing made him more enemies. "Look at this bourgeois, look at this snob," they said, "pretending to be scornful of the very best of all *food*, sausage and sauerkraut! Oh, what a rotten fellow! What conceit! What eternal damnation!"

"Alas!" Julien cried, in his moments of discouragement, "the ignorance of these young peasants, my classmates, is an immense advantage for them! When they entered the seminary, their teachers didn't have to free them from the fearful number of worldly ideas I bear, and which they can see on my face no matter what I do."

With an attentiveness bordering on jealousy, Julien studied the coarsest of the peasant seminarians. When they'd stripped off their ratteen jackets, so they could put on their black garments, their education had been limited to a limitless respect for money—*hard or soft*, as folk in Franche-Comté phrase it.

This is the holy, epic way of expressing that sublime conception, *cash.*

Happiness, for these seminarians, as for the heroes of Voltaire's novels, is above all else a good dinner. Julien found in almost all of them an innate respect for anyone who wore *cotton broadcloth* clothing. Such an attitude values *distributive justice,* the sort we receive in our courts of law, at exactly its true worth—or perhaps a bit less than that. "What good does it do," they kept saying among themselves, "suing a *big shot?*"

That's the phrase they use in the valleys of the Jura, when they refer to a rich man. Imagine their respect for the wealthiest of the wealthy—the government!

In these Franche-Comté peasants' eyes, not to smile respectfully, when the governor's name was mentioned, was sheer recklessness. After all, a poor man's recklessness is quickly punished by an absence of food.

After having virtually suffocated early on, in his feelings of contempt, Julien ended by experiencing pity. Most of his classmates' fathers well knew what it was like, coming home to their cottage on a winter night and finding no bread, no potatoes, no chestnuts. "Why should it seem surprising," Julien said to himself, "if in their eyes a happy man is, first of all, someone who's just had a good meal, and next to that someone who wears decent clothes? My classmates have a fixed vocation, or in other words they see in the priesthood a long continuation of exactly that happiness—eating well and having warm clothes in the winter."

Once, he heard a young seminarian, blessed with an imagination, saying to a companion:

"Why shouldn't I become pope, just like Sextus VI, who was a swineherd?"

"Only Italians get to be pope," said his friend. "But I'm sure they'll pick some of us, the lucky ones, for posts as vicar-generals, canons, and maybe bishops.... Father P., Bishop of Châlons, is a barrel-maker's son, and that's what my father does."

One day, during a dogma lesson, Father Pirard summoned Julien. The poor young man was thrilled to leave the physical and moral atmosphere in which he was immersed.

The director gave him exactly the kind of welcome he'd experienced, and been so terrified by, the day he'd entered the seminary.

"Explain what's written on this playing card," he said, and the way he looked at Julien made him wish he could sink down into the ground.

Julien read:

"Amanda Binet, at the Giraffe Café, before eight o'clock. Say you're from Genlis, and my mother's cousin."

Julien saw at once what danger he was in: Father Castaneda's spies had sniffed out this address, and stolen it.

"The day I entered the seminary," he said, looking at Father Pirard's forehead, because he could not endure those terrible eyes, "I was trembling. Father Chélan had warned me this was a place full of denunciations and all kinds of wickedness. Spying on your classmates, and denouncing them, were encouraged. Heaven wishes it to be that way, to show young priests life as it really is, and to inspire them with disgust for the world and all its displays."

"And you use your rhetoric even on me!" cried Father Pirard, furious. "You little rascal!"

"At Verrières," Julien replied coldly, "my brothers beat me any time they were jealous."

"Get to the point! the point!" Father Pirard shouted, almost beside himself.

Not in the least intimidated, Julien went on with his story.

"The day I came to Besançon, about noon, I was hungry, I went into a café. I felt intense repugnance for such a profane place, but I thought my lunch would cost me less there than in an inn. A lady, who seemed to be the proprietress, took pity on me, an obvious newcomer in the city. 'Besançon is full of crooks,' she told me. 'I fear for you, sir. If any harm comes to you, just seek my help, send me word before eight o'clock. If the porter at the seminary won't send your note, tell him you're my cousin, and like me a native of Genlis' . . ."

"All this jabbering will be looked into," cried Father Pirard, unable to stay in one place, walking up and down his room.

"Back to your cell!"

The director followed him in and locked the door. Then he set himself to inspecting Julien's trunk, at the bottom of which the fatal playing card had been carefully hidden. There was nothing missing from the trunk, but things had gotten disarranged—and yet he had always kept the key with him. "What good luck," Julien told himself, "that during those days of my blindness, I never made use of permission to go out of the seminary, so often offered by Father Castaneda, and with a goodwill that, now, I quite understand. If I'd been weak enough to change my clothes and go see pretty Amanda, I'd have been lost. When they gave up on using their information that way, and not wanting to just throw it away, they denounced me."

Two hours later, the director summoned him again.

"You were not lying," he said, not looking at him as harshly. "But holding on to an address like this is careless beyond your conception, and profoundly serious. You miserable child! Ten years from now, who knows? It might disgrace you."

CHAPTER TWENTY-SEVEN

FIRST EXPERIENCE OF LIFE

The present age, oh Lord! It's like the Ark of the Covenant.
Woe to anyone who touches it.
—DIDEROT

The reader will allow us to skip over most of the clear, precise facts of this time in Julien's life. It's not that we don't have them—quite the contrary. But it may be that what he saw, there in the seminary, was entirely too black for the more moderate coloring we seek in these pages. Those who have suffered certain things can only remember them with a horror that paralyzes every other pleasure—even that of reading a story.

Julien did not make much progress in his attempts at an externalized hypocrisy. He lapsed into moments of disgust and even of complete discouragement. He had not been successful, even in this sordid career. Any help at all, from anywhere or anyone, would have been enough to lift his heart; the difficulties he needed to conquer would not have seemed so enormous. But he was as alone as an abandoned ship in the middle of the ocean. "And if I did succeed," he said to himself, "to have all the rest of my life to spend in such company! Gluttons who think only of the bacon omelet they gobble down at dinner, or those like Father Castaneda, for whom there's no such thing as a crime too black! They'll get the power they're after, but oh great God, at what a price!

"Man has a powerful will; I read this everywhere. But can it be powerful enough to overcome such disgust? Great men's tasks used to be easy. No matter the danger, they appreciated its beauty. But who can understand, except me, this ugliness all around me?"

It was, for his life, the acid test. It would have been so easy to enlist in one of the fine regiments garrisoned at Besançon! Or he could have become a Latin teacher: he needed so little to live on! But then, no more career, no more future for him to imagine. That would be death.

Here are the details of just one of his depressing days.

"I've congratulated myself, often, for thinking I was different from the other young peasants! Well, I've lived long enough to see that *difference creates hatred*," he told himself one morning. This great truth had just been demonstrated by one of his most stinging failures. He had labored for a week, making himself pleasant to one of the seminarians who lived as if already canonized. He walked with him in the courtyard, humbly listening to stupid prattle until he couldn't keep his eyes open. Suddenly the weather turned stormy, thunder rumbled, and the saintly one called out, pushing Julien away in the rudest fashion:

"Listen, it's everyone for himself in this world. I'm not interested in being burned up by a thunderbolt. God might strike you down as an infidel, just like Voltaire."

His teeth clenched in rage, and his wide-open eyes staring at a sky streaked by lightning: "I'd deserve to be swept away, if I fell asleep during a storm!" Julien cried to himself. "Let's try to win over some other righteous snot!"

The bell announced Father Castaneda's class in ecclesiastical history.

Instructing these young peasants, terrified by hard work and their fathers' poverty, Father Castaneda taught, that day, that the government, which seemed to them so terrifying, only had true and legitimate power because the pope delegated it.

"Make yourselves worthy of the pope's kindness and goodwill by the saintliness of your lives, by your obedience. Become *like a rod in his hands*," he added, "and you will ascend to some noble post where you will be in charge, beyond anyone's control, permanently in power, where the government pays a third of your salary, and the faithful, molded by your teaching, the other two-thirds."

Leaving his classroom, Father Castaneda stopped in the courtyard.

"It is truly said of a parish priest that whatever the man is worth will decide how much his post is worth," he said to the students standing in a circle around him. "I have myself known, I who here speak to you, of mountain parishes where the supplemental fees were worth far more than those of parish priests in the city. The nominal salaries were the same, but without counting the fat capons, the eggs, the fresh butter, and a thousand other details, equally attractive. And in the mountains the parish priest ranks highest, no doubt about it. There's no good dinner to which he won't be invited, no celebration, etc."

Father Castaneda had hardly gone up to his room when the students divided into groups. Julien was not in any of them: he was ignored, a black sheep. In every group, he saw someone toss a coin in the air, and if heads or tails was guessed correctly, everyone said the coin tosser would soon have a parish rich in supplemental fees.

Then they swapped stories. A certain young priest, ordained barely a year, had given a pet rabbit to the old parish priest's maidservant. He was asked to serve in that parish and, not more than a month later, when the parish priest died a quick death, the young one inherited the parish. Another young priest had managed to be named successor to the parish priest of a big, wealthy town, because he'd sat at table, every meal, with the paralyzed old parish priest, and gracefully cut up his chicken for him.

Like young people in all walks of life, the seminarians dramatized the effects of these little maneuvers, which are colored in unusual hues and strike the imagination.

"I've got to participate in these conversations," Julien told himself. "When they're not talking about sausages and good old priests, they chatter about the worldly side of Church doctrine, like quarrels between bishops and governors, or between mayors and parish priests." Julien saw the concept of a second God emerging, but a new God far more frightening and more powerful than the other one. This second God was the pope. They would say, but in low voices and when they were very sure Father Pirard could not hear them, that the pope didn't bother naming all the governors and mayors in France, only because he'd given this responsibility to the French king when he'd declared him the Church's elder son.

It was just about this time when Julien thought, using de Maistre's book *On the Pope,* he might be able to get himself into one of the groups. He truly astonished his classmates—but it was still a disaster. He annoyed them by presenting their opinions better than they did. Father Chélan had been as careless of Julien's welfare as he had been of his own. Having trained him to think clearly, and not let himself settle for empty verbiage, he'd neglected to explain that, for someone not well respected, this habit is criminal, for in any case logical thinking is always offensive.

Julien's elegant rhetoric thus gave rise to a new crime. On further reflection, his classmates compressed into a single phrase all the horror he inspired in them: they nicknamed him "Martin Luther"— above all, they said, because of this diabolic logic, of which he was so proud.

A number of young seminarians had fresher complexions, and might have been considered better looking than Julien, but he had pale hands and could never hide certain delicate habits. This apparent advantage was nothing of the kind, in this sad dwelling into which fate had thrown him. The unwashed peasants with whom he lived said he was clearly of loose morals.

We do not wish to bore the reader by reciting our hero's thousand misfortunes. For example, the strongest of his classmates regularly tried beating him up: he took as a weapon a double-pointed metal protractor and notified them, by gestures rather than words, that he'd use it. When spies write up their reports, it's hard to make as much out of gestures as words.

CHAPTER TWENTY-EIGHT

A PROCESSION

Every heart was moved. God's presence seemed to have descended into
the narrow, Gothic streets, extending in every direction and well sanded
by the efforts of the faithful.

—YOUNG

Julien had tried in vain to make himself small and stupid: he could not
be liked; he was far too different. "But," he told himself, "all our professors are notable people and one in a thousand. Why aren't they happy
about my humility?" Just one of them seemed willing to waste his kindness by believing in and being fooled by everything. This was Father
Chas-Bernard, director of ceremonials at the cathedral, where for fifteen years he'd been led to expect a post as canon, and where, while he
waited, he taught sacred eloquence at the seminary. In Julien's blind period, this was one of the classes where he was regularly the top student.
Father Chas had demonstrated affection for this prize pupil; when class
was over, he would take Julien's arm and walk in the garden with him.

"What's he after?" Julien asked himself. He noted, with astonishment, that for hours on end Father Chas would talk to him about the
vestments owned by the cathedral. There were seventeen chasubles,
all trimmed with lace, not to mention mourning garments. They were
expecting more from President de Rubempré's widow. Now ninety
years old, this lady had, for at least seventy years, preserved her wedding clothes, superb Lyons silk, brocaded in gold. It was universally
believed, in Besançon, that by the terms of the president's will the
cathedral's *treasures* would be enriched by more than ten chasubles,
not counting four or five long mantles for high festivals. "I'd go even
further," added Father Chas, lowering his voice. "I have reason to believe the president left us eight magnificent candlesticks, of gilded silver, which are said to have been bought in Italy by Charles the Bold,
Duke of Burgundy, a favorite minister of whose was one of the president's ancestors."

"But what's he after, with all this old-clothes stuff?" thought Julien. "He's been building this up, like a master, for a hundred years, and there's still nothing in sight. It's got to be that he really mistrusts me! He's smarter than all the others: in two weeks you can easily figure out their secret goal. But I understand: this fellow has been putting up with it for fifteen years!"

One evening, in the middle of a fencing lesson, Julien was summoned by Father Pirard, who said:

"Tomorrow's the Feast of Corpus Christi. Father Chas-Bernard needs your assistance in decorating the cathedral. Go, and obey him."

Then Father Pirard called him back.

"You can decide for yourself, if you want to make this an occasion for wandering around the city."

"*Incedo per ignes,* I have secret enemies," Julien thought.

Early the next day, Julien made his way to the cathedral, walking with lowered eyes. It felt good to see the streets and the bustle beginning everywhere in the city. Everywhere, they were hanging handsome cloth across house fronts. All the time he'd spent in the seminary seemed to him no more than a mere flicker. His thoughts were of Vergy, and of pretty Amanda Binet: he might meet her again, since her café was not far away. As he approached the cathedral, he could see Father Chas-Bernard in the distance, in the doorway. He was a fat man with a joyous face and a straightforward look. Right now, he seemed triumphant.

"I've been waiting for you, my dear son," he cried when he saw Julien coming. "You're most welcome. Our task, today, will be long and trying, so let us fortify ourselves with an early breakfast. We'll have another at ten, during high mass."

"It is my wish, sir," Julien said gravely, "not to be alone for an instant. Be so good as to note," he added, pointing toward the cathedral clock above their heads, "that I've come at one minute to five."

"Ah! Those naughty fellows at the seminary have made you afraid! It's very decent of you to remember them," said Father Chas. "Is a road less lovely because there are thorns in the hedges alongside it? Travelers go their way and let the nasty thorns wither where they are. For the rest, to work, my dear friend, to work!"

Father Chas had been right when he'd said the work would be trying. The previous night the cathedral had been the site of a large funeral; nothing could be put in readiness for Corpus Christi. It was thus necessary, in just one morning, to wrap every one of the Gothic pillars, along the three main aisles, in a kind of cloak of red damask, thirty feet high. The bishop had brought in, by mail coach, four Parisian decorators, but these gentlemen could not take care of everything—and rather than encourage their local helpers, less experienced and a good deal clumsier, they made matters worse by laughing at them.

Julien realized he'd have to go up the ladders himself; his nimbleness clearly came in handy. He took charge of the local decorators. Father Chas, delighted, watched him flying from one ladder to the next. Once all the pillars were wrapped in damask, huge feather clusters, five in all, had to be set above the main altar canopy. It was a rich, crowning work, in gilded wood, supported by eight great columns of Italian marble, spiraling from top to bottom. But to reach the center of the canopy, it was necessary to walk along an ancient wooden cornice, which was perhaps worm-eaten but was certainly forty feet high.

Seeing this risky road, the Parisian decorators lost their merry brightness. They stood looking up at it, saying a great deal and staying right where they were. Julien snatched the feather clusters and fairly ran up the ladder. He shaped the clusters like a beautiful crown, directly in the center of the canopy. When he came down the ladder, Father Chas threw his arms around him.

"*Optime,* superb," cried the good priest. "I'll tell the bishop about this."

Their ten o'clock breakfast was a very happy one. Father Chas had never seen his church so lovely.

"My dear disciple," he told Julien, "my mother used to do the chair rentals in this venerable basilica, so in a sense I was nurtured in this splendid edifice. Robespierre's Terror ruined us, but at the age of eight, which I then was, I was already assisting at private masses, and on those days I was fed. No one was better at folding a chasuble: the gold braid never got frayed. Ever since Napoleon reestablished holy services, I have had the good fortune to run everything, here in this ancient cathedral. Five times every year, my eyes see it adorned with such wonderfully beautiful ornamentation. But it has never been so resplendent—the widths of damask have never been so well tied as they have been today; never have they been so well fitted to the pillars."

"Finally," thought Julien, "he's going to tell me his secret. He's telling me about himself, it's pouring out of him. But even though he's obviously excited, he hasn't spoken a careless word. He's worked hard, yes, and he's happy," Julien said to himself, "and he's been putting away a lot of this first-class wine. What a man! What an example for me! He's way ahead of all the others." (He'd learned this slangy talk from the old surgeon-major.)

As the *Sanctus* of the high mass began, Julien said he'd like to put on a surplice and follow behind the bishop in this marvelous procession.

"The thieves, my dear, the thieves!" cried Father Chas. "You're not thinking about the thieves! The procession will go out of the church, and it will be empty—but we'll watch over it, you and I. We'll be very lucky if there aren't a couple of yards missing from that beautiful braid, wrapped around the base of the pillars. That was yet another gift from Madame de Rubempré. It came from her great-grandfather, the famous count: it's pure gold, my dear," the priest added, bending toward Julien's ear and speaking very softly, plainly very excited, "not some kind of fake. You keep watch on the north aisle: don't leave it for an instant. I'll take the middle aisle and the whole central part. Keep an eye on the confessionals: that's where the women hide, the ones who spy for the thieves. They watch for the very second our backs are turned."

As he finished speaking, the bells sounded a quarter to twelve, and the great clock could be heard as well. It gave a great peal. All these clear, solemn sounds moved Julien. His mind no longer felt tied to the earth.

The scent of incense, and of the rose petals that little children, dressed as Saint John, had strewn in front of the holy tabernacle, completed his excited state.

All that the clock's somber tolling should have awakened in Julien, really, was the thought of twenty men toiling for half a franc, helped perhaps by fifteen or twenty of the faithful. He should have contemplated the ropes and their wear and tear, as well as the vulnerable wooden portions of the building, and the risky state of the clock itself, which fell down every other century, and he should at the very least have thought of some way of paying the bell ringers less, or of paying them by an indulgence or two, or some other blessing drawn from the Church's rich treasure, and thereby keeping its cash resources intact.

But instead of these wise reflections, Julien's soul, exalted by these clear, bold sounds, wandered in imaginary places. He'll never make a good priest, nor a great administrator. Souls stirred like this are good, at best, for making artists. Here, Julien's vanity bursts into the full light of day. Perhaps fifty of his fellow seminarians—whom public opinion had made mindful of living reality, as had the Jacobinism showing itself to them, lying in ambush behind every bush—would have heard the great clock and thought of nothing but the bell ringers' wages. They would then have considered, with all of Barême's mathematical genius, whether the extent of public emotion justified what the bell ringers were paid. Had Julien cared to think about the cathedral's material interests, his imagination might even have soared so far that it could have devised a way to save forty francs of Church funds, and how to avoid expenses of twenty-five pence.

All this time, on the most beautiful day the world has ever seen, the procession proceeded slowly through Besançon, pausing at the temporary altars built, in competition, one with the other, by the authorities, and the church remained profoundly silent. It was in half darkness, and there was a pleasant, cool freshness; the fragrance of flowers and the scent of incense still hung in the air.

The hushed quiet, the deep solitude, the cool freshness of the long aisles—everything made Julien's daydreaming sweeter. He was not worried about Father Chas, who would not bother him, busy as he was elsewhere in the building. His soul had very nearly deserted its mortal shell, which was slowly walking down the north aisle, assigned to him for surveillance. He was still more tranquil because he'd made sure that all there was in the confessional booths was a scattering of pious women. His eyes looked but did not see.

However, his abstraction was half broken by the sight of two women, extremely well dressed and on their knees, one already in a confessional, and the other close by, on a prayer stool. He was looking without seeing, but still, whether from some vague sense of his responsibilities, or perhaps admiring the two ladies' fine, simple clothes, he noticed that there was no priest in the confessional. "Strange," he thought. "Why aren't these fine ladies on their knees at some temporary altar, if they're in fact so devout? Or else set advantageously in the front row of a balcony, if they're worldly women? How well designed that dress is! How charming!" He slowed down, trying to see it better.

The woman who was on her knees, inside the confessional, turned her head a bit, hearing—in the midst of all the deep silence—the sound of Julien's steps. Suddenly, she cried out and fainted.

As she began to fall, tumbling backward, her friend, who was close by, hurried to her assistance. At the same time, Julien saw the neck and shoulders of the fallen woman. A twisted rope of fine, large pearls, terribly familiar to him, caught his eye. Who can say what he felt, recognizing Madame de Rênal's hair! And it was she. The lady trying to hold up her head, and keep her from falling full on the ground, was Madame Derville. Quite beyond thought, Julien ran to them: Madame de Rênal's fall might well have carried down her friend had Julien not kept them both from the floor. He saw Madame de Rênal's pallor, her blank face, loose against his shoulder. He helped Madame Derville support this charming head on a straw-bottomed chair; he was on his knees.

Madame Derville turned and recognized him:

"Leave, sir, leave!" she said, intensely angry. "Above all, don't let her see you again. The sight of you surely shocked and horrified her: she'd been so happy, until you appeared. Your behavior is abominable. Leave—go away, if there is any decency left in you."

She spoke with such authority, and at that moment Julien felt so weak, that he went away. "She always hated me," he said of Madame Derville.

Just then, the nasal chanting of the lead priests resounded in the church. The procession was returning. Father Chas-Bernard called Julien, then called again; Julien did not at first hear him. Finally, the priest came and touched his arm, having found Julien behind a pillar where he had hidden himself, half dead. Father Chas had meant to present him to the bishop.

"You're ill, my child," the priest said, seeing him pale and almost unable to walk. "You've worked too hard." He gave Julien his arm to lean on. "Come, sit down on this little bench, behind me. It's for the giving of blessings, with holy water. I'll stand in front of you, so you won't be seen." They were standing near the main entrance. "Calm yourself. We still have twenty solid minutes before the bishop appears. Try to get a grip on yourself. When he comes by, I'll help you up, because I'm good and strong, despite my age."

But when the bishop came past, Julien was shaking so hard that Father Chas gave up the idea of presenting him.

"Don't worry," he said to Julien. "I'll find another opportunity."

That night, he sent the seminary chapel ten pounds of the candles he'd saved up, he said, because Julien had been so careful, and so quick, in snuffing them out. Nothing could have been less truthful. The poor young fellow was himself snuffed out. There had been absolutely nothing in his head since he'd seen Madame de Rênal.

CHAPTER TWENTY-NINE

THE FIRST FORWARD STEP

He knew his own time, he knew his own district, and he's rich.
—*THE PRECURSOR* [NEWSPAPER]

Julien had not yet recovered from the profound trance, brought on by what had happened in the cathedral, when one morning harsh Father Pirard summoned him.

"I have here a very favorable letter about you, from Father Chas-Bernard. All in all, I'm basically pleased by your behavior. You are extremely reckless, even harebrained, though you don't appear to be. To this point, however, your heart's been good, even generous. Your mind is superior. In sum, I see a spark in you that must not be neglected.

"After fifteen years as director, I am about to leave this institution.

My crime has been allowing our students freedom to make decisions for themselves, rather than championing or assisting that secret society, about which you spoke when you knelt in the confessional. Before I go, I want to do something for you. I would have done it two months sooner, because you deserve it, had it not been for the denunciation based on Amanda Binet's address, found in your possession. I hereby make you assistant master for both the New and the Old Testaments."

Overwhelmed with gratitude, Julien thought of dropping to his knees and thanking God, but he yielded to a more genuine gesture: he went to Father Pirard, took his hand, and brought it to his lips.

"What's this?" exclaimed the director as if annoyed. But Julien's eyes spoke even more clearly than his deed.

Father Pirard looked at him, astonished, like a man who many years ago lost the habit of dealing with tender feelings. His face, his whole manner, betrayed him; his voice became different.

"Well then! Yes, my child, I am fond of you. Heaven knows it's entirely in spite of myself. I've been charged with being fair, and not manifesting either dislike or affection for anyone. Your career will be painful. I see something in you which offends coarse souls. Jealousy and slander will hound you. Wherever Providence may place you, your colleagues will never see you without hating you, and they will pretend to love you, the better to betray you. For which there is just one remedy: put all your hope in God, for He has caused you to be hated, in punishment for your vanity. Let your behavior be pure: it is the only resource I see for you. If you hold to the truth, with an unyielding grip, sooner or later your enemies will be confounded."

It had been so long since Julien heard a friendly voice, he was forced to forgive himself his weakness: he dissolved in tears. Father Pirard threw open his arms; it was a wonderfully sweet moment for them both.

Julien was wild with happiness. This was the first promotion he'd gotten; the advantages were immense. To properly understand, you must be condemned for months on end never to know solitude, placed in close contact with colleagues, at best tiresome, for the most part unendurable. Their loud voices would be enough to upset a delicate constitution. The noisy delight of these well-nourished, well-fed peasants could not be contained, or even believed in, unless they yelled as loud as their lungs would let them.

Julien now ate by himself, or very nearly so, an hour later than the other seminarians. He had a key to the garden and could walk there during the hours when no one else was about.

To his great surprise, Julien perceived that he was not as hated as before: he had anticipated, in fact, that hatred for him would be doubled. His secret wish that no one speak to him, which had earned him many enemies, was no longer perceived as a sign of ridiculous arrogance. To the coarse peasants who surrounded him, this was now a proper feeling of self-worth. Hatred faded quite significantly, especially among the youngest of his classmates, who had now become his students; he treated them with great civility. Little by little he even acquired supporters; it became bad taste to refer to him as Martin Luther.

What does it accomplish, mentioning his friends, his enemies? It's all incredibly ugly, and uglier still because the picture is entirely true. Yet for ordinary people, these men are the only teachers of morality they possess—and without those men, what would happen to ordinary people? Can the newspaper ever replace the parish priest?

Now that Julien had achieved his new dignity, Father Pirard was careful never to speak to him unless others were present. This was sensible conduct for the master, as it was for the disciple, but above all it was *proof.* As a harsh Jansenist, Father Pirard's fixed principle was: Do you think someone is deserving? Then put obstacles between him and everything he desires, everything he tries to do. If he is truly deserving, he'll surely know how to overcome or transform those obstacles.

It was hunting season. Fouqué conceived the notion of sending the seminary a stag and a wild boar, in the name of Julien's parents. The dead animals were placed in the corridor between the kitchen and the dining room. This was to let everyone see them when they went to eat. They were all very curious. Dead as he was, the wild boar frightened the youngest of the seminarians: they reached out and touched his tusks. For a whole week, no one talked of anything else.

This gift, putting Julien's family into a social category that had to be respected, was a mortal blow to jealousy. His became a superiority consecrated by wealth. Chazel and the most distinguished among his classmates made overtures, almost as if they were upset because he had not warned them of his parents' riches, thus allowing them to seem deficient in the respect due to wealth.

Military conscription was enacted; as a seminary student, Julien was exempted. This strongly affected him. "There goes forever the moment when, had it been twenty years earlier, I might have begun an heroic life!"

He was walking alone, in the seminary garden, and overheard a conversation between two masons working on one of the cloister's walls.

"Well, I've got to go, we got ourselves a new conscription."

"In that *other one's* day, hey, it was great! A mason could get to be an officer, even a general. It happened."

"Just look at it now! There's only poor folks going. Those what's *worth something,* they stay home."

"You're born poor, you stay poor, and that's that."

"Hey, is it really true, like they say, the *other one's* dead?" a third mason asked.

"It's the stuffed shirts who say that, believe me! He scared them."

"What a difference for workingmen, in his day! And I hear his own generals turned traitor on him! There's traitors for you!"

This talk comforted Julien. As he went past them, he repeated, sighing:

"The only king the people still remember!"

Examination time arrived. Julien replied to the questions brilliantly; he saw that even Chazel tried to show how much he knew.

After the first day, the examiners named by the famed Vicar-General de Frilair were very annoyed, always having to put first on their list, or at worst second, Julien Sorel; they had been told he was Father Pirard's favorite. There had been bets made in the seminary that Julien would stand first on the examination list; whoever placed first was rewarded by a dinner with the bishop. But at the end of one session, when he had been examined on the Church Fathers, a clever examiner who'd first questioned him about Saint Jerome and that saint's passion for Cicero, turned the subject to Horace, Virgil, and other profane writers. Julien's classmates did not know it, but he had memorized a great many passages from these authors. Carried away by his success, Julien forgot where he was and, when the examiner repeated his question, he passionately recited several of Horace's odes and then gave an analytical summary of each. The examiner gave him twenty minutes to bury himself in his own trap, then suddenly turned severe and issued a sharp scolding for the time Julien had wasted on these profane studies, and the useless, or sinful, ideas they had put in his head.

"I am a fool, sir, and you are right," said Julien modestly, recognizing the clever stratagem by which he'd been victimized.

This was clearly a dirty trick; even the seminarians said so. But that did not stop Father de Frilair—that shrewd man who'd so knowledgeably organized the Congregation of the Holy Virgin's network in Besançon, and whose communications with Paris caused trembling among the judges, the governors, and even the higher officers in the garrison—from placing, in his imposing handwriting, "grade-level 198" next to Julien's name. It gave him pleasure to thus mortify his enemy, Pirard the Jansenist.

His major concern, for a full ten years, had been to remove Pirard as director of the seminary. Obedient to the precepts he'd explained to Julien, Father Pirard had been honest, pious, involved in no intrigues, devoted to his duty. But heaven's wrath had fallen on him, giving him a choleric disposition, inclined to react strongly to insults and hatred. Every offense against this fiery soul hit home. He would have handed in his resignation a hundred times over, but he considered himself useful in the post to which Providence had assigned him. "I'm blocking the advance of Jesuitism and idolatry," he told himself.

At examination time, it had been roughly two months since he'd spoken to Julien, and yet he was sick for an entire week when he got the official letter, announcing the final results, and saw "grade-level 198" assigned to this student, in his judgment the glory of the institution. Given his severe nature, his only consolation was to concentrate on Julien every form of surveillance he could command. He was thrilled when he discovered no anger in the young man, no plan for revenge, no discouragement.

Some weeks later, receiving a letter, Julien shuddered; the post-mark was Paris. "At last," he thought, "Madame de Rênal has remembered her promises." Someone who signed his name Paul Sorel, and said he was a relative, was sending him a bill of exchange in the amount of five hundred francs. It was noted that, should Julien continue to study the finest Latin authors, and with such success, a similar sum would be sent him annually.

"It's her, it's her generosity!" Julien told himself, his heart softening. "She wants to comfort me. But why not a single affectionate word?"

He deceived himself about the letter: Madame de Rênal, guided by her friend, Madame Derville, was completely lost in her profound remorse. In spite of herself, she often thought of the unusual being who, once he'd come into her life, had turned it upside down. But she would have been exceedingly careful about writing to him.

If we spoke the seminary's language, we could call this dispatch of five hundred francs a miracle; we could say the gift was from Father de Frilair himself, who had been made heaven's instrument for that purpose.

Twelve years earlier, Father de Frilair had come to Besançon, carrying a suitcase holding very little indeed, and what it did contain, according to the chronicle, was in fact all he owned. He found himself, now, one of the richest landholders in the district. In the course of this prosperous advance, he had invested in one half of a property, the other half of which had been left to Monsieur de La Mole. This led to a protracted lawsuit between these two.

Despite his prominence in Paris, and the position he occupied at the king's court, Marquis de La Mole felt it might be risky to fight, on his home grounds, against a vicar-general who had a reputation for making and unmaking governors. But instead of seeking a fifty-thousand-franc public gratuity—to be hidden in the budget under any authorized name—and withdrawing from this paltry fifty-thousand-franc lawsuit, the marquis got angry. He thought he was right—as if this had anything to do with legal matters.

Now, if I may say so: Where will we find a judge without a son, or at least a cousin, to push forward in the world?

To make matters clear enough even for the blind: a week after obtaining a preliminary decree, Father de Frilair borrowed the bishop's carriage and went, in person, to bring his lawyer the medal of the Legion of Honor. Monsieur de La Mole, a bit dizzied by his adversary's attitude, and sensing some yielding on the part of his own lawyers, sought Father Chélan's advice, whereupon the marquis was introduced to Father Pirard.

At the time of our story, the relationships just recounted had gone on for several years. Father Pirard brought his fiery temperament to this business. He had endless contact with the marquis's lawyers; he studied the marquis's cause; and, finding it just, he took the Marquis de La Mole's side against the all-powerful vicar-general. Father de Frilair was outraged by such insolence—and from a little Jansenist!

"Just see these court noblemen, who claim to be so powerful!" Father Frilair would say to his close friends. "Monsieur de La Mole hasn't even sent a miserable medal to his Besançon agent, and he's simply going to let him lose his post. Still, as I hear from Paris, this fine peer of the realm never lets a week go by without showing off his wonderful medals and ribbons, in the keeper of the seal's drawing room—whoever he may be."

In spite of Father Pirard's energetic support, and even though Monsieur de La Mole was, as ever, on the very best of terms with the minister of justice, and above all with the minister's subordinates, all he'd been able to accomplish, after six years of effort, had been to keep from definitively losing his lawsuit.

In constant correspondence with Father Pirard, in this business that both of them passionately pursued, the marquis came to appreciate how the priest's mind worked. Bit by bit, despite the immense difference in social standing, their letters took on a friendly tone. Father Pirard would tell the marquis how they were trying to force him, by means of insults and affronts, to resign his post. In his anger at the disgraceful stratagem (as he put it) used against Julien, he told the marquis Julien's history.

Rich as he was, the noble lord was no miser. He could never persuade Father Pirard to accept so much as reimbursement for the lawsuit's postal expenses. He leaped at the idea of sending five hundred francs to the priest's favorite pupil.

Monsieur de La Mole set himself to writing the letter of transmittal. And this made him think about Father Pirard.

One day, the good priest received a brief note, asking him to call, on urgent business and without delay, at an inn on the outskirts of Besançon. There he found the Marquis de La Mole's steward.

"Monsieur de La Mole has commissioned me to bring you his closed carriage," said the man. "He hopes that, after reading the letter he sends you, by me, you'll agree to leave for Paris in four or five days. I propose to use this time, the duration of which you will be so good as to make known to me, in checking on the marquis's properties, here in Franche-Comté. After which, on whatever day is convenient for you, we will leave for Paris."

The letter was short:

Shake off, my dear sir, all the difficulties of provincial life; come breathe the calm air of Paris. I send you my carriage, which has been ordered to await, for four days, your fixing the day of departure. I myself will wait for you, here in Paris, until Tuesday. All I would need from you, sir, is a "yes," in order to accept, in your name, one of the best parishes in the vicinity of Paris. The richest of your future parishioners has never seen you, but he is more devoted to you than you might believe. He is the Marquis de La Mole.

Without suspecting it, harsh Father Pirard had loved the seminary, full of his enemies; he had consecrated to it, for fifteen years, all his thoughts. Monsieur de La Mole's letter seemed to him like the arrival of a surgeon, come to perform a painful, necessary operation. His dismissal was certain. He told the steward to return in three days.

For forty-eight hours, he was in a frenzy of doubt. In the end, he wrote to Monsieur de La Mole and composed a letter for the bishop, a masterpiece of ecclesiastical prose, though a trifle long. It would have been difficult to find language equally beyond reproach and exuding a more sincere respect. And at the same time, this letter, intended to give Father de Frilair a difficult hour, in dealing with his immediate superior, spelled out all the matters of grave complaint, and got down to the dirty little tricks which, after enduring them all, resignedly, for six years, were forcing Father Pirard to leave the diocese.

Wood had been stolen from his woodshed; his dog had been poisoned; etc., etc.

Having finished this letter, he had Julien awakened: at eight o'clock, he was already asleep, as were all the seminarians.

"Do you know where the bishop's palace is located?" he asked in the very best Latin. "Bring him this letter. I will not conceal the fact that I am sending you into a pack of wolves. Be all eyes and all ears. Let there be no lies when you are asked questions, but be aware that those who question you may perhaps truly relish the power to do you harm. I am very pleased, my child, to give you this experience before I leave you: I will not hide from you that the letter you're carrying is my resignation."

Julien did not move; he loved Father Pirard. Discretion tried to tell him:

"Once this honest man leaves, the Sacred Heart people are going to take away my post, and may even expel me."

He could not think of himself. What made matters awkward was something he wanted to say politely, but in fact he could not focus his mind.

"Well, my dear! Aren't you going?"

"I've heard it said, sir," Julien began shyly, "that all through your long administration you've never saved a thing. I've got six hundred francs."

His tears kept him from continuing.

"That will be noted, too," the former director of the seminary declared coldly. "Go to the bishop's. It's getting late."

As luck would have it, that night Father de Frilair was on duty in the bishop's drawing room. The bishop was dining with the governor. Although Julien did not know it, it was thus to Father de Frilair himself that he delivered the letter.

Julien watched, astonished, as this priest boldly opened a letter addressed to the bishop. The vicar-general's handsome face first expressed surprise, mixed with lively pleasure, and then became extremely somber. While he was reading, Julien—struck by his fine appearance—

had the time to consider him more carefully. His face might have seemed a good deal more sober, had it not been for the sharp keenness notable in certain of its features, so marked that they would have been an indication of duplicity, if the possessor of so handsome an appearance had ever, even for an instant, stopped thinking of himself. His nose, quite prominent, was shaped in an unbroken straight line, creating a profile—though otherwise eminently distinguished—unfortunately and irremediably like that of a fox. For the rest, this ecclesiastic, who seemed so utterly absorbed in Father Pirard's letter of resignation, was dressed with an elegance that Julien found most attractive, and that he had never seen on any other priest.

Julien was not aware, until afterward, of Father de Frilair's special gift. He knew how to amuse his bishop, a pleasant old fellow, made for life in Paris, who regarded Besançon as a place of exile. The bishop's eyesight was very bad, and he was most passionately fond of fish. Father de Frilair filleted every fish served to His Lordship.

Julien was watching, silently, as the priest read the letter once again, when suddenly the door was noisily thrown open. A richly dressed servant passed rapidly through the room. Julien barely had time to turn toward the door; he saw a little old man wearing a large cross on his breast. He dropped to his knees and lowered his head: the bishop gave him a kindly smile and continued on his way. The handsome priest followed him, and Julien was left alone in the drawing room, where he was able to admire, at his leisure, its pious magnificence.

The Bishop of Besançon, a man whose spirit had been sorely tried, but not snuffed out, by the long, hard years of life abroad during the Revolution, was over seventy-five and not particularly concerned about what might happen in ten years' time.

"Who is this seminarian, with such a lively face, whom I seemed to see as I went by?" the bishop asked. "Aren't they supposed to be asleep by now, according to the rules I laid down?"

"This one is wide-awake, I assure you, my lord, and he is the bearer of wonderful tidings: a letter of resignation from the only Jansenist still in your diocese. Terrible Father Pirard finally managed to take the hint."

"Ah!" said the bishop, laughing. "I challenge you to replace him with someone just as good. And to show you how good the man truly is, I'm inviting him to dinner, tomorrow."

The vicar-general tried to slip in a few words about who that successor might be. The bishop, not much interested in business matters, at the moment, said:

"Before we put someone else *in,* let's learn a little about why this one is going *out.* Bring that seminarian in here: truth comes from the mouths of babes."

Julien was summoned. "I'm going to have an inquisitor on each side of me," he thought. But he had never felt braver.

As he entered, two valets, better dressed than Monsieur Valenod himself, were disrobing the bishop. Before he got to the question of Father Pirard, His Lordship felt it his duty to inquire into Julien's studies. He mentioned a few issues of dogma, and was surprised by what he heard in response. Soon he turned to the humanities, to Virgil, to Horace, to Cicero. "These writers," thought Julien, "earned me my one-hundred-ninety-eighth place. I've got nothing to lose: Why not try to shine?" He succeeded. The bishop, himself a fine humanist, was enchanted.

Earlier that evening, when the bishop had dined with the governor, a young woman, deservedly celebrated, had recited a contemporary poem on Mary Magdalene. He was more than ready to discuss literature, and at once forgot about Father Pirard and everything connected with him, so he could consider, together with this seminarian, whether Horace had been rich or poor. The bishop quoted from several odes, but sometimes his memory was sluggish, and Julien each time promptly recited, always modestly, the entire ode. What particularly struck the bishop was that, when thus reciting, Julien maintained his conversational tone: he would speak twenty or thirty Latin verses exactly as he might have told what went on in his seminary. They spoke at length about Virgil, and about Cicero. Finally, the bishop could not help but pay the seminarian a compliment.

"To have pursued your studies better would be impossible."

"My lord," Julien said, "your seminary can present you with one hundred and ninety-seven students much less unworthy of such high approval."

"What?" said the bishop, astonished at this figure.

"What I've had the honor to tell Your Lordship can be fully supported, by official proof.

"At our annual examinations, responding to questions on precisely these matters, for which Your Lordship has just praised me, I was placed one hundred ninety-eighth."

"Ah," the bishop cried, laughing and glancing over at Father de Frilair, "you're Father Pirard's favorite. I should have realized. But it's an amusing war. Isn't it true, my young friend," he added, turning back to Julien, "that you had to be awakened in order to be sent here?"

"Yes, my lord. I have left the seminary unaccompanied only once before, to assist Father Chas-Bernard in decorating the cathedral, the day of Corpus Christi."

"*Optime,* wonderful," said the bishop. "But was that you, who had the courage to put those feather clusters on top of the canopy? Every year, they make me shudder: I always worry they'll cost me someone's life. My friend, you'll go far—but I have no desire to check your career, which will be brilliant, by making you die of hunger."

And at the bishop's order, biscuits and Malaga wine were brought, to which Julien did honor, and Father de Frilair even more so, for he knew his bishop loved to see people eating happily and with a good appetite.

Happier and happier with how his evening was ending, the bishop spoke for a bit about Church history. He saw that Julien did not understand. He went on to the moral condition of the Roman Empire, under the emperors of Constantine's time. Paganism's fall had been accompanied by the same uncertainty and doubt that, in the nineteenth century, afflicted sorrowful, weary minds. His Lordship noted that Julien barely knew Tacitus's name.

Julien replied frankly, to the bishop's astonishment, that this author was not to be found in the seminary's library.

"That really makes me feel better," said the bishop cheerfully. "You've saved me from an embarrassment: for the past ten minutes I've been trying to think of a way of thanking you for the pleasant evening you've given me, and certainly most unexpectedly. I did not expect a student in my seminary to be an accomplished scholar. Although it may not be a particularly canonical gift, I'd like to give you a Tacitus."

The bishop had them bring in eight volumes, beautifully bound, and on the title page of the first he wrote, in his own hand, a Latin inscription for Julien Sorel. He prided himself on his fine command of Latin. And he finished by saying, in a serious manner, totally different from that he had displayed all through the evening:

"Young man, *if you're sensible,* one day you'll have the best parish in my diocese, and it won't be a hundred miles from this palace. But you *must be sensible.*"

Burdened with these books, Julien left the palace, still in shock, just as midnight was sounding.

His Lordship had not said a word about Father Pirard. Julien was especially startled by the bishop's extraordinary politeness. It had never occurred to him that such formal courtesy could coexist with an equally natural, dignified bearing. This contrast seemed particularly striking, seeing somber Father Pirard, who was waiting for him so impatiently.

"*Quid tibi dixerunt?* What did they say to you?" he called out, loudly, as soon as he saw him, in the distance.

Julien got himself rather tangled up, translating the bishop's discourse into Latin.

"Speak French, and repeat His Lordship's own words, without adding or omitting a thing," said the former director of the seminary in his harsh way, his manners profoundly inelegant.

"What a queer gift for a bishop to give a young seminarian," he said, leafing through the superb Tacitus, the gilt edging of which seemed to fill him with horror.

Two o'clock was sounding when, after an exceedingly detailed account had been supplied, he allowed his favorite pupil to return to his room.

"Leave me the first volume of your Tacitus, with the inscription from the Lord Bishop," Father Pirard said. "This line in Latin will be your lightning rod, here, after I leave.

"*Erit tibi, fili mi, successor meus tanquam leo quaerens quem devoret.* Because for you, my son, my successor will be like a raging lion, hunting someone to devour."

The next morning, Julien noticed something strange in the way his classmates spoke to him. It made him even more reserved. "Here we have," he thought, "the effect of Father Pirard's resignation. They all know it, and I'm supposed to be his favorite. There must be something nasty about this behavior." But he could not see anything of the sort. On the contrary: he saw no hatred in the eyes of those he met, walking through the dormitory. "What does this mean? It must be a trap. Let me play this very close to the vest." Then the little seminarian from Verrières shouted, laughing: "*Corneli Taciti opera omnia,* the complete works of Tacitus!"

Everyone overhead these words, and they began to outdo each other, complimenting Julien not only for the magnificent gift he'd received from His Lordship, but also on the two-hour conversation with which he'd been honored. They knew everything, down to the smallest details. And after this, there was no more jealousy; they all paid him the most servile court; Father Castaneda, who had treated him, the evening before, with the utmost insolence, came and took him by the arm, inviting Julien to have lunch with him.

But there was a fatal flaw in Julien's character. Insolence from these coarse beings had caused him a great deal of pain; their abasement of themselves left him disgusted. There was nothing pleasant about it.

Toward midday, Father Pirard left his pupils, but not before making a stern speech: "Is it worldly honors you want?" he said to them. "All the social advantages? The delights of giving orders, of paying no attention to the law and being safely insolent to everyone? Or is it eternal salvation you long for? Even the least advanced among you need only open his eyes, to see the difference between these two paths."

He had barely left the building when the devotees of the Sacred Heart chanted a Te Deum in the chapel. No one in the seminary paid any attention to the former director's speech. "He's in a sour mood, because he's lost his job," was what most of them said. Not a single seminarian was simple enough to believe in a voluntary resignation, not from a post that offered so many contacts with large suppliers.

Father Pirard went to stay at the very best inn in Besançon. Under the pretext of unfinished business, of which he had none whatever, he planned to stay there for two days.

The bishop had indeed invited him to dinner: to have fun with his vicar-general, Father de Frilair, he sought to have Father Pirard shown to the best advantage. They were at dessert when the strange news came from Paris: Father Pirard had been named priest to the magnificent parish of N——, six miles from the capital. The good bishop congratulated him most sincerely. He saw in this whole business a *capital joke*, which put him in a fine mood and gave him the highest opinion of Father Pirard's abilities. He gave him a splendid testimonial of character, in Latin, and, when Father de Frilair ventured to object, ordered him to be silent.

That evening, His Lordship brought his news and his admiration to the house of Marquise de Rubempré. This was a great event in Besançon's high society; everyone wondered at such an extraordinary mark of favor. They considered Father Pirard already as good as a bishop. The most subtle among them believed Marquis de La Mole had been made a cabinet minister, and allowed themselves, that day, to smile at the imperial airs put on, in society, by Father de Frilair.

The next morning, Father Pirard had something of a following out in the streets, and merchants stood in the doorway of their shops when he went visiting the judges in Marquis de La Mole's lawsuit. For the very first time, they received him politely. The harsh Jansenist, outraged by everything he'd seen, put in a long day's work with the lawyers he'd chosen for the Marquis de La Mole. And then he left for Paris. He was weak enough to tell two or three of his own classmates, who escorted him to the carriage, that after directing the seminary for fifteen years, he was leaving Besançon with savings amounting to five hundred and twenty francs. These friends embraced him, weeping, and said, among themselves: "The good Father might have spared himself this falsehood. It really makes him look foolish."

Those of more vulgar minds, blinded by the love of money, simply could not understand that it was his honesty that had given Father Pirard the strength to fight, for six long years, against Marie Alocoque and the order she had founded, the Sacred Heart of Jesus, and against the Jesuits, and against his own bishop.

CHAPTER THIRTY

AN AMBITIOUS MAN

There's only one true nobility, and that's someone who's a *duke;* being a
"marquis" is a joke, but people turn their heads at the word *duke.*
—*EDINBURGH REVIEW*

The Marquis de La Mole received Father Pirard without any of those
"great man" mannerisms, so very very polite and yet so rude to those
who understand them. This would have been a waste of time, and the
marquis was sufficiently deep in matters of high import that, truthfully, he had no time to waste.

For six months he'd been scheming to have both the king and the
country accept a certain ruling ministry, which would then, in gratitude, have him made a duke.

For many years, the marquis had been asking, in vain, to have his
Besançon lawyer give him a clear, precise analysis of his Franche-
Comté lawsuit. But how could the famous lawyer have explained to
him what he did not understand himself? Father Pirard gave him a little slip of paper that explained everything.

"My dear Father," said the marquis, after complying, in less than
five minutes, with all the formulas of politeness and queries about personal matters, "my dear Father, in the midst of my so called prosperity, I don't have the time to seriously concern myself with two
minor matters, which are however of some importance: namely, my
family and my finances. I look after my family's fortune, and most in-
tensively: I can accomplish a lot, in these regards. I look after my own
pleasures, which ought to be most important of all, at least to me," he
added, surprising and even astonishing Father Pirard. Although a sensible man, the priest was amazed to hear an old man speaking so
frankly of his pleasures.

"There are people who work, here in Paris," continued the great
man, "but only those roosting high on the fifth floor. As soon as I establish relations with a man, he gets himself an apartment on the sec-

ond floor, and his wife announces a day for receiving visitors, and then there's no more working, and no doing anything more than being—or appearing to be—a man of the world. That's all they care about, as soon as they have enough to eat.

"As for my lawsuit, to tell the truth, and even more for each one among them, separately considered, I have lawyers who are killing themselves: one of them died of consumption just the day before yesterday. But as to my financial affairs in general, would you believe, sir, that three years ago I gave up all hope of finding a man who, as he writes my letters, bothers to think seriously, even just a little, about just what he's doing? Now, this is simply a preface.

"I think very well of you and, I dare say, although I'm seeing you for the first time, I like you. Would you become my secretary, with a salary of eight thousand francs—or even double that? I will still come out ahead, I swear to you, and I'll make it my business to save your fine new parish for you, in case there comes a day when we don't get along anymore."

The priest declined. But toward the end of the conversation, the marquis's very real difficulty made him think of an alternative.

"Back in my seminary, I've left a poor young man who, unless I deceive myself, will be harshly persecuted. If he were no more than a simple monk, he'd already be *in pace* [at peace: i.e., dead].

"To this point, all this young man knows is Latin and the Holy Scriptures, but it is not impossible that, some day, he'll show very large abilities as a preacher or perhaps as a spiritual guide. I don't know what he'll do, but he has a sacred passion; he's capable of going far. I had planned to assign him to our bishop—if one ever came to us who had even a little of your way of viewing men and their affairs."

"Where does your young man come from?" asked the marquis.

"He's said to be the son of a carpenter, from our mountains, but I'd sooner believe him the illegitimate son of some wealthy man. I saw him receive an anonymous, or perhaps a pseudonymous, letter, containing a bill for five hundred francs."

"Ah! That's Julien Sorel," said the marquis.

"How do you know his name?" said the astonished priest, and then he blushed at his question.

"I'm not prepared to tell you that," answered the marquis.

"In any case," the priest went on, "you might try him as your secretary. He has energy, and he has a mind. In a word, it's an experiment worth attempting."

"Why not?" said the marquis. "But would he be the sort who'd let the chief of police, or someone else, grease his paws for spying on me? That's the only difficulty I see."

After positive assurances from Father Pirard, the marquis picked up a thousand-franc note.

"Send this to Julien Sorel, as travel money. Let him come to me."

"It's very clear," said Father Pirard, "that you're a resident of Paris. You don't understand the tyranny that oppresses us all, we poor provincials, and presses especially on priests who are not allies of the Jesuits. They won't let Julien go; they know how to cover themselves with the cleverest excuses; they'll tell me he's sick, the letters were lost in the post, etc., etc."

"Some day soon," said the marquis, "I'll bring the bishop a letter from the minister."

"I forgot one warning," said the priest. "Although he's of low birth, the young man has a noble heart. He won't be of any use if his pride is wounded. You'll turn him into an idiot."

"I like that," said the marquis. "I'll make him my son's companion. Will that do it?"

Sometime afterward, Julien received a letter, written in an unknown hand and bearing a postmark from Châlons. It contained a money order drawn on a merchant in Besançon, and a notice to proceed, without delay, to Paris. The letter was signed with a made-up name, but in opening it Julien had been thrilled: a leaf had fallen at his feet, and this was the sign he'd agreed upon with Father Pirard.

Less than an hour later, Julien was summoned to the bishop's palace, where he was greeted with entirely paternal benevolence. Even as he was quoting Horace, His Lordship paid him wonderfully shrewd compliments, on account of the high destiny awaiting him in Paris, which, in return, deserved further explanation. But Julien could not tell him a thing, primarily because he knew nothing about it, and His Lordship was abundantly considerate. One of the minor clerics at the palace wrote to the mayor, who came hurrying over with a passport, signed, but with the name of the traveler left blank.

At midnight, Julien was at Fouqué's, whose knowing mind was more astonished than excited by the future apparently awaiting his friend.

"You'll end up," said this liberal voter, "with a place in the government, which will compel you to do something for which the newspapers will run you down. That's how I'll hear news about you—by seeing you disgraced. Remember, even financially speaking, it's better to earn four hundred francs in the solid timber business, where you're your own boss, than to get four thousand francs from a government, even were it that of King Solomon."

All Julien saw in this was the petty spirit of a provincial bourgeois. He was finally going to make his appearance in the theater of great events. The happiness of going to Paris—which he imagined peopled by cleverly scheming minds, distinctly hypocritical, but as polished as the Bishop of Besançon, or the Bishop of Agde—overshadowed thoughts of anything else. He explained to his friend that Father Pirard's letter left him no other choice.

The next day, about noon, and the happiest of men, he came to Verrières. He was counting on seeing Madame de Rênal once again. But first he went to see his original protector, Father Chélan. He met with a harsh reception.

"Do you think you owe me something?" Father Chélan said, not responding to his greeting. "Come to lunch with me, and during that time someone will lend you another horse, and you'll leave Verrières, *without seeing anyone else.*"

"To hear is to obey," replied Julien, like a seminarian, and as if all they were discussing were theology and classically correct Latin.

He mounted his horse, rode a mile or two, at which point he saw a wood and nobody around to see him ride into it, so in he went. When the sun went down, he sent back the horse. Later, he walked into a peasant's house, where the man agreed to sell him a ladder and follow after him, carrying it, until they reached the little wood overlooking Loyalty Walkway, in Verrières.

"I've been walking along behind some poor conscript, who's deserted . . . or maybe a smuggler," the peasant said, taking leave of him.

"But who cares? I've gotten a good price for my ladder, and in all these years I've had to do some pretty fancy *stepping,* myself."

It was now pitch dark. At about one o'clock in the morning, carrying his ladder, Julien entered Verrières. As quickly as he could, he went down into the old streambed, now enclosed by two walls and crossing Monsieur de Rênal's magnificent gardens at a depth of ten feet. Julien climbed up easily, on his ladder. "How will the guard dogs react to me?" he wondered. "That's the whole question." The dogs barked and started to dash at him, but he whistled softly, and they wagged their tails and licked his hands.

Climbing up from terrace to terrace, though all the gates were locked, he quite easily found himself underneath Madame de Rênal's bedroom window; overlooking the garden, it was no more than eight or ten feet above the ground.

The shutters had a small, heart-shaped opening, which Julien knew well. He was deeply disappointed: no glow from a night-light shone through this little opening.

"Good Lord!" he said to himself. "Madame de Rênal isn't using the room tonight. Where could she be sleeping? The family must be at Verrières, since the dogs were on guard outside, but if I went into the dark room, I might meet up with Monsieur de Rênal himself, or some stranger—and then, what a scandal!"

The most prudent thing would be to leave, but to Julien that seemed a horrible choice. "If it's a stranger, I can save myself by running as fast as my legs will carry me, leaving my ladder behind. But if it's her, what sort of reception will I find? She's fallen into deep remorse, and become incredibly pious: that's for sure. Still, her memory of me is still alive: she's just written to me." That argument settled the matter.

His heart trembling, but determined to see her or to perish, he threw pebbles at the shutters. There was no response. He leaned his ladder against the wall, alongside the window, and tapped on the shutters, softly at first, but then harder. "No matter how dark it is, they could shoot at me," he thought. That idea reduced the whole wild affair to a question of courage.

"Either there's no one in the room, tonight," he pondered, "or else whoever may be sleeping there is now awake. So I don't need to go on tiptoes anymore. All I have to worry about is not being heard by people sleeping in the other rooms."

He climbed down, repositioned the ladder directly against one of the shutters, climbed back up, and put his hand through the heart-shaped opening. He was lucky, and quickly located the wire from which hung a hook: this hook locked the shutter. He pulled on the wire, and felt an inexpressible joy, realizing that the shutter had been released, and could now be opened. "I have to open it gently, a little at a time, and let her recognize my voice." He opened it enough so he could put his head past the shutter, then said, very softly, "It's a friend."

He could tell, listening carefully, that the silence remained unbroken. But he could also see that there was indeed no night-light set above the fireplace, not even one turned very low. This was truly a bad sign.

"Watch out for gunshots!" He considered matters for a bit, then tapped on the glass pane. There was no response. He tapped harder. "Well, even if I have to break the glass, I need to get this done." When he tapped very forcefully indeed, he thought he glimpsed, in the middle of the intense darkness, something like a white shadow coming across the room. And then he was sure of it: there was a shadow, and it was coming very slowly toward him. Suddenly, he saw a cheek, leaning against the glass he was peering through.

He shivered and pulled his head back a little. But so dark was the night that, even at so short a distance, he could not tell if it was Madame de Rênal. He worried about a sudden, alarmed cry: he could hear the dogs circling around the foot of the ladder, growling nervously. "It's me," he repeated, quite loudly, "a friend." There was no response. The white phantom had disappeared. "Please let me in, I have to talk to you, I'm miserable!" And he rapped almost hard enough to crack the glass.

He heard a quick, faint sound; the rod was pulled back. He pushed the window open and jumped nimbly into the room.

The white phantom withdrew; he grasped its arms; it was a woman. All his brave ideas vanished. "If it's her, what's she going to say?" How did he feel when she gave a faint cry and he realized it was indeed Madame de Rênal?

He held her tightly. She trembled, and barely had the strength to push him away.

"Wretch! What are you doing?"

Her choked voice could scarcely shape the words. Julien could hear her very real indignation.

"After fourteen months of bitter separation, I've come to see you."

"Go away, leave me immediately! Ah, Father Chélan, why did you stop me from writing to him? I could have prevented this horror." She pushed him again, with extraordinary force. "I repent my sin, heaven has graciously shed its light on me," she repeated, her voice breaking. "Leave! Go away!"

"I don't intend to leave without speaking to you, not after fourteen months of misery. I want to know everything you've done. Ah, surely I've loved you deeply enough to deserve that much trust. . . . I want to know everything."

In spite of herself, his firm voice still ruled her heart.

Julien had been clasping her tightly, not letting her push him away, but now loosened his arms. This somewhat reassured her.

"I'll pull up the ladder," he said, "so you won't be compromised, should some servant, wakened by the noise, come to inspect."

"Ah, go away, go away instead," she told him, truly angry. "What do other people matter? It's God who sees the ghastly scene you're inflicting on me, and it's He who will punish me. You're taking cowardly advantage of feelings I once had for you, but which I have no longer. Do you hear me, Monsieur Julien?"

He pulled up the ladder, slowly and carefully, making no noise.

"Is your husband in town?" he asked, using the intimate form of the word *you*, not intending to annoy her but falling into old habits.

"Don't talk to me like that, for mercy's sake, or I'll summon my husband. I'm already more than guilty, not having chased you away, no matter what. I pity you," she told him, trying to wound the pride she knew was so prickly.

These rejections, this sharp way of snapping so tender a tie, one he still counted on, drove Julien almost to the height of passionate delirium.

"Ah! You really don't love me anymore? Is that possible?" he said amorously, the sort of talk it was difficult to hear dispassionately.

She did not reply, and he, he wept bitter tears.

Indeed, he no longer had the strength to say anything.

"And so," he thought, "I've been completely forgotten by the only one who's ever loved me! What's the point to living?" All his courage had deserted him, from the moment he no longer had to worry about encountering, in this dark room, not a familiar woman but a man. There was only one thing left in his heart, and that was love.

He cried, silently, for a long time. He took her hand; she tried to pull it away, but then, after several very nearly convulsive movements, she left it where it was. The darkness was absolute; they found themselves sitting, side by side, on Madame de Rênal's bed.

"How changed from fourteen months ago!" Julien thought, and his tears flowed faster. "So this is how absence inevitably destroys all human feelings!"

"Please: tell me what's happened to you," he finally said, embarrassed by his silence, and in a voice broken by tears.

"Surely," Madame de Rênal replied, her voice brittle and freighted with dry reproach, "at the time you left here, the whole town knew my erring ways. You behaved so recklessly! Later, when I'd fallen into despair, worthy Father Chélan came to see me. This accomplished nothing because, for a long time, he tried to get me to confess. One day, he thought of bringing me to the church in Dijon, where I'd made my first communion. There, for the first time, he ventured to speak—" Madame de Rênal broke off, weeping. "What a shameful moment! That wonderful man didn't bother to heap his indignation on my head: he grieved with me. Every day I wrote you letters, back then, but I didn't dare send them. I hid them, very carefully, and when I was too miserable to endure it, I locked myself in my room and reread my letters.

"In the end, Father Chélan persuaded me to give them all to him. . . . A few, written more sensibly, were sent to you, but you never answered."

"I swear to you, I never received any letters from you, when I was in the seminary."

"My God, who could have intercepted them?"

"Imagine my sorrow before that day I saw you in the cathedral. I didn't know if you were still alive."

"God gave me the grace to understand how deeply I sinned against Him, against my children, against my husband," answered Madame de Rênal. "He has never loved me, not the way I used to believe you loved me."

Julien fairly threw himself into her arms, not thinking anything, but simply beside himself. Yet Madame de Rênal once again repulsed him, and continued, with considerable determination:

"My worthy friend, Father Chélan, has helped me to understand that, in marrying Monsieur de Rênal, I committed to him all my affections, even those I did not know I possessed, and which, before a fatal liaison, I had never experienced. . . . Since the huge sacrifice of those letters, so terribly dear to me, my life has flowed on, perhaps not happily, but at least more or less calmly. Don't disturb it: be my friend . . . my best friend.

"Now it's your turn: tell me what you've been doing."

Julien could not speak.

"I want to know what your life in the seminary was like," she repeated, "and after that, you'll go away."

Not thinking what he was saying, Julien recounted the endless scheming and jealousy he'd encountered, at the start, then the quieter life he'd lived since having been made an assistant master.

"That was when," he added, "after a long silence, surely intended to make me understand what, today, I'm seeing, which is that you no longer love me and that I've become of no concern to you . . ." Madame de Rênal clasped his hands. "That was when you sent me five hundred francs."

"Never," said Madame de Rênal.

"It was a letter postmarked in Paris and signed Paul Sorel, to avoid suspicion."

A brief discussion arose on the letter's possible origin. The moral positions shifted. Without being aware of it, Madame de Rênal had abandoned her grave approach and returned to their former tenderness. They could not see each other, in the complete blackness. But the sound of their voices said everything. Julien put his arm around his beloved's waist, clearly a risky thing. She tried to remove his arm, but he skillfully began to recount a particularly interesting episode, and she was distracted. His arm was totally forgotten and stayed where it was.

After many attempts to guess at the letter's origin, Julien had resumed his account. In speaking of the life he'd been leading, he became more master of himself, for it interested him remarkably little, compared to what was happening at the moment. His sole concern was how this visit was going to end. "You'll go away," she kept saying, from time to time, and rather curtly.

"How I'll be shamed, if I'm sent packing! Such a failure would poison my entire life," he told himself. "She'll never write to me. God only knows when I'll come back to this part of the country!" Then and there, whatever admixture of the celestial there had been in Julien's attitude, and in his heart, rapidly disappeared. Sitting next to a woman he adored, virtually holding her in his arms, in this very room where, once, he had been so happy, wrapped in total darkness, very much aware that a brief moment ago she had begun weeping, sensing her sobs from her heaving breast, he became, alas! a cold schemer, almost as calculating and cold as when, in the seminary courtyard, he'd found himself the target of some nasty joke, played by a classmate much stronger than he was. Julien dragged out his story, and spoke of the miserable existence he'd led since leaving Verrières. "So," said Madame de Rênal to herself, "after a year away, almost completely deprived of any sign that he was remembered, and while I was forgetting him, all he thought about were the happy days he experienced at Vergy." Her sobs grew stronger. Julien saw how successful his story had been. He understood that, now, he had to deploy his final resource: he turned, swiftly, to the letter he'd just received from Paris.

"I've said my farewell to the bishop."

"What? You're not going back to Besançon? You're leaving us for good?"

"Yes," Julien answered, his voice firm. "I'm abandoning a place where I've been forgotten even by the one, in all my life, that I've loved the best, and I leave with no intention of ever coming back. I'm going to Paris. . . ."

"You're going to Paris!" she exclaimed, rather loudly. Her voice was almost choked by tears, and clearly showed how deeply she was affected. Julien needed this encouragement. He was about to take a step that might decide everything against him. Before this stifled cry, and being unable to see her, he'd had absolutely no idea what effect he'd produced. He hesitated no longer. Fear of failure gave him supreme control over himself. He rose, and spoke coldly:

"Yes, madame, I'm leaving you forever. Be happy. Farewell."

He took several steps toward the window; he had it open. Madame de Rênal rushed toward him and threw herself into his arms.

Thus, after talking for three hours, Julien obtained what, with so much passion, he'd desired for the first two of those hours. Had it happened a bit sooner, this reversion to tender emotions, this casting off of Madame de Rênal's remorse, would have been divine happiness. Attained as it was, by artful skill, it was merely a pleasure.

Julien was determined, despite his beloved's protests, to turn on the night-light.

"Do you want me," he said to her, "to have no memory of having seen you? Love, surely delightful to you, will be forever lost to me. For me, the whiteness of this pretty hand will remain invisible? Remember, I'm leaving you for a very long time!"

There was no way Madame de Rênal could resist these ideas, which made her dissolve in tears. But dawn began to clearly outline the pine trees on the mountain, east of Verrières. Instead of leaving, Julien, drunk with sensual delight, asked Madame de Rênal to spend the whole day with her, shut in her room, which she would not leave until darkness fell once more.

"And why not?" she answered. "This fatal relapse completely destroys my self-respect and makes me forever miserable." She pressed herself against his breast. "My husband has never been the same, he's suspicious; he thinks I've been lying to him through this whole business, and he's clearly angry at me. If he hears the slightest noise, I'm lost: he'll throw me out like the wretch I am."

"Ah, you learned those words from Father Chélan," said Julien. "You'd never have spoken to me like that before I was so cruelly sent off to the seminary. You loved me, then."

Julien was rewarded for the cool calm with which he'd said these things. He saw his beloved swiftly forget the risks inherent in her husband's presence, becoming aware of the even greater risk that Julien doubted her love. The sun rose rapidly and lit up the room. Julien recovered all the delights of pride, seeing in his arms, and almost at his feet, this charming woman, the only one he'd ever loved and who, just a few hours earlier, had been completely overcome by fear of a terrible God, and by love of her duty to Him. Resolutions strengthened by an entire year of constancy had been unable to withstand his courage.

Soon, there were noises heard in the house. One thing which she had not thought of began to worry Madame de Rênal.

"That wicked Elisa will come in here. What can we do with this enormous ladder?" she asked her lover. "Where can I hide it? I'll put it up in the attic!" she suddenly cried, with a kind of playfulness.

"But you'll have to go through the valet's bedroom," said Julien, astonished.

"I'll leave the ladder in the corridor, then I'll call him in here and send him to do something somewhere else."

"Think of what you can tell him, in case he notices the ladder as he goes by," he told her.

"Yes, my angel," said Madame de Rênal, giving him a kiss. "And you, you think of quickly hiding under the bed, in case Elisa comes in while I'm away."

He was surprised at this sudden gaiety. "So," he thought, "the possibility of serious danger, rather than upsetting her, makes her gay, because she's forgotten all that remorse! What a supreme woman! Ah, ruling a heart like that is truly glorious." Julien was in ecstasies.

Madame de Rênal approached the ladder; it was clearly too heavy for her. Julien went to help her. He was admiring her elegant waist, which did not indicate any serious strength, when suddenly, unaided, she picked up the ladder and carried it as she might have lifted a mere chair. She took it quickly down the corridor and laid it along the wall. Then she called for the valet, and in order to give him time to get dressed, went up to the pigeon house. Five minutes later, when she came back along the corridor, the ladder was gone. What had become of it? If Julien had been out of the house, this would hardly have mattered. But, just then, if her husband saw that ladder! That could be disastrous. She ran all over the house. Finally she found the ladder up under the roof, where the valet had carried and even hidden it. This was strange, and at any other time it would have been alarming.

"What difference does it make to me," she thought, "what happens twenty-four hours from now, when Julien will be gone? For me, won't everything be horror and remorse?"

The vague notion came to her: Should she leave this mortal life? But what did it matter? After a separation she had thought would be eternal, he'd been restored to her; she'd seen him again, and what he'd done to reach her demonstrated such love!

As she told Julien about the ladder, she asked him:

"What shall I say to my husband, if the valet tells him he found the ladder?" She considered for a moment. "They'll need twenty-four hours to find the peasant who sold it to you." And throwing herself into Julien's arms, hugging him exceedingly tightly: "Oh, to die, to die like this!" she exclaimed, covering him with kisses. Then she laughed: "But there's no need for you to die of hunger," she said.

"Come. First I'll hide you in Madame Derville's room, which stays locked all the time." She stood guard at the end of the corridor, and Julien went running down. "Be careful: if anyone knocks, don't open the door," she told him, turning the key. "Anyway, it would just be the children, playing their games."

"Take them into the garden, under the window," said Julien, "so I can have the pleasure of seeing them. Get them to talk."

"Yes, yes," cried Madame de Rênal, hurrying off.

She soon returned with oranges, and biscuits, and a bottle of Malaga wine. It had been impossible for her to steal any bread.

"What's your husband doing?" asked Julien.

"He's writing up marketing plans with some peasants."

But now it was eight o'clock, and the house was very noisy. If they had not seen Madame de Rênal, they'd have been looking everywhere for her; she had no choice but to leave him. Soon she returned, defying all prudence, bringing him a cup of coffee: she shuddered that he might be dying of hunger. After lunch, she managed to lead the children under the window of Madame Derville's room. He saw how big they were, but had they become too much like all the rest? Or had his own ideas changed?

Madame de Rênal talked to them about Julien. The oldest responded warmly, and with regrets, but Julien saw that the younger one had very nearly forgotten him.

Monsieur de Rênal did not go out that morning. He was constantly going up and down the house, doing business with peasants to whom he was selling his potato crop. Until lunchtime, Madame de Rênal did not have a moment to give her prisoner. Lunch having been announced, and served, she conceived the notion of stealing a bowl of hot soup for him. As she walked noiselessly toward the door of the room he was occupying, carefully carrying a bowl, she found herself face-to-face with the valet who, that morning, had hidden the ladder. Just then he too was going quietly along the corridor, and as if listening. Julien had probably been walking around, incautiously. The valet went away, a bit embarrassed. Madame de Rênal went boldly in to Julien; hearing what had just taken place, he shuddered.

"You're afraid," she told him. "But me, I'd risk all the dangers in the world, and never blink. There's only one thing I'm afraid of, and that's the moment when I'll be alone, and you'll have gone away." She ran off and left him.

"Ah," said Julien, swept away. "The only danger this sublime soul fears is remorse."

Evening finally came. Monsieur de Rênal went to the casino.

His wife had announced herself ill with a frightful migraine. She retired to her room, she hurriedly sent Elisa away, and then she quickly rose to release Julien.

He realized that, in truth, he was dying of hunger. Madame de Rênal went down to the pantry, in search of bread. Julien heard a loud scream. Madame de Rênal returned, and told him that, going into the dark pantry and approaching a sideboard where the bread was kept, she put out her hand and touched a woman's arm. It was Elisa whose scream Julien had heard.

"What was she doing there?"

"Stealing some sweets. Or maybe she was spying on us," Madame de Rênal replied with utter indifference. "But luckily I found a meat pie and a loaf of bread."

"And what's in there?" said Julien, pointing to her apron pockets.

She'd forgotten that, since lunchtime, they'd been stuffed with bread.

Julien took her in his arms with the liveliest passion: she had never seemed so beautiful. "Even in Paris," he told himself, more than a little bewildered, "I'll never find anyone with such a noble heart." She had all the awkwardness of a woman not accustomed to waiting on others, and at the same time the true courage of someone who feared only perils of a very different sort, and very much more terrible.

While Julien ate, with a keen appetite, and his beloved was teasing him about the sparseness of his meal—for she had a horror of speaking seriously—suddenly the locked door was shaken back and forth, with great force. It was Monsieur de Rênal.

"Why have you locked yourself in?" he shouted at her.

Julien barely had time to slip under the sofa.

"Hah! You're all dressed," said Monsieur de Rênal as he came in. "You're eating, but you've locked the door!"

Such a question, delivered with the abruptness of married conversation, would on any ordinary day have bothered Madame de Rênal. But she knew that all her husband had to do was lower his glance, and he would see Julien, for Monsieur de Rênal had thrown himself into the chair that Julien had left only a moment before, and this chair faced the sofa.

She used her headache to explain everything. As her husband recounted, at some length, exactly how he had won the billiards prize at the casino—"worth nineteen francs, by God!" he added—she saw, on a chair three feet away, Julien's hat. Her cool calm soared, she started taking off her clothes, and in a moment, as she walked quickly behind her husband, she dropped her dress across the revelatory chair.

Finally, Monsieur de Rênal left. She begged Julien to resume his account of life at the seminary. "I didn't really hear you, yesterday; I kept thinking, while you were talking, how I could make myself send you away."

She was rashness itself. Their voices were quite loud, and at about two o'clock that morning they were interrupted by a violent knock at the door. Once more, it was Monsieur de Rênal.

"Open the door right away, there are burglars in the house!" he called. "Saint-Jean found their ladder this morning."

"It's the end of everything!" cried Madame de Rênal, throwing her arms around him. "He'll kill us both, he doesn't believe it's burglars. I'll die in your arms, happier when I die than I've ever been in my life."

She gave her husband no answer at all; he grew angry. She held Julien in a passionate embrace.

"Save Stanislas's mother," he told her, his glance authoritative. "I'm going to jump to the courtyard, through your dressing room window, and I'll run into the garden. The dogs know me. Roll up my clothes as fast as you can and throw them into the garden. Let him break down the door, in the meantime. Above all, admit absolutely nothing—I forbid it. Better for him to have suspicions than certainties."

"You'll kill yourself, jumping!" It was the only thing she said, her only concern.

She went to the window with him; she carefully hid his clothing. And at last she opened the door for her husband, who was boiling mad. He searched the bedroom, and her dressing room, without a word, and disappeared. She threw down Julien's clothes, he took the bundle and ran quickly toward the lower part of the garden, beside the Doubs.

As he ran, he heard a bullet whistle by, and immediately after the sound of a gunshot.

"That's not Monsieur de Rênal," he thought. "He's too poor a shot for that." The dogs ran beside him, silently. A second shot apparently hit one of them in the paw; he began to howl piteously. Julien jumped over a terrace wall, stayed under cover for another fifty feet, then turned and ran in a different direction. He heard voices calling back and forth, and he distinctly saw the valet, his enemy, firing a gun. A farmer fired, too, from the other side of the garden. But Julien had already gotten to the bank of the Doubs, where he put on his clothes.

An hour later, he was three miles from Verrières, on the road to Geneva. "If they're looking anywhere," he thought, "they'll be hunting for me on the road to Paris."

PART TWO

She's not pretty,
she's not wearing rouge.
—SAINTE-BEUVE

CHAPTER ONE

COUNTRY PLEASURES

Oh country scenes, when shall my eyes behold you!
—VIRGIL [IN FACT, BY HORACE]

"The gentleman is surely waiting on the coach for Paris?" said the proprietor of an inn, where he'd stopped for lunch.

"Today's coach or tomorrow's, it doesn't matter to me," said Julien.

As he was pretending indifference, the coach arrived. There were two available seats.

"What! It's you, my poor Falcoz," said the traveler who'd arrived from Geneva, speaking to the passenger who got on when Julien did.

"I'd thought," said Falcoz, "you'd settled in the Lyons area, in a delightful little valley near the Rhône?"

"Very happily settled. I'm running away."

"Really! You're running away? You, Saint-Giraud, you who seem so reasonable, so wise—have you committed a crime?" said Falcoz, laughing.

"By God, pretty much the same thing. I'm running away from the ghastly life one leads in the provinces. I love the freshness of the woods and the peacefulness of the fields, exactly as you say. You've often accused me of being a romantic. For the whole rest of my life I don't want to hear anything about politics, and yet it's politics that's chasing me away."

"But what party do you belong to?"

"None, and that's been my ruination. Here's my politics: I love music, painting; a good book is sensational, for me; I'm going on forty-four. How much longer do I have? Fifteen—twenty—thirty years at the most. So! It strikes me that, in thirty years, government ministers will be a little smarter, but just as decent fellows as the ones we have now. English history, I think, is a mirror for looking into our future.

There'll always be a king trying to increase his power, and people trying to get into Parliament—and Mirabeau's reputation, plus the hundreds of thousands of francs he made, will go on keeping rich provincials from sleeping at night. They'll label themselves liberals, and claim they're on the people's side. There'll always be right-wingers desperately trying to become noblemen, or gentlemen of the king's chambers. When it comes to the Ship of State, everyone wants to steer, because the job pays so well. But will there ever be some little spot that's open to an ordinary passenger?"

"Yes, yes—and by the way, that should all really please someone as peace loving as you. Is it these most recent elections driving you out of the provinces?"

"My problem goes back a lot further. Four years ago, I was forty, and I had five hundred thousand francs. I'm four years older, today, and probably worth fifty thousand francs less. That's what I'm going to lose, when I sell my château, Montfleury, near the Rhône—a superb location.

"I got tired of the perpetual comedy we're forced to play, in Páris, by what you call nineteenth-century civilization. I was thirsty for goodwill and simplicity. I bought a place in the mountains, near the Rhône, lovelier than anything under the sun.

"For six months, the village priest and the local squires kept courting me. I gave them dinners. 'I've left Paris,' I told them, 'so I'd never hear another word about politics the whole rest of my life. As you've noticed, I don't take a newspaper. The fewer letters the postman brings me, the happier I am.'

"That wasn't what the priest had in mind. Pretty soon I was being harassed by a thousand prying questions and nuisances, etc. I wanted to give two or three hundred francs a year to the poor; they wanted my money for pious organizations—for Saint Joseph, the Virgin Mary, etc. I wouldn't do it. So then they insulted me in a hundred different ways. I was stupid enough to get annoyed. I could no longer go out in the morning, relishing the beauty of our mountains, without some vexation pulling me out of my reveries, bringing me back to thoughts of men and their wickedness. In the processions, for example, just before Ascension Day—and I like the chant, it's probably a Greek melody—they stopped blessing my fields, because, said the priest, they belong to a blasphemer. An old peasant lady, very devout, lost her cow, and she said it died from drinking out of my pond—me, a blasphemer from Paris. And a week later I found all my fish belly up, poisoned by lime. I was surrounded by vexations, in every form imaginable. The justice of the peace, a decent man but worried about losing his post, always ruled against me. For me, the peace of the countryside was a hell. Once they saw that the priest had turned away from me—he was head of the local Congregation of the Holy Virgin—and that the head of the local liberals, a retired army captain, wouldn't back me up, they all descended on me, even the mason I helped support, for an entire year, even down to a wheelwright who kept cheating me royally, in the most barefaced fashion, every time he repaired my plows.

"To get some support, and to prevail in at least some of my lawsuits, I took up with the liberals—but, just as you said, those devilish elections came along, and they wanted my vote."

"For some unknown fellow?"

"Oh no, no, for a man I knew only too well. So I refused: what terrible rashness! From then on, with the liberals as well on my hands, my position became intolerable. I believe, so help me, that if the priest had taken it into his head to accuse me of murdering my servant, there would have been twenty witnesses, from both political parties, swearing they saw me committing the crime."

"You'd like to live in the country without indulging your neighbors' passions, without even listening to their jabbering? Oh, how offensive..."

"I've finally taken care of that. My château is for sale, I'll lose fifty thousand francs, if I have to, but I'll be overjoyed: I'm getting out of that inferno of hypocrisy and petty troublemaking. I propose to look for the peace and solitude of the countryside in the only place in France where those things can be found, a fourth-floor apartment overlooking the Champs-Elysées. But I'm still wondering if, perhaps, I won't begin my political career in Paris, selling consecrated bread to a neighborhood parish."

"All that wouldn't have happened, under Bonaparte," said Falcoz, his eyes shining with sorrow and anger.

"That may be true, but why couldn't he keep himself in power, your Bonaparte? Everything I endure today stems from what he did."

At this point, Julien began listening even more closely. He had understood from the very first word that Falcoz, the Bonapartist, was Monsieur de Rênal's old childhood friend, repudiated by him in 1816, just as the philosophical Saint-Giraud had to be brother to that department head, in the ———— district, who knew how to get city properties knocked down to him for a song.

"It's all your Bonaparte's work," Saint-Giraud went on. "A decent man, as harmless as they make them, who's forty years old and has five hundred thousand francs, can't settle down in the provinces and find peace there. The priests and the country aristocracy chase him off."

"No, don't say such awful things about him," Falcoz exclaimed. "France never stood so tall, in the eyes of the world, as it did in the thirteen years of his reign. Back then, there was something grand about everything we did."

"Your emperor, may the devil take him," replied the forty-four-year-old man, "was only grand on the field of battle and when he put our finances on a sound footing, in 1802. What did it all mean, after that? With his fancy chamberlains, his pompous displays, and his receptions at the Tuileries, he gave us a new edition of all that kingly twaddle. It was a corrected edition; it might have lasted a century or two. The aristocracy and the priests, they wanted to bring back the old one, but they didn't have the iron hand they needed to sell it to the people."

"Now there's an old printer talking!"

"Who was it who drove me off my property?" the angry printer went on. "The priests, brought back by Napoleon and his concordat, instead of dealing with them the way government deals with doctors, lawyers, astronomers, viewing them simply as citizens, rather than harassing the trade by which they try to earn their bread. Would there be arrogant noblemen, today, if your Bonaparte hadn't created barons and counts? No, that was already out of fashion. Next to the priests, it was the petty provincial aristocrats who gave me the most trouble and made me turn myself into a liberal."

The conversation went on and on: it was a text that France would be busy with for another half century. When Saint-Giraud said, once again, how impossible it was to live in the provinces, Julien shyly offered the example of Monsieur de Rênal.

"By God, young man, that's an example indeed!" exclaimed Falcoz. "He's turned himself into a hammer, so he won't become an anvil—and a really terrible hammer. But I suspect he'll be pushed aside by Valenod. Do you know that scoundrel? He's the real thing. What's your Monsieur de Rênal going to say, early some morning, when he finds himself thrown out and Valenod taking his place?"

"He'll be left looking at all the crimes he's committed," said Saint-Giraud. "So you know what's going on in Verrières, young man? Well! It's Bonaparte—may heaven close its doors against him and his monarchist rubbish—who put the Rênals and Chélans in power, and it's them who gave us the Valenods and the Maslons."

This dark political dialogue astonished Julien, disrupting his voluptuous daydreams.

He paid little attention to the first view of Paris, seen in the distance. Constructing castles in the air had been warring against lingering, still palpable memories of the twenty-four hours just spent in Verrières. He silently swore never to abandon his beloved's children; he'd leave everything in order to protect them, should priestly arrogance ever bring on a republic and persecution of the aristocracy.

What would have happened, the night he came to Verrières, had he leaned his ladder against the casement of Madame de Rênal's bedroom window, and found the room occupied by a stranger—or by Monsieur de Rênal?

But then, those delightful first two hours, when his beloved honestly wanted to send him away, and he'd argued for his cause, sitting next to her in the darkness!

A soul like Julien's remains wrapped in such memories: they last a lifetime. All the rest of the encounter had already been blended into thoughts of this love's early stages, fourteen months before.

Julien was awakened from these deep daydreams: the carriage had stopped. They had just entered the mail-coach yard, on J.J. Rousseau Street.

"I'd like to go to Malmaison," he told a cabdriver who approached him.

"At this hour, sir? Why?"

"None of your business! Go."

Real passion always thinks of nothing but itself. This is why, it seems to me, passions are so ridiculous in Paris, where your neighbor acts as if you're always deeply attentive to him. I'll spare you a description of Julien's ecstasies at Malmaison, where Napoleon had held court. He wept. (What! In spite of the ugly white walls, just recently put up, chopping the whole property into tiny morsels? Yes, my dear reader: for Julien, as for posterity, the Battle of Arcola and Saint Helena and Malmaison were as good as one and the same.)

That evening, Julien hesitated a long time before allowing himself to go to the theater: he had strange notions about these hellish places.

Deep mistrust kept him from admiring Paris as he now saw it; the monuments left by his heroes were all that moved him.

"Here I am, in the very center of scheming and hypocrisy! This is where Father de Frilair's patrons exercise their power."

The third evening, curiosity obliged him to give up his plan of seeing everything before presenting himself to Father Pirard. The priest explained, his manner distant, what sort of life he should expect to lead, employed by Monsieur de La Mole.

"After a few months, if you've not proven useful, you'll go back to the seminary, but through the front door. You'll be living at the marquis's house: he is one of France's greatest noblemen. You will wear black, but as a man does when he's in mourning, not like an ecclesiastic. I will require you, three times a week, to continue your theological studies, at a seminary to which I will present you. Every day, at noon, you will be in the marquis's library, where your employer intends to have you write whatever letters are necessary for his lawsuits and his other business. The marquis will make a brief notation, on each letter he receives, as to the sort of response required. I have assured him that, after three months, you will be prepared to write these replies in such a fashion that, of any twelve you present to the marquis for his signature, he will be able to sign eight or nine. Every evening at eight, you will put his desk in order. And at ten you will be free.

"It may be," continued Father Pirard, "that some ancient lady, or some man with a gentle voice, will draw to your attention certain immense advantages, or flagrantly offer you money to show him letters received by the marquis—"

"Ah! Sir!" exclaimed Julien, blushing.

"How strange," said the priest with a bitter smile, "that poor as you are, and after a year in the seminary, you still feel such virtuous indignation. You really must have been quite blind!

"Could this be caused by heredity?" Father Pirard murmured under his breath, and as if talking to himself.

"Now, it is odd, but the marquis seems to know you. . . . I have no idea how. To begin with, he will pay you four hundred francs a month. This is a man who regularly indulges his whims: this is his flaw. He will compete with you, in the matter of childish pranks. If he is pleased, your salary may rise, in time, to eight thousand francs.

"But as you know perfectly well," the priest resumed sourly, "he's not going to pay you all that money on account of your beautiful eyes. It all depends on being useful. Were I in your place, I would speak very little—and above all, I would never talk about things I knew nothing about.

"Oh yes," the priest said. "I have looked into things for you. I was forgetting Monsieur de La Mole's family. He has two children, a daughter, and a nineteen-year-old son, extraordinarily stylish and a kind of fool, never certain at noon what he's likely to be doing at two o'clock. He's spirited, he's brave; he fought in the war with Spain. The marquis hopes, I have no notion why, that you might become the young Count Norbert's friend. I've told him you were a fine Latinist, so perhaps he expects you'll teach his son some ready-made phrases from Cicero and Virgil.

"In your place, I should never allow this fine young man to trifle with me. And before yielding to his advances, no matter how perfectly polite (though marred by a bit of irony), I would make him ask more than once.

"I will not hide from you that, at first, young Count de La Mole is surely going to look down at you, since you're only a petty bourgeois. One of his ancestors was a courtier, and had the honor of being beheaded in the Place de Grève, on the twenty-sixth of April, 1574, for his participation in a political intrigue. You, you're the son of a Verrières carpenter who, what's even worse, began by working for his father. Consider these differences carefully, and read this family's history, in Moreri's biographical dictionary—a book to which all the sycophants who dine there will, from time to time, make what they call discerning references.

"Be careful how you respond to jests made by Count Norbert de La Mole, who is a major in a cavalry regiment and a future peer of France, and don't come complaining to me, afterward."

"It would seem to me," said Julien, turning very red, "that I need not reply at all to a man who shows himself contemptuous of me."

"You have no experience of this sort of contempt; it manifests itself only in exaggerated compliments. If you were a fool, you could take it at face value. If you're eager to make your fortune, you ought to let it take you in."

"When I can't tolerate that sort of thing anymore," said Julien, "will I look like an ingrate if I go back to my little cell, number one oh three?"

"Of course," said Father Pirard. "All the fawners and flatterers who fill the house will slander you, but me, I will be there. *Adsum qui feci,* I'm the one who did it. I'll say it was entirely my decision."

Julien had been hurt by the bitter, almost nasty voice in which Father Pirard had been speaking. This virtually ruined, for him, the priest's last response.

The truth is that Father Pirard felt qualms of conscience about his affection for Julien, and he experienced a kind of religious terror, interfering so directly in another person's fate.

"You will also be seeing," he added, with the same unpleasantness, as if fulfilling a painful duty, "you'll also be seeing the Marquise de La Mole. She's a tall, blonde woman, pious, haughty, perfectly polite, and still more completely insignificant. She's the old Duke of Chaulnes's daughter, a man celebrated for his aristocratic prejudices. This great lady is more or less a three-dimensional epitome of what, at bottom, the women of her rank truly are. She makes no attempt to conceal, indeed, that having had ancestors who journeyed out on the Crusades is the only form of honor she values. Money didn't come until much later: Does that surprise you? We're no longer in the provinces, my friend.

"You will find, in her drawing room, a number of great lords who speak of our present royalty with a curious kind of indulgence. Madame de La Mole herself lowers her voice, most respectfully, whenever she speaks of a prince and especially of a princess. I would not advise you to say, in her presence, that Philip II or Henry VIII were monsters. They were *kings,* which gives them imperishable right to everyone's respect, and above all to the respect of those who do not have high birth, like you and me. However," Father Pirard added, "we are priests—for she will take you to be one. Given this title, she considers us a form of house servant necessary to her salvation."

"It seems to me, sir," said Julien, "that I won't be in Paris for long."

"Fine. But note that, for anyone wearing our sort of clothing, no fortune is available except through these great lords. With that indefinable something—indefinable, at least, by me—which I find in your nature, if you do not make your fortune, you will be persecuted. For you, there is no middle way. Don't deceive yourself. People see you're not pleased when they speak to you. In a country as social as ours, you dedicate yourself to misfortune if you do not earn respect.

"What would you have become, in Besançon, absent this caprice of the Marquis de La Mole? Someday you'll understand just how odd it is, what he is doing for you, and unless you're a monster you'll be eternally grateful to him and his family. How many poor priests, more learned than you, have lived in Paris for years, on fifteen pence a day for the masses they say and ten pence a day for the classes they give at the Sorbonne! . . . Remember what I told you, last winter, about the early years of that rascal, Cardinal Dubois. Does your pride persuade you, by any chance, that you're more talented than him?

"Take me, for example, a quiet, mediocre man: I counted on dying in my seminary. I had the childishness to grow attached to it. Well! I'd have been poverty-stricken when I handed in my resignation. Do you know the extent of my fortune? I had a total of five hundred and twenty francs, neither more nor less, not a friend in the world, barely two or three acquaintances. Monsieur de La Mole, whom I'd never met, pulled me out of so tight a corner. All he had to say was a single word, and I was given a parish in which everyone is rich, set far above the worst vices, with a salary that embarrasses me, so out of proportion is it to the labor involved. I've said this much only to get a bit of ballast into your head.

"But one word more. I have the misfortune of being short-tempered. It could happen that you and I break off all communication. If the marquise's haughtiness, or her son's unpleasant jests, make this house impossible for you, I advise you to finish your studies at some seminary a hundred miles from Paris, and rather to the north than to the south. There is more civilization to the north, and less injustice. And," he added, lowering his voice, "I have to admit it: being in the neighborhood of Paris newspapers strikes fear into petty tyrants.

"If we continue to have the pleasure of seeing each other, and the marquis's house does not suit you, I offer you a post as the assistant priest in my parish, and I will divide the salary I receive with you, half to us each. I owe you that, and more," he added, interrupting Julien's thanks, "for the unusual offer you made me, in Besançon. If instead of five hundred and twenty francs I had had none, you would have saved me."

Father Pirard's voice had lost its harshness. To his great shame, Julien felt tears in his eyes. He felt an incredible urge to throw himself into his friend's arms. He could not keep himself from saying, in as masculine a voice as he could manage:

"From the time I was in my cradle, I've hated my father. It has been one of my greatest misfortunes. But I can complain of my luck no longer: sir, I have found a father in you."

"Good! That's good," said the priest, embarrassed. Then, happening on a phrase appropriate for the director of a seminary: "Never say 'luck,' my child. Always say 'providence.'"

———

The cab stopped. The coachman raised the bronze knocker on a huge door: it was THE DE LA MOLE RESIDENCE—and so that passersby could not be in any doubt, the words were legible, in black marble, above the door.

This affectation displeased Julien. "How afraid of the Jacobins they are! They see a Robespierre with his guillotine-bound tumbrel behind every hedgerow. It makes you want to die of laughter. And they post their names in front of their houses so the rabble will know where to find them, in case they come rioting and pillaging." He offered this thought to Father Pirard.

"Ah! Poor child: you'll soon be my assistant priest. What a dreadful thought that is!"

"It seems to me utterly straightforward," said Julien.

The porter's solemnity, and above all the cleanliness of the courtyard, drew his admiration. It was a lovely sunny day.

"What magnificent architecture!" he said to his friend.

He was talking about one of those great Faubourg Saint-Germain houses with even-faced façades, built at about the time of Voltaire's death. Never have fashion and beauty existed at such opposite poles.

CHAPTER TWO

ENTERING SOCIETY

A ridiculous, moving memory: the first drawing room in which, at eighteen, one appeared, alone and without any support! A woman's glance was enough to intimidate me. The more I wanted to please, the more awkward I became. I argued for all the silliest ideas: either I jabbered senselessly, or I felt that every man who looked at me seriously was my enemy. But just the same, buried by my shyness in frightful misery, how fine a fine day could be!

—KANT

Julien stopped, dumbfounded, in the middle of the courtyard.

"Try to at least *look* sensible," said Father Pirard. "Horrible ideas come to you and then you're simply a child! What happened to Horace's *nil mirari*, never show your enthusiasm? Think how this horde of servants, seeing you pitch your tent right there, will work at making fun of you. They'll see you as one of their equals, mistakenly set above them. Pretending to be kind, to be giving you good advice, from a desire to help and guide you, they'll get you to fall into the most grotesque stupidities."

"Just let them try," said Julien, biting at his lips; he drew deep on his sense of mistrust.

The rooms through which these gentlemen walked, on the ground floor, before arriving at the marquis's private office, would have seemed to you, oh my reader, quite as melancholy as they were magnificent. If they were offered to you, exactly as they are, you'd refuse to live in them: this is the land of yawning and dreary formalisms.

Julien's enchantment grew still stronger. "How can anyone be un-happy," he thought, "when they live in such splendor!"

The gentlemen finally came to the ugliest of all the rooms in this magnificent place: daylight scarcely reached it. And there they found a small, lean man, with sparkling eyes and a blond wig. Father Pirard turned to Julien and presented him. It was the marquis. He was so courteous that Julien was hard put to recognize him. He was no longer the high and mighty lord of Upper Bray, who carried himself so haughtily. Julien thought there was too much hair in his wig, and this impression helped him lose his shyness. At first, this descendant of Henry III's friend seemed to him distinctly shabby. He was really very lean and rather excitable. But he soon noticed that the marquis spoke to people so politely that, indeed, it was pleasanter than even the Bishop of Besançon himself. The interview took no more than three minutes. As they left, Father Pirard said to Julien:

"You were staring at the marquis as one stares at a picture. I am not particularly adept at what people here call good manners, and you will soon know more than I do, but nevertheless your bold staring seemed to me not really polite."

They got back into the cab; the coachman pulled up near the boulevard; the priest brought Julien to a suite of large sitting rooms. Julien observed that there was no furniture. He was looking at a huge gilt clock, adorned in what seemed to him gross indecency, when a most elegant man came cheerfully over to him. Julien made him a faint bow.

The man laughed and put his hand on the young man's shoulder. Julien winced and jumped back. He was red with anger. Father Pirard, for all his sobriety, laughed until he cried. The man was a tailor.

"You are now free for two days," Father Pirard said as they were leaving. "Only then can you be presented to Madame de La Mole. Someone else might watch over you as if you were a young girl, in these initial moments of your stay in this new Babylon. Ruin yourself right away, if you need to ruin yourself, and then I'll be released from this weakness of thinking about you. The day after tomorrow, in the morning, this tailor will deliver two suits of clothing; give five francs to the young fellow who'll see how they fit you. For the rest, don't let these Parisians hear the sound of your voice. Say one word, and they'll know exactly how to make fun of you. It's their special gift. Come to me at noon, that day. . . . Go, ruin yourself. . . . I've been forgetting: go order some boots, and shirts, and a hat, at these addresses."

Julien looked at the handwriting.

"The marquis wrote these," the priest said. "He's an active man who thinks of everything, who likes to do things rather than order that they be done by others. He's hiring you to spare him all that trouble. Will you be intelligent enough to properly do all the things this lively man will tell you to do, in only a very few words? Only time will tell. Be careful!"

Julien went to the craftsmen at the addresses he'd been given, not saying a word. He noted how respectfully they received him, and how the bootmaker, recording his name in an account book, wrote "Monsieur Julien de Sorel."

At the Père Lachaise Cemetery, a most obliging man, and even more assertively a liberal, offered to show Julien the tomb of Marshall Ney, Napoleon's general, to whom wise politicians have denied an epitaph. But after leaving this liberal gentleman, who embraced him tightly, tears in his eyes, Julien no longer had his watch. Two days later, at noon, enriched by these experiences, he presented himself to Father Pirard, who carefully looked him over.

"You're well on the way to becoming a fop," the priest told him, severely. Julien looked like a very young man in deep mourning. He seemed quite presentable, but the good priest was himself too much of a provincial to be aware that Julien still hunched his shoulders, which in the provinces is considered a sign of both elegance and importance. When the marquis saw the young man, he evaluated Julien's gracefulness very differently. He said to Father Pirard:

"Would you mind if Monsieur Sorel took dance lessons?"

The priest stood dumbfounded.

"No," he said at last. "Julien's not a priest."

Going up two steps at a time, the marquis ascended a small, secret staircase, in order to personally show our hero a pretty attic room that looked out on the building's huge garden. Then he asked Julien how many shirts he'd bought at the linen shop.

"Two," Julien answered, self-conscious at seeing so great a lord descend to such details.

"Very good," the marquis went on, seriously and in a distinctly commanding, curt voice that left Julien thinking. "Very good! Get another twenty-two. Here's your first quarter's salary."

When they went down the staircase, the marquis summoned an old man: "Arsène," he said, "you will wait on Monsieur Sorel." A few minutes later, Julien found himself alone in a magnificent library; it was a delightful moment. So no one would come on him, excited as he was, he hid himself in a dark corner. From there, he looked out at the books' glittering spines. "I could read every one of them," he told himself. "How could I be unhappy here? Monsieur de Rênal would think himself dishonored, had he done for me a hundredth part of what Marquis de La Mole has just done.

"But first, let's see what I'm supposed to copy." That finished, Julien ventured over to the books. He was wildly happy, finding an edition of Voltaire. He ran and opened the library door, so no one could come on him by surprise. Then he gave himself the pleasure of opening each of the eighty volumes. They were superbly bound: this set of Voltaire was the masterpiece of the best binder in London. Nothing else was needed to carry Julien to the heights of wonder.

An hour later, the marquis came in, looked over the copies, and noticed, with astonishment, that Julien had misspelled a very simple word, dropping the "t" from the end of "that." "Everything Father Pirard told me about his learning is simply a fairy tale." Deeply discouraged, the marquis said to him, gently:

"You're not sure of your spelling?"

"That's true," said Julien, not thinking in the slightest of how much harm he was doing himself. He was stirred by the marquis's benevolence, which made him think of Monsieur de Rênal's arrogant tone.

"My experiment with this little Franche-Comté priest is all a waste of time," thought the marquis. "But I so badly need a man who knows what he's doing!"

"There is a 't' at the end of 'that,'" he said. "When you've finished your copies, use the dictionary and look up the words you're not sure of."

At six o'clock, the marquis had him called. He looked with obvious distress at Julien's boots. "It's my fault," he said. "I didn't tell you that, every day at five-thirty, you need to be dressed."

Julien looked at him, not understanding.

"I mean, you need to put on stockings and shoes. Arsène will remind you: for today, I will apologize on your behalf."

Having said this, Monsieur de La Mole showed Julien into a drawing room, resplendent in its gilded decor. On similar occasions, Monsieur de Rênal had never failed to walk very fast, so he could go through the door first. His former employer's petty vanity now caused Julien to step on the marquis's feet, and give him a good deal of pain, on account of his gout. "Ah, to top it all off, he's a clumsy oaf," he said to himself. Julien was presented to a tall lady of imposing appearance. This was the marquise. Julien thought her insolent, rather like Madame de Maugiron, wife of the deputy governor of the Verrières district, when she'd attended the Saint Charles feast day dinner. A bit bothered by the drawing room's excessive splendor, Julien did not listen to what Monsieur de La Mole was saying. The marquise scarcely troubled herself to look at him. There were a few men in attendance, among whom Julien recognized, with inexpressible pleasure, the young Bishop of Agde, who had been good enough to say a few words to him before the ceremony at Upper Bray. The young bishop was surely startled by the soft, shy glances fixed on him by Julien, and had no interest in recognizing this provincial.

All the men assembled in the drawing room struck Julien as rather somber and constrained. "People speak softly, in Paris, and they don't make much of unimportant things."

A handsome young man, wearing a mustache, very pale and slender, came in at about six-thirty. He had an extremely small head.

"You always make us wait for you," said the marquise, whose hand he kissed.

Julien understood that this was Count de La Mole. From the start, Julien thought him charming.

"Is it really possible," he asked himself, "that this is the man whose offensive jokes are supposed to chase me out of the house!"

As he considered Count Norbert, Julien noticed that he was wearing boots and spurs. "And I have to be in shoes, since I'm an inferior."

They sat down to dinner. Julien heard the marquise say something harsh, raising her voice a bit. At almost exactly the same time, he saw a young woman, very blonde and with a fine figure, who seated herself directly across from him. She did not attract him. However, when he looked at her more carefully, he thought he'd never seen such beautiful eyes, though they spoke of an enormously cold heart. Afterward, he decided they simply expressed her boredom at everyone there, though they obviously never forgot how imposing they were supposed to appear. "However, Madame de Rênal had quite beautiful eyes," he said to himself. "Everyone compliments her. But they're absolutely different from these." Julien lacked the experience to realize that what he saw, from time to time, gleaming in Mademoiselle Mathilde's eyes (he had heard her thus addressed) was a passionate wit. When Madame de Rênal's eyes grew bright, it was with emotion, or with compassionate indignation, hearing an account of some malicious act. Toward the end of dinner, Julien found words for the kind of beauty he saw in Mademoiselle Mathilde's eyes. "They're sparkling," he said to himself. But, for the rest, she unfortunately resembled her mother, who increasingly displeased him; he stopped looking at her. On the other hand, Count Norbert seemed to him entirely admirable. Julien was so captivated that it never occurred to him to be jealous and dislike the count, even though he was infinitely richer and nobler.

To Julien's eyes, the marquis seemed bored.

As they came to the second course, he said to his son:

"Norbert, let me ask for your kindness toward Monsieur Julien Sorel, who has just joined my staff, and of whom I intend to make a man—if *that* is possible.

"He's my secretary," said the marquis to the person seated next to him, "and he writes 'that' without the final 't.' "

Everyone looked at Julien, who bowed a bit extravagantly to Norbert. But in general, people were pleased at his appearance.

The marquis had probably been talking about how Julien had been educated, because one of the guests challenged him on the subject of Horace. "It was precisely discussing Horace with the Bishop of Besançon," Julien said to himself, "which made me successful with that prelate. These people don't seem to know any other authors." From then on, he had himself under complete control. It had become even easier because he'd just decided that, for him, Mademoiselle de La Mole could never seem a woman. After having been in the seminary, people could simply do their worst: he would not let anyone intimidate him. He might have been still calmer had the dining room been less magnificently furnished. Indeed, there were two mirrors, each eight feet high, in which from time to time he observed the man questioning him about Horace. He still found these mirrors rather commanding. But he did not frame his replies, for a provincial, in sentences of excessive length. He had beautiful eyes, which shone even more brilliantly, either with shyness or, when he had answered particularly well, with joy. He was found acceptable. This kind of testing added a little interest to their somber dinner. The marquis gave his questioner a sign to push him even harder. "Might it be possible," he was thinking, "that he actually knows something?"

Julien answered, improvising ideas as he went along, and losing enough of his shyness so that he demonstrated—not exactly wit, an impossibility for anyone not in command of Paris's way of speaking—but an originality, not to be sure set out gracefully, or properly ordered, but proving that he had a perfect grasp of Latin.

His adversary, a member of the Paleographic Academy, who by chance knew Latin, seeing that Julien was a first-rate humanist, no longer worried about embarrassing him; he began a really serious interrogation. In the heat of combat, Julien was finally able to forget about the dining room's decorations, and to bring forth ideas about the Roman poets that his questioner had never seen so much as mentioned in print. As an honest man, he was obliged to respect the young secretary. Luckily, they got into a discussion of whether Horace had been poor or rich. Had he been a friendly fellow, voluptuous and carefree, throwing off poems to amuse himself, like Chapelle, friend of Molière and La Fontaine, or was he a poor devil of a poet laureate, connected to court and turning out odes for the ruler's birthday, like Southey, Byron's attacker? They spoke of the state of society under Augustus and George IV, in both of which epochs the aristocracy had been all-powerful, though Maecenas, in Rome—not the simple knight he'd seemed—had stripped away that power, while in England the aristocracy had reduced George IV almost to the level of the Doge of

Venice. This discussion appeared to draw the marquis out of the torpid state into which, when dinner had started, boredom had plunged him.

Julien knew nothing whatever about these moderns—Southey, Lord Byron, George IV—whose very names he was hearing for the first time. But no one could doubt that, whenever events in Rome were at issue, knowledge of which could be gathered from the works of Horace, Martial, Tacitus, etc., he was unquestionably the superior. Julien unceremoniously drew on ideas he'd acquired from the Bishop of Besançon, in the jolly discussion he'd had with that prelate. Nor were these the least appreciated.

When they were weary of talking about poets, the marquise, who made it a rule to admire whatever amused her husband, condescended to give Julien a passing glance. "The truly gauche manners of this young priest," remarked the academician to her, he being seated beside her, "may well conceal a genuinely learned man." Julien overheard part of this. The mistress of the house was fond of ready-made phrases, and she adopted this one, about Julien, very pleased at having invited an academician to dine with them.

"He amuses Monsieur de La Mole," she thought.

CHAPTER THREE

The First Steps

This immense valley, filled with glittering lights and so many thousands of men, dazzles my eyes. Not one of them knows me, but they're all my superiors. My head whirls.

—Poems of *Reina*, the lawyer

Next day, very early, Julien was in the library, copying letters, when Mademoiselle Mathilde came in, using a small, secret door, extremely well hidden by books. As Julien was admiring this device, Mademoiselle Mathilde seemed both surprised and distinctly annoyed at meeting him there. She had stiff curling paper in her hair; he found her haughty and almost masculine. Mademoiselle de La Mole was in the habit of taking books from her father's library, without anyone's knowledge. Julien's presence, on this particular morning, made her errand impossible, which was all the more annoying since she had come to seek out the second volume of Voltaire's *Princess of Babylon,* an indelicate book eminently suited to someone who had been educated in a deeply monarchist and religious institution—an educational masterpiece produced by the Sacred Heart of Jesus! At nineteen, this poor girl's imagination already needed spicing, for her to find a novel interesting.

Count Norbert appeared in the library toward three o'clock. He had come to scrutinize a newspaper, so he'd be able to talk politics that night, and was quite pleased to find Julien, whose existence he had forgotten. He behaved admirably toward him; he offered to take him riding.

"My father will let us out until dinner."

Julien appreciated his "us," and found him charming.

"My God," said Julien. "Were it a question of cutting down a fifty-foot tree, squaring it off, and sawing it into planks, I dare say I might manage very well. But I've been on horseback half a dozen times in my life."

"Fine," said Norbert. "This will be the seventh."

In fact, Julien was recalling the King of ———— and his entry into Verrières, and thought himself an accomplished horseman. But in returning from the Bois de Boulogne he fell, right in the middle of Du Bac Street, while trying to suddenly avoid a carriage, and got himself covered with mud. It was fortunate that he'd bought two suits. At dinner, trying to make conversation, the marquis asked how his excursion had gone. Norbert hastily replied in very general terms.

"The count exhibits great goodwill toward me," said Julien. "I thank him, and deeply appreciate his kindness. He was good enough to give me the gentlest, prettiest horse, but after all he could not tie me on and, failing that precaution, I fell right in the middle of that long street, near the bridge."

Mademoiselle Mathilde tried, unsuccessfully, to hide her fit of laughter, and then indiscreetly requested a more detailed account. Julien behaved with great straightforwardness; he was gracious without knowing it.

"I expect good things of this little priest," said the marquis to the academician. "A provincial, and straightforward about such an event! This is something never seen before, and which will never be seen again. And to tell about his misfortune even in the presence of *ladies*!"

Julien made those who heard him feel so comfortable about his mishap that, when dinner was over, and the general conversation had taken a different direction, Mademoiselle Mathilde put more questions to her brother about the unlucky occasion. Her questions were elaborate, and took a very long time to deal with. Julien several times made eye contact with her and did not hesitate, though he had not been directly queried, to give her plain replies, and all three of them, in the end, were laughing, just like three young villagers in the woods.

The next day, Julien attended two theology classes, and returned, in order to transcribe twenty letters. He found seated very near him, in the library, a young man carefully but shabbily dressed, and a face stamped with envy.

The marquis came in.

"What are you doing here, Monsieur Tanbeau?" he said to the newcomer, his voice harsh.

"I was thinking . . ." began the young man, smiling unpleasantly.

"No, sir, you *were not thinking*. This is clearly a test of some sort, but a very unfortunate one."

Young Tanbeau got up, furious, and disappeared. He was the academician's nephew, the man who was Madame de La Mole's friend, and planned to take up literary work. The academician had arranged for the marquis to hire him as a secretary. He'd been working in an isolated room and, having learned of the favors granted to Julien, wanted to share them. That morning he had come and set up his writing desk in the library.

At four o'clock, after some hesitation, Julien ventured to go to Count Norbert. The latter, already mounted, was embarrassed but perfectly polite.

"I imagine," he said to Julien, "you'll soon be going to riding school and, after a few weeks, I'll be delighted to go riding with you."

"I wanted to thank you, most gratefully, for all the kindness you've shown me. Believe me, sir," added Julien most seriously, "I am deeply aware of how much I owe you. If your horse was not injured by my clumsiness yesterday, and is available, I should like to ride him today."

"My dear Sorel, of course, but at your risk. Let's pretend I've given you all the necessary reasons against it, as prudence requires. The fact is, it's already four o'clock and we have no time to lose."

Once they were mounted:

"What do I need to do, to keep from falling?" Julien asked the young count.

"A great deal," replied Norbert, roaring with laughter. "Among other things, hold yourself farther back."

Julien went at a brisk trot. They were in Louis XVI Square.

"Ah, you foolhardy youngster," said Norbert. "There are too many vehicles, and they're driven by such reckless fellows! Once you fall to the ground, they'll ride right over you. They have no interest in pulling up short and damaging their horses' mouths."

Twenty times, Norbert saw Julien almost fall, but they returned without an accident. As they came in, the young count said to his sister:

"Let me introduce you to a bold daredevil."

At dinner, speaking to his father, at one end of the table, he did full justice to Julien's bravery. That was all one *could* praise about his horsemanship. The young count had overheard, that morning, stable hands grooming horses in the courtyard and having great fun over Julien's fall, mocking him outrageously.

For all their great kindness, Julien soon felt totally isolated in the middle of this family. All their customs struck him as peculiar, and he was deficient in virtually everything. His blunders were the joy and delight of all the valets.

Father Pirard had gone to take up his parish duties. "If Julien is a slender reed, let him perish. If he has the courage, let him figure this business out, all by himself," he thought.

CHAPTER FOUR

THE DE LA MOLE MANSION

What's he doing here? Is he happy here?
Does he think they'll ever like him?
—RONSARD

If everything seemed peculiar to Julien, in the de La Moles' splendid drawing rooms, this pale, black-robed young man seemed, in turn, extremely peculiar to those who bothered noticing him. Madame de La Mole suggested to her husband that, on days when they had important people to dinner, Julien should be sent away on errands.

"I wish to carry the experiment to its completion," replied the marquis. "Father Pirard assures me that we're wrong to crush the self-respect of those we allow into our household. *You can only push against something that pushes back*, etc. The young man is unseemly only because his is not a face with which we are familiar. For the rest, he's deaf and dumb."

"In order to properly locate myself, here," Julien thought, "I need to keep a written record of the names and the natures of the people I find in these drawing rooms."

He set on the first line five or six friends of the house, people who, just in case, had been paying him court, thinking he was the marquis's latest whim. They were poor wretches, more or less servile and colorless. But it must be said, in praise of this class of people (to be found, these days, in all aristocratic drawing rooms), that they were not deferential to everyone. Some of them would allow the marquis to browbeat them, but would rebel against a single harsh word if addressed to them by Madame de la Mole.

The masters of the house suffered, at bottom, from too much pride and too much boredom; they were too accustomed to insulting others, in order to relieve their own boredom, to expect their visitors to be genuine friends. Still, except on rainy days, and at moments of truly fierce boredom, which did not occur very often, they were always perfectly polite.

If these five or six flatterers, who showed Julien such paternal friendship, were to desert the de La Mole house, the marquise would have been left vulnerable to long periods of solitude, and, to women of her social rank, solitude is ghastly. It is, indeed, the very symbol of *disgrace.*

The marquis was exactly right for his wife; he made sure her drawing room was sufficiently garrisoned. Not however with people of their own rank: he viewed his new associates as insufficiently noble to be received as friends, nor sufficiently amusing to be admitted to his home as inferiors.

Julien did not decipher these puzzles until a good deal later. The government's political decisions, much discussed among wealthy bourgeois families, were never broached by those in the marquis's social class, except in serious emergencies.

And still, despite this century's reigning boredom, the need for amusement is such that, even on days when the de La Moles invited people for dinner, the marquis had barely left the room when everyone hurried away. In the marquis's dining room, provided that you did not makes jokes about God, or priests, or the king, or those holding government posts, or artists patronized by the court, or all established ideas and institutions—provided that you did not praise the satirist Béranger, or the opposition newspapers, or Voltaire, or Rousseau, or anyone who indulged himself, even a very little bit, in freedom of speech—and provided, above all, that you never discussed politics— in the marquis's dining room, you were free to talk about anything you liked.

No income of a quarter of a million francs, nor the possession of the noblest decoration awarded by the state, had the power to oppose the de La Moles' house rules. Any idea with a scrap of vitality seemed gross coarseness. Despite polished manners, complete courtesy, and a desire to please, boredom could be seen on every face. Young people who came because it was their duty, terrified at the prospect of saying something that might dimly resemble an idea, or that might disclose their knowledge of a banned book, said a few elegant words about Rossini, or about the weather, and then said nothing at all.

Julien observed that conversation was usually kept alive by two viscounts and five barons, all of whom Monsieur de La Mole had known during their exile, during the Revolution. These gentlemen had incomes ranging from six to eight hundred thousand francs; four of them favored *Today's News,* and three preferred *The French Gazette.* One told a story, every day, about the sixteenth-century court of Charles IX, in which the word *wonderful* was freely used. Julien noted that this man wore five decorations; in general, the others limited themselves to three.

On the other hand, there were regularly ten uniformed servants in attendance, and every quarter of an hour the diners were offered tea and ices. Just before midnight, they were served a sort of supper, with champagne.

This was why, sometimes, Julien stayed to the very end; mostly, he could not quite fathom how anyone could listen, seriously, to the conversation regularly heard in this magnificently gilded dining room. Occasionally, he would watch the people who were talking, to see whether they were making fun of what they themselves were saying. "My de Maistre," he thought, "whose book I know by heart, is a thousand times better, and still he's quite boring."

Julien wasn't the only one aware of the moral asphyxiation. Some took comfort in eating a great many ices, others in saying, the whole rest of the night, "I've just left the de La Moles, where I understood that Russia," etc., etc.

One of the hangers-on told Julien that, just six months ago, after twenty years of regular attendance at her dinners, Madame de La Mole had repaid poor Baron Le Bourguignon, an assistant governor since the Revolution, by having him promoted to a governorship.

This noble event had strengthened the zeal of all these gentlemen: if they'd been irritated, before, by almost anything, now they were irritated by nothing. Lack of respect for them was seldom blunt, but Julien had already been startled, two or three times, by brief exchanges between the marquis and his wife, which were hard on those seated around them. These aristocrats never disguised their honest scorn for everyone not descended from those *who rode in the king's carriage.* Julien could see that the word *Crusade* was the only one at which their faces took on an expression of deep seriousness, blended with respect. Usually, their respect carried with it a flavor of condescension.

In the midst of such magnificence, and such boredom, Julien concerned himself with nothing but Monsieur de La Mole. He was pleased, one day, to hear the marquis protest that he was in no way involved in poor Le Bourguignon's promotion. This was out of consideration for the marquise: Julien had heard the truth from Father Pirard.

One morning, the priest was working with Julien in the marquis's library, on the interminable lawsuit against Father de Frilair:

"Sir," Julien asked suddenly. "Is dining every day with madame and the marquis one of my duties, or is it their kindness toward me?"

"It's an extraordinary honor!" replied Father Pirard, shocked. "Monsieur N————, the academician, who has paid faithful court for fifteen years, has never succeeded in obtaining such an honor for his nephew, Monsieur Tanbeau."

"I find it, sir, the most painful part of my job. The seminary didn't bore me so completely. Sometimes, I've even seen Mademoiselle de La Mole yawning, though she ought to be used to the attentions of the regular guests. I worry about falling asleep. Can you please arrange it so I eat a forty-pence dinner in some out-of-the-way inn?"

Father Pirard, a true social climber, was deeply aware of the honor of dining with a great lord. While he was struggling to understand Julien's feelings, a slight noise made them both turn their heads. Julien saw that Mademoiselle de La Mole had been listening. His face reddened. She had come looking for a book and had heard everything. It gave her some reason to think well of Julien. "That one isn't down on his knees," she thought, "like the old priest. God, but the priest's ugly!"

At dinner, Julien did not dare look at Mademoiselle de La Mole, but she kindly spoke to him. That day they were expecting many fashionable people, and she urged him to remain. Young Parisian girls have no great liking for people of a certain age, especially when they're not well dressed. Julien did not need much cleverness to realize that Baron Le Bourguignon's colleagues, who remained in the dining room, had the honor of being the butt of Mademoiselle de La Mole's jests. That day, whether she was putting on a show or not, she was savage about bores in general.

Mademoiselle de La Mole was at the center of a small group, which came together almost every night behind the marquise's immense easy chair. Among them were the Marquis de Croisenois, Count de Caylus, Vicomte de Luz, and two or three other young officers, friends either of Norbert or of his sister. These gentlemen seated themselves on a great blue sofa. At one end of the sofa, facing gay Mathilde, Julien sat silently on a small, rather low straw chair. His modest position was the envy of all the flatterers. Norbert came to the aid of his father's young secretary, making remarks to him and, once or twice in the course of the evening, mentioning his name. Mademoiselle de La Mole asked Julien, that night, how high the mountain might be, on which stood the Besançon fort. Julien did not know whether it was higher or lower than Montmartre. He often laughed cheerfully at what those around him, in this little group, were saying, but he felt quite unable to say anything of the sort himself. It was like a foreign language that he could understand, but which he could not speak.

That day, Mathilde's friends were having great fun, continually mocking those arriving in the huge room. Their preferred targets, initially, were the friends of the house, since they were better known. You can imagine whether Julien was paying close attention: it all interested him, both what they were talking about and their way of poking fun.

"Ah!" said Mathilde. "Here comes Monsieur Descoulis. He's not wearing a wig anymore. Does he think he can get to be a governor by genius alone? He's showing off that bald head, which according to him is stuffed with lofty thoughts."

"He's a man who knows everyone," said the Marquis de Croisenois. "My uncle, the cardinal, sees him at his table all the time. He's good at keeping lies about his friends alive for years, and he has two or three hundred friends. He understands how to nourish friendship: it's his special talent. You'll see him just like that, in the wintertime, starting at seven in the morning, in front of a friend's door, splattered with mud just the way he is now.

"He gets into quarrels, from time to time, and writes seven or eight angry letters. Then he makes it up, and writes seven or eight letters about the delights of friendship. But he shines to best advantage when he's spewing out stuff about how frank and sincere he is, just an honest man who has no secrets hidden away in his heart. When he's playing that game, you know he has a favor to ask. One of my uncle's vicar-generals is wonderfully good at telling Monsieur Descoulis's life, since the Restoration. I'll bring him here."

"Bah!" said Count de Caylus. "I don't trust a word of these tales. It's professional jealousy between unimportant people."

"Monsieur Descoulis will have a place in history," replied de Croisenois. "It was he who brought about the Restoration, along with Talleyrand and Pozzo di Borgo, not to mention Father de Pradt."

"Millions have passed through that man's hands," said Norbert, "and I've never understood why he comes here and lets my father insult him—sometimes very nastily. 'How many times have you betrayed your friends, my dear Descoulis?' he called out to him the other day, from one end of the table to the other."

"But has he really betrayed anybody?" asked Mademoiselle de La Mole. "Anyway, who hasn't?"

"Ho-ho," said Count de Caylus to Norbert. "That famous liberal, Monsieur Sainclair, is here, and why the devil has he come? I've got to go over and talk to him, make him talk to me. They say he's really got a brain."

"But how would your mother like that?" said Monsieur de Croisenois. "His ideas are so extravagant, so bountiful, so independent...."

"Look," said Mademoiselle de La Mole, "just see that independent man bowing almost to the ground as he greets Monsieur Descoulis. Look, he's clasping his hand. I almost thought he was going to kiss it."

"So Descoulis gets on with the government, and better than we'd thought," replied Monsieur de Croisenois.

"Sainclair's come here to lobby himself into the academy," said Norbert. "Croisenois, just see how he's greeting Baron L———."

"It would be less vulgar if he went down on his knees," said Monsieur de Luz.

"My dear Sorel," said Norbert, "you've got such a good head on your shoulders, but since you've just come from the mountains, make sure you never bow to anyone the way our great poet just has, even if it's God Himself."

"Ah," said Mademoiselle de La Mole, vaguely imitating how the servant announced newcomers, "here comes the Great Brain Himself, Baron Bâton."

"I think even your servants make fun of him," said Monsieur Caylus. "Baron Bâton! What a name."

" 'Names don't mean a thing!' he was telling us the other day," said Mathilde. "Just imagine 'Le Duc de Bouillon,' the Duke of Hot Beef Broth, announced for the first time. I think people only need to get used to it. . . ."

Julien walked away. Still not very receptive to clever irony, charmingly delicate, he assumed that, before you could laugh at such a jest, it had to make some sense. He could not see the chatter of these young people as anything but universal insult, and he was shocked. His provincial (or English?) prudery even thought they were denigrating people out of jealousy, but there he was certainly mistaken.

"Count Norbert," he told himself, "whom I have seen write three drafts for a twenty-line letter to his colonel, would certainly be very pleased to have written, in his whole life, a single page as good as Monsieur Sainclair's work."

His departure unnoticed, he being of no importance, Julien first went over to another group, and then another still. He tracked Baron Bâton from a distance, and wished he could hear him. A most intelligent man, Baron Bâton seemed restless, only recovering a bit, Julien saw, when he'd managed three or four sharp remarks. "That kind of mind," Julien thought, "needed a good deal of room."

The baron could not simply speak *words:* to be brilliant, he had to have at least four sentences, each of six lines.

"That man doesn't talk, he expatiates," said someone behind Julien. Turning around, he blushed with pleasure as he heard Count Chalvet's name. His was the best mind of the century. Julien had often come across his name, both in *Memories of Napoleon on Saint-Helena* and in the historical fragments dictated by Napoleon. Count Chalvet clearly did not waste words: his observations were clear, balanced, lively, profound. If he spoke of something, then and there the discussion progressed. He brought in facts; he was a delight to hear. But beyond that, in matters political he was a brazen cynic.

"I'm a freethinker, I really am," he was saying to a man wearing three decorations; he appeared to be mocking his listener. "Why should anyone expect me, today, to hold the same opinions I had six weeks ago? If I did, my opinions would be tyrannical."

Four serious young men, standing around him, frowned: these gentlemen did not care for witty remarks. The count saw he'd gone too far. Luckily, he noticed decent Monsieur Balland—an absolute hypocrite of decency. The count walked over and began talking to him; people drifted over, knowing poor Balland was going to be roasted alive. Wielding moralisms and morality, after having begun his break into society in ways difficult to discuss in print, Balland had managed to marry an exceedingly rich wife (though he was horribly ugly), who died. He then married a second rich woman, who never appeared in society. He enjoyed, most humbly, an income of sixty thousand francs, and had flatterers of his own. Showing him no mercy, Count Chalvet rehearsed all these matters. Soon, there was a circle of thirty people around them. They were all smiling, even the serious young men—the great hope of the century.

"Why does he come here?" thought Julien. "At Monsieur de La Mole's, he's everybody's target." He went over to Father Pirard, to ask him.

Monsieur Balland slunk away.

"Good!" said Norbert. "There's one of my father's spies gone. The only one left is little lame Napier."

"Is that the answer to the riddle?" wondered Julien. "But if it is, why does Monsieur de La Mole have Monsieur Balland in the house?"

Harsh Father Pirard was in a corner of the room, listening to new arrivals being announced, and frowning.

"It's a regular smugglers' den," he said, sounding like Basilio in Rossini's *Barber of Seville.* "Everyone I see coming here is a degenerate."

Stern-faced Father Pirard knew nothing about high society. But he'd acquired, from his Jansenist friends, very accurate notions about men who got into aristocratic drawing rooms only because they maneuvered so very deftly, in the service of any political party whatever, or because their fortunes were of scandalous origin. For several minutes, that night, he spoke from the heart, answering questions Julien put to him, and then suddenly broke off, deeply contrite for having spoken ill of so many people. He felt himself guilty of having sinned. Fretful, Jansenist, and convinced of the duty of Christian charity, his life in society was a perpetual struggle.

"What a face on that Father Pirard!" said Mademoiselle de La Mole as Julien returned to her little group.

Julien was annoyed, but she was right. Certainly, no one could deny that Father Pirard was the most respectable man in the entire room, but his blotchy complexion, racked by his pangs of conscience, at that moment did make him hideous. "Better believe what faces tell you!" thought Julien. "It's precisely when Father Pirard's scrupulousness scolds him for some little sin that he looks atrocious, while on Napier's face—that universally recognized spy—all you see is pure, calm happiness." But Father Pirard had made some large concessions to his new role: he had hired a manservant, and he dressed very well.

Julien noticed something odd: every eye was turned toward the door, and the great room was almost silent. The servant was announcing famous Baron de Tully, on whom the elections had just focused universal attention. Julien stepped forward and saw him very well. The baron had been in charge of one of the electoral districts, and had had the bright idea of spiriting off the little slips of paper bearing every vote belonging to one of the parties. In compensation, however, he had replaced them, in proper proportion, with other little scraps of paper, bearing a name that better suited him. This peremptory maneuver had been noticed by a number of voters, who promptly congratulated Baron de Tully. The good man was still pallid from this great affair. A few wicked tongues had talked about jail cells.

Monsieur de La Mole welcomed him with an intense coldness. The poor baron left in rather a hurry.

"If he's leaving us so quickly, he must be going to see that magician, Monsieur Comte," said Count Chalvet, and everyone laughed.

Poised right in the middle of some great lords (standing silent, yet schemers all, and among the most corrupt of the lot, though men of high intelligence) who, that night, had followed one another into Monsieur de La Mole's drawing room—there being talk of making him a government minister—little Tanbeau drew his social fencing sword for the first time. If he did not wield it particularly deftly, he made up for that, as you'll see, by the forcefulness of his words.

"Why hasn't that man been sent to prison for ten years?" he was saying, just as Julien approached his group. "Reptiles like that ought to be thrown into the deepest dungeons. Let them die down in the darkness: otherwise their venom gets puffed up and becomes even more dangerous. What's the point to fining him a few thousand francs? Maybe he's poor—all right, so much the better. But his party will pay the fine. He should have been fined five hundred francs and sent to the dungeons for ten years."

"My God!" thought Julien. "Who is the monster they're talking about?" He admired his colleague's vehement tone and wild gestures. Just then, the lean, drawn face of the academician's favorite nephew was ghastly to look on. Julien discovered, soon enough, that he was talking about the greatest poet of their time, Béranger.

"Oh, you monster!" Julien murmured, great tears rolling down his cheeks. "You little beggar! I'll get you for that."

"But just see," he thought, "these last hopes of Monsieur de La Mole's party, a party he helps lead! And that famous poet who Tanbeau is slandering—what medals, what sinecures he couldn't have had, if he'd sold himself—not to Prime Minister de Nerval's completely colorless government, but to one of the others, more or less respectable, that have since taken power!"

Father Pirard, from far off, beckoned to Julien; Monsieur de La Mole had just said something to him. But by the time Julien was free to make his way over, finally able to slip away from a bishop's moaning and groaning, to which he'd been listening with lowered eyes, he found him cornered by that vile little Tanbeau. The little monster, who detested Father Pirard as the source of Julien's special favor, had now come to pay court to him.

"When will death free us from that withered old rottenness?" With biblical energy, this is how the little man of letters spoke of worthy, but Whiggish, Lord Holland. His special skill was to have accumulated biographies of everyone alive; he had just been making a rapid review of

everyone who might aspire to any influence, in the reign of William IV, the new King of England.

Father Pirard went into the next room; Julien followed him.

"I must warn you: the marquis does not care for scribblers. It's his only aversion. If you're versed in Latin; in Greek, if you can; if you know Egyptian history, and Persian, etc., he'll honor and protect you as a scholar. But go and write a single page of French, especially on matters which are serious and above your social position, he'll label you a scribbler and you'll be out of luck. Living as you do in a great lord's house, remember what the Duke de Castries said of d'Alembert and Rousseau: 'They argue about everything, and don't have any income worth talking about.'"

"They find out everything," Julien thought, "here, too, just as in the seminary." He had written eight or ten rather rhetorical pages, a kind of eulogy of the old surgeon-major who, he always said, had made a man of him. "And that little notebook," he reminded himself, "has always been locked away!" He went up to his room, burned the manuscript, and returned to the drawing room. The radiant rogues were all gone; only the men with medals were left.

Around the table, just brought in by the servants, with everything set out and ready, there were seven or eight distinguished women of thirty or thirty-five, deeply devout, very conceited. Madame de Fervaques, a gay and shining marshall's widow, came in, busily making excuses for her late arrival. It was after midnight; she went to sit next to the marquise. Her appearance moved Julien: she had Madame de Rênal's eyes, and her look.

Mademoiselle de La Mole's group was still well populated. She and her friends had been making fun of the unlucky Count de Thaler. This was the only son of the famous Jew, celebrated for the wealth he'd acquired, lending money to kings so they could oppress their own people. The old Jew had just died, leaving his son an income of three hundred thousand francs a month and a name, alas, only too well known! This peculiar position would require a mind of great simplicity, or one with a powerful will.

Unfortunately, the count was only a nice man, totally wrapped in pretensions created by his flatterers.

Monsieur de Caylus declared they had puffed him up with a determination to seek Mademoiselle de La Mole's hand (to whom the Marquis de Croisenois, who would be a duke, but with an income of only fifteen thousand francs, was paying court).

"Ah, don't accuse him of being determined," said Norbert, woefully.

What was most lacking in poor Count de Thaler, in all likelihood, was indeed willpower. Looking at this aspect of the young man, he would have made a worthy king. Endlessly taking advice from all sides, he did not have the tenacity to follow any suggested course to its end.

His face, Mademoiselle de La Mole declared, was in itself sufficient to inspire her with eternal joy. It was an odd blend of nervousness and disappointment, though from time to time it clearly displayed flushes of self-importance and of the sharp voice to be expected from the richest man in France, who after all was rather good-looking and not yet thirty-six. "He's shyly insolent," said Monsieur de Croisenois. Count de Caylus, Norbert, and two or three other young men with mustaches joked as they liked about him, bantering back and forth, without his knowing what they were up to. And then, as one o'clock sounded, they sent him on his way:

"Are your famous Arab horses waiting at the gate, and in this weather?" Norbert asked him.

"No, these are new, and cost a lot less," replied Monsieur de Thaler. "The left-hand horse cost me five thousand francs, and that on the right was only three thousand. But do please understand that I use the latter only at night, because his trot perfectly matches the other one's."

Norbert's question had made the count think it was proper for a man like him to really care about his horses, and not leave them out to get soaked. He left, and the other men soon went as well, still making fun of him.

"So," reflected Julien, hearing their laughter as they went down the stairs, "they've let me see the other extreme of my situation! I don't have an income of four hundred francs, and here I am, side by side with a man who has an income of four hundred francs an hour—and they're making fun of him. . . . Seeing such things can cure you of jealousy."

CHAPTER FIVE

SENSITIVITY AND A DEVOUT ARISTOCRATIC LADY

There, an idea with any life in it seems gross, they're so used to flat, dull
language. Watch out, if you let them hear you talk well!
—FAUBLAS

After several months of being on trial, here is where Julien had gotten
to, the day the house steward handed him his third-quarter salary.
Monsieur de La Mole had given him responsibility for his properties in Brittany and Normandy; Julien had to make frequent trips.
He was also put in charge of correspondence dealing with the celebrated case against Father de Frilair. Father Pirard gave him the help
he needed.

Using short marginal notes scribbled by the marquis, Julien dealt
with documents of every sort; of the letters he composed, virtually all
were signed and sent.

His professors at the theological school complained he did not
work hard enough, but still viewed him as their best student. All these
labors, performed with the ardor of stifled ambition, had quickly
sapped the fresh complexion he'd brought from the provinces. In the
eyes of the young seminarians who were his classmates, Julien's pallor
was a sign of worthiness; he found them a good deal less wretched, and
much less worshipful of money, than those in Besançon; and they
thought him a consumptive. The marquis had given him a horse. Worried that his classmates might see him out on horseback, Julien told
them this was exercise, and had been prescribed by his doctors.

Father Pirard had taken him to several Jansenist communities.
Julien was astonished: religion was inextricably tied, in his mind, to
hypocrisy and the hope of acquiring riches. He admired these pious,
stern men who did not concern themselves with making ends meet.
Several Jansenists had become friendly, and given him advice. It was a
new world opening in front of him. At one Jansenist community he
met Count Altamira, nearly six feet tall, devout and a liberal, who had

been condemned to death in his native country. He was struck by the strange contrast between piety and love of liberty.

Julien's relationship with Count Norbert was somewhat strained. Norbert had seen Julien overreacting to some of his friends' jests. His manners having once or twice been proven inadequate, Julien never allowed himself to speak to Mademoiselle de La Mole. Everyone was perfectly polite to him, but he felt himself less well regarded. His provincial good sense explained what had happened by the vulgar proverb: *New meat, new appetite.*

Perhaps he had learned a bit, since those early days, or more likely his initial enchantment with Parisian urbanity had worn off.

He had no sooner put down his pen than he fell into the grip of deadly boredom. It was the withering effect of a politeness that was wonderful, but never unguarded, perfectly calibrated to social status: this was the mark of high society. But no feeling heart could ignore its artificiality.

Of course, provincial society is rather common, and impolite. But provincials let themselves go a bit when they answer you. In the de La Mole house, no one ever violated Julien's self-respect, but quite often, at the end of the day, he wanted to weep. In the provinces, a café waiter takes a genuine interest if you hurt yourself coming in, but if the nature of your accident in some way shames you, he will repeat ten times over the words you cannot bear to hear. In Paris, people are careful to hide their laughter, but you remain forever a stranger.

Let us pass over in silence the many petty events that might have made Julien look ridiculous, had he not been, after a fashion, beneath ridicule. His insane sensitivity made him commit thousands of blunders. His amusements were entirely precautionary: he practiced with his pistol, every day, and was one of the best pupils of the very best fencing master. The moment he had a bit of free time, instead of spending it with a book, as he used to do, he hurried to the riding school, requesting that he be given the most vicious horses they had. When he rode with the director of the school, he was regularly thrown by his horse.

The marquis found him handy, because he worked so doggedly, he was silent, and he had a good mind; gradually, everything difficult to untangle was entrusted to him. The marquis himself, when his high ambitions did not claim his attention, was an excellent man of business: positioned as he was to know what would be happening, he played the market well. He bought houses, he bought woodland, but he had a quick temper. He gave away thousands of francs, and fought lawsuits over hundreds. Passionate rich men go into business for amusement, not for results. What the marquis needed was a head steward who would clarify his finances and put them in order, ready to hand.

Madame de La Mole, though by nature restrained, sometimes made fun of Julien. Anything *unexpected,* spawned by sensitivity, is every great lady's nightmare, since it is the direct opposite of propriety. Two or three times, the marquis defended him: "He may seem silly in your drawing room, but at his desk he's heroic." For his part, Julien fancied he knew the marquise's secret. She took the trouble to find everything of interest the moment Baron de La Joumate was announced. She was cold, her face totally inexpressive. He was small, slim, ugly, very well dressed, lived his life at court and, for the most part, said nothing about anything. That was how his mind worked. Madame de La Mole would have been passionately happy, for the first time in her life, had she been able to make him her daughter's husband.

CHAPTER SIX

PRONUNCIATION

Their lofty mission is to calmly judge the petty events of which nations' daily lives are composed. Their wisdom is expected to keep great anger from coming out of petty issues, or out of events which rumor transforms, in carrying them abroad.

—GRATIUS

For someone who had in a sense just landed, whose pride kept him from ever asking a question, Julien did not make many truly serious mistakes. One day, thrust into a café on Saint-Honoré Street, when a sudden shower struck, a tall man in a heavy frock coat, made of wool interwoven with beaver hair, was so startled by Julien's somber stare that he stared right back, exactly as Mademoiselle Amanda's lover had done, one day in Besançon.

Julien had too often blamed himself for allowing that insult to go by to tolerate this stare. He demanded an explanation. The frock-coated man replied with the filthiest insults. Everyone in the café gathered around them; passersby stopped in the doorway. As a cautious provincial, Julien never went out without his pistols; his hand closed convulsively on them, in his pocket. But he was sensible, and limited himself to repeating, regularly, "Sir, your address? You are despicable."

At last, his firmness in employing only these six words made an impression on the crowd.

"Damn! That man who's talking all the time has got to give him his address."

The frock-coated man, hearing other people say the same thing, threw five or six calling cards at Julien. Luckily, none of them hit our hero, and he had vowed not to use his pistols unless he was touched. The frock coat left, though not without coming back, over and over, shaking his fist and hurling insults.

Julien was soaked in perspiration. "So scum like him can do this to me!" he said to himself, furious. "How can I smother this humiliating sensitivity?"

Where would he find a second? He had no friends. He had had a few acquaintances, but after six weeks they had all dropped him. "I am unsocial, and I'm being harshly punished for it," he thought. At last he remembered a man named Liéven, who had been a lieutenant in the Ninety-sixth, a poor devil with whom he had often fenced. He was honest with this man.

"I'll be glad to be your second," Liéven said, "but on one condition. If you don't wound your man, you'll fight with me, on the spot."

"Agreed," said Julien, delighted, and they went to find Monsieur C. de Beauvoisis, at the address shown on his cards, in the heart of Faubourg Saint-Germain.

It was seven in the morning. Not until he was being announced at the man's house did Julien reflect that this might well be Madame de

Rênal's young relative, formerly of the French Embassy at Rome, or Naples, who had given the singer, Géronimo, a letter of recommendation.

Julien had handed the tall servant one of the cards thrown at him the night before, and one of his own.

They were kept waiting, he and his second, for a full three-quarters of an hour; finally they were ushered into a wonderfully elegant room. There they found a tall young man, dressed up like a tailor's dummy; his face displayed both the beauty and the insignificance of the Greek ideal. His remarkably narrow head bore a pyramid of intensely blond hair, elaborately curled, not a hair out of place. "This damned fop," thought the lieutenant of the Ninety-sixth, "made us wait so he could get himself all curled." The man's striped dressing gown, his morning trousers, everything right down to his embroidered slippers, was absolutely in fashion and wonderfully trim. His face, noble and empty, indicated that his ideas were proper, and very rare: he was the absolute model of the amiable good fellow, horrified by the unexpected and by all witty remarks; he was steeped in sobriety.

The lieutenant of the Ninety-sixth having explained that keeping a man waiting so long, especially after having thrown your card in his face, was yet another insult, Julien stalked into Monsieur de Beauvoisis's rooms. He meant to be insolent, though at the same time he wished to preserve good form.

He was so startled by Monsieur de Beauvoisis's gentle good manners, his demeanor at once formal, weighty, and pleased with himself, and by the admirable elegance which surrounded him, that in the twinkling of an eye he dropped all thought of insolence. This was not the man he'd encountered the night before. He was so stunned to find someone thus distinguished, instead of the coarse fellow he'd met in the café, that he was unable to say a thing. He handed over one of the cards that had been thrown at him.

"It is my name," said the stylish man, in whom Julien's black garments and the wickedly early hour of seven in the morning inspired very little respect. "But I don't understand, on my honor. . . ."

The way he pronounced these last words partially restored Julien's annoyance.

"I'm here to fight with you, monsieur." And he quickly explained the whole thing.

Monsieur Charles de Beauvoisis, after more mature reflection, was satisfied by the cut of Julien's black clothing. "That's from Staub, I see it quite clearly," he said to himself while he listened. "That vest is in good taste; his boots are fine. But on the other hand, those black clothes at this hour of the morning! . . . They'll give him a better chance of dodging the bullet," said the Chevalier de Beauvoisis to himself.

Having determined these matters, he resumed his perfect politeness, and treated Julien almost as if they were equals. It was rather a long conversation, and a delicate business, but in the end Julien could not deny the evidence. The very well-born young man he was facing did not in any way resemble the coarse person who, the night before, had so insulted him.

Julien found it very hard to leave; he felt obliged to prolong the discussion. He noted the Chevalier de Beauvoisis's self-sufficiency—and he had carefully described himself as "chevalier," in speaking to Julien, shocked at having been addressed simply as "monsieur."

Our hero admired the sobriety, mixed with a certain modest conceit, that de Beauvoisis never discarded for an instant. Julien was startled to see the odd way his tongue moved, as he pronounced his words. . . . But in the end, no matter what, there was not the slightest reason to quarrel with him.

With immense courtesy, the young diplomat offered nevertheless to do battle, but the former lieutenant of the Ninety-sixth, having sat there for an hour, his legs parted, his hands on his legs, his elbows akimbo, had decided that his friend Monsieur Sorel had no interest whatever in picking a German-style quarrel with a man, because someone else had stolen that man's calling cards.

Julien left in a bad mood. The Chevalier de Beauvoisis's carriage was waiting in the courtyard, in front of the steps. By chance, Julien looked up and recognized the coachman as his man from the night before.

Seeing him, grasping at his heavy coat, throwing him down from the driver's seat, and covering him with blows from his own whip, was a moment's work. Two servants decided to defend their comrade; they hit at Julien and, at the same time, Julien drew one of his pistols and fired at them; they ran off. All this, too, took only a moment.

The Chevalier de Beauvoisis came down the steps with amusing somberness, repeating in his lordly accent, "What's this? What's this?" He was clearly anxious to know, but diplomatic aloofness did not permit him to show any greater interest. Once he knew what had been going on, hereditary arrogance was still visibly mixed with the cool, casual good humor that ought never to leave a diplomat's face.

The lieutenant of the Ninety-sixth understood that Monsieur de Beauvoisis now wanted to fight, and he tried, diplomatically, to preserve for his friend the advantages of taking the initiative.

"This time," he exclaimed, "there's cause for a duel!"

"More than enough, I should think," replied the diplomat.

"This rascal is dismissed," he told his servants. "Let someone else climb up." The carriage door was opened; the chevalier absolutely insisted that Julien and his second precede him. They hunted up one of Monsieur de Beauvoisis's friends, who directed them to a quiet spot. There was a most pleasant conversation, on the way. The only odd aspect was the diplomat's dressing gown.

"These gentlemen," thought Julien, "although they're noblemen, are not anything like so boring as those who dine with Monsieur de La Mole. And I see why," he added, a moment later. "They allow themselves indecorous talk." Some dancers were mentioned, who had been honored by the audience, at a ballet given the previous evening. The gentlemen told certain spicy stories that neither Julien nor his second, the lieutenant of the Ninety-sixth, had ever heard. Julien was not so stupid that he pretended to know them; he openly admitted his ignorance. His candor pleased the chevalier's friend; he had told these stories in very substantial detail, and told them extremely well.

One thing infinitely astonished Julien. A temporary altar, being erected in the middle of the street, for the Corpus Christi procession, forced the carriage to stop for a moment. The gentlemen permitted themselves several witticisms: the parish priest, as they told it, was an archbishop's son. Nothing of the sort could possibly have been said under the roof of the Marquis de La Mole, who wanted to become a duke.

The duel lasted only a moment. Julien had been shot in the arm; they tied it up with handkerchiefs; they moistened it with brandy; and the Chevalier de Beauvoisis very politely requested that he be allowed to bring Julien home, in the same carriage that had brought them. When Julien gave his address as the de La Mole residence, he saw the young diplomat and his friend exchange glances. Julien's cab was still where he had left it, but he found these gentlemen's conversation infinitely more amusing than that of the good lieutenant of the Ninety-sixth.

"My God!" thought Julien. "A duel—that's all there is to it! How glad I am to have recognized that coachman! How miserable I'd have been to endure yet another insult in a café!" The amusing conversation went on almost without interruption. Julien realized that diplomatic affectation had some purpose.

"So boredom," he told himself, "isn't built into conversation among people of high birth! These two joke about the Corpus Christi procession; they let themselves tell rather scabrous stories, with lots of vivid details. Really, they fall short only when it comes to rationality in political matters, and they more than compensate with their gracious speech and the perfect rightness of what they say." Julien felt a strong liking for them. "How happy I'd be, seeing them often!"

They had barely driven away when the Chevalier de Beauvoisis went hurriedly in search of information. There was not much to learn.

The chevalier was most anxious to know with whom he had fought a duel. Might it be proper to pay him a call? What little he had learned was not encouraging.

"This is perfectly awful!" he said to his second. "How could I possibly admit to having fought a duel with Monsieur de La Mole's *secretary*, and all because my coachman stole those calling cards."

"Certainly, this would offer an opportunity for ridicule."

That same evening, the Chevalier de Beauvoisis and his friend began to say, everywhere they went, that Monsieur Sorel, in addition to being an irreproachable young man, was the natural son of one of the Marquis de La Mole's close friends. There was no difficulty having the tale accepted. Once it was properly in place, the young diplomat and his friend could condescend to pay visits to Julien, during the two weeks he spent in his room. Julien admitted to them that he'd never in his life been to the opera.

"That's awful," he was told. "There's nowhere else to go. The first time you're allowed out, you must come to Rossini's *Count Ory*."

At the opera, Chevalier de Beauvoisis introduced him to the famous singer, Géronimo, who was then having a great success.

Julien virtually courted the chevalier. He was enchanted by the young man's self-respect, blended with a mysterious weightiness and foppishness. For example: the chevalier stammered a bit, having often been honored by the company of a very great lord who suffered from this defect. Julien had never known, united in one person, such entertaining ridiculousness and such perfect manners, of the sort a poor provincial could only try to imitate.

Julien was seen at the opera with the Chevalier de Beauvoisis; the relationship made people talk about him.

"Well!" Monsieur de La Mole said to him, one day. "So now you're the natural son of a wealthy man from Franche-Comté, who happens to be my close friend?"

The marquis cut off Julien's reply; our hero wanted to protest that he had not in any way contributed to, or sanctioned, this rumor.

"Monsieur de Beauvoisis was not anxious to be known for fighting duels with a carpenter's son."

"I realize that, I quite realize that," said Monsieur de La Mole. "Now it's up to me to regularize this tale, which I find useful. But I have a favor to ask of you, and it won't cost you more than a slender half hour of your time. Every day there is to be an opera, go and watch as high society makes its exit. I still see in you some provincial mannerisms, which you need to be rid of. Besides, it's not a bad thing to know, even by sight, some of the important people to whom, some day, I might send you on an errand. Go by the box office so they'll know who you are. They'll admit you without any difficulty."

CHAPTER SEVEN

AN ATTACK OF GOUT

*And so I was promoted, not because I deserved it,
but because my master had the gout.*
—BERTOLOTTI

The reader may well be startled by this free and almost friendly tone, but we've forgotten to mention that, for six weeks, the marquis had been confined to his home by an attack of gout.

Mademoiselle de La Mole and her mother were at Hyères, visiting the marquise's mother. Count Norbert saw his father only at intervals: they were on excellent terms, but had nothing to say, one to the other. Monsieur de La Mole, thus reduced to Julien, was amazed to find that his secretary really had ideas. He had Julien read the newspapers; the young secretary was soon able to pick out the interesting passages. There was a new paper, which the marquis loathed; he had sworn never to read it, but talked about it every day. Julien laughed. Annoyed at the contemporary world, the marquis had him read Livy; Julien's improvised translation from the Latin pleased him.

One day the marquis said, his voice taking on the overpoliteness that often simply irritated Julien:

"My dear Sorel, allow me to present you with a blue suit. When you've had a chance to fetch it, come back here. You'll have become, in my eyes, the younger brother of Count de Chaulnes—that is, the son of my old friend, the duke."

Julien did not particularly understand what this was all about, but that same night he paid a visit, wearing the blue suit. The marquis treated him like an equal. Julien was quite sensitive enough to appreciate true politeness, but he did not understand its subtler aspects. He would have sworn, before this new whim, that the marquis could not possibly have received him with greater respect. "What a gifted man!" Julien said to himself. When he rose to leave, the marquis apologized, since his gout prevented him from showing Julien to the door.

The whole strange business was troubling. "Is he making fun of me?" Julien wondered. He sought Father Pirard's advice; less polite than the marquis, the good priest responded only by whistling and changing the subject. Next morning, Julien wore his black suit when he went to the marquis, carrying a letter case full of letters to be signed. He was received just as, before this new development, he had always been received. That evening, wearing the blue suit, the marquis once again behaved differently, exactly as polite as he'd been the first time Julien wore blue.

"Seeing that you're not too profoundly bored, making these kind visits to a poor old man," the marquis told him, "why don't you tell him all the trifling episodes of your life, but straightforwardly and without thinking about anything except telling them clearly and in such a fashion that they'll be entertaining? Entertainment is essential," the marquis continued. "That's life's only reality. A man can hardly save my life each and every day, or be perpetually giving me gifts of a million francs. But if I had old Rivarol here, every day, right here next to my couch, he'd take away an hour of boredom and pain. I knew him well, in Hamburg, when we were in exile."

And the marquis told Julien tales of Antoine Rivarol among the locals of Hamburg: it took four of them to understand one witty remark.

Reduced to the company of his little ecclesiastic, Monsieur de La Mole sought to liven him up. He pushed at Julien's pride. Since he'd been asked to tell the truth, Julien made up his mind to tell everything. But he was silent about two matters: his fanatical adoration of a man whose very name would put the marquis in a foul mood, and his own utter lack of faith, which did not fit well with a priestly future. The episode with the Chevalier de Beauvoisis fitted very well indeed. The marquis laughed until he cried, hearing the scene at the café in Saint-Honoré Street, when the coachman had covered our hero with filthy insults. It was a time of perfect, frank openness between protector and protected.

Monsieur de La Mole grew more interested in this strange person. To start with, he indulged Julien's absurdities, in order to be entertained by them, but soon found it even more interesting to gently correct the young man's faulty sense of the world. "Other provincials who come to Paris," the marquis thought, "admire everything. This one hates everything. They're dreadfully affected; he's not affected enough, so the fools take him for a fool."

Winter's cold chills prolonged his attack of gout; it lasted some months.

"One grows attached to a fine spaniel," the marquis said to himself, "so why do I feel ashamed of growing attached to this little ecclesiastic? He's odd, but fresh. I treat him like a son. All right: What harm does that do? This whim, if it lasts, will cost me a two-thousand-franc diamond, in my will."

Having once understood Julien's steadiness, the marquis gave him new responsibilities every day.

Julien was frightened to discover that this great lord sometimes gave him contradictory instructions on the same subject.

This could seriously compromise him. Accordingly, Julien regularly brought along an account book, in which he wrote down his orders, and the marquis initialed them. Julien hired a clerk, who copied every directive, in each and every instance, into a private notebook. All letters were copied into the same book.

It seemed, at first, the most ridiculous, boring procedure in the world. But in less than two months the marquis became aware of its advantages. Julien suggested that they hire another clerk, with banking experience, who would maintain double-entry accounts for all receipts, and all expenses, in connection with Julien's property administration.

These procedures so enlightened the marquis about the actual state of his affairs that he could, with great pleasure, undertake two or three new speculations without the assistance of his usual intermediary, who had been swindling him.

"Take yourself three thousand francs," the marquis told his young assistant one day.

"That could be misunderstood, sir."

"So how would you prefer it?" asked the marquis, annoyed.

"I'd like you to write an order and set it down, signed, in the account book. The order ought to give me three thousand francs. In any case, it was Father Pirard who thought up all this accounting." With an expression every bit as bored as that of the actor who plays the Marquis de Moncade, while he listens to his steward, Monsieur Poisson, giving his report, the marquis wrote the order.

That evening, when Julien appeared in his blue suit, no business matters were even mentioned. The marquis's benevolence was so flattering to our hero's perpetually painful self-respect that, in spite of himself, he soon felt a degree of affection for the pleasant old man. Not that, in Parisian terms, Julien possessed any sensibility, but simply that he was not a monster, and that no one, since the old surgeon-major's death, had spoken to him so kindly. And he was startled to realize that the marquis was more deftly discreet, in dealing with our hero's sense of self-worth, than the old surgeon-major had been. It came to him, at last, that the surgeon-major was prouder of his small medal than the marquis was, wearing the noblest award in all France. The marquis's father had been a very great lord.

One day, when they had finished their morning business, Julien being dressed in business black, he stayed on for two hours, so entertaining the marquis that he insisted Julien absolutely had to accept a sheaf of banknotes, just brought from the Stock Exchange by Monsieur de La Mole's intermediary.

"I trust, Monsieur Marquis, I will not seem deficient in that deep respect which I owe you, if I request you to permit me a few words."

"Speak, my friend."

"I should prefer that Monsieur Marquis graciously allow me to decline this gift. It is not meant for the man in black, and it would entirely destroy the behavior so kindly permitted to the man in blue." He bowed with great respect, and left without a glance.

This was very entertaining to the marquis. He told it to Father Pirard that night.

"I must finally admit to something, my dear Father. I am aware of Julien's birth, and I authorize you not to keep any of this secret."

"He behaved nobly, this morning," the marquis thought, "so I hereby ennoble him."

Not long afterward, the marquis was able to go out once more.

"Go spend some months in London," he told Julien. "Special couri-

ers, and others, will bring you what letters I receive, bearing my nota-
tions. You will compose the replies and send them back to me, along
with the original letters. I calculate that the delay will be no more than
five days."

Riding toward Calais, in the post carriage, Julien was shocked by
the trivial, so-called business on which he had been dispatched.

We will say nothing of the intense hate, virtually horror, that he
felt, setting foot on English soil. You are well aware of his insane passion for Bonaparte. In every officer he saw Sir Hudson Lowe, commander at Saint-Helena; in every great lord he saw Lord Bathurst,
war secretary, giving orders for the infamies Napoleon experienced in
this island prison, and for that being rewarded by ten years in the government.

At London, he finally understood high foppishness. He became
friendly with young Russian noblemen, who initiated him.

"My dear Sorel, you're absolutely born to it," they told him. "Nature has given you that cold bearing, *a thousand leagues from feeling anything,* which we have to work so hard to attain."

"You've not understood your own time," Prince Korasoff told him.
"*Always do the opposite of what people expect from you.* That, upon my honor,
is our time's only religion. Avoid foolishness, and affectation, which
would cause people to expect foolery and affectation from you, and
you'd no longer be observing the rules."

Julien covered himself with glory, one day, in the Duke de Fitz-
Folke's drawing room, where he and Prince Korasoff had been invited
to dine. They waited for an entire hour. There were twenty people, all
waiting: Julien's demeanor, in this small, suspended throng, is still referred to by young diplomats in London.

Despite his foppish friends, he longed to meet the celebrated Philip
Vane, the only philosopher England has had, after Locke. He found
him finishing his seventh year in prison. "You don't fool with the aristocracy, in this country," thought Julien. Moreover, Vane had been dishonored, vilified, etc.

Julien saw that he was a merry fellow; aristocratic anger amused
him. "Now there," said Julien to himself, as he left the prison, "there is
the only cheerful man I've yet to see in England."

"A tyrant's most useful idea is God," Vane had said to him. . . .

We suppress the remainder of his philosophy as pure *cynicism.*

When he returned to France: "What entertaining notions have you brought me, out of England?" the marquis asked him. . . . Julien was silent.

"What ideas have you brought, entertaining or not?" the marquis said again, briskly.

"First of all," said Julien, "the wisest man in England is insane for an hour every day. He's troubled by the demon of suicide, which is the country's deity.

"Second, intelligence, and even genius, are depreciated by twenty-five percent, at the moment of landing in England.

"Third, nothing in the world is as beautiful, as fine, as moving as the English countryside."

"Now it's my turn," said the marquis:

"First, what made you say, at the Russian ambassador's ball, that France boasts of three hundred thousand young men, twenty-five years old, who passionately long for war? Does that seem to you properly respectful of royalty?"

"How can we chat with important diplomats?" said Julien. "They have a mania for serious debate. If you stick to the usual newspaper formulae, they think you're a fool. If you allow yourself to say something true, and new, they're astonished. They don't know how to answer, and the next day, at seven in the morning, they have the embassy's first secretary announce that you've been objectionable."

"Not bad, not at all bad," said the marquis, laughing. "But in any case, I'll wager, Monsieur Profundity, that you haven't figured out what you were sent to England to do."

"Excuse me," replied Julien. "I had dinner every week at our ambassador's home, and he is the most polite of men."

"You went to look for this medal," the marquis said, handing it to him. "I don't want you to leave off wearing black, but I'm also used to the more entertaining tone I employ with the man in blue. Until further orders, here's what you're to do: pay attention. When I see you wearing this medal, you'll be the younger son of my friend, the Duke of Chaulnes, who plainly has for the last six months been functioning

as a diplomat. Please note," added the marquis, speaking very seriously and cutting off any expression of gratitude, "that I do not wish
to raise you above your proper station. That is always a mistake, and
just as unfortunate for the protector as for the protected. When my
lawsuits begin to bore you, or when you're no longer acceptable to me,
I'll find you a good parish, like that of our friend Father Pirard, and
that's all," added the marquis, rather curtly.

The medal comforted Julien's pride; he spoke more readily and
more often. He took offense less often, and no longer thought himself
butt of the sort of remarks, susceptible to less polite interpretation,
that occur in animated conversations and are sometimes spoken by
us all.

The medal earned him an extremely odd visit, that of the Baron de
Valenod, who had come to Paris to thank the minister for making him
a baron and for consenting to meet with him. He was going to become
mayor of Verrières, replacing Monsieur de Rênal.

Julien roared with laughter, though only inwardly, when Monsieur
de Valenod informed him that they'd just discovered Monsieur de
Rênal to be a Jacobin. The truth was that a new election was to be
held, and the freshly minted baron was the government's candidate,
as he was of the district's electoral college, as strongly right-wing as
anything could be, and Monsieur de Rênal was supported by the liberals.

Julien tried in vain to learn anything about Madame de Rênal; the
baron appeared to well remember their former rivalry, and was impenetrable. Indeed, in the end he asked Julien to seek his father's vote.
Julien promised to write him.

"Really, Monsieur Chevalier, you ought to introduce me to the
Marquis de La Mole."

"Indeed, *I ought to!*" Julien thought. "But he's such a rascal! . . ."

"In point of fact," he answered, "I'm much too unimportant, in the
de La Mole household, to take it on myself to introduce anyone."

He told all this to the marquis.

That evening, he told him of Valenod's ambitions, as well as what
he'd been doing, and how, ever since 1814.

"Not only," replied Monsieur de La Mole, most seriously, "will you present the new baron to me tomorrow, but afterward I will invite him to dinner. His will be one of our new districts."

"In that case," said Julien coolly, "I should like my father to have the post of director of the Pauper's Bureau."

"Good, good!" said the marquis, becoming cheerful once more. "Agreed. I was expecting a morality lesson. You're shaping up."

Baron de Valenod informed Julien that the lottery licensee in Verrières had just died. It seemed to our hero a good joke to give the job to Monsieur de Cholin, that old imbecile whose illiterate petition he had found, once, in cleaning the room occupied by the Marquis de La Mole. The marquis laughed heartily, as Julien recited that petition to him, while he was signing a letter seeking this post from the minister of finance.

Monsieur de Cholin had just been nominated when Julien learned that the post had been sought by the district delegation, on behalf of Monsieur Gros, the eminent mathematician. This noble, generous man had an income of only fourteen hundred francs, and every year lent six hundred to the license holder who'd just died, to help him raise his family.

Julien was stunned by what he'd done. "It's nothing," he told himself. "I'll have to be unjust many times over, if I want to get to the top, and somehow cover them up with pretty, sentimental phrases. Poor Monsieur Gros! He deserves this medal, and I have it, and I'm bound to follow the lead of the government which gave it to me."

CHAPTER EIGHT

WHICH MEDALS ARE HONORABLE?

"Your water does not refresh me," said the thirsty demon. "Yet it's the coolest well in all of Turkestan."

—PELLICO

Julien came back, one day, from the charming estate of Villequier, bordering on the Seine, to which Monsieur de La Mole was especially attracted, for of all his properties it was the only one that had been owned, once upon a time, by his famous ancestor, Boniface de La

Mole. Julien found the marquise and her daughter, newly returned from Hyères.

Julien had become a dandy, and understood the art of life in Paris. His cool demeanor toward Mademoiselle de La Mole was perfection itself. He appeared to have no memory whatever of her asking, so gaily, for the details of his tumble from a horse.

She found him taller and paler. Neither his figure nor his clothing retained anything of the provincial. But this was not true of his conversation, in which there remained, still, entirely too much of the serious, of the assertive. In spite of such intellectual traits, he showed no signs of inferior status, thanks largely to his pride: one simply felt that, still, he viewed too much as important. Yet he was clearly a man who would back up what he said.

"His touch needs an improving lightness, but not his mind," Mademoiselle de La Mole told her father, teasing him about the medal he'd given Julien. "For the last year and a half, my brother's been asking you for one—and he's a de La Mole! . . ."

"Yes. But Julien can surprise you, which is not something one can say of the de La Mole in question."

The Duke de Retz was announced.

An irresistible fit of yawning descended on Mathilde; she was aware of the old, gilt-covered objects in her father's drawing room, and the old visitors who came there. She had a vivid sense of the life she was resuming, here in Paris, in all its perfect boredom. Yet when she'd been in Hyères, she had missed Paris.

"And I'm still only nineteen!" she thought. "This is the time for happiness, according to all these gilt-edged morons!" She was looking at eight or ten brand-new books of poetry that had accumulated on the long, narrow table, fixed to the drawing room wall during her days in Provence. Unfortunately, she was smarter than Messieurs de Croisenois, de Caylus, de Luz, and her other friends. She could just imagine what they'd be telling her about the lovely skies of Provence, and poetry, and the South, etc., etc.

Her beautiful eyes, full of the most intense boredom—and, worse still, despair of ever being happy—lingered on Julien. At least he was not exactly like all the others.

"Monsieur Sorel," she said, speaking briskly, curt, and in no way feminine (as all high society's young women were expected to speak), "Monsieur Sorel, will you come to the Duke de Retz's ball, tonight?"

"Mademoiselle, I've never had the honor of being introduced to the duke." (It might be said that these words, and especially the ducal title, ripped the skin off this proud provincial's mouth.)

"He has asked my brother to bring you and, if you do come, you might tell me all about Villequier. There's some talk of going there, this spring. I'd like to know if the house is livable, and whether the neighborhood is as pretty as they say. So many reputations are so totally undeserved!"

Julien did not reply.

"Come to the ball with my brother," she added, very dryly.

Julien bowed respectfully. "And this," he thought, "even at a ball, is what I owe every member of this family. I'm paid to handle the family's business, am I not? God only knows if what I'll say to the daughter might not conflict with the father's plans, or the brother's, or the mother's! This is exactly like a ruling prince's court. You need to be an absolute nothing, and yet no one should have any reason to complain about you.

"How I dislike this towering little girl!" he thought, watching mademoiselle walk over to where her mother had summoned her, so she could be presented to the wives of some of their friends. "Whatever fashion she assumes, she overdoes it; her dress is falling off her shoulders. . . . She's even paler than before she went on that trip. . . . Her hair is absolutely colorless, it's so blonde! You could say the daylight goes right through it! . . . And what arrogance, when she greets people, when she just looks at them! She holds herself, she moves, like a queen!"

Mademoiselle de La Mole had just called to her brother, precisely when he was leaving the drawing room.

Count Norbert came over to Julien.

"My dear Sorel," he said, "where would you like me to fetch you from, at midnight, when I come to escort you to Monsieur de Retz's ball? He himself asked me, in very plain terms, to bring you."

"I'm well aware to whom I owe so many kindnesses," replied Julien, bowing very deeply.

His mood was so foul that, there being nothing to take offense at, in Norbert's polite, even concerned, manner of speech, he directed his annoyance toward his own response. It seemed to him clouded by a vulgar servility.

That evening, arriving at the ball, he was struck by the magnificence of the de Retz mansion. The entranceway courtyard was roofed over by a huge, crimson-colored canvas awning, dotted with golden stars. Nothing could have been more elegant. Underneath the awning, the courtyard had been transformed into an orange-tree grove, with flowering oleanders in bloom. All the containers had been carefully set very deep, so orange trees and oleanders seemed to be growing right out of the ground. The pathway on which the carriages drove had been sanded.

The whole thing seemed, to our provincial hero, utterly extraordinary. This kind of splendor was new to him: in a flash his mood changed from foul to fair. Norbert had been happy, as they traveled to the ball, but Julien had seen nothing but darkness. The moment they drove into the courtyard, they switched places.

Norbert paid attention only to those few details, in the midst of such magnificence, which no one had been able to take care of. He calculated the cost of everything, and the higher the total went, the more jealous he seemed to grow—and, as Julien noticed, the worse his mood became.

Our hero, already enchanted, admiring, and almost shy from so great a flood of emotion, reached the first drawing room, where people were dancing. The press of the crowd was so great, on the way to the second drawing room, that he had to stay where he was. (This second room was decorated to look like Grenada's Alhambra.)

"She's the queen of the ball, you can't deny it," a young, mustached man was saying; his shoulder was pressed against Julien's chest.

"Mademoiselle Fourmont, who's been the reigning beauty all winter," said the man next to him, "knows she has to settle for second place. Just see what a face she's making."

"Really, Fourmont's set all her sails, determined to please. Look— look at that gracious smile, the instant the dance sets her off by herself. On my honor, that's simply hysterical."

"Mademoiselle de La Mole keeps her pleasure extremely well in hand, even though she's fully aware what a triumph she's having. She seems to be trying not to appear too pleasant, if she does speak to anyone."

"Now there's the art of seduction!"

Julien tried, unsuccessfully, to catch a glimpse of this seductive woman: seven or eight taller men blocked his view.

"There's a good deal of the coquette in that terribly grand modesty," said the young man with a mustache.

"And those big blue eyes, which she lowers so slowly, just when you think they're about to betray her," said his neighbor. "My Lord, how very cunning."

"Notice how, next to her, the lovely Mademoiselle Fourmont seems downright common," said a third man.

"That modesty is really saying: 'How nice I could be to you, if you were the man worthy of me!' "

"And just who could be worthy of the sublime Mathilde?" said the first man. "Some royal prince, handsome, witty, strong, a military hero, and no older than twenty."

"The Emperor of Russia's natural son . . . for whom, in recognition of such a marriage, a kingdom would be created . . . or perhaps, in the end, Count de Thaler, who looks like a dressed-up peasant. . . ."

The doorway had opened. Julien was able to go in.

"If she strikes these toy soldiers as so remarkable," he thought, "she's worth having a look at. I'll find out what these fellows imagine is true perfection."

While he was trying to catch her eye, Mathilde looked at him. "Duty calls," Julien told himself. But he was not feeling wretched, though his enjoyment could not be told from his face. His curiosity grew, the nearer he came, and it grew still quicker on account of Mathilde's gown, extremely low on her shoulders—a sensation, however, that did not do much for his self-esteem. "She's lovely, yes, but she's also very young," he thought. There were still five or six young men, among them those he had heard discussing her, between him and Mathilde.

"You, sir," she said to Julien, "you've been here the entire winter. Isn't this really the best ball of the season?"

He did not reply.

"I think," she went on, "this is a fine Coulon they're dancing, and these ladies are doing it to perfection."

The other young men turned around to see who might be the happy man from whom, clearly, she wanted to have an answer. It was not an encouraging one.

"I wouldn't know how to properly judge, mademoiselle. I spend my life writing: this is the first ball of such magnificence I've ever seen."

The young, mustached men were horrified.

"How wise you are, Monsieur Sorel," came her reply, her interest more marked. "You see all these balls, all these festivities, like a philosopher—like Jean-Jacques Rousseau. Such extravagance astonishes, but it does not seduce you."

The mention of Rousseau cooled his mind and drove all illusions from his heart. His mouth framed a look of disdain, perhaps a bit exaggerated.

"Jean-Jacques Rousseau," he answered, "is simply a fool when he tries to analyze high society. He knows nothing about it; he displays the soul of an upstart servant."

"He wrote *The Social Contract*," she said worshipfully.

"But even as he argues for a republic, and the overthrow of monarchical ranks and stations, this upstart is absolutely drunk with joy if a duke condescends to alter his after-dinner walk so he can accompany one of his friends."

"Oh, yes: at Montmorency, when the Duke de Luxembourg walked toward Paris, with a certain Monsieur Coindet..." replied Mademoiselle de La Mole, with the unrestrained delight of her very first bookish pedantry. Her knowledge intoxicated her, almost like the scholar who proves the existence of King Feretrius. Julien's glance remained piercing, severe. Mathilde had experienced a rush of enthusiasm; her coparticipant's chilliness deeply shocked her. Even more, she was astonished, because she was accustomed to having exactly this effect on others.

Just then, Marquis de Croisenois pushed his way toward Mademoiselle de La Mole. He paused for a moment, three feet away, unable to get through the crowd. He looked at her, laughing at how he was being hindered. Young Marquise de Rouvray was near him; she was Mathilde's cousin. She held on to her husband's arm; they had been married only two weeks before. Marquis de Rouvray, quite as young as his wife, loved her with all the wild affection that overcomes a man who, entering upon a marriage of convenience, arranged from beginning to end by lawyers, finds a wonderfully beautiful bride. Monsieur de Rouvray was to become a duke, on the death of an exceedingly old uncle.

As the Marquis de Croisenois, unable to move toward her, looked at Mathilde, laughing, she let her big eyes, celestially blue, linger on him and his neighbors. "Could anything be as tepid," she was saying to herself, "as the whole lot of them! There's Croisenois, who'd like to marry me; he's sweet, polite, his manners are as perfect as de Rouvray's. Except for how boring they are, these are impressive people. He'd go to balls with me, looking exactly this narrow-minded, this perfectly pleased. A year after the wedding, my carriage, my hair, my clothes, my house sixty miles from Paris—it would all be as fine as it could be, precisely what ought to make an upstart, like perhaps the Countess de Roivelle, simply die of envy. And then . . . ?"

Just thinking about it bored her. Marquis de Croisenois reached her and began a conversation, but she was lost in dreams and did not listen. For her, the sound of his words mingled with the droning noise of the ball. Her eyes followed mechanically after Julien, who had moved off, respectful but proud and discontented. She noticed, off in a corner, away from the circulating crowd, Count Altamira, under a death sentence in his own country; the reader has already heard of him. In the reign of Louis XIV, one of his ancestors had married a Prince de Conti; this connection helped protect him against the Congregation of the Holy Virgin's police.

"Nothing can so distinguish a man as a death sentence," thought Mathilde. "It's the only thing one can't buy.

"Ah! What I just said to myself was indeed very well said! What a pity it didn't pop out when it could have earned me a reputation!" She had too much taste to toss a prefabricated witticism into a conversation, but she also had too much vanity not to be delighted at herself. An expression of pleasure replaced that of boredom. Marquis de

Croisenois, who had gone on talking to her, felt he was being successful, and his glibness was heightened.

"What could a spiteful person find to criticize, in this maxim of
mine?" Mathilde asked herself. "I'd tell this critic: 'A baron's title, a vicomte's, these are things that can be bought. A medal they simply give
you: my brother just got one, and what has he ever done? A promotion
isn't hard to get. Ten years in the garrison, or a relative who's minister
of war, and you're a squadron leader, like Norbert. Or an immense fortune! . . . That's the hardest to get, so it's the worthiest.' How funny! It's
exactly the opposite of everything they tell you, in books. . . . So! If
it's wealth you want, you marry Rothschild's daughter.

"My witticism really has some depth. A death sentence is still the
only thing no one will suggest that you look for."

"Do you know Count Altamira?" she asked Monsieur de Croisenois.

She seemed to be coming back from very far away, and this query
had so little connection with everything the poor marquis had been
saying to her, for the past five minutes, that his poise was shaken. But
he was a man of spirit, and well known on that score.

"Mathilde's rather odd," he thought. "That's a nuisance—but she'll
bring her husband such a superb social position! I don't know how the
Marquis de La Mole manages it. He's got ties to the best people in
both parties; he's a man who really couldn't be pulled down. Anyway,
Mathilde's strangeness might well pass for genius. When there's such
noble birth, and so much money, genius is not at all ridiculous—and
how distinguished she is! Also, when she wants to, she can exhibit such
intelligence, mixed with character and a fine sense of social timing,
that her manners, really, are quite perfect. . . ."

Doing two things at the same time, and doing them well, is difficult,
so the marquis answered her question with a blank face, as if reciting
back a lesson:

"Who doesn't know poor Altamira?" And then he told her about his
failed conspiracy—a ridiculous, absurd affair.

"Highly absurd," said Mathilde, as if speaking to herself. "But he
has *acted*. I'd like to see a *man*. Bring him to me," she said to the deeply
shocked marquis.

Count Altamira was one of the most open admirers of Mademoiselle de La Mole's haughtiness, which approached impertinence. He thought her one of the most beautiful women in Paris.

"How lovely she'd look, on a throne!" he said to Monsieur de Croisenois, letting himself be brought to her without the slightest opposition.

There is no shortage, in this world, of people wanting to create a fixed rule, which declares that nothing is so unfashionable as a conspiracy: it smells of Jacobinism. And could there be anything uglier than a failed Jacobin?

Mathilde glanced at Monsieur de Croisenois as if amused by Altamira's liberalism. But she listened to him with pleasure.

"A conspirator at a ball, that's a nice contrast," she thought. This one, with his thick black mustache, seemed to her like a sleeping lion. But she soon realized that his mind supported only a single intellectual position: *utility, admiration for whatever is useful.*

Altamira, who was still a young man, thought nothing so worthy of his attention as something, anything, that could bring bicameral legislative government to his country. So he cheerfully left Mathilde, the most seductive woman at the ball, when he saw, coming into the room, a Peruvian general.

Despairing of Europe, poor Altamira had been reduced to imagining that, when the United States of South America grew large and powerful, they would be able to give Europe back the liberty that Mirabeau, and the French Revolution, had given it.

A whirlwind of young men with mustaches was approaching Mathilde. She was very much aware that Altamira had not been seduced, and was irritated by his departure; she could see his black eyes gleaming as he talked to the Peruvian general. She contemplated the crowd of young Frenchmen with a profound seriousness none of her rivals could imitate. "Which of them," she thought, "might be capable of having himself sentenced to death, even under the most favorable of circumstances?"

The look on her face flattered the stupid among them, but made the rest uncomfortable. They dreaded an explosion of sharply pointed words, extremely hard to respond to.

"Noble birth gives a man a hundred qualities, the absence of which would offend me. I can see this in Julien, for example," thought Mathilde. "But good birth weakens those characteristics of the soul which can get a man sentenced to death."

Just then, someone near her said: "Count Altamira is the Prince of San Nazaro-Pimentel's second son. It was a Pimentel who tried to save Conradin, decapitated in 1268. It's one of the noblest families in Naples."

"There," said Mathilde to herself. "That's a really lovely proof of my maxim. High birth deprives a man of the strength of character without which no one can get himself condemned to death! So I'm fated, tonight, to babble nonsense. Since I'm a mere woman, no different from the others, well! I've got to dance." She yielded to the Marquis de Croisenois's urging: he'd been asking her for the last hour to dance with him. To keep from thinking about her bad luck as a philosopher, Mathilde wanted to be perfectly seductive. Monsieur de Croisenois was rapturously happy.

But neither dancing, nor any desire to please one of the most handsome men at court—nothing could distract her. No one could have had a greater success. She was the queen of the ball, and she knew it, but to her it did not matter.

"What a washed-out life I'd experience, with someone like Croisenois!" she said to herself as, an hour later, he led her back to her place. . . . "Where am I to find pleasure," she added sorrowfully, "if, after six months away, I can't find it right at the center of a ball which every woman in Paris would envy me? And yet, I'm surrounded by tokens of high respect from the very best society I can possibly imagine. Only a very few of these noblemen come from the bourgeosie, and there may be one or two Juliens. And then," she added, her sadness swelling, "what advantages Fate has given me—celebrity, wealth, youth! Alas! I've been given everything, except happiness.

"The most dubious of my advantages, still, are exactly those of the people who've been talking to me all night long. I have a brain, I think, because it's quite clear I make everyone afraid of me. If they have the nerve to broach a serious topic, five minutes later they're completely out of breath, as if they've discovered something truly momentous, when it's something I've been saying over and over for an hour. I'm beautiful, that's an advantage I have, for which Madame de Staël would have abandoned everything—and yet, for all that, I'm dying of boredom. Is there any reason why I'd be less bored, if I changed my name to the Marquise de Croisenois?

"But, God in heaven!" she added, very close to tears, "isn't he a perfect man? He's this century's masterpiece of education: you just look at him, and he finds something lovable, even spiritual, to tell you. He's brave. . . . But Sorel is peculiar," she told herself, and her eyes exchanged their sorrowful appearance for an angry one. "I let him know I had something to tell him, and he can't take the trouble to come back!"

CHAPTER NINE

THE BALL

Splendid, costly clothes, bright candles, perfume: so many pretty bare arms, lovely shoulders; flowers, rousing Rossini melodies, Ciceri's paintings! I'm beside myself!

UZERI, *TRAVELS*

"You're in a terrible mood," the Marquise de La Mole told her. "I warn you: at a ball, that's most ungracious."

"I just have a headache," answered Mathilde indifferently. "It's horribly warm in here."

Just then, as if to justify Mademoiselle de La Mole, old Baron de Tully got sick and collapsed; they had to carry him out. People mentioned apoplexy; it was distinctly disagreeable.

Mathilde did not care. It was her fixed prejudice never to so much as look at old men, or anyone else well known for saying sad things.

She danced in order to get away from talk about apoplexy, which this surely wasn't, because two days later the baron reappeared.

"But Monsieur Sorel has not," she said to herself, after her dancing was done. She was virtually hunting him, with her glance, when she saw him in another drawing room. Quite extraordinarily, he had apparently shed the impassive coldness that, to him, was so natural. He no longer looked like an Englishman.

"He's chatting with Count Altamira, my death-sentence man!"

Mathilde saw. "There's a dark fire in his eyes; he looks like a prince in disguise; he seems twice as proud."

Julien drifted back toward her, constantly in conversation with Altamira. She looked at him, fixedly, studying his face for signs of those high qualities that, in a man of honor, might make him worthy of a death sentence.

As he passed close by her:

"Yes," he was saying to Count Altamira, "Danton was a *man*!"

"Oh heavens! Might he be a Danton," she wondered. "But his face is so noble, and that Danton was so terribly ugly—a butcher, I think." Julien was still quite nearby; she had no hesitation about calling him over. Her conscience and her pride impelled her to ask, for a young girl, a truly extraordinary question.

"Wasn't Danton a butcher?" she said to him.

"Yes, as far as certain people are concerned," Julien told her, with a poorly masked expression of contempt, his eyes still burning from his conversation with Altamira. "But unfortunately for the aristocracy, he was in fact a lawyer at Méry on the Seine. In other words, mademoiselle," he added spitefully, "he began just like several of the peers I see here. It is true that Danton labored, in the eyes of beauty, under an enormous disadvantage: he was very ugly."

He spoke these last words rapidly, with an air both extraordinary and, without question, not very polite.

Julien waited a moment, bent slightly forward, in humble pride. He seemed to be telling her: "I am paid to answer you, and I live on what I am paid." He did not trouble to raise his eyes toward her. And she, her lovely eyes open very wide, and fixed on him, seemed to be his slave. Finally, as the silence remained unbroken, he glanced at her, just as a valet glances at his master, awaiting further orders. His eyes peered straight into hers, strange, fixed, and steady, but then he moved quickly away, with obvious haste.

"He's really so handsome," Mathilde said to herself, emerging from her half-dream state, "and he eulogizes ugliness! He's always looking out, not in! He's not like Caylus or Croisenois. This Sorel looks a good deal like my father when he does such a good imitation of Napoleon, at a ball." She'd completely forgotten Danton. "I'm most definitely bored tonight." She grasped her brother's arm and, to his great regret, forced him to walk around the ballroom. She conceived the notion of listening in on Julien's conversation with Altamira, the man under a death sentence.

There was a huge crowd. She managed to come up to them just when Altamira was about to take an ice from a tray. He was still speaking to Julien, but half turned away. Seeing a man's arm, clothed in an embroidered suit, taking the ice directly next to his, he grew excited. He turned completely around, the better to see the person to whom this arm belonged. And immediately his eyes, so noble and so naïve, took on an expression of casual disdain.

"You see that man?" he said to Julien, his voice very low. "That's the Prince d'Araceli, the Ambassador of ———. This morning he requested that your minister of foreign affairs, Monsieur de Nerval, grant my extradition. Look, there the minister is, right over there, playing whist. Monsieur de Nerval is likely to hand me over, since back in 1816 we gave you some of your conspirators. If they do send me back to my king, I'll be dead in twenty-four hours. And it will be one of these handsome fellows with mustaches who *will arrest me.*"

"Scoundrels!" exclaimed Julien, rather more loudly.

Mathilde had not lost a syllable of their conversation. Her boredom had vanished.

"Not such scoundrels," replied Count Altamira. "I've been talking to you about myself, so I could conjure up a living picture. Look at Prince d'Araceli. Every five minutes he stares at his Golden Fleece medal. He's never recovered from his delight, seeing that geegaw on his chest. When you come right down to it, this poor fellow's an anachronism. A hundred years ago, a Golden Fleece was a genuine mark of distinction, but in those days it would have been far above his reach. Today, among well-born people, you really have to be an Araceli to be so immensely pleased. To get it for himself, he'd have killed everybody in an entire city."

"And is this the price he paid?" Julien asked nervously.

"Not quite," said Altamira coldly. "He probably tossed into the river thirty or so of the richest landowners in his country, who passed as liberals."

"What a monster!" Julien said once again.

Mademoiselle de La Mole, bending her head toward them, fascinated, was so near him that her lovely hair came very close to brushing against his shoulder.

"You're terribly young!" Altamira responded. "I've told you that I have a married sister, living in Provence. She's still pretty, and good, and sweet; she's an excellent mother to her children, faithful to all her responsibilities, pious but not a fanatic."

"Where is he going with this?" wondered Mademoiselle de La Mole.

"She's happy," Count Altamira went on. "She was happy in 1815. I was hiding at her house, at the time, on her estate near Antibes. Well, as soon as she heard of Marshall Ney's execution, she began to dance."

"Is such a thing possible?" asked Julien, thunderstruck.

"It's simply political," Altamira answered. "We no longer have genuine passions, in the nineteenth century. That's why there's so much boredom, here in France. We do the most incredibly cruel things, but without cruelty."

"So much the worse!" said Julien. "At the very least, crimes ought to be committed with pleasure. That's the only good about them: How can we even begin to justify them for any other reason?"

Having completely forgotten her position, herself, and everything else, Mademoiselle de La Mole was now standing almost directly between Altamira and Julien. Her brother, whose arm she still grasped, was in the habit of doing whatever she wanted: he kept looking around the room and, to make matters look proper, was pretending that he'd been stopped by the crowd.

"You're right," said Altamira. "We do everything without pleasure, and without bothering to remember what we've done, even committing crimes. I could probably show you ten men, here in this room, who'll go to hell as assassins. They've forgotten all about it, and so has the world.

"They're often moved when their dog breaks its paw. When flowers are thrown onto these people's graves—as you put it so cheerfully, in Paris—we'll be told they embodied all the virtues of the bravest knights, and we'll hear about the grand deeds of their ancestor, who lived under Henri IV. If, in spite of the best efforts of Prince d'Araceli, I'm not about to be dead, and if I ever make my fortune in Paris, I'll be pleased to have you to dinner, together with eight or ten murderers, all honored men, all without any remorse.

"You and I, at such a dinner, will be the only ones without blood on our hands, but I'll be scorned and virtually despised, as a sanguinary monster and a Jacobin, and you, you'll be scorned just because you're a man of the people who's intruded himself into good company."

"Nothing could be truer," said Mademoiselle de La Mole.

Altamira looked at her, startled; Julien would not grant her a glance.

"Note that, in the revolution which I found myself leading," Count Altamira continued, "we failed only because I refused to have three heads cut off, and I would not distribute to our supporters seven or eight millions, deposited in a box to which I had the key. My king, who today is burning to grab me, and who before the revolt had been on first-name terms with me, would have given me the greatest medal in the land, had I cut off those three heads and handed out the money, because then I would have been at least half successful, and my country would have had a sort of constitution. . . . That's how the world works, it's all a chess game."

"But then," responded Julien, his eyes blazing, "you didn't know how to play. Now . . ."

"You mean, now I'd cut off those heads, and I wouldn't be the Girondin you made me out to be the other day? . . . I'll answer you," said Altamira sadly, "after you've killed a man in a duel, which is at least not so ugly as having him killed by an executioner."

"My Lord!" said Julien. "The man who desires a goal, also desires the way of accomplishing it. If I had any power, instead of being, as I am, a mere atom, I'd have three men killed if I could save the lives of four."

His glance glowed with moral fire, and with contempt for men's senseless decisions. His eyes met those of Mademoiselle de La Mole, so extremely close by, and his contempt, far from shifting to graciousness and civility, became even stronger.

She was profoundly shocked, but she was not capable, not anymore, of disregarding Julien. She went away, resentfully, dragging her brother behind her.

"I need a glass of punch, and I have to dance and dance," she told herself. "I'll pick the best dancer here and, no matter what, I'll make an impression. Fine: There's that notoriously rude fellow, the Count de Fervaques." She accepted his invitation; they danced. "It's still an open question," she thought, "which of us will be the rudest: if I intend to really show him up, I need to make him talk." All the rest of them, soon, were simply walking through the steps: no one wanted to risk losing any of Mathilde's keen-edged responses. Monsieur de Fervaques grew restless. He could not summon up neatly elegant phrases and, instead of ideas, resorted to letting himself look as angry as he felt. Mathilde, who was in a foul mood, treated him so savagely that she made herself an enemy. She danced until dawn, and finally left, incredibly weary. But as her carriage rolled away, whatever strength she had left was busily making her sad and miserable. She had been scorned by Julien, and she could not reply in kind.

Julien was as happy as he could be, in his ignorance thrilled by the music, the flowers, the beautiful women, the universal elegance and, above all else, by his imagination, which dreamed of all the honors he would receive, and of freedom for everyone.

"What a gorgeous ball!" he said to the count as the carriage drove away. "There's nothing missing."

"Except thought," responded Altamira.

And his face showed his scorn, which was no less barbed because it was obvious that politeness obliged him to mask it.

"But *you're* here, my dear count. And isn't any thought as good as a conspiracy?"

"I'm here because of the name I bear. But in these drawing rooms, thought is utterly hateful. They don't dare rise above the level of a vaudeville song: that's what pays, here. But a thinking man, if his insights are forceful and original, gets labeled a *cynic*. Isn't that the way one of your judges spoke of the great Hellenist, Courier? He was sent to prison, just like Béranger. The Congregation of the Holy Virgin sees to it, in France, that everyone whose mind is worth anything gets thrown into the criminal courts, and all the really good people applaud.

"That's because this withered old society of yours always puts propriety first. . . . France will never lift itself any higher than bravery in battle. You'll always have Murats, but never a Washington. All I see in France is vanity. A creative man, talking easily, slips into a brilliant impropriety, and the master of the house thinks he's been insulted."

At this point, the count's carriage, which was bringing Julien home, stopped in front of the de La Mole mansion. Julien had become fond of his conspiratorial acquaintance. Altamira had paid him a fine compliment, obviously born of deep conviction: "You don't have a Frenchman's trifling mind, and you understand the principle of *utility.*" It happened that, the night before, Julien had seen Casimir Delavigne's tragedy *Marino Faliero.*

"Isn't it true that the conspirator, Israel Bertuccio, has more character than all the noble Venetians he's plotting against?" our worker revolutionary asked himself. "Yet these are the established nobility, dating back to 700, a century before Charlemagne, while the most noble of those at the Duke de Retz's ball tonight go back—and pretty limply—only as far as the thirteenth century. Well! Among all these Venetian nobles, of such lofty birth, the only one we remember is Israel Bertuccio.

"A revolution cancels all a capricious society's titles and distinctions. In a revolution, a man assumes whatever rank he earns by his behavior in the face of death. The brain itself gives up much of its supremacy. . . .

"What would Danton be today, in this century of Valenods and Rênals? Not even a deputy attorney general . . .

"What am I talking about? He'd have sold himself to the Congregation of the Holy Virgin. He'd be a government minister, because the great Danton, after all, did his share of stealing. Mirabeau sold himself, too. Napoleon stole millions, in Italy, and without that wealth, poverty would have stopped him in his tracks, according to General Pichegru. Only Lafayette never stole. Is stealing required? Is selling yourself inevitable?" Julien wondered. The question stopped him in his tracks. He spent the rest of the night reading the history of the French Revolution.

Next day, as he wrote letters in the library, all he could think of, still, was his conversation with Count Altamira.

"In fact," he told himself, after meditating a long time, "if these Spanish liberals had compromised the people's cause by committing crimes, they would not have been so easily swept away. These were arrogant children, and mere talkers . . . like me!" he suddenly exclaimed, as if waking with a start. "What difficult things have I ever done, to give myself the right to judge these poor devils, who in the end, once in their lifetimes, actually dared, actually started to *act*? I'm like a man who, rising from the table, cries out: 'I won't eat dinner, tomorrow; it would only keep me from being as strong and happy as I am today.' Who knows how you'll deal with some grand deed, once it's under way? . . ." These lofty thoughts were disturbed by the arrival of Mademoiselle de La Mole, who came walking into the library. Julien had gotten so excited, admiring the great qualities of Danton, and Mirabeau, and Carnot, who had known how to escape defeat, that his eyes were checked by Mademoiselle de La Mole's appearance, though he was not thinking of her at all, and barely saw her. When his wide-open eyes realized she was there, their glow faded away. Mademoiselle de La Mole noticed it, bitterly.

It was no good, asking him for a volume of de Vély's *History of France,* which was sitting as high on the shelves as books could go, and which required Julien to go looking for the taller of the two library ladders. He went up the ladder, he found the book, he brought it down to her, still without being able to think of her. While putting the ladder back, he was so preoccupied that his elbow crashed into one of the glass shelf doors; the shattered pieces, falling to the floor, finally woke him up. He apologized to Mademoiselle de La Mole, hurriedly; he meant to be polite, but that was all he was. It was obvious to Mathilde that he was unsettled, and that, rather than talking to her, he would much prefer to keep thinking about whatever had been occupying his mind before she came. She looked at him most carefully, then slowly went away. Julien watched her walk off. He took a good deal of pleasure in the contrast between how she was dressed at the moment,

and her elegant magnificence, the night before. The difference between the face she now wore, and the one she'd worn then, was almost
equally striking. This young woman, who had seemed so haughty at
the Duke de Retz's ball, right now looked almost like a suppliant.
"Really," Julien said to himself, "this black dress makes her beautiful
figure even more apparent. She carries herself like a queen. But why is
she wearing mourning?

"But if I ask someone this question, I may just be blundering all
over again." Julien had now emerged from the depths of his rapture.
"I'll have to reread the letters I've written this morning: God only
knows all the words I've misspelled, and the mistakes I'll find." As he
read over the letters, concentrating hard, he heard just behind him the
rustle of a silk dress. He turned around rapidly. Mademoiselle de La
Mole was no more than two feet away, and she laughed. This second
interruption annoyed him.

Mathilde had just become vividly aware that, to this young man,
she did not matter a bit. She'd laughed in order to hide her embarrassment, and in that she succeeded.

"You're obviously thinking the most interesting thoughts, Monsieur Sorel. Might it be some strange tale of the conspiracy that sent
Count Altamira to us, here in Paris? Tell me, please, if that's what it is;
I'm most anxious to know; I'll be discreet, I promise you!" Hearing
herself saying these words, she was stunned. What was happening, that
she found herself begging favors of an underling! Her embarrassment
mounting, she added, lightly:

"What could have made you, usually so reserved, an inspired creature, a kind of Michael Angelo sort of prophet?"

This sharp, indiscreet query deeply wounded Julien, and his craziness came back.

"Was Danton right to steal?" he told her rudely, and in a manner
that quickly became more and more savage. "Should the revolutionaries of Piedmont, of Spain, have committed crimes that compromised the people? Should they have given even totally unworthy
people all the commissions in the army, and all the medals? Wouldn't
the people wearing these medals have worried that the king might retake his throne? Should they have let the hordes loose, on the treasures

of Turin? In short, mademoiselle," he said, coming over to her, his face frightening to behold, "must the man who wants to eliminate ignorance and crime from the earth—must he sweep across the earth like a hurricane and do evil however it happens to take place?"

Mathilde was afraid, unable to endure the way he was looking at her; she stepped two paces back. She glanced at him for just a moment, and then, ashamed of her fear, she left the library, walking with light unconcern.

CHAPTER TEN

QUEEN MARGUERITE

Love! What madness won't you descend to, in
order to bring us pleasure?

—*LETTERS OF A PORTUGUESE NUN*

Julien reread his letters. When the dinner bell was heard: "How ridiculous I must have seemed, to this Parisian doll," he said to himself. "What idiocy to tell her what I was actually thinking! Speaking the truth, here, was truly worthy of me.

"But why come and ask me such private questions? She was acting most indiscreetly. It's bad manners. My thoughts on Danton are no part of the work her father pays me for."

Coming into the dining room, Julien's ill humor was shunted to the side, seeing Mademoiselle de La Mole wearing such deep mourning, which was all the more remarkable because no one else in the family was wearing black.

After dinner, he realized that the flooding enthusiasm he had felt the entire day had completely left him. Luckily, the academician who knew Latin had been dining with them. "Here's a man who wouldn't likely make fun of me," Julien told himself, "if, as I suspect it is, asking Mademoiselle de La Mole about her mourning would be a stupid blunder."

Mathilde had been looking at him very strangely. "Here, then, is female flirtatiousness, Parisian style, exactly as Madame de Rênal described it for me," he told himself. "I wasn't pleasant to her this morning. I didn't give in to the silly notion of having a chat with her. And that made her think better of me. I have no doubt there'll be the devil to pay on that score! Later on, her arrogant contempt will know exactly how to take vengeance. Let her do her worst. How different she is from the woman I've lost. What natural charm that was! What innocence! I knew her thoughts before she did, I saw them as they were being born. The only enemy I had, in her heart, was the fear that her children might die. It was rational, natural affection, kind and gentle even for me, though it made me suffer. I've been a fool. The ideas I'd formed about Paris stopped me from appreciating that sublime woman.

"God in heaven, what a difference! What do I find here? Dry, arrogant vanity, every shade of narcissism, and nothing more."

The diners rose from the table. "Let's not have anyone else snaring my academician," Julien said to himself. He went over to him, as they were going into the garden, took on a pleasant, dutiful air, and shared his fury at the success of Victor Hugo's modernist drama, *Hernani*.

"If only we still lived in the era when bad art could be banned! . . ." he said.

"Then Hugo would never have dared," exclaimed the academician, with a gesture worthy of the great tragedian, Talma.

As they were discussing flowers, Julien quoted lines from Virgil's *Georgica,* and affirmed that nothing was so fine as the tame, mediocre verse of Jacques Delille. In short, he flattered the academician right and left. This accomplished, he noted, most casually: "I dare say Mademoiselle de La Mole has had some money from a deceased uncle, for whom she's wearing mourning."

"Ha! You live in this house," said the academician, suddenly interrupting their stroll, "and you don't know how crazy she is? Really, it's most peculiar that her mother allows her to do such things." He resumed their walk. "But it's not exactly by strength of character that one shines, in this household. Mademoiselle de La Mole has enough of that for the whole lot of them, and leads them around by their noses. Today is the thirtieth of April!" And he stopped, once more, looking at Julien and smiling ironically. Julien smiled as knowingly as he could.

"But what connection can there possibly be," he said to himself, "between making marionettes out of everyone in the house, and wearing a black dress, and the thirtieth of April? I must be even denser than I'd supposed."

"I confess . . ." he told the academician, pursuing the question with the look in his eyes.

"Let's walk in the garden," said the academician, delighted, sensing the opportunity for telling a long, elegant tale. "Really! Is it actually possible you don't know what happened on the thirtieth of April, in 1574?"

"Where?" asked Julien, amazed.

"In the Place de Grève."

Julien was so perplexed that the name meant nothing to him. Curiosity, and the prospect of a fine tragic story—so deeply in harmony with his own nature—made his eyes sparkle in exactly the way a storyteller loves to see, in his listener's expression. Delighted to have found a virgin ear, the academician unwound a long tale about how, on the thirtieth of April, 1574, the handsomest young man of that time, Boniface de La Mole, along with Annibal de Coconasso, a gentleman of Piedmont, and de La Mole's friend, had been beheaded in the Place de Grève. De La Mole had been the adored lover of Queen Marguerite de Navarre—"and note," added the academician, "that Mademoiselle de La Mole's name is *Mathilde-Marguerite*. Young de La Mole was also the Duke d'Alençon's favorite, and the King of Navarre's close friend—his mistress's husband, afterward Henry IV. On the day of Mardi Gras, in 1574, the royal court was at Saint-Germain, with poor King Charles IX, who was dying. De La Mole wanted to rescue his friends, the royal princes, held captive at the court by Queen Catherine de Médici. He brought two hundred horsemen to the very walls of Saint-Germain, the Duke d'Alençon was frightened, and de La Mole was thrown to the executioner.

"But what so deeply touches Mademoiselle de La Mole, as she told me herself, seven or eight years ago, when she was twelve—because she has a mind, a mind! . . ." And the academician raised his eyes toward heaven. "What struck her the most, about this political catastrophe, is that Queen Marguerite de Navarre, hidden in a house on

Place de Grève, dared to ask the executioner for her lover's head. And the next night, at midnight, she took the head in her carriage, and she herself buried it in a chapel at the foot of Montmartre Hill."

"Really?" exclaimed Julien, moved.

"Mademoiselle de La Mole is scornful of her brother, since as you've seen he has no interest whatever in all this ancient history, and never puts on mourning for the thirtieth of April. Ever since this famous execution, and in order to commemorate de La Mole's close friendship with Coconasso—who, being Italian, was named Annibal— every man in the de La Mole family bears that name. And," added the academician, lowering his voice, "this Coconasso, according to Charles IX himself, was one of the most savage of all the murderers, in the Saint Bartholomew's Day massacres of twenty-four August, 1572. . . . But how can it be possible, my dear Sorel, that you've not known these things, you who live in this house?"

"You've just explained to me why, twice, at dinner tonight, Mademoiselle de La Mole called her brother Annibal. I thought I'd misheard her."

"She was scolding him. What odd tricks she plays!"

He followed these remarks with five or six ironical observations. Julien was shocked by the glow of high intimacy in the academician's eyes. "Here we have two servants being malicious about our masters," he thought. But nothing this academic might say would have surprised him.

One day, Julien had stumbled on him, down on his knees in front of the Marquise de La Mole, begging that a nephew of his, who lived in the provinces, be given a collectorship of the tobacco tax. And that night, a young chambermaid of Mathilde's who, just like Elisa, had been wooing him, put in his head the idea that her mistress's mourning garb was not at all a way of getting attention. This extremely queer notion reached right to the depths of his soul. Mathilde actually loved the long-dead de La Mole, dearly beloved of the most intelligent queen of her time, and a man who had died while trying to liberate his friends. And what friends! The first Prince of the Blood, and the future King Henry IV.

Accustomed to the perfect simplicity that glowed in everything

Madame de Rênal said and did, all Julien had seen in Parisian women was affectation; and, whenever his mood was melancholic, he had nothing to say to them. Mademoiselle de La Mole was an exception.

He began to understand that the standard for beauty, as he could observe it among aristocratic women, did not necessarily involve coldness of heart. He had long after-dinner conversations with Mademoiselle de La Mole, who would sometimes walk in the garden with him, by the drawing room's open windows. She told him, one day, that she was reading d'Aubigné's history, and the stories of Brantôme. "What strange things for her to read," thought Julien, "when the marquise won't let her have Walter Scott's novels!"

One day she told him, her eyes gleaming with pleasure—showing how sincerely she admired it—the tale of what a young woman had done, in the days of Henry III. She had just been reading the story, in l'Etoile's *Memoirs:* finding her husband unfaithful, the young woman had stabbed him.

Julien's vanity was flattered. A woman raised in an environment so full of honor and respect, and someone who, according to the academician, led her whole family around by their noses, had thought it worthwhile to talk to him, and in a way that came rather close to friendliness.

"No, I was wrong," he thought, later on. "This isn't intimacy. All I am is someone to whom she can tell this tragedy: she needs to speak about it. I'm considered a scholar, in this family. Well, I'm going to read Brantôme, d'Aubigné, l'Etoile. Then I'll be able to argue about some of these stories Mademoiselle de La Mole's been telling me. I want to stop playing this role of passive confidant."

Gradually, these conversations with the girl—who carried herself with such a sense of importance, and at the same time with such ease— became more interesting. He forgot his sorrowful role as a working-class revolutionary. He found her knowledgeable, and even rational. The opinions she held, in the garden, were very different from those she exhibited in the drawing room. At times she showed him an enthusiasm, and an openness, that were in absolute contrast to her usual manner, so lofty and so cold.

"Those sixteenth-century Wars of the League are France's heroic era," she was saying to him one day, her eyes glittering with intelligence and spirit. "Everyone was fighting for something they wanted, trying to make their party triumphant, and not just to ploddingly earn a medal, the way they did in your emperor's time. You'll surely agree there was less egoism, and less pettiness. I love that time."

"And Boniface de La Mole was its hero," he said.

"At least he was loved, as perhaps it's sweet to be loved. What woman alive today wouldn't be horrified to touch her lover's chopped-off head?"

Madame de La Mole called to her daughter. To be useful, hypocrisy must be hidden, and Julien, as we have seen, had made Mademoiselle de La Mole more or less a confidante of his Napoleon worship.

Now alone in the garden: "There's the huge advantage they have over us," Julien told himself. "Their ancestors' history lifts them above vulgar feelings, and they don't always have to focus on where their bread is coming from! What misery!" he added, bitterly. "I'm not worthy of thinking about these great matters. My life is nothing but a succession of hypocrisies, because I haven't got an income of a thousand francs, with which to buy my bread."

"And what are you dreaming about, sir?" asked Mathilde, who had come running back.

Julien was tired of self-contempt. His pride led him to tell her, frankly, the thoughts he'd been having. It made him blush quite violently, speaking of his poverty to someone so very rich. He tried to make clear, by his proud tone, that he was not asking for a thing. Mathilde had never thought him so handsome; his expression conveyed a sensitivity and an openness he'd often lacked.

Less than a month later, Julien was walking, intensely thoughtful, in the de La Mole garden; his face no longer bore the hardness, the philosophic arrogance, imprinted on it by long-continued feelings of inferiority. He had just brought Mademoiselle de La Mole to the drawing room door: she was claiming to have hurt her foot, running with her brother.

"She leaned on my arm in such a peculiar way!" Julien said to himself. "Am I an arrogant puppy, or can she really have taken a liking to me? She listens to me so sweetly, even when I'm telling her what suffering my pride causes me! She, who's so haughty with everyone! They'd be truly startled, in the drawing room, if they could see that look on her face. That sweetness, that goodness, isn't something she ever shows, not to anybody."

Julien tried not to exaggerate this odd friendship. He described it to himself as a relationship at gunpoint. Every day, when they found themselves together again, and before they could resume the previous night's almost intimate tone, they virtually had to ask themselves: "Will we be friends today, or enemies?" Julien was very well aware that, if he ever let himself be insulted, with impunity, by this haughty girl, everything was all over. "If I have to quarrel with her, wouldn't it be better, in a proper defense of my pride, if I started it, instead of just repelling the signs of contempt that, surely, will follow right behind the very smallest surrender of my personal dignity?"

Several times, when they were not in good moods, Mathilde tried to play the great lady with him. She made these attempts with rare skill, but Julien roughly pushed them aside.

One day he interrupted her sharply: "Has Mademoiselle de La Mole some order to transmit to her father's secretary?" he said. "He is obliged to obey the marquis's orders, and to respectfully carry them out. But, otherwise, the marquis's secretary has nothing to say to mademoiselle. He is not paid to communicate his thoughts to her."

This kind of behavior, and his strange doubts, drove away the boredom once so regularly afflicting him, in that resplendent drawing room where he'd been afraid of everything, and where it had never felt proper to joke about anything.

"It would be a good joke, if she loved me! But whether she does or she doesn't," Julien went on, "I have for my friend a girl who's intelligent, in front of whom the whole house trembles, and most of all the Marquis de Croisenois—that infinitely polished young man, so gentle, so courageous, who has all the advantages of birth and fortune, either one of which would put my heart so completely at ease! He's wildly in love; he'll surely marry her. Just consider all the letters Monsieur de La Mole has had me write to the lawyers on both sides, to settle the terms of the marriage contract! And I, who see myself so much the underling, with my pen in my hand, here I am, two hours later, in the garden again, victorious over this fine, good young man—for her preference is striking, utterly plain to see. And perhaps she dislikes him as a possible husband. She's arrogant enough for that. And all the kindnesses she shows me, they come to me in my role as an employee-confidant!

"But no: Either I'm crazy, or she's paying court to me. The colder and more respectful I am to her, the more she comes looking for me. It might be a pretense, an affectation—but I can see her eyes light up when I appear without warning. Do Parisian women know how to go that far, with their game-playing? But what difference does it make to me! Here I've got all the appearances: let's savor them. And Lord, how pretty she is! How I relish those big blue eyes, seen so close, and looking at me as they often do! What a difference between this spring and last year's, in Besançon, when I was miserable and sustained myself only by force of character, in the middle of three hundred nasty, dirty hypocrites! I was almost as nasty as they were."

When he fell victim to mistrust: "She's making fun of me, that girl," Julien would think. "She and her brother have made a pact to bamboozle me. But she really seems to despise her brother's listlessness! 'He's courageous, and that's all he is,' she told me. 'He hasn't got a single thought bold enough to defy fashion! *I* am always required to defend *him*. I'm a girl, I'm only nineteen! How can I be forever faithful, day after day, to the hypocrisy they demand of us?'

"On the other hand, when Mademoiselle de La Mole looks so fixedly at me, with that strange expression in her big blue eyes, Count Norbert always looks away. That strikes me as suspicious. Shouldn't he be indignant if his sister so honors a household *servant*? And I've heard the Duke de Chaulnes talk of me that way." Remembering this, anger replaced every other feeling. "Is that peculiar old duke just crazy about old-fashioned ways of speech?

"Lord, Lord, but she's pretty!" Julien resumed, a tigerish look on his face. "I'll have her, I'll leave afterward, and anyone who chases after me had better watch out!"

He became preoccupied with the idea; he was unable to think of anything else. Days went by, for him, as if they'd been hours.

Over and over, as he tried to focus on some serious business, his mind would let everything else fall away, and for a quarter of an hour he'd be lost in dreams, his heart beating hard, his head hurting, and always wondering about the exact same thing: "Does she really love me?"

CHAPTER ELEVEN

A YOUNG GIRL'S IMPERIAL DOMINION

I admire her beauty, but I'm afraid of her mind.
—MÉRIMÉE

Had Julien tried to analyze what went on in the drawing room, with the same intensity with which he set himself to dramatizing her beauty, or getting himself excited about the family's natural arrogance—which she put aside for him—he would have understood how she ruled over everyone around her. The moment anyone displeased Mademoiselle de La Mole, she knew exactly how to strike back with a jest so carefully calculated, so well chosen, so apparently decent and decorous, hurled with such perfect timing, that the wound kept growing worse and worse, the more the victim thought about it. Bit by bit, she would become increasingly destructive of the offending party's self-esteem. Since she had absolutely no interest in most of the things so very seriously sought by the rest of the family, to them she seemed forever cool and calm. Aristocratic drawing rooms are pleasant to discuss, when you've escaped from them, but that's about all: sheer politeness, never progressing beyond politeness, is worth very little after first meetings. Julien had experienced this, too, after an initial enchantment, an initial surprise. "Politeness," he told himself, "is merely the absence of that anger which creates bad manners." Mathilde was frequently bored; it may well have been that she would have been bored wherever she was. Accordingly, honing an epigram was for her both a distraction and a genuine pleasure.

It may have been in order to have victims a bit more amusing than her grandparents, the academician, and the five or six underlings who composed their court, that she had encouraged the Marquis de

Croisenois, Count de Caylus, and two or three other young men of the highest rank. All they were to her was new targets for epigrams.

It pains us to admit, since we love Mathilde, that she had received letters from several of these young men, and had sometimes replied to them. We hasten to add that, in so doing, she was an exception to the rules of her time. Lack of prudence is not usually ascribable to young women who have been students at the noble Convent of the Sacred Heart of Jesus.

One day, the Marquis de Croisenois sent her back a significantly compromising letter that, the previous night, she had written him. This demonstration of great prudence seemed to him quite helpful, as a way of furthering his cause. But recklessness was what Mathilde liked in her correspondence. She took real pleasure in games of that sort. She did not speak to him again for a full six weeks.

These young men's letters amused her, but according to her they were all alike, always heavy with "the most profound passion," with "infinite melancholy."

"They're each and all the same perfect man, ready to leave on another Crusade," she said to her cousin, Mademoiselle de Sainte-Hérédité. "Have you ever seen anything more insipid? And these are the letters I'm going to receive, all the rest of my life! Letters like this can only change every twenty years, when the world changes to a new way of keeping itself busy. Letters had to be less colorless, in the days of Napoleon. All young aristocrats, back then, had seen or been involved in *really* grand deeds. My uncle, the Duke of N———, was at the Battle of Wagram."

"What has force of character got to do with swinging a saber? And when they do it, they're always talking about it!" said her cousin.

"Well! I like those stories. To be in a *genuine* battle, one of Napoleon's, where ten thousand soldiers were killed, that really tests your courage. Exposing yourself to danger lifts the soul, preserves it from the boredom in which, alas, my poor worshipers are immersed. And boredom is contagious. Have they ever thought of doing anything extraordinary? They're trying to win me: now there's a wonderful adventure! I'm rich, and my father will push his son-in-law. Ah, if only my father could find me, instead, someone who was just a tiny bit amusing!"

As you can see, Mathilde's way of looking at things, lively, candid, picturesque, had a bad effect on how she talked. Her remarks often seemed to her exceedingly polite friends in rather poor taste. Had she been less in fashion, they might almost have said that her way of talking was a bit overcolored to be true feminine delicacy.

For her part, she was certainly unfair to the handsome cavaliers who filled the Bois de Boulogne. She did not look to the future with terror—that would phrase it too forcefully—but with a disgust distinctly rare at her age.

What could she hope for? Wealth, noble birth, intelligence, beauty, all had been heaped on her by the hands of Fate, or so people said to her, and so she believed.

So this was how she thought, she who was the most envied heiress of the Faubourg Saint-German, at the time when she began to take pleasure in walking with Julien. His pride amazed her; she admired the shrewdness of this petty bourgeois. Just as Father Maury had done, she assured herself, he'd know how to make himself a bishop.

During these walks, the fashion in which our hero criticized some of her ideas, his honest, earnest opposition, soon began to preoccupy her; she thought about what he said; she told her cousin every little detail of their conversations, though she found herself unable to do justice to their full flavor.

And suddenly an idea flashed on her: "I'm lucky enough to be in love," she told herself, in an incredible ecstatic joy. "I'm in love, I'm in love, I am, I am! A young girl at my age, beautiful, spirited, where could I find such emotion, except in love? There's no point even trying, I could never fall in love with Croisenois, Caylus, and all the others. They're perfect, maybe too perfect, but—in a word—they all bore me."

She reviewed in her head all the descriptions of passion she'd read in *Manon Lescaut*, in *La Nouvelle Héloïse*, in *The Letters of a Portuguese Nun*, etc., etc. Of course, it could only be a grand passion: a frivolous love was unworthy of a girl her age, a girl of her birth. For her, the only thing that deserved the name *love* was the heroic emotion occurring, in the whole of French history, during the days of Henry III and of Bas-sompierre, Richelieu's antagonist. Such love never wavered, vulgarly, when it met with obstacles: quite to the contrary, obstacles led to truly great deeds. "How wretched that there's no real court, like Catherine de Médici's or Louis XIII's! I think I could do anything, no matter how bold, no matter how grand. What wouldn't I do if a passionate king, like Louis XIII, were sighing at my feet! I'd lead him straight into that peasant revolt, the Vendée, as Baron de Tully always says, and he'd go on from there, he'd reconquer his whole kingdom, there'd be an end to any more Constitutions . . . and Julien would help me. What is he missing? Name and fortune. He'd make himself a name, he'd win himself a fortune.

"Croisenois isn't missing anything. For the rest of his life, all he'll be is a sort of right-wing duke, a sort of liberal, a wobbly-minded man, forever avoiding extremes, and *as a result, forever coming in second.*

"What great deed isn't *extreme* when it's first begun? Only when it's been accomplished can it seem possible in the eyes of ordinary men. Yes—it has to be love, with all its miracles, that now will rule my heart: I feel its quickening fire. Heaven owes me this sign of favor. My happiness will be worthy of me. The days of my life will no longer, one by one, each coldly resemble the one before it. There's already grandeur, and true audacity, in daring to love someone so far beneath me in social standing. We'll see: Will he continue to deserve me? The first time I see weakness in him, I'll give him up. A girl of my birth, and with the courtly nature they've been good enough to concede me [this was one of her father's favorite expressions] must not behave like an idiot.

"And isn't that the role I'd be playing if I loved the Marquis de Croisenois? I would be nothing more than a new edition of my cousins, for whom I feel such utter contempt. I know in advance everything the poor marquis would say to me, everything I'd then have to say to him. What kind of love makes you yawn? You might as well be pious and devout. There'd be the same kind of ceremony my youngest cousin had, when her marriage contract was signed, with all the grandparents there—unless they'd been upset by some clause the lawyer for the other side had put, in the night before."

CHAPTER TWELVE

WILL HE BE ANOTHER DANTON?

A craving for excitement: *that was my aunt's nature, the beautiful Marguerite de Valois, who soon married the King of Navarre, now ruling France as Henry IVth. Gambling was the basic underlying, but secret, force in this likable princess' character, as it had been in all the quarrels and the reconciliations she'd had with her brothers, from the age of sixteen on. Now, with what can a young girl gamble? With her most precious possession, her reputation, the thing she must look after for her entire life.*

—DUKE D'ANGOULÊME, NATURAL SON OF CHARLES IX, *MEMOIRS*

"There will be no signing a contract, for Julien and me, no lawyers: it's all heroic, everything open to chance. Except for noble status, which he lacks, this is exactly Marguerite de Valois's love for the young de La Mole, the most distinguished man of his time. Is it my fault that the young men of the court are such intense partisans of *acceptability,* starting to shake at the very idea of anything even a little bit different? To them, a little trip to Greece, or to Africa, is the height of daring, and even then they only know how to march in step with everyone else. The minute they're alone, they're afraid—not of a Bedouin's spear, but of being made to look ridiculous, and that fear drives them crazy.

"My little Julien, on the other hand, only likes to act by himself. This privileged creature never so much as thinks of seeking support or assistance from others! He despises everyone, which is why I don't despise him.

"If Julien were noble, poor as he is, my love would be nothing but vulgar stupidity, an act of out-and-out miscegenation. I want nothing of the kind; it would have none of the qualities of a grand passion, none of the immense difficulties to be conquered, and the black uncertainty of what might come."

Mademoiselle de La Mole was so preoccupied with this fine chain of reasoning that, the next day, not thinking what she was saying, she praised Julien to the Marquis de Croisenois and her brother. Her eloquence soared so high that they grew annoyed.

"Watch out for that young fellow, with all that energy," exclaimed her brother. "If the Revolution ever starts up again, he'll have every one of us guillotined."

She stopped herself from answering, and quickly began to tease both her brother and the Marquis de Croisenois about how afraid they were of anything or anyone energetic. At bottom, this was simply fear of encountering the unexpected, the terror of falling short in its presence. . . .

"Always, gentlemen, always, this same fear of ridicule—a monster which, unluckily, died in 1816."

"There is no more ridicule," Monsieur de La Mole liked to say, "not in a country where there are only two parties."

His daughter had grasped the idea.

"And so, gentlemen," she said to Julien's enemies, "you'll have lived your whole lives in great fear, and afterward they'll tell you:

"It wasn't a wolf, but just its shadow."

Mathilde soon walked away. Her brother's words had filled her with horror. He'd left her very much worried; but by the next day, she saw it as the most handsome of compliments.

"In this nineteenth century, when all energy has died, Julien's makes them afraid. I'll tell him what my brother said; I want to see his response. But I'll pick a moment when his eyes are gleaming. He won't lie to me, then.

"He'll be a Danton!" she added, after a long, vague reverie. "Well! So the Revolution starts up again. What roles will Croisenois and my brother be playing? It's been written out in advance: sublime resignation. They'll be heroic sheep, they'll let themselves be swallowed up without a word. Their only fear, as they die, will still be to do everything in good taste. My little Julien would blow out the brains of the Jacobin who comes to arrest him, no matter how small his hope of getting away. He's not afraid of being in bad taste, not him."

This last observation made her thoughtful; it roused painful memories and wiped away all her boldness. It brought back the jests of Messieurs de Caylus, de Croisenois, de Luz, and her brother. These gentlemen had unanimously reproved Julien for his *priestly* airs: humble and hypocritical.

"But," she suddenly responded, her eyes bright with happiness, "the bitterness and frequency of these jests proves that, despite themselves, he's the most distinguished man we've seen all winter. What do his faults matter, his absurdities? He has grandeur, and they're shocked by it, these young men so good and so forgiving in other respects. He's poor, yes, and he's studied to be a priest; they're squadron chiefs, and they don't need to study anything. It's all very easy, for them.

"For all the drawbacks of his eternal black suit, and his priestlike expression—which he truly needs, the poor boy, to keep from dying of hunger—what makes them afraid is how fine he is. It couldn't be more obvious. And that priestly look, he doesn't have it anymore, once we've been alone together for even a moment. And when these gentlemen say something that seems to them subtle and unexpected, don't they immediately look toward Julien? I've often seen it. And still they know very well that he never speaks to them unless they ask him a question. He only speaks to me, he thinks I have a noble soul. When they object to something, he says only enough to be polite. Then he quickly turns respectful. But he talks to me for hours, and he doesn't insist when I have even a slight objection. And all winter long, there haven't been any duels: it's only by his words that he's been drawing attention to himself. And my father, a superior man who's doing wonderful things for the family fortune, he respects Julien. Everybody else hates him, but no one despises him, except my mother's pious friends."

Count de Caylus had, or pretended to have, a great passion for horses; he spent his life in his stables, and often had his lunch there. This great passion, together with his habit of never laughing, made him highly regarded among his friends: he was the eagle of their little circle.

The next day, when they met behind Madame de La Mole's easy chair, Julien not being present, Monsieur de Caylus, supported by de Croisenois and by Norbert, strongly criticized Mademoiselle de La Mole's high opinion of Julien, without any preliminaries, and virtually at the moment he saw her. She knew at once what he was up to, and found it delightful.

"There they are, all banded together," she said to herself, "against a man of genius who doesn't have an income of thirty francs, and who can only answer them when they ask him a question. They're afraid of what's under that black suit. How would it be if he wore epaulettes?"

Her wit had never shone so brightly. As her attack got under way, she showered de Caylus and his allies with sarcastic jests. When their witty counterfire had been thoroughly snuffed out:

"If, tomorrow, some gentlemanly country bumpkin, in the Franche-Comté mountains, were to make it known that Julien is his natural child, and give him his name and some thousands of francs, in six weeks he'd have mustaches exactly like yours, gentlemen; in six months he'd be a cavalry officer, exactly like you, gentlemen. And then the grandeur of his character would no longer be subject to your ridicule. I can imagine you forced to retreat, Monsieur Duke-to-be, to this old and empty argument: the superiority of court nobility to provincial nobility. But where would you stand if I were wicked enough to push you still further, if I were spiteful enough to make Julien's newly discovered father a Spanish duke, a prisoner of war in Besançon, dating from Napoleon's time, and who, motivated by his conscience, recognized his son on his deathbed?"

These suggestions of illegitimate birth seemed to Messieurs de Caylus and de Croisenois in very poor taste. That was all they saw in Mathilde's argument.

However dominated by his sister Norbert might be, her remarks had been so plain that he assumed a very sober tone, though it went quite poorly, it must be admitted, with his laughing, pleasant face. He risked a few words to her.

"Are you ill, my dear?" Mathilde answered him, appearing pertly serious. "You must really feel poorly, to answer jests with moralities.

"Moralities, from you! Are you looking for a post as a district governor?" Mathilde soon forgot Count de Caylus's irritation, Norbert's sulky mood, and the silent despair of Monsieur de Croisenois. She'd made up her mind about a fateful idea just now gripping her soul.

"Julien is basically honest with me," she said to herself. "At his age, obliged to be an underling, miserably driven as he is by astonishing ambition, he needs a lover. Perhaps I can be the one. But I see no sign of love in him. Reckless and bold as he is, he would surely have told me, had he been in love."

This uncertainty, and the debate within herself, which from then on constantly occupied her mind, and which acquired new arguments every time Julien spoke to her, completely dispelled the periods of boredom to which she had been so vulnerable.

As the daughter of a man of sense and sensibility, who might become a government minister and give its wooded lands back to the Church, Mademoiselle de La Mole had been the subject of extraordinary flattery, at the Sacred Heart of Jesus convent. This was a misfortune never redressed: she'd been persuaded that, because of all her advantages of birth, of fortune, etc., she ought to be happier than other people. This is the source of princes' boredom, and of all their foolishness.

Mathilde had never escaped the deadly effect of such ideas. No matter how intelligent a child may be, it cannot be capable, at age ten, of overcoming the flattery of an entire convent, especially when so apparently well founded.

The moment she'd decided she loved Julien, she was no longer bored. She felt self-congratulatory, every day, at having decided to throw herself into a great love affair. "This kind of amusement contains a good many risks," she thought. "So much the better! A thousand times better!

"Without a grand passion, I'd be languishing from boredom, right at the most beautiful time in my life, these years from sixteen to twenty. I've already lost the most beautiful of those years, compelled to take my only pleasure from listening to my mothers' friends and their idiotic chatter. They weren't anything like so rigid and moralistic as they are today, from what I've heard, back in 1792, at Coblenz."

While Mathilde was struggling with these intense doubts, Julien was bewildered by the long, lingering glances she lavished on him. He was experiencing vastly increased coldness from Count Norbert, and new onslaughts of arrogance from Messieurs de Caylus, de Luz, and de Croisenois. He was used to that. Sometimes it happened on days when, the evening before, he'd been more brilliant than suited his position. Without the unusual reception Mathilde gave him, and the curiosity inspired in him by this entire circle of young aristocrats, he would have refrained from following the shining young fellows with mustaches into the garden, after dinner, as they went walking with Mademoiselle de la Mole.

"Yes, I can't possibly ignore it," Julien told himself. "Mademoiselle de La Mole looks at me so very strangely. Yet even when those beautiful blue eyes are fixed on me, wide with utmost abandon, I always see a basically analytical stance, a cool calmness, and a maliciousness. Can these really be expressions of love? How differently Madame de Rênal looked at me!"

After dinner, once, having first followed Monsieur de La Mole into his office room, Julien hurried back down to the garden. As he came close to the group around Mathilde, without warning he was struck by loudly pronounced words. Mathilde was giving her brother a very difficult time. Julien heard his own name, twice, each time very distinctly. He came over to them; suddenly there was total silence, though assorted unsuccessful attempts were made to break it. Both Mademoiselle de La Mole and her brother were too worked up to find another topic of conversation. Messieurs de Caylus, de Croisenois, de Luz, and one of their other friends, were as cold as glass to Julien. He left them.

CHAPTER THIRTEEN

A Conspiracy

Random words, heard by chance, turn to hard facts in the eyes of a man of imagination, if there's any fire burning in his heart.
—Schiller

Again the next day, he surprised Norbert and his sister, who had been speaking of him. As he joined them, a deathly silence fell, exactly like the previous evening. He was hugely suspicious. Are these pleasant young people planning a way to make fun of me? He had to admit this was far more likely, and much more natural, than Mademoiselle de La Mole's pretended passion for a poor devil of a secretary. "In any case, do these people ever experience passion? Mystification is their specialty. They're jealous of my tongue's miserable little superiority. Jealousy remains one of their weaknesses. They're transparently clear. Mademoiselle de La Mole wants me to think she's interested in me, quite simply so she can turn me into a spectacle for her intended husband."

This bitter suspicion shifted Julien's entire moral framework. The destructive idea confronted a budding love in his heart; it had no difficulty killing it off. His love had been based only on Mathilde's rare beauty, or more likely on her queenly manner and the wonderful way she dressed. In such things, Julien was still a self-made social climber. It's always said that a pretty aristocratic woman is the most astonishing thing of all, for a spirited peasant, when he reaches the higher rungs of society. It was hardly Mathilde's character, all this time, that had set Julien to dreaming. He was sensible enough to understand that, in fact, he knew nothing about her character. Everything he'd been seeing of it might be no more than a pretense.

For example: Nothing could make Mathilde miss Sunday mass; she went to church with her mother virtually every day. If some careless fellow, in the de La Mole drawing room, happened to forget where he was and allowed himself even a distantly barbed remark about the true or pretended interests of either church or state, Mathilde immediately turned seriously icy. Her glance went from liveliness to all the impenetrable haughtiness of an old family portrait.

But Julien knew for sure that she always had, in her room, one or two of Voltaire's most philosophical books. He himself had often secretly borrowed volumes of that magnificently bound edition. He would separate somewhat the remaining books, concealing what he had borrowed, but soon realized that someone else was reading Voltaire. He fell back on a seminary trick, putting a few strands of hair in volumes he imagined might well interest Mademoiselle de La Mole. As the weeks went by, all the hair disappeared.

Monsieur de La Mole grew impatient with his bookseller, who was sending him all the so-called *Memoirs,* and ordered Julien to buy whatever new volumes were moderately racy. But to keep the poison from spreading through the house, the secretary had been directed to place these in a small bookcase right in the marquis's room. Julien was soon positive that if any of these new volumes were, to any degree, hostile to the interests of church or throne, it did not take long for them to disappear. He was equally certain that it was not Norbert who was reading them.

Considerably dramatizing this experience, Julien believed Mademoiselle de La Mole possessed of the conniving nature of Machiavelli. A pose of such wickedness was, in her eyes, quite charming—almost the only moral charm she enjoyed. Boredom, generated by hypocrisy and all his virtuous talk, threw him into such immoderate judgments.

It was his imagination he was exciting, rather than letting himself be swept away by love.

Only when he'd fallen into long reveries about Mademoiselle de La Mole's lovely figure, and about her superb taste in clothing, her exceedingly white hands, her beautiful arms, the *disinvoltura*, the easy indifference of all her movements, did he find himself in love. Then, to round off her charms, he thought her a Catherine de Médici. There could be nothing too profound, or too wicked, for the nature he assigned her. It was the ideal of all the Maslons, the de Frilairs, the Castanedas, the ideal he'd admired as a child. In other words, it was Paris's ideal.

Has there ever been anything more amusing than believing Parisians either profound or wicked?

"It's possible that this trio is making fun of me," thought Julien. You can't know him very well, reader, if you haven't long since noticed the dark, cold expression his face took on when Mathilde looked at him. Bitter irony repelled her friendly assurances, as the amazed Mademoiselle de La Mole discovered, when she two or three times risked such gestures.

Stung by this sudden strangeness, the young girl's cold, bored, over-intellectual heart became as passionate as her nature could be. But Mathilde's character also contained a great deal of pride, and the birth of an emotion that made all her happiness depend on someone else gave rise, as well, to a somber sadness.

Julien had by now learned enough, since he'd come to Paris, to recognize what was and what wasn't the dry sadness of boredom. Instead of being greedy for evening parties, for shows and any sort of distraction, as she had been, she avoided them.

Music sung by Frenchmen bored Mathilde to death, yet Julien, whose regular duty it was to attend high society's exits from the opera, noted that she made sure to have herself escorted to the opera just as often as she could. He fancied he could tell that she had lost some of that perfection, always so evident, before, in everything she did. Her remarks to her friends were sometimes outrageously sharp, to the point of nastiness. He thought she'd fallen onto hard times with the Marquis de Croisenois. "This young man must be desperately in love with money, not to throw over the girl, no matter how rich she might be," Julien thought. He himself, indignant at such affronts to masculine dignity, turned even colder to her. He often gave her answers bordering on the impolite.

However determined he might be not to let himself be deceived by Mathilde's shows of interest, on certain days they were so obvious that Julien, whose eyes had begun to be wide open, found her very pretty and was almost bowled over.

"These young aristocrats are so shrewd, and so long-suffering," he told himself, "that in the end they'll defeat my terribly limited experience." He had to leave all this, for a while. The marquis had just put him in charge of a number of small estates, and some châteaux, in lower Languedoc. A trip to the south of France was required; the marquis gave his grudging consent. Except in matters concerning the marquis's highest ambitions, Julien had become his second self.

"After all, they haven't snared me," Julien said to himself as he got ready for his departure. "Whether Mademoiselle de La Mole's witticisms about these gentlemen were genuine, or only intended to make me trust her, it's been amusing. If there's no conspiracy against this carpenter's son, I simply can't fathom Mademoiselle de La Mole. But she's even less understandable to the Marquis de Croisenois. Yesterday, for example, her bad temper was clearly real, and I had the pleasure of seeing a young nobleman, just as rich as I am penniless and plebian, forced to give up and acknowledge me the favored one. That's the greatest triumph I've had; it will still amuse me as I ride along the plains of Languedoc."

He had kept his departure secret, but Mathilde had known for a long time that, the next day, he was to leave Paris. She resorted to a severe headache, made worse by the dining room's stuffy air. She walked up and down the garden, and her quips so bloodied Norbert, the Marquis de Croisenois, de Caylus, de Luz, and several other young men who had dined with the de La Moles, that she finally drove them away. She was looking very strangely at Julien.

"Her expression is perhaps part of the comedy," thought Julien, "but that rapid breathing—all that agitation! Bah!" he told himself. "Who am I to pass judgment on all this? This is the Parisian woman at her most sublime, her most subtle. This quick breath, which almost moved me, is something she must have learned from Léontine Fay, that actress she loves so much."

They had been left alone; their conversation visibly faded away. "No! Julien feels nothing for me," Mathilde was telling herself, truly miserable.

As he was saying good night, she gripped his arm:

"You'll have a letter from me, tonight," she told him, her voice so changed that he could not recognize it.

This immediately moved him.

"My father," she went on, "quite properly values the services you render him. *You must not* leave tomorrow. Find some excuse." And then she ran away.

Her figure was charming. It would be impossible to have prettier feet; she ran so gracefully that Julien was entranced. But who could imagine his next thought, after she had disappeared? He was offended by the imperative tone with which she had said: "You must not." Louis XV, as he was dying, was deeply offended at the words "you must not," spoken most awkwardly by his chief physician. And Louis XV was hardly a social climber.

An hour later, a servant brought Julien a letter. It was a plain declaration of love.

"Her style isn't too terribly affected," Julien said to himself, trying to make use of literary observations to restrain a joy that made him suck in his cheeks and, in spite of himself, laugh out loud.

"So!" he cried suddenly, his emotions too strong to be held in. "I, a poor peasant, I've gotten a declaration of love from a great lady!

"Me, I haven't done so badly," he added, checking his joy as much as he could. "I've been able to preserve my personal dignity. I've not said I love her." He set himself to studying her writing: Mademoiselle de La Mole employed an extremely well-shaped English hand. He felt the need for something physical, to distract him from a joy that was very nearly delirium.

"Your departure compels me to speak. . . . It would be beyond my endurance not to see you any longer."

A thought struck Julien; it was like making a discovery. He broke off his examination of Mathilde's letter, and his joy swelled. "I'll bring it to the Marquis de Croisenois!" he cried silently. "I who say nothing but serious words! And he's so handsome! He has a mustache, a wonderful uniform. He's never at a loss for words, and at exactly the right time, something witty and subtle."

Julien experienced a delightful moment. He went wandering up and down the garden, crazed with happiness.

Later, he went up to the Marquis de La Mole's office room, for the marquis had fortunately not gone out that night, and explained that, happily, he wouldn't have to leave Paris. He was able to demonstrate, fairly easily, by showing the marquis some documents newly arrived from Normandy, that taking care of the Normandy lawsuits would force him to defer his departure for Languedoc.

"I'm very relieved you're not going," the marquis informed him when they were done talking business. *"I like seeing you."* Julien left; the remark embarrassed him.

"And I'm going to seduce his daughter—me! Perhaps her marriage to de Croisenois will be impossible—a marriage that glows in Monsieur de La Mole's future. He may not become a duke himself, but his daughter will be a duchess." Julien thought about leaving for Languedoc, in spite of Mathilde's letter, in spite of the excuses he'd made to the marquis. That ray of virtue quickly flickered out.

"How good of me," he told himself, "me, a plebeian, to take pity on a family of such high rank! Me, who the Duke de Chaulnes calls a mere servant! How does the marquis build up his immense fortune? By mortgaging some of his income as soon as he learns, at court, that the next day there'll be what looks like a coup d'état. And I, thrown to the lowest rungs by that harsh stepmother, Providence, me to whom she gave a noble heart and absolutely no income—which means no bread, *to put it exactly, no bread at all*—me, to turn down pleasure when it's offered to me! Clear water seeking to quench my thirst, in this burning desert of mediocrity which I cross so painfully! Good Lord, I'm not so stupid as that! Everyone for himself, in this desert of egoism, better known as life."

And he recalled looks of disdain cast on him by Madame de La Mole, and especially by the *ladies,* her friends.

The pleasure of triumphing over the Marquis de Croisenois was the final touch: his memory of virtue vanished.

"Oh, how I wish he were furious!" said Julien. "How confidently I'd slash him with a sword, now." And he performed a deft maneuver with an imaginary weapon.

"Before I could do that, I was a pedant, taking vulgar advantage of what little courage I had. After that letter, I am his equal.

"Yes," he told himself, with infinite delight and slowly measuring out his unspoken words, "our worth, de Croisenois and I, has now been weighed, and the scale favors the poor carpenter from the Juras.

"Fine!" he exclaimed to himself. "That will be the signature on my reply. Don't you go thinking, Mademoiselle de La Mole, that I'm forgetting what I am. I'm going to make you understand, and make you feel in your very bones, that you're betraying a fine descendant of the famous Guy de Croisenois, who followed Saint Louis to the Crusades, in favor of a carpenter's son."

Julien could not restrain his joy. He had to go down to the garden. His room, into which he had locked himself, seemed too narrow for him to draw a breath.

"Me, a poor peasant from the Juras," he repeated over and over to himself, "me, forever condemned to wearing this dreary black suit! Alas! Twenty years ago, I'd have worn a uniform like theirs! In those days, a man like me was either dead, or else he was *a general at age thirty-six*." The letter, which he held folded in his hand, endowed him with the height and bearing of a hero. "Of course, these days it's true that, wearing such a black suit, at age forty you have a salary of a hundred thousand francs and you wear the noblest decoration in the land, like the Bishop of Beauvais.

"Oh yes!" he told himself, laughing like Mephistopheles, "but I'm smarter than they are; I've chosen this century's uniform." He felt a surge, both in his ambition, and in his affection for ecclesiastical garb. "How many cardinals were born even lower than me, and have risen to authority! My countryman, Granvelle, for example."

Gradually, Julien grew calmer; caution came floating to the surface. He recited to himself the words of his model and master, that great hypocrite, Molière's Tartuffe:

> "I could believe these words, a decent trick. . . .
> I won't trust anything that seems so sweet,
> Except a taste of her, and then I'll sigh,
> Knowing she told the truth, and I have proof.

"Tartuffe was ruined by a woman, too, and he was as good as anyone else. . . . Other eyes may see my reply . . . for which there will be the following remedy," he said slowly, and with controlled ferocity: "We'll begin with the choicest phrases from the sublime Mathilde's own letter.

"Yes, but suppose four of Monsieur de Croisenois's servants throw themselves at me and snatch away the original.

"No, because I am well armed, and I've been known, as they say, to shoot at servants.

"So! One of them is brave; he jumps at me. He's been promised two thousand francs. I kill him, or perhaps I wound him—wonderful: it's just what they want. They throw me into prison, all very legally. And then I appear in court, and the judges sentence me, with vast justice and infinite equity, to live at the penitentiary at Poissy with Messieurs Fontan and Magalon. I lie down at night, there, with four hundred beggars, everybody on top of everybody else. . . . And I show pity to these people!" he exclaimed to himself, standing bolt upright. "And do they show it to the members of the Fourth Estate, the common people, when they've got them where they want them?" This was the last breath of his gratitude for Monsieur de La Mole, for in spite of himself that had been, till then, tormenting him.

"Gently, dear gentlemen: I understand this minor aspect of Machiavellianism. Neither Father Maslon nor Monsieur Castaneda at the seminary could have done it better. Take this *provocative* letter away from me—and, like Colonel Caron, at Colmar, I'll stroll to the firing squad.

"One moment, gentlemen: I plan to send the fatal letter to be deposited, well hidden, by Father Pirard. He's a very decent man, a Jansenist, and as a Jansenist immune to fiscal temptation. Yes, but he opens letters ... so I'll send them to Fouqué."

I concede that Julien's expression was ghastly, his face truly hideous. He fairly breathed of unadulterated criminality. He was a miserable man at war with all of society.

"To arms!" Julien exclaimed to himself. Then he went out the front door, leaped down the steps, and went straight to the copyist stall at the corner. The man was frightened by his appearance. "Copy it," he said, giving him Mademoiselle de La Mole's letter.

While the man did his work, Julien himself wrote to Fouqué; he begged him to take care of this precious deposit. "But no," he said to himself, breaking off. "The secret police at the post office will open my letter ... no, gentlemen." He went to the Protestant bookseller, bought an enormous Bible, hid Mathilde's letter, carefully and ingeniously, in the binding, had everything wrapped up, and sent his package via stagecoach, addressed to one of Fouqué's workmen; even the man's name was unknown to anyone in Paris.

That done, he went happily, light-footedly back to the de La Mole house. *"Our turn, now!"* he exclaimed silently, as he turned the key and locked himself into his room. He threw off his black suit.

"Really, Mademoiselle," he wrote to Mathilde, "Mademoiselle de La Mole writes, and uses her father's servant, Arsène, to deliver an exceedingly seductive letter to a poor carpenter from the Juras, surely to have fun at his simpleminded expense...." And then he copied out the plainest, most revealing sentences from the letter he'd just received.

His letter would have done honor to the cautious diplomatic skills of the Chevalier de Beauvoisis. It was still only ten o'clock. Drunk with happiness and a sense of his own power, all very new to a poor devil, Julien went to the Italian Opera House. He heard his friend Géronimo singing. Never had music exalted him to such heights. He was godlike.

CHAPTER FOURTEEN

A YOUNG GIRL'S THOUGHTS

Such bepuzzzlement! What sleepless nights! God in heaven! Am I going
to make myself contemptible? He himself will scorn me. But he's leaving, he's going away.

—ALFRED DE MUSSET

It had not been easy for Mathilde to write. No matter what had awakened her interest in Julien, he'd soon come to dominate that pride
which, from the first moment she'd become aware of it, had ruled, solitary, in her heart. Her haughty, cold spirit had been carried, for the
very first time, into passionate feeling. But if it dominated over her
pride, it remained loyal to that pride's customary behavior. Two months
of internal struggle, and of new sensations, in a word, renovated her
entire moral existence.

Mathilde believed she was reaching happiness. This vista, all-
powerful for courageous hearts bound to superior minds, had long been
struggling against both her personal dignity and her sense of everyday
responsibilities. One day she went to her mother, at seven in the morning, asking for permission to hide herself at Villequier. The marquise
didn't bother to answer, suggesting only that the girl go back to bed.
This was a final effort by ordinary common sense and deference to
received notions.

Fear of doing wrong and offending against the most sacred beliefs
of the de Cayluses, the de Luzes, and the de Croisenoises, were hardly
deeply seated in her soul. She did not think such people had been
fashioned to understand her; had it been a question of buying a carriage, or a piece of property, she would have consulted them. Her true
fear was that Julien might be disappointed in her.

And perhaps she also worried: Was he only apparently rather than
truly superior?

She detested lack of character: this was her single objection to the
handsome young men who surrounded her. The more gracefully they

made jokes about whatever was not in fashion (or which tried to be fashionable, but did it badly), the lower they fell in her eyes.

They were courageous, and that was all. "And still, just how brave, really?" she asked herself. "In duels, but duels are only a ritual. Duels are totally predictable, even as to what one says, falling to the ground. Stretched out on the green grass, hand on heart, the other combatant must be most nobly pardoned, and final words sent to a lovely one left behind (often an imaginary) beloved, who's likely to go to a ball on the day the fallen one dies, to keep from arousing suspicion.

"It's one thing to face danger bravely, leading a squadron into battle, shining steel all around, but what about danger that's solitary, strange, unpredictable, and genuinely ugly?

"Alas!" Mathilde told herself. "At Henry III's court there were men whose characters were as lofty as their birth! Ah, if Julien had fought at Jarnac, or at Montcontour, I'd have no doubts. In those strong, forceful times, the French were not dressed-up dolls. The day of battle, really, was the least of their problems.

"Their lives were not all wrapped around, like an Egyptian mummy, confined in some common covering, shared by everyone, always the same. Yes," she added, "it took more genuine courage to go home alone, an hour before midnight, leaving the Soissons mansion where Catherine de Médici lived, all thronging with cutthroats, than it does today to go running off to Algeria. A man's life, then, involved taking one chance after another. Civilization has now eliminated risks, especially unexpected ones. If anyone talks about such things, he's smothered in witticisms; if they actually occur, no cowardliness is too low to accommodate our fears. Whatever insanity fear makes us commit, it's forgiven. A degenerate, boring epoch! What would Boniface de La Mole have said, lifting his severed head out of his tomb, if he had seen seventeen of his descendants letting themselves be herded off like sheep, to be guillotined two days later? Death was absolutely certain, but it would have exhibited a lack of taste to defend themselves and, at least, kill a Jacobin or two. Ah! In France's heroic age, in Boniface de La Mole's time, Julien would have been a squadron leader, and my brother would have been the young priest, with very good manners, and caution in his eyes, reason in his mouth."

Several months earlier, Mathilde had given up hope of meeting anyone even faintly out of the ordinary. She had taken some pleasure in letting herself write to some of these young aristocrats. This inappropriate boldness, so reckless in a young girl, might well have dishonored her in the eyes of Monsieur de Croisenois, as it might also to his father, the Duke of Chaulnes, and all their family, friends, and followers, who would have seen the intended marriage broken off and would have wanted to know why. When she'd written such a letter, in those days, she'd been unable to sleep. But those letters were nothing but replies.

Now she'd dared to say she was in love. It was she who had written *first* (such a shocking word!), and to a man from the lowest levels of society.

This would guarantee, if she should be discovered, eternal dishonor. Which of the women who came to see her mother would dare take her side? What words could they use, repeating them from one drawing room to another, to soften society's frightful scorn?

Even to say these things would have been ghastly, but to write them! *"There are things one does not write,"* exclaimed Napoleon when he heard that Bailen had been surrendered to the Spanish, and on what terms. And it was Julien who had told her this story, as if teaching her a lesson in advance.

But all this was more or less trivial: Mathilde's anguish had other causes. Putting aside the awful effect on society, the ineradicable, totally open stain of social contempt (since she had grossly offended against her class), Mathilde had written to a creature of a totally different sort than the de Cayluses, the de Luzs, or the de Croisenoises.

The depths, the *mysteriousness* of Julien's character would have been frightening, even in striking up an ordinary, everyday relationship. But she was going to make him her lover, perhaps her master!

"What won't he demand, if he ever has me under his thumb? Well! I'll say, as Medea did: 'In the midst of all these perils, I remain *me!*'

"Julien has absolutely no reverence for noble blood," she believed. What's more, quite possibly he had no love whatever for her!

In these final moments of terrible doubt, ideas of womanly pride occurred to her. "Everything has to be unique, for the kind of girl I am," she exclaimed impatiently. Then the pride they'd instilled in her, from her very cradle, began to struggle against virtue. And at just that moment, Julien's departure accelerated everything.

(Characters like hers, fortunately, are very rare indeed.)

That evening, very late, Julien was malicious enough to have the porter bring down an exceedingly heavy trunk, and the servant he summoned was Mademoiselle de La Mole's footman. "Perhaps this won't accomplish anything," he said to himself, "but if it succeeds, she'll think I've gone." He went to bed happy, extremely pleased at his little stratagem. Mathilde never closed her eyes.

The next day, very early in the morning, Julien went out without being noticed. But he came back before eight o'clock.

He'd barely walked into the library when Mademoiselle de La Mole appeared at the door. He gave her his written reply. He thought he ought to speak to her, and certainly there'd be no more convenient time, but Mademoiselle de La Mole refused to listen, and disappeared. Julien found this captivating: he would not have known what to say to her.

"If this isn't just a game that she and Count Norbert are playing, then the fire of such a strange love, which this girl of high birth conceives she feels for me, must have been lit by the icy-cold looks I've showered on her. I'd be a hopelessly stupid idiot if I ever let myself actually *like* this tall blonde doll." Thinking this way let him be colder and more calculating than ever before.

"In the coming combat," he added, "pride of birth will be like a tall hill, constituting a military position between her and me. There's where we'll have to maneuver. I was very wrong to stay in Paris: putting off my departure is detrimental, and it leaves me vulnerable, if all this is indeed merely a game. What risk was there in going away? I'd be making fools of them, if they were making a fool of me. If she's really interested in me, I'd be heightening it a hundredfold."

Mademoiselle de La Mole's letter had so intensely gratified Julien's vanity that, while relishing what had happened, he'd forgotten to think very seriously about the utility of removing himself from the scene.

It was a fatal flaw in his character, this extraordinary sensitivity to his mistakes. This one deeply upset him; he'd almost stopped thinking of the incredible victory he'd had just before this minor setback, when, toward nine o'clock, Mademoiselle de La Mole appeared, barely inside the library door; after throwing a letter to him, she ran off.

"It looks as if this is going to be an epistolary novel," he said, picking it up. "This is an enemy feint; me, I'm going to respond with coldness and virtue."

With a haughtiness that fueled his inner delight, the letter asked for a decisive reply. He amused himself, as he wrote his two pages, by playfully toying with the people who might be trying to make a fool of him and, still in this humor, toward the end of his response, announced that he would be leaving the following morning.

His letter was done. "The garden will do very well for sending it to her," he thought, so there he went. He looked up at Mademoiselle de La Mole's window.

It was on the second floor, next to her mother's rooms; but underneath her window there was a large mezzanine.

The ground floor had been raised high enough so that, walking along the line of linden trees, his letter in his hand, Julien could not have been seen from Mathilde's window. The tall, arching trees got in the way. "Really!" Julien said to himself, annoyed. "Yet another risky development! If someone's trying to make a fool of me, just having me seen with a letter in my hand will do very nicely; my enemies will be pleased."

Norbert's room was just above his sister's, and if Julien were to walk out from under the arching vault of the tall trees, Norbert and his friends would be able to follow his every movement.

Mademoiselle de La Mole appeared behind the glass; he let her have a quick glimpse of his letter; she bent her head in acknowledgment. He turned at once and ran back to his room and, as it happened, met on the stairs the lovely Mathilde, who snatched up the letter, completely at her ease, her eyes laughing.

"What passion there was in poor Madame de Rênal's eyes," Julien said to himself, "if, even after six months of our relationship, she dared accept a letter from me! Never in her life, I think, did she ever look at me with laughing eyes."

The rest of his reaction was not anything like so clear: Was he ashamed of how petty he was being? "But what a difference, too," his thought continued, "in the elegance of her dressing gown, the elegance of everything she wears!" Just seeing Mademoiselle de La Mole, from thirty feet away, any man of taste could guess her social standing. That was definitely a positive thing.

Caught up in his jesting, Julien still did not admit all he was thinking. There had been no Marquis de Croisenois for Madame de Rênal to sacrifice for him. His only rival had been that lowly deputy governor, Monsieur Charcot, who'd given himself the name de Maugiron, since there were no more de Maugirons.

At five, Julien received a third letter; she'd thrown it to him, from the library door. Once again, Mademoiselle de La Mole ran away. "What a mania for writing!" he said to himself, laughing, "when conversation is so readily available! The enemy wants my letters, that's obvious—and they want more than one!" He was in no hurry to open this one. "Still such elegant phrases," he was thinking, but then he turned pale as he read on. There were only eight lines:

> I need to talk to you; I must talk to you, and tonight. When the clock sounds an hour after midnight, be in the garden. Take the gardener's big ladder from near the well; place it against my window and climb up to me. There'll be a full moon: it doesn't matter.

CHAPTER FIFTEEN

IS IT A CONSPIRACY?

What a bitter space between conceiving and executing a noble project! What empty terrors! What indecision! It's life and death—but it's far more: it's honor!

—SCHILLER

"This is becoming serious," Julien thought, . . . "and a bit too clear," he added after further thought. "Hmm! This beautiful lady can talk to me in the library, with a freedom that, by the grace of God, is absolute. The marquis is so afraid I might show him my accounts, he never walks in. Hah! Monsieur de La Mole and Count Norbert, the only people who ever appear here, are away virtually all day long. It's perfectly easy to see them, when they're returning—and my sublime Mathilde, for whose hand a ruling prince would not be too noble, wants me to be guilty of something so abominably rash.

"Plainly, they either want to ruin me or, at least, to make fun of me. First they wanted me to ruin myself with my letters; my letters were too cautious. Well! They've got to have something clearer than daylight. These handsome little fellows think I'm either extremely stupid or a hopeless fop. The devil! In full moonlight, to climb up a ladder, like that, to a second story twenty-five feet high! They'd have plenty of time to see me, even from the neighboring houses. How handsome I'll look, up on my ladder!" Julien went up to his room and, whistling, began to pack his trunk. He'd made up his mind to leave, and not to bother replying.

But this sensible solution did not put his heart at ease. "Suppose, by some odd chance," he suddenly said to himself, his trunk now closed, "suppose Mathilde is acting in good faith! Then, in her eyes, I'd be playing the role of a perfect coward. I have no noble birth, so I have to have a great character—cash on demand, and no easy little forgeries—and that character has to be solidly proven: the deeds need to speak for themselves. . . ."

He spent a quarter of an hour in reflection. "Why try to deny it?" he finally said. "I'll be a coward in her eyes. I'd give up not only the most brilliant woman in high society, as everyone said at Duke de Retz's ball, but also the divine pleasure of seeing the Marquis de Croisenois, a duke's son who will himself be a duke, sacrificed for me. A charming young man, with all the qualities I lack: quick wit, birth, money.

"I'll be sorry the rest of my life—not for her, there are lots of mistresses! 'But there's only one honor!' as Corneille's old Don Diego says—and here, facing the first danger I've been offered, I clearly and simply pull back—because that duel with Monsieur de Beauvoisis was almost a joke. This is entirely different. I might be shot by a servant, at point-blank range, but that's not the most serious risk. I might be disgraced.

"This is getting serious, my boy," he added, clownishly, brightly.

"It's all about '*onor*, it is. What poor devil, thrown so far down by chance, ever gets an opportunity like this? I'll do well with other women, yes, but never one so high up. . . ."

He thought for a long time, walking rapidly up and down his room, from time to time stopping abruptly. A magnificent marble bust of de Richelieu was kept in the room; in spite of himself, he found himself drawn to it. De Richelieu seemed to be looking at him rather harshly, as if scolding him for lacking the audacity so proper and natural to the French character. "In your time, you great man, would I have hesitated?

"At the worst," he finally told himself, "let's suppose this is all a trap; it remains very dark and exceedingly compromising for a young girl. They know I'm not someone who'll stay silent. They'd have to kill me. That was fine in 1574, the days of Boniface de La Mole, but today's de La Moles would never risk it. This family is no longer what it was. They're so jealous of Mademoiselle de La Mole! Tomorrow there'd be four hundred drawing rooms ringing with her shame—and with such pleasure!

"The servants gossip among themselves about the obvious preference I've been shown. I know it, I've heard them. . . .

"On the other hand, her letters! . . . They might believe I'll have them on me. If they can surprise me in her room, they could take them. I'd have to deal with two, three, four men—who knows? But where would they find such men? Where can you find discreet servants, here in Paris? The law frightens them. . . . By God! the de Cayluses, the de Luzes, the de Croisenoises themselves! Being there just then, and the stupid figure I'd cut, in the middle of them—that might tempt them. Watch out for what happened to Abélard, Monsieur Secretary!

"So, by God! Gentlemen, you'll carry the scars of our combat; I'll slash your faces, as Caesar's soldiers cut up Pompey's men, at Pharsalia. . . . And as for the letters, I can find them a safe hiding place."

Julien made copies of the last two, hid them in a volume of the library's beautiful Voltaire, and brought the originals to the post.

When he returned: "What madness am I throwing myself into?" he asked himself, surprised and alarmed. He had spent an entire quarter of an hour without looking straight ahead, facing what was to happen next, that same night.

"But if I don't do it, I'll despise myself afterward. This will linger on, my whole life long, as something questionable—and for me that sort of uncertainty is the bitterest misery of all. Wasn't that what I felt about Amanda's lover? I think I'd be far readier to forgive myself some simple crime: once I admitted it, I'd stop thinking about it.

"Hah! I'll have been competing against a man bearing one of the best names in all France—and then cheerfully, of my own volition, I'll have said he was the better, I was the inferior one! It's plain enough: not to do this is cowardice. And that settles it," Julien exclaimed silently, jumping to his feet. . . . "Besides, she's so very pretty.

"If this isn't a betrayal, what madness she's committing for my sake! . . . It's a puzzle, by God! So, gentlemen, it's up to me, just me, to turn the joke into a serious affair, and that's what I intend to do.

"Yet what if they tie up my arms, as I'm coming into the room. Maybe they've set up some ingenious device.

"Well, it's like a duel," he assured himself, laughing. " 'There's a riposte for every sword stroke,' as my fencing teacher says, 'but God, who wants it over and done with, makes one of the two forget how it's done.' In any case, here's how I'll deal with them." He pulled his pistols out of his pocket and, even though they were charged and loaded, he readied them all over again.

He still had several hours of waiting. In order to be doing something, Julien wrote to Fouqué:

My friend: Don't open the letter, here enclosed, unless there's been an accident and you hear that something strange has happened to me. In that event, erase the names from the manuscript I'm sending you, and make eight copies, to be sent to the newspapers in Marseilles, Bordeaux, Lyons, Brussels, etc. Ten days later, have the manuscript printed and send the first copies to the Marquis de La Mole. And fifteen days later, strew the other copies, at night, along the streets of Verrières.

The short manuscript he had enclosed, explaining and justifying, and which Fouqué was only to read in case of accident, had been written as a narrative; he had made it as minimally compromising as possible for Mademoiselle de La Mole, but nevertheless it clearly stated his own position.

Julien had finished sealing this package just as the dinner bell sounded; it made his heart beat. Preoccupied with the narration he had just been composing, his imagination was full of tragic foreboding. He could see himself seized by the servants, tied, carried down to a cellar, a gag in his mouth. Once there, one of the servants would stand guard over him, and if the honor of the noble family required a tragic ending, it would be easy to finish him off with a poison that left no traces. Then they could say he'd died of some illness, and they'd bring him back to his room, dead.

Moved by his own narrative, like a playwright by his drama, Julien entered the dining room with a feeling of genuine fear. He looked at all the servants, in their full regalia. He examined their faces. "Which of these people have been picked for tonight's expedition?" he asked himself. "In this family, memories of Henry III's court are so much alive, so often recalled, that if they believe there has been an outrage against the family, they're likely to be more decisive than other people of their rank." He looked at Mademoiselle de La Mole, trying to read the family's plans in her eyes. She was pale and looked thoroughly medieval. He'd never seen her looking so noble and grand; she was truly beautiful, and imposing. He almost fell in love with her. "*Pallida morte futura,* her pallor prophesies death," he said to himself.

After dinner, though he pretended to spend time walking in the garden, it was useless; Mademoiselle de La Mole did not appear. Had he been able to talk to her, just then, it would have taken a great weight from his heart.

Why not admit it? He was afraid. Since he was determined to go ahead with it, he shamelessly indulged his fear. "Provided that, when it's time to act, I have the courage to carry me through," he told himself, "what difference does it make what I'm feeling right now?" He checked the location, hefting the ladder to be sure of its weight.

"This is a tool," he said to himself, laughing, "which it seems to be my destiny to make use of! Here, just as, before, in Verrières. But what a difference! Then," he continued, sighing, "there was no need to mistrust the person for whom I endangered myself. And what a difference, also, in the danger!

"I might have been killed, in Monsieur de Rênal's gardens, without necessarily being dishonored. They could perfectly well have made my death unexplainable. Here, what abominable stories they're going to be telling, at the de Cayluses, the de Chaulneses, the de Retzes, etc.—indeed, everywhere. I will go down in history as a monster.

"Or maybe only for two or three years," he answered himself, laughing once again, but this time at himself. But the thought made him feel suddenly weak. "And I, where will I find anyone to argue for me? Supposing Fouqué prints my little pamphlet, posthumously, why, that will be yet another infamy. What! I'm welcomed into the house, and to pay back the hospitality they gave me, the kindness they showered on me, I print a pamphlet about what happened! I attack a woman's honor! Ah, let me be betrayed—a thousand times better, that way."

It was a ghastly evening.

CHAPTER SIXTEEN

ONE O'CLOCK IN THE MORNING

The garden was very big, designed fairly recently and in perfect taste. But the trees were more than a century old. The effect was somewhat rustic.

—MASSINGER

He was about to write a counterorder to Fouqué, when one o'clock sounded. He locked the door to his room noisily, as if he were shutting himself in for the night. Then he loped around the whole house, like a wolf, especially on the top floor, where the servants were quartered. He saw nothing unusual. One of Madame de La Mole's maids was having a party, and the servants were happily emptying the punch bowl. "The ones who are laughing like that," thought Julien, "can't be the ones participating in a nocturnal expedition. They'd be more serious."

At last he went and stood in a dark corner of the garden. "If their plan is to hide themselves from the de La Mole servants, the ones who are supposed to surprise me will have to come in over the garden walls.

"If Monsieur de Croisenois has any sense about all this, he has to know how much less compromising it would be, for the young woman he wants to marry, to surprise me before I've reached her room."

He performed a very precise military reconnaissance. "This is a question of my honor," he thought. "If I let something slip by me, it won't be an excuse—not to me—if I tell myself: 'I never thought of that.'"

The weather was depressingly fine. The moon had risen about eleven o'clock; by twelve-thirty, the side of the house facing the garden was fully lit.

"She's insane," Julien told himself. When one o'clock sounded, there was still light in Count Norbert's windows. Never in all his life had Julien been so terrified: all he saw were the risks he was taking, nor was he enthusiastic about taking them.

He went to get the big ladder, waited five minutes so she had time to countermand her instructions, and at five after one set the ladder against Mathilde's window. He climbed up quietly, pistol in hand, astonished not to have been attacked. As he reached the window, she threw it open, noiselessly.

"There you are, sir," Mathilde said to him, very emotionally. "I've been following your movements for the last hour."

Julien was deeply embarrassed; he did not know how to behave; he felt no love whatever. In his embarrassment he thought he might as well act the lover, so he tried to kiss Mathilde.

"For shame!" she said, pushing him away.

Very happy to have been repulsed, he quickly glanced around him. The moon was so bright that the shadows it cast in Mathilde's room were black. "But there could well be men so well hidden that I can't see them," he thought.

"What's that in your side pocket?" Mathilde asked, delighted to have found a subject for conversation. She was feeling strangely tormented: all those feelings of restraint and shyness, so natural to a well-bred girl, had resumed their sway and were torturing her.

"I've got all sorts of weapons, as well as pistols," Julien replied, equally happy to have something to say.

"The ladder has to be removed," said Mathilde.

"It's huge, and it might break the glass in the room down below, or the ones in the mezzanine."

"The glass mustn't be broken," Mathilde answered, trying unsuccessfully to speak in an ordinary conversational tone. "You could, I should think, lower the ladder, using a rope tied to the first rung. I always keep ropes in my room."

"And this is a woman in love!" thought Julien. "She has the nerve to say she's in love! Such calm, such sensible precautions, show me very plainly that I'm not triumphing over Monsieur de Croisenois, as I so foolishly believed. I've simply become his successor. Really, what does it matter? Am I in love with her? I've won a victory over de Croisenois, because he'll be exceedingly angry, having a successor at all, and angrier still to have that successor be me. How arrogantly he looked at me, yesterday night, at Café Tortoni, pretending he didn't even know me! How nastily he greeted me, afterward, when he couldn't get out of it any longer."

Julien had tied a rope to the ladder; it went down quietly, leaning far enough out from the balcony to keep from touching the glass panes. "Just the time to kill me," he thought, "if there's someone hidden in Mathilde's room." But a profound silence still hung over everything.

The ladder touched the ground; Julien managed to lay it down in a bed of exotic flowers, along the wall.

"What will my mother say," said Mathilde, "when she sees her beautiful flowers all crushed? . . . You've got to throw the rope down, too," she added with immense calm. "If anyone sees it leading back to the balcony, it won't be easy to explain."

"And how me go 'way?" Julien said wryly, assuming a Creole accent. (One of the chambermaids had been born in San Domingo.)

"You, you'll leave by the door," said Mathilde, fascinated by the idea.

"Ah, this is a man fully worthy of my love!" she thought.

Julien had just dropped the rope into the garden; Mathilde took him by the arm. He thought he'd been seized by some enemy, and turned around quickly, drawing a dagger. She'd thought she heard a window opening. They stood motionless, not even breathing. The moon fell full on them. There was no other sound, no further cause for alarm.

Then they were once again seriously embarrassed, both of them. Julien made sure that the door had been properly closed, all the bolts thrown. He'd thought of looking under the bed but did not dare; there could be a servant or two under there. In the end, he was so worried that prudence would make him regret the omission, at some future date, that he looked.

Mathilde had been gripped by all the torments of extreme shyness. This horrified her.

"What have you done with my letters?" she asked at last.

"Just the time to shake up these gentlemen, if they're listening, and to avoid a battle!" thought Julien.

"The first one is hidden in a huge Protestant Bible, which the mail coach carried away, last night, and will be taking far away."

He spoke very clearly, as he gave her all the details, so he could be heard by anyone who might be hidden, perhaps, in the two big mahogany armoires, which he hadn't dared look into.

"The other two are in the mail, going to the same place as the first."

"Good Lord! Why all these precautions?" asked Mathilde, astonished.

"Is there some reason for lying to her?" thought Julien. And he told her all his suspicions.

"That's why your letters were so cold!" Mathilde exclaimed, sounding more irrational than tender, but suddenly, devastatingly, changing to a pronoun implying familiarity, even intimacy.

Julien was no longer listening closely. Once he had heard her use conclusively intimate language, he lost his head—or, at least, he lost all his suspicions. He found the courage to embrace this wonderfully beautiful girl, for whom he felt immense respect. She only partly pushed him away.

He fell back on his memory, as he had done once before, in Besançon, with Amanda, and recited some of the loveliest phrases of *La Nouvelle Héloïse*.

"You have a man's heart," she said endearingly, without really listening to his words. "I wanted to test your courage; I admit it. Your early suspicions and your determination show me that you're even braver than I could have believed."

Mathilde was consciously trying to keep using intimate language; she was obviously paying more attention to this new and unfamiliar way of speech than to what she was actually saying. Intimate words, devoid of any tenderness, did not please him: he was stunned by the complete absence, in his heart, of any sign of happiness. At last, trying to feel it, he fell back on rationality. He could see that this exceedingly proud young girl thought very well of him, and he knew she never praised anyone or anything unreservedly. This argument satisfied his self-esteem.

It was not, indeed, that same intensity of sensual pleasure he had experienced, several times, with Madame de Rênal. He felt no tenderness whatever: this was the vigorous happiness of ambition, for Julien was ambitious, above all else. Once again, he talked about the people he had suspected, and the precautions he had devised. As he spoke, he thought how best to take advantage of his triumph.

Still deeply embarrassed, and apparently staggered by what she had done, Mathilde seemed delighted to have found a topic for conversation. They discussed how they might be able to meet again. Julien was thoroughly enjoying the wit and courage he had proved, once more, as they were talking. They were dealing with extremely clear-sighted people; little Tanbeau was certainly a spy; but he and Mathilde were not exactly fools, either.

What would be easier than to meet in the library, the most convenient place of all?

"I can appear, without creating any suspicion, in any part of the house," added Julien, "and very nearly in Madame de La Mole's room." Crossing through that room, to get to her daughter's, was completely unavoidable. If Mathilde thought it better that he always arrive by ladder, he would expose himself to that trivial danger, his heart drunk with joy.

Listening to him speak, Mathilde was shocked by his sense of triumph. "He's already my master!" she told herself. She felt remorse gripping her; her rational mind was horrified by the remarkable act of madness she'd committed. Had she been able to, she would have annihilated both herself and Julien. When by sheer force of will she could momentarily beat back remorse, shyness and suffering modesty made her wretchedly miserable. She had had no idea of the frightful state in which she would find herself.

"But, still, I need to talk to him," she finally told herself. "That's understood: you speak to your lover." And then, to fulfill this obligation, and with a tenderness that was still more in the words she used than in the tone of her voice, she told him several decisions she had made, these last few days.

She had decided that if he were courageous enough to come to her, via the gardener's ladder, as she had directed he should, she would be entirely his. But never were such tender words spoken more coldly and politely. To this point, their rendezvous had been utterly frigid. It was almost enough to turn love into something detestable. What a lesson in morality, for a young, careless girl! Was a moment like this worth the pain of losing one's whole future?

After long hesitation, which an observer might have thought caused by strong distaste—so hard is it for a woman to abandon her sense of what she owes herself, even in yielding to a will equally strong— Mathilde ended by becoming his loving mistress.

In truth, their ecstasies were a bit *willed*. Passionate love was still a model they were imitating, rather than something real.

Mademoiselle de La Mole felt that she had fulfilled her duty to herself and to her lover. "The poor boy," she told herself, "has demonstrated perfect bravery; he ought to be happy; or else I'm the one with a deficient character." But she wished she could buy off, in return for an eternity of misfortunes, the cruel necessity in which she found herself caught up.

In spite of the horrible violence she was doing to herself, she remained absolutely in control of her words.

There was no regret, no reproach, to spoil this night that seemed to Julien strange rather than happy. What a difference, Good Lord! from his final twenty-four hours in Verrières! "These lovely Parisian manners have acquired the secret of spoiling everything, even love," he told himself, most unfairly.

He shaped these reflections while standing in one of the large mahogany armoires, which he'd gone into at the first sounds heard in the adjoining rooms, which belonged to Madame de La Mole. Mathilde went to mass with her mother, the maids were soon out of the rooms, and Julien escaped quite easily, before they returned to finish their work.

He mounted his horse and hunted up the most solitary parts of a forest close to Paris. He remained far more amazed than happy. The sort of happiness that now and then filled his heart was like that of a young second lieutenant, who, after an astonishing battle, has just been made a colonel, on the spot, by the commanding general. He felt himself borne to an immense height. Everything that had been above him, the night before, was now at his level or even below him. Little by little, the farther he got from Paris, the more his happiness grew.

If he had no tenderness in his soul, it was because—however strange the words may seem—Mathilde, in everything she had done with him, had been fulfilling a duty. She had experienced nothing unforeseen in all that happened during their night together, except the misery and shame she'd found, instead of the absolute felicity of which novels had told her.

"Was I wrong? Was I *not* in love with him?" she asked herself.

CHAPTER SEVENTEEN

AN OLD SWORD

> I now mean to be serious; —it is time,
> Since laughter nowadays is deemed too serious.
> A jest at vice by virtue's called a crime.
> —BYRON, *DON JUAN*

She did not come down to dinner. Later, she appeared in the drawing room, very briefly, but did not look at Julien. Her conduct seemed to him strange. "But," he thought, "I don't know their customs; she'll give me some good reason for these things." All the same, impelled by the strongest curiosity, he studied Mathilde's expression, and could not conceal from himself that she seemed wry and nasty. This was obviously not the same woman who, the night before, had enjoyed—or had feigned—an ecstatic happiness far too great to be real.

The next day, and the day after that, her coldness remained the same; she did not look at him; she was not aware of his existence. Gripped by intense discomfort, Julien was a thousand miles from the triumphant feelings which, that first day, had been all there was in his heart. "Could this, by any chance," he asked himself, "be a return to virtue?" But this was too bourgeois a word for haughty Mathilde.

"In everyday life," Julien thought, "she has hardly any religious belief. She approves of it as useful to the interests of her class.

"But couldn't plain female delicacy be reproaching her for the sin she's committed?" Julien now believed he had been her first lover.

"Still," he told himself, at other moments, "it must be conceded that there is nothing naïve, simple, or tender in her whole manner of being. I've never seen her haughtier. Does she despise me? It would be like her to reproach herself for what she's done for me, strictly on account of my low birth."

While Julien, full of preconceived judgments, drawn from books as well as his memories of Verrières, was haunted by the chimera of a tender mistress who, from the moment she had made her lover happy, was no longer concerned with his existence, Mathilde's vanity was wildly angry with him.

Since she had not been bored in two months, she was no longer worried about boredom; thus, without having the slightest suspicion of it, Julien had lost his greatest advantage.

"I've given myself a master!" Mademoiselle de La Mole told herself, succumbing to the blackest, most sorrowful regret. "He's enormously honorable, for what that's worth, but if I push his vanity over the edge, he'll take his revenge by letting the world know our relationship." Mathilde had never had a lover, and being in a state which makes even the sourest souls dream tender illusions, she was consumed by the bitterest of black thoughts.

"He has immense power over me, since he rules by terror and can punish me with tremendous pain if I push at him too hard." This alone was enough to lead Mademoiselle de La Mole to show him stern disrespect: her character's primary attribute was courage. Nothing could have set her in restless motion, and cure her of her endless boredom, without forever quickening her sense that she was gambling for the highest of all stakes, her very existence at risk.

On the third day, with Mademoiselle de La Mole stubbornly refusing to acknowledge him, after dinner Julien followed her, clearly against her will, into the billiard room.

"So, sir, you feel possessed of some mighty power over me," she said, with barely restrained anger, "since, quite directly against my wishes, unmistakably expressed, you intend to speak to me? . . . Are you aware that no one in the world has ever dared do that?"

Nothing could be so amusing as the dialogue between these two lovers, unaware that they were each driven by intensely passionate hatred of the other. Neither of them endowed with much patience, and both being accustomed to the ways of good society, they were soon flatly declaring eternal enmity.

"I am forever bound to secrecy, I swear it!" said Julien. "I might add that I'd never speak to you again, except that such a marked change could damage your reputation." He bowed respectfully and left.

He had performed, without much difficulty, what seemed to him his duty, it would never have occurred to him that he was in love with Mademoiselle de La Mole. There was no question he hadn't loved her three days earlier, when he'd been hidden in the big mahogany armoire. But his soul suffered a sharp sea change the moment he saw he'd broken with her forever.

His relentless memory made him retrace every detail of that night, which in truth had left him so cold.

The very next night after the decisive rupture, Julien almost drove himself mad, forced to admit that he was in love with Mademoiselle de La Mole.

Ghastly struggles followed on this discovery: his emotions had been tossed every which way.

Two days later, instead of being haughty with Monsieur de Croisenois, he came close to tearfully embracing him.

He was accustomed to misery, and that lent him a whiff of common sense: he decided to leave for Languedoc, packed his trunk, and went to arrange his trip.

He felt faint when, arriving at the mail-coach office, he found that by a strange coincidence there was an available seat, for the next day, in the coach going to Toulouse, the capital of Languedoc. He bought his ticket and returned to inform the Marquis de La Mole of his departure.

Monsieur de La Mole had gone out. More dead than alive, Julien went to the library to wait for him. How did he feel, when he there encountered Mademoiselle de La Mole?

Seeing him, she put on a nasty expression, which he could not possibly misunderstand.

Carried away by his misery, confused and surprised, Julien had the weakness to say to her, in the tenderest voice, and truly from the heart: "So you don't love me anymore?"

"I'm horrified that I gave myself to the first one who came along," Mathilde said, weeping with self-directed fury.

"The first one who came along!" Julien exclaimed, running over to where, hung in the library as a curiosity, there was an ancient, medieval sword.

His misery, which he had thought at its height when he spoke to her, was intensified a hundredfold, seeing her tears of shame. He would have been the happiest of men if he could have killed her.

Just as, with some difficulty, he'd drawn the sword from its ancient sheath, Mathilde, thrilled by this wonderfully new sensation, came toward him, haughtily; her tears had stopped.

The thought of the Marquis de La Mole, his benefactor, came vividly into his mind. "I'd be killing his daughter!" he told himself. "How awful!" He started to throw the sword down. "Certainly," he thought, "she's going to howl with laughter, seeing this melodramatic gesture," and that idea made him once more calm and quite collected. He looked at the ancient sword's blade, suddenly curious: it was as if he were trying to find some rusty spot. Then he put the sword back in its sheath and, with immense, quiet poise, set it on the gilded brass nail from which it had been hung.

The whole process, very slow toward the end, lasted a solid minute. . . . Mademoiselle de La Mole was looking at him, stunned. "I've really been at the point of being killed by my lover!" she told herself.

The idea carried her back to the most beautiful times of Charles IX's and Henry III's century.

Julien had just replaced the sword; she stood immobile in front of him, and there was no longer any hate in her eyes. It must be admitted that she was exceedingly seductive just then; certainly, no woman had ever less resembled a Paris doll (this being Julien's major objection to Parisian women).

"I'm going to fall back into caring for him," Mathilde thought. "And he'll be convinced, here and now, he's my lord and master, once I let myself relapse—and just when I've been speaking to him so strongly." She fled.

"My God, but she's lovely!" said Julien, watching her run off. "Here's this creature who threw herself into my arms, just a week ago, and with such passion! . . . And those moments will never return! And it's my fault! Right then, at such an extraordinary moment, so fascinating, I let myself be insensitive! . . . I must confess I was born insipid and incredibly wretched."

Monsieur de La Mole came in. Julien quickly told him of his departure.

"For where?" asked the marquis.

"For Languedoc."

"No, if you please. I'm saving you for higher matters. If you do leave, it will be to the North. . . . Accordingly, in military terms, I confine you to quarters. You will oblige me by never being absent for more than two or three hours. I may need you on very short notice."

"So," he thought, "I can't even take myself away! God knows how long the marquis is going to keep me here in Paris. Good God! What's going to become of me? And I haven't got a friend I can look to for advice. Father Pirard wouldn't let me finish the first sentence; Count Altamira would suggest that I join him in some conspiracy.

"But I'm insane, I know it. I'm out of my mind!

"Who could help me, what's going to happen?"

CHAPTER EIGHTEEN

TERRIBLE TIMES

And she admits it to me! She tells me everything, every little detail! Her beautiful eyes, watching me so intently, show me the love she feels for someone else!

—SCHILLER

Thrilled to the bottom of her soul, Mademoiselle de La Mole could think of nothing but the happiness of having almost been killed. She even said it to herself: "He's worthy of being my master, having been about to kill me. How many handsome young society men would have to be melted into one, to reach such a fit of passion?"

She had to admit how really handsome he'd been when he'd climbed up on a chair, replacing the sword exactly as the decorator had so picturesquely hung it! "After all, I wasn't so crazy, falling in love with him."

Just then, had she been offered some more or less honorable way of restarting their love affair, she'd gladly have taken it. Julien, who'd double-locked himself into his room, was overcome by the most violent despair. Among other crazy notions, he thought of throwing himself at her feet. If, instead of hiding himself in a secluded place, he had gone wandering in the garden and around the house, so he could be ready for whatever might happen, he might conceivably, in no more than a second, have changed his frightful misery into the liveliest happiness.

But we're now reproaching him for being deficient at what, had he not been thus lacking, would also have kept him from the sublime act of seizing the ancient sword which, at that very moment, had made him so handsome in Mademoiselle de La Mole's eyes. So favorable to Julien, this whim lasted the whole day. Mathilde painted a charming picture for herself, composed of the brief moments when she had loved him; she mourned them.

"Really," she said to herself, "my passion for the poor boy only lasted, as far as he's concerned, from one in the morning, when I saw him coming up his ladder, his pistols stuffed into his pocket, until eight the next morning. It was fifteen minutes later, as I was hearing mass at Sainte-Valerie, that I began to think he'd fancy himself my master, and might well try to force me into obeying him, using terror as his weapon."

After dinner, far from fleeing Julien, Mademoiselle de La Mole spoke to him and, as it were, coerced him into following her to the garden; he acquiesced. For him, it was a new sort of test. Not fully aware what she was doing, Mathilde yielded to the love she was beginning to feel for him once more. She took great delight in walking beside him, looking with great interest at his hands, which that morning had taken up the sword, intending to kill her.

After that, and everything else that had happened, there could no longer be any question of conversing as once they had.

Mathilde gradually began to talk to him, trustingly, intimately, about the state of her heart. She found an odd, sensual pleasure in this sort of talk; she began to tell him about her passing fancies for Monsieur de Croisenois, for Monsieur de Caylus . . .

"No! For Monsieur de Caylus too!" Julien exclaimed, all the bitter jealousy of a discarded lover ringing in his words. That was how Mathilde took it, and was not a bit offended.

She went on torturing Julien, detailing her sometime feelings in the most graphic fashion, and speaking both intimately and truthfully. He could tell she was describing what had really taken place. It was painful for him, noticing that as she spoke she was learning what was truly in her heart.

Jealousy's miseries cannot get much worse.

Suspecting that a rival is loved is horrible enough, but having the details of that love confessed to you, in detail, by the woman you adore is, surely, the worst of all miseries.

How Julien was being punished for his arrogance, thinking himself favored over de Caylus and de Croisenois! With what intimate wretchedness and emotion he now exaggerated, to himself, every single one of their trifling advantages! With what ardent good faith he despised himself!

Mathilde seemed to him adorable; words alone are too feeble to express his adoration. While walking beside her, he cast furtive glances at her hands, her feet, her queenly bearing. He was ready to fall at her feet, overpowered, annihilated by love and misery, and crying: "Have pity!"

"And this bewitchingly beautiful woman, so far above all others, who once loved me, will surely soon be in love with Monsieur de Caylus!"

Julien could not have doubted Mademoiselle de La Mole's sincerity: the tone of truth was too obvious in everything she was saying. So that his misery might be absolutely complete, there were moments when, because she was remembering so intently what, at one time, she had felt for Monsieur de Caylus, Mathilde would speak as if she were in fact still in love with him. Plainly, there was love in her voice. Julien could hear it very clearly.

Had his chest been filled with boiling lead, he would have suffered less. How could the poor fellow, brought to this pitch of misery, possibly have imagined that, precisely because she was speaking to him, Mademoiselle de La Mole took such great pleasure in summoning up the old love fancies she had felt, once upon a time, for Monsieur de Caylus or Monsieur de Luz?

Nothing can describe Julien's anguish. He was listening to these confiding, intimate details of the love she'd felt for others, even as they walked along the same row of lindens where, so few days before, he'd been waiting for the clock to sound and summon him to her room. No human soul can experience any greater misery.

This kind of intimate cruelty went on for eight long days. Mathilde would sometimes seem to hunt for opportunities to speak to him, and would sometimes seem to do no more than keep herself from avoiding him. And the subject of their conversations, to which they both seemed to return, in a sort of ecstatic savagery, was the tale of her feelings for other men. She told him the letters she'd written, recalling even the precise words employed, sometimes reciting whole sentences from memory. Toward the end, she appeared to be contemplating Julien with a kind of malign pleasure. His sorrows were shining joys to her.

It's clear that Julien had no experience of life; he had not even read novels. Had he been a bit less gauche, and had he been able to say, coolly and calmly, to this young girl he so adored, and who told him such intimate and strange secrets: "Let's face it; I may not be as lofty as all these other gentlemen, but just the same the one you love is me...."

Perhaps she might have been happy to be understood. At least, his success would have been entirely dependent on the grace with which he'd expressed the idea, and the exact moment he'd chosen to say it. No matter what, he would have freed himself, and with positive effects for him, from a situation bound to become monotonous for her.

"And you no longer love me, and I adore you!" Julien told her one day, frantic with love and misery. This stupidity was very nearly the worst he could have committed.

His words destroyed, in the twinkling of an eye, all the pleasure Mademoiselle de La Mole had been finding, talking to him about the state of her heart. She began to be amazed that, after all of that, he had not taken offense at her accounts; she had started to think, just when he made this doltish remark, that perhaps he no longer loved her. "His pride has surely extinguished his love," she had told herself. "He's not a man to quietly listen to himself being compared, unfavorably, to the likes of de Caylus, de Luz, de Croisenois, and admitting they're better than he is. No, I won't see him at my feet anymore!"

In the days leading up to this moment, in all the innocence of his misery, Julien had often, and most sincerely, silently praised the brilliant qualities of these gentlemen; he even exaggerated them. This tendency had not escaped Mademoiselle de La Mole. It had amazed her. But she had not guessed its cause. Julien's frantic soul, by praising a rival he thought loved, was identifying with the other's happiness.

His deeply candid, and totally stupid, remark changed everything in an instant. Certain of being loved, Mathilde utterly despised him.

She had been walking with him when he'd spoken those blundering words; she left him on the spot, and her final glance expressed the most awful disgust. Back in the drawing room, she never looked at him again. The next day, scorn had completely taken over her heart. There was no longer any question of the urge that, for an entire week, had made her treat Julien as her most intimate friend. The very sight of him seemed disagreeable. Her feelings bordered on utter disgust; there can be no way to express the extraordinary contempt she felt when her eyes happened to fall on him.

Julien had not understood anything of what had been going on in Mathilde's heart, the past week, but he understood her contempt. He had the good sense to let himself be as invisible as he could, and never so much as glanced at her.

But there was deadly pain in so completely depriving himself of her presence. He felt that his misery was constantly growing. "A man's heart contains only so much courage," he said to himself. He spent his days looking out his little window, up in the attic. He kept the blinds carefully though not fully closed; he could at least see Mademoiselle de La Mole when she went into the garden.

How he felt, after dinner, when he saw her walking with Monsieur de Caylus, Monsieur de Luz, or someone else for whom, once upon a time, she had felt vague stirrings of love!

Julien had not known such misery existed. He found himself at the edge of crying aloud; his once steady soul had been turned upside down, shaken awry from top to bottom.

Thinking of anything other than Mademoiselle de La Mole had become obnoxious; he'd become incapable of composing even the simplest of letters.

"You've gone crazy," the marquis told him.

Trembling at the thought of being found out, Julien spoke of sickness and even began to believe it. Luckily for him, the marquis amused himself at dinner, teasing Julien about his coming trip: Mathilde understood it might be a very long one. There had already been days when he simply fled from her, and the brilliant young gentlemen, possessing everything missing in this pale, grave person, previously so attractive to her, were quite unable, now, to distract her from her meditative reveries.

"Any ordinary girl," she told herself, "would have hunted among these young men for the one she wanted; they draw all the girls' glances, in drawing rooms. But it is characteristic of genius not to let its thoughts be dragged into ruts ordinary minds have created.

"When I'm with someone like Julien, who is deficient only in wealth, as I am not, I will always draw people's attention; I will not go through life unnoticed. Far from endlessly worrying about a revolution, as all my cousins do—they're so afraid of the common people that they won't scold a coachman who takes them where they don't want to go—I'll make sure I play a role, and a great one, because the man I've chosen has real character, and boundless ambition. What is he lacking? Friends, money? I'll give him all that." But in her mind she rather tended to treat Julien as an inferior, someone to be loved when she felt like it.

CHAPTER NINETEEN

COMIC OPERA

O how this spring of love resembleth
The uncertain glory of an April day,
Which now shows all the beauty of the sun
And by and by a cloud takes all away!
—SHAKESPEARE

Busy with thoughts of the future, and the special role she expected to play, Mathilde soon began to long for the dry, metaphysical discussions she had often had with Julien. She could be wearied by such lofty notions, but sometimes she also missed the happy moments spent in his company. Nor did she remember these without feeling remorse, and at certain times it overwhelmed her.

"But even having a weakness," she told herself, "a girl like me deserves to forget her duty only for a man who's worthy. It mustn't be said that his handsome mustache, or the graceful way he mounts his horse, were what seduced me, but his far-seeing thoughts on France's future, his perception of similarities between what's going to swoop down on us and the British Revolution of 1688. And, yes, I've been seduced," she replied to her sense of remorse, "I was a weak woman, but at least I wasn't misled by merely external matters, like a brainless doll.

"If there is another revolution, why couldn't Julien play the role of

Roland, and I the part of that Girondin leader, Madame Roland? I'd prefer being her to being Madame de Staël: in our time, personal immorality will be an obstacle. No one's ever going to reproach me for falling twice; I'd die of shame."

Mathilde's reveries weren't all as somber as the notions just transcribed: that must be conceded.

She looked at Julien, finding a charming grace in everything he did, no matter how unimportant.

"No question about it," she said to herself. "I've managed to crush out of him even the slimmest sense that he has any rights.

"The wretched look, the profound passion with which the poor fellow told me he loved me, a week ago, surely proves it. Yes, it's true, it was quite extraordinary how I flared up at words so glowing with respect, and spoken with such passion. I'm his wife, am I not? What he said was perfectly reasonable and, I must say, I found it pleasant. Julien still loves me, even after those endless conversations when all I talked to him about, and so cruelly—I agree—were just vague stirrings of love, born out of the boredom of my existence, love that I imagined I felt for those young aristocrats: he's so jealous of them. Ah, if he knew how little danger they represent for me! how, when I compare them to Julien, they seem bloodless, all of them copies of one another."

As her mind shaped these notions, Mathilde was drawing random lines, in pencil, on a page in her sketchbook. One of the profiles she'd produced both amazed and delighted her: it was strikingly like Julien. "It's the voice of heaven! This is one of love's miracles," she exclaimed to herself, ecstatically. "Now I'll surely draw his portrait."

She ran up to her room, shut herself in, and set to work, trying hard to really draw a portrait of Julien. But she could not: the profile she'd drawn by accident always resembled him most closely. She was utterly enchanted: it seemed to her proof positive of a great passion.

She didn't close her sketchbook until much later, when her mother called her to go to the Italian opera. There was only one idea in her head: catch Julien's attention, so she could get her mother to have him accompany them to the performance.

He did not appear; the only people with whom the ladies shared their box were some dull commoners. During the opera's first act,

Mathilde dreamed most passionately of the man she loved. But in the second act—sung, it must be admitted, to a melody worthy of Cimarosa—she heard a maxim about love, and it pierced her to the heart. The heroine was proclaiming: "I must be punished for loving him so wildly; I love him far too much!"

From the moment Mathilde heard this sublime aria, the whole world seemed to disappear for her. She was spoken to; she did not reply. Her mother was scolding her, but Mathilde could barely see the marquise. Her ecstasy reached an exalted, passionate state comparable to the most violent sensations that, for some time, Julien had been feeling for her. The divinely graceful aria, in which she heard the strikingly apposite maxim, filled every moment when she was not thinking directly of Julien. Her love of music, that night, left her feeling as Madame de Rênal always had, when thinking of Julien. Mind-made love is of course subtler than true love, but its moments of enthusiasm are limited: it understands itself too well; it is always evaluating, passing judgment. Rather than deranging the mind, it throbs only to the beating of thought.

Returning to the house, no matter what Madame de La Mole might say, Mathilde claimed she was feeling feverish, and spent much of the night playing the melody, over and over, on her piano. She sang the words of the famous aria that had so charmed her:

> *Devo punirmi, devo punirmi,*
> *Se troppo amai,*
>
> etc.

> I must be punished, I must be punished,
> I love him too much.

After that wild night, she believed she'd managed to triumph over her love.

(Writing these things, I know, will still further injure this unfortunate author. Prigs and prudes will accuse me of indecency. But it does no harm to young women, shining so brilliantly in Parisian drawing rooms, to suggest that one, just one, among them might be susceptible to the insane acts disfiguring Mathilde's character. She's a completely imaginary person, and indeed conceived well outside the manners and mores which, in the pages of history, will secure such a distinguished place for our nineteenth-century civilization.

(It is, after all, not prudence that might be thought deficient, among the young girls who have ornamented this winter season's dances and balls.

(Nor do I think anyone can accuse them of excessive scorn for glittering fortunes, horses, handsome estates, and everything that guarantees a fine position in the world. Far from feeling bored by all such advantages, these are usually precisely what they have their hearts most set upon. And if there is passion in their hearts, it is these things that have aroused it.

(Nor is it love that beclouds the fortunes of gifted young men like Julien. They tie themselves by unbreakable bonds to some coterie and, when the coterie makes its fortune, society rains down on them all the good things it has to offer. But woe to the learned man who belongs to no coterie: even his minor, distinctly doubtful successes will be criticized, and noble virtue will be victorious, stealing them away.

(Ah, my dear sir: a novel is a mirror, taking a walk down a big road. Sometimes you'll see nothing but blue skies; sometimes you'll see the muck in the mud piles along the road. And you'll accuse the man carrying the mirror in his basket of being immoral! His mirror reflects muck, so you'll accuse the mirror, too! Why not also accuse the highway where the mud is piled, or, more strongly still, the street inspector who leaves water wallowing in the roads, so the mud piles can come into being.

(Then we're all agreed: Mathilde's character is impossible, in this time we live in, this age no less prudent than virtuous. I suspect you'll find it less irritating, now, as I continue telling the tale of this lovable girl's foolishness.)

All the next day, she watched for chances to reaffirm her triumph over wild passion. Her central goal was to offend Julien in every possible way; still, nothing she did escaped him.

Julien was too miserable, and above all too shaken, to comprehend so complicated a passionate maneuver; still less was he able to understand how strongly positive were her feelings about him. Her maneuver still further defeated him: never, in all probability, had his misery been so extreme. His mind had so little control over his actions that, if some sour-tongued philosopher had said to him—"Think how you can quickly take advantage of any favorable inclinations. In this sort of mind-made love, as one sees it in Paris, no state of being lasts longer than two days"—Julien would not have understood him. But however excited, however exalted he might be, he retained his sense of honor. His primary responsibility was discretion; he understood that. To seek advice, to tell his suffering to the first person who came along, would have been, for him, happiness like that experienced by the lost soul who, crossing a burning desert, is blessed by a falling drop of ice-cold water. He knew the danger, he was sure he'd reply to any indiscreet questioner with a flood of tears; he shut himself in his room.

He saw Mathilde walking in the garden, at some length. When she left, he went down. He went over to a bush from which she had plucked a flower.

It was a dark night; he could let himself feel all his misery without fear of being seen. It was obvious to him that Mademoiselle de La Mole was in love with one of the young officers; she had just been talking and laughing with a group of them. She had loved him, but she had recognized how unworthy of her he was.

"And, really, I'm not worth very much," Julien told himself, with deep conviction. "All in all, I'm exceedingly dull, very common, terribly boring to other people, unbearable to myself." He was fatally revolted by every one of his good qualities, by everything he had once loved with such enthusiasm, and in this state of *inverted imagination* he set himself to judging life in terms of imagination. This is decidedly a superior man's mistake.

Several times the idea of suicide came to him. It had many attractions, it was like some delicious sleep, it was a whole glass of ice water offered to the wretch who, in a desert, is dying of thirst and heat.

"My death would make her despise me even more!" he cried to himself. "What a memory I'd leave behind me!"

Fallen into this final abyss of misery, the only resource a human being has left is courage. Julien wasn't clever enough to tell himself: "I have to keep trying." But as he looked up at the window of Mathilde's room, he saw through the blinds that she had put out her light. He pictured to himself that charming room, which he had seen, alas, only once in his life. His imagination could reach no further.

He heard the clock sounding one, and he listened, and then he said, in a flash: "I'm going to climb up the ladder."

This was a stroke of genius; good arguments came flocking after. "Could I be more miserable?" he asked himself. He ran over to the ladder; the gardener had chained it in place. Breaking the cocking hammer off one of his pistols, and working, now, with superhuman strength, he twisted a link from the chain and, in minutes, had the ladder set against Mathilde's window.

"She's going to be furious, she'll pour scorn on me, but who cares? I'll kiss her, a final kiss, then I'll go up to my room and I'll kill myself . . . my lips will touch her cheek before I die!"

He flew up the ladder, he knocked on the blinds. In a few moments Mathilde heard him, she tried to open the blinds, but the ladder was in the way. Julien clamped his fingers around the iron hook (meant to hold the blinds open) and, at the continuing risk of dashing himself to the ground, shook the ladder so violently that it moved to one side. Mathilde was able to open the blinds.

He threw himself into the room, more dead than alive.

"So it's you!" she said, as she ran into his arms. . . .

———

Who could describe Julien's overflowing happiness? Mathilde's was almost as great.

She became her own enemy; she denounced herself to him:

"Punish me for my horrible pride," she told him, wrapping him so tightly in her arms that she nearly suffocated him. "You're my master, I'm your slave, I need to beg your pardon, on my knees, for having revolted against you." She left his arms and fell at his feet. "Yes, you're my master," she told him, still drunk with happiness and love. "Rule over me forever; punish your slave, harshly, when she tries to revolt."

The next minute, she pulled herself away from him, lit a candle—

and then Julien had to struggle hard, to keep her from cutting off her hair, all down the one side.

"I want to remember," she told him, "that I'm your servant. If I'm ever overwhelmed by my disgusting pride, just show me this hair and say: 'It's no longer a question of love, nor is it a matter of what emotion you feel in your heart, at this moment. You have sworn to obey: On your honor, obey.'"

But it's better to suppress the details of such frenzy, such happiness.

Julien's valor matched his happiness. "I must go back down the ladder," he told Mathilde, "when we can see dawn shining on the distant chimneys, off to the east, on the other side of the gardens. The sacrifice I impose on myself is worthy of you. I will be depriving myself of hours spent in the most amazing happiness the human heart can taste, but it's a sacrifice I make on behalf of your reputation. If you know my heart, you know the violence I'm doing to myself. Will you always be to me what you are at this moment? But honor speaks for you; it is enough. Let me inform you that, since we were first together, suspicion has not been directed solely at burglars. Monsieur de La Mole has set up a watch in the garden. Monsieur de Croisenois is surrounded by spies; they know everything he does, each and every night. . . ."

Hearing this, Mathilde roared with laughter. Her mother and one of the maids were awakened; suddenly Mathilde was being spoken to, through the closed door. Julien looked at her: she was pale, even as she scolded the maid and refused to speak to her mother.

"But if they think of opening their windows, they'll see the ladder!" he told her.

He wound her one final time in his arms, then threw himself down the ladder, sliding rather than climbing down; he was on the ground almost instantly.

Three seconds later, the ladder was under the arching linden trees, and Mathilde's honor had been preserved. Julien came back to his senses and found himself covered with blood and very nearly naked: he had been hurt, letting himself slide down so precipitously.

Surging happiness had given him all his rightful energy: twenty men might have come at him, and to attack them by himself would, just then, have been only one more delight. Luckily, his military valor was not put to the proof. He set the ladder back in its usual place; he replaced the chain he'd taken off, nor did he forget to erase, in the bed of exotic flowers under Mathilde's window, the imprint left by the ladder.

As, in the darkness, he wiped his hand along the soft earth, making sure the imprint had indeed been completely effaced, he felt something fall on his hands. It was her hair, all down one side, which she had cut off and thrown to him.

She was at her window.

"Here's what your servant sends you," she told him, not at all softly. "It's the sign of eternal obedience. I surrender my capacity to make judgments: be my master."

Overcome, Julien was ready to pick up the ladder and climb back up to her. At last, reason prevailed.

Getting back into the house, from the garden, was not at all easy. He finally managed to force a cellar door; when he reached the main part of the house he had to break open, as quietly as he could, the door to his room. In his concern and excitement, he had left everything in the little room he'd fled from so rapidly, including the key, which was in his suit pocket. "Just as long," he thought, "as she thinks of hiding all those fatal clothes!"

At last, weariness overcame happiness and, just as the sun was rising, he fell into a deep sleep.

It was not easy for the lunchtime bell to awaken him; he appeared in the dining room. Mathilde came in shortly afterward. Julien's pride flared with happiness, seeing the love shining in the eyes of this extraordinarily beautiful woman, surrounded as she was by such homage. But prudence soon had reason to be frightened.

Pretending that she'd not had time to do her hair properly, Mathilde had so arranged it that he could see, at a glance, the full extent of the sacrifice she'd made for him in cutting off her hair the night before. If so beautiful a face could be spoiled by anything, Mathilde had managed it. One whole side of her ash blonde hair had been cut within half an inch of her head.

During lunch, Mathilde's behavior fully lived up to this initial recklessness. It might have been supposed that she was determined to let the whole world know her wild passion for Julien. Fortunately, the Marquis and Marquise de La Mole were preoccupied, that day, with a list of high decorations to be awarded, and which did not include Monsieur de Chaulnes. Toward the end of the meal, it happened that Mathilde, who was speaking to Julien, called him *my master*. He reddened to the white of his eyes.

Whether by chance, or because Madame de la Mole had been careful to arrange it that way, Mathilde was not left alone at any time during the entire day. But that evening, as they were going from the dining room into the drawing room, she found a moment to say to Julien:

"Don't think this is an excuse, on my part, but my mother has just decided that one of her maids is going to spend nights in my room."

The day went by like lightning. Julien was bursting with joy. Starting at seven in the morning, the next day, he was at his place in the library. He hoped Mademoiselle de la Mole would take the trouble to come there: he had written her an enormously long letter.

He did not see her until hours later, at lunch. She'd done her hair, this time, with immense care: with incredible artfulness, all the hair she had cut off seemed never to have disappeared. She looked at Julien, once or twice, but her eyes were polite and calm, and there was no longer any question of calling him *my master*.

Julien's astonishment stopped him from breathing. . . . Mathilde was reproaching herself for virtually everything she had done for him.

After more mature thought, she'd decided he was someone, not perhaps completely common, but at least not sufficiently extraordinary to deserve all the strange foolishness she had dared on his behalf. All in all, she was scarcely thinking about love; she was wearied by love, that day.

Julien's heart was leaping like that of a boy of sixteen. Terrible doubt, amazement, despair, all took their turn, during lunch, which seemed to him to last forever. As soon as he could decently rise from the table, he very nearly threw himself, rather than merely running, toward the stable, saddled his horse without waiting for a stable hand, and left at a gallop. He dreaded dishonoring himself by some show of weakness. "I need to kill my heart with physical exertion, with fatigue," he said to himself as he galloped in the Meudon woods. "What have I done, what have I said, to deserve such a disgrace?

"Today, I must do nothing, I must say nothing," he thought, as he returned. "I'm just as dead physically as I am mentally. Monsieur Julien is no longer alive. This is his corpse that keeps on moving."

CHAPTER TWENTY
THE JAPANESE VASE

> His heart did not understand, at first, the full extent of his misery; he was more upset than moved. But as his mind was restored, slowly, to rationality, he came to feel the depth of his misfortune. For him, life's pleasures were completely annihilated: all he could feel was the sharp point of despair, as it cut into him. But what's the use of speaking about physical pain? What merely bodily suffering is the equal of this?
>
> —JEAN-PAUL

The dinner bell was sounding; Julien barely had time to dress. When he reached the dining room, he found Mathilde, who was pleading with her brother and Monsieur de Croisenois not to attend the party at Suresnes, the home of Madame de Fervaques, the marshall's widow.

It would have been difficult for her to be more captivating or pleasant. After dinner, they were joined by Messieurs de Luz, de Caylus, and several of their friends. It might have been said that Mademoiselle de La Mole had resumed, not merely her worship of fraternal affection, but also the most demanding observance of social convention. Though the weather was lovely that night, she insisted they should not go into the garden; she wished them to stay near the easy chair in which, as usual, Madame de La Mole was sitting. The blue sofa was clearly to be the group's center, as it had been that winter.

Mathilde was ill disposed to the garden, or at least it left her totally indifferent: it was connected to memories of Julien.

Misery weakens the mind. Our hero was awkward enough to stand close to the little straw chair, which had once witnessed such brilliant victories. No one said a word to him, today; his presence was imperceptible—or worse. Those of Mademoiselle de La Mole's friends seated at the far end of the sofa, near him, tried to turn their backs to him, or at least he had that impression.

"I've fallen out of favor at court," he thought. He wanted to study, for a moment, these people who were pretending to crush him with their disdain.

Monsieur de Luz's uncle held a high position, close to the king, so as newcomers joined the group, the handsome young officer began the conversation, each and every time, with striking news: his uncle had departed for Saint-Cloud at seven that morning, and expected to be there that evening, and to stay there that night. This information was conveyed in what seemed complete geniality, but it was always set forth.

Watching Monsieur de Croisenois with the harsh eye of misery, Julien noticed the extraordinary importance which that friendly, and so very handsome, young man attributed to occult forces. He carried this so far that his face darkened and he turned sullen when he saw even a mildly important event explained by some simple, entirely natural cause. "He's more than a bit crazy," Julien said to himself. "This sounds strikingly like Emperor Alexander of Russia, as Prince Korasoff described him to me." During his first year in Paris, after leaving the seminary, dazzled by the utterly novel graces of all these genial young gentlemen, Julien could not help admiring them. Their real character was just beginning to reveal itself.

"I'm playing an unworthy role, here," he suddenly thought. How was he to get away from his little straw chair without being horribly clumsy? He tried to think of a way, but this was setting novel problems for a mind already elsewhere occupied. He fell back on his memory, which was, it has to be admitted, not very rich in resources of this kind. The poor fellow was still uneasy with social custom, so he seemed perfectly clumsy, as well as perfectly obvious, when he rose to leave the drawing room. Misery was all too obvious in everything he did. He had played, for three-quarters of an hour, the role of a supplicant underling, from whom no one bothers to hide exactly what they think of him.

The critical observations he had just made about his rivals, however, kept him from treating his misery too tragically, and to solace his pride he had the memory of what had taken place two nights earlier. "Whatever advantages they may have over me," he thought, walking alone in the garden, "Mathilde has never been to any of them what, twice in her life, she's been willing to be for me."

It was as far as his wisdom went. He had absolutely no comprehension of this bizarre woman's character, she whom Fate had made complete mistress of his happiness.

He spent the day trying to kill, by way of weariness, both himself and his horse. In the evening, he carefully stayed away from the blue sofa, to which Mathilde remained faithful. He noticed that Count Norbert would not so much as look at him, when they crossed paths in the house. "It must be violently difficult," he thought, "for such a naturally polite man."

For Julien, sleep would have been happiness. Despite his fatigued body, wonderfully alluring memories began to take over his imagination. He was not clever enough to see that long days of riding through the woods near Paris affected him, and him only; they had no effect on Mathilde's heart, or on her mind. He was leaving his destiny entirely up to chance.

He fancied that there was one thing which would be infinitely soothing to his sorrows: it would be to speak to Mathilde. And yet, what could he dare say to her?

And this is what, at seven in the morning, he was dreamily considering when, suddenly, he saw her come into the library.

"I'm aware, sir, that you wish to speak to me."

"Good Lord! Who said that to you?"

"I know it: why does it matter how? If you're not a man of honor, you can destroy me, or at least attempt to. But such a danger, which I do not consider real, will certainly not prevent me from being honest. I no longer love you, sir. My insane imagination deluded me. . . ."

After this terrible blow, frantic with love and misery, Julien attempted to argue himself back into favor. Nothing could have been more absurd. Argue yourself out of being disliked? But reason no longer had any control over his actions. Blind instinct compelled him to delay this final determination of his fate. He felt that, while he was still talking, it would not be all over. Mathilde did not listen to him; the sound of his words irritated her. She could not have believed he'd have the audacity to interrupt her.

Remorse, caused by virtue and by pride, had made her, that morning, equally wretched. To some extent, she was overwhelmed by a frightful idea: she had given claims on herself to a petty priest, a peasant's son. "This is almost the same," she told herself, in moments of exaggerating her misery, "as if I had to reproach myself, having had a weakness for one of the servants."

For proud, bold spirits, it's a short step from anger at themselves to anger at others. Wild fury is, in such cases, a lively pleasure.

In a flash, Mathilde soared into action, covering Julien with furiously exaggerated contempt. She had immense resources, especially in the arts of torturing people's vanity and inflicting the most savage wounds.

For the first time in his life, Julien found himself subjected to the workings of a superior mind, motivated by extraordinary hatred, and entirely directed at him. He was unable even to think of defending himself; indeed, he began to share her burning contempt. As he heard Mathilde heaping up her disdain, her cruelties, all cleverly calculated to destroy whatever good opinion he might have had of himself, he felt she was right, and she could not have said enough of such things.

She herself felt a delicious, thrilling pride in thus punishing herself, and him, for the worship of him that, several days earlier, had so overcome her.

There was no need for her to create out of nothing, or to plan for the first time, the cruel things she spoke with such satisfaction. All she had to do was repeat what the anti-love forces, deep in her heart, had already been saying for a week.

The things she said kept multiplying Julien's terrible misery. He tried to run off; Mademoiselle de La Mole held him where he was, with an authoritative grip on his arm.

"Take notice, please," he said, "that you're speaking very loudly. You'll be heard in the next room."

"I don't care!" she responded haughtily. "Who's going to dare tell me they've overheard me? I want to cure—forever!—any ideas your petty vanity may have had about me."

When Julien was able to leave the library, he was so stunned that he actually could not feel his misery so deeply as before. "Well! She doesn't love me anymore," he kept repeating aloud, as if to help himself determine his position. "She has apparently loved me for a week or so—and I, I'll love her forever.

"How can it be possible that, just a few days ago, she had absolutely no place in my heart, none whatever!"

Mathilde's heart was flooded with delighted pride. She had managed to break with him forever! To triumph so completely, over so powerful a passion, made her perfectly happy. "Now this little gentleman will understand, once and for all, that he neither has nor will have the slightest dominion over me." She was so intensely happy that, truthfully, at that moment there was no love left in her.

After such an awful scene, as humiliating as it was dreadful, love would have become impossible for anyone less impassioned than Julien. Without forgetting for an instant what she owed herself, Mademoiselle de La Mole had directed distasteful remarks at him, deftly calculated to seem truths even when remembered more calmly.

The conclusion Julien had drawn, in the first moments that followed such an astonishing scene, was that Mathilde's pride was boundless. He believed firmly that, between them, everything was finished forever, and yet the next day, at lunch, he was awkward and shy in her presence. It was not a failing that, until then, he could have been reproached with. In little as in large matters, he knew precisely what he was owed, and what he wanted to do, and he did it.

That day, after lunch, when Madame de La Mole was asking him for a seditious and distinctly rare pamphlet, brought to the library that morning by her parish priest, Julien knocked over an old vase, in blue porcelain, and almost inconceivably ugly.

Madame de La Mole stood up, uttering a cry of distress, and came nearer, to look at the shattered pieces of her precious vase. "This was from old Japan," she said. "It came to me from my great aunt, the Abbess at Chelles. It had been a present from the Dutch to the Duke d'Orléans, when he was Regent of France, and he had given it to his daughter. . . ."

Mathilde had been watching her mother, delighted to see the blue vase broken; it had always seemed to her horribly ugly. Julien said nothing, not particularly upset. He saw Mademoiselle de La Mole quite near him.

"This vase," he told her, "has been destroyed forever, as has also been destroyed a feeling that used to be master of my heart. Please accept my apologies for all the stupidities I have committed." And he left.

"One might say, really," said Madame de La Mole as he walked out, "that this Monsieur Sorel is both proud and pleased by what he's just done."

Her words fell directly on Mademoiselle de La Mole's heart. "It's true," she said to herself. "My mother has guessed correctly: that was exactly how he felt." And then the joy she had been feeling, because of the scene she'd created for him the night before, ceased to exist. "So, it's all over," she told herself, apparently quite calmly. "What remains to me is a frightful warning. This is a ghastly mistake, and humiliating! It ought to be enough to keep me sensible, and for the whole rest of my life."

"Why didn't I speak the truth?" thought Julien. "Why does the love I had for this crazy female still torment me?"

This love, far from flickering out, as he had hoped it would, made rapid progress. "She's crazy, of course she is," he told himself. "But does that make her less adorable? Is it possible to be prettier? Isn't every vivid pleasure the most elegant of civilizations can offer—isn't all of it absolutely, perfectly united in Mademoiselle de La Mole?" These memories of past happiness overwhelmed Julien, and rapidly tore down what reason had tried to erect.

Reason fights in vain against memories of this kind. Its hardest labors only add to their charm.

Twenty-four hours after the old Japanese vase was broken, Julien was without question one of the most miserable men on earth.

CHAPTER TWENTY-ONE

THE SECRET NOTE

Because everything I'm telling you, I've seen for myself. And if I might
have been deceiving myself, seeing it, I certainly won't deceive you,
telling it.

—A LETTER TO THE AUTHOR

The marquis summoned him. Monsieur de La Mole seemed rejuve-
nated, his eyes were sparkling.

"Let's talk about that memory of yours," he said to Julien. "I'm told
it's prodigious! Could you learn four pages by heart, and go to London, and recite them back? But not changing a word . . ."

The marquis was irritably crumpling up that day's *The Legitimist,*
and trying, unsuccessfully, to disguise an intense seriousness, unlike
anything Julien had ever seen in him, even when they'd been dealing
with the de Frilair lawsuit.

Julien had seen enough of how these things were done; he felt
sure he was supposed to appear taken in by all the marquis's casual
talk.

"That issue of *The Legitimist* may not be very interesting. But, if
monsieur will allow me, tomorrow morning I will have the honor to
recite it back to you, complete and entire."

"Ha! Even the advertisements?"

"Word for word, and not one missing."

"On your honor?" replied the marquis, suddenly very serious indeed.

"Yes, sir. What might trouble my memory, and only this, would be
worrying that I might somehow fail to keep my word."

"It's only that, yesterday, I forgot to ask you the question. Nor need
I ask you to swear never to repeat what you're going to hear: I know
you too well to thus insult you. I have answered for you. I'm going to
conduct you to a drawing room, in which there will be twelve people.
You will take notes on what each of them says.

"Don't be concerned: this will not be a disorderly conversation; each will speak when his turn arrives. I don't mean in some formal sequence," the marquis added, returning to the light, subtle way so natural to him. "While we are speaking, you will write perhaps twenty pages. We'll come back here, you and I, and we'll reduce those twenty pages to four. These are the four pages you will recite back to me, tomorrow morning, instead of the whole issue of *The Legitimist.* You'll leave for London soon afterward. You will have to travel as a young pleasure seeker. Your goal: not to be noticed by anyone. In London, you will go to a very great person. Once there, you'll need a good deal more skill. It will be a question of deceiving all those who surround him: whether among his secretaries, or whether among his servants, there are people who have been bought by our enemies, and who are on the watch for our agents, whenever they come, so as to intercept them.

"You will carry a letter of recommendation, of no significance.

"The moment His Excellency looks at you, you will take out my watch, which I hereby lend you for this trip. Take it, now, while we're on the subject, and let me have yours.

"The duke himself will be prepared to write down, while you dictate to him, the four pages you will have memorized. That done, but—note this carefully—not before, you may, if His Excellency questions you, tell him about the meeting you are going to attend.

"It may help you to avoid boredom, along the way, to be aware that, between Paris and the minister's house, there are people who would ask for nothing better than to put a bullet into Father Sorel. For then his mission would be over, and everything would be much delayed—you see, my dear fellow, how would we know you're dead? Your zeal won't be much help, then, in sending us notice.

"Go, right now, and buy yourself totally new clothes," the marquis continued seriously. "Make yourself look like a fashionable young man of two years ago. For tonight, you must seem rather unkempt. Once you're on your way, on the other hand, you will dress as you usually do. Are you startled? Will your sense of mistrust help you guess? Yes, my friend: one of the venerable people you're going to be listening to, telling us his opinions, is very capable of sending out information, as a result of which you might very well be given a dose of opium, tonight, in some nice little inn where you'll have ordered yourself supper."

"It might be better," said Julien, "to go forty or fifty miles farther, rather than by the direct route. It's Rome I'll be going to, I suppose. . . ."

The marquis looked at him with a haughtiness, and a dissatisfaction, that Julien had not seen since Upper Bray.

"You'll know that, sir, when I consider it proper to tell you. I don't like questions."

"That wasn't a question," Julien replied volubly. "I swear it, sir. I was thinking out loud, trying in my head to find the safest route."

"Yes, it did seem that your mind was far away. Do not forget that an ambassador, and above all one of your age, should never seem to be seeking information he has not been offered."

Julien was deeply mortified: he had been wrong. His vanity hunted for some excuse, and found none.

"Realize, also," added Monsieur de La Mole, "that we always tend to appeal to our hearts, when we've done something foolish."

An hour later, Julien came back to the marquis, dressed like a very junior employee, in old clothes, with a tie not entirely white, and a generally priggish appearance.

The marquis roared with laughter, seeing him, and only then was Julien's vindication complete.

"If this young man betrays me," Monsieur de La Mole said to himself, "in whom might I trust? Yet when it comes to doing what must be done, somebody has to be trusted. My son and his glowing friends are every one of them brave, they've got loyalty enough for a hundred thousand men. If they have to fight, they'll die on the steps of the throne. They understand everything . . . except exactly what, right now, needs to be done. I'll be damned if I can see one of them who's capable of memorizing four pages and traveling a hundred and fifty miles without being sniffed out. Norbert would know how to get himself killed, as his ancestors did—but so can a peasant drafted into the army. . . ."

The marquis dropped into deep thoughtfulness: "And still, when it comes to getting himself killed, perhaps this young Sorel would do that as well as my son. . . ."

"Let's get into the carriage," said the marquis, as if repelling an unwelcome idea.

"Sir," said Julien, "while they were mending this suit, I memorized the first page of today's *Legitimist*."

The marquis took the paper; Julien recited it, without a word out of place. "Good," said the marquis, very diplomatic that evening. "While we've been doing this," he thought, "the young man has been paying no attention to the streets we're traveling along."

They came to a large, rather dismal drawing room, one part of it paneled and another draped in green velvet. In the center of the room, a sullen servant finished setting up a large table, meant for dining, which, by means of a huge green tablecloth, heavily ink-spotted, plainly discarded by some minister's office, he then changed into a table at which business could be conducted.

The master of the house was an enormous man, never named; Julien thought both his face and his speech showed someone who was slow to act, concerned mostly with his own digestive processes.

The marquis had signaled Julien to remain at the lower end of the table. To keep from seeming out of place, he busied himself, sharpening quill pens. Out of the corner of his eyes he counted seven participants, though he could see only their backs. Two of them were speaking to Monsieur de La Mole as if they were his equals; the others seemed more or less deferential.

A new participant entered; there was no announcement. How odd, Julien thought: no one is ever announced in this drawing room. Is this a precaution taken in my honor? To welcome this latest attendee, everyone rose. Like three others, he wore the most exalted of all medals. Conversation was hushed. All Julien could go on, as he sought to shape an opinion of the newcomer, was his face and his bearing. He was short, stocky, of very high color; his eyes sparkled and showed no expression but the malice of a wild boar.

Julien's attention was diverted by the immediate arrival of someone utterly different. This was a tall and exceedingly thin man, wearing three or four vests. His eyes were gentle, his movements polished.

"He looks a lot like the old Bishop of Besançon," thought Julien. He was obviously an ecclesiastic, apparently of no more than fifty or fifty-five: no one could have looked more paternal.

The young Bishop of Agde appeared, and seemed distinctly surprised, looking down the table, to see Julien. He had not spoken a word to our hero since the ceremony at Upper Bray. His startled glance embarrassed and irritated Julien. "Lord!" he said to himself. "Is knowing someone always going to be a disaster? All these great lords, none of whom I've ever seen, don't intimidate me a bit, and yet this young bishop's glance freezes my bones! I'm obliged to agree with him; I'm an odd fellow, and a most unfortunate one."

A very short man with exceedingly dark skin soon came in, accompanied by a good deal of noise and fuss. He began speaking the moment he was inside the door. His complexion was yellowish; he seemed rather mad. As soon as this unstoppable talker entered, the earlier arrivals clustered in groups, apparently to avoid the boredom of having to listen to him.

As they moved away from the fireplace, they came closer to the end of the table where Julien sat. He grew more and more embarrassed: in the end, no matter what efforts he made, he could not fail to understand their words, and no matter how little experience he possessed, he could not fail to understand, and quite fully, the importance of the things they were very openly discussing. Yet how strongly these seemingly lofty persons, though under his surveillance, must desire their proceedings to remain secret!

Working slowly, carefully, Julien had already sharpened twenty quill pens. His supply of pens was going to run out. He tried to see some directive in Monsieur de La Mole's glance, but the marquis had forgotten him.

"What I'm doing is ridiculous," Julien told himself while sharpening his pens. "But people with rather mediocre faces, and given—by others or by themselves—such huge responsibilities, are surely highly sensitive. There's something unfortunately too inquisitive, and too little respectful, about the way I look at people, and obviously I annoy them. But if I sit here with my eyes lowered, it will seem as if I'm trying to soak up their words."

His embarrassment was intense: he was hearing some bizarre things.

CHAPTER TWENTY-TWO

THE DISCUSSION

The Republic: for each person, today, prepared to sacrifice everything for the public good, there are thousands—millions—who acknowledge nothing but their pleasure, their vanity. Your reputation, in Paris, is based on your horse and carriage, and not on your virtue.

—NAPOLEON, *MEMOIRS*

A servant hurried in, calling: "Monsieur the Duke of ———."

"Shut up: you're nothing but a fool," said the duke as he came in. He spoke these words so well, and so majestically that, in spite of himself, Julien understood that knowing how to display anger at a servant was all the knowledge this great man possessed. Julien raised his eyes, then quickly lowered them. He had so well grasped the new arrival's importance that, trembling, he hoped his glance had not been an indiscretion.

The duke was a man of fifty, dressed like a dandy, with a jaunty step. His head was narrow, his nose was large and aquiline, as was his face: it would have been difficult to have a bearing nobler or less significant. His coming signaled the meeting's start.

Julien's psychophysiological observations were interrupted by Monsieur de La Mole's voice:

"Let me introduce you to Monsieur Sorel," the marquis said. "He has been endowed with an astonishing memory. I spoke to him only an hour ago, about the mission with which he's to be honored, and in order to give me proof of his memory, he learned by heart the first page of today's *Legitimist.*"

"Ah, the news from abroad, about that poor fellow, N———," said the master of the house. He picked up the newspaper, hurriedly, and gave Julien an amused glance, wanting to demonstrate his importance: "Speak, sir," he directed.

There was total silence; all eyes were fixed on Julien, who recited so accurately that, after twenty lines: "That will do," said the duke. The very short man with the eyes of a wild boar sat down. He was to preside, and was hardly in his chair when he pointed out, for Julien, a card table, and gestured that it be brought near. Julien set himself at this smaller table, with his writing materials. He counted twelve people sitting around the green cloth.

"Monsieur Sorel," said the duke. "Please retire to the adjoining room. You will be summoned."

The master of the house grew excited. "The shutters haven't been closed," he murmured to his neighbor. "You'll learn nothing by peering through the window!" he shouted, stupidly, at Julien. "Here I am," thought our hero, "caught up in a conspiracy, or maybe something more. Luckily, it's not the sort that leads to the executioner's block. But even if there's danger, I owe the marquis that, and more. Happily, I'll have the chance to atone for all the sorrows I may bring him, some day."

Julien went into the next room.

His mind occupied with his own sorrows, and his misery, he stared all around him, so intently that he'd never forget the place. Only then did he recall not having heard the marquis tell the coachman where they were to go, and that the marquis had ordered a cab, which he'd never done before.

Julien spent a long time alone with his thoughts. He was in a drawing room hung with red velvet, striped with gold braid. A side table along the wall bore a large ivory crucifix; on the fireplace mantel was de Maistre's *On the Pope,* with gilt edges and magnificently bound. Julien opened it, in order not to seem as if he'd been listening. From time to time they spoke quite loudly, in the next room. Finally, the door was opened; he was called.

"Say to yourselves, gentlemen," said the chairman, "that as we speak we are in the presence of the Duke of ———. This gentleman," he said, gesturing toward Julien, "is a young cleric, devoted to our holy cause, who will readily repeat, by means of his amazing memory, even the least of our remarks.

"You have the floor, sir," he said, indicating the man with the fatherly appearance, the one who wore three or four vests. To Julien, it would have seemed most natural to call him "the triple-vested man." Julien took a sheet of paper and wrote, and wrote.

(The author would have preferred, at this point, to insert a page consisting of nothing but ellipses. "That would look awful," said the publisher, "and, for such a lightweight book, looking bad is, quite simply, death." — "Politics," the author replied, "is a stone tied around literature's neck, and in less than six months, it sinks under the weight. Politics set among the imagination's concerns is like a pistol shot fired at a concert. The noise mangles without energizing. It does not harmonize with the sound of any instrument in the orchestra. Politics will mortally offend half your readers, and bore the other half, who would have found the discussion fascinating, and wonderfully lively, in the morning newspaper. . . ." — "If your characters don't talk politics," responded the publisher, "they'll cease to be the Frenchmen of 1830, and your book will no longer be a mirror, as you claim it is. . . .")

Julien had twenty-six pages of notes. What follows are some thoroughly pallid excerpts, since it has been necessary, as always, to suppress absurdities, for too many of them would have seemed obnoxious, or even unreal (see *Reports from the Law Courts*).

The triple-vested man, who bore a paternal look (a bishop, more than likely), laughed a good deal, and when he laughed his eyes, under their wavering lids, turned very bright and far less indecisive than usual. This man, the first to speak, after the duke was done ("but duke of what?" Julien asked himself), apparently so he could express the general opinion and serve the function of an assistant public prosecutor, seemed, to Julien's mind, to fall into the vagueness and absence of definite conclusions for which, so often, such officers of the court are reproved. As the discussion continued, indeed, the duke went so far as to scold him on just that account.

After several remarks of a moral nature, rather glibly philosophical, the triple-vested man declared:

"Noble England, led by so great a man as the immortal Pitt, spent forty billion francs to check the Revolution. If my colleagues will allow me to broach, with a certain degree of frankness, a melancholy notion, England did not clearly understand how, with a man like Bonaparte—especially when all one has with which to oppose him are an assemblage of good intentions—only personal measures can be decisive. . . ."

"Ah!" said the master of the house, looking uncomfortable. "So we're still praising assassination!"

"Spare us your sentimental sermons," exclaimed the chairman, distinctly annoyed. His wild boar eyes glittered ferociously. "Go on," he said to the triple-vested man. The chairman's cheeks and forehead had turned purple.

"Noble England," the speaker resumed, "has been crushed, today, because every Englishman, before he buys his bread, is compelled to pay the interest on the forty billion francs which were employed against the Jacobins. They no longer have a Pitt—"

"They have the Duke of Wellington," said a military-looking man, assuming a stance of high importance.

"Please: silence, gentlemen," exclaimed the chairman. "If we keep on arguing, there'll be no point to bringing in Monsieur Sorel."

"We are aware that the gentleman has many ideas," said the duke, irritated; he stared at the interrupter, a former Napoleonic general. Julien could tell that these words referred to something personal and deeply offensive. Everyone smiled; the turncoat general appeared outraged beyond belief.

"There is no longer a Pitt, gentlemen," the speaker said again, with the discouraged air of a man desperate to lead his listeners to reason. "Were there a new Pitt in England, it would not be possible to hoax a nation, a second time, by the same methods—"

"And that is why a conquering general, a Bonaparte, is forever impossible in France," cried the military interrupter.

This time, neither the chairman nor the duke dared show their anger, although Julien thought he could see in their glances that they certainly wished to. They lowered their eyes, and the duke satisfied himself by sighing so loudly that he was heard by everyone.

But the speaker had grown annoyed.

"You're pressuring me to be done," he said angrily, and putting completely aside his smiling politeness, and the measured language that Julien had thought was an expression of his character: "You're pressuring me to be done, you're ignoring all the efforts I've been making to keep from offending anyone's ears, no matter how long they may be. So, gentlemen, I will be brief.

"And I will tell you in blunt language: England no longer has a penny for the good cause. Pitt himself could return, and even with his genius he couldn't manage to hoax the small landowners of England, because they know that even the short Waterloo campaign, all by itself, cost them a billion francs. Since what you want is blunt talk," the speaker added, growing more and more excited, "let me tell you: *Help yourselves*—because England hasn't got a guinea to give you, and when England won't pay, then Austria, Russia, Prussia, who only have courage, but have no money, can do nothing against France, beyond a campaign or two.

"You may expect that the young soldiers mustered by Jacobinism will be beaten in the first campaign, and perhaps in the second, but by the third—though I may seem, to your prejudiced eyes, too much like a revolutionary—in the third campaign you'll have the soldiers of 1794, who were no longer the peasant conscripts of 1792."

At this point, the interruptions came from three or four voices, speaking at the same time.

"Sir," said the chairman to Julien, "go into the next room and make a fair copy of the beginning of your notes, as you have so far written them." Julien left, to his great regret. The speaker had just launched into probabilities that Julien had long been accustomed to ponder.

"They're afraid I'll make fun of them," he thought.

When he was called back, Monsieur de La Mole was saying, with a seriousness that seemed to Julien, who knew him so well, decidedly sarcastic:

". . . Yes, gentlemen, it's above all those miserable people who just might say, as La Fontaine had his sculptor wondering:

"Will it be a god, a table, or a washbowl?"

"*It will be a god!*' proclaims the great writer of fables! These words, so noble and so profound, seem to describe *you,* gentlemen. Act by yourselves, and France will reappear, almost as noble as our ancestors made it, and as we ourselves actually saw it before the death of Louis XVI.

"England—or at least its noble lords—find this unspeakable Jacobinism as abominable as we do. Without English gold, Austria, Russia, and Prussia will produce only two or three campaigns. Will that be enough to lead to a successful occupation, like that which Monsieur de Richelieu squandered, so stupidly, in 1817? I do not think so."

At this point there was an interruption, but it was stifled by a "Hush!" from everyone else. Once more, the interrupter had been the former general, who longed for the nation's grandest medal, and wanted his name to appear prominent among the authors of the secret note.

"I do not think so," Monsieur de La Mole repeated when the noise died down. He stressed "I," with an insolence that charmed Julien. "That's well played," he said to himself, even as he made his pen fly almost as rapidly as the marquis's words. With a single, well-said word, Monsieur de La Mole had wiped out the turncoat general's twenty campaigns.

"It's not only foreigners," the marquis continued, his words carefully measured, "to whom we may owe a new military occupation. All the young fellows who write incendiary articles in *The Globe* may provide you with three or four thousand young captains, among whom, perhaps, might be found a Kléber, a Hoche, a Jourdain, a Pichegru, but not so well meaning."

"We haven't known how to make him glorious," said the chairman. "Pichegru should have been kept immortal."

"Finally: France must have two parties," resumed Monsieur de La Mole, "two parties not only in name, but two clearly defined parties, distinct and separate. We need to be aware of who and what must be crushed. On the one hand, journalists, voters, public opinion—in short, youth and all who admire it. While they stupefy themselves with the noise of their empty words, we—we have the clear advantage of consuming the budget."

Here there was another interruption.

"You sir," said Monsieur de La Mole to the interrupter, with admirable arrogance and facility, "if the word shocks you, then you don't 'consume' the budget: you devour forty thousand francs, as a line item in the state budget, and eighty thousand which you receive from the king's budget.

"Well, sir, since you compel me, let me use you, boldly, as an example. Like your noble ancestors, who followed Saint Louis to the Crusades, you really should be able to show us, for those thousands of francs, at least a regiment, a company—what am I saying! Half a company, if it were composed of fifty combat-ready men, all dedicated to the good cause, to life, and to death. All you have is servants who, in case there's a revolution, will make you afraid of *them*.

"The throne, the altar, the nobility may perish tomorrow, gentlemen, as long as you have still not created, in every district, a force of five hundred *dedicated* men. Dedicated, let me say, not only with the courage of Frenchmen, but also with the steadiness of the Spanish.

"Half of this troop should be composed of our children, our nephews—in a word, of real gentlemen. Each of them will have at his side, not some word-crazed petty bourgeois, ready to hoist the tricolor flag if another 1815 gives him yet another chance, but a good peasant, simple, frank, like Cathelineau. Our young sons and nephews will have taught them—the peasants ought to be sons of the women who nursed their betters. Each of us ought to give up *one-fifth* of our income, in order to form this little, dedicated troop of five hundred in each district. And then you'll be able to rely on a foreign occupation. Foreign soldiers will never get as far as Dijon, on their own, if they can't be sure of finding five hundred friendly soldiers in every department.

"Foreign kings will only listen to you when you inform them of twenty thousand gentlemen, ready to take up arms, on their behalf, and open the ports of France. This will be painful, you may say. Gentlemen, it's the price of keeping ourselves alive. Between liberty of the press, and our existence as gentlemen, it is war to the death. Turn yourself into manufacturers, or peasants—or pick up your guns. Be timid, if you so choose, but do not be stupid. Open your eyes.

"*Formez vos battalions,* get your battalions ready, I say to you, in the words of the 'Marseillaise,' that Jacobin song. Then you'll have some noble King Gustavus Adolphus, moved by an imminent threat to the very principle of monarchy, who will come five hundred miles from his own country, and do for us what that Gustavus did for the Protestant princes. Do you prefer to go on talking, and never act? In fifty years all there will be, in Europe, is the presidents of republics—not a king left. And when those four letters—K-I-N-G—disappear, so too will all the priests and all the gentlemen. All I can see is *candidates* paying court to dirt-covered *majorities.*

"In spite of there being, right now, as you have said, no proven general in all of France, known to and loved by everyone, and our army being organized solely in the interests of the throne and the altar, and all our good old soldiers having been discharged from the ranks, every single Austrian and Prussian regiment contains fifty junior officers who have seen combat.

"And there are two hundred thousand young men, petty bourgeois all of them, who long for war. . . ."

"Leave off these unpleasant truths," said a sober dignitary, in an imposing voice; he was clearly someone high on the list of ecclesiastical worthies, for Monsieur de La Mole smiled pleasantly, instead of becoming angry. To Julien, this was a very plain sign.

"Enough of these unpleasant truths," the dignitary repeated. "Let us sum up, gentlemen: a man, facing amputation of a gangrenous limb, would make a serious mistake, were he to tell his surgeon: 'This sick limb is perfectly healthy.' Forgive me the expression, gentlemen: the noble Duke of ——— is our surgeon."

"There's the key word, it's finally been said," thought Julien. "Tonight I'll be galloping toward ———."

CHAPTER TWENTY-THREE

THE CLERGY, THEIR WOODLANDS, AND FREEDOM

The first law of existence is self-preservation, staying alive. You sow
hemlock seed and expect to see ripening corn!
—MACHIAVELLI

The sober dignitary went on. He was clearly knowledgeable; he set
forth large verities with a gentle, measured eloquence that Julien
found infinitely pleasant:

"First: England hasn't got a guinea to help us; thriftiness and Hume
are all the fashion, there. Even their noncomformist *Saints* will give us
nothing, and Mister Henry Brougham will only laugh at us.

"Second: It will be impossible to obtain more than two campaigns
from Europe's kings, absent English money; and two campaigns against
the petty bourgeoisie will not be enough.

"Third: We must form an armed party in France, without which
the chief European monarchies will not risk even those two campaigns.

"The fourth point I venture to propose to you, as something quite
obvious, is this:

"*No armed party can be formed in France without the clergy.* I tell you this
boldly, gentlemen, because I'm going to prove it to you. The clergy
must be given everything.

"Primarily because the Church conducts its business night and day,
and is guided by men of high capacity who are positioned, far from
any exposure to storms, nine hundred miles from your frontiers—"

"Ah! Rome, Rome!" exclaimed the master of the house.

"Yes, my dear sir, *Rome!*" the cardinal replied proudly. "Whatever
witticisms, more or less ingenious, may have been fashionable when
you were young, I will say to you, emphatically, that in 1830 the
clergy, guided by Rome, are the common people's only voice.

"Fifty thousand priests say the same things, on the day decreed by
their leaders, and the people—who after all supply the soldiers—are

more affected by the voices of their priests than by all the little poetry in the world. . . ."

(This very personal remark evoked murmurs.)

"The Church's genius is superior to yours," the cardinal went on, raising his voice. "Every step already taken toward that central achievement, *having an armed party in France*, has been accomplished by us." He produced the facts: "Who sent eighty thousand guns to the Vendée? . . ." etc., etc.

"But while the clergy are not in possession of their woodlands, they have nothing. As soon as war starts, the minister of finance writes to his agents that no one has any more money, except for the priests. France truly has no faith, and it loves war. Whoever can give her war will be doubly popular, because war—to use the common phrase—means starving the Jesuits. Making war means freeing those prideful monsters, the French, from the threat of foreign intervention."

The cardinal's remarks were positively received.

"Monsieur de Nerval," he declared, "must resign from the government. His name is senselessly provoking."

At these words, they all rose and began speaking at the same time. "They're going to send me away again." Julien thought. But even the wise chairman had forgotten Julien was there, or that he even existed.

Everyone was looking toward a man Julien recognized. This was Monsieur de Nerval, the prime minister; Julien had seen him at Duke de Retz's ball.

Confusion was at its height, as the newspapers say, reporting on Parliament. After a long quarter of an hour, silence was partially restored.

Then Monsieur de Nerval rose, speaking apostolically:

"I will not tell you," he said, his voice quite odd, "that I don't enjoy being prime minister.

"It has been indicated, gentlemen, that my name significantly intensifies Jacobinism, by making many moderates oppose us. Accordingly, I would gladly retire from my post, but our Lord's ways can only be seen by a very few. Still," he added, staring directly at the cardinal, "I have a mission. Heaven has said to me: 'Either you will bring your head to the scaffold or else you will reestablish monarchy in France, and reduce Parliament to what it was under Louis XV'—and, gentlemen, *I will do exactly that.*"

He fell silent, he sat down once more, and there was not a sound to be heard.

"Now there's a fine actor," thought Julien. He deceived himself, as he usually did, in seeing more in other people than was really there. Excited by an evening of such lively debate, and above all by the sincerity of the discussion, at that moment Monsieur de Nerval believed in his mission. He was wonderfully courageous, but not endowed with much common sense.

Midnight sounded, during the silence that followed those fine words: *"I will do exactly that."* It seemed to Julien that there was something imposing and funereal in the striking pendulum. He was moved.

The discussion soon resumed, with heightened energy and, above all, incredible naïvité. "These gentlemen will have to have me poisoned," Julien thought, at some points. "How can they say such things in front of a working-class man?"

Two o'clock sounded, and they were still talking. The master of the house had been asleep for a long time; Monsieur de La Mole had to summon a servant to bring in new candles. Monsieur de Nerval, the prime minister, had left at one forty-five, not without having paid considerable attention to Julien's face, employing a pocket mirror he had with him. Everyone relaxed, once he had gone.

While candles were being replaced: "God only knows what that man will say to the king!" the triple-vested man said in a low voice, to the man next to him. "He's capable of making us seem utterly foolish and destroying our future."

"But you have to concede that he's unusually conceited, and even impudent, coming here. He used to come, before he rose to be prime minister. But power changes everything, washes away whatever a man once cared about. He really ought to be aware of that."

The prime minister had barely walked out of the room, when Bonaparte's former general closed his eyes. Then he talked about his health, his wounds, looked at his watch, and went away.

"I would wager," said the triple-vested man, "that our general is running after the prime minister. He'll be excusing himself for having been found here, and claiming he can pull us this way and that."

When the half-asleep servants had finished with the candles:

"Let us now consult, gentlemen," said the chairman, "without further attempts at persuading one another. Let us turn to that note which, forty-eight hours from now, will be read by our foreign friends. We've talked about government ministers. We can now say that Monsieur de Nerval has broken with us—and what do ministers matter? We'll do with them as we will."

With a delicate smile, the cardinal agreed.

"There is nothing easier, it strikes me, than to sum up our position," said the young Bishop of Agde, with the intensely focused, passionate compulsion of the most exalted fanaticism. He had been silent, until now. His eyes, Julien had noted, were at first mild and calm; they had been aflame ever since the discussion's first hour. By this point, his soul was bubbling over like lava at Vesuvius.

"From 1806 to 1814, England made only one mistake," he said, "which was not to act directly and personally against Napoleon. Once that man created dukes and high court officers, once he'd reestablished the throne, the mission God had entrusted to him was done. He was good for nothing but the flames. The Holy Scriptures teach us, in many ways, how to do away with tyrants." (Here there were several quotations in Latin.)

"Today, gentlemen, it's not a man we need to burn, but Paris. France follows Paris in everything. What good will it do to arm your five hundred men, in every administrative department? That's a risky task, and it will be endless. Why entangle France in a matter which depends entirely on Paris? Paris alone, with its newspapers and its drawing rooms, has created the evil. Let this modern Babylon perish.

"Let us be done, at last, with the question of Paris or the Church. This immense destruction would actually serve the worldly interests of the throne. Why did Paris never emit so much as a puff, under Bonaparte? Go ask the artillerymen of Saint-Roch. . . ."

———

Only at three in the morning did Julien leave, with Monsieur de La Mole.

The marquis was ashamed and weary. For the first time, in speaking to Julien, there was something like entreaty in his voice. He asked that Julien give him his word, never to reveal the excessive zeal—if that was the correct word—which, by chance, he had witnessed. "Only mention these things to our foreign friend if he insists, most seriously, on knowing about our young wildmen. Do these hotheads worry about the state being overthrown? They'll become cardinals; they'll take refuge in Rome. But us, in our great houses, we will be massacred by the peasants."

The secret note, which the marquis composed on the basis of Julien's large report, all twenty-six pages of it, was not ready until four forty-five.

"I'm tired to death," the marquis said, "and that's perfectly obvious in this note, which toward the end lacks clarity. I'm less satisfied with this than I've ever been, really, with anything in my life. See here, my friend," he added, "go take a few hours of rest. And because I worry about your being kidnapped, I will come with you and lock you in your room."

The next day, the marquis brought Julien to an isolated country house, rather far from Paris. There were strange people in residence; Julien took them for priests. He was given a passport, under a fictitious name, which indicated the true destination of his trip, something he had always pretended not to know. He climbed into a carriage, alone.

The marquis was not worried about his memory. Julien had several times recited the secret note. What did worry Monsieur de La Mole was fear of Julien's being intercepted.

"Never stop looking like a fop, traveling to kill time," he told Julien, just as the younger man was leaving. His voice was friendly. "There may have been more than one false friend at our meeting, last night."

Traveling was rapid and extremely dismal. Julien was barely out of the marquis's sight when he'd forgotten the secret note, and his mission, only daydreaming about Mathilde's contempt.

In a village not far distant from Metz, the postmaster came to tell him there were no horses available. It was ten o'clock at night. Much vexed, Julien requested supper. He walked along, in front of the post house, and gradually, without being seen, got into the stables. There was not a horse in sight.

However, Julien told himself, the postmaster had seemed strange. "He was studying me with his vulgar eyes."

He had begun, as you see, not to fully believe everything he'd been told.

He thought about escaping, after supper. In order to learn something about the place, he left his room and went down to warm himself at the kitchen fire. How happy he was to discover, there, Signor Géronimo, the famous singer!

Settled in an easy chair, which he'd brought up to the fire, the Neapolitan was groaning louder, and talking more, all by himself, than the twenty German peasants who stood around, gaping at him.

"These people here are ruining me," he declared to Julien. "I've promised to sing tomorrow, in Mayence. Seven sovereign princes have hurried to hear me. But let's go for a walk," he added, with a knowing look.

When they were a hundred paces down the street, and beyond any chance of being overheard:

"Do you know what this is all about?" he asked Julien. "Our postmaster is a scoundrel. I came out and walked around, earlier, and gave twenty pence to a young rascal who told me the whole story. There are more than a dozen horses, in a stable at the other side of town. They're trying to slow down some courier."

"Do you think so?" Julien said innocently.

Uncovering the fraud did not solve their problem. They had to be able to leave. And this, Géronimo and his friend could not arrange. "We'll wait till daylight," the singer finally said. "They don't trust us. Maybe it's you or me they're after. Tomorrow morning we'll order a good meal. While they're fixing it, we'll go for a little walk, we'll rent horses, and we'll go on to the next mail-coach stop."

"And your baggage?" said Julien, who was wondering if perhaps Géronimo himself could have been sent to intercept him. They had to eat and go to bed. Julien was still in his first sleep when he was wakened, with a start, by the voices of two men who were talking, right in his room, without even pretending to be quiet.

He recognized the postmaster, equipped with a muffled lantern. Its light was directed at his traveling trunk, which had been brought up to his room. Standing next to the postmaster was a man, calmly rummaging through the opened trunk. Julien could only make out the sleeves of his suit, which were black and exceedingly tight.

"It's a cassock," he told himself, and quietly picked up the pistols he'd set under his pillow.

"Don't worry about him waking up, Father," said the postmaster. "I gave him the wine you yourself prepared."

"There's not a trace of any papers," said the priest. "A lot of linen, perfume, soap, nonsense like that. He's a young man of our time, only concerned with his pleasures. The courier must be the other one, putting on that Italian accent."

They came closer to Julien, so they could look in the pockets of his traveling suit. He was powerfully tempted to kill them, as burglars. There could not be any serious consequences. He felt very attracted to the idea. . . . "But what a fool I'd be," he told himself. "I'd compromise my mission." After looking through Julien's pockets: "This is no diplomat," the priest said. He moved away, and it was an excellent thing that he did. "If they touch me, here in this bed, they'll be sorry indeed!" Julien said to himself. "They might be coming to stab me, and I'm not about to give them that opportunity."

The priest turned his head, and Julien half opened his eyes. What an astonishing sight! It was Father Castaneda! And indeed, though the two men had tried to keep their voices down, he had thought from the first that he recognized one of the voices. Julien experienced a fierce desire to rid the earth of one of its most cowardly scoundrels.

"But my mission," he told himself.

The priest and his acolyte left. A quarter of an hour later, Julien pretended to wake up. He cried out, waking the whole house.

"I've been poisoned!" he called. "I'm in terrible pain!" He wanted some pretext to go to Géronimo's assistance. He found him half suffocated by the opium the postmaster had put in his wine.

Fearing some trick of this sort, Julien had drunk only the chocolate he'd brought from Paris. He was barely able to sufficiently waken Géronimo, so they could discuss whether to stay or to leave.

"Give me the whole kingdom of Naples," said the singer, "but right now I cannot give up the delights of sleep."

"But the seven sovereign princes!"

"Let them wait."

Julien left by himself, and without any further incident came to the great personage he was to see. He wasted an entire morning, soliciting an audience, and in vain. Luckily, at about four o'clock the duke wanted a breath of fresh air. Julien saw him leaving, and on foot; he immediately went after him and asked for alms. When he was two steps away, he drew the Marquis de La Mole's watch and carefully displayed it. "Follow me, but not too closely," said the duke, not looking at him.

Three-quarters of a mile farther along, the duke walked briskly into a small coffeehouse. In one of the rooms of this fourth-rate establishment, Julien was privileged to recite for the duke his four pages. When he had finished: "Start again, and go more slowly," he was told.

The duke took his notes. Then:

"Go to the next post stop, on foot. Leave everything there, including your trunk. Go to Strasbourg, as best you can, and on the twenty-second of the month (it was then the tenth) return here, to this same coffeehouse, at twelve-thirty. Don't leave for half an hour. Be silent!"

These were the only words Julien heard. They were enough to imbue him with the highest admiration. "This is how to do business," he thought. "What would this great statesman say, had he heard those wild magpies chattering, three days ago?"

It took Julien two days to get to Strasbourg. Having no business to conduct there, he took a leisurely route. "If that devil, Father Castaneda, recognized me, he's not a man to easily give me up. . . . And how happy he'd be to mock me, and to ruin my mission."

Happily, Father Castaneda, the Congregation of the Holy Virgin's police chief for the entire northern frontier, had not recognized him. And the Strasbourg Jesuits, though wonderfully zealous, never dreamed of keeping watch on Julien, who in his blue frock coat, and wearing his honored medal, seemed most like a young officer, totally self-concerned.

CHAPTER TWENTY-FOUR

STRASBOURG

Spell-binding charmer! You have all love's energy, all its sweeping sorrow. Only its enchanting pleasures, its sweet joys, are beyond your sphere. But I could not say, watching her sleep: "She's all mine, her angelic beauty, her lovely weaknesses! There she is, completely in my power, exactly as Heaven in its gracious mercy made her, to bewitch a man's heart."

—SCHILLER

Obliged to spend a week in Strasbourg, Julien tried to distract himself with notions of military glory and patriotic devotion. Was he in love? He knew nothing: all he found, in his tormented heart, was Mathilde, absolute mistress of both his happiness and his imagination. All the energy of his character was required to keep from falling into despair. Thinking of anything that had no connection to Mademoiselle de La Mole was beyond his powers. Once, his ambition, and the lesser triumphs of vanity, had distracted him from feelings like those Madame de Rênal had inspired in him. Mathilde had absorbed everything; wherever he looked, in his future, he saw only her.

And everywhere, in that future, he saw failure. This young person who, at Verrières, had been so full of presumption, so arrogant, had succumbed to ridiculously overzealous modesty.

Three days earlier, he would have been delighted to kill Father Castaneda. But if, in Strasbourg, a child had quarreled with him, he would have taken the child's side. Thinking back to his adversaries, the enemies he had encountered all through his life, in each and every instance he judged himself, Julien, to have been in the wrong. His implacable enemy, now, was precisely that powerful imagination, once so interminably busy, painting for him a future full of brilliant successes.

The absolute solitude of a traveler's life added to the reign of his dark imagination. What a treasure a friend would have been! "But," Julien asked himself, "is there any heart that beats for me? And if I should find a friend, wouldn't honor oblige me to keep eternally silent?"

He was on horseback, riding sadly around the countryside near Kehl, a town on the banks of the Rhine, immortalized by the hard-fought victories of Desaix and Gouvion Saint-Cyr, making their way over the river under heavy fire. A German peasant showed him the little streams, the roads, the small islands in the Rhine, made famous by these great generals' courage. Leading his horse with his left hand, Julien had spread open, with his right, the superb battlefield map adorning Marshall Saint-Cyr's *Memoirs*. Then he lifted his head, startled by a cheerful exclamation.

It was Prince Korasoff, his London friend, who some months earlier had revealed to Julien the basic principles of high foppishness. Faithful to this noble art, Korasoff, who no more than an hour ago had set foot in Kehl, riding from Strasbourg, and who had never in his life read a line about the siege of 1796, set himself to explaining everything about it. The German peasant stared at them, astonished, for he knew enough French to make out the enormous blunders the prince was falling into. Julien's mind was far away. He was watching the handsome young nobleman, amazed; he was admiring the grace with which he mounted his horse.

"What a happy nature!" he told himself. "How well his riding clothes fit him; how elegantly his hair has been cut. Oh, had I looked like him, perhaps she wouldn't have taken such a dislike to me, after three days of loving me."

When the prince had finished off the siege of 1796: "You're looking like a Trappist monk," he said to Julien. "The principles I gave you, in London, should not be applied so rigorously. To seem sorrowful is perhaps not quite in good taste: you're supposed to seem bored. If you're sad, there's something deficient about you, something you haven't yet conquered.

"*It's a demonstration of inferiority.* If you really are bored, on the other hand, this sort of thing would show that whoever's been trying hard to please you is *your* inferior. Understand me, my dear friend: showing contempt is a serious business."

Julien tossed a gold coin to the peasant, who had been listening, his mouth hanging open.

"Good," said the prince. "Now that was graceful—a noble disdain! Very good!" And he set his horse to galloping. Julien followed him, overwhelmed by dull, stupefied admiration.

"Ah, had I been like him, she wouldn't have preferred de Croisenois!" The more shocked he was by the prince's absurdities, the more he despised himself for not admiring them, and the more miserable he judged himself for not sharing them. Self-loathing can go no further.

The prince was aware of Julien's genuine misery. "What's all this, my friend," he said, as they rode back to Strasbourg. "Have you lost your money, or perhaps you've fallen in love with some little actress?"

Russians imitate French manners, but they're always fifty years behind. Right now, they've reached the era of Louis XV.

This fooling with love brought tears to Julien's eyes. "Why shouldn't I turn to this friendly fellow for advice?" he suddenly asked himself.

"Yes, yes, old boy," the prince said. "You'll see, when we're back in Strasbourg, that I myself am madly in love, and decidedly rejected. A charming woman, who lives in a nearby city, has dropped me, after three days of passion, and this reversal is killing me."

Julien described for the prince, using fictitious names, both Mathilde's actions and her character.

"Don't bother going on," said Korasoff. "To give you proper confidence in your physician, I'll finish your intimate tale myself. Either the young woman's husband revels in an immense fortune, or, much more likely, she herself belongs to your country's highest class. She really must have something to be proud of."

Julien nodded; he no longer had the courage to speak.

"Very good," said the prince. "Here are three rather bitter pills, which you're going to have to take, and without delay:

"First, make sure, every single day, that you see Madame . . . what's her name?"

"Madame de Dubois."

"What a name!" said the prince, roaring with laughter. "But, forgive me: for you, it must be sublime. But you have to see Madame de Dubois every day; above all, don't let her think you're being cold or angry. Remember the great principle of this century: be the opposite of what you're expected to be. Let her see you exactly as you were a week before she honored you with her favors."

"Ah! Then I was calm," Julien exclaimed despairingly. "I thought I was being sorry for her...."

"The moth burns itself on the candle," the prince went on, "a metaphor as old as the world.

"So: first, you'll see her every day.

"Second: you'll pursue some lady in high society, but not displaying any sign of passion—do you follow me? I won't conceal it from you: your role will be a difficult one. You'll be acting in a comedy, and if they guess you're only acting, you're done for."

"She's so smart, and I'm not! I'm done for," said Julien, sorrowfully.

"No, it's simply that you're more in love than I'd thought. Madame de Dubois is profoundly concerned with herself, like all the women blessed by heaven either with an excess of nobility, or an excess of money. She thinks about herself instead of thinking about you, and so she knows nothing about you. During the two or three small fits of love she's granted you, she made a huge imaginative effort to see in you the hero she's always dreamed of, not you as you actually are....

"Good Lord, these are such utterly basic matters, my dear Sorel. Are you no more than a schoolboy? ...

"By God! Let's go in this shop. Look at that charming black tie. You'd think it was from John Anderson of Burlington Street. Make me happy: take it, and then throw just as far away as you can that horrible bit of black rope you've got around your neck.

"Carry on," said the prince, as they left Strasbourg's very best shop for men's accessories. "Now, with whom does your Madame de Dubois associate? My Lord, what a name! Don't be annoyed at me, my dear Sorel: it's stronger than I am.... Just whom will you pursue?"

"A magnificent prude," said Julien, "daughter of an immensely rich provincial merchant. She has the loveliest eyes in the world, which I find infinitely delightful; she surely is of the highest rank in France; but even with such social standing, she blushes almost to distraction if anyone tries to talk to her about business and shopkeeping. Her bad luck, but her father happened to be one of the best-known merchants in Strasbourg."

"And so," said the prince, laughing, "if there's talk about *business,* you'll be sure this lovely creature is thinking about herself, and not you. This is divine and highly useful absurdity: it will keep you from even the tiniest flicker of insanity when you're looking into those lovely eyes. Victory will be yours."

Julien had been thinking of Marshall Fervaques's widow, who often came to visit the de La Moles. She was a beautiful foreigner who'd been married to the marshall just a year before his death. Her only goal in life appeared to be erasing any awareness of herself as a *businessman*'s daughter; to create a name for herself, in Paris, she'd become a leader of the virtue party.

Julien sincerely admired the prince: what he wouldn't have given to possess the man's wit! The two friends chatted on, and Korasoff was delighted: no Frenchman had ever listened to him for so long. "So I've finally succeeding in being heard," he told himself, utterly enchanted, "by giving lessons to my teachers!"

"We're agreed, then," he repeated to Julien for the tenth time. "Not a flicker of passion, when you're in Madame de Dubois's presence and talking to this young beauty, daughter of a stocking salesman in Strasbourg. On the other hand, let your passion absolutely burn when you write to her. Reading a well-written love letter is a prude's greatest delight; it's an interlude of relaxation. She's no longer acting in *her* comedy; she can allow herself to listen to her heart. Accordingly, two letters a day."

"Never, never!" said Julien, discouraged. "I'd rather be pounded to death in a mortar than write three sentences. I'm a corpse, my dear friend; don't expect anything from me. Let me die out on the street."

"And why are you talking about writing sentences? I carry in my luggage six manuscripts of love letters. They're for all kinds of women; I've got plenty for the nobly virtuous sort. Didn't Kalisky pay court, at Richmond—you know the place, it's not ten miles from London—and to the prettiest Quakeress in all of England?"

By the time he left his friend, at ten in the morning, Julien felt less miserable.

Next day, the prince summoned a copyist, and two days later Julien had fifty-three love letters, neatly numbered, constructed to appeal to the most sublime, the most dismal, of virtuous women.

"I haven't got fifty-four," said the prince, "because Kalisky was turned down. But you won't be worrying about being misused by the stocking seller's daughter, since all you're after is Madame de Dubois's heart."

They went riding every day; the prince was extraordinarily fond of Julien. Not knowing how to demonstrate his sudden friendship, he ended by offering Julien a cousin's hand, she being a rich heiress in Moscow. "And once you're married," he added, "my influence, and the medal you're wearing, will make you a colonel in less than two years."

"But I didn't get this from Napoleon; that makes a difference."

"Why?" said the prince. "He created that medal, didn't he? And it remains the highest decoration in all Europe."

Julien was almost ready to accept the offer, but called to mind his duty to the great nobleman. When he left Korasoff, he promised to write. The response to his secret note arrived, and he hurried toward Paris. But barely two days later, the thought of leaving France, and Mathilde, seemed to him more painful than death itself. "I won't marry the millions Korasoff offered," he said to himself. "But I will take his advice.

"After all, seduction's the Russian's profession. He hasn't thought about anything else since he was fifteen, and he's thirty by now. It can't be said he's stupid: he's subtle, he's crafty. You can't expect raptures, or poetry, from such a man. He's really a pimp—which is yet another reason he can't afford to be wrong.

"It's got to be done. I'll pursue Madame de Fervaques.

"She'll probably be something of a bore, but I'll keep looking into her really lovely eyes, which so closely resemble those I love best in the world.

"She's a foreigner: that will be something new to consider.

"I'm crazy, I'm drowning, I have no choice but to take my friend's advice and not expect to know what I'm doing, left to myself."

CHAPTER TWENTY-FIVE

THE MISTRESS OF VIRTUE

But if I sought pleasure with such prudence and care,
for me it wouldn't be pleasure.

—LOPE DE VEGA

He'd barely gotten back to Paris, presented his dispatches to Monsieur de La Mole, who appeared greatly distressed by them, and left the marquis in his office, than our hero went hurrying to see Count Altamira. In addition to having being sentenced to death, this handsome foreigner was also a man of great sobriety, and lucky enough to be deeply devout. These two assets, and more than anything else his high birth, completely suited Madame de Fervaques, who saw a good deal of him.

Julien confessed, most soberly, that he was deeply in love with the lady. "Hers is the purest kind of virtue, and the noblest," Altamira responded, "though rather Jesuitical and a bit grandiloquent. There are days when I understand each and every word she says, but I don't understand a single sentence in its entirety. She often makes me think I don't understand French as well as they say I do. Knowing her will bring your name forward; she'll give you weight in the world. But first, let's go see Bustos," the count added. "He's tried paying court to her."

Don Diego Bustos let them explain the whole affair at some length, saying nothing, like a lawyer in consultation. He had a monk's fat face, with a thick black mustache, and unmatchable sobriety—in other words, just like a perfect Italian conspirator.

"I understand," he finally told Julien. "Has Madame de Fervaques had lovers, or hasn't she? Accordingly, is there any hope of your succeeding? That is the question. This is a way of telling you that, as for myself, I failed. Now that I'm no longer angry, I try to rationalize it like this: she's often irritable, and as I'll explain in a moment, she can be quite spiteful.

"I don't think her bilious temper is a sign of high intelligence, which can put a passionate varnish on everything. I think, on the contrary, she owes her unusual beauty, and her fresh complexion, to a phlegmatic, calm Dutch temperament."

Julien grew impatient with the Spaniard's slow, stolid speech. From time to time, in spite of himself, small monosyllabic sounds escaped him.

"Do you wish to hear me?" Don Diego Bustos said to him solemnly.

"Forgive me this *furia francese*, this French frenzy. I am all ears," said Julien.

"Madame de Fervaques, as I have said, is strongly inclined to hatred. She pursues, unpityingly, people she's never seen—lawyers, and poor devils like Charles Collé, literary men who've written songs—you know.

> "*J'ai la marotte*
> *D'aimer Marote*, etc.
>
> "I'm in the habit
> Of loving Rabbit..."

And then Julien had to listen, as Don Diego went through the entire song. The Spanish love to sing in French.

This divine song had never been heard with such impatience. And when he'd finished: "Madame de Fervaques," said Don Diego, "had the author of another song dismissed from his post—it begins 'Un jour l'amour au cabaret,' 'One day a lover was half-seas over.'"

Julien shuddered: Bustos might want to sing this one, too. But Don Diego was satisfied with analysis. In fact, it was blasphemous and rather indecent.

"When Madame de Fervaques got angry about this song," Don Diego went on, "I felt obliged to tell her that a woman of her standing should never read all the stupidities put into print. Whatever progress piety and sobriety may make, in France there will always be barroom literature. When she had this writer, a poor devil on half pay, thrown out of his post, worth eighteen hundred francs: 'Watch out,' I told her. 'You've attacked this rhymester with your weapons; he can answer you with his. He'll write a song about virtue. The gilt drawing rooms will support you; those who relish laughter will be repeating his epigrams.' Do you know, sir, what she answered? 'In the service of the Lord, the whole of Paris can watch me proceed to my martyrdom: it would be a new sort of spectacle for France. The people would learn to respect those of higher standing. It would be the most beautiful day of my life.' Her eyes had never been lovelier."

"And she has superb eyes," exclaimed Julien.

"I see you are amorously inclined. . . . So," Don Diego resumed gravely, "she's not the constitutionally bilious type, simply swept into vengeance. Yet if, all the same, she likes doing harm, it's because she's unhappy. I suspect some *inner misery*. Might she be a moral prude who's weary of her profession?"

Silently, and for a long minute, the Spaniard looked at him.

"That's the whole question," he added soberly, "and there's where you can find some hope. I have done a great deal of reflecting on those two years, when I was very humbly in her service. Your whole future, sir lover, hangs on this basic problem: Is she a prude who's tired of being prudish, and nasty because she's miserable?"

"Or else," said Altamira, finally breaking his profound silence, "could it be what I've told you twenty times? French female vanity, in a word. It's the memory of her father, the celebrated drapery merchant, which makes a naturally cheerless, dried-out constitution descend into misery. The only happiness she can find would be to live in Toledo, and be tormented, day after day, by a confessor who shows her the gaping doors of hell."

As Julien was leaving: "Altamira tells me you're one of us," Don Diego told him, as ever somber. "One day you'll help us win back our freedom, so I've tried to help you in this little diversion. It would be good for you to be familiar with Madame de Fervaques's style: here are four letters written in her hand."

"I'll have them copied," exclaimed Julien, "and then return them."

"And you'll never tell anyone a word of what we've been saying?"

"Never, on my honor," exclaimed Julien.

"May God come to your aid!" the Spaniard added, as he silently escorted Altamira and Julien to the stairs.

The scene had somewhat cheered our hero: he was close to smiling. "And here's pious Altamira," he said to himself, "helping me along the road to adultery."

While Don Diego had been droning soberly on, Julien was listening to the house clock, striking the hours.

The time for dinner grew nearer; he was going to see Mathilde again! He went home and dressed with considerable care.

"Stupidity number one," he told himself, as he went down the stairs. "The prince's instructions must be followed to the letter."

He went back up to his room and put on the simplest travel clothes he owned.

"And now," he thought, "the next question is how to look at her." It was only five-thirty; dinner was at six. He thought he'd go to the drawing room; he found it empty. The sight of the blue sofa moved him almost to tears; soon his cheeks were burning. "This idiotic sensitivity must be controlled," he told himself angrily. "It's betraying me." He picked up a newspaper, to help him look more assured, and walked three or four times from the drawing room to the garden.

Only trembling, and completely hiding himself behind an oak tree, did he dare raise his eyes toward Mademoiselle de La Mole's window. The shutters were very tightly closed; he thought he might collapse, and stood for a long time, leaning against the oak. Then, walking unsteadily, he went to look at the gardener's ladder.

The iron link, which he'd forced open, alas! under very different circumstances, had not been repaired. Carried away by a surge of madness, Julien pressed it to his lips.

After wandering for some time, between the drawing room and the garden, Julien felt unbearably weary: this was an initial success of which he was very aware. "My glances will be half dead and won't give me away!" Gradually, the guests appeared in the drawing room: each time the door opened, a deadly anxiety shot through Julien's heart.

They went into the dining room and seated themselves. At last, Mademoiselle de La Mole appeared, faithful as ever to her habit of keeping people waiting. She blushed quite deeply, seeing Julien: she had not been told he'd come back. Following Prince Korasoff's suggestion, Julien looked only at her hands. They were trembling. Although this discovery bothered him more than he could have said, he was still pleased to seem simply fatigued.

Monsieur de La Mole spoke very highly of him. The marquise spoke to him, immediately thereafter, remarking, pleasantly, that he looked tired. Julien kept saying to himself: "I can't let myself stare at Mademoiselle de La Mole, though I mustn't seem to be avoiding her glance. I need to really look just as I did a week before my misfortune. . . ." He had reason to believe he'd been successful, and went into the drawing room after dinner. Attentive for the first time to the mistress of the house, he devoted himself to speaking to the other men and to keeping the conversation moving along.

His politeness was rewarded: at eight o'clock, Madame de Fervaques was announced. Julien slipped away and soon returned, dressed with the greatest care. Madame de La Mole was profoundly grateful, observing that he'd shown her guest such respect, and, wishing to testify to her pleasure, began to speak to Madame de Fervaques about his trip. Julien took a position near the marshall's widow, making sure that, from where he was, it was impossible for Mathilde to see his eyes. So situated, and obeying all the rules of the game, Madame de Fervaques was able to furnish him with a source of dazzled admiration. He expressed these sentiments in a speech, drawn from the opening paragraph of the first of the fifty-three letters, generously presented to him by Prince Korasoff.

The marshall's widow had declared her intention of going to the opera buffa. Julien hurried over, and found the Chevalier de Beauvoisis, who conducted him to a box set aside for the king's gentlemen-in-waiting, which was next to Madame de Fervaques's private box. Julien never took his eyes off her. "I need," he said to himself, when he left, "to begin a siege journal; otherwise I'll forget my onslaughts." He compelled himself to write two or three pages on this boring topic, and thus very nearly succeeded—what a wonderful thing!—in not thinking of Mademoiselle de La Mole.

Mathilde had almost forgotten him while he was away on his trip. "He's nothing but a commoner, after all," she thought. "His name will always remind me of the greatest mistake of my life. I need to follow, most faithfully, all those popular notions of wisdom, restraint, and honor: a woman has everything to lose, forgetting them." She finally showed herself ready to conclude the arrangements with the Marquis de Croisenois, drafted and ready for a very long time. He was wildly happy; it would have thoroughly astonished him, had he been informed that what underlay Mademoiselle de La Mole's changed attitude, which made him so proud, was resignation.

Seeing Julien had altered all her ideas. "Really, he's my husband," she said to herself. "If I make a good-faith return to believing in wisdom and honor, obviously it's him I ought to marry."

She expected Julien to come pleading to her, she expected him to act miserable; she had her responses all prepared, because he would surely try to say something to her, as they left the table after dinner. He did nothing of the sort. He stayed steadily where he was, not even glancing toward the garden—God only knows with what painful effort! It would be better, having our explanations quickly said and done, thought Mademoiselle de La Mole. She went into the garden, alone. Julien did not follow her. Mathilde set herself to walking near the drawing room windows. She saw him deeply occupied, describing for Madame de Fervaques's benefit the old ruined châteaux, crowning the hills along the banks of the Rhine and lending them so much character. He was beginning to do not too badly, developing the sentimental, picturesque phrases that in certain drawing rooms are called *spirited,* even *witty.*

Prince Korasoff would have been very proud of him, had he happened to be in Paris: the evening had gone precisely as he'd predicted.

He would also have approved of how Julien conducted himself in the days that followed.

An intrigue among the members of the hidden government-behind-the-government would soon lead to the award of a number of supreme medals. Madame de Fervaques insisted that her great-uncle receive one. The Marquis de La Mole had made the same claim for his father-in-law; they began to work together, and the marshall's widow came to the house virtually every day. It was she who told Julien that the marquis was to join the government and become a minister: the marquis had proposed, to the powers behind the throne, a highly ingenious plan for eliminating the Constitution, without any fuss, in another three years.

If Monsieur de La Mole became a minister, it might be possible for Julien to become a bishop, but for him all these large concerns could be glimpsed only as if through a veil. His mind mostly perceived them vaguely, at best, and as it were from a distance. His horrible misery, which had turned him into a maniac, made him see all aspects of life in terms of their connection to Mademoiselle de La Mole. He had estimated that, after five or six years of trying, he would get her to love him again.

His cold, distant mind, as we have seen, had disintegrated into a state of utter irrationality. Of all the qualities that had distinguished him, once, only a modicum of firmness remained. Totally bound, in body, to the plan dictated by Prince Korasoff, he placed himself, every night, carefully close to Madame de Fervaques's armchair, but he could not find a single word to say to her.

The exertions he inflicted on himself, trying to make Mathilde think he'd been cured, absorbed all the strength his soul possessed: he fixed himself near Madame de Fervaques like someone barely alive. Even his eyes—as eyes can, under severe physical strain—had lost all their fire.

Since Madame de La Mole's opinions neither were, nor ever had been, anything more than a direct reflection of her husband's—he who was likely to make her a duchess—for the past few days she had been praising Julien to the skies.

CHAPTER TWENTY-SIX

LOVE OF A MORAL SORT

> There also was of course in Adeline
> That calm patrician polish in the address,
> Which ne'er can pass the equinoctial line
> Of anything which Nature would express:
> Just as a Mandarin finds nothing fine,
> At least his manner suffers not to guess
> That anything he views can greatly please.
> —BYRON, *DON JUAN*

"There's something a bit insane about this whole family's perspective," thought Madame de Fervaques. "They're infatuated with their little priest, who understands nothing except listening—with, it's true, rather beautiful eyes."

For his part, Julien found the lady's behavior almost a perfect example of *patrician calm,* which radiates an exact politeness and, even more, the impossibility of vibrant emotion. A spontaneous movement, a lack of self-control, would have scandalized Madame de Fervaques almost as much as a failure to condescend to one's inferiors. The least sign of sensitivity would have been, in her eyes, like a form of *moral drunkenness,* which ought to make one blush, and would be harmful indeed to what a person of high standing owed herself. Her great happiness was to talk about the king's most recent hunt; her favorite book was *Memoirs of the Duke de Saint-Simon,* especially the genealogical parts.

Julien understood the exact spot where, because of the lighting arrangements, Madame de Fervaques's sort of beauty shone the most brilliantly. He would post himself there, in advance, but taking considerable pains to face so he could not see Mathilde. Stunned by his persistence in hiding from her, she abandoned the blue sofa, one day, and took her needlework to a small table near the armchair beside which he was posted. Julien saw how near she'd come, looking out from under Madame de Fervaques's hat. Seeing those eyes, which held the key to his fate, was initially frightening. But then he wrenched himself out of his usual apathy and spoke extremely well.

He was speaking to Madame de Fervaques, but his only aim was to affect Mathilde's soul. He grew so animated that his conversational partner could no longer understand what he was saying.

That was a positive development. If Julien had been able to think of rounding off his success, employing a few quotations from German mysticism, or from high Jesuitical theology, he would have elevated himself, in the lady's eyes, to the ranks of those superior men who, she considered, were called upon to regenerate the era.

"Since he's displaying such bad taste," Mademoiselle de La Mole said to herself, "spending so much time talking—and with such vigor—to Madame de Fervaques, I won't listen to him anymore." And she didn't take in a word he said for the rest of the evening, although the task was not an easy one.

At midnight, when Mathilde was carrying her mother's candle-holder, while escorting her to her room, Madame de La Mole paused, on the staircase, and delivered herself of a full-scale panegyric on Julien's high merits. This put Mathilde in a foul mood, and she was unable to sleep. One idea alone calmed her: "He for whom I feel such contempt can still seem a man of high merit, in Madame de Fer-vaques's eyes."

But Julien, who had now taken action, was less miserable. Back in his room, he happened to glance at the leather binder Prince Korasoff had given him to hold his gift of fifty-three love letters. Julien saw the prince's annotation, below the first letter: "to be sent a week after you first meet her."

"I'm late!" he exclaimed to himself. "It's been a very long time since I met Madame de Fervaques." He quickly set to copying the first let-ter: it was a sermon, full of virtuous observations, and incredibly bor-ing. He was lucky enough to fall asleep, by the second page.

Some hours later, he was awakened by bright sunshine. One of the most painful moments in his life occurred, every morning, when he woke and was once again aware of his misery. But on this day, he com-pleted his copy of the letter, laughing. "Is it really possible," he was saying to himself, "that a young man truly exists, capable of writing

like this!" He noted several sentences that ran a full nine lines each. At
the close of the original, he saw a note, in pencil:

These letters must be delivered by you: on horseback, wearing a black tie
and a blue frock coat. You are to hand the letter to the porter, looking as if
you felt guilty of something; your eyes must be full of profound melancholy. If some maid servant notices you, wipe your eyes, rather furtively.
Say a few words to the servant.

Julien faithfully followed his orders.

"This is all very bold of me," Julien thought as he was leaving
Madame de Fervaques's mansion, "but all the worse for Korasoff.
Imagine daring to write love letters to such a celebrated prude! I'll be
treated with the utmost contempt, and nothing could please me more.
And, really, this is the only kind of comedy I care for. Yes: To cover
this disgusting creature I call *me* in ridicule, that will please me. If I
took myself seriously, I'd commit a crime, just for the distraction."

For the past month, Julien's most satisfying moments had been
when he brought his horse back to the stable. Korasoff had forbidden
him, in the most explicit terms, from using any pretext whatever to
look at the mistress who'd rejected him. But the clatter of this horse's
hooves, a sound that she knew so well, and the way Julien rapped
his whip on the door, to summon a stable hand, sometimes brought
Mathilde to stand behind her window curtain. The chiffon was so thin
he could see right through it. If he held himself just so, he could see
her, from underneath his riding hat, without having to meet her
eyes. "Which means," he assured himself, "that she can't see my eyes,
either, so this doesn't constitute *looking*."

Madame de Fervaques's demeanor that night betrayed no sign
that, earlier in the day, she had received the philosophical-mystical-
religious dissertation he'd handed, with such utter melancholy, to her
porter. Chance had shown Julien, the night before, how he might make
himself eloquent: he arranged his chair so he could see Mathilde's
eyes. And she, for her part, rose from the blue sofa only moments after
Madame de Fervaques's arrival: it was open desertion of her usual
evening company. Monsieur de Croisenois seemed disturbed by this

latest whim; his obvious sorrow eased Julien's misery of its most painful agonies.

Such unexpected occurrences made him speak like an angel. And since vanity worms its way, even into hearts serving as temples of the most solemn virtue: "Madame de La Mole was right," Madame de Fervaques said to herself as she stepped back into her carriage. "That young priest is a man of distinction. It must be that, at first, being in my presence intimidated him. And it is true that everyone I meet in that house tends to be frivolous. The only virtue I find there is the sort that age brings with it, and which the frosts of growing old have immensely assisted. This young man, surely, knows the difference. He writes well, but I strongly suspect that the request he made in his letter, that I give him my advice, must really be founded in feelings of which he is himself not fully aware.

"All the same, how often conversions begin this way! What makes me expect good things from this one is how differently he writes, compared to the other young men whose letters I've come upon. It's impossible not to see spirituality, and deep seriousness and profound conviction, in this young ecclesiastic's prose. He will become a master of sweet virtue, like Massillon himself."

CHAPTER TWENTY-SEVEN

THE CHURCH'S BEST JOBS

Service? Talent? Merit? Bah!
Belong to a clique.
—FÉNELON, *TÉLÉMAQUE*

And so the notion of a bishopric was joined, for the first time, with ideas about Julien, in the mind of a woman who, sooner or later, would be bestowing the most powerful, the most lucrative posts in the French Church. This honor would scarcely have concerned Julien: just then, his mind was not capable of reaching toward anything but his current misery. All things intensified it: the view from his room, for example, had become unendurable. When he walked upstairs with his candle at night, every piece of furniture, every trifling ornament, seemed to him to become vocal and proclaim some new detail of his affliction.

"Today," he told himself, returning to his room with a liveliness he'd not felt in a long time, "I've got some compulsory labor. Let's hope the second letter will be as boring as the first."

It was worse. The stuff he was copying struck him as so absurd that he began reproducing it line by line, without any regard to sense.

"This is even more bombastic," he said to himself, "than the official documents of the Munster Treaty, which my diplomacy professor made me copy out in London."

And then, for the first time, he thought of Madame de Fervaques's letters, the originals of which he'd forgotten to return to that sober Spaniard, Don Diego Bustos. He hunted them up; they were in fact virtually as obscure and rambling as those of the young Russian nobleman. They possessed a perfect vagueness, wishing to say everything, and saying nothing. "This is the Aeolian harp of style," Julien thought. "Set among the highest thoughts of nothingness, of death, of infinity, etc., the only real thing I see is a horrible fear of appearing ridiculous."

The monologue we have just summarized was repeated over and over, for the following two weeks. Falling asleep while copying a kind of commentary on the Apocalypse; the next day, going to deliver a letter, with the prescribed melancholic mien; bringing his horse back to the stable, and hoping to catch a glimpse of Mathilde's dress; attending the opera, that evening, when Madame de Fervaques did not visit the de La Mole house: these events comprised the monotonous moments of Julien's life. Things were more interesting when Madame de Fervaques visited Madame de La Mole: he could catch glimpses of Mathilde's eyes, under cover of the brim of Madame de Fervaques's hat, and then he spoke eloquently. His picturesque and sentimental language began to take on more striking and more elegant forms.

He realized that, to Mathilde, he was speaking absurdities, but he was anxious to impress her with the elegance of his diction. "The more falsehoods I speak, the more pleased she should be," Julien thought. And then, with frightful boldness, he heightened and exaggerated certain aspects of physical nature. It had not taken him long to understand that, to keep Madame de Fervaques from thinking him vulgar, it was necessary above all other things to avoid simple, rational ideas. He maintained that standard, shortening the amplifications he would give to these notions, depending on the successful or the indifferent reactions he could observe in the great ladies he was trying to please.

On the whole, his life was less horrible than when he had passed his days in purely passive misery.

"But," he said to himself one night, "here I am, copying out the fifteenth of these awful disquisitions. The first fourteen have been faithfully delivered to Madame de Fervaques's doorman. I'll achieve the high honor of filling all the storage slots in her desk. And still, she treats me exactly as if I had never written a word! Where will all of this end? Is my persistence as boring to her as it is to me? It must be said, surely, that this Russian, Korasoff's friend, was a dreadful man in his day: there has never been anyone more deadly dull."

Like all mediocre men, placed by chance amid the maneuvers of some great general, Julien understood nothing of the young Russian's attack on the lovely English Quakeress. The only purpose of the first forty letters had been to excuse his boldness in daring to writing at all. It had been necessary to create, in this sweet young woman (who may well have become infinitely bored), the habit of receiving letters just a little less insipid, perhaps, than her everyday existence.

One morning, a letter came for Julien. He recognized Madame de Fervaques's coat of arms, and broke the seal with a speed that, only a few days earlier, would have seemed to him impossible. It was simply an invitation to dinner. On such points, where he ought to have been clear and direct, the young Russian had been as casual as Claude Dorat, legendarily remiss: Julien was unable to calculate exactly what moral stance he was supposed to assume at this dinner.

The drawing room was the ultimate in magnificence, gilded like the great Galleries of Diana, at the Tuileries, and with large, descriptive oil paintings hung on the paneled walls. These canvases bore oddly placed clear spots. Julien learned, later, that the lady of the house, thinking the paintings a bit indecent, had had certain portions blotted out. *"This moral age!"* he thought.

He noted the presence of three people who had helped prepare the secret note. One of them, the Bishop of ———, Madame de Fervaques's uncle, was in charge of placing priests in parishes and, it was said, would deny his niece nothing. "What an immense step I've taken," Julien said to himself, with a melancholy smile, "and how little it means to me! Here I am, dining with the famous Bishop of ———."

The dinner was mediocre; the conversation irritating. "It's a bad book's table of contents," Julien thought. "They proudly tackle all the important themes of human thought. But after you listen for three minutes, you have to ask yourself which stands out more clearly, the speaker's sheer bombast or his abominable ignorance."

The reader has surely forgotten that minor man of letters, Tanbeau by name, the academician's nephew, and a professor-to-be: he seemed actively employed, here, in vulgar slander aimed at the de La Mole drawing room.

It was this little fellow who first gave Julien the idea that, in spite of not having answered his letters, Madame de Fervaques might well look favorably on the sentiment that had led them to be written. Monsieur Tanbeau's black heart was torn apart, contemplating Julien's success. "But on the other hand," the diminutive future professor said to himself, "neither a worthy man nor a fool can manage to be in two places at the same time. If Sorel should become the sublime Fervaques's lover, she'll get him well placed in the Church, and then I'll be rid of him in the de La Mole drawing room."

Father Pirard, too, delivered himself of long sermons, admonishing Julien for his success at this dinner. There was *sectarian jealousy*, as between the austere Jansenist and the Jesuitical drawing room, reactionary and monarchical, of Marshall de Fervaques's virtuous widow.

CHAPTER TWENTY-EIGHT

MANON LESCAUT

Now, once he was thoroughly convinced of the priest's ignorant stupidity, he usually managed quite well by calling black whatever was white, and white whatever was black.

—LICHTENBERG

His Russian instructions prescribed, imperiously, that the woman to whom he was writing should never be conversationally contradicted. Under no pretext whatever was he to set aside his role of ecstatic admirer. Every one of the letters began with this assumption.

One evening, at the opera, in Madame de Fervaques's box, Julien was praising to the skies the ballet *Manon Lescaut*. His only reason for such praise was that he himself thought it trivial.

Madame de Fervaques observed that the ballet was much inferior to the novel of the same name, by Abbé Prévost, on which it was based.

"Ha!" thought Julien, surprised and amused. "A woman of such soaring virtue praising a novel!" Madame de Fervaques regularly testified, two or three times a week, to her utter contempt for writers who, by means of such low works, sought to corrupt young people—alas, only too inclined to sensual error.

"Among the books in this immoral and dangerous category," Madame de Fervaques continued, "it is said that *Manon Lescaut* occupies a very high place. The weaknesses and well-deserved anguish of an assuredly guilty heart, it is said, are there drawn with a truthfulness that attains to profundity—which did not keep your Bonaparte from proclaiming, at Saint-Helena, that it was a novel written for servants."

This observation restored full vigor to Julien's soul. "Someone has been trying to ruin me with Madame de Fervaques. She's been told of my enthusiasm for Napoleon. It annoys her enough so she's willing to give in and show me her annoyance." The realization amused him, all night long, and made him entertaining. As he was taking leave of her, in the opera lobby: "Remember, sir," she told him, "that people who love me cannot also love Bonaparte. The most I can allow is that they accept him as a necessity imposed by Providence. In any case, the man lacked a soul sufficiently flexible for appreciating artistic masterpieces."

"People who love me!" Julien was repeating. "Either that means nothing, or it means everything. Here are the secrets of language, unavailable to us poor provincials." And as he copied out an immense letter, meant for the marshall's widow, he spent much of the time thinking about Madame de Rênal.

"How does it happen," Madame de Fervaques asked him the next day, with an assumed indifference he thought unconvincing, "that you mention 'London' and 'Richmond' in a letter you wrote me, I suspect, after leaving the opera?"

Julien was deeply embarrassed. He had been copying line by line, without paying attention to what he was writing, and apparently had forgotten to substitute "Paris" and "Saint-Cloud" for the original's "London" and "Richmond." He began an explanation, and then another, but could not finish either; he felt like laughing wildly. At last, hunting for something to say, he arrived at this idea: "Exalted by so sublime a discussion, dealing with the greatest concerns of the human soul, my own soul, while I was writing to you, might have suffered some distraction."

"I'm making an impression," he told himself, "so for the rest of the night I can spare myself any more boredom." He hurriedly left the de Fervaques mansion. Later, looking at the letter he'd been copying, the night before, he quickly spotted the fatal place where the young Russian spoke of London and Richmond. Rereading the letter, Julien was astonished to find it almost tender.

It was the contrast between the surface frivolity of his conversation, and the letters' profound, almost apocalyptic sublimity, that made him stand out. The length of his sentences, above all, pleased the marshall's widow: this was not the hopping and jumping style made fashionable by Voltaire, that terribly immoral man! Although our hero did everything he could, striving to eliminate any good sense from his conversation, it still struck notes of antimonarchism and impiety, nor did that escape Madame de Fervaques's notice. Surrounded as she was by eminently moral people, who often passed an entire evening without having a single idea, the lady was deeply impressed by something that seemed novel, though at the same time she considered it her duty to herself to be offended. She termed these radical notions a lack of judgment, *bearing the stamp of the era's frivolity.*

But frequenting drawing rooms like hers is only useful when there's something you want to ask for. The boredom of that meaningless life, as Julien was living it, is surely shared by the reader. These are the barren moors and heaths of our journey.

During the time carved out of Julien's life by Madame de Fervaques, Mademoiselle de La Mole had to try not thinking of him. There was a violent struggle in her soul: sometimes she was proud of despising someone so woebegone, but in spite of herself she found his conversation captivating. What especially amazed her was its perfect falsity: every word he said to Madame de Fervaques was either a lie or, at least, a horrific camouflaging of his real thought, with which, on virtually every subject imaginable, Mathilde was completely familiar. She found this Machiavellianism striking. "What depth!" she told herself. "How different from the grandiloquent simpletons, or the vulgar rascals who, like Monsieur Tanbeau, use exactly the same language!"

Nevertheless, Julien experienced some frightful days. His daily appearances in Madame de Fervaques's drawing room were dedicated to duties of the most painful sort. His role-playing labors sucked all the strength from his soul. Often, at night, walking across her huge courtyard, only the force of willpower and rationality held him, but just barely, above the pit of despair.

"I conquered despair at the seminary," he told himself. "And yet what ghastly things lay in front of me, back then! I'd either make my fortune, or I wouldn't, and in either case I expected to spend the rest of my life, most intimately, in company with those who seemed to me the most untrustworthy and disgusting in the world. The next spring, only eleven brief months later, I may have been the happiest young person of this entire era."

But all too often, these fine arguments were useless, in the face of horrid realities. Every day, at lunch and at dinner, he saw Mathilde. After he'd composed uncountable numbers of letters for Monsieur de La Mole, he thought how she was soon to marry Monsieur de Croisenois. That pleasant young man was already appearing, twice a day, at the de La Mole residence: the jealous eye of a rejected lover did not overlook a single one of his visits.

When he'd seen Mademoiselle de La Mole treating her future husband particularly well, Julien would return to his room, unable to keep from loving glances at his pistols.

"Ah! How much smarter it would be," he said to himself, "to cut the identifying marks from my clothes and go to some lonely forest, thirty miles from Paris, and end this wretched life! No one would know me, there; my death would be a secret for two weeks—and who would ever think of me, after two weeks!"

This was eminently good thinking. Yet the next day, a glimpse of Mathilde's arm, displayed between the sleeve of her dress and her glove, was all it took to plunge our young philosopher into cruel recollection, which all the same linked him, once again, to life. "All right!" he then said to himself. "I'll pursue this Russian diplomacy till it finishes. How will it end?

"As far as Madame de Fervaques is concerned, once I've copied out the fifty-third letter, I certainly won't be writing any more.

"As for Mathilde, these six weeks of exceedingly painful comedy will produce no change in her anger, or else they'll bring me a moment of reconciliation. Good Lord! I'd die of happiness!" And then he had to stop thinking.

After a long reverie, once more he was able to pick up the thread of his thought: "So," he told himself, "I'll win one day of happiness, after which her harshness will start all over, founded as it is, alas! in how little ability I have to please her, and then I'll have nothing to turn to, I'll be destroyed, perhaps forever. . . .

"With a character like hers, how could she give me guarantees? Alas, the only answer is that I wouldn't be worth it. My manners will still lack proper elegance, my speech will still be heavy and monotonous. My God! Why am I *me*?"

CHAPTER TWENTY-NINE

BOREDOM

Sacrificing yourself to your passions, fine. But to nonexistent passions?
O sad nineteenth century!

—GIRODET

Having read the first of Julien's long letters without pleasure, Madame de Fervaques now began to find them interesting. But there was something making her unhappy: "What a shame that Monsieur Sorel is not determined to be a priest! He could then be admitted to a certain intimacy. But wearing that medal, and with his virtually bourgeois clothing, cruel questions might be asked—and how could they be answered?" Her mind did not carry that question any further. "Some wicked friend might imagine things, and even spread a rumor that he was a minor relation, from my father's family, a businessman who got the medal for service in the National Guard."

Until she'd met Julien, Madame de Fervaques's greatest pleasure had been to write *Marshall Fervaques's widow* next to her name. But after Julien's appearance, a social climber's vanity, morbid and quick to take offense, struggled with growing interest.

"It would be easy enough," she told herself, "to have him made vicar-general of some diocese near Paris! But plain Monsieur Sorel, still employed as Monsieur de La Mole's little secretary! That is distressing."

Her soul, *afraid of everything,* was for the first time stirred by something foreign to her social ambitions and social superiority. The old porter noticed that, when he brought her a letter from this handsome young man, whose demeanor was so sorrowful, he was sure to see the disappearance of that distracted, discontented air with which his mistress always, and most carefully, greeted her servants.

The weariness of living a life completely dependent on public performance, without, at bottom, taking any real joy in such success, had become so intolerable, since she'd begun thinking about Julien, that it was enough to keep her chambermaids from being mistreated, the entire day, if she'd spent a single hour, the night before, with this odd young man. His standing, constantly increasing, withstood some extremely well-written anonymous letters. Little Monsieur Tanbeau worked hard, and in vain, supplying Messieurs de Luz, de Croisenois, and de Caylus with two or three very clever slanders, which these gentlemen took pleasure in amplifying, though not so wildly as to cast doubt on the reliability of their accusations. The marshall's widow, whose mind was not capable of withstanding such vulgar onslaughts, would tell Mathilde her doubts, and was always reassured.

One day, after having three times asked whether any letters had come, Madame de Fervaques suddenly decided to reply to Julien. This victory was attributable to boredom. By the second word, the marshall's widow was almost brought to a halt by the indelicacy of having to write, in her own hand, an address so vulgar as *To Monsieur Sorel, in care of the Marquis de La Mole.*

"It will be necessary," she said to Julien that evening, very wryly, "for you to bring me some envelopes bearing your address."

"And thus," thought Julien, "I've been made a footman-lover," and he bowed, taking a certain pleasure in making himself look like old Arsène, the marquis's manservant.

He brought the envelopes that same evening, and the next day, very early indeed, he had a third letter from her. He read five or six lines at the beginning, and two or three toward the end. She'd written four pages, in an extremely small hand, squeezed very tight.

Gradually, they got into the sweet habit of writing almost every day. Julien replied with exact copies of the Russian letters and, this being an advantage of grandiloquence, Madame de Fervaques was not at all surprised that his responses did not in any way match her letters.

How tiny Tanbeau's pride would have suffered, having constituted himself an unpaid spy on Julien's proceedings, had he learned that all her unopened letters were tossed, at random, into the drawer of Julien's desk.

One morning, her porter came to him, in the library, bringing a letter from Madame de Fervaques. Mathilde recognized the man, saw the letter, and noted the address, as written in Julien's hand. She came into the library just as the porter left; the letter was still on the edge of the table; Julien, busily writing, had not yet put it in his desk drawer.

"Now this I cannot endure," cried Mathilde, seizing the letter. "You're completely forgetting me—I, who am your wife. Your behavior is frightful, monsieur."

At these words, her pride, stunned by the dreadful indelicacy of her behavior, choked her. She dissolved in tears, and soon it seemed to Julien as if she had ceased to breathe.

Astonished, confused, Julien had very little notion just how excellent, how fortunate, this scene was for him. He helped Mathilde to a chair; she virtually surrendered herself to his arms.

His first reaction to this was extraordinary joy. His second was a thought derived from Korasoff: "Just one word, and I may be utterly ruined."

His arms grew rigid, so painfully difficult was the effort imposed by diplomacy. "I must not even let myself press this soft, lovely body to my heart, or she will scorn me, she will mistreat me. What a horrible person!"

And as he cursed Mathilde's character, he loved her a hundred times more. It seemed to him he had a queen in his arms.

Julien's impassive coldness redoubled the prideful sickness tearing at Mademoiselle de La Mole's heart. She did not possess the calm to try to see from his eyes how, at that moment, he actually felt about her. She could not bring herself to look at him, so afraid was she of seeing him scornful.

Seated on the library couch, unmoving, her head turned away from Julien, she was gripped by the sharpest sorrow pride and love can make a human heart feel. What horrible behavior she had fallen into!

"He's aloof, unfortunate creature that I am! To see the most indecent advances repulsed! And repulsed by one of my father's servants."

"This is what I will not endure," she said loudly.

And, furious, she pulled open the drawer of Julien's writing desk, only two feet away. She stood as if frozen in horror, seeing eight or ten unopened letters, exactly like the one the porter had just delivered. She recognized Julien's handwriting, more or less disguised, on all of them.

"So," she cried, absolutely beside herself, "not only are you in her good graces, but you despise her just the same. You, a man who has nothing, you're contemptuous of Marshall de Fervaques's widow!

"Ah, forgive me, my dear," she continued, throwing herself to her knees, "despise me if you wish, but love me. I cannot live any longer, deprived of your love." And she fell at his feet, in a faint.

"And there's the proud creature, at my feet!" Julien told himself.

CHAPTER THIRTY

A BOX AT THE OPERA

As the blackest sky
Foretells the heaviest tempest.
—BYRON, *DON JUAN*

In the middle of these immense fluctuations, Julien was more astonished than overjoyed. Mathilde's insults had shown him just how wise Russian diplomacy was. "*Say little, do little:* this is, for me, the only road to salvation."

He lifted Mathilde and, not saying a word, set her back on the couch. Slowly, gradually, she fell into weeping.

To help restore herself, she picked up Madame de Fervaques's letters; she slowly opened them. She started, nervously and markedly, as she recognized the handwriting. She turned over all the pages, without reading them; most were six pages long.

"At least answer me," Mathilde said at last, in the most suppliant of voices, not yet daring to look at Julien. "You know very well how proud I am: it's the sickness of my position, and even of my character. I admit it. So Madame de Fervaques has stolen your heart from me. . . . Has she made the same sacrifices for you, as this fatal love swept me into doing?"

A mournful silence was Julien's only reply. "By what right," he thought, "does she ask of me such a dishonorable indiscretion, unworthy of any honest man?"

Mathilde tried to read the letters; her tear-filled eyes made that impossible.

She had been miserable for a month, but her haughty heart was far from ready to admit it. Chance alone had led to this explosion. In an instant, jealousy and love had swept away pride. She was seated on the couch, very near him. He saw her hair and her alabaster neck. In that moment he forgot everything he was supposed to do: he put his arms around her waist and pressed her against his chest.

Slowly, she turned her head toward him. He was surprised by the extraordinary sorrow in her eyes; he could scarcely recognize her.

Julien felt his strength leaving him, so mortally painful was the courageous act he imposed on himself.

"Soon," he said to himself, "these eyes will express nothing but cold disdain, if I let the happiness of loving her carry me away." Meanwhile, her voice weak, and in words she was barely able to articulate, in this moment of reassurance she repeated her regret for everything her excessive pride had led her to do.

"I, too, am proud," Julien told her, his voice muffled, his face exhibiting the signs of utter prostration.

Mathilde turned quickly toward him. Hearing his voice was a joy for which she had almost given up hope. At that moment, all she could remember of her arrogance were curses directed at it. She wished she could think of some extraordinary behavior, something truly incredible, to show him how much she adored him and, simultaneously, how much she detested herself.

"It is probably because of your pride," Julien went on, "that you briefly honored me. It is surely because of that courageous resolve, worthy of a man, that right now you respect me. Perhaps I am in love with Madame de Fervaques...."

Mathilde shook; her eyes suddenly looked very strange. She had heard her sentence pronounced. None of this escaped Julien; he felt his courage ebbing.

"Ah," he said to himself, hearing the empty words his mouth had pronounced, as if he had been emitting strange noises, "if I could cover those pale cheeks with kisses, and you never felt them!"

"I may be in love with Madame de Fervaques," he continued ... and his voice grew steadily weaker, "but then, I have as yet no decisive proof of her interest in me."

Mathilde looked at him. He did not waver—at least, he hoped his face had not betrayed him. He felt love penetrating to the most intimate depths of his heart. He had never so adored her; he was almost as crazed as Mathilde. Had she found the calm, and the courage, to maneuver her way through the situation, he would have fallen at her feet, disavowing all this empty comedy. He had just enough strength to go on talking. "Ah, Korasoff!" he exclaimed inwardly, "why aren't you here! How desperately I need a word to guide me!" As he was thinking this, his voice was saying:

"Lacking any other sentiment, gratitude would be sufficient to tie me to Madame de Fervaques. She has been indulgent; she has comforted me when people have been scornful. I cannot put unlimited faith in certain appearances, doubtless extremely flattering, but perhaps, just as likely, of no great durability."

"Oh, Good Lord!" cried Mathilde.

"So! What guarantee can I expect from you?" Julien resumed, his voice now firm and lively, apparently abandoning, for a moment, the cautious forms of diplomacy. "What guarantee? What God will tell me that the stance you appear to be taking toward me, right now, will last more than two days?"

"The intensity of my love and of my misery, if you no longer love me," she said, taking his hands and turning toward him.

The sudden movement had slightly displaced her neck scarf: Julien could see her lovely shoulders. Her faintly disordered hair brought back delicious memories.

He was going to yield. "One careless word," he told himself, "and I go back to that long sequence of days spent in despair." Madame de Rênal found reasons to do what her heart dictated. This young girl of the highest society let her heart be moved only when, for good reasons, she felt she ought to be moved.

He glimpsed this truth, in the twinkling of an eye, and in another instant rediscovered his courage.

He withdrew the hands Mathilde had been pressing in hers, and with marked respect moved a bit away from her. A man's courage can go no further. Then he busied himself, gathering up all of Madame de Fervaques's letters, which had been scattered on the couch, doing all this with a politeness quite extraordinary—and, as he then added, a politeness savagely cruel:

"If Mademoiselle de La Mole will be so good as to permit me to reflect on these matters." He moved quickly away and left the library. She heard him closing all the doors, one after the other.

"The monster isn't a bit disturbed," she said to herself. . . .

"But what am I saying: monster! He's wise, cautious, good. It's I who am wrong, wronger than anyone could possibly imagine."

This view of things lasted. That day, Mathilde was almost happy, because she was completely in love. You might have said this was a heart that had never been moved by pride—and by what pride!

She shivered with horror when, in the dining room that night, a servant announced Madame de Fervaques: the very sound of the man's voice seemed to her sinister. She could not endure seeing the marshall's widow, and hurriedly left. Julien, not particularly proud of his painful victory, had been afraid his own appearance might betray him, and had not dined with the family.

His love and his happiness grew rapidly, the more distant became the time of the battle; he had already begun to criticize himself. "How could I have resisted her?" he asked himself. "What if she won't ever love me anymore? One instant can change that haughty heart, and it must be plain that I treated her abominably."

That evening, he felt he absolutely had to appear in Madame de Fervaques's box at the opera. She had expressly invited him, and Mathilde would certainly learn if he'd been there or if, impolitely, he had stayed away. It was persuasive reasoning, but he did not have the strength, when the hour came and the drawing rooms were opening their doors, to plunge into society. Just by talking, he'd lose half his happiness.

Ten o'clock sounded: he absolutely had to be there.

Luckily, he found Madame de Fervaques's box full of women, and was relegated to a place near the door, completely obscured by the ladies' hats. This position saved him from embarrassment: the divine sounds of Caroline's despair, in *Il Matrimonio segreto*, made him dissolve in tears. Madame de Fervaques saw the tears; they were in such sharp contrast to his usual masculine steadiness that the heart of this great lady, so long steeped in all the most corroding effects of social-climber pride, was moved. What little remained in her of a woman's heart led her to speak to him. At that moment, she wanted the pleasure of hearing his voice.

"Have you seen the de La Mole ladies?" she asked him. "They're on the third level, tonight." Julien immediately bent forward, leaning rather impolitely on the front of the box. He saw Mathilde; her eyes were shining with tears.

"But it isn't their night for the opera," Julien thought. "What eagerness!"

Mathilde had talked her mother into coming, in spite of the unsuitability of the box that an amiable patron had been urged to offer them. She wanted to see if Julien would indeed spend the evening with Madame de Fervaques.

CHAPTER THIRTY-ONE

MAKE HER AFRAID

So there's your civilization's fine miracle! You've turned love into
something ordinary.

—BARNAVE

Julien hurried off to Madame de La Mole's box. The first thing he saw was Mathilde's tear-filled eyes. She wept without restraint: the other people in the box were of no consequence, being only the woman who had lent them the box and some others the woman knew. Mathilde set her hand on Julien's; she had apparently lost all fear of her mother. Nearly suffocated by her tears, she said only one word to him: "Guarantees!"

"At least, let me say nothing to her," Julien told himself, deeply moved, and hiding his eyes, as well as he could, behind his hand, as if to shield them from the glare of the chandelier, which, on the third level, shone directly into the box. "If I speak, she can't help but know how strongly I feel. The sound of my voice would betray me. And, once again, everything would be ruined."

His struggles were more painful than they had been that morning; his heart had had time to be roused. He was afraid of seeing Mathilde's vanity awakened. Drunk with love and sensual ecstasy, he forced himself to say nothing.

As far as I'm concerned, reader, this is one of the finest traits of his character. Anyone capable of compelling himself to make such an effort can go far—*si fata sinat,* if the fates grant it.

Mademoiselle de La Mole insisted on taking Julien back with them. Luckily, it was raining hard. But the marquise put him across from her, spoke to him without stopping, and made sure he could not say a word to her daughter. It might have seemed she was showing concern for Julien's happiness, but no longer fearful he would ruin everything by showing how deeply he'd been moved, he readily surrendered himself.

Do I dare say that, returning to his room, Julien threw himself on his knees and covered Prince Korasoff's gift of love letters with kisses?

"Oh, great man! How could I have doubted you?" he silently exclaimed, in his madness.

Gradually, his calm came back. He compared himself to a general who had just half won a great battle. "My advantage is clear, it's immense," he said to himself. "But what will happen tomorrow? One moment can destroy everything."

With a passionate gesture, he opened Montholon's *Memories of Napoleon on Saint-Helena,* and for two long hours forced himself to read: only his eyes were really reading, but that made no difference, he kept them at it. All during this strange sort of reading, both his head and his heart, climbing as high as they could go, worked without his being at all aware. "This woman's heart is certainly different from Madame de Rênal's," he said to himself, but he let his mind go no further.

"Make her afraid!" he suddenly cried, tossing his book away. "The enemy will obey me only if I make him afraid. And then there'll be no more contempt shown me."

He paced up and down his little room, drunk with joy. Truthfully, there was more pride in this happiness than there was love.

"Make her afraid!" he kept repeating proudly, and he had reason to be proud. Even in their happiest moments, Madame de Rênal had always doubted that his love equaled hers. "I'm subduing a demon, here, which must be *subdued*."

He knew very well that, at eight the next morning, Mathilde would be at the library; he did not come until nine, burning with love, but his head in charge of his heart. Virtually every single minute he repeated to himself: "Always compel her to deal with this immense uncertainty: 'Does he love me?' Her brilliant social position, the perpetual flattery from everyone she talks to, make her *a bit over confident*."

She was pale, calm; she was sitting on the couch, but seemed unable to move from that position. She held out her hand:

"My love, I've offended you, I know I have. Might you be angry at me? . . ."

Julien was not prepared for this plain, direct approach. He was about to betray himself.

"You want guarantees, my dear," she added, after a silence she had hoped would be broken. "That's fair. Carry me off; let's go to London. . . . I'll be ruined forever, dishonored. . . ." She managed to take her hand from Julien's and set it over her eyes. All her modesty, her sense of feminine virtue, flooded back into her heart. . . . "All right, dishonor me," she said at last, sighing. "That's a *guarantee*."

"I was happy, yesterday," Julien thought, "because I had the courage to be hard on myself." After a short interval of silence, he took enough control of his heart to say, his voice exceedingly cold:

"Once we're en route to London, once you've been dishonored—as you phrase it—who's to say you'll still love me? Will my presence in the mail coach still seem important to you? I'm not a monster: having your reputation destroyed would be nothing more than another wretchedness. Neither your rank, nor your position in society, creates the obstacle, but—unfortunately—your own character. Can you tell yourself: in a week, you'll still love me?"

("Ah, if she loves me for a week, just a week," Julien murmured to himself, "I'll die of happiness. Who cares about the future? Who cares about life or death? And that divine happiness could begin right at this moment, if I want it to. It all depends on me!")

Mathilde looked at him, thoughtfully.

"So I'm completely unworthy of you," she said, taking his hand once more.

Julien embraced her, but duty's iron hand immediately seized his heart. "If she sees how I adore her, I lose her." Even before stepping away from her arms, he had resumed a man's full and fitting dignity.

That day, and those which followed it, he managed to conceal his immense happiness. There were moments when he refused even the pleasure of holding her in his arms.

At other moments, the delirium of happiness swept away all of caution's counsels.

There was an arbor of climbing honeysuckle, meant to hide the gardener's ladder, near which he had taken to placing himself so he could stare from afar at the blinds in Mathilde's window, and weep at her inconstancy. Close by, there was a huge oak, and its trunk had kept him from being seen by curious eyes.

Walking by this spot with Mathilde, and remembering so vividly the enormity of his miseries, the contrast of past despair and present felicity was too strong for him. Tears flooded into his eyes and, pressing his lips to his beloved's hand: "Here is where I lived, thinking of you. Here I stood, looking at those blinds, waiting for hours at a time for the blessed moment when I could see your hand opening them. . . ."

His weakness was total. He drew his portrait in true colors, none of them merely imagined, depicting the state of despair he had endured. A few quick interjections bore witness to his current happiness, which had brought an end to that horrible suffering. . . .

"Good Lord, what am I doing!" Julien said to himself, suddenly recovering his senses. "I'm lost."

His alarm was so intense that he imagined Mademoiselle de La Mole's eyes showing, even now, less love for him. This was illusory, but Julien's face rapidly turned color, and he became mortally pale. His eyes lost their brilliance, for an instant, and a haughty expression, with a trace of nastiness, immediately took the place of the truest, most abandoned look of love.

"What's wrong, my dear?" asked Mathilde, tenderly concerned.

"I'm a liar," Julien said irritably, "and I was lying to you. I reproach myself, and God knows I sufficiently respect you not to tell you lies. You love me, you're devoted to me, and there's no point to making up fine phrases just to please you."

"Good God! Are all those ravishing things you've been telling me, the last ten minutes, just fine phrases?"

"And I most sternly reproached myself, my dear. I composed them, once, for a woman who loved me, who also bored me. . . . It's a defect in my character: I openly accuse myself. Forgive me."

Tears were running down Mathilde's cheeks.

"Every time something startles me, I'm inevitably thrown into a fantasy," Julien continued, "and my ghastly memory—which at the moment I execrate—offers me something from its stockpiles, and I take advantage of it."

"Have I just stumbled into doing something, all unawares, that displeases you?" Mathilde asked, with charming naïveté.

"I remember, one day, walking by this honeysuckle, you picked a flower and Monsieur de Luz took it, and you let him have it. I was two steps away."

"Monsieur de Luz? That can't be," said Mathilde, with the haughtiness so natural to her. "I don't do such things."

"I'm sure you did," Julien replied, forcefully.

"Well, then it's true, my dear," said Mathilde, sadly lowering her eyes. She'd been positive that, for many months, she'd not permitted Monsieur de Luz to do anything of the kind.

Julien looked at her with inexpressible tenderness: "No," he told himself. "She does not love me *less*."

She laughingly teased him, that night, for his interest in Madame de Fervaques: "A bourgeois in love with a social climber! Those kinds of hearts may be the only ones my Julien can't drive wild. She's turned you into a real dandy," she said, playing with his hair.

While Mathilde had so totally scorned him, Julien had become one of the best-dressed men in Paris. But he still had an advantage over men of that sort: once he was dressed, he thought no more about it.

One thing irritated Mathilde. Julien continued to copy out the Russian letters and send them to the marshall's widow.

CHAPTER THIRTY-TWO

THE TIGER

Alas! Why these things, and not others?
—BEAUMARCHAIS

An English traveler tells how he lived on familiar terms with a tiger: he had raised it, and he stroked it, but on his table he always kept a fully loaded pistol.

Julien surrendered himself to the heights of happiness only when Mathilde could not see the expression in his eyes. He did his duty with dedication, from time to time saying harsh things to her.

Any time Mathilde's gentle sweetness, which he watched, astonished, and his suddenly swelling devotion came close to making him lose control, he had the courage to brusquely turn away and leave her.

It was the first time Mathilde had ever been in love.

Life had always dragged along, for her, at a tortoiselike pace; now, it flew.

But since her pride had to somehow manifest itself, she tried to fearlessly expose herself to all the risks her love could create. Julien was the cautious one, and only when risks were involved would she refuse to let him make the decisions. Submissive and even humble as she was with him, she was even haughtier with everyone who came near her, whether family or servants.

In the evening, in the drawing room, surrounded by sixty people, she would call Julien over to talk to him alone, and for extended periods.

Little Tanbeau having come and seated himself beside her, one day, she asked him to go hunt for her, in the library, the book by Smollett in which he discusses the British Revolution of 1688. When he hesitated: "Don't rush yourself," she added, with an arrogantly insulting look that was balm to Julien's soul.

"Did you notice the little monster's face?" he told her.

"His uncle had ten or twelve years of service, in this drawing room; otherwise I'd get rid of him on the spot."

Her conduct toward Messieurs de Croisenois, de Lutz, etc., though in form perfectly polite, was at bottom scarcely less provoking. Mathilde seriously reproached herself, on account of the amatory confidences she had once made to Julien—even more so because, though she did not dare tell him this, she had exaggerated the almost entirely innocent signs of interest of which these gentlemen had been the object.

For all her good resolutions, her womanly pride kept her from ever saying to Julien: "It was talking to you: that's why I took such pleasure, describing my weakness in not withdrawing, that once, when Monsieur de Croisenois put his hand on a marble table and it just barely brushed against mine."

Now these gentlemen could barely speak to her for a few moments when, suddenly, she simply had to ask Julien a question, and made that an excuse to keep him near her.

She realized she was pregnant, and joyfully told this to Julien.

"Can you doubt me, now? Isn't this a guarantee? I am your wife forever."

This news profoundly astonished Julien. He was at the point of forgetting the principles of his behavior toward her. "How can I be willingly cold and rude to this poor young girl, who is ruining herself for me?" When she seemed the least bit indisposed, even on days when wisdom's awful voice made itself heard, he no longer had the courage to address those cruel remarks to her—words so indispensable, as he had learned, for the preservation of their love.

"I plan to write to my father," Mathilde told him one day. "He's been more than merely a father to me; he's been a friend. How unworthy I would feel, both of you and of myself, if I tried to deceive him even for an instant."

"My God!" said Julien, terrified. "What are you doing?"

"My duty," she replied, her eyes shining with joy.

She felt she was being nobler than her lover.

"But he'll dismiss me, most disgracefully!"

"That's his right: we need to respect it. I'll give you my arm and we'll leave by the front door, in full daylight."

Stunned, Julien begged her to wait a week.

"I can't," she answered. "Honor calls. I have seen my duty and I must observe it—and immediately."

"Very well! I order you to wait," Julien finally said. "Your honor is protected: I'm your husband. This truly major step will change everything, for both of us. I too am within my rights. Today is Tuesday; next Tuesday will be the Duke de Retz's day to receive visitors. That evening, when Monsieur de La Mole returns, the porter will hand him the fatal letter. . . . All he thinks about is making you a duchess: I know it. Think how miserable he'll be!"

"Do you mean: think what vengeance he'll take?"

"I am capable of commiserating with my benefactor, and being deeply sorrowful at hurting him. But I neither am, nor will I ever be, afraid of anyone."

Mathilde yielded. This was the first time, since she had told him of her new state, that he had spoken to her authoritatively. He had never loved her so deeply. The tender part of his heart accepted her present condition, most happily, as good reason not to speak to her harshly. But her confession to Monsieur de La Mole made him exceedingly nervous. Would he be separated from Mathilde? And no matter what sadness his departure might cause her, would she still think of him, a month afterward?

His dread was almost as severe as the thoroughly justified reproaches the marquis might direct at him.

That evening, he confessed to Mathilde how concerned he was, on this second score—and then, swept on by love, he also admitted the first.

She changed color.

"Really?" she asked. "Six months away from me would be misery?"

"Immensely—the only sorrow I can imagine that absolutely terrorizes me."

Mathilde was happy. Julien had played his role so studiously that, by now, she'd come to believe her love greater than his.

The fatal Tuesday came. At midnight, on his return, the marquis was given a letter that had been marked for him alone to open, and for him to read only when alone:

MY FATHER,

All merely social connections have been broken, as between us: all that remain are those created by Nature. After my husband, you are and always will be most dearest to me. My eyes fill with tears, I imagine the pain I cause you, but to keep my shame from becoming public I could no longer withhold the confession I owe you, so you will have the opportunity to think, and to act. If your affection for me, which I know is strong, leads you to grant me some small allowance, I will go and live wherever you like, perhaps in Switzerland, with my husband. His name is so little known that no one will recognize your daughter as Madame Sorel, daughter-in-law of a carpenter from Verrières. There is the name it so hurts me to write. I dread, on Julien's behalf, the anger which will seem to you so just. I will not be a duchess, my father, but I knew that from the moment I loved him—and it was I who first fell in love, it was I who seduced him. It is from you that I come by a soul too lofty to linger over matters that are, or which seem to me to be, coarse. I tried unsuccessfully, as you wished, to please you and contemplate Monsieur de Croisenois. Why did you set true merit right under my eyes? You yourself said to me, when I returned from Hyères: "This young Sorel is the only person I find entertaining." The poor fellow is every bit as distressed as I am, if that is possible, at the pain this letter will cause you. I cannot keep you from being angry, as a father, but love me, always love me, as a dear friend.

Julien always respected me. If he sometimes spoke to me, that was only due to his profound gratitude toward you, because natural pride allowed him only to respond in formal terms to everything he knew was beyond him. He is keenly, inherently aware of the difference in our social positions. It was I—I confess this to my best friend, blushing, nor is this a confession I will ever make to anyone else—it was I who, in the garden one day, took his arm.

Twenty-four hours from now, why should you be angry with him? My offense is irreparable. If you so require, I will be the one to transmit to you his assurances of the most profound respect, and his despair at having displeased you. You need not see him, but I will join him, once again, wherever he may go. That is his right, and it is my duty: he is my child's father. If in your kindness you wish to give us six thousand francs to live on, I would be grateful. Otherwise, Julien plans to reside in Besançon, where he will become a teacher of Latin and of literature. No matter how low his beginning may be, I am positive he will rise. I am not worried about obscurity, living with him. If there is a revolution, I am confident he will play a leading role. Could you possibly say such a thing of any of the others who have sought my hand? They possess fine lands and estates! That alone does not seem to me reason to admire them. Even under the regime now in power, my Julien will rise to high position, if he had a million and my father's support. . . .

Knowing her father to be a man who regularly acted, and at once, on the first thought that came to him, Mathilde had written him a full eight pages.

"What can I do?" Julien was asking himself, while Monsieur de La Mole read this letter. "What, first of all, is my duty? And second, what would be best for me? My debt to him is immense. Without him, I might have been a worthless rogue, and not enough of a rogue to prevent my being hated and persecuted. He made me a man of the world, on which account my *necessary* rascalities will be, first, less frequent, and second, less unworthy. That's a good deal more than if he'd given me a million. I owe him this medal, and some show of diplomatic activity, which set me on equal terms with the world.

"If he were, right now, to write out rules for my behavior, what would he write. . . ?"

Julien was cut short by Monsieur de La Mole's old manservant.

"The marquis wants you, right now, dressed or not."

As he walked at Julien's side, the valet added, his voice low: "He's beside himself. Watch out."

CHAPTER THIRTY-THREE

THE HELL OF WEAKNESS

Cutting this diamond, a clumsy jeweler took away some of its greatest
brilliance. In the Middle Ages—no, even under Richelieu—a Frenchman had *willpower.*

—MIRABEAU

The marquis was furious. For the first time in his life, perhaps, this
noble lord acted unacceptably: he showered Julien with every insult
he could think of. Our hero was astonished, irritated, but his gratitude
was in no way shaken. What wonderful plans, long cherished deep in
the poor man's heart, came crashing down in a tumbled heap! "But I
ought to answer him: my silence will make him angrier." His response
was provided by Molière's Tartuffe.

"I'm not an angel.... I've served you well, and you've paid me generously. . . . I was grateful, but I'm twenty-two years old. . . . In this
house, you were the only one who understood my thoughts, and that
lovable lady—"

"Monster!" cried the marquis. "Lovable! Lovable! The day you
found her lovable, you should have fled."

"And I tried to. I asked you, at the time, to let me go to Languedoc."

Weary of pacing angrily up and down, subdued by sorrow, the marquis threw himself into an armchair. Julien heard him mutter: "That
does show he's not malicious."

"No, that's not what I've been to you," exclaimed Julien, falling to
his knees. But that made him feel deeply shamed, and he rose at once.

The marquis was truly unhinged. Seeing Julien on his knees, he
began to heap insults on him, horrible and quite worthy of a taxi
driver. Hearing such unheard-of things from his own lips may have offered a degree of distraction.

"What! My daughter to be known as Madame Sorel! What! My
daughter is not to be a duchess!" Every time these two ideas plainly
presented themselves, Monsieur de La Mole's soul was racked; his

mind was no longer under control. Julien feared the marquis might beat him.

In lucid intervals, and when he began to grow more habituated to his misery, the marquis spoke quite reasonably of Julien's behavior:

"You had to flee, sir," he said. . . . "Your duty was to flee. . . . You're the lowest of men. . . ."

Julien went to a desk and wrote:

"My life has long been unbearable: I here end it. I beg Marquis de La Mole to accept, along with an expression of boundless gratitude, my regret for the embarrassment which my death, under his roof, may cause him."

"If monsieur will trouble himself to read this. . . . Kill me," said Julien, "or have your valet kill me. It's now one in the morning. I'm going to walk in the garden, near the far wall."

"Go to the devil," cried the marquis as he left.

"I quite understand," Julien thought. "He wouldn't regret it, if I spared his valet the trouble of killing me. . . . All right, let him kill me himself: I offer him that reparation. . . . But, damn it, I love life. . . . I owe myself to my son."

This idea, for the first time clearly presenting itself to his mind, took over his thoughts, after the first few minutes of his walk, which had been filled with the sense of danger.

This brand-new concern made him a prudent man. "I need to get advice, to deal with this wildly insane man. . . . He's lost his mind; he's capable of anything. Fouqué is too far off. Besides, he has no sense for what the heart of someone like the marquis would be feeling.

"Count Altamira . . . Can I be sure of eternal silence? The advice I seek must not involve performance of an action: that would complicate my position. Alas: the only one I can turn to is somber Father Pirard. . . . His spirit has been shrunken by Jansenism. . . . Some rascally Jesuit would understand the world, and would suit me better. . . . Father Pirard is capable of beating me, the instant he hears what I've done."

Tartuffe's genius came to Julien's aid: "Yes, I'll go and make my confession to him." After walking in the garden for two whole hours, that was the last decision he came to. He no longer expected to be surprised by a gunshot. Sleep prevailed.

The next day, very early in the morning, Julien was miles from Paris, knocking at the harsh Jansenist's door. He discovered, to his immense astonishment, that Father Pirard was not particularly surprised by what he heard.

"I ought perhaps to reproach myself," he said, more worried than annoyed. "I should have been able to predict this love affair. My affection for you, my miserable little one, kept me from warning the father. . . ."

"What's he going to do?" Julien asked anxiously.

(At this moment, he loved the priest, and any kind of quarrel would have been, for him, extremely painful.)

"I myself envisage three choices," Julien went on. "First, Monsieur de La Mole can sentence me to death." He described the suicide letter he had left with the marquis. "Second, he can have me shot at point-blank range by Count Norbert, who would challenge me to a duel."

"You'd accept?" said the priest, furious, and he rose from his chair.

"You're not letting me finish. Most assuredly, I could never fire at my benefactor's son.

"Third, he might send me away. If he says: 'Go to Edinburgh, to New York,' I'd obey him. Then they might be able to hide Mademoiselle de La Mole's condition. But I would not permit them to do away with my son."

"And that will be—have no doubt—," said Father Pirard, "—this corrupt man's first idea. . . ."

At Paris, Mathilde was in despair. At seven o'clock, she had seen her father. He had shown her Julien's letter: she shivered, thinking he might have considered that putting an end to his life would be a noble deed. "And without my permission," she said to herself, with a sadness that was also anger.

"If he is dead," she told her father. "I will die. And you'll be the cause of his death. . . . It might make you happy. . . . But I swear by his departed ghost, I'd first put on mourning, and in every public place I will be known as *the widowed Madame Sorel,* and I'll send out death notices: you can count on it. You'll find me neither timid nor cowardly."

Love drove her almost mad. For his part, Monsieur de La Mole was stunned.

He began to see what had happened with some degree of rationality. Mathilde did not come to lunch. The marquis felt himself freed of an enormous weight, and above all flattered, when he realized she'd said nothing to her mother.

Julien dismounted. Mathilde had him called, and threw herself into his arms, almost in sight of her chambermaid. Julien was not terribly gratified by this demonstration, having left his long conference with Father Pirard in an intensely diplomatic and calculating state of mind. Turning all the possibilities over and over in his mind, his imagination had worn itself down. Mathilde, tears in her eyes, told him she'd seen his suicide letter.

"My father might change his mind. Please, for my sake, leave this very instant for Villequier. Get back on your horse and leave, before they rise from the table."

Julien still seemed amazed, and cold; she shed enormous quantities of tears.

"Let me manage our business," she exclaimed ecstatically, holding him tightly in her arms. "You know very well I'm not separating us of my own choice. Write to me, using my chambermaid's name, and have the address written by someone else. Me, I'll write you volumes. Farewell! Flee!"

This last word offended Julien, but he obeyed. "It's nothing less than fated," he thought, "that, even in their best moments, these people know how to hurt me."

Mathilde was completely firm, resisting every one of her father's *prudent* plans. She refused to negotiate on any other bases than these: she would be Madame Sorel and live in poverty, with her husband, in Switzerland, or else at her father's great house in Paris. The proposal that her delivery be a clandestine one was totally out of the question: "That would open the door for possible slander and dishonor. Two months after my marriage, I'll go traveling with my husband, and then, to suggest that my son was born at the proper time will be extremely simple."

Greeted, at first, by fits of anger, her steadiness ended by shaking the marquis.

Once, in a tender moment:

"Look here," he told his daughter. "This is a registered certificate, good for a yearly income of ten thousand francs. Send it to your Julien, and let him hide it somewhere so I can't take it back."

In order to *obey* Mathilde, whose passion for giving orders he knew only too well, Julien had made a useless hundred-and-twenty-mile journey. He had been staying in Villequier, putting the farmers' accounts in order; the marquis's gift brought him back. He went to seek asylum with Father Pirard, who in his absence had become Mathilde's most useful ally. Every time the marquis sought his advice, Father Pirard demonstrated that any choice, other than a public marriage, would be a sin in the eyes of God.

"And luckily," the priest would continue, "the world's wisdom is, in this matter, completely in accord with that of the Church. Could one rely for a single moment, given Mademoiselle de La Mole's fiery character, on the sanctity of a secret she would not impose on herself? If you do not take the frank step of a public marriage, society will be busy, for a long time to come, with this strange mismatch. Everything must be said and done at the same time, without any display, or any reality, of the mysterious and unknown."

"That's true," the marquis acknowledged somberly. "That way, talk about the marriage, after three days, would become the boring gossip of empty-headed people. We will have to take advantage of some great anti-Jacobin proposals from the government, and slide along, unseen, right behind that."

Two or three of Monsieur de La Mole's friends agreed with Father Pirard. To their minds, the great obstacle was Mathilde's notorious willfulness. Yet for all these finely tuned arguments, the marquis's soul found it hard to abandon hope of a duchess's title for his daughter.

His memory, and his mind, were equally well stocked with tricks and pretenses of every kind, for in his earlier days they had all been possible. To give in to necessity, to be afraid of the law of the land, seemed absurd and dishonorable for a man of his rank. He was paying dearly, now, for those enchanting daydreams about his daughter's future in which, for ten long years, he had indulged himself.

"Who could have foreseen it?" he told himself. "A girl of such a haughty nature, of so fine a mind, prouder even than I am of the name she bears! whose hand had been sought of all of the most illustrious men in France!

"All prudence must be renounced! This century was born to overwhelm everything! We are marching into chaos."

CHAPTER THIRTY-FOUR

A MAN OF SPIRIT

The governor was riding along on his horse, saying to himself: "Why can't I be a government minister? President of the Privy Council? A duke? Here's how I'd wage war. . . . And this is how I'd lock away all innovators, chain them up. . . ."

—*THE GLOBE*

Ten years of dreaming take such complete control of a man's mind that no argument can destroy them. The marquis did not think it reasonable to be angry, but neither could he make up his mind to forgive. Sometimes he said to himself: "If this Julien could have a fatal accident . . ." This was how his gloomy mind found a bit of solace, pursuing the most absurd fantasies. His wild fancies numbed the effect of Father Pirard's wise reasoning. And so an entire month went by, and negotiations did not advance a single step.

In this family business, as in politics, the marquis formulated brilliant insights, his enthusiasm for which lasted three days. No plan pleased him, merely on the basis that it was supported by excellent arguments: he approved only of those arguments which favored whatever, at that moment, his favorite plan happened to be. For three days, he labored with a poet's ardor and enthusiasm, bringing everything to a certain posture. The next day, he wouldn't hear of it any longer.

Julien was initially disconcerted by all the marquis's delaying actions. After several weeks, however, he began to understand that, in this business, Monsieur de La Mole had no fixed approach whatever.

Madame de La Mole, like everyone else in the house, believed that Julien had gone to the provinces to supervise family properties. He was in fact staying, secretly, with Father Pirard, and saw Mathilde almost every day. Every morning, she spent an hour with her father, but sometimes they went for weeks without mentioning the business that remained central in their minds.

"I don't want to know where that man is," the marquis told her, one day. "Just send him this letter." Mathilde read it:

> My Languedoc properties bring in 20,600 francs. I give 10,600 francs to my daughter, and 10,000 francs to Monsieur Julien Sorel. This means, of course, that I hereby give the property as well as the income therefrom. Tell the lawyer to draw up two separate deeds of gift, and have them brought to me tomorrow. From then on, there will be no relationship between us. Ah! Sir, should I have expected all this?
>
> MARQUIS DE LA MOLE

"I thank you very much," said Mathilde gaily. "We'll be staying at Château d'Aiguillon, between Agen and Marmande. I'm told it's every bit as beautiful as Italy."

The gift was an immense surprise to Julien. This was not the cold, severe marquis he had known. Julien's own thoughts were taken up, well in advance, with his son's future. This unexpected and, for a man as poor as himself, rather considerable fortune made him ambitious for his child. He anticipated, either on his wife's account or his own, an income of thirty-six thousand francs. All Mathilde's emotions were absorbed in adoration of her husband—as pride always caused her to refer to Julien. Her great, her sole ambition was to have her marriage made known. She spent her days in exaggerating to herself the high wisdom she had shown, linking her destiny to that of so superior a man. Personal merit had become her preoccupation.

Almost continuous separation, the great number of business matters to be dealt with, the shortage of time for talking of love, completed the healthy effect of wise diplomacy, conceived originally by Julien.

Mathilde finally became impatient at seeing so little of the man she had, in fact, truly learned to love.

In a fit of bad humor, she wrote to her father, beginning her letter like Othello:

The fact of my choice sufficiently demonstrates, in itself, that I have preferred Julien to the pleasures society offered to the daughter of Marquis de La Mole. The delights of esteem and rank, and of petty vanity, are as nothing to me. I have lived, separated from my husband, for nearly six weeks. This should be sufficient to demonstrate my filial respect. Before this coming Wednesday, I will have left my father's house. Your benefactions have enriched us. No one knows my secret, except worthy Father Pirard. I will go to him; he will marry us, and an hour after the ceremony we will be en route to Languedoc, and we will not return to Paris unless you so order. But what pierces my heart is that all this will make a juicy story aimed at me, and at you. Might not the witticisms of some public fool compel our excellent Norbert to pick a quarrel with Julien? In that case, I know Julien too well to think I'd have any control over him. We should see that his soul is that of a plebeian in revolt. I beg you on bended knees, oh my father! come and attend our marriage, which will be next Thursday, in Father Pirard's church. The nasty stories will have their spice smoothed away, and the life of your only daughter and her husband will be saved, etc., etc.

The marquis's heart was thrown into a strange quandary. Finally, he had to make a choice. All his petty customs, all his coarse friends, had lost their influence.

In these unusual circumstances, lofty characteristics, born out of the events of his youth, came once again to the fore. The miseries of forced emigration had made him an imaginative man. For a brief two years he had enjoyed the benefits of a huge fortune and all manner of court distinctions, and then 1790 had thrown him into frightful suffering. It was a hard school and had changed a twenty-two-year-old's soul: he was still encamped in the middle of his wealth, rather than ruled by it. But this same imagination, which had protected his soul from the gangrene of gold, had plunged him into a mad passion to see his daughter dignified by a glorious title.

In the past six weeks, which had been dominated by his whims, the marquis first wanted to make Julien rich. Poverty seemed to Monsieur de La Mole unworthy, dishonorable to him personally, utterly impossible in his daughter's husband. He threw money at Julien. The next day, his mind took a different direction: he was sure Julien would come to understand the silent language in which all this gold was speaking, and would change his name, exile himself to America, write to Mathilde, saying he was now dead, as far as she was concerned. . . . Monsieur de La Mole imagined this letter written, received, read; he traced out its effect on his daughter's character. . . .

On the day when Mathilde's *real* letter drew him out of such childish dreams, instead of fancies about killing Julien, or making him disappear, he imagined creating for him a truly brilliant fortune. He would have him take the name of one of his estates, and saw no reason why the de La Mole peerage should not descend to Julien. His own father-in-law, the Duke of Chaulnes, had more than once spoken to him—after the duke's only son was killed in Spain—of his wish that Norbert succeed to the title. . . .

"How could we deny Julien his marked aptitude for business, his boldness, perhaps even his *brilliance*," the marquis said to himself. "But there is something frightening, deep down in his character. This is the effect he always has on others, so it must stem from something real." (The more difficult it was to be sure just how real, the more the old marquis's imaginative soul took fright.)

"The other day, my daughter told me, very cleverly [this letter has been deleted]: 'Julien has not joined any social group, nor any intellectual one.' He hasn't mustered any support against me, not even the smallest resources, were I to turn my back on him. . . . But is this simple ignorance of how things actually work? . . . I've said to him, two or three times: 'The only real, the only profitable, society to join is society itself.' . . .

"No, he lacks the lawyer's fawning shrewdness, which never loses a minute or wastes an opportunity. . . . He's not a bit like someone from Louis XI's time. On the other hand, I see in him a most striking lack of generosity. . . . I can't fathom him. . . . Does he say such things simply to dam up his passions?

"Still, one thing stands out: he cannot tolerate contempt. That gives me a grip on him.

"He has no faith in high birth; that's a fact. He has no instinctive respect for us. . . . That's a drawback—yet, ultimately, a seminarian's soul should be impatient only with shortages of pleasure and money. He is totally different, incapable of enduring scorn, no matter what the price."

Pressured by his daughter's letter, Monsieur de La Mole saw that he had to make up his mind: "In the end, this is the central question: Was Julien's boldness, his daring in courting my daughter, founded in his knowledge that I love her more than anything in the world—and that I have an income of a quarter of a million francs?

"Mathilde directly challenges this. . . . No, my Julien; this is a matter about which I cannot afford to entertain any illusions.

"Is what we have here a genuine love, unforeseen, unplanned? Or merely a low desire to rise into a higher social standing? Mathilde sees things very clearly. She knew from the very beginning that, for me, this could be the issue on which he ruins himself, and so she made her confession, saying it was she who was the first to think of love . . .

"A girl of such lofty character, so far forgetting herself that she makes physical advances! Clutching at his arm, in the garden, one night: how ghastly! As if she hadn't a hundred less indecent ways of letting him know she was thinking of him.

"*He who excuses himself, accuses himself.* I don't believe Mathilde." On this day, the marquis's thoughts were more conclusive than usual. But habit prevailed; he decided to gain time by writing to his daughter, since they had been corresponding back and forth, from one part of the house to the other. Monsieur de La Mole did not dare engage in a face-to-face discussion with Mathilde; he would not be able to hold his own. He was afraid of ending it all by some sudden surrender:

Beware of any new foolishness. Here is a commission as a cavalry lieutenant, for Chevalier Julien Sorel de La Vernaye. You can see what I'm doing for him. Don't oppose me; don't ask me any questions. Let him leave in twenty-four hours, to report at Strasbourg, where his regiment is stationed. Here too is a draft on my banker. See to it that I am obeyed.

Mathilde's love, and her joy, were boundless. She wanted to take due advantage of her victory, and replied immediately:

Monsieur de La Vernaye would be at your feet, wild with gratitude, if he knew what you are willing to do for him. But, so immersed has my father been in his generosity, he has forgotten his daughter, whose honor is at risk. One single indiscretion can result in an everlasting stain, which sixty thousand francs of income would never wipe away. I will not send his commission to Monsieur de La Vernaye unless you give me your word that, sometime next month, my marriage will be celebrated in public, at Villequier. Shortly thereafter—and I beg you not to exceed the stipulated period—your daughter will appear in public, under the name Madame de La Vernaye. How grateful I am to you, dear Papa, for having saved me from the name Sorel, etc., etc.

The reply was unexpected:

Obey me, or I'll take back everything. Be careful, rash young woman. I still do not know what your Julien truly is, and you yourself know even less than I do. Let him leave for Strasbourg, and let him do what he ought to do. I will let you know my wishes in two weeks' time.

This strict response stunned Mathilde. *"I don't know who Julien is."* These words threw her into a reverie, which soon ended in the most enchanting of imaginary events. But she thought they were real. "My Julien's spirit hasn't worn the drawing rooms' shabby *uniform*, and my father doesn't believe in his superiority, precisely on these grounds, which in fact prove it . . .

"Just the same, if I don't give in to this characteristic whim, I can see the real possibility of a public quarrel. A scandal would lower my social position, and might well make me less lovable to Julien. After a scandal . . . ten years of poverty—, and the madness of choosing a husband because of his merit, and nothing else, can only be rescued from ridicule by the most gleaming opulence. If I live far away from my father, at his age he might forget me. . . . Norbert will marry some lovable, clever woman: old Louis XIV was seduced by the Duchess of Burgundy."

She decided to obey, but was careful not to let Julien see her father's letter. His fierce nature might lead him to do something foolish.

That evening, when she told Julien he was a cavalry lieutenant, his joy was unrestrained. One can easily picture it, knowing his lifelong ambition, and also his new passion for his son. The name change absolutely struck him dumb.

"After all," he thought, "this romantic story is over, and the glory is all mine. I've learned how to love this prideful monster," he added, looking at Mathilde. "Her father can't live without her, nor she without him."

CHAPTER THIRTY-FIVE

A THUNDERSTORM

My God, give me mediocrity.
—MIRABEAU

His soul was lost in thought; he only partially responded to her eager tenderness. He remained silent, somber. He had never seemed to her so noble, so adorable. She worried that his pride might fall into some subtlety, which would end by jumbling up everything.

Virtually every morning, she saw Father Pirard come to the house. Couldn't he have helped Julien discover something of what her father meant to do? Might the marquis himself, moved by an eccentric impulse, have written to the priest? Following on such intense happiness, how explain Julien's somber behavior? She did not dare ask him.

She *did not dare!* She, Mathilde de La Mole! From then on there was something vague, unpredictable, almost terror-stricken in her feelings about Julien. Her dry heart experienced all the passion possible, for someone brought up in the midst of the extravagant civilization worshipped by Paris.

The next day, very early, Julien was at Father Pirard's. A team of mail-coach horses arrived in the priest's courtyard, pulling a dilapidated carriage, rented from the nearby mail office.

"This kind of thing is no longer appropriate," the harsh priest told him, sourly. "Here's twenty thousand francs, given you by Monsieur de La Mole. He expects you to spend this in the course of a year, but is also expecting you not to look any more ridiculous than you have to." (The priest also saw, in so large a sum thrown to so young a man, the commission of a sin.)

"The marquis also writes," Father Pirard went on, "that Monsieur Julien de La Vernaye has had this money from his father, who needs no further designation. It will be up to Monsieur de La Vernaye to decide if he wants to give something to Monsieur Sorel, a carpenter in Verrières, in whose charge he was, as a child. . . . I can take care of that part of the commission," the priest added. "I have finally brought Monsieur de La Mole to the point of settling with Father de Frilair, that ultimate Jesuit. His influence is definitely stronger than ours. The implicit recognition of your high birth, by that man who rules Besançon, will be one of the tacit terms of the settlement."

Unable to control his excitement, Julien embraced the priest. He saw himself acknowledged.

"What nonsense!" said Father Pirard, pushing him away. "What's the meaning of such worldly vanity? As for Sorel and his sons, I will offer them, in my name, an annual pension of five hundred francs each, to be paid so long as I hear no evil of them."

Julien had already become cold and distant. He expressed his thanks, but in the vaguest language, and without committing himself to anything. "Might it be possible," he was asking himself, "that I could be the natural son of some great lord, exiled to our mountains by the dreaded Napoleon?" The more he considered it, the idea seemed to him less and less improbable. . . . "My hatred for my father would be one thing that proved it. . . . And I wouldn't be a monster!"

A few days later, the Fifteenth Cavalry Regiment, one of the army's shining units, was in battle formation on the Strasbourg parade ground. Chevalier de La Vernaye rode the finest horse in all Alsace, which had cost him six thousand francs. He had been mustered in as a lieutenant, without ever having been a second lieutenant, except on the rolls of a regiment he'd never heard of.

His imperturbable demeanor, his severe and almost malicious eyes, his pallor, and his invariable calm coolness began to frame his reputation. Soon, his perfect, measured politeness, his swordsmanship and skill with his pistol, which he neither hid nor affectedly advertised, eliminated the possibility of open, audible jesting about him. Matters hung in the balance for five or six days, but then regimental opinion publicly declared itself in his favor. "This young fellow has everything," pronounced bantering senior officers, "except youth."

From Strasbourg, Julien wrote to Father Chélan, formerly parish priest at Verrières, who was reaching the outer limits of extreme old age:

> You will have heard, with a joy I cannot doubt, of the events which have induced my family to make me rich. I enclose five hundred francs which I beg you to distribute, very quietly, and with no mention of my name, to such miserable wretches as, once, I myself used to be, people you are surely helping as once you helped me.

Julien was drunk with ambition, not with vanity, but all the same most of his attention was devoted to his appearance. His horses, his and his servants' uniforms, received such care as would have done honor to the fastidiousness of a great English lord. Though very newly commissioned, just two days since, and by preferential treatment, he was already calculating that to be commander in chief by, at the latest, age thirty (as all great generals were), by the time he was twenty-three he must be more than a mere lieutenant. All he thought about were glory and his son.

It was thus in the midst of the most ungoverned ecstasies of ambition that he was surprised by a young de La Mole footman, who came bearing a letter:

> We're completely ruined [Mathilde wrote]. Hurry as fast as you can, sacrifice everything, desert if necessary. When you come, wait for me in a taxi, near the garden's little door, at number —— of ——— Street. I'll come and speak with you; perhaps I can bring you into the garden. We're ruined, I believe, beyond any hope whatever. You can count on me: you'll see that, in adversity, I am both devoted and constant. I love you.

In a matter of minutes, Julien obtained a leave from his colonel and left Strasbourg at full gallop. But he was too horribly upset, consumed by anxiety, to continue this mode of travel any farther than Metz. He threw himself into a mail coach and, with a speed that seemed almost incredible, reached the place she had indicated, near the little door to the de La Mole garden. The door was opened. And in a moment, forgetting all concern for what others might see, Mathilde dashed into his arms. Fortunately, it was only five in the morning, and the street was still deserted.

"We're completely ruined. My father, afraid of my tears, left Thursday night. For where? No one knows. Here is his letter. Read it." And she got into the cab with him.

> I could pardon anything, but not a plan to seduce you because you're rich. That, my ill-fated daughter, is the ghastly truth. I give you my word of honor that I will never consent to your marrying this man. I promise him an income of ten thousand francs, if he wishes to live abroad, outside the borders of France, or best of all in America. Read the letter I received, in response to the inquiries I made. The shameless fellow himself is responsible for my writing to Madame de Rênal. If you write to me about him, I will never read a line of it. I loathe both Paris and you. Try to keep totally secret that which will be happening. Renounce—renounce *sincerely*—this vile man, and you will regain a father.

"Where is Madame de Rênal's letter?" Julien asked, coldly.
"Here it is. I didn't want you to see it till you were ready."

> My duty to the sacred cause of religion and morality requires me, sir, to proceed with the painful step I am about to take, in writing to you. An infallible law now orders me to do harm to my neighbor, but in order to prevent an even greater disgrace. The sorrow I feel must yield to my sense of duty. It is entirely true, sir, that the person in question's conduct, about which you seek full and accurate information, might be considered inexplicable, or even honorable. I might have thought it proper to hide, or to disguise, some part of the truth; prudence might so desire, as might, also, religion. But the conduct about which you inquire has in fact been extraordinarily blameworthy—indeed, more than I can tell you. Poor and voraciously greedy, this man sought position and reputation by the most consummate hypocrisy, as well as by the seduction of a weak and miserable woman. One part of my painful duty is to add, here, that I believe Monsieur J——— has absolutely no religious beliefs. In good conscience,

I am obliged to believe that one of his roads to success, in any house into which he comes, is to search for and seduce the woman whose assets are the greatest. Cloaked by a pretense of unselfishness, and by romantic talk, his great, and his sole, goal is to enable himself to make use of the master of the house and of his fortune. He leaves behind him misery and eternal regret, etc., etc.

This extremely long letter, partially erased by tears, had in fact been written by Madame de Rênal. She had written it, indeed, more carefully than usual.

"I can't blame Monsieur de La Mole," said Julien when he had finished reading. "He is fair and sensible. What father would give his beloved daughter to such a man! Farewell!"

Julien jumped down from the cab and ran to a mail coach, which had stopped at the end of the street. He appeared to have forgotten Mathilde, who took several steps as if to follow after him. But staring merchants, coming to the doors of their shops—people very well aware of who she was—forced her to turn and hurriedly go back into the garden.

Julien was going to Verrières. During this rapid trip, he was unable to write to Mathilde, as he had planned: the only marks he made on paper were illegible scribblings.

It was Sunday morning when he reached Verrières. He went into a local gunsmith's shop, where he was covered with compliments for his recent good fortune. Everyone was talking about it.

It was not easy for Julien to make the man understand that what he wanted was a pair of pistols. At his request, the gunsmith loaded and charged them.

He heard three bells tolling: it was a familiar signal, in French villages. After the various morning bells had been rung, this announced that mass would soon be said.

He went into Verrières's new church. All the building's high windows were draped with crimson curtains. He found himself standing a few steps behind Madame de Rênal's pew. He thought she was praying quite fervently. Seeing this woman, for whom he had felt such love, made Julien's limbs tremble so much that, at first, he could not do what he had planned. "I can't do it," he was saying to himself. "It's physically impossible, shaking like this."

Just then, the young priest who was saying mass rang the little bell, announcing *elevation of the Host*. Madame de Rênal bent her head, and for a moment she was completely hidden beneath the folds of her shawl. Julien could no longer see her as plainly as he had. He fired the first pistol at her, and missed. He fired the second, and she fell.

CHAPTER THIRTY-SIX

Somber Details

Don't expect me to show weakness. I have taken my revenge. I deserve death, and here I am. Pray for my soul.
—Schiller

Julien remained motionless; he could not see. When he came back to himself, just a little, he became aware that all the faithful had fled from the church. The priest had left the altar. Julien began to walk, very slowly, behind several women who were screaming as they ran. One woman, wanting to run faster than the others, shoved him, roughly, and he fell. His feet became entangled in a chair, knocked over by the rushing crowd. As he rose, he felt his neck tightly gripped. It was a policeman, in full uniform, who was holding him. Automatically, Julien tried to reach for his pistols, but a second policeman grasped his arms.

He was brought to prison. They came into a room; chains were put on his wrists. He was left all alone. The door had been double-locked. Everything had happened quickly, and he had no idea what was going on.

"My God, it's all over," he said out loud, as he came back to himself. . . . "Yes, fifteen days, and then the guillotine . . . or I kill myself, between now and then."

His thinking could go no further. His head felt as if it had been violently compressed. He looked around to see if someone had hold of it. Almost immediately afterward, he fell into a very deep sleep.

Madame de Rênal had not been fatally wounded. The first ball had gone through her hat. The second shot had been fired as she was turning around. The ball had hit her in the shoulder and, astonishingly, had been redirected by the shoulder bone which, however, it had cracked; the ball had ended by striking a Gothic pillar, from which it had split off an enormous sliver of stone.

Later, after a long, painful dressing and bandaging, when the serious-faced surgeon told her, "I answer for your life as I would for my own," she was profoundly distressed.

For a long while, she wished sincerely for death. The letter, written to Monsieur de La Mole on the order of her current confessor, had been the final blow to a creature weakened by unremitting misery. This misery was Julien's absence; she called it, she herself, *remorse.* Her confessor, a young, fervently virtuous priest, newly arrived from Dijon, was not taken in.

"To die this way, but not by my own hand: that's not a sin," thought Madame de Rênal. "God will perhaps pardon me for rejoicing in my death." She did not dare add: "And to die at Julien's hand, that is the very height of bliss."

She was barely free of the surgeon, and all the friends crowding around, when she summoned Elisa, her chambermaid.

"The jailer," she told her, blushing deeply, "is a savage man. He will surely mistreat Julien, believing I would want that. . . . I cannot endure the idea. Might you yourself go and bring the jailer this little package, which contains some gold coins? You'll tell him that religion does not allow him to mistreat a prisoner. . . . Above all, he must not go around talking about receipt of this money."

And this, which we have just been recounting, was responsible for the Verrières jailer's humanity to Julien. This was, as ever, Monsieur Noiroud, the perfect bureaucrat, in whom we have seen Monsieur Appert's presence strike such notable fear.

A judge came to the prison. "I killed by premeditation," Julien told him. "I bought the pistols from, and had them loaded and charged by, Monsieur So-and-So, a gunsmith. Article 1342 of the Code is clear: I deserve a sentence of death, and I expect it." Astonished by this kind of response, the judge wanted to ask a whole batch of questions, so that the accused might have an opportunity to give *conflicting* answers.

"But don't you see," said Julien, smiling, "that I'm making myself as

guilty as you could ever want? Face it, sir: there'll be no difficulty nab-
bing the victim you're chasing. You will have the pleasure of sentenc-
ing him. Spare me, please, having to deal with you."

"I have one boring duty to fulfill," Julien thought. "I must write to
Mademoiselle de La Mole."

> I have had my revenge [he told her]. Unfortunately, my name will appear
> in the newspapers; I cannot escape, incognito, from this world. I will die in
> two months. It was a revenge entirely ghastly, as is my sorrow at being
> separated from you. From this moment on, I forbid myself either to write
> or to speak your name. Never speak of me, even to my son: silence is
> the only way of honoring me. For the vulgar herd, I will be a coarse assas-
> sin. . . . Let me be allowed to speak the truth, at this supreme moment: you
> will forget me. This immense catastrophe—as to which I advise you never
> to say a word, not to any living being—will for several years have drained
> away everything romantic and adventurous, so far as I can see, in your na-
> ture. You were made to dwell with the heroes of the Middle Ages: exhibit
> that same firmness in your own character. What must take place will be
> done in secret, without in any way compromising you. You will take an
> assumed name, and you will confide in no one. If you absolutely need a
> friend's help, let me leave you Father Pirard.
>
> Speak to no one else, and above all not to people of your own class: the
> de Cayluses, the de Luzes.
>
> When I've been dead a year, marry Monsieur de Croisenois: please, I
> am commanding you, as your husband. Do not write to me; I will not
> reply. Since I'm not as evil as Iago, at least in my own mind, I'm going to
> say to you, as he said: "From this time forth I never will speak word."
>
> I will not speak or write to anyone. You alone will have my final words,
> as also my final adoration.
>
> J.S.

Only after having sent this letter, and for the first time, was Julien,
now a bit more himself, very miserable. All the expectations and
hopes of ambition had to be yanked out of his heart, one after the
other, by those immense words: I am going to die. Death did not seem
to him, in and of itself, *horrible*. His whole life had been nothing but a
long prelude to misery, nor did he have to worry that he might forget
what commonly passed as the greatest event of all.

"Well then!" he told himself. "Suppose in sixty days I had to fight a duel against a truly magnificent swordsman, would I be so weak-minded that I'd never think of anything else, terror-stricken at heart?"

He spent more than an hour trying to learn where he stood on this matter.

When he could see clearly into his soul, and the truth was as plain as the prison's stone pillars, which he saw very clearly indeed, he turned to thoughts of remorse!

"Why should I be remorseful? I was atrociously offended against. I killed, I deserve death, but that's all there is to it. I die, having first settled my accounts with humankind. I'm leaving no obligations unsatisfied, I owe no one anything: the only shameful aspect of my death is the instrument which will cause it. That alone, of course, will do more than nicely for the Verrières bourgeoisie, but from an intellectual perspective what could be more contemptible! In their eyes, all I have left is a single road to importance—and that would be to scatter pieces of gold among the crowd, as I go to the gallows. Thus joined to the idea of *gold*, my memory would be, for them, a truly resplendent thing."

A minute after this internal discussion, which seemed to him quite obvious: "I have nothing more to do on this earth," Julien told himself, and fell deeply asleep.

Toward nine, that night, the jailor woke him, bringing in his supper.

"What's being said, in Verrières?"

"Monsieur Julien, the oath I took in front of the holy cross, right in the king's courtroom the day I was installed in my place here, forces me to remain silent."

He was silent, but he did not leave. This coarse hypocrisy amused Julien. "I have to keep him waiting a long time," he thought, "for the five francs he wants, so he can sell me his conscience."

The jailer saw the meal concluded without any attempt at bribery:

"My regard for you, Monsieur Julien," he said, smoothly hypocritical, "compels me to speak, even if they say it's not in the interests of justice, because maybe it would let you better settle your defense. . . . Monsieur Julien, who's a good fellow, will be very glad to hear Madame de Rênal's getting better."

"What! She's not dead?" cried Julien, beside himself.

"Ah, you didn't know that?" said the jailer stupidly; in another moment he had turned happily greedy. "It would only be fair if Monsieur Julien felt like giving something to the surgeon, who according to law and justice should never say anything. But just to please you, sir, I went to see him, and he let me know everything, strictly in confidence...."

"You mean, the wound wasn't fatal?" Julien said impatiently. "You'd stake your life on that?"

The jailer, a giant of a man, was afraid, and backed toward the door. Julien saw he'd taken the wrong road to get at the truth; calming himself, he threw a five-franc gold piece to Monsieur Noiroud.

As the jailer's account began to convince Julien that Madame de Rênal's wound had not been fatal, he felt himself overwhelmed by tears. "Get out," he said sharply.

The jailer left. The door had barely closed behind him: "Good God! She's not dead!" Julien exclaimed. And he fell to his knees, weeping hot tears.

At that supreme moment, he was a true believer. "What difference does priestly hypocrisy make! Are they capable of depriving the idea of God of its truth and sublimity?"

Only then did Julien begin to repent the crime he'd committed. Purely by coincidence, he escaped from despair: beginning at that very moment, he no longer felt physically inflamed and half mad, the state into which he had been plunged after his departure from Paris.

His tears had sprung from a noble source; he had not the slightest doubt about the sentence awaiting him.

"So she'll live!" he was saying to himself.... "She'll live, so she can forgive me, and so she can love me...."

The jailer woke him, late the next morning:

"You've got to have a first-rate heart, Monsieur Julien," he said. "I've been here twice, and I didn't want to wake you up. Here's two bottles of good wine, that our good parish priest, Father Maslon, sends you...."

"Really? That rascal's still here?" said Julien.

"Yes, sir," answered the jailer, lowering his voice. "But don't speak so loud. It might not be good for you."

Julien had a good laugh.

"From where I'm standing, my friend, you're the only one who could hurt me, if you stopped being gentle and humane. . . . You'll be well paid," Julien said, breaking off and resuming his imperious air. And he justified himself, immediately thereafter, by a golden gift.

Monsieur Noiroud told him, once again, and in much greater detail, everything he had learned about Madame de Rênal, but he never said a word about Mademoiselle Elisa's visit.

The man was as deferential and tame as he could possibly be. An idea came into Julien's head: "This deformed giant earns, at most, three or four hundred francs a year, because this jail's not a very busy place. I could guarantee him ten thousand, if he were willing to save himself, and me, by going to Switzerland. . . . The problem would be convincing him I really meant it." The thought of the long discussion he'd have to endure, with such a vile creature, disgusted Julien. He turned his mind to other things.

There was no more time for such diversions, after that night. At midnight, a mail coach arrived to take him away. He was very pleased with the policemen who made the trip with him. In the morning, when he arrived at the Besançon prison, they were kind enough to lodge him on the upper floor of a Gothic tower. He estimated the date of construction to be early fourteenth century; he admired the tower's grace, and the striking lightness of its design. Through a narrow space between two walls, on the far side of a great courtyard, he had a glimpse of the superb view.

He was interrogated the next day, after which, for several days, he was left in peace. His soul was calm. All he could see in the whole affair was perfectly simple: "I wanted to kill; I ought to be killed."

There was no point to even thinking about it, beyond this. The trial, the boredom of having to appear in public, his defense—all of those things seemed to him trivial embarrassments, boring ceremonies he need not think about, until the day came. The moment of his death hardly concerned him any more than these matters: "I'll think about it after the trial's over." He did not find life boring: he found himself considering things from a new perspective. He had no more ambition. He seldom thought of Mademoiselle de La Mole. Remorse preoccupied him, and often presented him with the image of Madame de

Rênal, especially during the nighttime silence, only disturbed, in his high tower, by the shrieking of an osprey.

He thanked heaven he had not fatally wounded her. "Astonishing!" he said to himself. "I felt that her letter to Monsieur de La Mole had destroyed, and forever, all my future happiness, and now, less than fifteen days after the date of that letter, I no longer think of what was then filling my mind. . . . An income of two or three thousand francs, to live peacefully up in the mountains, some place like Vergy . . . I was happy, then. . . . I didn't realize how happy I was!"

Other times, he leaped up from his chair. "If I had fatally wounded Madame de Rênal, I would have committed suicide. . . . I need to know that without a doubt, so I'm not horrified by myself.

"Kill myself! That's the really big question," he told himself. "These terribly formalist judges, so relentless toward the poor accused, who'd have the worthiest of citizens strung up on a rope so they could earn themselves a medal. . . . I'd take myself out of their control, to the insults they frame in their awful French, which the regional newspapers will call eloquence. . . .

"Anyway, I like being alive. This vacation resort is peaceful. There aren't any boring people in here," he added, laughing, and began noting the books he'd like sent on to him, from Paris.

CHAPTER THIRTY-SEVEN

THE TOWER

A friend's tomb.

—STERNE

He heard a loud noise in the corridor. It wasn't the right time for people to be visiting the prison. The osprey flew off, screaming, the door opened, and old Father Chélan, trembling all over, walking cane in hand, flung himself into his arms.

"Ah, Lord in heaven! Is it possible. My child . . . You monster, I really ought to say."

And the good old man could not manage another word. Julien was afraid he'd collapse. He had to lead him to a chair. Time's hand lay heavily on this man, once so energetic. He seemed to Julien no more than a shadow of himself.

When the old man could breathe again: "I got your letter, from Strasbourg, just the day before yesterday, and the five hundred francs for the poor in Verrières. They've taken me up to the mountains, where my nephew Jean lives, and I'm staying up there. Yesterday I heard about the catastrophe. . . . Oh heaven! Is it possible?" And he was not crying anymore; he seemed blank, and went on, mechanically: "You'll need your five hundred francs. Here."

"What I need is seeing you, my Father!" exclaimed Julien, deeply moved. "I've still got money."

But there was no coherent response. Now and then Father Chélan dropped a few tears, which crawled slowly down his cheeks; then the old man looked at Julien, and seemed astonished to see his hands clasped in Julien's, and lifted to Julien's lips. His once-lively face, which had portrayed so many noble feelings, and with such vivid energy, remained apathetic. A peasantlike man came looking for him. "We mustn't let him get too tired," he told Julien, who realized this was the nephew.

This ghostly visit left Julien profoundly upset; he wept. Everything struck him as gloomy and comfortless; he felt his heart frozen in his breast.

This was the hardest moment he'd experienced since his crime. He had just seen death, in all its ugliness. All his illusions of soulful heights and nobility of feeling were blown away, like clouds in a wind.

This horrible situation lasted for several hours. After having been morally poisoned, he needed physical remedies, and some good wine. Julien felt it was cowardly to fall back on such measures. Toward the end of this ghastly day, spent walking up and down his narrow tower: "What a fool I am!" he cried. "If I were to die as other people do, then seeing this poor old man ought to throw me into this frightful misery. But to die quickly, and in the flower of my life, is exactly what preserves me from this sad decrepitude."

But whatever arguments he set forth, Julien felt himself full of pity, like some chicken-livered fellow, and so was made miserable by the visit.

There was nothing rough and grandiose left in him, nothing of high Roman stoicism. Death seemed to be descending on him from some immense height, and was no longer so easily faced.

"This will be my thermometer," he told himself. "Tonight I'm ten degrees below the courage that can carry me to the guillotine. This morning, I had that courage. Nothing else matters, except lifting myself back, when I need to be there!" He found this metaphoric thermometer an amusing notion, and was at last able to turn his thoughts elsewhere.

When he woke, the next day, he felt shamed by what had taken place the day before. "My happiness, my peace of mind, are threatened." He was almost resolved to write to the prosecutor and ask that nobody at all be permitted to visit. "And Fouqué?" he thought. "If he decides to come to Besançon, how painful that would be!"

It was two months, probably, since he'd thought of Fouqué. "I was a stupendous idiot, at Strasbourg: my mind stopped when it got to the collar on my coat." He lingered over his memories of Fouqué, which left him feeling more tender. He walked nervously up and down. "By now I'm definitely twenty degrees below my death-level. . . . If this weakness gets worse, it would be better to kill myself. What pleasure I'd give the likes of Father Maslon and Monsieur de Valenod if I die like a slob!"

Fouqué came. This simple, good man was frantic with grief. His only idea—if he had an idea—was to sell everything he owned, to bribe the jailer and save Julien. He spoke at length about Count de Lavalette's escape from the guillotine, in 1815.

"You're upsetting me," Julien told him. "Monsieur de Lavalette was innocent, and me, I'm guilty. You don't mean to, but you're making me think about the difference. . . .

"But really?" he continued. "Really? You'd sell everything?" Suddenly, Julien was once again watchful, suspicious.

Thrilled to see his friend responding to his great idea, Fouqué went into immense detail, down to the last hundred francs, of what he could get for each bit of property.

"What a sublime effort for a country landowner!" Julien thought. "What scraping and saving, what petty scrimping—which used to make me blush when I'd see him do it—he'd sacrifice for me! One of those handsome young fellows I saw at the de La Moles, wallowing in *René*, wouldn't do all the ridiculous things that Fouqué does. But except for the terribly young ones who came into all their money by inheriting it, and have no idea what money is worth, which of those young Parisians would be capable of such a sacrifice?"

All Fouqué's grammatical errors, his country bumpkin manners, disappeared: Julien threw himself into his arms. Never have the provinces, set in comparison to Paris, received a handsomer homage. Seeing the flaring of enthusiasm in his friend's eyes, Fouqué was ecstatic; he took it as consent for an escape.

Seeing this *sublimity* restored all Julien's strength, lost after Father Chélan's ghostly visit. He was still very young, reader, but as I see him, he was already a fine growth. Instead of proceeding, as most men do, from tender youth into crooked sticks, age would have endowed him with a kindness easily roused; he would have been cured of his insane mistrust. . . . But is there any point to such empty predictions?

Interrogations became more frequent, no matter how hard Julien tried: all his responses were intended to shorten the whole business. "I killed, or at least I tried to kill, with premeditation," he repeated every day. But above all else, the judge was a formalist. Julien's statements in no way shortened the interrogations. The judge's vanity had been roused. Julien had no knowledge of their plan to transfer him to a dark, frightful dungeon: only Fouqué's efforts forced them to leave him in his pleasant little room, reached by climbing a hundred and eighty steps.

Father de Frilair was one of the many important men who bought their supply of wood from Fouqué. The good-hearted timber merchant went to see the all-powerful vicar-general. To his inexpressible delight, Father de Frilair assured him that, moved by Julien's good qualities, and by the services he had, in the past, performed for the seminary, Father de Frilair could be counted upon to commend him to the judge. Fouqué saw some chance, here, of saving his friend, and as he left he prostrated himself, begging the vicar-general to accept ten gold coins, to be expended in masses said for the accused's acquittal.

Fouqué had oddly misunderstood. Father de Frilair was no Valenod.

He would not take Fouqué's money; he even tried to make the good peasant understand that he'd do better to hold on to his gold. Seeing how impossible it was to be perfectly clear, without becoming seriously imprudent, he finally advised Fouqué to donate this sum as alms for poor prisoners—who lacked, in truth, everything.

"This Julien is a bizarre creature, quite inexplicable," thought Father de Frilair, "though, for me, nothing ought to be that. . . . Perhaps it will be possible to turn him into a martyr. . . . In any case, I intend to probe this business to the *bottom*. Perhaps I can find a way to strike fear into this Madame de Rênal, who does not think highly of us and, underneath it all, simply detests me. . . . Perhaps I can find, in all this, some dazzling road to reconciliation with Monsieur de La Mole, who has a weakness for this little seminarian."

The lawsuit settlement had been signed some weeks earlier, and Father de Frilair had returned to Besançon, the day of the unfortunate attempt to kill Madame de Rênal, in the Verrières church; he had said nothing about Julien's mysterious birth.

Only one disagreeable event remained, as Julien saw it, between him and his death, and that would be his father's visit. He consulted Fouqué about writing to the prosecutor, to be excused from receiving any more visitors. His horror at the idea of seeing his father, at such a moment, profoundly shocked the timber merchant's honest, bourgeois heart.

He believed he could understand why so many people passionately hated his friend. Out of respect for the miserable fellow, he hid his feelings.

"In any case," he replied stiffly, "such an order would not apply to your father."

CHAPTER THIRTY-EIGHT

A POWERFUL MAN

But she moves so mysteriously, and her figure is so elegant!
Who can she be?
—SCHILLER

The tower doors opened very early, the next day. Julien woke with a start.

"Oh, Good God!" he thought. "Here's my father. What unpleasant-ness!"

Just then, a woman dressed like a peasant threw herself into his arms; he could just barely recognize her. It was Mademoiselle de La Mole.

"You're wicked! I couldn't tell from your letter where you were. This crime, as you call it, is simply a noble act of vengeance, and shows me all the loftiness of the heart beating in your breast. I only found out in Verrières. . . ."

Despite his bias against Mademoiselle de La Mole (which, inciden-tally, he never directly admitted to himself), Julien found her ex-tremely pretty. How could he not see, in everything she did, and everything she said, noble, unaffected feelings far beyond what a petty, vulgar soul could have dared? He still believed he had loved a queen; after a few moments, he said to her, with a rare nobility of both speech and thought:

"I saw the future wonderfully clearly. After my death, I saw you re-married to Monsieur de Croisenois, who would be marrying a widow. The noble but a bit romantic soul of this charming widow had been so shocked by a bizarre occurrence, for her both tragic and great, that she became a convert to the cult of common prudence, and took the trouble to understand the real worth of the young marquis. You would have been resigned to everyday happiness: respect, wealth, a lofty rank. . . . But, my dear Mathilde, your coming here, should it be sus-pected, would be a fatal blow for Monsieur de La Mole, and for that he will never forgive me. I've already caused him so much sorrow! The academician will be saying he nourished a serpent in his breast."

"I confess I did not expect so much cold reasoning, so much concern for the future," said Mademoiselle de La Mole, almost angry. "My chambermaid, virtually as cautious as you are, took herself a passport, and I've been traveling, as fast as I could, under the name Madame Michelet."

"And Madame Michelet was able to arrive where she now is, just as easily as that?"

"Ah, you're always the superior man I favored! First, I offered a hundred francs to a judge's secretary, who acted as if my getting in here was an impossibility. But once the money was in his hand, this respectable man kept me waiting, and raised all sorts of objections. I wondered if he was thinking of robbing me. . . ." She stopped.

"And?" said Julien.

"Don't be angry, my little Julien," she said, hugging him. "I had to give the secretary my name: he thought I was some young working girl from Paris, who'd fallen in love with handsome Julien. . . . In fact, those are his words. I swore I was your wife, and I have permission to see you every day."

"The idiocy is complete," thought Julien. "I haven't been able to stop it. But after all, Monsieur de La Mole is such a great lord that the newspapers, and their readers, will know how to invent excuses when a young colonel marries this charming widow. My imminent death will muffle everything else." He abandoned himself, delighted, to Mathilde's love, which contained madness, greatness of soul, everything strangest and most remarkable. She seriously proposed dying with him.

After the first ecstasies, and when her happiness at seeing Julien had been sated, a lively curiosity suddenly seized her mind. She looked her lover over and found him far beyond what she had been imagining. Boniface de La Mole seemed to be resuscitated in him, but even more heroic.

She visited the region's leading lawyers, and offended them by offering gold rather too crudely. But they ultimately accepted the case. She quickly decided that, in Besançon, any dealings of a doubtful nature, in which important matters were at stake, were completely dependent on Father de Frilair.

Using her obscure assumed name, she at first experienced insurmountable difficulties, and could not reach the Congregation of the Holy Virgin's all-powerful agent. But rumors had soon spread all over town about the beautiful, young, fashionable dressmaker, come to Besançon from Paris, wild with love, to console the young ecclesiastic, Julien Sorel.

Mathilde hurried, alone and on foot, along the streets of Besançon; she hoped no one would recognize her. In any case, she thought it unwise for her cause to produce a great impression on ordinary people. She was foolish enough to dream of starting a revolution, to rescue Julien as he was going to his death. Mademoiselle de La Mole fancied herself dressed simply, as befitted a woman who was suffering; she was in fact dressed to catch every eye.

In Besançon, she was the center of attention everywhere she went, until finally, after a week of petitioning, she obtained an audience with Father de Frilair.

No matter how courageous she might be, two ideas—powerful men in the Congregation of the Holy Virgin, and foxlike wickedness—were so strongly linked in her mind that she shook as she stood at the episcopal palace door and rang the bell. She could barely walk when she had to climb the stairway leading to the vicar-general's rooms. The palace's empty silence gave her chills. "I'll sit in an armchair, and the chair will take hold of me. I'll disappear. To whom can my chambermaid go, seeking news of me? The police captain will be careful not to do anything. . . . I am totally alone in this great town!"

Her first glimpse of the vicar-general's rooms reassured her. First, the door was opened by a servant in very elegant livery. The drawing room where one waited displayed a subtle, delicate luxury to be found, in Paris, only in the best houses. The moment she saw Father de Frilair, who approached her most paternally, all her notions of horrible criminality disappeared. The appearance of this handsome man did not in the least evoke a sense of energetic virtue, more than a little barbaric, so obnoxious to Paris society. The half smile on the priest's face—he who controlled everything in Besançon—proclaimed a man of good manners, the learned prelate, the crafty administrator. Mathilde felt herself back in Paris.

It did not take more than a few moments before Mathilde admitted that she was the daughter of his powerful adversary, Marquis de La Mole.

"I am not in fact Madame Michelet," she said, resuming her haughty bearing, "and that admission costs me very little, for I have come to consult you, sir, about the possibility of arranging Monsieur de La Vernaye's escape. First of all, he is guilty of nothing more than thoughtlessness: the woman he fired at is doing well. Secondly, in order to bribe underlings I will give you, here and now, fifty thousand francs, and pledge myself to doubling that. And, finally, my gratitude and that of my family will find nothing impossible for whoever saves Monsieur de La Vernaye."

The vicar-general was astonished at this name. Mathilde showed him several letters from the minister of war, addressed to Monsieur Julien Sorel de La Vernaye.

"You can see, sir, that my father has made himself responsible for the accused's fortunes. I married him, in secret: my father wished him to be a commissioned senior officer before announcing this marriage—not at all a usual one for a de La Mole."

Mathilde saw the kindly, pleasantly sweet-tempered expression fade swiftly away, step by step, as Father de Frilair made these important discoveries. Shrewdness, blended with profound duplicity, settled onto his face.

The vicar-general was uncertain; he reread the official documents, slowly.

"How should I act, in the face of these strange revelations? This sets me in a familiar relationship, all of a sudden, with a woman who is a friend of the famous Madame de Fervaques, niece of the all-powerful Bishop of ——, he who creates bishops here in France.

"That which has seemed to be the remote future has unexpectedly materialized. This could lead me to everything I have wished for."

Mathilde was initially frightened, seeing how this powerful man's face kept changing: she was alone with him in a secluded room. "But Good Lord!" she soon told herself. "Wouldn't it be the worst thing that could have happened, had I made no impression at all on the cold egotism of a power- and pleasure-glutted priest?"

Dazed by the swift, unexpected vision of actually becoming a bishop, stunned by Mathilde's quick intelligence, for a moment Father de Frilair's defenses were no longer fully operational. Mademoiselle de La Mole saw him virtually at her feet, ambitious and eager to the point of nervous trembling.

"It's all quite apparent," she thought. "Nothing will be impossible, here, for Madame de Fervaques's friend." Although still moved by gloomy jealousy, she was courageous enough to explain that Julien was on intimate terms with Marshall de Fervaques's widow, and had met, almost daily, the Bishop of ————.

"Any list of thirty-six jurors, drawn by chance even four or five times over, and representative of the most important residents of this district," said the vicar-general, grasping ambition visible on his face as he carefully stressed each and every word, "would be extremely unlikely not to include eight or ten of my friends, who would be the most sensible of the whole lot. I would usually have a majority—even more than that, indeed—of the necessary votes. You see, mademoiselle, I can very easily pardon and exonerate—"

He suddenly stopped himself, as if amazed by what he was saying: he'd been admitting things never spoken of in front of secular people.

Then Mathilde was stunned, in turn, when Father de Frilair disclosed that, above all other things, what had astounded, and interested, Besançon society about Julien's bizarre adventures was that he had begun by inspiring a grand passion in Madame de Rênal, and for a long time had reciprocated it. The priest had no trouble seeing how this account produced a strong reaction.

"Now I can even the score!" he thought. "Finally, I have a way of managing this very determined little lady: I was quivering, afraid of not finding one." The noble and rather unmanageable charm of this beautiful woman doubled, in his eyes, as he saw her virtually a supplicant. He recovered his cold collectedness, and did not hesitate to twist the dagger in her heart.

"I wouldn't be surprised, in the end," he said casually, "if we learned that jealousy was behind Monsieur Sorel's having fired two shots at this woman, once so dearly beloved. It's not likely that she has deprived herself of all human pleasures, and of late she very often saw a certain young priest from Dijon, a kind of Jansenist without manners or morals, as of course they all are."

Father de Frilair took vast sensuous delight in torturing, very slowly, this pretty young girl, whose weak side he took by surprise.

"And why," he said, fastening his burning eyes on Mathilde, "why would Monsieur Sorel have chosen a church, if it hadn't been because, at exactly that moment, his rival was there, celebrating mass? Everyone agrees on the vast intelligence, and even more on the good sense, of this happy man you are shielding. What could be simpler than to hide himself in Monsieur de Rênal's gardens, which he knew so well? There, with the virtual certainty of not being seen, or arrested, or even suspected, he could have killed the woman who had made him so jealous."

This argument, apparently so legitimate, drove Mathilde out of control. Her soul was lofty, but saturated in the sterile prudence which, in sophisticated society, is considered an accurate depiction of the human heart: it had not been fashioned to understand, quickly or easily, the joy of mocking such prudence, which to a burning soul can be so inspiriting. In the upper ranks of Paris high society, where Mathilde had always dwelled, passion can only very rarely cut through prudence. People who throw themselves out of windows always leap from the upper stories.

The vicar-general was finally sure he had everything under control. He let Mathilde know (and was surely lying) that he could do as he liked, in dealing with the public official who was prosecuting Julien's case.

If he had not thought Mathilde so very pretty, Father de Frilair would not have spoken to her so openly until, at least, the fifth or sixth interview.

CHAPTER THIRTY-NINE

PLOTTING

Castres, 1676: A man had just murdered his sister, in the house next to mine; this gentleman had previously been guilty of murder. His father, by having five hundred francs distributed, in secret, among the town councillors, saved his son's life.

—LOCKE, *A TRIP TO FRANCE**

Leaving the bishop's palace, Mathilde had no hesitation about sending a courier to Madame de Fervaques: fear of compromising herself did not hold her back for a second. She begged her rival to secure a letter for Father de Frilair, handwritten by the Bishop of ———. She went so far as to plead that Madame de Fervaques herself hurry to Besançon. For a soul so jealous, and so proud, this was an heroic act.

Following Fouqué's advice, she had been careful not to tell Julien about any of these proceedings. Her presence sufficiently disturbed him, without adding more. Far more respectable in the face of death than ever before in his life, Julien felt remorseful not only toward Monsieur de La Mole, but toward Mathilde as well.

"What's this?" he said to himself. "I find myself paying no attention to her, and even feeling bored. She's ruining herself for me, and this is how I repay her! Am I as bad as all that?" He had not been much concerned about this, when he'd been ambitious: in those days, the only shame he felt was for not achieving success.

His moral discomfort, when he was with Mathilde, was even more marked because, at those very moments, he was inspiring in her the most extraordinary and most insane passion. All she talked about was the wild, exotic sacrifices she wished she could make to save him.

Excited by feelings that she cherished, and that swept before them all her pride, she wished she could fill every second of her life with some dramatic development. The weirdest plans, and the most

* Retranslated from the French

perilous for her, filled her long sessions with Julien. The jailers, who had been well paid, let her do what she liked. Mathilde's ideas did not stop at the sacrifice of her reputation: she did not care if every member of good society knew how things were with her. Falling on her knees in front of the king's carriage, as it galloped along, and begging for Julien's pardon, catching the king's eye at the risk of being crushed a thousand times over, was one of the least extravagant daydreams concocted by her exalted, courageous heart. By making use of friends with posts close to the king, she was sure she could get into areas of the castle closed to the public.

Julien did not consider himself worth this much devotion: to tell the truth, he was tired of heroism. Simple tenderness, unsophisticated and even shy, would have made an impression on him, but Mathilde's proud soul always required a public, the presence of *all those other people.*

In the middle of all her suffering, and all her fears for her lover's life (she did not want to survive him), she had a hidden need to astonish the public with the utter extravagance of her love, and the sublimity of everything she was trying to do.

Julien was not happy, finding himself indifferent to all this heroism. How would he have felt had he known all the craziness she piled on that devoted, but thoroughly reasonable—as well as limited—spirit, good Fouqué?

Fouqué was bewildered, and could not really criticize Mathilde's devotion, since he too would have sacrificed everything he had, exposing himself to the greatest perils in order to save Julien. He was staggered by the quantities of gold she dispensed. In the beginning, he had been impressed by the vast sums she spent, having a provincial's absolute veneration of money.

He finally discovered that Mademoiselle de La Mole's plans were not always fixed, and, to his immense relief, he devised a way of describing this utterly wearying person: she was *changeable.* To proceed from this label to that of *scatterbrained*—a provincial's most damning criticism—was no great leap.

"How strange," Julien told himself one day as Mathilde was leaving his prison, "that so violent a passion, directed toward me, leaves me so cold! And just two months ago, I adored her! I've read, certainly, that death's approach turns you away from everything. But to feel myself an ingrate and be unable to change! Am I an egotist?" He subjected himself to the most humiliating censure.

In his heart, ambition had died, but from its ashes another passion had emerged: he called it remorse for having tried to kill Madame de Rênal.

In fact, he was frantically in love with her. He experienced an odd happiness, left absolutely alone and not worried about being interrupted, completely surrendering himself to memories of the happy days he had once passed, at Verrières and at Vergy. The smallest incidents from those times, which had flown past far too rapidly, had a freshness, an irresistible charm for him. He never thought of his successes in Paris: he was weary of them.

These tendencies, which grew rapidly, were to some extent perceptible to Mathilde's jealousy. She saw very clearly how she had to struggle against his desire to be alone. Sometimes, in her terror, she spoke Madame de Rênal's name. She could see Julien shiver. After that, her passion was unlimited, unrestrained.

"If he dies, then I will die, too," she said to herself, as sincerely as such things can be said. "What will they say, in the drawing rooms of Paris, seeing a girl of my rank so adore a lover about to die? To find such sentiments, you'd have to return to the day of heroes: it was love of this kind that made hearts flutter, in the time of Charles IX and Henry III."

In the middle of the most intense ecstasies, when she pressed his head to her heart: "Oh!" she told herself, horrified, "this lovely head is going to be chopped off! All right!" she went on, inflamed by a heroism that contained its own happiness. "My lips, now pressed against his beautiful hair, will be cold as ice, less than twenty-four hours later."

Thoughts of these heroic moments, and of a ghastly eroticism, held her in an invincible grip. The idea of suicide, itself so engrossing, and before then so entirely foreign to her haughty soul, made its way into her mind and soon ruled it with iron control. "No," she said to herself proudly, "my ancestors' blood hasn't become lukewarm, as it has come down to me."

"I have a favor to ask of you," her lover said to her one day. "Let your child's nurse be someone in Verrières. Madame de Rênal would watch over the nurse."

"That's a very difficult thing to ask of me...." And Mathilde grew pale.

"You're right, and I beg your pardon, a thousand times over," exclaimed Julien, shaking off his reverie and clasping her in his arms.

Having dried her tears, he came back to his notion, but more skillfully. He colored the conversation with philosophical melancholy. He spoke of the future, which was to close, for him, so very soon. "You surely agree, my dearest, that passions are accidental, in these lives of ours, but they are accidents that happen to superior souls.... My son's death, in the end, would be a blessing for your family's pride: that's what underlings would think. Disregard will be the fate of this child of misery and shame.... I hope that on a day I have no wish to set, but which I am strong enough to foresee, you will obey my last wishes: you will marry Monsieur de Croisenois."

"Once I've been dishonored!"

"Dishonor cannot adhere to a name like yours. You'll be a widow, the widow of a lunatic, and that's all. I'll go further: my crime, for which there is absolutely no monetary motive, will not be dishonorable. In those times, perhaps, some philosophical legislator will have secured, despite his contemporaries' prejudices, the abolition of the death penalty. Then some friendly voice will cite an example: 'Consider: Mademoiselle de La Mole's first husband was crazy, yes, but not a wicked man, not a scoundrel. It was absurd to cut off his head....' And then my memory won't be infamous, at least after a certain length of time.... Your position in the world, your wealth and, if you'll permit me to say so, your first-rate mind, will allow Monsieur de Croisenois, after he's become your husband, to play a role which, on his own, he'd lack the ability to achieve. All he has is birth and bravery, and these qualities, by themselves, which gave a man the reputation of being accomplished, in 1729, are anachronisms a century later, and only lead to pretentiousness. There must be other qualities, before you can lead our French youth.

"You'll bring a firm, adventuresome character to the assistance of whatever political party you choose for your husband. You could be the successor to women like Madame de Chevreuse and the Duchess of Longueville, in the great Fronde wars of the seventeenth century. . . . But then, my beloved, the heavenly fire which burns in you, now, will have cooled a little. . . .

"Permit me to say to you," he added, after many more preparatory observations, "that in fifteen years you'll perceive as an excusable folly, but nevertheless a folly, the love you now feel for me. . . ."

He stopped abruptly, and returned to his daydreams. He faced, as he had earlier, the thought that had so shocked Mathilde: "In fifteen years, Madame de Rênal will adore my son, and you will have forgotten him."

CHAPTER FORTY

TRANQUILLITY

It's because I was foolish, then, that I'm wise today. Oh you philosopher, seeing nothing but the things of this moment, how shortsighted you are! Your eye was not made for tracing the subterranean labor of the passions.

—MADAME GOETHE

Their time together was interrupted by an interrogatory, followed by a conference with the lawyer responsible for Julien's defense. These were the only truly unpleasant moments in a life without cares, filled with tender daydreams.

"It was murder, and premeditated," Julien said to the judge as well as to the lawyer. "I'm sorry, gentlemen," he added, smiling, "but this reduces your job to a very small affair."

"After all," Julien said to himself, when he had freed himself from both of them, "I have to be brave—and apparently braver than either of these two. They take as the height of all misfortune, as *the king of all terrors*, this duel that has an unfortunate ending, and I will only take it seriously when the day arrives.

"It's because I've known greater misery," Julien continued, philosophizing with himself. "I was suffering far more, on my first trip to

Strasbourg, when I thought I'd been abandoned by Mathilde. . . . And how I longed, with such passion, for that perfect intimacy which, today, leaves me so cold! . . . In fact, I am happier alone than when this wonderfully beautiful girl shares my solitude. . . ."

The defense lawyer, a man of rules and formalities, thought Julien was crazy; like the public at large, he thought it was jealousy that had made him pick up his pistols. He tried, one day, to make Julien understand that such a plea, whether true or false, would serve him very well in the trial. But the accused was instantly transformed back into a fiery and mordant creature.

"On your life, sir," cried Julien, beside himself, "be careful, never utter that abominable lie again!" The cautious lawyer was afraid, for just a moment, that he might be killed, too.

He polished his address to the court, because the decisive time was fast approaching. Besançon and the entire region talked about nothing but this celebrated case. Julien paid no attention: he had requested that things of this sort never be mentioned to him.

That day, Fouqué and Mathilde wanted to tell him about some much-discussed rumors, quite likely, according to them, to raise his hopes. Julien had stopped them at the first word.

"Let me live my imaginary life. Your petty concerns, your details of real existence, all of them more or less irritating to me, pull me away from heaven. Each of us has to die as best we can: me, I prefer to think about death exclusively in my own way. What do *other people* mean to me? My relationships to *other people* are going to be abruptly cut off. Please, don't talk to me anymore about such people. It's more than enough, having to see the judge and the lawyer."

"Indeed," he said to himself, "it seems my destiny is to die dreaming. An unknown, like me, certain of being forgotten in less than two weeks, would be a real fool, wouldn't he, if he tried being dramatic. . . .

"How strange, all the same, that I never learned the art of enjoying life until I could see its end closing in on me."

He spent these final days walking on the narrow terrace, at the very top of the tower, smoking some first-rate cigars Mathilde had brought for him, by courier, from Holland; more than likely his appearance was looked for and watched, every day, through all the telescopes in town. His thoughts were at Vergy. He never mentioned Madame de Rênal to Fouqué, but two or three times his friend told him she was recovering quickly, and the words resounded in his heart.

While Julien lived almost completely in his inner world, Mathilde, deeply concerned with reality (as an aristocratic heart ought to be), had brought the correspondence between Madame de Fervaques and Father de Frilair to such a point of direct intimacy that the great words *diocese* and *bishopric* had already been pronounced.

Madame de Fervaques's elderly uncle, responsible for the assignment of Church preferments, had added, in a footnote to a letter he wrote her, "That poor Sorel is simply a fool; I hope he can be returned to us."

Seeing these words, Father de Frilair was incredibly excited. He had no doubts about saving Julien.

"Without that Jacobin law, requiring an absolutely endless list of possible jurors, with no other purpose, actually, but to strip away all the influence of well-born people," he told Mathilde, the evening before lots were drawn for the thirty-six jurors, "I could have already told you the *verdict*. I certainly arranged Father N————'s acquittal. . . ."

The next day he was delighted to find, among the names pulled from the lottery box, five Besançon members of the Congregation of the Holy Virgin, and among those from outside the city, Messieurs de Valenod, de Moirod, and De Cholin. —"I can speak for these eight jurors," he told Mathilde. "The first five are no more than *machines*. Valenod is my agent, Moirod owes me everything, and De Cholin is an idiot and afraid of everyone." Newspapers spread the jurors' names all over the district, and Madame de Rênal, to her husband's inexpressible terror, decided to go to Besançon. Her husband was barely able to convince her that, if she went, she should at least not leave her bed, to save herself the unpleasantness of being called as a witness. "You don't understand my situation," said the former mayor of Verrières. "I have now *defected* to the liberals. Certainly, that dissolute rascal, de Valenod, and the vicar-general, won't have much trouble getting the prosecutor and the judges to make things unpleasant for me."

It was not hard for Madame de Rênal to agree to her husband's request. "If I appear in court," she told herself, "it would look as if I were seeking revenge."

But in spite of all the promises she'd made, to her confessor and to her husband, about being cautious and sensible, she had barely reached Besançon when she wrote, in her own hand, to each of the thirty-six jurors:

I will not appear at the trial, sir, because my presence might prejudice Monsieur Sorel's case. There is only one thing in the world I passionately desire, which is that he be saved. Please be in no doubt: the frightful idea that, because of me, an innocent man has been consigned to death, would poison the rest of my life and, without any doubt, would shorten it. How could you condemn him to death, while I live on? No, surely society has no right to strip away life, and above all the life of someone like Julien Sorel. Everyone in Verrières has known some of his wilder moments. This poor young man has many powerful enemies, but even among his enemies (and how many of them there are!) is there anyone who doubts his wonderful gifts and his profound learning? This is not an ordinary citizen, sir, the man on whom you will be passing judgment. For nearly eighteen months we have all known him to be pious, wise, hardworking. Yet two or three times a year, he was overtaken by fits of melancholy that approached aberration. The whole town of Verrières, all our neighbors at Vergy, where we spend our summers, our whole family, and the deputy governor of the district himself, will affirm his exemplary piety: he knows the Holy Bible by heart. Would anyone lacking in piety have worked so hard, over the years, to memorize the holy book? My sons will have the honor of bringing you this letter: they are children. Take the trouble to question them, sir: they will give you whatever details, about this poor young man, that might yet be needed to convince you of how barbarous it would be to convict him. Far from revenging me, you would be killing me. What can his enemies say to contradict me? There is not much danger in the wound, caused by one of those wild moments that even my children noticed in their tutor: after less than two months I have been able to take the mail coach from Verrières to Besançon. Should I learn, sir, that you hesitate in any way whatever to release someone so minimally guilty from the law's barbarity, I will rise from my bed, where I remain only because my husband has so ordered me, and I will come and throw myself at your feet.

Determine, sir, that premeditation is not a fixed and unwavering affair, and you will not have the blood of an innocent man on your conscience, etc., etc.

CHAPTER FORTY-ONE

THE TRIAL

The whole region will long remember this celebrated case. Concern for the accused heightened into agitation, because his crime, though astonishing, was not horrible. And even had it been, the young man was so handsome! His immense good fortune, brought to an end so soon, swelled people's pity. Will he be found guilty, women asked the men they knew? And they grew pale as they waited for the answer.

—SAINTE-BEUVE

The day finally came, the day so dreaded by Madame de Rênal and Mathilde.

The town's strange appearance heightened their terror; even Fouqué's steady soul was troubled. The whole province had come hurrying to Besançon, to see this romantic case tried.

For several days, all the inns were filled to the brim. The presiding judge had to deal with a storm of ticket requests; every lady in town wanted to be there; portraits of Julien were being sold in the streets, etc., etc.

Mathilde had been holding in reserve, for exactly this moment, a letter written in its entirety in the hand of the Bishop of ————. This prelate, administrator of the Church throughout France, and creator of bishops, took the trouble to ask for Julien's acquittal. The night before the trial, Mathilde brought this letter to the all-powerful vicar-general.

When the interview had ended, and she was leaving in tears: "I will vouch for the jury's verdict," said Father de Frilair, finally shedding his diplomatic reserve, and himself almost moved. "Among the dozen persons charged with determining if the crime, alleged to have been committed by the man you have been assisting, has been proven, and above all whether there was premeditation, there are six who are dedicated to my good fortune, and I have informed them that it is up to them whether or not I become a bishop. Baron de Valenod, whom I made mayor of Verrières, has complete control of his two subordinates, Messieurs de Moirod and de Cholin. Admittedly, fate has given us two jurors, in this matter, whose intentions are likely to be exceedingly poor. On the other hand, although they are ultraliberals, on high occasions they are faithful to my orders, and I have asked them to vote with Monsieur de Valenod. I have been informed that a sixth juror, an immensely wealthy manufacturer, and a long-winded liberal, is secretly angling for a Ministry of War contract, and surely he would not want to annoy me. I have told him that Monsieur de Valenod has my final orders."

"And just who is this Monsieur de Valenod?" Mathilde asked, concerned.

"If you were acquainted with him, you could not doubt our success. He possesses a bold tongue, he is rude, coarse—in short, ideal for leading fools by the nose. He was plucked out of misery, in 1814, and I intend to make him governor of the district. He is quite capable of striking the other jurors, if they refuse to vote as he wishes."

Mathilde was somewhat reassured.

She was to have another discussion that evening. In order not to prolong an unpleasant scene, the final result of which was, in his eyes, completely certain, Julien had resolved not to take the witness stand.

"My lawyer will speak: that is surely sufficient," he said to Mathilde. "I have no desire to be exposed to all my enemies, as a spectacle, for any longer than necessary. These provincials have been stunned by my rapid rise, which I owe to you, and, believe me, there isn't one of them who doesn't want me convicted, though they'll all weep like idiots as I'm taken to my death."

"They want to see you humiliated: that's very true," Mathilde replied, "but I hardly think they're savages. My presence in Besançon, and the sight of my sorrow, has awakened interest in all the women. Your handsome face will do the rest. If you say anything, when you appear before the judges, the whole audience will be on your side, etc., etc."

The next day, at nine in the morning, when Julien came down from the tower, on his way to the great hall of the Palace of Justice, the gendarmes almost could not clear away an immense crowd crammed into the courtyard. Julien had slept well; he was very calm, and felt nothing but philosophic compassion for this envious mob that, without the slightest cruelty, would be applauding his death sentence. He was intensely startled, having been detained more than a quarter of an hour, surrounded by the crowd, finding himself forced to admit that his presence stirred the public to affectionate pity. He did not hear a single unpleasant word. "These provincials are not as nasty as I believed," he said to himself.

Entering the courtroom, he was struck by the elegant architecture. It was true Gothic, with a host of lovely little columns of carved stone, fashioned with the greatest of care. He felt as if he were in England.

But soon his attention was captured by twelve or fifteen pretty women who, seated directly across from the prisoner's bench, filled the three galleries over the judges and jurors. Looking once more at the audience, he saw that the circular gallery all around the hall was full of women. Most were young and seemed to him very pretty; their eyes shone and were filled with concern. In the rest of the auditorium, the crowd was enormous: those outside were beating on the doors, and the guards could not keep them quiet.

As all the eyes that had been looking for Julien saw him there, and observed him ascend to the slightly elevated spot designated for the accused, he was greeted by a murmur both surprised and tender.

That day, it might have been said he was not yet twenty. His clothing was very simple, but perfectly graceful; his hair and his face were charming: Mathilde had herself presided over his grooming. He was extremely pale. He had hardly taken his seat when he heard, from all sides: "My Lord! How young he is! . . . He's nothing but a child. . . . He's even better-looking than his picture."

"Defendant," said the policeman sitting to Julien's right, "do you see those six ladies, sitting in the gallery over there?" The policeman pointed out a small gallery, protruding into the hall just above the jurors. "That's the governor's wife," the policeman went on, "next to Marquise de M———, the one who thinks so well of you; I heard her speaking to the chief judge. And next to her is Madame Derville. . . ."

"Madame Derville!" Julien exclaimed, blushing fiercely. "When she leaves here," he thought, "she'll go and write to Madame de Rênal." He did not know that Madame de Rênal had come to Besançon.

The witnesses were thoroughly examined. From the very first words of the prosecutor's statement, two of the ladies in the small gallery, directly facing Julien, dissolved in tears. "Madame Derville is not as moved as they are," thought Julien. But he noted that her face had turned quite red.

The prosecutor heaped up pathos, in bad French, about the barbarity of the crime. Julien observed that the ladies sitting near Madame Derville looked very disapproving. Several jurors, apparently people known to these women, spoke to them, and they seemed to be reassured. "That cannot help but be a good omen," Julien thought.

To that point, he felt himself overwhelmingly, and unmitigatedly, contemptuous of everyone on the prosecution side. The platitudinous eloquence of the prosecutor added to his disgust. But bit by bit Julien's tepid soul quickened, in the face of the signs of interest obviously directed at him.

He was pleased by his lawyer's firm bearing. "No fancy phrases," Julien directed, as the lawyer prepared to speak.

"All this empty eloquence, stolen from Bossuet and pointed at you, has in fact helped you," the lawyer told Julien as he rose. In fact, Julien's lawyer had not been speaking for five minutes when all the women's handkerchiefs were out. Encouraged, the lawyer made some very emphatic remarks to the jurors. Julien shivered, feeling himself at the point of tears. "Good God! What will my enemies be saying?"

He was prepared to yield to the tenderness creeping up on him when, luckily for him, he caught an overbearing glance from Baron de Valenod.

"This pig's eyes are blazing," he said to himself. "How victorious his vulgar soul must feel! Even if my crime had produced nothing but this, I'd have to curse it. Lord knows what he'll tell Madame de Rênal about me!"

This idea erased everything else from his mind. But not too long afterward, Julien was brought back to himself, hearing the sounds of public approval. His lawyer had just ended his speech. Julien reminded himself that it was proper to shake the lawyer's hand. The time had gone by very quickly.

Refreshments were brought to the lawyer and to his client. Only then was Julien struck by something: not a single woman had gotten up and left, in order to have dinner.

"Ah, I'm dying of hunger," said the lawyer. "And you?"

"Exactly the same," Julien replied.

"See? The governor's wife has just had her dinner delivered," said the lawyer, gesturing to the small gallery. "Have courage, everything went well."

The trial resumed.

As the presiding judge presented his summation, midnight sounded. The judge was forced to interrupt himself: in the midst of a silence born of universal anxiety, the tolling of the clock filled the hall.

"This is how my last day on earth begins," thought Julien. And soon he felt himself burning with the idea of duty. He had controlled his emotions, to that point, and his resolve to remain silent had been firm. But when the presiding judge asked him if he had anything to say, he rose. He saw, right opposite him, Madame Derville's eyes; in the light of the many lamps, they seemed unusually brilliant. "Is she by any chance crying?" he wondered.

"Gentlemen of the Jury:

"My loathing for being disdained, which I thought I could control till the moment of death, now obliges me to speak. Gentlemen, I do not have the honor of belonging to your class. What you see in me is a peasant, in revolt against the barrenness of his fate.

"I ask no mercy of you," Julien continued, his voice growing steadier. "I have absolutely no illusions: what awaits me is death, and it will be a just verdict. I have tried to kill a woman eminently worthy of respect, and of homage. Madame de Rênal was like a mother to me. My crime is atrocious—and it was *premeditated*. I thoroughly deserve death, gentlemen of the jury. But even were I less guilty, what I see, here, is men who, not stopping to consider whatever pity my youth may merit, wish to punish—in me—and to discourage forever all young people born into an inferior class, and in one way or another oppressed by poverty, who wish for themselves the happiness of a good education, young people who might have the audacity to mingle among those who are labeled, by the arrogance of the rich, 'society.'

"There is my crime, gentlemen, and it will be punished even more severely if, in truth, I am not judged by my peers. I do not see, on these jury benches, a single wealthy peasant, but only the angry and indignant bourgeoisie."

For twenty minutes, Julien spoke like this, saying everything that had been in his heart. The prosecutor, who longed for aristocratic favor, was bouncing on his bench. But in spite of the somewhat abstract turn of phrase Julien employed, all the women melted in tears. Before he finished, Julien came back to the issue of premeditation, and to his repentance, and to the respect, the adoration—filial and limitless—that he felt for Madame de Rênal. Madame Derville gave a cry and fainted away.

One o'clock was sounding as the jurors retired to their room. Not a single woman had left her place; numbers of men had tears in their eyes. Conversation was, at first, very lively, but gradually, as they waited for the jury's decision, universal weariness began to quiet the audience. It was a solemn moment; the lamps were not burning as brightly as before. Julien, very weary indeed, heard people discussing, near him, whether the jury's delay was a good or a bad omen. He saw with pleasure that everyone wished him well. The jury did not return, and still not a single woman left.

Two o'clock had just sounded, and much stirring about was heard. The little door to the jury room swung open. Baron de Valenod came forward, walking gravely, theatrically; the other jurors followed him. He coughed, then announced, on his soul and conscience, the jury's unanimous decision that Julien Sorel was guilty of murder, and murder with premeditation. This verdict carried with it the death sentence, which was pronounced a moment later. Julien looked at his watch, and was reminded of Count de Lavalette, who had escaped the guillotine. It was a quarter after two. "Today is Friday," he thought.

"Yes, but it's a happy day for that Valenod, who just sentenced me to death. . . . I am far too closely watched; Mathilde can't possibly save me, as de Lavalette's wife saved him. Accordingly, in three days, at this same time, I will know what to think about the *great perhaps*."

At that moment, he heard a cry and was recalled to the things of this world. All the women around him were crying: he saw every face turned toward a small gallery, built into the highest part of a Gothic column. He learned, later, that Mathilde had been hidden there. There being no further cry, everyone turned to look at Julien again: policemen were leading him through the crowd.

"Let's give that scoundrel de Valenod nothing he can laugh about," Julien thought. "With what a glib, contrite face he announced his verdict, and the death penalty! And the chief judge, though he's been on the bench I don't know how many years, had tears in his eyes as he said the words. How happy Valenod was, taking revenge for our old rivalry over Madame de Rênal! And now I'll never see her again! It's over. . . . A last farewell is impossible, I know it. . . . But how good it would have been to tell her how horrified I am, for what I did!

"And these words only: I've been rightly condemned."

Chapter Forty-Two

Returned to prison, Julien was put into a cell meant especially for those sentenced to death. Ordinarily, he took in every small detail of his surroundings, but was not aware he'd not come back to his tower. He was imagining what he'd say to Madame de Rênal, if at the last moment he was fortunate enough to see her. He thought she'd cut him off, and wanted his first words to fully express repentance. Having done what he'd done, how could he persuade her he loved her and her only? "And, really, it was ambition that made me want to kill her, or else it was love for Mathilde."

Getting into bed, he realized the sheets were made of coarse cloth. His eyes were opened. "Ah, I'm in solitary confinement," he told himself, "having been sentenced to death. That's quite right. . . .

"Count Altamira told me that Danton, the night before he was to die, said in his rough voice: 'How odd: the verb "to guillotine" can't be conjugated in all the tenses. You can say "I will be guillotined, you will be guillotined," but you can't say "I have been guillotined." '

"But why not?" Julien responded, "if there is another life? . . . Oh, if what I find is the Christian God, I'm ruined. He's a despot, so He's obsessed with revenge: all His Bible talks about is atrocious punishments. I've never loved Him; I've never even wanted to believe anyone honestly loved Him. He's utterly devoid of pity (and here Julien remembered several passages from the Bible). He'll punish me with abominations.... But if what I find is Fénelon's God! He might tell me: 'Much will be forgiven thee, since thou hast loved much....'

"Have I loved much? Ah, yes, I loved Madame de Rênal, but I behaved atrociously. There, as I always did, I abandoned simple, modest worthiness in favor of what was brilliant....

"And yet, what a future!... A cavalry colonel, if we had a war—an embassy secretary, in peacetime, and then an ambassador... because I'd have quickly learned all about diplomacy... and if I were an absolute idiot, what rival would the Marquis de La Mole's son-in-law need to be afraid of? All my stupidities would have been forgiven, or more likely thought worthy. A man of high repute, enjoying high life in Vienna or London....

"Not exactly, sir: you'll be guillotined in three days."

Julien laughed heartily at his own mordant wit. "Really, we all have two personalities," he thought. "What devil thought up that nasty joke?

"All right! Yes, my friend, guillotined in three days," he replied to whoever or whatever had interrupted him. "Monsieur de Cholin will rent a window, for watching the show; he'll go halves with Father Maslon. And then, to pay themselves back, which one of these two worthies will rob the other?"

Suddenly, he thought of these lines from Rotrou's play, *Venceslas:*

LADISLAS: My soul is prepared and ready.
THE KING, LADISLAS'S FATHER: So is the scaffold. Bring it your head.

"A fine reply!" he thought, and went to sleep. Someone woke him, the next morning, gripping him hard.

It was Mathilde. "Good: she didn't understand me." That realization restored his calm coolness. Mathilde looked as if she'd been sick for six months: indeed, she was not recognizable.

"That vile de Frilair betrayed me," she told him, wringing her hands. Anger kept her from crying.

"Wasn't I wonderful, yesterday, when I made my speech?" Julien replied. "For the first time in my life, I was improvising! Of course, it may well be the last time, too."

Julien was playing on Mathilde's character with all the calm skill of a trained pianist seated at a keyboard. . . . "I don't have the advantage of illustrious birth: true. But," he went on, "Mathilde's lofty soul has raised her lover to her level. Do you think Boniface de La Mole would have done better, facing these judges?"

That day, Mathilde was unaffectedly tender, like some poor girl who lived high on the fifth story, but she could not get him to speak more straightforwardly. He did not realize it, but he was paying her back for the torments she had often inflicted.

"We have no idea where the Nile begins," he said to himself. "No human eye has ever been allowed to see the king of rivers as a simple little brook; so, too, no human eye will see Julien weak, first of all because he isn't. But my heart is easily moved: perfectly ordinary words, if said truly, can affect my voice and even make my tears fall. How many times have dried-out hearts scorned me for this defect! They think I'm begging for mercy—and I can't endure that.

"It's said Danton was moved by thoughts of his wife, even at the foot of the scaffold, but Danton had given strength to a nation of conceited puppies, and kept the enemy out of Paris. I'm the only one who knows what I might have been able to do. . . . For everyone else, I'm pretty much a *perhaps*.

"If Madame de Rênal were here in my cell, instead of Mathilde, could I have answered for what I've done? The intensity of both my despair and my repentance would be seen by the Valenods, and all the Franche-Comté patricians, as vulgar fear of death. They're so proud, these feeble-hearted men, because their wealth sets them above temptation! 'See what it's like,' Messieurs de Moirod and de Cholin would say—the men who have just condemned me to death—'to be born a carpenter's son! You can make yourself learned, and skillful—but ah, the spirit! . . . That cannot be learned.' Not even by this wretched Mathilde, who's crying, right now," he said to himself, looking at her reddened eyes . . . and then he put his arms around her. Seeing real sorrow made him forget his philosophizing. . . . "Perhaps she's been crying all night," he said to himself. "But, some day, how ashamed she'll be, remembering this! She'll see herself, in her early youth, having been led astray by the base ideas of a plebeian. . . . De Croisenois is weak enough to marry her and, damn it, he'll do very well. She'll give him a role to play:

> "By the rights a steady spirit enjoys, all filled with high
> Ideals, against the coarser spirit of vulgar humans.

"Now that's amusing: since I knew I had to die, all the poetry I've ever known has been coming back to me. This indicates a failing mind. . . ."

Mathilde was repeating, her voice faint: "He's there, in the next room." He finally paid attention to what she was saying. "Her voice may be weak," he thought, "but her imperious manner is still there. She's keeping her voice down, so she can hold in her anger."

"And who's there?" he said to her, gently.

"The lawyer, so you can sign the appeal."

"I won't appeal."

"What do you mean, you won't appeal?" she said, raising her voice, her eyes blazing with anger. "And why, if you don't mind telling me?"

"Because right now I think I've got courage enough to die, without too many people laughing at my expense. And who can promise that, two months from now, after a long stay in this damp cell, I'll be just as willing? I can see meeting with priests, with my father. . . . Nothing in the world could be as disagreeable. Let me die."

This unexpected opposition roused all Mathilde's lofty pride. She hadn't been able to see the vicar-general before the cells were opened: her anger fell on Julien. She adored him but, for a full quarter of an hour, as she cursed his very nature, and swore she regretted ever having loved him, he saw once again the same haughty soul that, in other days, had covered him with such poisonous insults, in the de La Mole library.

"Heaven should have glorified your race by making you a man," he said. "But for myself," he thought, "I'd be a wretched fool, believing I could stand two months in this disgusting place, the butt of slanders and humiliations invented by the patricians,* with

---

* This is a Jacobin speaking [Stendhal's note].

my only consolation being the curses of this crazy woman. .... All right, two mornings from now I'll fight a duel with a fellow known for his calm collectedness and remarkable skill.... 'Very remarkable,' said his Mephistophelian side. 'He never misses.'

"All right, so be it, fine (Mathilde's eloquence flowed on). Damn it, no," he told himself. "I won't appeal."

Having made this decision, he fell into a reverie. . . . "The mail carrier, making his rounds, will bring the newspaper at six o'clock, as usual. At eight, after Monsieur de Rênal has read it, Elisa will go up, on tiptoes, and put it on her bed. Later, she'll wake up: suddenly, as she reads, she'll be upset, her pretty hand will tremble; she'll read as far as: *At five minutes after ten, he ceased to exist.*'

"She'll shed hot tears, I know she will. Never mind that I tried to kill her: everything will be forgotten. And she who I wanted to deprive of her life will be the only one honestly crying over my death.

"Ah, what an antithesis!" he thought—and for the rest of a long quarter of an hour, as Mathilde went on with her scene, all he thought about was Madame de Rênal. In spite of himself, and even though he often replied to what Mathilde was saying to him, he could not pull his soul away from the memory of her bedroom, in Verrières. He saw the Besançon *Gazette* lying on the orange taffeta quilt. He saw that whitest of white hands clutching it, in a convulsive movement. He saw Madame de Rênal weeping. . . . He followed the path of each of her tears, down that charming face. . . .

Unable to get anything out of Julien, Mademoiselle de La Mole had the lawyer brought in. Luckily he had been a captain in the army, during the Italian campaign of 1796, where he had been the illustrious Jacques Manuel's comrade. Good form required him to oppose the condemned man's decision. Wishing to treat him respectfully, Julien set out all his reasons.

"On my faith, it's possible to think that way," Monsieur Félix Vaneau—that being the lawyer's name—finally said. "But you have three full days to file an appeal, and it's my duty to return on each of those days. Then, if a volcano erupted under the prison, you'd be saved. You could die of illness," he said, watching Julien.

Julien shook his hand. "Let me thank you. You're a thoroughly decent man. I'll think about it."

And when Mathilde at last left, together with the lawyer, he felt a good deal friendlier to him than to her.

CHAPTER FORTY-THREE

An hour later, as he was sleeping deeply, he was awakened by tears falling on his hand. "Ah! It's Mathilde again," he thought, only half awake. "She's come, faithful to her theory, attacking my decision with tenderness." Bored by the prospect of yet another scene of the pathetic variety, he did not open his eyes. La Fontaine's lines about Belphégor fleeing from his wife came into his mind.

He heard an odd sigh, and opened his eyes. It was Madame de Rênal.

"Ah! I'm seeing you before I die. Is this an illusion?" he cried, throwing himself at her feet.

"But excuse me, madame. To you, I'm only a murderer," he said quickly, getting control of himself.

"Sir, I come to beg that you appeal. I know you do not wish to—" Her sobs choked her; she could not speak.

"Can you forgive me?"

"If you want me to forgive you," she said, rising and throwing herself into his arms, "appeal the death sentence—at once."

Julien covered her with kisses.

"Will you come and see me every day, for the next two months?"

"I swear it. Every day, unless my husband forbids it."

"I'll sign!" Julien cried. "Really? You forgive me? Is it possible!"

He held her tightly; he was wild with joy. She gave a faint cry.

"It's nothing," she said. "You hurt me."

"Your shoulder!" exclaimed Julien, bursting into tears. He stepped back a bit, covering her hand with burning kisses. "Who could have told me all this, the last time I saw you, in your room, in Verrières?"

"Who could have told me, then, I'd write Monsieur de La Mole that scandalous letter?"

"Believe me, I've always loved you, I've never loved anyone else."

"Is that really true?" cried Madame de Rênal, equally overjoyed.

She leaned against Julien, who was on his knees, and for a long time they wept in silence.

Julien had never known anything like it, never in all his life.

Much later, when they could speak:

"And that young Madame Michelet," said Madame de Rênal. "Or, rather, Mademoiselle de La Mole, because I'm beginning to believe this strange story."

"It's only true on the surface," Julien replied. "She's my wife, but she's not my beloved. . . ."

And interrupting each other, a hundred times over, they each managed, though with difficulty, to tell the other what had not been known. The letter sent to Monsieur de La Mole had been composed by the young priest, now her confessor, and she had copied it out. — "The horror that religion has made me commit!" she told him. "But, still, I toned down the most ghastly parts of that letter. . . ."

Julien's ecstasy, and his happiness, proved to her how completely she had been forgiven. He had never been so wildly in love.

"Still, I consider myself pious," Madame de Rênal told him, as they were talking. "I believe most sincerely in God, and I believe, just as fervently, that the sin I'm committing is frightful—and the very moment I see you, even after you've twice fired a pistol at me—" And at this point, in spite of her, Julien covered her with kisses.

"Let me go," she went on. "I need to argue with you, before I forget. . . . As soon as I see you, my whole sense of duty disappears, all I am is my love for you—though the word *love* is much too feeble. What I feel for you is what I ought to feel only for God: a mixture of respect, and love, and obedience. . . . But, really, I don't know what you make me feel. If you told me to attack the jailer with a knife, the crime would have been done before I even knew I was doing it. Explain that to me, very clearly, before I leave here: I want to see right into my heart, since in another two months we'll be separated. . . . And speaking of which, do we really need to be separated?"

"I take back my promise," cried Julien, rising. "I will not appeal the death sentence if you try by any means to end your life—poison, a knife, gas, a pistol—or if you seek in any other way to stop yourself from living."

Madame de Rênal's face suddenly changed. The most vivid tenderness gave way to a profound reverie.

"And if we were to die right now?" she finally said.

"Who knows what we'll find, in that other life?" Julien answered. "Perhaps suffering, perhaps nothing at all. Can't we spend two months together, delightfully? Two months: that's a great many days. I'll never have been so happy!"

"You'll never have been so happy?"

"Never," Julien repeated ecstatically. "And I'm speaking to you as I speak to myself. God save me from exaggeration."

"When you speak like that, I feel myself compelled to obey you," she said, smiling timidly and sadly.

"Very well! Do you swear, on the love you feel for me, not to attempt your life in any way, direct or indirect. . . . Imagine," he added, "that you need to live for my son's sake. For Mathilde will abandon him to the servants as soon as she's the Marquise de Croisenois."

"I swear," she said calmly. "But I plan to take with me your appeal, written in your hand, and signed. I will bring it to the prosecutor myself."

"Be careful. You'll compromise yourself."

"Having taken the step of coming to see you in prison, I'll forever be, for Besançon and all Franche-Comté, the heroine of endless anecdotes," she said, seeming deeply sorrowful. "The boundaries of strict modesty have been crossed. . . . I am a woman without honor and, truly, it has been for you. . . ."

Her voice was so sad that Julien embraced her with a happiness utterly new to him. This was not love's drunkenness, but extraordinary gratitude. He had just seen, for the first time, the full extent of the sacrifice she'd made for him.

Some charitable soul, without a doubt, informed Monsieur de Rênal of the long visits his wife was making to Julien's prison, because after three days he sent his carriage, along with an express order that she return at once to Verrières.

That cruel separation began a cruel day for Julien. Two or three hours later, he learned that a certain scheming priest (who had not been able to wheedle himself into the Jesuit order in Besançon) had, that morning, set himself in the street outside the prison gates. It was raining heavily, and he stayed there, intending to play a martyr's role. Julien was not a bit in the mood: this stupidity profoundly troubled him.

He had already, that morning, refused to see this priest. But the man had gotten it into his head that he would hear Julien's confession and thus give himself a reputation among the young women of Besançon, especially for the secrets he could then pretend to have been told.

He declared, loudly, that he would spend day and night at the prison gates. "God has sent me to move the heart of this new apostate. . . ." And the common people, always curious about any dramatic spectacle, began to gather around him.

"Yes, brethren," he told them, "I will spend the day here, and the night, every day the same, and every night the same. The Holy Spirit has called to me. I have a mission from on high. I am the one who must save young Sorel's soul. Join me in my prayers, etc., etc."

Julien had a horror of scandal, and of everything that might draw attention to him. He thought about seizing this moment to escape, incognito, but he still hoped to see Madame de Rênal again, and he was frantically in love.

The prison gate opened onto one of the town's busiest streets. The very thought of this mud-spattered priest, creating crowds and scandal, was torturing his soul. "And surely, he keeps repeating my name!" It was more painful than death.

He called two or three times, an hour apart, to a guard who was devoted to him, sending him to see if the priest was still out there.

"Sir, he's on his knees in the mud," the guard told him, each time. "He prays in a loud voice, and says prayers for your soul. . . ." "The bare-faced rascal!" thought Julien. And just then, in fact, he heard a dull droning: it was the people calling out the litany's responses. To add to his annoyance, he saw the guards themselves moving their lips, as they repeated the Latin words. "People are starting to say," they told him, "you must have a really hard heart, to refuse the help of this saintly man."

"O my country! How barbarous you still are!" cried Julien, wildly angry. And he continued to argue aloud, without a thought to the guards' presence:

"This man wants an article in the papers, and this is sure to get it for him.

"Ah, accursed provincials! In Paris, I'd never be submitted to such annoyances! There, they know more about charlatans.

"Bring in this holy priest," he finally said to the guards, sweat pouring down his forehead. The guards made the sign of the cross and hurried out, all of them joyful.

The saintly priest turned out to be horribly ugly; he was even dirtier. The cold rain that had been falling added to the darkness and the humidity in Julien's cell. The priest tried to embrace him, and set himself to speaking tenderly. The lowest form of hypocrisy was only too obvious: Julien had never been so angry in his life.

A quarter of an hour after the priest came in, Julien suddenly felt himself turn into a coward. For the first time, death seemed to him horrible. He thought of the state of putrefaction his body would be in, two days after his execution, etc., etc.

He would either betray himself, by some sign of weakness, or he'd throw himself on the priest and strangle him with his chain. Then, suddenly, he conceived the idea of asking this holy man to go and say a mass for him, a good forty-franc mass, that very same day.

Since it was already almost noon, the priest took his forty francs and hurried away.

CHAPTER FORTY-FOUR

As soon as he had gone, Julien wept for a long time, and it was death that made him weep. He gradually realized that, if Madame de Rênal had been in Besançon, he would have admitted his weakness to her. . . .

Just when he was most regretting this adored woman's absence, he heard Mathilde coming.

"The worst of all prison's miseries," he thought, "is not being able to close the door." Everything Mathilde said to him was irritating.

She told him that, on the day of the trial, since Monsieur de

Valenod already had, in his pocket, his nomination as governor, he had dared to scoff at the vicar-general and give himself the pleasure of passing a death sentence on Julien.

" 'What could have been in your friend's mind,' Father de Frilair was just saying to me, 'setting out to rouse and attack the petty vanity of that *aristocratic bourgeois*! Why talk about *class*? He showed them what they had to do, in their own political interest: these simpletons hadn't ever thought of that; they were ready to weep for him. Raising the idea of class masked their eyes to the horror of passing a death sentence. It must be admitted that Monsieur Sorel is very much a novice in these matters. If we can't save him, now, by an act of pardon, his death will be a sort of *suicide*. . . .' "

Mathilde was careful not to tell Julien something she no longer doubted, namely, that Father de Frilair, seeing Julien lost, believed it would be helpful to his ambitions if he sought to replace him in her affections.

Virtually beside himself with impotent anger and irritation: "Go hear a mass for me," he told her, "and let me have a little peace." Mathilde, already very jealous about Madame de Rênal's visits, having just heard of her rival's departure, understood Julien's sullen mood and melted into tears.

Her sorrow was real. Julien saw that, and was only more irritated by it. He had a desperate need for solitude, but how obtain it?

Finally, having tried to soften him by every argument she could muster, Mathilde left him alone. But at almost that same moment, Fouqué appeared.

"I really need to be alone," Julien told his faithful friend. . . . And seeing how his friend hesitated: "I'm composing a memorandum, to advance my appeal for a pardon . . . besides . . . do me a favor: don't ever talk to me about death. If I need some special help, that day, let me ask, first."

When Julien finally had his solitude, he found he was even more overwhelmed and cowardly than before. Whatever strength there had been in his weakened soul had been used up, trying to hide his state of mind from both Mademoiselle de La Mole and from Fouqué.

Toward evening, he had an idea that consoled him:

"Supposing, this morning, just when death seemed so awful, I'd been warned to ready myself for execution: *the public's eyes would have spurred me to glory.* My walk might have been rather heavy, like some timid fop going into a drawing room. Some clear-sighted people, if there are any among these provincials, might have guessed my weakness . . . but nobody *would have seen it.*"

And he felt himself freed of some part of misery. "Right now I'm a coward," he was repeating to himself, chanting the words, "but nobody will know that."

The next day, there was something almost more unpleasant waiting for him. His father had long since said he would be making a visit, and that day, before Julien woke up, the old white-haired carpenter appeared in his cell.

Julien felt weak; he was expecting reproaches of the nastiest sort. To finish off the pain he was experiencing, that very morning he had been feeling the most intense remorse for not loving his father.

"Pure chance put us near each other on this earth," he was saying to himself, as the guards did a bit of tidying up, in the cell, "and we've done each other just about all the harm we could. Here he comes, at the moment of my death, to deal me the final blow."

The old man's reproaches began just as soon as there was no one else to hear him.

Julien could not hold back his tears. "What shameful weakness!" he said to himself, furious. "He'll go everywhere, exaggerating my failed courage. What a triumph for Valenod and all the dull hypocrites who run Verrières! They're truly powerful, in France: they combine in themselves every social advantage. Till now I could at least tell myself: they take in all the money, it's true; all the honors are heaped on them; but me, I have nobility of heart.

"And here's a witness no one will doubt, who will certify to everyone in Verrières—and exaggerate it, too—that in the face of death I was a coward! That's what I'll have become, in this great test that they can all understand!"

Julien was close to despair. He did not know how he could send his father away. And to invent some pretense that would deceive this sharp-sighted old man was, at that moment, completely beyond his strength.

His mind ran quickly through all the possibilities.

"I've saved some money!" he suddenly cried.

These inspired words changed the old man's face, and changed Julien's status.

"How should I take care of it?" Julien went on, more calmly. The effect he'd produced took away all his feelings of inferiority.

The old carpenter was burning, longing not to let this money get away from him: he thought Julien wanted to leave something to his brothers. He talked at length and strongly. Julien felt he could scoff at him.

"All right, then! God's given me an inspiration. In my will I'll leave a thousand francs to each of my brothers, and the rest to you."

"Very good," said the old man. "I deserve all the rest. But since God has been good enough to move your heart, you have to pay your debts if you really want to die as a good Christian. There are still expenses for your food, and your education—moneys I have advanced, on your behalf, though you've never thought about it. . . ."

"And here we have fatherly love!" Julien said to himself when he was alone once more, and he said it again, and again, cut to the heart. Soon the jailer appeared.

"Sir, after a visit from relatives, I always bring my guests a bottle of good wine. It's a bit expensive, six francs a bottle, but it soothes the heart."

"Bring three glasses," Julien told him with childlike haste, "and bring in the two prisoners I hear walking in the corridor."

The jailer brought in two convicts, who had fallen back into their old ways and were getting ready to return to the penitentiary. They were the gayest of rascals, and really quite remarkable for their sharpness, their courage, and their calm collectedness.

"If you give me twenty francs," one of them said to Julien, "I'll tell you, in detail, the story of my life. It's a *blast*."

"But you'll be telling me a lot of lies?" asked Julien.

"Not at all," was the answer. "My friend here, who's jealous about my twenty francs, will squeal on me if I don't tell the truth."

It was a horrible story, showing a brave heart, which knew only one passion, and that was money.

When they'd left, Julien was no longer the same man. His anger at himself had completely vanished. The ghastly sorrow, inflamed by cowardliness, that had been gripping him ever since Madame de Rênal's departure, had been turned into straightforward melancholy.

"As I've become less deceived by mere appearances," he told himself, "I've learned that Paris drawing rooms are inhabited by respectable people just like my father, or by clever rogues like these old convicts. They're right: society people will never wake up, in the morning, with this agonizing thought: 'How am I going to eat?' And they boast about how honest they are! And when they serve on juries, they fiercely condemn a man who stole a set of silver tableware because he thought he'd die of hunger.

"But whether it's a courtroom, or the question of getting or losing a ministerial appointment, my honest society folk fall into crimes strictly parallel to the ones, inspired by the necessity of eating, that these two convicts have committed. . . .

"There is no such thing as *natural law*. Such terms are nothing more than ancient twaddle, worthy of the public prosecutor who was hunting me, the other day: his grandfather's wealth came from a forfeiture in the days of Louis XIV. There are no *rights*, unless there's a law forbidding you to do this or that, or else you'll be punished. Before there's a law, there's nothing *natural* except a lion's strength, or the needs of someone who's hungry, who's cold—who, in short, *needs*. . . . No, those we honor are simply rascals who've been lucky enough not to get caught with their hands in the cookie jar. The prosecutor who society hurled at me was made wealthy by a disgraceful act. . . . I tried to kill, and I have been justly condemned, but if you put aside this one thing, the Valenod who condemned me is a hundred times more harmful to society.

"All right!" Julien added, sadly but without anger. "In spite of his greed, my father's worth more than all these fellows. He never loved me. I'm going to fill that cup to overflowing, dishonoring him with an infamous death. His fear of not having money, that exaggerated view of human wickedness which is called *greed*, made him see a gigantic source of consolation, and of security, in the sum of a few thousand francs which I can leave him. Some Friday, after dinner, he'll show his gold to all his jealous friends in Verrières. At this price, his look will tell them, which of us would not be charmed to have a son guillotined?"

This approach might be valid, but it was the sort that makes death seem desirable. And so five long days went by. He was polite and gentle to Mathilde; he could tell she was driven by the liveliest furies of jealousy. One evening, Julien thought seriously about killing himself. His soul had been worn down, ever since Madame de Rênal's departure, by the deepest misery. Nothing would have pleased him more, neither in reality nor in his imagination. Having no exercise began to affect his health, giving him the lofty-minded, wan nature of a young German student. He lost the masculine haughtiness that rejects, with a decisive oath, the less-than-decent ideas that swarm up at miserable souls.

"I used to love truth. . . . What's happened to it? . . . Hypocrisy is everywhere, or charlatanism, at least, even among the most virtuous, even among the most honored." His lips took on an expression of disgust. . . . "No: Man cannot be proud of men.

"Madame de ——— took up a collection for poor orphans; she told me such-and-such a nobleman had just given her ten gold coins. She lied. But what am I saying? Napoleon at Saint-Helena . . . Pure charlatanism. A proclamation for his son, the King of Rome.

"Good Lord! If such a man, even when misery ought, by rights, to sharply recall him to his duty, lowers himself to charlatanism, what should we expect from the rest of the species? . . .

"Where can we find truth? In religion . . . Oh yes," he added, his smile bitter with the most intense contempt. "In the mouths of Maslon, de Frilair, Castaneda . . . Perhaps in real Christianity, where priests wouldn't be paid, any more than the Apostles were? . . . But Saint Paul was paid because he loved giving orders, and public speaking, and getting people to talk about him. . . .

"Ah! If there were a true religion . . . Idiot that I am! I see a Gothic cathedral, with ancient stained-glass windows; my feeble heart pictures the priest's face, in those images. . . . My heart understands him, my soul needs him. . . . But all I find is a fop with filthy hair—aside from the pleasant amenities, a Chevalier de Beauvoisis.

"But a true priest, a Massillon, a Fénelon . . . Massillon consecrated

Dubois as a bishop. *The Memoirs of Saint-Simon* spoiled Fénélon for me. But, finally, a *real* priest . . . Then the world's sensitive hearts would have a place to come together. . . . We would not be isolated. . . . This good priest would talk to us about God. But which God? Not the one in the Bible, a cruel, petty tyrant, thirsting for vengeance . . . but Voltaire's God, just, good, infinite . . ."

He was troubled by all his memories of that Bible, which he knew by heart. . . . "Yet, if there are *three in one,* how can we believe in that great name, GOD, after the frightful abuse, acting in that name, the priests have committed?

"To live in isolation! . . . What torture! . . .

"I'm becoming crazy and unjust," Julien told himself, striking his forehead. "I am completely alone in this cell, but on this earth I have not *lived in isolation.* I had a powerful idea of *duty.* That duty, which rightly or wrongly was prescribed for me . . . It's been like a solid tree trunk, and I have leaned on it when it stormed. I staggered, I was shaken. In the end, I've never been anything more than a man. . . . But I wasn't swept away.

"The damp air in this cell is what's making me think about isolation. . . .

"And why be a hypocrite, even as I'm cursing hypocrisy? It isn't really death, nor this cell, nor its damp air—it's Madame de Rênal's absence that's crushing me. If, in Verrières, just to see her I had to live for whole weeks, hidden in the cellars, would I be complaining?

"I'm overwhelmed by my contemporaries' influence," he said haughtily and with a bitter laugh. "Speaking only to myself, and two steps from death, I'm still a hypocrite. . . . Oh you nineteenth century!

". . . A hunter in a forest fires his gun, his prey falls, he comes to get it. His boot smashes into an anthill, two feet high, and destroys the ants' home; ants are scattered far and wide, their eggs. . . . The best ant philosopher could never understand this huge black thing, immense, horrible—the hunter's boot—which suddenly broke into their dwelling, with incredible speed, and just before that happened there had been a dreadful noise, together with a shower of reddish sparks. . . .

". . . So too death, life, eternity: matters terribly simple to whoever has organs vast enough to have any conception of them. . . .

"A mayfly born at nine in the morning, during the summer's long days, and dying at five that evening: How could it comprehend the word *night?*

"Let it live another five hours, and it sees and understands what night is.

"As for me, I will die in twenty-three hours. Give me five more years of life, to be with Madame de Rênal."

And then he began to laugh like Mephistopheles. "What stupidity, trying to think my way through such huge questions.

"First of all, I'm just as much a hypocrite, all alone, as I would be were there anyone to listen to me.

"Second, I'm forgetting living and loving, though I have so very few hours left to live. . . . Alas, Madame de Rênal is not here. Maybe her husband won't let her come back to Besançon, to continue dishonoring herself.

"That's what's isolating me, not any lack of a just God, good, all-powerful, not a bit evil-minded, not at all greedy for revenge. . . .

"Ah, but if He existed . . . Alas, I'd fall at His feet. 'I deserved death,' I'd tell Him. But Almighty God, kind God, indulgent God: give me back the woman I love!"

The night was well along. After an hour or two of peaceful sleep, Fouqué arrived.

Julien felt as strong and resolved as a man who can see clearly into his soul.

CHAPTER FORTY-FIVE

"I can't do such a thing to poor Father Chas-Bernard; it would be a shabby trick to ask him," he told Fouqué. "He wouldn't eat his dinner for three days. But try to find me a Jansenist, some friend of Father Pirard, immune to plots and scheming."

Fouqué had been waiting, most impatiently, for this overture. Julien had done decently everything public opinion requires, in the provinces. Thanks to Father de Frilair, and in spite of having chosen the wrong kind of confessor, Julien had been protected, in his cell, by the Congregation of the Holy Virgin: had he behaved with more spirit, he might have been able to escape. But as the damp air of the cell worked on him, his mind seemed to shrink. He was even happier when Madame de Rênal returned.

"My primary responsibility is to you," she said, embracing him. "I've escaped from Verrières. . . ."

Julien felt no petty vanity: he told her all his weaknesses. She was kind, and she was charming.

That evening, as soon as she'd left the prison and gone back to her aunt's house, she summoned the priest who, like a hunting animal, had fastened himself onto Julien. Since all he wanted was to establish a reputation among Besançon's young society women, it was not difficult to hire him for a novena at Upper Bray, in the old abbey.

Julien's mad love was beyond anything words can express.

Employing gold, and both using and abusing her aunt's influence, Madame de Rênal got permission to see him twice a day.

Hearing this, Mathilde's jealousy rose to the point of insanity. Father de Frilair had sworn that all his influence could not so defy the rules that she might see her beloved more than once a day. Mathilde had Madame de Rênal followed, so she could learn everything she did. Father de Frilair expended every ounce of his ingenuity, which was very considerable, trying to persuade her that Julien was not worthy of her.

And in the midst of these torments, she had never loved him more; virtually every day she staged a ghastly scene for his benefit.

Julien wanted with all his strength to behave, right to the very end, as decently as possible to this young girl he had so strangely compromised. But over and over, his ungovernable love for Madame de Rênal swept him away. When he could not truly persuade Mathilde (the reasons he gave her were not good enough) that her rival's visits were entirely innocent: "Well," he told himself, "the end of the drama isn't very far off: that's the best excuse I have, if I can't think of better ones."

Mademoiselle de La Mole learned that de Croisenois had died. The exceedingly rich Monsieur de Thaler had allowed himself some unpleasant comments about Mathilde's disappearance. Monsieur de Croisenois requested that he publicly deny these statements. Monsieur de Thaler showed him certain anonymous letters he had received, full of details so skillfully juxtaposed that poor de Croisenois could not tell what was false and what was true.

Monsieur de Thaler then permitted himself some distinctly unsubtle jests. Drunk with misery and anger, de Croisenois demanded such extravagant amends that the millionaire preferred a duel. Stupidity was victorious, and one of the most lovable men in Paris was found dead, at age twenty-four.

His death had a strange and morbid effect on Julien's affable soul.

"Poor de Croisenois," he said to Mathilde, "was really very reasonable and decent to us. He was obliged to hate me when you behaved so incautiously in your mother's drawing room, and so he wanted a quarrel, since the hate that follows after contempt is usually a furious one."

Monsieur de Croisenois's death changed all of Julien's ideas about Mathilde's future. He spent several days proving to himself that, after all, she ought to accept Monsieur de Luz. "He's rather shy, but not too Jesuitical," he told her, "and he'll surely try to marry you. His ambitions are duller than poor de Croisenois's, but they're steadier, and since there's no dukedom in his family, he won't hesitate about marrying Julien Sorel's widow."

"And a widow who despises grand passions," Mathilde answered coldly, "since she's lived long enough to have seen, six months later, that her lover prefers another woman, and indeed the very woman who brought about all his misfortunes."

"You're not being fair. Madame de Rênal's visits will supply our Paris lawyer, who's trying to win me a pardon, with invaluable information. He'll be able to show the murderer being honored by his victim's attentions. That might work, and maybe, someday, you'll see me the subject of a melodrama, etc., etc."

Furious jealousy, which could not be avenged; a continuous, hopeless misery (because even assuming Julien were saved, how would she win back his heart?); the shame and sorrow of loving her unfaithful lover more than ever before—all this had plunged Mademoiselle de La Mole into a mournful silence, from which neither Father de Frilair's eager courtship, nor Fouqué's rough honesty, could help her escape.

Aside from time stolen away by Mathilde, Julien lived a life of love in which there did not need to be a future. By a strange working of this passion, now that it was at fever pitch and without the slightest pretense, Madame de Rênal almost shared his jauntiness, his gentle gaiety.

"It used to be," Julien told her, "when I was so happy, walking with you in the woods at Vergy, fiery ambition would carry my soul into imaginary places. Instead of clasping to my heart this charming arm, which was so near my lips, the future swept me away from you. I was fighting endless battles, which had to be fought so I could build a colossal fortune. . . . No, I would have died without knowing happiness, if you hadn't come to see me, here in prison."

Two things occurred to trouble this peaceful existence. Julien's confessor, even being the devout Jansenist he was, could not help being the screen for a Jesuit scheme, and, without knowing it, becoming the Jesuits' instrument.

One day he came to tell Julien that, to avoid the frightful sin of suicide, he needed to do everything he could to secure a pardon. Now, the Church having great influence with the Ministry of Justice, in Paris, there was a singularly open road: he needed to make as big a show as possible about having reformed his sinful soul. . . .

"A show!" Julien echoed. "Oh, I see: you're playing the missionary game, Father, just as the others do."

"Your youth," the Jansenist answered somberly, "the attractive face with which Providence has blessed you; even the motive for your crime, which remains inexplicable; the prodigious measures Mademoiselle de La Mole has so lavishly engaged in, on your behalf; and, finally, the astonishing friendliness your victim has shown you—all this contributes to the young women of Besançon having made you into a hero. They have forgotten everything else for you, even politics. . . .

"Your awakening will find an echo in their hearts and will make a profound impression. You can be of major importance to religion, and the trifling reasoning of the Jesuits, in similar situations, does not give me pause. Even in this special case, which has escaped their rapacity, they would still act destructively. They should not be allowed to. . . . The tears that your awakening will cause to flow will wipe out the corrosive effect of ten editions of Voltaire's impious works."

"And what will I have left," Julien responded coldly, "if I turn, contemptuously, against myself? I have been ambitious, but I have no intention of calling that blameworthy: I was simply following the conventions of my time. Now I live from day to day. But as people here see these things, I would be making myself seriously miserable, were I to surrender to such cowardice...."

The other episode, which was far more painful to Julien, stemmed from Madame de Rênal. I have no idea, reader, which of her lady friends managed to persuade this naïve and shy soul that it was her duty, now, to go to Saint-Cloud and throw herself on her knees in front of King Charles X.

She was prepared to make the sacrifice of tearing herself away from Julien, which was an immense struggle. Her distaste at making a spectacle of herself, which at any other time would have been worse than death itself, was now, in her eyes, of no consequence whatever.

"I'll go to the king; I will proclaim loudly that you are my lover. A man's life, and especially such a man as you, must prevail over all other considerations. I will say that it was jealousy which caused you to seek my life. There are many instances where young men have been saved, in such a case, either by the jury's humanity or by the king's—"

"I'll never let you in here again. I'll have the door of my cell shut against you," cried Julien, "and without any question I'll kill myself, in despair, the day after you leave, unless you swear you'll do nothing to make the two of us a public spectacle. This notion of going to Paris cannot be your own. Tell me the name of the schemer who proposed it to you....

"Let us be happy, in the few days left to this short life. Let's hide our existence; my crime is already too conspicuous. Mademoiselle de La Mole has powerful friends at court: believe me, she's doing what can humanly be done. Here in the provinces, all the rich and respected men are against me. If you go to Saint-Cloud, they'd be bitterer still, and especially the moderates who lead such easy lives. . . . Let's not give an opportunity for mocking laughter to the Maslons, the Valenods, and a thousand better men than them."

The cell's foul air had become unbearable. Fortunately, on the day they told him he was to die, the sun was making all of nature rejoice, and Julien was in a courageous mood. Walking in the open air was, for him, a delightful sensation, as walking on the firm ground is for the sailor, long at sea. "Let's go, everything's fine," he said to himself. "I have more than enough courage."

Never had that head felt more poetic than now, when it was going to be cut off. The sweetest times he had known, once, in the woods of Vergy, came crowding back into his mind, and with wonderful force.

Everything happened simply, decently, and on his part without the slightest affectation.

The night before, he had said to Fouqué:

"As far as emotions are concerned, I can't predict. This ugly, damp cell gives me feverish moments when I can't recognize myself. But fear—no. They won't see me turning pale."

He had arranged matters, in advance, for this last day. Fouqué was to leave, afterward, with Mathilde and Madame de Rênal.

"Take them in the same carriage," Julien had instructed. "Make sure the horses never stop galloping. Either they'll fall into each other's arms, or they'll show mortal hatred. In either case, the poor women will be a little distracted from their frightful sorrow."

Julien had exacted from Madame de Rênal her oath that she would live on, so she could care for Mathilde's son.

"Who knows? Maybe we still feel things, after our death," he'd said to Fouqué one day. "I'd like to rest, considering that 'rest' is the right word, in that little cave up on the tall mountain, overlooking Verrières. I spent the night there more than once, as I've told you, and I could see in the distance the richest provinces in all France. My heart was burning with ambition: that was my true passion, then ... Anyway, that cave is dear to me, and no one can argue it isn't situated where a philosopher might envy me. . . . All right! These fine Besançon fanatics, these Congregationalists of the Holy Virgin, are good at making money out of anything. If you handle it properly, they'll sell you my mortal remains. . . ."

Fouqué was successful, in this grim negotiation. He was spending the night in his room, alone with his friend's body, when to his great surprise he saw Mathilde come in. Just a few hours earlier, he had left her, fifteen miles from Besançon. She looked distraught, her eyes were wild.

"I want to see him," she said.

Fouqué did not have the courage either to speak or to rise. He pointed to a large blue cloak, lying on the floor, in which what remained of Julien was wrapped.

She dropped to her knees. The memory of Boniface de La Mole and Marguerite de Navarre surely gave her superhuman courage. Her trembling hands opened the cloak. Fouqué turned away his eyes.

He heard Mathilde walking rapidly around the room. She was lighting candles. When Fouqué had the strength to look at her, she had set on a marble table, in front of her, Julien's head, and she was kissing his forehead. . . .

Mathilde followed her lover to the tomb he had chosen for himself. There were a great many priests escorting the bier. No one knew it but, alone in her covered carriage, she carried on her knees the head of the man she had so loved.

So, when they reached the highest point of one of the highest of the Jura mountains, in the middle of the night, in the little cave, lit by an enormous number of candles, twenty priests celebrated the service for the dead. All those who lived in the little mountain villages along their route had followed them, drawn by the bizarre nature of this strange ceremony.

Mathilde was in their midst, wearing long mourning robes. At the end of the service, she had thousands of five-franc pieces scattered among the villagers.

Left alone with Fouqué, she insisted on burying her lover's head with her own hands. Fouqué was almost insane with grief.

Mathilde had this wild grotto ornamented with marble sculptures, brought at great expense from Italy.

Madame de Rênal was faithful to her promise. She did not try in any way to shorten her life, but three days after Julien, she died while hugging her children.

NOTES

TRANSLATOR'S NOTE

P. xxii, L. 8. *and notoriously unreliable:* Professor Jean-Jacques Hamm has concluded that only fifteen of the seventy-three epigraphs in *The Red and the
Black* are correctly and verifiably attributed. For the rest, it is virtually
impossible to determine precisely which are playful inventions, mistakes, or intentional misattributions by Stendhal. As a rule, citations attributed to English, Latin, and Italian writers were given in the original
languages—which Stendhal knew—those of German origin were translated into French.

PART ONE

P. xxv, LL. 1–3. *Notice . . . the great events of July:* the Revolution of July 1830,
which brought down the increasingly conservative government of
Charles X and effectively ended the Bourbon monarchy and the period
known as the Restoration. The Duke d'Orléans became King Louis-
Philippe and began what is known as the July Monarchy.
L. 5. *1827:* There is no question that Stendhal began writing *The Red and
the Black* in 1829 and completed the novel in 1830.

P. 1, EPIGRAPH. *Danton:* Georges-Jacques Danton (1759–94) was a celebrated
revolutionary orator; leader of the radical Cordeliers and then the
Jacobins; minister of justice during the first republican government

(1792–93); and member of the infamous Committee for Public Safety during the Terror. Danton was imprisoned and then guillotined when he and his onetime ally Robespierre turned on each other. There is no record of Danton ever having made this statement.

CHAPTER ONE. A SMALL TOWN

P. 3, EPIGRAPH. *Hobbes:* The epigraph was given in English, and arranged as if from a poem by Stendhal. The English philosopher Thomas Hobbes (1588–1679) wrote no poetry.

LL. 1–5. *Verrières . . . built by the Spanish:* The geography and description of Verrières suggests the town of Besançon, historic capital of the Franche-Comté region, which was a possession of the Spanish Hapsburgs until it was conquered by Louis XIV in 1678. Stendhal was born and raised in the small mountain town of Grenoble, which he despised.

L. 14. *Mulhouse:* a small Alsatian town known for its textile production.

P. 4, L. 35. *1815:* The year of Waterloo marked the permanent—so it was thought—restoration of the Bourbons to the throne.

P. 5, LL. 26–27. *Père Sorel:* literally, Father Sorel, not a religious but a folksy and familiar form of address, more respectful than *le vieux Sorel* (old man Sorel) but less than *Monsieur.*

CHAPTER TWO. A MAYOR

P. 6, EPIGRAPH: *Barnave:* Antoine Barnave (1761–93) quickly earned a reputation as the finest young orator of the National Assembly in 1789. A native of Grenoble, he had been an acquaintance of Stendhal's (Marie-Henri Beyle's) grandfather. Barnave was a moderate supporter of constitutional monarchy; he was an early victim of the Terror.

P. 7, L. 15. *monarchist . . . liberal:* "Monarchist" is given here for *ultra.* The *ultra-royalistes* were a faction that were said to be more monarchist than the monarch, and opposed the moderate constitutionalism of King Louis XVIII, younger brother of Louis XVI. They gained increasing political power with the advent of the third brother, Charles X (reigned 1824–30), whose attempts to turn back the historical clock eventually led to the July Revolution. "Liberal" is a broader term, covering everyone from constitutional monarchists to republicans.

L. 35. *An old surgeon-major:* This character is based on Dr. Gagnon, Stendhal's maternal grandfather, to whom the author was extremely close as a child. Gagnon was a surgeon, if not a soldier, and a political progressive, if not actually a Jacobin. Like Julien Sorel, Marie-Henri Beyle lost his mother at a young age, and had a difficult relationship with his lawyer father.

P. 8, L. 1. *Jacobin:* The most radical faction of the National Assembly, the Jacobin Club took its name from the former monastery that served as their headquarters. Danton and Robespierre were leading members. Throughout the early nineteenth century, "Jacobin" became an epithet for anyone suspected of political radicalism, even in Britain and the United States.

LL. 5–6. *Legion of Honor:* founded by Bonaparte in 1802 to recognize service to the nation; although maintained by the restored Bourbons, the Legion of Honor was necessarily scorned by conservatives such as Monsieur de Rênal.

L. 25. *Adolphe: Adolphe* was the title of Benjamin Constant's very popular sentimental novel of 1816, which tells the story of a young man's unhappy affair with an older woman. A suggestion of sentimentality on Madame de Rênal's part?

CHAPTER THREE. A PRIEST

P. 9, EPIGRAPH. *Fleury:* the name suggests two very different early-eighteenth-century ecclesiastics: Claude Fleury (1640–1723) was confessor to Louis XV and a Church historian, principal author of the thirty-six-volume *Histoire écclésiastique;* André-Hercule, Cardinal de Fleury (1653–1743), was a skillful politician who served as de facto prime minister for Louis XV from 1726 until his death.

P. 12, L. 13. *Buonaparté:* Royalists, even before 1815, would use the Italian pronunciation of the "usurper's" name to emphasize the Corsican-born dictator's foreignness. *Italian campaigns:* The youthful General Bonaparte made his name by driving the Austrians out of northern Italy in 1796–97. The Italian campaigns included such famous battles as Rivoli and the Lodi bridge. These campaigns concluded in 1797 with the Treaty of Campo Formio, where the young general virtually dictated terms to the Holy Roman emperor before returning to a hero's welcome in Paris.

L. 14. *"he even voted against the Empire":* Citizen First Consul Bonaparte became the Emperor Napoleon by virtue of a plebiscite in 1804. The total vote of 3,572,329 *for* to 2,569 *against* reflected intimidation, corruption, and massive abstention.

P. 13, L. 3. *"a hundred gold crowns":* for ecus, a coin worth three francs in the nineteenth century.

P. 14, L. 7. *Duke d'Orléans,* et al.: these are curious allusions for the conservative Monsieur de Rênal: In the last years of the ancien régime, the Duke d' Orléans (1747–93) and his Paris residence, the Palais-Royal, were centers of political opposition. The duke was a cousin of Louis XVI, First Prince of the Blood Royal, and was an ambitious and thoroughly unprincipled man. Hungry for power, he attempted to put himself at the head of the Revolution, abandoning his name (but not his inheritance) and calling himself Philippe Égalité. In spite of this ostentatious radicalism, he ended up being guillotined during the Terror.

L. 9. *Madame de Montesson,* morganitic second wife of Philippe Égalité's father, introduced the young duke to her niece, the Countess de Genlis (1746–1830). This intellectual and progressive thinker was briefly the duke's mistress; he later scandalized conservatives and thrilled the philosophes by making her tutor to his children, including the future king, Louis-Philippe d'Orléans. Madame de Genlis fled to England after the arrest of the Royal family, and eked out her living by writing her memoirs and also novels.

L. 10. *Royal Palace* [*Palais-Royal*]: Parisian palace to the north of the Louvre, built by Cardinal de Richelieu and later acquired by the Orleans family. In the last years of the ancien régime, under the future Philippe Égalité, the Palais-Royal was known as a hotbed of liberal politics and libertine society. With the help of Marquis Ducrest [*sic,* né *du Crest*], brother of Madame de Genlis, the duke turned the palace into a public gathering place by renting out space in the public galleries to shops and cafés. The galleries and gardens of the Palais-Royal were frequented by prostitutes and by radical orators such as Camille Desmoulins.

CHAPTER FOUR. A FATHER AND SON

P. 14, EPIGRAPH. *Machiavelli:* Niccolò Machiavelli (1469–1527) is best known for *The Prince,* his masterpiece of cynical realpolitik. However, these precise words are not found in Machiavelli's work.

L. 28. *peasant:* should be understood to refer to social rather than economic status.

P. 15, LL. 12–13. *the* fedayin *of Egypt:* the peasants of ancient Egypt.

P. 17, LL. 9–10. Memories of Napoleon on Saint-Helena: *Le Mémorial de Sainte-Hélène,* by Comte Emmanuel de Las Cases, was the author's recounting of Napoleon's life in exile and the deposed emperor's oral history of his extraordinary career. Las Cases, Napoleon's chamberlain, followed his master to Saint-Helena and lived with him until, in November 1816, the British ordered him to leave. *Le Mémorial* appeared in 1822 and 1823 and contributed greatly to the already growing Napoleonic legend.

L. 34. *half-pay military pension:* One of the politically clumsy moves of the Restoration government was to cut by 50 percent the pensions of all veterans of the Revolutionary and Napoleonic armies. Perhaps economically necessary, this move increased resentment toward the Bourbons and contributed to the popularity of Napoleon among the military and the lower classes.

CHAPTER FIVE. A NEGOTIATION

P. 18, EPIGRAPH. *Ennius:* Quintus Ennius (239–169 B.C.), a Roman poet whose work survives largely through quotations in the works of other writers, such as Cicero.

P. 19, L. 1. *"who will I be eating with?":* an important question for the time. To eat with the family was a sign of status; only servants ate in the kitchen.

LL. 26–27. *Rousseau's* Confessions: the autobiographical masterpiece of Jean-Jacques Rousseau (1712–78). Published posthumously, 1782–88, the sentimental and introspective *Confessions* became one of the inspirational texts of European romanticism.

L. 28. *Grand Army bulletins:* These weekly bulletins, first appearing in 1805, were the official record of the military exploits of the emperor and his troops. Blatantly propagandic—soldiers used the expression "to lie like the bulletin"—they were nonetheless an effective tool for Napoleon. Stendhal appreciated their crisp, journalistic prose.

P. 20, L. 1. *Monsieur de Maistre's* On the Pope: Joseph-Marie de Maistre (1753–1821) was a leading writer of the counterrevolutionary movement; his royalism was heavily influenced by his deeply mystical Catholicism. His 1819 book, *Du Pape,* was an argument in favor of papal infallibility.

P. 22, LL. 15–16. *at Lodi bridge, at Arcoli, and at Rivoli:* all victories in Bonaparte's Italian campaigns of 1796–97.

L. 23. *the Congregation of the Holy Virgin:* "La Congrégation" and similar secret organizations—on the left and the right—preoccupied the popular imagination of early-nineteenth-century France. In *The Red and the Black,* the Congregation obliquely refers to the Jesuits—who were widely resented as a secretive, power-hungry shadow government—and their allies. A royalist organization known as La Congrégation actually existed; formed in 1801, dissolved by order of Napoleon in 1814, they regrouped under the Restoration and broke up in 1830. A similar group was the

Chevaliers de la Foi (The Knights of the Faith), a group of devout royalists formed under the Empire who exercised some influence under the Restoration. Many Chevaliers were also members of the Congrégation, which contributed to the reputation of the latter for secretive political activism.

LL. 30–31. The Constitutional: First published in 1815, this newspaper was the voice of the liberal opposition throughout the Restoration.

P. 23, L. 17. *Madame de Beauharnais:* The future empress, Joséphine de Beauharnais (1763–1814), widow of a general, was a celebrated beauty in the libertine high society of the Directory when she met the young General Bonaparte. It is a matter of some dispute how much she actually loved him when they were married in 1796.

P. 24, L. 19. Louis Jenrel: This odd-sounding name is an anagram of Julien Sorel. Stendhal was very fond of anagrams, which frequently figure in the ludic threads that run through his fiction.

P. 25, L. 10. *Stanislas-Xavier:* another meaningful name for a Rênal child? Louis-Xavier-Stanislas was the full name of King Louis XVIII (born 1755, reigned 1814–15, 1815–24). The ultra Monsieur de Rênal would have chosen this name.

CHAPTER SIX. BOREDOM

P. 25, EPIGRAPH. Figaro: Mozart's *Figaro,* as every French reader knew, was based on the character from Beaumarchais's wildly popular play, *Le Mariage de Figaro.* This quote comes from the act 1 aria in which Chérubin sings of his adolescent desires. Mozart and Cimarosa (*see note for p. 341, l. 3*) were Stendhal's favorite composers.

CHAPTER SEVEN. ELECTIVE AFFINITIES

P. 33, L. 9. *Feast of Saint Louis:* August 25; the feast days of Catholic saints were very important in France. Saint Louis, the canonized King Louis IX, was especially important to the French, particularly after the execution (martyrdom, for royalists) of Louis XVI in 1793.

P. 35, L. 21. *the Jesuits:* became increasingly unpopular in France throughout the sixteenth and seventeenth centuries, and were ultimately expelled from the kingdom in 1764. Allowed to return under the Restoration, they retained their reputation as secretive, power-hungry intriguers. Napoleon in particular hated the Jesuits.

P. 38, L. 33. *the late Prince de Condé:* the princely Condé family were cousins of the Bourbons, Princes of the Blood Royal. The most famous member of the family, le Grand Condé, was a famous general and leader of the Fronde rebellions against Cardinal Mazarin during the minority of Louis XIV (*see note for p. 453, l. 3*).

LL. 35–36. *Besenval's memoirs:* The Baron de Besenval was a soldier and courtier at Versailles. He became an intimate and a defender of Marie-Antoinette. Stendhal had read his unreliable *Mémoires,* which gave a very biased view of life at the last royal court of the ancien régime.

CHAPTER EIGHT. MINOR OCCASIONS

P. 43, EPIGRAPH. *Byron,* Don Juan: Stendhal had met Lord Byron while living in Milan.

P. 47, L. 6. *Gabrielle:* The medieval romance of Gabrielle de Vergy tells the story of a virtuous young peasant girl, beloved by a virtuous young peasant boy. The Duchess of Burgundy falls in love with Gabrielle's lover and, when he rejects her, accuses him, before her husband the duke, of having assaulted her. In despair, Gabrielle commits suicide, and her distraught lover stabs himself to death over her body.

P. 48, L. 4. *Monsieur Godart:* a naturalist who published a popular illustrated study of butterflies.

CHAPTER NINE. AN EVENING IN THE COUNTRY

P. 50, EPIGRAPH. *Monsieur Guérin's . . . Dido:* Pierre-Narcisse Guérin (1774–1833), a popular and successful painter during the Empire. His *Aeneas Telling Dido of the Disasters of Troy* (1817) hangs in the Louvre. Dido was the Carthaginian queen who killed herself when deserted by Aeneas in Virgil's epic *The Aeneid. Strombeck:* a German friend of Stendhal.

P. 52, L. 36. *Charles the Bold:* Charles le Téméraire (1433–77), the last of the great Valois dukes of Burgundy, who for four generations ruled Burgundy and Flanders and rivaled the power of their cousins and putative feudal lords, the kings of France. Charles's fierce military skills proved no match for the shrewd, patient, and unprincipled statecraft of Louis XI.

P. 54, L. 34. *the Robespierres of the world:* a reference to Maximilien de Robespierre (1758–94), the fanatically anti-aristocratic Jacobin politician who controlled France through the Terror until he was himself guillotined.

CHAPTER TEN. A LARGE HEART AND A SMALL FORTUNE

P. 60, LL. 31–32. *fifty gold crowns:* or ecus, 150 francs.

CHAPTER ELEVEN. AN EVENING

P. 65, L. 20. The Legitimist: *La Quotidienne*, a conservative daily paper, virtually an organ for the conservative ultra party.

CHAPTER TWELVE. A JOURNEY

P. 65, EPIGRAPH. *Sieyès:* Emmanuel-Joseph Sieyès (1748–1836) was an important political figure during the Revolution. A priest and vicar-general of Chartres under the ancien régime, in 1789 he published a political pamphlet, *Qu'est-ce que le tiers état?* (*What Is the Third Estate?*), which was seen as a political manifesto for liberal reforms desired by the Third Estate. A shrewd and crafty politician, after serving in the legislatures of the revolutionary and Directory governments, Sieyès became one of five directors. Hoping to grab power himself, he joined forces with General Bonaparte in plotting the 1799 coup, hoping to become the *éminence grise* of the young military hero. Like all others who hoped to dominate Napoleon, he soon found himself eclipsed and out of power.

P. 70, LL. 30–31. *Bonaparte . . . greatest of things:* Born in 1769, Bonaparte at age twenty-eight was the hero of the revolutionary armies; he had not yet seized power or declared himself emperor, moves that disillusioned many early supporters, like the old surgeon-major.

CHAPTER THIRTEEN. FISHNET STOCKINGS

P. 71, EPIGRAPH. *Saint-Réal:* suggests the César Vichard, Abbé de Saint-Réal (1639–92), historian, novelist, and diplomat. He was criticized for novelizing history; one of his novels, *The Spanish Conspiracy Against Venice*, was in fact long believed to be a work of history. The statement given is not found in his writings.

CHAPTER FOURTEEN. ENGLISH SCISSORS

P. 76, EPIGRAPH. *Polidori:* John Polidori was physician and secretary to Lord Byron, whom Stendhal had met in Milan in 1816. A very similar quote is also attributed to Sainte-Beuve at the beginning of part 2 (*see note for p. 217, Epigraph*).

P. 79, L. 2. *Corneille:* With the comic playwright Molière and the great tragedian Jean Racine, Pierre Corneille (1606–84) was one of the triumvirate of great playwrights of the seventeenth century. Corneille in his tragedies was greatly concerned with notions of duty and honor, while his comedies often deal with problems of love and marriage.

CHAPTER FIFTEEN. COCK CROW

P. 79, EPIGRAPH. Blason d'Amour: A poetic form based on "the minute description of the qualities of an object" (*Oxford Companion to French Literature*).

P. 81, L. 8. *the cock woke Saint Peter:* Stendhal frequently used this biblical reference to describe a moment of awakening.

CHAPTER SEVENTEEN. THE FIRST DEPUTY

P. 87, EPIGRAPH. *Two Gentlemen of Verona:* Stendhal was a great admirer of Shakespeare; he wrote a study entitled *Racine and Shakespeare* (1825), forcefully attacking the traditional stature given to Racine and setting up Shakespeare, instead, as a model for young writers (of the third decade of the nineteenth century) to emulate.

P. 89, LL. 28–29. *Voltaire and Louis XV:* The great philosophe Voltaire (1694–1778) and the legendarily debauched King Louis XV (born 1710, reigned 1715–75) personify here the enlightenment and the excesses of eighteenth-century France.

P. 90, L. 24. *Battle of Fontenoy:* a great French victory in 1745; at Fontenoy, in Belgium, the French, commanded by the Marshal de Saxe, defeated the combined forces of the British, Dutch, and Austrians.

CHAPTER EIGHTEEN. A KING IN VERRIÈRES

P. 94, L. 27. *a heretic:* A Jansenist, used here as a sort of generic epithet, refers to the seventeenth-century Catholic sect known for their austere and strict devotion, as illustrated by Father Pirard. Similar to the Calvinists, believing like them in predestination and the need for divine grace, they were strictly Catholic in their belief in the papal hierarchy, relics, miracles, etc. The Jansenists were great enemies of the more political and indulgent Jesuits, and Stendhal plays on that historical rivalry in *The Red and the Black.*

P. 96, L. 24. *Leipzig and Montmirail:* The defeat at Leipzig (October 1813) and the victory at Montmirail (February 1814) were part of Napoleon's long and ultimately doomed efforts to preserve his throne after the disastrous campaign against Russia (1812).

P. 97, L. 4. *revolutionary vandalism:* Anticlerical feeling ran strong during the Revolution; many churches and other religious buildings were badly damaged.

P. 101, L. 11. Agde: a port on the Mediterranean, west of Marseilles. Stendhal may have been thinking of the Cardinal de Retz, who had begun his career as Bishop of Adge. Retz (1613–79) is a notorious figure in French history. His libertinism and ambition are frankly discussed in his *Mémoires,* which recount his career, especially his participation in the Fronde, the aristocratic rebellion during the minority of Louis XIV (*see note for p. 453, l. 3*).

P. 104, L. 5. *Philip the Good:* Third Valois Duke of Burgundy (1396–1467), father of Charles the Bold, had a reputation as a philanthopist and patron of the arts.

CHAPTER NINETEEN. THINKING LEADS TO SUFFERING

P. 104, EPIGRAPH. *Barnave: See note for p. 6, Epigraph.*

LL. 22–23. *Lyons . . . in '93, of wretched memory:* In 1793, a popular uprising against the revolutionary government was brutally surpressed in Lyons.

CHAPTER TWENTY-ONE. CONVERSATION WITH THE HEAD OF THE HOUSE

P. 117, L. 16. *1814:* the year of the first fall of Napoleon, and the initial return of the Bourbons, before the Hundred Days and Waterloo. Ancien régime class distinctions became important again, at least among aristocrats of the stripe of Monsieur de Rênal. The names of Rênal's old friends come from two Grenoble acquaintances of young Stendhal, whom the author remembered fondly: Falcoz was a bookseller and Ducros a librarian.

P. 119, L. 30. *casino and at the gentlemen's club:* Monsieur de Rênal's social clubs. In France, especially in the nineteenth century, "casino" referred not necessarily to a gambling establishment but more generally to a place designated for public entertainments, i.e., concerts, dancing, cards, etc.

P. 126, L. 1. *In 1816:* sometimes referred to as the "White Terror," after the color of the royal family; the early years of the Restoration inevitably brought the arrest and prosecution of revolutionaries and imperialists.

L. 5. *"And I was never made a peer!":* Under the Restoration, the upper house of the legislature was the Chambre des Pairs. Monsieur de Rênal believes his efforts in 1816 merited a peerage.

CHAPTER TWENTY-TWO. PATTERNS OF BEHAVIOR, IN 1830

P. 128, EPIGRAPH. *R. P. Maladriga:* Italian Jesuit who spent thirty years as a missionary in Brazil. He returned to Europe to assist victims of the Lisbon earthquake of 1755. Accused of plotting to assassinate the king of Portugal, he was burned at the stake in 1761. The quotation is usually attributed to Talleyrand, the legendarily agile diplomat (*see note for p. 245, l. 9*), to whom it is far more appropriate.

P. 129, L. 21. *King Philip:* refers to Philip II of Macedonia, who had the good fortune to find in his neighborhood Aristotle, who became preceptor to his son, the future Alexander the Great.

P. 132, L. 29. *yellow gloves:* the hallmark of the young dandy in fashionable salons, full of Romantic idealism and utterly ineffectual.

P. 133, L. 1. *the Besançon Academy:* Provincial academies gave intellectuals and amateur scholars a forum for presenting and publishing the fruits of their labors. Such academies tended to sponsor conservative scholarship. L. 31. *Ligorio:* a possible reference to Saint Alphonsus Liguori, an eighteenth-century Italian theologian who had been beatified in 1816.

P. 134, LL. 6–7. *La Fontaine:* The verse *Fables* of Jean de La Fontaine (1621–95) have, since their publication, been a staple of the French education system, schoolchildren committing them to memory and reciting them (*see note for p. 136, ll. 34–35*). Master Jean Chouart is a character in one of the fables, notable for its anticlericalism. La Fontaine's *Contes* (*Tales*) tended toward ribaldry.

P. 135, L. 21. *a mathematician named Gros:* a nod to Marie-Henri Beyle's own mathematics tutor in Grenoble, who helped his student gain entry to the École Polytechnique and thus escape Grenoble for Paris.

P. 136, LL. 34–35. *"the crow . . . the fox, picks up":* The Fox and the Crow, or *Le Corbeau et le Renard*, one of La Fontaine's most popular fables: The clever, hungry fox, envying the crow's hunk of cheese, flatters the bird by praising his beautiful singing voice and begging for a song. The crow opens his beak to squawk, and drops the cheese.

P. 137, L. 20. legitimate *authority:* words loaded with political significance in France and Europe of the early nineteenth century; legitimists being a broad term describing supporters of the Bourbon monarchy, and the doctrine of legitimacy being the guiding principle of the Congress of Vienna in 1815.

P. 138, L. 35. *vicar-general:* or *Grand Vicaire*, was a priest who served as auxiliary to a bishop. When many bishops were still aristocratic political appointees, a vicar-general could wield considerable influence within a diocese.

CHAPTER TWENTY-THREE. A CIVIL SERVANT'S SORROWS

P. 140, EPIGRAPH. *Casti:* Casti refers to a licentious poet of eighteenth-century Italy.

P. 141, L. 17. *François I:* King Francis I was the great model of the Renaissance prince for the French; the verses quoted would not have been out of character. Francis's amorous activities inspired Victor Hugo's play *Le Roi s'amuse* (*The King Takes His Pleasure*), which in turn inspired Verdi's opera *Rigoletto.*

P. 143, L. 15. *ultra:* short for *"ultra royaliste";* the ultra party longed for a return to absolute monarchy, including the reinstatement of feudal laws and customs.

P. 146, L. 13. *Pulcinella:* The fool or clown Pulcinella was a stock character in European theatre, opera, etc.

P. 149, L. 30. *"that peasant, killed on a roof":* See p. 126, ll. 1–2, and note for p. 126, l. 1.

CHAPTER TWENTY-FOUR. A CAPITAL CITY

P. 153, EPIGRAPH. *Barnave:* a revolutionary politician and acquaintance of Stendhal's family *(see note for p. 6, Epigraph).*

P. 154, L. 6. *1674:* the year that Louis XIV took the Franche-Comté from Spain.

P. 157, LL. 2–3. La Nouvelle Héloïse: Rousseau's sentimental romance of 1761. The novel was an immediate success and continued to be widely read for generations.

CHAPTER TWENTY-FIVE. THE SEMINARY

P. 163, L. 15. *of Bossuet, of Arnauld, of Fleury:* three highly regarded theologians of recent French history. Jacques-Bénigne Bossuet (1627–1704), Bishop of Meaux and tutor to the Dauphin, was one of the leading religious intellectuals of Louis XIV's court; he engaged in running religious quarrels with the more liberal Fénelon *(see note for p. 391, Epigraph).* Antoine Arnauld (1612–94), *le grand Arnauld,* was the leading scholar and defender of Jansenism in France; exiled by Louis XIV, he spent the last years of his life writing pamphlets against Protestantism. Claude Fleury, principal author of the *Histoire ecclésiastique* (*see note for p. 9, Epigraph*).

P. 164, LL. 21–22. *Saint Jerome, Saint Augustine, Saint Bonaventura, Saint Basil:* all fathers of the ancient Church, with the exception of Bonaventura (ca. 1221–74), who was a theologian and adviser to Pope Gregory X.

L. 37. *de Maistre: See note for p. 20, l. 1.*

P. 166, L. 4. *Pope Pius V:* (1504–74); "Unam Ecclesiam": an invention of Stendhal's.

CHAPTER TWENTY-SIX. THE WORLD, OR WHAT THE RICH MAN IS MISSING

P. 167, EPIGRAPH. *Young:* The quotation given corresponds to no known author named Young. Although Stendhal typically quotes English authors in their original language, this quote appears in French.

L. 24. *Jansenism:* a rigid, austere sect of Catholicism (*see note for p. 94, l. 27*).

P. 168, L. 12. *Saint Theresa, or Saint Francis:* Saint Theresa Avila and Saint Francis of Assisi.

P. 169, LL. 13–14. *Sieyès . . . Grégoire:* two priests who rejected the Church in favor of the Revolution. For Sieyès, *see note for p. 65, Epigraph.* Henri Grégoire (1750–1831), known as *l'abbé Grégoire,* was a deputy to the Third Estate from Grenoble in 1789, and a member of all the revolutionary assemblies. He voted for the execution of Louis XVI and against the Empire. He was a leader in the antislavery movement in France. In 1989, his remains were brought to a place of honor in the Pantheon, in Paris.

P. 170, L. 30. The Constitutional: a liberal daily newspaper, founded in 1815 in opposition to the Bourbon government.

P. 172, L. 4. *Sextus V:* a Renaissance pope (1520–90) better known for his administrative skills than his piety.

L. 31. *Delille:* an obscure country priest who found sudden fame when he published a translation of Virgil's *Georgica;* he was adopted as a protégé by the very rich and very literary Madame Geoffrin, in whose elegant salon he was something of a fish out of water. There is no record of the egg incident.

P. 173, L. 19. *Guercino* [from Stendhal's footnote]: "See, at the Louvre Museum, *François, Duke of Aquitaine, laying down his armor to take the monk's habit.*" Guercino (1591–1666), an Italian painter, pupil of Caravaggio. Stendhal had a great interest in Italian art; one of his early books was *A History of Painting in Italy* (1817).

CHAPTER TWENTY-SEVEN. FIRST EXPERIENCE OF LIFE

P. 176, EPIGRAPH. *Diderot:* Denis Diderot (1713–84), with Voltaire and Rousseau, was one of the greatest of the philosophes. Diderot was founder of the *Encyclopédie;* novelist; playwright; author of *Jacques the Fatalist and His Master, Rameau's Nephew,* and the scandalous *The Nun.* This quote is not to be found in his writings.

CHAPTER TWENTY-EIGHT. A PROCESSION

P. 180, EPIGRAPH. *Young:* Again, in the original, the quote is given in French, and again the text cannot be identified.

L. 7. *canon:* a post within a Church carrying greater authority—and receiving greater pay—than a simple priest.

L. 16. *President:* refers here to a presiding judge of a royal court. Members of the magistrature were referred to as the *noblesse de robe,* as opposed to the *noblesse de l'épée,* typified in this novel by the La Mole family and their titled Parisian friends.

P. 181, L. 9. *Feast of Corpus Christi:* in France, the Fête Dieu, a religious celebration marked by the procession of the Eucharist through the streets for the adoration of the faithful.

P. 182, L. 31. *Robespierre's Terror:* 1793–94.

P. 184, L. 13. *Jacobinism:* here referring rather generically to political radicalism and anticlericalism (*see note for p. 8, l. 1*).

L. 16. *Barême:* seventeenth-century mathematician whose name became a byword for mathematical accuracy.

CHAPTER TWENTY-NINE. THE FIRST FORWARD STEP

P. 186, EPIGRAPH. The Precursor: a newspaper published in Lyons.

P. 189, L. 13. "*that* other one": or *l'autre,* a politically prudent way of referring to Napoleon under the Restoration. Napoleon died on Saint-Helena in 1821, but rumors circulated, especially among veterans and the lower classes, that this was a lie propagated by the frightened Bourbons. Many of Napoleon's generals had working-class origins, and many of them did in fact rally to the Bourbons when Napoleon returned from Elba, prudent enough to realize that the great European powers would never tolerate his retaking the throne.

L. 25. "The only king the people still remember!": "the people" here for *le peuple,* the commoners or lower classes, among whom the cult of Napoleon was strongest.

P. 192, L. 18. *"keeper of the seal's":* or *Garde des Sceaux,* effectively the minister of justice.

P. 195, L. 26. *hard years of life abroad:* The bishop was an émigré, the name given to those aristocrats who fled France during the Revolution. The first notable émigré was Louis XVI's brother, the Comte d'Artois, who fled almost immediately after the fall of the Bastille, and in 1824 had become King Charles X. Many émigrés returned after Robespierre's downfall, many more when Bonaparte declared an amnesty in 1801. Among ultras, it was a badge of honor, a sign of right-thinking loyalty, to have remained in exile until 1814.

P. 196, L. 22. *poem on Mary Magdalene:* "La Madeleine" was written by young Delphine Gay, the future wife of Emile de Girardin—the famous publisher—and a literary figure in her own right.

P. 197, L. 26. *Constantine:* Constantine I (ca. 275–337), the Roman emperor who converted to Christianity.

P. 199, L. 29. *Te Deum:* ceremony of thanksgiving to God.

P. 200, L. 32. *Marie Alacoque:* Saint Marguerite-Marie; a Burgundian peasant girl (1647–90) who entered a convent and there had a vision of the Sacred Heart of Jesus, who ordered her to establish a feast day in honor of the Sacred Heart. She succeeded in 1686.

CHAPTER THIRTY. AN AMBITIOUS MAN

P. 201, EPIGRAPH: Edinburgh Review: The quotation given is an invention, but the *Edinburgh Review* was a real newspaper that featured Romantic writers and which Stendhal read regularly.

P. 201, L. 26–P. 202, L. 1. *fifth floor . . . the second floor:* In Paris, the best apartments were located on the first floor—one flight above ground level—and the fifth floor was the proverbial garret. Monsieur de La Mole's protégés, appropriately, move to the second floor, not quite the best.

PART TWO

P. 217. EPIGRAPH. *Sainte-Beuve:* Charles-Augustin Sainte-Beuve (1804–69) had already begun his long career as a writer and critic when Stendhal wrote *The Red and the Black.* The two writers knew each other. This quote is not to be found in Sainte-Beuve's writings.

CHAPTER ONE. COUNTRY PLEASURES

P. 219, EPIGRAPH. *Virgil:* Although Virgil wrote the *Georgica,* odes to the country life, this quote is in fact from Horace's *Satires,* in which an avaricious usurer hypocritically sings the praises of the simple country life.

P. 220, L. 2. *Mirabeau's reputation:* Honoré-Gabriel Riqueti, Comte de Mirabeau (1749–91), was already a scandalous figure when he deserted his class and got himself elected as a deputy for the Third Estate in 1789. Through his gift for oratory and the force of his personality, he quickly became one of the most powerful members of the National Assembly. Always corrupt and deeply in debt, Mirabeau was receptive when the court opened secret negotiations with him; he also sincerely feared the Revolution was getting out of control. He was supposed to calm the more radical tendencies of the Assembly, but his sudden death put an end to this possibility. Mirabeau was the first national hero to be entombed in the Pantheon, the disaffected church near the Sorbonne that was turned into a patriotic shrine by the revolutionary government. One year later, his correspondence with the court was discovered and his remains were disinterred and thrown into a common grave.

P. 222, L. 28. *concordat:* the 1801 agreement between the Pope and First Consul Bonaparte that reestablished the Catholic Church in France.

LL. 32–33. *barons and counts:* In 1807, Napoleon decided to create a new Imperial nobility in order to create loyalty and to aggrandize his Empire.

P. 223, L. 35. *Malmaison:* a small château just west of Paris, bought by Joséphine Bonaparte soon after her marriage to Napoleon. It was their home until he took power in 1799 and appropriated for himself the royal residences in Paris and the countryside. Joséphine retired there after the 1809 divorce, and died there in 1814, after Napoleon's first exile to Elba.

P. 224, LL. 8–9. *Arcola* was the site of one of General Bonaparte's Italian triumphs, in 1796. *Saint-Helena* is the Atlantic island where the deposed emperor spent the last six years of his life in exile.

P. 225, L. 21. *the war with Spain:* In 1820, a liberal revolution arose against the reactionary Spanish Bourbons, seeking a stable, constitutional monarchy. The French Bourbons, in the person of the Duke d'Angoulême, intervened in the name of legitimacy, and secured the throne for Ferdinand VII in 1823.

L. 33. *Place de Grève:* on the right bank of the Seine, the site of public tortures and executions in Paris until the guillotine was set up in the Place Louis XV, which was then renamed Place de la Revolution, today's Place de la Concorde.

L. 37. *Moreri's biographical dictionary:* the work of Louis Moreri (1643–80).

P. 226, L. 26. *Duke of Chaulnes:* a name Stendhal borrowed from French history; the ducal Chaulnes family was prominent in the last centuries of the ancien régime and died out in the eighteenth century.

P. 227, L. 1. *Philip II:* the Spanish king who aggressively interfered in French politics and attempted (unsuccessfully) to suppress a rebellion in the Spanish Netherlands with brutal force. *Henry VIII:* English King who is called a monster, no doubt as much for his abandonment of the Catholic faith as for his beheaded wives.

P. 228, L. 25. THE DE LA MOLE RESIDENCE: The great *hôtels particuliers,* the town houses of the French aristocracy, were a sign of wealth and status.

P. 229, L. 5. *Faubourg Saint-Germain:* Roughly corresponding to today's seventh arrondissement on the Left Bank, the Faubourg Saint-Germain was the most aristocratic neighborhood in Paris. The neighborhood became a metaphor for aristocratic society and ultra politics.

CHAPTER TWO. ENTERING SOCIETY

P. 229, CHAPTER TITLE. *Society:* in French, the *monde*, the exclusive and almost purely aristocratic high society of Paris.

EPIGRAPH. *Kant:* As those familiar with Kant's philosophy will immediately deduce, this citation is nowhere to be found among his writings.

P. 230, L. 11. *Henri III:* (born 1551) reigned briefly during the turbulent second half of the sixteenth century. He was the third son of Henri II and Catherine de Médici to take the throne of France, becoming king after the death of his brother, Charles IX. Some of the worst battles of the Wars of Religion took place under his reign. He was assassinated by the fanatical Catholic monk Jacques Clément. His friends, known as *mignons*, were his companions in debauchery.

P. 231, LL. 14–15. *Monsieur Julien de Sorel:* The marquis has awarded Julien an aristocratic *de*, the particule (sometimes *des, de la*, or *du*) that was indicative of noble birth.

L. 16. *Père Lachaise Cemetery:* on the east side of Paris, where many cultural and political notables have been buried since 1803.

LL. 17–18. *Marshal Ney:* Michel Ney (1769–1815), whom Napoleon called *le brave des braves*, made his name with the revolutionary armies; he was named Duke d'Elchingen in 1808 and then Prince de la Moskova after the Russian campaign. He pledged his loyalty to the Bourbons and was sent by Louis XVIII to arrest Bonaparte when he returned from Elba in 1815. Ney famously promised to bring his former emperor back to Paris "in an iron cage." His resolution could not withstand the sight of his former general, and he defected to the imperial cause at Châlons-sur-Marne. Arrested after Waterloo—where many believe he deliberately sought death once defeat became inevitable—he was tried and convicted of treason by the Chamber of Peers, and shot by firing squad in 1815.

P. 234, L. 11. *Mathilde:* Stendhal almost certainly took this name from Mathilde Dembowska, the beautiful Italian wife of a Polish officer with whom he had fallen passionately in love in Milan.

P. 235, LL. 29–30. *Chapelle, friend of Molière and La Fontaine:* Chapelle was a wealthy bourgeois who composed light satirical verse for the amusement of friends like the playwright Molière (*see note for p. 79, l. 2*) and the fabulist La Fontaine (*see note for p. 134, ll. 6–7*).

L. 32. *Southey:* Robert Southey (1774–1843), minor English poet and biographer, friend of Coleridge. He and Byron, differing in literary and political opinion, engaged in a public feud.

LL. 33–34. *Augustus and George IV . . . Maecenas:* George IV, King of England (1820–30); Maecenas is best remembered as the great patron of the arts under the golden age of Augustus's reign.

P. 235, L. 36–P. 236, L. 1. *Doge of Venice:* The Doges were the elected leaders of the aristocratic oligarchy of the Venetian Republic.

CHAPTER THREE. THE FIRST STEPS

P. 236, EPIGRAPH. Reina: Francesco Reina (1772–1826), a lawyer and amateur poet whom Stendhal met in Milan.

P. 237, L. 3. *Voltaire's* Princess of Babylon: considered scandalous by conservatives.

L. 6. *Sacred Heart of Jesus:* a fashionable Paris convent school for aristocratic girls.

L. 23. *Bois de Boulogne:* Then on the outskirts of Paris, these woods were a fashionable place to ride (and to see and be seen) for the Parisian élite.

LL. 23–24. *Du Bac Street:* or Rue du Bac, one of the main roads in the Faubourg Saint-Germain.

CHAPTER FOUR. THE DE LA MOLE MANSION

P. 240, EPIGRAPH. *Ronsard:* Pierre de Ronsard (1524–85), one of the greatest of French poets and a leading figure in the Pléiade school.

P. 241, L. 22. *Béranger:* Pierre-Jean de Béranger (1780–1857), immensely popular songwriter whose satirical songs reflected, and some said encouraged, the political discontent that led to the July Revolution of 1830.

L. 28. *the noblest decoration:* the cordon bleu (*see note for p. 264, ll. 14–15*).

L. 35. *Rossini:* The operas of Gioacchino Antonio Rossini (1792–1868) gained popularity in Paris throughout the Restoration. Stendhal, although he preferred Mozart and Cimarosa, wrote a pamphlet defending Rossini's work.

P. 242, L. 4. Today's News: for the conservative *La Quotidienne, see note for p. 65, l. 20.* The *Gazette de France,* the official organ of the court, was equally conservative.

LL. 34–35. *those* who rode in the king's carriages: This was one of the cherished privileges accorded to the highest nobility of the ancien régime.

P. 245, L. 9. *Talleyrand; Pozzo di Borgo; Father de Pradt:* Prince Charles-Maurice de Talleyrand Périgord (1754–1838) was the renegade bishop and legendarily agile politician and diplomat who served virtually every government from the Revolution through the July Monarchy. After having been Napoleon's principal adviser and foreign minister in the early years of his reign, Talleyrand turned on the emperor and became an active agent for the Bourbons in the closing months of the Empire, in 1814. As Louis XVIII's foreign minister, he represented France at the Congress of Vienna. Pozzo di Borgo (1764–1842) was a Corsican and royalist who fled France during the Revolution and subsequently joined the government of the Russian Czar, Alexander I. Pozzo's family had been political adversaries of the Bonapartes in Corsica, and he carried the feud to the much larger stage of European politics. As one of Alexander's principal advisers at Vienna, in 1815, and then as Russia's ambassador to France (1814–34), Pozzo worked to support the doctrine of legitimacy and maintain the Bourbons on the throne after the Hundred Days. The inclusion of Father de Pradt (1759–1837), who was mostly an agent of Talleyrand's, is rather surprising and possibly ironic.

P. 246, L. 7. *Duc de Bouillon:* one of the oldest names in France, *Bouillon* is also a homonym for bouillon, broth.

P. 247, L. 29. *Basilio:* a bitter, jealous hypocrite in *The Barber of Seville*, in both Beaumarchias's play of 1775 and Rossini's opera of 1816.

P. 248, L. 32. *Monsieur Comte:* an allusion to Monsieur de Tolly's own magic act, making ballots disappear.

P. 249, L. 23. *Nerval:* a possible allusion to Comte Joseph de Villèle (1773–1854), who rose to power as an ultra in 1821, but proved insufficiently reactionary and was forced out in 1828. He was replaced by the fanatical and politically incompetent Jules de Polignac (1780–1847), whose extremism provoked the July Revolution.

L. 35. *Lord Holland:* Charles James Fox (1749–1806), rival of William Pitt (*see note for p. 361, l. 31*) and leader of the opposition Whig party in the House of Commons and then the House of Lords. He supported both the American and—early on—French revolutions and sought a rapprochement with Bonaparte until 1804, when he became persuaded of the new emperor's dangerous ambitions.

P. 250, LL. 1–2. *William IV:* took the throne on the death of his brother, George IV, in 1830.

L. 10. *Duke de Castries:* a powerful aristocrat and accomplished soldier under the ancien régime. This phrase appears to be Stendhal's, though it does typify the attitude of many nobles (as well as bourgeois) toward poets and artists.

L. 10. *d'Alembert:* Jean Le Rond d'Alembert (1717–83), philosophe, collaborator of Diderot's in the *Encyclopédie* project.

L. 28. *Count de Thaler:* proabably modeled on the Baron de Rothschild. *Thaler* was an old German currency, the origin of the word *dollar.*

CHAPTER FIVE. SENSITIVITY AND A DEVOUT ARISTOCRATIC LADY

P. 252, EPIGRAPH. *Faublas:* a character in the novel *Les Amours du chevalier de Faublas,* by Louvret de Couvray, published in 1787. The chevalier's comic adventures in love lead to a tragic ending.

L. 27. *Altamira:* Many scholars believe Altamira to be based on the Neapolitan Count di Fiore, who was a friend of Stendhal's.

CHAPTER SIX. PRONUNCIATION

P. 254, EPIGRAPH. *Gratius:* This quote cannot be identified with any known Latin author named Gratius.

P. 257, L. 4. *Staub:* a fashionable tailor in the rue de Richelieu.

P. 260, L. 7. Count Ory: A success for Rossini, it debuted in 1828.

CHAPTER SEVEN. AN ATTACK OF GOUT

P. 261, EPIGRAPH. *Bertolotti:* a politically active Italian poet (1784–1860).

L. 4. *Hyères:* a fashionable spa on the Mediterranean, between Toulon and St. Tropez.

P. 262, L. 17. *Rivarol:* Count Antoine de Rivarol (1743–1801), a writer and aristocrat famous for his wit and conversation. A fierce opponent of the Revolution, he had to flee in 1792 because of his published attacks. Hamburg was one of the many German cities where émigrés (*see note for p. 195, l. 26*) awaited the fall of their enemies.

P. 264, L. 3. *Moncade... Poisson:* characters from a 1728 play, *L'école des bourgeois.*

LL. 14–15. *his small medal... the noblest award:* The first is the Cross of the Legion of Honor (*see note for p. 8, ll. 5–6*), which was preserved by the Bourbons but which became depreciated by its proliferation. The second is the *cordon bleu,* the decoration that denoted membership in the Ordre du Saint-Esprit (Order of the Holy Spirit), founded by Henri III in 1578.

P. 265, L. 9. *Sir Hudson Lowe:* Napoleon engaged in a series of constant and petty squabbles with Lowe, whose rules and conditions the former emperor found insulting. Lowe and Bathurst are the villains of *Le Mémorial de Sainte-Hélène* (*see note for p. 17, ll. 9–10*).

L. 10. *Philip Vane:* an invention of Stendhal's; Stendhal had studied several English philosophers, probably including Locke.

P. 267, LL. 13–14. *Baron de Valenod:* It appears that Valenod has aquired an aristocratic particle (*de*) along with his title.

CHAPTER EIGHT. WHICH MEDALS ARE HONORABLE?

P. 268, EPIGRAPH. *Pellico:* Silvio Pellico (1789–1854), Italian patriot and poet, whose liberal political activities against the Austrian government of northern Italy earned him both a long jail term and a death sentence during the 1820s. He titled his 1832 memoir *My Prisons.*

P. 269, L. 20. *Duke de Retz:* Stendhal has again borrowed a name from French history for his duke (*see note for pg. 101, l. 11*).

P. 273, L. 20. The Social Contract: A strange object of veneration for the very aristocratic Mathilde. *Du contrat social* is Rousseau's 1762 essay analyzing the development of government in primitive societies.

L. 25. *Montmorency:* lush country region just north of Paris where many nobles owned country houses, including the Duke de Luxembourg, who was something of a patron of the philosophes. The incident Julien and Mathilde refer to is recounted in Rousseau's *Confessions.*

L. 29. *King Feretrius:* a sly reference to an incident in which an amateur scholar invented an ancient Roman king named Feretrius so that he could deliver a lecture on him.

P. 274, LL. 27–28. *a Prince de Conti:* The Conti family were a branch of the Condé family (*see note for p. 38, l. 33*), Princes of the Blood Royal.

P. 276, L. 24. *Mirabeau:* a great but controversial figure of the early Revolution (*see note for p. 220, l. 2*).

L. 24. *had given it* [Stendhal's footnote]: "Cette feuille, composée le 25 juillet 1830, a été imprimée le 4 août. —Note de l'éditeur." [This page, written on July 25, 1830, was printed on August 4. —Editor's note.]

This is a reference to the July Revolution, which broke out on July 28. By July 30, Charles X had abdicated to his son and then his grandson. On August 4, Charles abandoned his quest to maintain the throne and agreed to leave France with his family.

P. 277, L. 6. *Conradin:* Conradin (1252–68), son of Conrad IV, king of Sicily, failed in an attempt to regain his father's throne and was executed.

L. 27. *"noblemen come from the bourgeoisie":* i.e., recently ennobled commoners.

P. 278, L. 1. *Madame de Staël:* Germaine Necker, Baroness de Staël-Holstein (1766–1817), author of *Corinne* and *Delphine.* Immensely rich, a successful and influential author, and probably the most famous nonroyal woman in Europe; it is true that Madame de Staël was not beautiful. Whether she would have traded all her advantages for Mathilde's beauty is highly debatable.

CHAPTER NINE. THE BALL

P. 278, EPIGRAPH. *Uzeri:* another invented quote, perhaps suggested by the

Zurich composer J. M. Usteri's *Schweizer-Reise (Swiss Travels)*, a collection of Swiss folk songs.

P. 279, L. 10. *Danton was so terribly ugly.* For Danton, *see note for p. 1, Epigraph.* Danton was in fact quite ugly, and guilty of complicity in much of the violence of the Terror before he himself became its victim.

P. 280, LL. 25–26. *Golden Fleece medal:* The knightly Order of the Golden Fleece was established by Philip the Good, Duke of Burgundy, in 1429. Charles V of Spain, grandson and heir of Charles the Bold, then carried it on in Spain.

P. 281, LL. 28–32. *C'est un mécontent qui parle* [Stendhal's footnote]: This is a malcontent speaking. *Tartuffe* is a Molière masterpiece, concerning the religious hypocrite Tartuffe, who uses an ostentatious show of extreme faith to ingratiate himself with a rich and naïve bourgeois, Orgon. There is no record of Molière ever making such a comment about *Tartuffe*.

P. 282, L. 1. *Henri IV:* The first Bourbon king (born 1553, reigned 1589–1610). He brought an end to the Wars of Religion when he converted to Catholicism in order to claim the throne. Legend has him declaring "Paris is well worth a mass!" He imposed his authority on fractious nobles, divorced his adulterous wife, Marguerite de Valois (*see note for p. 289, ll. 9–10)* to marry Marie de Médici—mother of Louis XIII—and was assassinated by the fanatical Ravaillac. This political martyrdom—plus his military skills and his rough-hewn ways—helped contribute to the legend of a great and popular king, which survived even the Revolution.

L. 26. *Girondin:* appellation given to the moderates in the convention. As the principle opponents of the Jacobins—their former allies—many Girondins, after 1792, were executed when the more radical party emerged victorious.

P. 283, L. 34. *Courier:* Paul-Louis Courier (1772–1825), a personal friend of Stendhal's and a vocal Republican as well as a Hellenist and political pamphleteer. The judge who called him a cynic knew that Courier would understand its original meaning of "dog."

P. 284, L. 5. *Washington:* The revolutionary and postrevolutionary generations greatly admired George Washington, chiefly for his Cincinattus-like abandonment of power on two occasions, after the end of the Revolutionary War and again in 1796.

L. 14. *Delavigne's tragedy* Marino Faliero: an 1829 play, controversial chiefly because it defied the traditional rules of the theater. *Marino Faliero* told the story of Israel Bertuccio, who plotted to assassinate the Venetian aristocracy in order to establish Faliero as reigning prince of Venice.

The Romantics were fascinated by the byzantine politics of medieval and Renaissance Italy, which furnished subject matter to many works, especially plays. Stendhal himself drew on such sources for his novel *La Chartreuse de Parme* (The Charterhouse of Parma) and the *Chroniques italiennes* (The Italian Chornicles).

LL. 32–35. *Danton; Mirabeau; Napoleon; Pichegru; Lafayette:* Danton (*see note for p. 1, Epigraph*) was arrested and executed on charges of embezzlement that, after his death, proved to be true. Mirabeau likewise was proven, after his death, guilty of accepting bribes (*see note for p. 220, l. 2*). Napoleon's looting in Italy was standard for the leader of a revolutionary army, and the government of the Directory profited more than Napoleon did personally. Jean-Charles Pichegru (1761–1804) rose through the ranks to become commander of the Army of the North. He conquered Holland in 1795, but was accused—probably truthfully—of accepting bribes from royalist agents and was forced to resign in 1796. Elected by the Royalists to the Council of the Five Hundred, under the Directory in 1797, he was soon exiled to Guyana after an antiroyalist sweep of the government by Barras. He later escaped to England and soon joined in the anti-Bonapartist plots among the émigrés in London. In 1804 he traveled secretly to Paris to take part in a British-sponsored plot to kidnap First Consul Bonaparte. Betrayed by a fellow conspirator, Pichegru was arrested and emprisoned in the Temple. He was found there, strangled by his own silk scarf; the official government report of suicide was never fully accepted. The Marquis de Lafayette's personal integrity was one character trait not even his worst enemies challenged.

P. 285, L. 18. *Carnot:* Lazare Carnot (1753–1823), revolutionary politician with remarkable survival skills. De facto war minister during the Convention and the Directory, he managed to survive his enemies in both governments as well as their downfalls. Named minister of war by Bonaparte in 1800, he was too independent to serve as a mere figurehead and soon resigned. An imperial senator who frequently opposed Napoleon, he devoted himself to scientific study after the Senate was suppressed in 1807. He returned to Napoleon's service in the last days of the Empire and again during the Hundred Days, when he was named minister of interior. Exiled by the Bourbons after Waterloo, he died in Prussia. His son and grandson were prominent in French politics, and another son was a prominent physicist.

P. 286, LL. 31–32. *revolutionaries of Piedmont, of Spain:* refers to the failed liberal uprisings in both countries in the early 1820s.

CHAPTER TEN. QUEEN MARGUERITE

P. 287, EPIGRAPH. *Letters of a Portuguese Nun:* The title of a novel by Diderot (1713–84) that does not contain the quotation given.

P. 288, L. 17. *Hernani:* The premiére of Victor Hugo's play (1830), which flouted the rules of classical French drama, caused such controversy that there were rhetorical feuds in the newspapers—and at least one brawl—between Romantics and the defenders of classicism. Seen as a manifesto of Romanticism, the play greatly offended conservatives, like those of the Académie Francaise.

P. 289, LL. 9–10. *thirtieth of April, in 1574:* The story of Boniface de La Mole (or La Molle) is set against the turbulent era of the Wars of Religion, or Wars of the League, in the second half of the sixteenth century. These complicated political circumstances merit some explanation. At the death of Henri II in 1559, Catherine de Médici wielded enormous influence during the reigns of her three sons. Francis II (born 1544, reigned 1559–60), married Mary, Queen of Scots. He was succeeded by Charles IX (born 1550), who at his mother's urging ordered the Saint Bartholomew's Day Massacre—August 24, 1572—when agents of the king murdered a great number of Huguenot nobles gathered in Paris for the marriage of Marguerite de Valois to Henri, King of Navarre (the future Henri IV of France [*see note for p. 282, l. 1*]). This act of calculated mass murder further inflamed the Wars of Religion. Charles died in 1574, and the throne passed to the third brother, Henri III (1551–89), who acknowledged his Protestant cousin Henri de Navarre as his heir presumptive. This enraged many Catholics who, under the leadership of the Duke de Guise, formed the Holy League (*Sainte Ligue*) to prevent Henri de Navarre's accession. Henri III himself was assassinated in 1589. Henri de Navarre became Henri IV of France, after converting to Catholicism.

L. 19. *Boniface de La Mole:* Joseph de Boniface, seigneur de La Mole, was, according to legend, one of Queen Marguerite's many lovers, and was executed with his friend Annibal Coconasso in the Place de la Grève on April 30, 1574. Marguerite de Valois became immortalized by Alexandre Dumas's 1845 novel, *La Reine Margot.* Henri had their marriage annulled in 1599.

L. 24. *Duke d'Alençon:* the fourth son of Henri II and Catherine de Médici; it was his death in 1584 that lead Henri III to name Henri de Navarre his heir.

P. 291, L. 9 *d'Aubigné... Brantôme:* Théodore-Agrippa d'Aubigné (1552–1630) was a Huguenot nobleman, historian, and poet; a friend of Henri de Navarre, he escaped the Saint Bartholomew's massacre only by chance. Pierre de Bourdeilles, seigneur de Brantôme (ca. 1540–1614), was a soldier who turned to writing; he is most famous for his *Memories* and his *Lives of Gallant Ladies,* both of which are rich with frank anecdotes about life at the Valois courts. Both authors confirm the liaison of Marguerite and Boniface.

L. 11, *Walter Scott:* The historical novels of Sir Walter Scott (1771–1832)— *Ivanhoe,* et al.—enjoyed immense popularity in France, contributing to the vogue of historical novels and plays in France.

L. 15. *l'Etoile:* Pierre de l'Etoile (1546–1611), a Parisian bourgeois, left a detailed diary of his time.

CHAPTER ELEVEN. A YOUNG GIRL'S IMPERIAL DOMINION

P. 295, EPIGRAPH. *Mérimée:* Prosper Mérimée (1803–70), one of the great French writers of the nineteenth century, was known especially for his short stories. He and Stendhal met in the late 1820s and became close friends.

P. 296, LL. 17–18: *profound passion . . . infinite melancholy:* clichés of Romantic literature, especially after Châteaubriand's immensely popular short novels, *René* and *Atala,* which Stendhal despised.

L. 27. *Wagram:* One of Napoleon's last significant victories was the Battle of Wagram, fought against Austria in 1809. The subsequent truce with Austria led to Napoleon's marriage with Archduchess Maria Louisa von Hapsburg.

P. 297, L. 33. Manon Lescant . . . The Letters of a Portuguese Nun: *Manon Lescaut,* by the abbé Prévost, Rousseau's *La Nouvelle Héloïse,* and Diderot's *Lettres d'une religieuse portugaise* were all eighteenth-century novels with vague reputations for immorality, especially among conservatives like the La Moles.

P. 298, LL. 4–5. *Catherine de Médici:* wife of Henri II and mother of three kings of France *(see note for p. 289, ll. 9–10).* She was said to have brought the culture of the Renaissance to the French court. Her legend as a cruel, manipulative, almost witchlike figure began in her own lifetime.

L. 5. *Louis XIII:* Louis's court was a constant center of intrigues both political and amorous.

L. 18. *Vendée:* an Atlantic coastal region just south of Brittany that was a center of counterrevolutionary insurrection. Motivated by deep Catholicism and funded by émigrés in England, as many as forty thousand, mostly peasant, Vendéens formed a "catholic and royal army," which conducted a fierce guerrilla war against the revolutionary government from 1793 to 1796, with flare-ups in 1799 and 1815.

LL. 9–10. *an end to any more Constitutions:* The *Charte*, or Constitution, of 1815 was a thorn in the side of the ultras despite the fact that they maintained power under it.

CHAPTER TWELVE. WILL HE BE ANOTHER DANTON?

P. 299, EPIGRAPH. Duke d'Angoulême: Charles de Valois (1573–1650).

P. 302, L. 18. *Spanish duke:* Many Spanish noblemen, including most of the royal family, were Napoleon's prisoners after he invaded the Iberian peninsula in 1808.

P. 303, L. 29. *in 1792, at Coblenz:* Coblenz, Germany, was the center of the émigré community in the early years of the Revolution. The so-called Army of the Princes, led by Louis XVI's brother and cousins, was headquartered at Coblenz.

CHAPTER THIRTEEN. A CONSPIRACY

P. 304, EPIGRAPH. *Schiller:* Friederich von Schiller (1759–1805), German Romantic writer.

P. 305, L. 33. *so-called* Memoirs: Fraudulent memoirs of famous personages of the revolutionary era proliferated in the early nineteenth century.

P. 308, L. 9. *Léontine Fay:* a famous actress of the Parisian theaters.

P. 310, L. 22. *Saint Louis:* King Louis IX (born 1214, reigned 1226–70), who led two crusades, one to Egypt, where he was captured and ransomed, the other to Tunis, where he died of the plague; he was canonized in 1296. The Bourbons often referred to themselves as the "sons of Saint Louis."

P. 311, L. 4. *My countryman, Granvelle:* Born in Besançon, the sixteenth-century prelate Antoine Perronet de Granvelle rose to become a trusted and influential minister to the Hapsburg Holy Roman Emperor Charles V and his son Philip II of Spain. Their influence made him a cardinal in 1561.

L. 12. *"Tartuffe was ruined by a woman, too":* "Tartuffe aussi fut perdu par une femme." A stunning sentence for anyone familiar with *Tartuffe*, as most of the French were and are. The lines quoted are from Tartuffe (*see note for p. 281, ll. 28–32*) as the hypocrite prepares to seduce Elmire, the virtuous wife of his preposterous benefactor, Orgon. Most people would say that Tartuffe was unmasked by Elmire, his "ruin" being richly deserved.

L. 26. *Fontan and Magalon:* Both were sent to prison for publishing a satirical antigovernment revue, *The Album*.

P. 312, L. 2. *Colonel Caron:* an officer executed for conspiring against the government. Stendhal saw Caron, like Fontan and Magalon, as a victim of the oppressive excesses of the Bourbons. *Colmar:* a small town in Alsace.

CHAPTER FOURTEEN. A YOUNG GIRL'S THOUGHTS

P. 313, EPIGRAPH. *Alfred de Musset:* An important figure in French romanticism, Musset (1810–57) was a poet, novelist, and playwright.

P. 314, L. 21. *the Soissons mansion:* or Hôtel de Nesle, a huge sixteenth-century town house that belonged to Catherine de Médici; the "cutthroats" swarming there are part of the legend of the woman and her times.

L. 23. *Algeria:* The French colonization of North Africa began in 1830. Algiers fell to the French on July 4, 1830.

P. 315, L. 20. *Bailen:* a defeat for the Imperial Army in Spain in July 1809. Napoleon was as infuriated by the treaty, by which the French accepted blame for starting the Spanish war, as he was by the loss.

L. 32. *Medea:* a misquotation of Corneille's *Médée.* (*For Corneille, see note for p. 79, l. 3.*)

CHAPTER FIFTEEN. IS IT A CONSPIRACY?

P. 319, L. 30. *Corneille's old Don Diego:* father of the hero in *Le Cid,* a noble old soldier who, as a true Cornelian, puts honor before everything.

P. 320, LL. 5–6. *de Richelieu:* the Cardinal de Richelieu (1585–1642), the great first minister of Louis XIII. Brought into the government by Louis's formidable mother, Marie de Médici, Richelieu studied the political terrain and switched his allegiance to the son. He dominated France for the rest of his life and for most of Louis's reign.

L. 28. *Abélard:* As a young priest, Pierre Abélard (1079–1142 or 44) was hired to tutor Héloïse (1101–64), the bright niece of a wealthy Parisian merchant. They fell in love, were secretly married, and, when the girl was found to be pregnant, her furious uncle had Abélard castrated. The two lovers were sent to distant cloistered monasteries, communicating only by letter. Their tragic love story became a touchstone in French literature, and their correspondence in Latin survives. Abélard went on to become one of the leading theologians in Europe, engaging in polemic battles with the Sorbonne and Saint Bernard of Clairvaux. Héloïse's letters reveal a woman of sharp and independent intellect.

L. 32. *Pharsalia:* According to Plutarch, Julius Caesar ordered his hardened veterans to slash at the faces of his enemy Pompey's soldiers, who were reputed to be vain young Roman patricians.

P. 322, L. 24. Pallida morte futura: From Virgil's *Aeneid,* the phrase describes Dido.

CHAPTER SIXTEEN. ONE O'CLOCK IN THE MORNING

P. 323, EPIGRAPH. *Massinger:* Philip Massinger (1583–1640), a British playwright, and a contemporary of Shakespeare.

P. 325, L. 20. *Café Tortoni:* A very successful and fashionable café in the Boulevard des Italiens, Café Tortoni opened in 1804 and specialized in ice cream.

L. 34. *San Domingo:* The French lost the colony of Saint-Domingue, now Haiti, to Toussiant Louverture's insurrection in 1791. Bonaparte sent his brother-in-law General Leclerc to retake the island in 1802; Leclerc captured Louverture, who died in France, but Haitians, under the leadership of Dessalines, drove the French troops off the island and declared independence in 1804.

P. 327, LL. 1–2. La Nouvelle Héloïse: Rousseau's sentimental novel of love, thought risqué in some circles. The title alludes to Abélard's Héloïse (*see note for p. 320, l. 28*).

CHAPTER NINETEEN. COMIC OPERA

P. 339, Epigraph. *Shakespeare: See note for p. 87, Epigraph.*

L. 22. *the British Revolution of 1688:* The political turbulence of seventeenth-century Britain—the execution of Charles I, Cromwell's protectorate, the return of the Stuarts under the protection of General Monck—was a constant point of reference for the revolutionary and postrevolutionary generations. The year 1688 was the time of the "Glorious Revolution," which drove James II into exile and brought to the throne the more conciliatory (and Protestant) William of Orange and Mary Stuart, James's daughter.

P. 340, L. 1. *Roland . . . Madame Roland:* Jean-Marie Roland de La Platière (1734–93) was a leader of the Girondin party (*see note for p. 282, l. 26*), minister of the interior in 1792; his wife, Jeanne-Marie (1754–93), was a highly educated woman whose influential salon was a gathering place for moderate Republicans. The Rolands opposed the execution of Louis XVI, which earned them the enmity of Robespierre and the Jacobins. Roland fled to Rouen in January 1793; hearing there of his wife's execution, he killed himself.

LL. 2–3. *Madame de Staël . . . personal immorality:* Madame de Staël's (*see note for p. 278, l. 1*) list of reputed lovers included Talleyrand, the Count de Narbonne, Joseph Bonaparte, and especially Benjamin Constant. The story of their stormy affair is told from his perspective in the novel *Adolphe*, and from hers in *Corinne*.

P. 341, L. 3. *Cimarosa:* Domenico Cimarosa (1749–1801), Italian composer. He and Mozart were Stendhal's favorite composers; his comic operas were very successful in Paris.

L. 22. *the famous aria:* Mathilde's aria has not been found in any known opera.

P. 344, L. 24. *"So it's you!": "C'est donc toi!"* in French; Mathilde uses the intimate *tu* form with Julien for the first time.

P. 347, L. 4. *high decorations:* again, the *cordon bleu* of the Order of the Holy Spirit (*see note for p. 264, ll. 14–15*).

P. 348, L. 2. *the Meudon woods:* forest west of Paris, near Saint-Cloud.

CHAPTER TWENTY. THE JAPANESE VASE

P. 348, EPIGRAPH. *Jean-Paul:* pen name of Johann Paul Friedrich Richter (1763–1825), German Romantic writer greatly influenced by Rousseau.

P. 349, L. 21. *Emperor Alexander:* Czar Alexander I (born 1777, reigned 1801–25), grew increasingly mystic and erratic in his later years. His death was never officially certified, and there were rumors that he had actually abdicated and withdrawn to a monastery.

P. 352, L. 35. *Chelles:* aristocratic convent east of Paris. The Regent Duke d'Or-léan's daughter Louise-Adélaïde was Abbess of Chelles in the early eighteenth century.

CHAPTER TWENTY-ONE. THE SECRET NOTE

P. 354, L. 6. The Legitimist: or *La Quotidienne,* a highly conservative daily newspaper (*see note for p. 65, l. 20*).

CHAPTER TWENTY TWO. THE DISCUSSION

P. 361, L. 31. *the immortal Pitt:* William Pitt the Younger (1759–1806) suc-ceeded his father as prime minister at age twenty-four; he took an inter-est in Continental politics when revolutionary armies conquered the Low Countries in 1796. Under his direction, the British subsidized the anti-French coalitions until 1801, when he resigned over Anglo-Irish politics. His successor sought conciliation with France, but Bonaparte's relentless ambitions renewed the Anglo-French conflict and brought Pitt back to power in 1804. He died in office in 1806, just after Napoleon's massive vic-tory over the Allies at Austerlitz.

P. 362, L. 11. *the Duke of Wellington:* Arthur Wellesley (1769–1852), hero of the battle of Waterloo. The "Iron Duke" had a long career in British politics, including prime minister in 1828–30. With Metternich, he was one of the great leaders and symbols of the effort to preserve a conservative status quo in Europe.

L. 16. *a former Napoleonic general:* Many of Napoleon's generals, whether out of political ambition or disgust with the emperor's relentless bellicosity, rallied to the Bourbons in 1814 and 1815.

P. 363, LL. 15–16. *soldiers of 1794 . . . 1792:* the revolutionary armies acquired skills and talented leaders in the two years of war against allied royalist forces.

P. 364, L. 5. *Monsieur de Richelieu:* The Duke de Richelieu in question (1766–1822), descendant of the great cardinal, was Louis XVIII's prime minister from 1815 to 1818 and from 1820 to 1822. Had the Allied occupation that he "stupidly squandered" in 1817 lasted much longer, civil war was a real possibility. The reactionaries at Monsieur de La Mole's secret meeting regret that the Allies did not help to reestablish absolutism; this is merely one aspect of their detachment from reality.

L. 20. The Globe: newspaper of the liberal opposition in the late Restoration. Stendhal was a contributor.

L. 22. *Kléber . . . Pichegru:* four non-nobles who rose quickly through the meritorious ranks of the revolutionary armies. The Alsatian Jean-Baptiste Kléber (1753–1800) made his name in the Vendée and in Germany, followed Bonaparte to Egypt, and was assassinated in Cairo after Bonaparte returned to France to seize power in 1799. Louis-Lazare Hoche (1768–97) fought in the Vendée and against the Austrians. Jean-Baptiste Jourdan (1762–1833) survived the revolutionary wars, served under Joseph Bonaparte in Italy and Spain, and switched allegiance to the Bourbons and ultimately to Louis-Philippe d'Orléans. Pichegru became a royalist and later plotted against Napoleon (*see note for p. 284, ll. 32–35*); it is probably these good intentions that the marquis is referring to.

P. 365, LL. 1–2. *the king's budget:* refers to the Civil List, a rich source of income for politically connected aristocrats ruined by the Revolution.

L. 17. *another 1815:* i.e., another revolution or threat to the Bourbons, referring to Napoleon's return from Elba in March 1815. The tricolor flag, still the official flag of France, was adopted by the Empire and banned by the Restoration.

L. 18. *Cathelineau:* a peasant leader in the Vendée rebellion (*see note for p. 298, l. 18*).

LL. 19–20. *be sons of the women who nursed their betters:* Under the ancien régime, wealthy parents sent their newborns to the country to be nursed, and then raised for up to five years. The marquis is referring to the supposedly unshakable lifelong loyalty of these foster families—*the frères et soeurs de lait,* literally milk-brothers and -sisters—to their young noble charges: part and parcel of the nostalgia of these men for the aristocratic golden age, when peasants knew their place and their duty to their betters.

L. 35. *the "Marseillaise":* like the tricolor flag, the "Marseillaise" was considered to be a symbol of the worst excesses of the Revolution. Banned by Bonaparte and the Restoration, it was not adopted as the French national anthem until 1879. The lyrics are in fact quite violent.

L. 36. *King Gustavus Adolphus:* Stendhal—or the marquis—seems to be blurring the lives of two kings of Sweden. Gustavus IV Adolphus (born 1778, reigned 1792–1809) fought against the French Revolution on monarchic principle, and was deposed by a palace coup in 1809. Gustavus II Adolphus (born 1594, reigned 1611–32) made himself the protector of German Protestant princes against the Catholic Hapsburgs of Austria (and thus in allegiance with the Catholic Louis XIII and the Cardinal de Richelieu) during the Thirty Years War.

CHAPTER TWENTY-THREE. THE CLERGY, THEIR WOODLANDS,
AND FREEDOM

P. 367. *Machiavelli:* author of *The Prince* (*see note for p. 18, Epigraph*).

L. 4. *Hume:* A rationalist and skeptic, the great Scottish philosopher David Hume (1711–76) was no friend to the sort of reactionary monarchism preached at his meeting.

L. 5. *Saints:* the Quakers; French Romantics were fascinated by their simplicity and devotion.

L. 6. *Mister Henry Brougham:* another troublesome Scot; a liberal leader in Parliament, notable for his opposition to the slave trade.

L. 23. *witticisms . . . fashionable:* The anticlericalism of the philosophes was widespread in the late eighteenth century, especially among the upper classes, even among certain aristocratic clergymen.

P. 368, L. 9. *woodlands:* Wood being the basic fuel and construction material of the time, woodlands (*bois*) were the most valuable real estate. The clergy had been the largest proprietors of woodlands under the ancien régime, and under the Restoration the Church sought compensation, if not actual restitution, for these assets.

L. 17. *Monsieur de Nerval: See note for p. 249, l. 23.* Nerval in this scene seems to resemble Jules de Polignac, the most reactionary of ultras and Charles

X's last prime minister. He was controversial when appointed in 1829, and became only more so as he sought to undermine the progress made by liberals since 1789. He had also become deeply devout, and saw his politics as a holy mission, as Nerval does in this chapter; he also resembles Charles X in this regard.

L. 35. *"I have a mission":* In the early years of the Consulate, many royalists hoped that Bonaparte would fulfill the role played by General Monck in England in 1660, leading the military to restore the monarchy. They were quickly disabused.

P. 370. L. 33. *Saint-Roch:* On October 5, 1795—*13 vendémiaire* according to the revolutionary calendar still in effect—troops under General Bonaparte fired on a crowd of royalists who had gathered near the Church of Saint-Roch, hoping to spark a counterrevolutionary coup. Bonaparte's actions established him as an agent of government authority and solidified his ties to Barras and the Directory government.

The meeting described accurately reflects the political mood and instability of the last months of the Restoration. Discontent was widespread and secret societies proliferated, on the right and the left, although not to the extent the public imagined. The politics of the Marquis de La Mole's group suggests the archconservative Chevaliers de la Foi *(see note for p. 22, l. 23),* an aristocratic, counterrevolutionary association founded in 1801, whose members included some of the greatest names of the French aristocracy (i.e., Montmorency, La Rochefoucauld). Many of the Chevaliers were also members of the Congrégation, thus giving the latter group an undeserved reputation for political activism. There are no historical indications that either the Chevaliers or any other group ever sought to overthrow the French government with the help of foreign invaders.

P. 371. L. 34. *Metz:* town in Lorraine, on the Moselle River near the German border.

L. 34. *postmaster:* The post in question is a relay stop, where coaches could changes horses and passengers could stop for a meal or a night's rest.

P. 372, L. 15. *Mayence:* Mainz, important German city at the confluence of the Rhine and the Main Rivers.

CHAPTER TWENTY-FOUR. STRASBOURG

P. 376, L. 4. *Kehl:* small town on the German side of the Rhine, just across from Strasbourg.

L. 5. *Desaix and Gouvion Saint-Cyr:* Louis-Charles-Antoine des Aix, nobleman who joined the revolutionary armies—and so altered the spelling of his name—made his reputation in Germany, performed impressively in Egypt, and was killed in the great French victory at Marengo (1800), a victory that some say was his, though Bonaparte took credit for it. Louis Jean-Baptiste de Gouvion Saint-Cyr, another nobleman who joined the Revolution, rallied to the Bourbons in 1814, briefly served Louis XVIII as minister of war. The two of them led a siege of Kehl in 1796.

P. 377. L. 12. *the era of Louis XV:* Certainly the great age of French *libertinage,* but the mode of rich men keeping actresses as their mistresses had by no means died out in 1830.

L. 31. *Madame de Dubois:* What a name, indeed; the combination of the aristocratic "de" with the quintessentially bourgeois "Dubois" is absurd and patently fictitious, hence the Russian prince's laughter.

P. 379, L. 29. *Richmond:* the site of a summer residence of the English royal family, known for its gardens along the Thames.

CHAPTER TWENTY-FIVE. THE MISTRESS OF VIRTUE

P. 381, EPIGRAPH. *Lope de Vega:* Spanish poet and playwright (1562–1635).

P. 382, L. 12. *Charles Collé:* a writer of popular songs in the eighteenth century.

CHAPTER TWENTY-SIX. LOVE OF A MORAL SORT

P. 388, L. 14. Saint-Simon: The famous memorialist of the court of Louis XIV and the Regency, the Duke de Saint-Simon (1675–1755) was greatly preoccupied with questions of rank, etiquette, and genealogy.

P. 391, L. 20. *Massillon:* Jean-Baptiste Massillon (1663–1742), priest and celebrated orator, delivered the funeral oration for Louis XIV.

CHAPTER TWENTY-SEVEN. THE CHURCH'S BEST JOBS

P. 391, EPIGRAPH. *Fénelon,* Télémaque: François de Salignac de la Mothe-Fénelon (1651–1715) was a clergyman and writer of mystical tendencies who took a great interest in education. A protégé of Madame de Maintenon, Fénelon in 1699 wrote *Télémaque* as an instructive parable for the Duke de Bourgogne, grandson of Louis XIV and heir presumptive to the throne; he would predecease the old king, and his son would become Louis XV at the age of five. Télémaque, or Telemachus, was the son of Odysseus; in Fénelon's tale, he makes a voyage in search of his long-lost father in the company of his tutor, Mentor. The lessons young Telemachus learns from his travels and from Mentor are intended as a model of governance and conduct for the future king. *Télémaque* was intended and understood as a critique of the reign of Louis XIV, and Fénelon was banished from court in 1699. The quote given cannot be found or imagined in Fénelon's work.

CHAPTER TWENTY-EIGHT. MANON LESCAUT

P. 395, CHAPTER TITLE. *Manon Lescaut:* the tragic heroine of the abbé Prévost's 1765 novel of the same name (*see note for p. 297, l. 33*). *Manon Lescaut* tells the story of the doomed love of the prostitute Manon and the Chevalier des Grieux.

EPIGRAPH. *Lichtenberg:* Georg Christoph Lichtenberg (1743–99), a German physicist and author of sharp satires of metaphysical and Romantic writings he found excessive.

L. 6. *the ballet* Manon Lescaut: a ballet-opera by Halévy and Scribe that debuted in 1830.

LL. 11–13. *praising a novel . . . such low works:* In the early nineteenth century, novels were still considered immoral and artistically inferior by political and literary conservatives.

CHAPTER TWENTY-NINE. BOREDOM

P. 399, EPIGRAPH. *Girodet:* Anne-Louis Girodet de Roucy, known as Girodet-Trioson (1767–1824), is more famous for his painting than his writing.

CHAPTER THIRTY. A BOX AT THE OPERA

P. 405, L. 34. Il Matrimonio segreto: opera by Domenico Cimarosa (*see note for p. 341, l. 3*); Stendhal's favorite opera.

CHAPTER THIRTY-ONE. MAKE HER AFRAID

P. 406. *Barnave: See note for p. 6, Epigraph.*

P. 407, LL. 22–23. *Memories of Napoleon on Saint-Helena:* as dictated to the Comte de Montholon, who published them in 1822–25.

CHAPTER THIRTY-TWO. THE TIGER

P. 411, EPIGRAPH. *Beaumarchais:* Pierre-Auguste Caron de Beaumarchais (1732–99), famous wit, financier, and literary celebrity of the late eighteenth century. Beaumarchais was best known as the author of two hugely successful comedies, *The Barber of Seville* and *The Marriage of Figaro*. The second was for a time banned for its perceived antiauthoritarian sentiments, which shocked Louis XVI. The hero of these two plays, the witty and slightly roguish Figaro, quickly became fixed in the French national imagination. Both plays inspired operas, better known to Anglophone audiences than the plays that inspired them.

LL. 24–25. *Smollett:* Tobias George Smollett (1721–71), versatile English writer known for his satirical novels and a multivolume *History of England;* he also translated *Don Quixote.*

P. 413, L. 7. *"the Duke de Retz's day to receive visitors":* Among the busy society of the Parisian monde, many aristocrats reserved one day a week when they received guests.

CHAPTER THIRTY-THREE. THE HELL OF WEAKNESS

P. 416, EPIGRAPH. *Mirabeau: See note for p. 220, l. 2.*

CHAPTER THIRTY-FOUR. A MAN OF SPIRIT

P. 421, EPIGRAPH. The Globe: *See note for p. 364, l. 20.*

P. 422, L. 34. *like Othello:* It is actually Desdemona who writes a letter.

P. 424, L. 29. *Louis XI:* Known as the Spider King, Louis XI (born 1423, reigned 1461–83) was a shrewd and ruthless politician who made great strides in increasing the centralized power of the French monarchy.

P. 426, LL. 30–31. *Louis XIV . . . the Duchess of Burgundy:* Wife of the old king's grandson, the Duchess of Burgundy became a favorite of—but certainly not a mistress to—Louis XIV.

CHAPTER THIRTY-FIVE. A THUNDERSTORM

P. 427, EPIGRAPH. *mediocrity:* This quotation is difficult to imagine from the mouth or pen of Mirabeau.

CHAPTER THIRTY-SIX. SOMBER DETAILS

P. 434, L. 25. *Iago:* the jealous false friend of Othello, who persuades him of the innocent Desdemona's betrayal. Julien implies that he is using sincerely the words Iago used to stoke the Moor's suspicions.

CHAPTER THIRTY-SEVEN. THE TOWER

P. 438, EPIGRAPH. *Sterne:* Laurence Sterne (1713–68), author of *Tristram Shandy,* a highly experimental novel read and appreciated by many French Romantic authors. *Tristram Shandy* makes use of many unconventional devices, such as an unreliable narrator, long digressions, and stories within stories.

P. 440, LL. 25–26. *Count de Lavalette:* Condemned to death by the Bourbon government for having rallied to Napoleon during the Hundred Days,

Lavalette escaped from prison by trading clothes with his wife and leaving her in his place.

P. 441, L. 3. René: the highly successful novel by François-Auguste-René de Châteaubriand (1768–1848), which was a key text of the early Romantic movement. Stendhal disliked the sentimentality of Châteaubriand's work and frequently tweaked the "noble vicomte" in his own writing.

CHAPTER THIRTY-NINE. PLOTTING

P. 449, EPIGRAPH. *Locke:* John Locke (1632–1704); his *Trip to France* is found in Peter King's 1676 *The Life of John Locke, with extracts from his Correspondance, Journals, and Commonplace Books.*

P. 453, L. 3. *the great Fronde wars:* Civil wars brought about by the power vaccuum of the minority of Louis XIV, from 1648 to 1653. Resentment against the late Cardinal de Richelieu and his political heir, Mazarin, spurred a quest for power among the great nobles and the parlements. In an era filled with larger-than-life figures, the Duchesses de Chevreuse and de Longueville stood out. The former (1600–79) was a lifelong plotter and political schemer, and was an ally of the Cardinal de Retz (*see note for p. 101, l. 11*), who was also her unmarried daughter's acknowledged lover. The Duchesse de Longueville (1619–79) was a Princess of the Blood Royal, cousin of Louis XIV, and one of the most beautiful women of the age. She brought her lover, the Duke de La Rochefoucauld—future author of the *Maximes*—into the party of her brother, the Grand Condé (*see note for p. 38, l. 33*), and had many picaresque adventures of her own in the course of the war. The word *Fronde* means slingshot, given to this conflict by contemporaries because of its opera bouffe qualities, but they inflicted five years of civil war on France.

CHAPTER FORTY. TRANQUILITY

P. 453, EPIGRAPH. *Madame Goethe:* In the original French, the word *foolish (fou)* appears in the masculine form in this quote attributed to Madame Goethe. Many editors have mistakenly replaced "Madame" with "J. W. von Goethe."

CHAPTER FORTY-TWO

P. 464, L. 5. *Fénelon: See note for p. 391, Epigraph.* Fénelon was a humanistic but devout Christian; the love Julien has felt was probably not the sort Fénelon would have professed.

L. 26. *Rotrou's play,* Venceslas: one of the most popular and enduring plays of Jean Rotrou (1609–50). Venceslas, aging King of Poland, abdicates in order to avoid having to carry out the execution of his son, Ladislas, who has been convicted of murder.

P. 466, LL. 5–6. *"By the rights . . . vulgar humans":* an inexact quotation from Voltaire's play *Mahomet.*

P. 467, L. 29. *Jacques Manuel:* a soldier (1775–1827) of the Revolution who became one of the leading orators of the liberal opposition under the Restoration.

CHAPTER FORTY-THREE

P. 468, LL. 9–10. *La Fontaine's . . . Belphégor:* an unhappily married man in a comic tale by La Fontaine.

CHAPTER FORTY-FOUR

P. 477, L. 21. *the King of Rome:* son of Napoleon and Marie-Louise, proclaimed "King of Rome" by his father even before his birth in 1811. He was known as the King of Rome to true believers in the Bonapartiste cause—who also called him Napoleon II, Napoleon having pointlessly abdicated in his favor in 1814. He was named Duke of Reichstadt by his grandfather, the Austrian emperor, and died in 1832, not having seen his father after the age of three.

P. 477, L. 36–P. 478, L. 1. *Massillon . . . Dubois:* The virtuous Massillon (*see note for p. 391, l. 20*) consecrated the dissolute abbé Dubois as a bishop at the command of the Regent Duke d'Orléans, whose political confidant and compagnon in debauchery Dubois was. Dubois ended his checkered ecclesiastical career as a cardinal.

L. 1. *The Memoirs of Saint Simon . . . Fénelon:* The Duke de Saint Simon (*see note for p. 388, l. 14, and note for p. 391, Epigraph*) was decidedly partisan in all his judgments, and he portrays Fenélon as a weak, obsequious courtier.

CHAPTER FORTY-FIVE

P. 484, LL. 9–10. *Everything happened . . . without the slightest affection:* Julien's story was inspired, in part, by the trial of Antoine Berthet, which took place in Grenoble in 1827. Berthet was the bright son of a blacksmith who entered the seminary and was later hired by the wealthy Michoud de La Tour family as a tutor. He and Madame Michoud had an affair, and Berthet was dismissed. Hired as a tutor by the Cordon family, he was fired for initiating a liaison with the eldest daughter of the family. When Madame Michoud then refused to renew their relationship,

Berthet followed her to church and shot her during Mass. Although the victim was only slightly wounded, Berthet was condemned to death, and was beheaded in Grenoble on February 27, 1828. In other writings, Stendhal compared this verdict to that in the 1829 Lafargue case, in which the defendant, Lafargue, slit the throat of a peasant girl. He was sentenced to five years in prison and pardoned after serving two.

BURTON RAFFEL is distinguished professor of humanities at the University of Louisiana at Lafayette. His many translations include Rabelais's *Gargantua and Pantagruel*, winner of the 1991 French-American Foundation Translation Prize; Chrétien de Troyes's Arthurian romances; Cervantes's *Don Quijote*; and Balzac's *Père Goriot*. His translation of *Beowulf* has sold more than a million copies.

A NOTE ON THE TYPE

The principal text of this Modern Library edition
was set in a digitized version of Janson, a typeface that
dates from about 1690 and was cut by Nicholas Kis,
a Hungarian working in Amsterdam. The original matrices have
survived and are held by the Stempel foundry in Germany.
Hermann Zapf redesigned some of the weights and sizes for
Stempel, basing his revisions on the original design.